KNIFE
OF
DREAMS

THE WHEEL OF TIME
by Robert Jordan

KNIFE
OF
DREAMS

ROBERT JORDAN

A TOM DOHERTY ASSOCIATES BOOK
NEW YORK

KNIFE OF DREAMS

Copyright © 2005 by The Bandersnatch Group, Inc.

The phrases "The Wheel of Time™" and "The Dragon Reborn™," and the snake-wheel symbol, are trademarks of Robert Jordan.

A Tor Book
Published by Tom Doherty Associates, LLC
175 Fifth Avenue
New York, NY 10010

www.tor.com

Tor® is a registered trademark of Tom Doherty Associates, LLC.

Maps by Ellisa Mitchell
Interior illustrations by Matthew C. Nielsen and Ellisa Mitchell

Library of Congress Cataloging-in-Publication Data

Jordan, Robert, 1948–
    Knife of dreams / Robert Jordan.— 1st ed.
        p.   cm.
    "A Tom Doherty Associates book."
    ISBN 0-312-87307-7 (regular edition) (acid-free paper)
    EAN 978-0-312-87307-3 (regular edition)
    ISBN 0-765-31053-8 (limited edition) (acid-free paper)
    EAN 978-0-765-31053-8 (limited edition)
    1. Rand al'Thor (Fictitious character)—Fiction.   I. Title.

  PS3560.O7617K58   2005
  813'.54—dc22

                                        2005018098

First Edition: October 2005

Printed in the United States of America

0 9 8 7 6 5 4 3 2 1

In memory of Charles St. George Sinkler Adams
July 6, 1976–April 13, 2005

CONTENTS

The sweetness of victory and the bitterness of defeat are alike a knife of dreams.

—From *Fog and Steel* by Madoc Comadrin

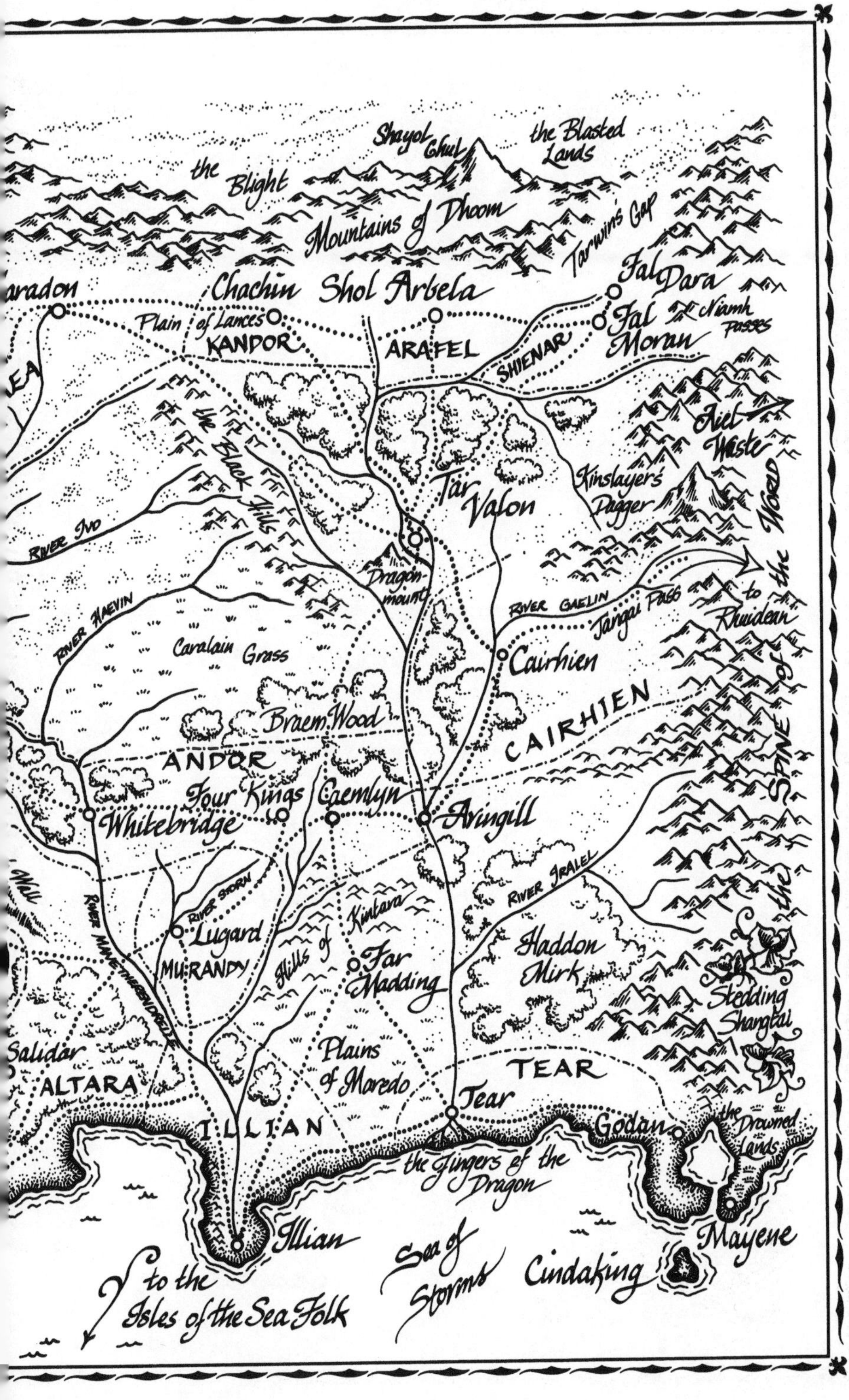
Shayol Ghul
the Blasted Lands
the Blight
Mountains of Dhoom
Tarwin's Gap
Fal Dara
Fal Moran
Niamh Passes
Chachin
Shol Arbela
Plain of Lances
KANDOR
ARAFEL
SHIENAR
the Black Hills
Aiel Waste
Kinslayer's Dagger
Tar Valon
RIVER IVO
Dragonmount
RIVER HAEVIN
RIVER GAELIN
Jangai Pass
to Rhuidean
Caralain Grass
Cairhien
CAIRHIEN
Braem Wood
ANDOR
Four Kings
Caemlyn
Aringill
Whitebridge
Spine of the World
RIVER STORN
RIVER IRALELL
RIVER MANETHERENDRELLE
Lugard
MURANDY
Hills of Kintara
Far Madding
Haddon Mirk
Stedding Shangtai
Salidar
ALTARA
Plains of Maredo
TEAR
Tear
ILLIAN
Godan
the Drowned Lands
the Fingers of the Dragon
Illian
Mayene
Sea of Storms
Cindaking
to the Isles of the Sea Folk

KNIFE
OF
DREAMS

PROLOGUE

Embers Falling on Dry Grass

T he sun, climbing toward midmorning, stretched Galad's shadow and those of his three armored companions ahead of them as they trotted their mounts down the road that ran straight through the forest, dense with oak and leatherleaf, pine and sourgum, most showing the red of spring growth. He tried to keep his mind empty, still, but small things kept intruding. The day was silent save for the thud of their horses' hooves. No bird sang on a branch, no squirrel chittered. Too quiet for the time of year, as though the forest held its breath. This had been a major trade route once, long before Amadicia and Tarabon came into being, and bits of ancient paving stone sometimes studded the hard-packed surface of yellowish clay. A single farm cart far ahead behind a plodding ox was the only sign of human life now besides themselves. Trade had shifted far north, farms and villages in the region dwindled, and the fabled lost mines of Aelgar remained lost in the tangled mountain ranges that began only a few miles to the south. Dark clouds massing in that direction promised rain by afternoon if their slow advance continued. A red-winged hawk quartered back and forth along the border of the trees, hunting the fringes. As he himself was hunting. But at the heart, not on the fringes.

The manor house that the Seanchan had given Eamon Valda came into view, and he drew rein, wishing he had a helmet strap to tighten for excuse. Instead he had to be content with re-buckling his sword belt, pretending that it had been sitting wrong. There had been no point to wearing armor. If the morning went as he hoped, he would have had to remove breastplate and mail in any case, and if it went badly, armor would have provided little more protection than his white coat.

Formerly a deep-country lodge of the King of Amadicia, the building was a huge, blue-roofed structure studded with red-painted balconies, a wooden palace with wooden spires at the corners atop a stone foundation like a low, steep-sided hill. The outbuildings, stables and barns, workmen's small houses and craftsfolks' workshops, all hugged the ground in the wide clearing that surrounded the main house, but they were nearly as resplendent in their blue-and-red paint. A handful of men and women moved around them, tiny figures yet at this distance, and children were playing under their elders' eyes. An image of normality where nothing was normal. His companions sat their saddles in their burnished helmets and breastplates, watching him without expression. Their mounts stamped impatiently, the animals' morning freshness not yet worn off by the short ride from the camp.

"It's understandable if you're having second thoughts, Damodred," Trom said after a time. "It's a harsh accusation, bitter as gall, but—"

"No second thoughts for me," Galad broke in. His intentions had been fixed since yesterday. He was grateful, though. Trom had given him the opening he needed. They had simply appeared as he rode out, falling in with him without a word spoken. There had seemed no place for words, then. "But what about you three? You're taking a risk coming here with me. A risk you have no need to take. However the day runs, there will be marks against you. This is my business, and I give you leave to go about yours." Too stiffly said, but he could not find words this morning, or loosen his throat.

The stocky man shook his head. "The law is the law. And I might as well make use of my new rank." The three golden star-shaped knots of a captain sat beneath the flaring sunburst on the breast of his white cloak. There had been more than a few dead at Jeramel, including no fewer than three of the Lords Captain. They had been fighting the Seanchan then, not allied with them.

"I've done dark things in service to the Light," gaunt-faced Byar said grimly, his deep-set eyes glittering as though at a personal insult, "dark as moonless midnight, and likely I will again, but some things are too dark to be allowed." He looked as if he might spit.

"That's right," young Bornhald muttered, scrubbing a gauntleted hand across his mouth. Galad always thought of him as young, though the man lacked only a few years on him. Dain's eyes were bloodshot; he had been at the brandy again last night. "If you've done what's wrong, even in service to the Light, then you have to do what's right to balance it." Byar grunted sourly. Likely that was not the point he had been making.

"Very well," Galad said, "but there's no fault to any man who turns back. My business here is mine alone."

Still, when he heeled his bay gelding to a canter, he was pleased to have them gallop to catch him and fall in alongside, white cloaks billowing behind. He would have gone on alone, of course, yet their presence might keep him from being arrested and hanged out of hand. Not that he expected to survive in any case. What had to be done, had to be done, no matter the price.

The horses' hooves clattered loudly on the stone ramp that climbed to the manor house, so every man in the broad central courtyard turned to watch as they rode in: fifty of the Children in gleaming plate-and-mail and conical helmets, most mounted, with cringing, dark-coated Amadician grooms holding animals for the rest. The inner balconies were empty except for a few servants who appeared to be watching while pretending to sweep. Six Questioners, big men with the scarlet shepherd's crook upright behind the sunflare on their cloaks, stood close around Rhadam Asunawa like a bodyguard, away from the others. The Hand of the Light always stood apart from the rest of the Children, a choice the rest of the Children approved. Gray-haired Asunawa, his sorrowful face making Byar look fully fleshed, was the only Child present not in armor, and his snowy cloak carried just the brilliant red crook, another way of standing apart. But aside from marking who was present, Galad had eyes for only one man in the courtyard. Asunawa might have been involved in some way—that remained unclear—yet only the Lord Captain Commander could call the High Inquisitor to account.

Eamon Valda was not a large man, but his dark, hard face had the look of one who expected obedience as his due. As the very least he was due. Standing with his booted feet apart and his head high, command in every inch of him, he wore the white-and-gold tabard of the Lord

Captain Commander over his gilded breast- and backplates, a silk tabard more richly embroidered than any Pedron Niall had worn. His white cloak, the flaring sun large on either breast in thread-of-gold, was silk as well, and his gold-embroidered white coat. The helmet beneath his arm was gilded and worked with the flaring sun on the brow, and a heavy gold ring on his left hand, worn outside his steel-backed gauntlet, held a large yellow sapphire carved with the sunburst. Another mark of favor received from the Seanchan.

Valda frowned slightly as Galad and his companions dismounted and offered their salutes, arm across the chest. Obsequious grooms came running to take their reins.

"Why aren't you on your way to Nassad, Trom?" Disapproval colored Valda's words. "The other Lords Captain will be halfway there by now." He himself always arrived late when meeting the Seanchan, perhaps to assert that some shred of independence remained to the Children—finding him already preparing to depart was a surprise; this meeting must be very important—but he always made sure the other high-ranking officers arrived on time even when that required setting out before dawn. Apparently it was best not to press their new masters too far. Distrust of the Children was always strong in the Seanchan.

Trom displayed none of the uncertainty that might have been expected from a man who had held his present rank barely a month. "An urgent matter, my Lord Captain Commander," he said smoothly, making a very precise bow, neither a hair deeper nor higher than protocol demanded. "A Child of my command charges another of the Children with abusing a female relative of his, and claims the right of Trial Beneath the Light, which by law you must grant or deny."

"A strange request, my son," Asunawa said, tilting his head quizzically above clasped hands, before Valda could speak. Even the High Inquisitor's voice was doleful; he sounded pained at Trom's ignorance. His eyes seemed dark hot coals in a brazier. "It was usually the accused who asked to give the judgment to swords, and I believe usually when he knew the evidence would convict him. In any case, Trial Beneath the Light has not been invoked for nearly four hundred years. Give me the accused's name, and I will deal with the matter quietly." His tone turned chill as a sunless cavern in winter, though his eyes still burned. "We are among strangers, and we cannot allow them to know that one of the Children is capable of such a thing."

"The request was directed to me, Asunawa," Valda snapped. His glare might as well have been open hatred. Perhaps it was just dislike of the other man's breaking in. Flipping one side of his cloak over his shoulder to bare his ring-quilloned sword, he rested his hand on the long hilt and drew himself up. Always one for the grand gesture, Valda raised his voice so that even people inside probably heard him, and declaimed rather than merely spoke.

"I believe many of our old ways should be revived, and that law still stands. It will always stand, as written of old. The Light grants justice because the Light is justice. Inform your man he may issue his challenge, Trom, and face the one he accuses sword-to-sword. If that one tries to refuse, I declare that he has acknowledged his guilt and order him hanged on the spot, his belongings and rank forfeit to his accuser as the law states. I have spoken." That with another scowl for the High Inquisitor. Maybe there really was hatred there.

Trom bowed formally once more. "You have informed him yourself, my Lord Captain Commander. Damodred?"

Galad felt cold. Not the cold of fear, but of emptiness. When Dain drunkenly let slip the confused rumors that had come to his ears, when Byar reluctantly confirmed they were more than rumors, rage had filled Galad, a bone-burning fire that nearly drove him insane. He had been sure his head would explode if his heart did not burst first. Now he was ice, drained of any emotion. He also bowed formally. Much of what he had to say was set in the law, yet he chose the rest with care, to spare as much shame as possible to a memory he held dear.

"Eamon Valda, Child of the Light, I call you to Trial Beneath the Light for unlawful assault on the person of Morgase Trakand, Queen of Andor, and for her murder." No one had been able to confirm that the woman he regarded as his mother was dead, yet it must be so. A dozen men were certain she had vanished from the Fortress of the Light before it fell to the Seanchan, and as many testified she had not been free to leave of her own will.

Valda displayed no shock at the charge. His smile might have been intended to show regret over Galad's folly in making such a claim, yet contempt was mingled in it. He opened his mouth, but Asunawa cut in once more.

"This is ridiculous," he said in tones more of sorrow than of anger. "Take the fool, and we'll find out what Darkfriend plot to discredit the Children he is part of." He motioned, and two of the hulking Questioners took a step toward Galad, one with a cruel grin, the other blank-faced, a workman about his work.

Only one step, though. A soft rasp repeated around the courtyard as Children eased their swords in their scabbards. At least a dozen men drew entirely, letting their blades hang by their sides. The Amadician grooms hunched in on themselves, trying to become invisible. Likely they would have run, had they dared. Asunawa stared around him, thick eyebrows climbing up his forehead in disbelief, knotted fists gripping his cloak. Strangely, even Valda appeared startled for an instant. Surely he had not expected the Children to allow an arrest after his own proclamation. If he had, he recovered quickly.

"You see, Asunawa," he said almost cheerfully, "the Children follow my orders, and the law, not a Questioner's whims." He held out his helmet to one side for someone to take. "I deny your preposterous charge, young Galad, and throw your foul lie in your teeth. For it is a lie, or at best a mad acceptance of some malignant rumor started by Darkfriends or others who wish the Children ill. Either way, you have defamed me in the vilest manner, so I accept your challenge to Trial Beneath the Light, where I will kill you." That barely squeezed into the ritual, but he had denied the charge and accepted the challenge; it would suffice.

Realizing that he still held the helmet in an outstretched hand, Valda frowned at one of the dismounted Children, a lean Saldaean named Kashgar, until the man stepped forward to relieve him of it. Kashgar was only an under-lieutenant, almost boyish despite a great hooked nose and thick mustaches like inverted horns, yet he moved with open reluctance, and Valda's voice was darker and acrid as he went on, unbuckling his sword belt and handing that over, too.

"Take a care with that, Kashgar. It's a heron-mark blade." Unpinning his silk cloak, he let it fall to the paving stones, followed by his tabard, and his hands moved to the buckles of his armor. It seemed that he was unwilling to see if others would be reluctant to help him. His face was calm enough, except that angry eyes promised retribution to more than Galad. "Your sister wants to become Aes Sedai, I understand, Damodred. Perhaps I understand precisely where this originated. There was a time I would have regretted your death, but not today. I may send your head to the White Tower so the witches can see the fruit of their scheme."

Worry creasing his face, Dain took Galad's cloak and sword belt, and stood shifting his feet as though uncertain he was doing the right thing. Well, he had been given his chance, and it was too late to change his mind, now. Byar put a gauntleted hand on Galad's shoulder and leaned close.

"He likes to strike at the arms and legs," he said in a low voice, casting glances over his shoulder at Valda. From the way he glared, some matter stood between them. Of course, that scowl differed little from his normal expression. "He likes to bleed an opponent until the man can't take a step or raise his sword before he moves for the kill. He's quicker than a viper, too, but he'll strike at your left most often and expect it from you."

Galad nodded. Many right-handed men found it easier to strike so, but it seemed an odd weakness in a blademaster. Gareth Bryne and Henre Haslin had made him practice alternating which hand was uppermost on the hilt so he would not fall into that. Strange that Valda wanted to prolong a fight, too. He himself had been taught to end matters as quickly and cleanly as possible.

"My thanks," he said, and the hollow-cheeked man made a dour grimace. Byar was far from likable, and he himself seemed to like no one save young Bornhald. Of the three, his presence was the biggest surprise, but he was there, and that counted in his favor.

Standing in the middle of the courtyard in his gold-worked white coat with his fists on his hips, Valda turned in a tight circle. "Everyone move back against the walls," he commanded loudly. Horseshoes rang on the paving stones as the Children and the grooms obeyed. Asunawa and his Questioners snatched their animals' reins, the High Inquisitor wearing a face of cold fury. "Keep the middle clear. Young Damodred and I will meet here—"

"Forgive me, my Lord Captain Commander," Trom said with a slight bow, "but since you are a participant in the Trial, you cannot be Arbiter. Aside from the High Inquisitor, who by law may not take part, I hold the highest rank here after you, so with your permission . . . ?" Valda glared at him, then stalked over to stand beside Kashgar, arms folded across his chest. Ostentatiously he tapped his foot, impatient for matters to proceed.

Galad sighed. If the day went against him, as seemed all but certain, his friend would have the most powerful man in the Children as his enemy. Likely Trom would have had in any event, but more so now. "Keep an eye on them," he told Bornhald, nodding toward the

Questioners clustered on their horses near the gate. Asunawa's under-
lings still ringed him like bodyguards, every man with a hand on his
sword hilt.

"Why? Even Asunawa can't interfere now. That would be against
the law."

It was very hard not to sigh again. Young Dain had been a Child
far longer than he, and his father had served his entire life, but the man
seemed to know less of the Children than he himself had learned. To
Questioners, the law was what they said it was. "Just watch them."

Trom stood in the center of the courtyard with his bared sword
raised overhead, blade parallel to the ground, and unlike Valda, he
spoke the words exactly as they were written. "Under the Light, we are
gathered to witness Trial Beneath the Light, a sacred right of any Child
of the Light. The Light shines on truth, and here the Light shall illu-
minate justice. Let no man speak save he who has legal right, and let
any who seek to intervene be cut down summarily. Here, justice will
be found under the Light by a man who pledges his life beneath the
Light, by the force of his arm and the will of the Light. The combat-
ants will meet unarmed where I now stand," he continued, lowering
the sword to his side, "and speak privately, for their own ears alone.
May the Light help them find words to end this short of bloodshed, for
if they do not, one of the Children must die this day, his name stricken
from our rolls and anathema declared on his memory. Under the Light,
it will be so."

As Trom strode to the side of the courtyard, Valda moved toward
the center in the walking stance called Cat Crosses the Courtyard, an
arrogant saunter. He knew there were no words to stop blood being
shed. To him, the fight had already begun. Galad merely walked out to
meet him. He was nearly a head taller than Valda, but the other man
held himself as though he were the larger, and confident of victory.

His smile was all contempt, this time. "Nothing to say, boy? Small
wonder, considering that a blademaster is going to cut your head off in
about one minute. I want one thing straight in your mind before I kill
you, though. The wench was hale the last I saw her, and if she's dead
now, I'll regret it." That smile deepened, both in humor and disdain.
"She was the best ride I ever had, and I hope to ride her again one day."

Red-hot searing fury fountained inside Galad, but with an effort
he managed to turn his back on Valda and walk away, already feeding
his rage into an imagined flame as his two teachers had taught him. A

man who fought in a rage, died in a rage. By the time he reached young Bornhald, he had achieved what Gareth and Henre had called the oneness. Floating in emptiness, he drew his sword from the scabbard Bornhald proffered, and the slightly curved blade became a part of him.

"What did he say?" Dain asked. "For a moment there, your face was murderous."

Byar gripped Dain's arm. "Don't distract him," he muttered.

Galad was not distracted. Every creak of saddle leather was clear and distinct, every ringing stamp of hoof on paving stone. He could hear flies buzzing ten feet away as though they were at his ear. He almost thought he could see the movements of their wings. He was one with the flies, with the courtyard, with the two men. They were all part of him, and he could not be distracted by himself.

Valda waited until he turned before drawing his own weapon on the other side of the courtyard, a flashy move, the sword blurring as it spun in his left hand, leaping to his right hand to make another blurred wheel in the air before settling, upright and rock steady before him, in both hands. He started forward, once more in Cat Crosses the Courtyard.

Raising his own sword, Galad moved to meet him, without thought assuming a walking stance perhaps influenced by his state of mind. Emptiness, it was called, and only a trained eye would know that he was not simply walking. Only a trained eye would see that he was in perfect balance every heartbeat. Valda had not gained that heron-mark sword by favoritism. Five blademasters had sat in judgment of his skills and voted unanimously to grant him the title. The vote always had to be unanimous. The only other way was to kill the bearer of a heron-mark blade in fair combat, one on one. Valda had been younger then than Galad was now. It did not matter. He was not focused on Valda's death. He focused on nothing. But he intended Valda's death if he had to Sheathe the Sword, willingly welcoming that heron-mark blade in his flesh, to achieve it. He accepted that it might come to that.

Valda wasted no time with maneuvering. The instant he was within range, Plucking the Low-hanging Apple flashed toward Galad's neck like lightning, as though the man truly did intend to have his head in the first minute. There were several possible responses, all made instinct by hard training, but Byar's warnings floated in the dim recesses of his mind, and also the fact that Valda had warned him of this very thing. Warned him twice. Without conscious thought, he chose another way, stepping sideways and forward just as Plucking the Low-hanging Apple became the Leopard's Caress. Valda's eyes widened in surprise as his stroke missed Galad's left thigh by inches, widened more as Parting the Silk laid a gash down his right forearm, but he immediately launched into the Dove Takes Flight, so fast that Galad had to dance back before his blade could bite deeply, barely fending off the attack with Kingfisher Circles the Pond.

Back and forth they danced the forms, gliding this way then that across the stone paving. Lizard in the Thornbush met Lightning of Three Prongs. Leaf on the Breeze countered Eel Among the Lily Pads, and Two Hares Leaping met the Hummingbird Kisses the Honeyrose. Back and forth as smoothly as a demonstration of the forms. Galad tried attack after attack, but Valda *was* as fast as a viper. The Wood Grouse Dances cost him a shallow gash on his left shoulder, and the Red Hawk Takes a Dove another on the left arm, slightly deeper. River of Light might have taken the arm completely had he not met the draw-cut with a desperately quick Rain in High Wind. Back and forth, blades flashing continuously, filling the air with the clash of steel on steel.

How long they fought, he could not have said. There was no time, only the moment. It seemed that he and Valda moved like men under water, their motions slowed by the drag of the sea. Sweat appeared on Valda's face, but he smiled with self-assurance, seemingly untroubled by the slash on his forearm, still the only injury he had taken. Galad could feel the sweat rolling down his own face, too, stinging his eyes. And the blood trickling down his arm. Those wounds would slow him eventually, perhaps already had, but he had taken two on his left thigh, and both were more serious. His foot was wet in his boot from those, and he could not avoid a slight limp that would grow worse with time. If Valda was to die, it must be soon.

Deliberately, he drew a deep breath, then another, through his mouth, another. Let Valda think him becoming winded. His blade lanced out in Threading the Needle, aimed at Valda's left shoulder and not quite as fast it could have been. The other man countered easily with the Swallow Takes Flight, sliding immediately into the Lion Springs. That took a third bite in his thigh; he dared not be faster in defense than in attack.

Again he launched Threading the Needle at Valda's shoulder, and again, again, all the while gulping air through his mouth. Only luck kept him from taking more wounds in those exchanges. Or perhaps the Light really did shine on this fight.

Valda's smile widened; the man believed him on the edge of his strength, exhausted and fixated. As Galad began Threading the Needle, too slowly, for the fifth time, the other man's sword started the Swallow Takes Flight in an almost perfunctory manner. Summoning all the quickness that remained to him, Galad altered his stroke, and Reaping the Barley sliced across Valda just beneath his rib cage.

For a moment it seemed that the man was unaware he had been hit. He took a step, began what might have been Stones Falling from the Cliff. Then his eyes widened, and he staggered, the sword falling from his grip to clatter on the paving stones as he sank to his knees. His hands went to the huge gash across his body as though trying to hold his insides within him, and his mouth opened, glassy eyes fixed on Galad's face. Whatever he intended to say, it was blood that poured out over his chin. He toppled onto his face and lay still.

Automatically, Galad gave his blade a rapid twist to shake off the blood staining its final inch, then bent slowly to wipe the last drops onto Valda's white coat. The pain he had ignored now flared. His left shoulder and arm burned; his thigh seemed to be on fire. Straightening took effort. Perhaps he was nearer exhaustion than he had thought. How long *had* they fought? He had thought he would feel satisfaction that his mother had been avenged, but all he felt was emptiness. Valda's death was not enough. Nothing except Morgase Trakand alive again could be enough.

Suddenly he became aware of a rhythmic clapping and looked up to see the Children, each man slapping his own armored shoulder in approval. Every man. Except Asunawa and the Questioners. They were nowhere to be seen.

Byar hurried up carrying a small leather sack and carefully parted the slashes in Galad's coatsleeve. "Those will need sewing," he muttered, "but they can wait." Kneeling beside Galad, he took rolled bandages from the sack and began winding them around the gashes in his thigh. "These need sewing, too, but this will keep you from bleeding to death before you can get it." Others began gathering around, offering congratulations, men afoot in front, those still mounted behind. None gave the corpse a glance except for Kashgar, who cleaned Valda's sword on that already bloodstained coat before sheathing it.

"Where did Asunawa go?" Galad asked.

"He left as soon as you cut Valda the last time," Dain replied uneasily. "He'll be heading for the camp to bring back Questioners."

"He rode the other way, toward the border," someone put in. Nassad lay just over the border.

"The Lords Captain," Galad said, and Trom nodded.

"No Child would let the Questioners arrest you for what happened here, Damodred. Unless his captain ordered it. Some of them would order it, I think." Angry muttering began, men denying they would stand for such a thing, but Trom quieted them, somewhat, with raised hands. "You know it's true," he said loudly. "Anything else would be mutiny." That brought dead silence. There had never been a mutiny in the Children. It was possible that nothing before had come as close as their own earlier display. "I'll write out your release from the Children, Galad. Someone may still order your arrest, but they'll have to find you, and you'll have a good start. It will take half the day for Asunawa to catch the other Lords Captain, and whoever falls in with him can't be back before nightfall."

Galad shook his head angrily. Trom was right, but it was all wrong. Too much was wrong. "Will you write releases for these other men? You know Asunawa will find a way to accuse them, too. Will you write releases for the Children who don't want to help the Seanchan take our lands in the name of a man dead more than a thousand years?" Several Taraboners exchanged glances and nodded, and so did other men, not all of them Amadician. "What about the men who defended the Fortress of the Light? Will any release get their chains struck off or make the Seanchan stop working them like animals?" More angry growls; those prisoners were a sore point to all of the Children.

Arms folded across his chest, Trom studied him as though seeing him for the first time. "What would you do, then?"

"Have the Children find someone, anyone, who is fighting the Seanchan and ally with them. Make sure that the Children of the Light ride in the Last Battle instead of helping the Seanchan hunt Aiel and steal our nations."

"Anyone?" a Cairhienin named Doirellin said in a high-pitched voice. No one ever made fun of Doirellin's voice. Though short, he was nearly as wide as he was tall, there was barely an ounce of fat on him, and he could put walnuts between all of his fingers and crack them by clenching his fists. "That could mean Aes Sedai."

"If you intend to be at Tarmon Gai'don, then you will have to fight alongside Aes Sedai," Galad said quietly. Young Bornhald grimaced in strong distaste, and he was not the only one. Byar half-straightened before bending back to his task. But no one voiced dissent. Doirellin nodded slowly, as if he had never before considered the matter.

"I don't hold with the witches any more than any other man," Byar said finally, without raising his head from his work. Blood was seeping through the bandages even as he wrapped. "But the Precepts say, to fight the raven, you may make alliance with the serpent until the battle is done." A ripple of nods ran through the men. The raven meant the Shadow, but everyone knew it was also the Seanchan Imperial sigil.

"I'll fight beside the witches," a lanky Taraboner said, "or even these Asha'man we keep hearing about, if they fight the Seanchan. Or at the Last Battle. And I'll fight any man who says I'm wrong." He glared as though ready to begin then and there.

"It seems matters will play out as you wish, my Lord Captain Commander," Trom said, making a much deeper bow than he had for Valda. "To a degree, at least. Who can say what the next hour will bring, much less tomorrow?"

Galad surprised himself by laughing. Since yesterday, he had been sure he would never laugh again. "That's a poor joke, Trom."

"It is how the law is written. And Valda did make his proclamation. Besides, you had the courage to say what many have thought while holding their tongues, myself among them. Yours is a better plan for the Children than any I've heard since Pedron Niall died."

"It's still a poor joke." Whatever the law said, that part had been ignored since the end of the War of the Hundred Years.

"We'll see what the Children have to say on the matter," Trom replied, grinning widely, "when you ask them to follow us to Tarmon Gai'don to fight alongside the witches."

Men began slapping their shoulders again, harder than they had for his victory. At first it was only a few, then more joined in, until every man including Trom was signaling approval. Every man but Kashgar, that was. Making a deep bow, the Saldaean held out the scabbarded heron-mark blade with both hands.

"This is yours, now, my Lord Captain Commander."

Galad sighed. He hoped this nonsense would fade away before they reached the camp. Returning there was foolish enough without adding in a claim of that sort. Most likely they would be pulled down and thrown in chains if not beaten to death even without it. But he had to go. It was the right thing to do.

Daylight began to grow on this cool spring morning, though the sun had yet to show even a sliver above the horizon, and Rodel Ituralde raised his gold-banded looking glass to study the village below the hill where he sat his roan gelding, deep in the heart of Tarabon. He did hate waiting for enough light to see. Careful of a glint off the lens, he held the end of the long tube on his thumb and shaded it with a cupped hand. At this hour, sentries were at their least watchful, relieved that the darkness where an enemy might sneak close was departing, yet since crossing from Almoth Plain he had heard tales of Aiel raids inside Tarabon. Were he a sentry with Aiel perhaps about, he would grow extra eyes. Peculiar that the country was not milling like a kicked antheap over those Aiel. Peculiar, and perhaps ominous. There were plenty of armed men to be found, Seanchan and Taraboners sworn to them, and hordes of Seanchan building farms and even villages, but reaching this far had been almost too easy. Today, the easiness ended.

Behind him among the trees, horses stamped impatiently. The hundred Domani with him were quiet, except for an occasional creak of saddle leather as a man shifted his seat, but he could feel their tension. He wished he had twice as many. Five times. In the beginning, it had seemed a gesture of good faith that he himself would ride with a force mainly composed of Taraboners. He was no longer certain that had been the right decision. It was too late for recriminations, in any event.

Halfway between Elmora and the Amadician border, Serana sat in a flat grassy valley among forested hills, with at least a mile to the trees in any direction save his, and a small, reed-fringed lake fed by two wide streams lay between him and the village. Not a place that could be surprised by daylight. It had been sizable before the Seanchan came, a stopping point for the merchant trains heading east, with over a dozen inns and nearly as many streets. Village folk were already getting about their day's tasks, women balancing baskets on their heads as they glided down the village streets and others starting the fires under laundry kettles behind their houses, men striding along toward their workplaces, sometimes pausing to exchange a few words. A normal morning, with children already running and playing, rolling hoops and tossing beanbags among the throng. The clang of a smithy rose, dim with the distance. The smoke from breakfast fires was fading at the chimneys.

As far as he could see, no one in Serana gave a second glance to the three pairs of sentries with bright stripes painted across their breast-plates, walking their horses back and forth perhaps a quarter of a mile out. The lake, considerably wider than the village, shielded the fourth side effectively. It seemed the sentries were an accepted matter of every day, and so was the Seanchan camp that had swollen Serana to more than twice its former size.

Ituralde shook his head slightly. He would not have placed the camp cheek-by-jowl with the village that way. The rooftops of Serana were all tile, red or green or blue, but the buildings themselves were wooden; a fire in the town could spread all too easily into the camp, where canvas store-tents the size of large houses far outnumbered the smaller tents where men slept, and great stacks of barrels and casks and crates covered twice as much ground as all the tents combined. Keep-ing lightfingered villagers out would be all but impossible. Every town had a few tickbirds who picked up anything they thought they could get away with, and even somewhat more honest men might be tempted by the proximity. The location did mean a shorter distance to haul wa-ter from the lake, and a shorter distance for soldiers to walk to reach the ale and wine in the village when off-duty, but it suggested a com-mander who kept slack discipline.

Slack discipline or not, there was activity in the camp, too. Sol-diers' hours made farmers' hours seem restful. Men were checking the animals on the long horselines, bannermen checking soldiers standing in ranks, hundreds of laborers loading or unloading wagons, grooms harnessing teams. Every day, trains of wagons came down the road into this camp from east and west, and others departed. He admired the Seanchan efficiency at making sure their soldiers had what they needed when and where it was needed. Dragonsworn here in Tarabon, most sour-faced men who believed their dream snuffed out by the Seanchan, had been willing to tell what they knew if not to ride with him. That camp contained everything from boots to swords, arrows to horseshoes to water flasks, enough to outfit thousands of men from the ground up. They would feel its loss.

He lowered the looking glass to brush a buzzing green fly away
from his face. Two replaced it almost at once. Tarabon teemed with
flies. Did they always come so early here? They would just have begun
hatching at home by the time he reached Arad Doman again. If he did.
No; no ill thoughts. When he did. Tamsin would be displeased, otherwise, and it was seldom wise to displease her too far.

Most of the men down there were hired workmen, not soldiers, and
only a hundred or so of those Seanchan. Still, a company of three hundred Taraboners in stripe-painted armor had ridden in at noon the day
before, more than doubling their numbers and requiring him to change
his plans. Another party of Taraboners, as large, had entered the camp at
sunset, just in time to eat and bed down wherever they could lay their
blankets. Candles and lamp oil were luxuries for soldiers. There was one
of those leashed women, a *damane*, in the camp, too. He wished he could
have waited until she left—they must have been taking her elsewhere;
what use for a *damane* at a supply camp?—but today was the appointed
day, and he could not afford to give the Taraboners reason to claim he
was holding back. Some would snatch at any reason to go their own
way. He knew they would not follow him much longer, yet he needed to
hold as many as he could for a few days more.

Shifting his gaze to the west, he did not bother with the looking
glass.

"Now," he whispered, and as though at his command, two hundred
men with mail veils across their faces galloped out of the trees. And
immediately halted, cavorting and jockeying for place, brandishing
steel-tipped lances while their leader raced up and down before them
gesturing wildly in an obvious effort to establish some semblance of
order.

At this distance, Ituralde could not have made out faces even with
the glass, but he could imagine the fury on Tornay Lanasiet's features
at playing out this charade. The stocky Dragonsworn burned to close
with Seanchan. Any Seanchan. It had been difficult to dissuade him
from striking the day they crossed the border. Yesterday he had been
visibly overjoyed finally to scrape the hated stripes indicating loyalty
to the Seanchan from his breastplate. No matter; so far he was obeying
his orders to the letter.

As the sentries nearest Lanasiet turned their mounts to speed toward the village and the Seanchan camp, Ituralde swung his attention
there and raised his looking glass once more. The sentries would find

their warning superfluous. Motion had ceased. Some men were pointing toward the horsemen on the other side of the village, while the rest
seemed to be staring, soldiers and workmen alike. The last thing they
expected was raiders. Aiel raids or no Aiel raids, the Seanchan considered Tarabon theirs, and safely so. A quick glance at the village showed
people standing in the streets staring toward the strange riders. They
had not expected raiders, either. He thought the Seanchan were right,
an opinion he would not share with any Taraboner in the foreseeable
future.

With well-trained men, shock could last only so long, however.
In the camp, soldiers began racing toward their horses, many still
unsaddled, though grooms had started working as fast as they could.
Eighty-odd Seanchan footmen, archers, formed into ranks and set off
running through Serana. At that evidence that there truly was a
threat, people began snatching up the smaller children and herding
the older toward the hoped-for safety of the houses. In moments, the
streets were empty save for the hurrying archers in their lacquered
armor and peculiar helmets.

Ituralde turned the glass toward Lanasiet and found the man galloping his line of horsemen forward. "Wait for it," he growled. "Wait
for it."

Again it seemed the Taraboner heard his command, finally raising
a hand to halt his men. At least they were still a half-mile or more from
the village. The hotheaded fool was supposed to be near a mile away,
on the edge of the trees and still in seeming disorder and easily swept
away, but half would have to suffice. He suppressed the urge to finger
the ruby in his left ear. The battle had begun, now, and in battle you
had to make those following you believe that you were utterly cool,
completely unaffected. *Not* wanting to knock down a putative ally.
Emotion seemed to leak from a commander into his men, and angry
men behaved stupidly, getting themselves killed and losing battles.

Touching the half-moon-shaped beauty patch on his cheek—a man
should look his best on a day like today—he took slow measured
breaths until certain that he was as cool inside as his outward display,
then returned his attention to the camp. Most of the Taraboners there
were mounted, now, but they waited for twenty or so Seanchan led by
a tall fellow with a single thin plume on his curious helmet to gallop
into the village before falling in behind, yesterday's latecomers trailing
at the rear.

Ituralde studied the figure leading the column, viewing him through the gaps between houses. A single plume would mark a lieutenant or maybe an under-lieutenant. Which might mean a beardless boy on his first command or a grizzled veteran who could take your head if you made one mistake. Strangely, the *damane*, marked by the shining silvery leash that connected her to a woman on another horse, galloped her animal as hard as anyone. Everything he had heard said *damane* were prisoners, yet she appeared as eager as the other woman, the *sul'dam*. Perhaps—

Abruptly his breath caught in his throat and all thought of *damane* fled. There *were* people still in the street, seven or eight men and women, walking in a cluster and right ahead of the racing column that they seemed not to hear thundering up behind them. There was no time for the Seanchan to stop if they wanted to, and good reason not to try with an enemy ahead, but it looked as though the tall fellow's hand never twitched on his reins as he and the rest rode the people down. A veteran, then. Murmuring a prayer for the dead, Ituralde lowered the glass. What came next was best seen without it.

Two hundred paces beyond the village, the officer started forming his command where the archers had already stopped and were waiting with nocked arrows. Waving directions to the Taraboners behind, he turned to peer at Lanasiet through a looking glass. Sunlight glinted off the tube's banding. The sun was rising, now. The Taraboners began dividing smoothly, lance heads glittering and all slanted at the same angle, disciplined men falling into ordered ranks to either side of the archers.

The officer leaned over to converse with the *sul'dam*. If he turned her and the *damane* loose now, this could still turn into a disaster. Of course, it could if he did not, too. The last of the Taraboners, those who had arrived late, began stretching out in a line fifty paces behind the others, driving their lances point-down into the ground and pulling their horsebows from the cases fastened behind their saddles. Lanasiet, curse the man, was galloping his men forward.

Turning his head for a moment, Ituralde spoke loudly enough for the men behind him to hear. "Be ready." Saddle leather creaked as men gathered their reins. Then he murmured another prayer for the dead and whispered, "Now."

As one man the three hundred Taraboners in the long line, *his* Taraboners, raised their bows and loosed. He did not need the looking

glass to see the *sul'dam* and *damane* and the officer suddenly sprout arrows. They were all but swept from their saddles by near a dozen striking each of them at once. Ordering that had given him a pang, but the
women were the most dangerous people on that field. The rest of that
volley cut down most of the archers and cleared saddles, and even as
men struck the ground, a second volley lanced out, knocking down the
last archers and emptying more saddles.

Caught by surprise, the Seanchan-loyal Taraboners tried to fight.
Among those still mounted, some wheeled about and lowered lances to
charge their attackers. Others, perhaps seized by the irrationality that
could take men in battle, dropped their lances and tried to uncase their
own horsebows. But a third volley lashed them, pile-headed arrows
driving through breastplates at that range, and suddenly the survivors
seemed to realize that they were survivors. Most of their fellows lay
still on the ground or struggled to stand though pierced by two or
three shafts. Those still mounted were now outnumbered by their op-
ponents. A few men reined their horses around, and in a flash the lot of
them were running south pursued by one final rain of bowshot that
toppled more.

"Hold," Ituralde murmured. "Hold where you are."

A handful of the mounted archers fired again, but the rest wisely
refrained. They could kill a few more before the enemy was beyond
range, but this group was beaten, and before long they would be
counting every arrow. Best of all, none of them went racing in pursuit.

The same could not be said of Lanasiet. Cloaks streaming, he and
his two hundred raced after the fleeing men. Ituralde imagined he
could hear them yelping, hunters on the trail of running prey.

"I think we've seen the last of Lanasiet, my Lord," Jaalam said,
reining his gray up beside Ituralde, who shrugged slightly.

"Perhaps, my young friend. He may come to his senses. In any case,
I never thought the Taraboners would return to Arad Doman with us.
Did you?"

"No, my Lord," the taller man replied, "but I thought his honor
would hold through the first fight."

Ituralde lifted his glass to look at Lanasiet, still galloping hard.
The man was gone, and unlikely to come to senses he did not possess.
A third of his force gone as surely as if that *damane* had killed them. He
had counted on a few more days. He would need to change plans again,
perhaps change his next target.

Dismissing Lanasiet from his thoughts, he swung the glass to glance at where those people had been ridden down, and grunted in surprise. There were no trampled bodies. Friends and neighbors must have come out to carry them away, though with a battle on the edge of the village that seemed about as likely as them getting up and walking away after the horses passed.

"It's time to go burn all those lovely Seanchan stores," he said. Shoving the looking glass into the leather case tied to his saddle, he donned his helmet and heeled Steady down the hill, followed by Jaalam and the others in a column of twos. Ruts from farm wagons and broken-down banks indicated a ford in the eastern stream. "And, Jaalam, tell a few men to warn the villagers to start moving what they want to save. Tell them to begin with the houses nearest the camp." Where fire could spread one way, it could the other, too, and likely would.

In truth, he had already set the important blaze. Breathed on the first embers, at least. If the Light shone on him, if no one had been overcome by eagerness or given in to despair at the hold the Seanchan had on Tarabon, if no one had fallen afoul of the mishaps that could ruin the best laid plan, then all across Tarabon, above twenty thousand men had struck blows like this, or would before the day was out. And tomorrow they would do it again. Now all he had to do was raid his way back across better than four hundred miles of Tarabon, shedding Taraboner Dragonsworn and gathering in his own men, then re-cross Almoth Plain. If the Light shone on him, that blaze would singe the Seanchan enough to bring them chasing after him full of fury. A great deal of fury, he hoped. That way, they would run headlong into the trap he had laid before they ever knew it was there. If they failed to follow, then at least he had rid his homeland of the Taraboners and bound the Domani Dragonsworn to fight for the King instead of against him. And if they saw the trap. . . .

Riding down the hillside, Ituralde smiled. If they saw the trap, then he had another plan already laid, and another behind that. He always looked ahead, and always planned for every eventuality he could imagine, short of the Dragon Reborn himself suddenly appearing in front of him. He thought the plans he had would suffice for the moment.

The High Lady Suroth Sabelle Meldarath lay awake on her bed, staring up at the ceiling. The moon was down, and the triple-arched windows that overlooked a palace garden were dark, but her eyes had adjusted so that she could make out at least the outlines of the ornate, painted plasterwork. Dawn was no more than an hour or two off, yet she had not slept. She had lain awake most nights since Tuon vanished, sleeping only when exhaustion closed her eyes however hard she tried to keep them open. Sleep brought nightmares she wished she could forget. Ebou Dar was never truly cold, but the night held a little coolness, enough to help keep her awake, lying beneath only a thin silk sheet. The question that tainted her dreams was simple and stark. Was Tuon alive, or dead?

The escape of the Atha'an Miere *damane* and Queen Tylin's murder spoke in favor of her death. Three events of that magnitude happening on one night by chance was pressing coincidence too far, and the first two were horrifying enough in themselves to indicate the worst for Tuon. Someone was trying to sow fear among the *Rhyagelle*, Those Who Come Home, perhaps to disrupt the entire Return. How better to achieve that than to assassinate Tuon? Worse, it had to be one of their own. Because she had landed under the veil, no local knew who Tuon was. Tylin had surely been killed with the One Power, by a *sul'-dam* and her *damane*. Suroth had leaped at the suggestion that Aes Sedai were to blame, yet eventually someone who mattered would question how one of those women could enter a palace full of *damane* in a city full of *damane* and escape detection. At least one *sul'dam* had been necessary to uncollar the Sea Folk *damane*. And two of her own *sul'dam* had disappeared at almost the same time.

In any case, they had been noticed as missing two days later, and no one had seen them since the night Tuon vanished. She did not believe they were involved, though they had been in the kennels. For one thing, she could not imagine Renna or Seta uncollaring a *damane*. They certainly had reasons enough to sneak away and seek employment far off, with someone ignorant of their filthy secret, someone like this Egeanin Tamarath who had stolen a pair of *damane*. Strange that, for one newly raised to the Blood. Strange, but unimportant; she could see no way to tie it to the rest. Likely the woman had found the stresses and complexities of nobility too much for a simple sailor. Well, she would be found and arrested eventually.

The important fact, the potentially deadly fact, was that Renna and Seta were gone, and no one could say exactly when they had left. If the wrong person noted their departure so close to the critical time and made the wrong calculation. . . . She pressed the heels of her hands against her eyes and exhaled softly, very near to a groan.

Even should she escape suspicion of murdering Tuon, if the woman was dead, then she herself would be required to apologize to the Empress, might she live forever. For the death of the acknowledged heir to the Crystal Throne, her apology would be protracted, and as painful as it was humiliating; it might end with her execution, or much worse, with being sent to the block as property. Not that it would actually come to that, though in her nightmares it often did. Her hand slid beneath the pillows to touch the unsheathed dagger there. The blade was little longer than her hand, yet more than sharp enough to open her veins, preferably in a warm bath. If time came for an apology, she would not live to reach Seandar. The dishonor to her name might even be lessened a little if enough people believed the act was itself an apology. She would leave a letter explaining it so. That might help.

Still, there was a chance Tuon remained alive, and Suroth clung to it. Killing her and spiriting the body away might be a deep move ordered from Seanchan by one of her surviving sisters who coveted the throne, yet Tuon had arranged her own disappearance more than once. In support of the notion, Tuon's *der'sul'dam* had taken all of her *sul'dam* and *damane* into the country for exercise nine days ago, and they had not been seen since. Exercising *damane* did not require nine days. And just today—no; yesterday, now, by a good few hours—Suroth had learned that the captain of Tuon's bodyguard also had left the city nine days ago with a sizable contingent of his men and not returned. That was too much for coincidence, and very nearly proof. Near enough for hope, at least.

Each of those previous disappearances, however, had been part of Tuon's campaign to win the approval of the Empress, might she live forever, and be named heir. Each time, some competitor among her sisters had been forced or emboldened to acts that lowered her when Tuon reappeared. What need had she of such stratagems now, here? Rack her brains how she would, Suroth could not find a worthy target outside Seanchan. She had considered the possibility that she herself was the mark, but only briefly and only because she could think of no one else. Tuon could have stripped her of her position in the Return with three words. All she needed to do was remove the veil; here, the Daughter of the Nine Moons, in command of the Return, spoke with the voice of the Empire. Bare suspicion that Suroth was *Atha'an Shadar*, what those this side of the Aryth Ocean called a Darkfriend, might have been enough for Tuon to have handed her over to the Seekers for questioning. No, Tuon was aiming at someone else, or something else. If she did still live. But she had to. Suroth did not want to die. She fingered the blade.

Who or what else did not matter, except as a clue to where Tuon might be, but that was very important. Immensely so. Already, despite the announcement of an extended inspection trip, whispers floated among the Blood that she was dead. The longer she remained missing, the more those whispers would grow, and with them the pressure for Suroth to return to Seandar and make that apology. She could only resist so long before she would be adjudged *sei'mosiev* so deeply that only her own servants and property would obey her. Her eyes would be ground into the dirt. Low Blood as well as High, perhaps even commoners, would refuse to speak to her. Soon after that, she would find herself on a ship whatever her wishes.

Without doubt Tuon would be displeased at being found, yet it seemed unlikely her displeasure would extend so far as Suroth being dishonored and forced to slit her wrists; therefore Tuon *must* be found. Every Seeker in Altara was searching for her—those Suroth knew of, at least. Tuon's own Seekers were not among the known, yet they must be hunting twice as hard as any others. Unless they had been taken into her confidence. But in seventeen days, all that had been uncovered was that ridiculous story of Tuon extorting jewelry from goldsmiths, and that was known to every common soldier. Perhaps. . . .

The arched door to the anteroom began to open slowly, and Suroth snapped her right eye shut to protect her night vision against the light of the outer room. As soon as the gap was wide enough, a pale-haired woman in the diaphanous robes of a *da'covale* slipped into the bedchamber and softly closed the door behind her, plunging the room into pitch blackness. Until Suroth opened her eye again, and made out a shadowy form creeping toward her bed. And another shadow, huge, suddenly looming in a corner of the room as Almandaragal rose noiselessly to his feet. The *lopar* could cross the room and snap the fool woman's neck in a heartbeat, but Suroth still gripped the hilt of her dagger. It was wise to have a second line of defense even when the first seemed impregnable. A pace short of the bed, the *da'covale* stopped. Her anxious breathing sounded loud in the silence.

"Working up your courage, Liandrin?" Suroth said harshly. That honey-colored hair, worked in thin braids, had been enough to name her.

With a squeak, the *da'covale* dropped to her knees and bent to press her face to the carpet. She had learned that much, at least. "I would not harm you, High Lady," she lied. "You know I would not." Her voice was rushed, in a breathy panic. Learning when to speak and when not seemed as far beyond her as learning how to speak with proper respect. "We are both bound to serve the Great Lord, High Lady. Have I not proven I can be useful? I removed Alwhin for you, yes? You said you wished her dead, High Lady, and I removed her."

Suroth grimaced and sat up in the dark, the sheet sliding down to her lap. It was so easy to forget *da'covale* were there, even this *da'covale*, and then you let slip things you should not have. Alwhin had not been dangerous, merely a nuisance, awkward in her place as Suroth's Voice. She had achieved all she had ever wanted in reaching that, and the likelihood of her risking it by so much as the smallest betrayal had been tiny. True, had she broken her neck falling down a flight of stairs, Suroth would have felt some small relief from an irritant, but poison that left the woman with bulging eyes and a blue face was another matter. Even with the search for Tuon, that had brought the Seekers' eyes to Suroth's household. She had been forced to insist on it, for the murder of her Voice. That there were Listeners in her household, she accepted; every household had its share of Listeners. Seekers did more than listen, though, and they might uncover what must remain hidden.

Masking her anger required surprising effort, and her tone was colder than she wanted. "I hope you did not wake me merely to plead again, Liandrin."

"No, no!" The fool raised her head and actually looked straight at her! "An officer came from General Galgan, High Lady. He is waiting to take you to the general."

Suroth's head throbbed with irritation. The woman delayed delivering a message from Galgan *and* looked her in the eyes? In the dark, to be sure, yet an urge swept over her to strangle Liandrin with her bare hands. A second death hard on the heels of the first would intensify the Seekers' interest in her household, if they learned of it, but Elbar could dispose of the body easily; he was clever in such tasks.

Except, she enjoyed owning the former Aes Sedai who once had been so haughty with her. Making her a perfect *da'covale* in every way would be a great pleasure. It was time to have the woman collared, however. Already irritating rumors buzzed of an uncollared *marath'-damane* among her servants. It would be a twelve-day wonder when the *sul'dam* discovered she was shielded in some way so she could not channel, yet that would help answer the question of why she had not been leashed before. Elbar would need to find some *Atha'an Shadar* among the *sul'dam*, though. That was never an easy task—relatively few *sul'-dam* turned to the Great Lord, oddly—and she no longer really trusted any *sul'dam*, but perhaps *Atha'an Shadar* could be trusted more than the rest.

"Light two lamps, then bring me a robe and slippers," she said, swinging her legs over the side of the bed.

Liandrin scrambled to the table that held the lidded sand bowl on its gilded tripod and hissed when she found it with a careless hand, but she quickly used the tongs to lift out a hot coal, puffed it to a glow, and lit two of the silvered lamps, adjusting the wicks so the flames held steady and did not smoke. Her tongue might suggest that she felt herself Suroth's equal rather than a possession, yet the strap had taught her to obey commands with alacrity.

Turning with one of the lamps in her hand, she gave a start and a choked cry at the sight of Almandaragal looming in the corner, his dark, ridge-ringed eyes focused on her. You would think she had never seen him before! Yet he was a fearsome sight, ten feet tall and near two thousand pounds, his hairless skin like reddish brown leather, flexing his six-toed forepaws so his claws extended and retracted, extended and retracted.

"Be at ease," Suroth told the *lopar*, a familiar command, but he stretched his mouth wide, showing sharp teeth before settling back to the floor and resting his huge round head on his paws like a hound. He did not close his eyes again, either. *Lopar* were quite intelligent, and plainly he trusted Liandrin no more than she did.

Despite fearful glances at Almandaragal, the *da'covale* was quick enough to fetch blue velvet slippers and a white silk robe intricately embroidered in green, red and blue from the tall, carved wardrobe, and she held the robe for Suroth to thrust her arms into the sleeves, but Suroth had to tie the long sash herself, and to thrust out a foot before Liandrin remembered to kneel and fit the slippers on. Her eyes, but the woman was incompetent!

By the dim light, Suroth examined herself in the gilded stand-mirror against the wall. Her eyes were hollow and shadowed with

weariness, the tail of her crest hung down her back in a loose braid for
sleeping, and doubtless her scalp required a razor. Very well. Galgan's
messenger would think her grief-stricken over Tuon, and that was true
enough. Before learning the general's message, though, she had one
small matter to take care of.

"Run to Rosala and beg her to beat you soundly, Liandrin," she said.

The *da'covale's* tight little mouth dropped open and her eyes widened
in shock. "But why?" she whined. "Me, I have done nothing!"

Suroth busied her hands with knotting the sash tighter to keep
from striking the woman. Her eyes would be lowered for a month if it
was learned that she had struck a *da'covale* herself. She certainly owed
no explanations to property, yet once Liandrin did become completely
trained, she would miss these opportunities to grind the woman's face
in how far she had fallen.

"Because you delayed telling me of the general's messenger. Because you still call yourself 'I' rather than 'Liandrin.' Because you meet
my eyes." She could not help hissing that. Liandrin had huddled in on
herself with every word, and now she directed her eyes to the floor, as if
that would mitigate her offense. "Because you questioned my orders
instead of obeying. And last—last, but most importantly to you—
because I wish you beaten. Now, run, and tell Rosala each of these reasons so she will beat you well."

"Liandrin hears and obeys, High Lady," the *da'covale* whimpered, at
last getting something right, and flung herself at the door so fast that
she lost one of her white slippers. Too terrified to turn back for it, or
perhaps even to notice—and well for her that she was—she clawed the
door open and ran. Sending property for discipline should not bring a
sense of satisfaction, but it did. Oh, yes, it did.

Suroth took a moment to control her breathing. To appear to be
grieving was one thing, to appear to be agitated quite another. She was
filled with annoyance at Liandrin, jolting memories of her nightmares,
fears for Tuon's fate and even more so her own, but not until the face in
the mirror displayed utter calm did she follow the *da'covale*.

The anteroom to her bedchamber was decorated in the garish Ebou
Dari fashion, a cloud-painted blue ceiling, yellow walls and green and
yellow floor tiles. Even replacing the furnishings with her own tall
screens, all save two painted by the finest artists with birds or flowers,
did little to relieve the gaudiness. She growled faintly in her throat at
sight of the outer door, apparently left open by Liandrin in her flight,

but she dismissed the *da'covale* from her mind for the moment and concentrated on the man who stood there examining the screen that held the image of a kori, a huge spotted cat from the Sen T'jore. Lanky and graying, in armor striped blue-and-yellow, he pivoted smoothly at the soft sound of her footsteps and went to one knee, though he was a commoner. The helmet beneath his arm bore three slender blue plumes, so the message must be important. Of course, it must be important to disturb her at this hour. She would give him dispensation. This once.

"Banner-General Mikhel Najirah, High Lady. Captain-General Galgan's compliments, and he has received communications from Tarabon."

Suroth's eyebrows climbed in spite of herself. Tarabon? Tarabon was as secure as Seandar. Automatically her fingers twitched, but she had not yet found a replacement for Alwhin. She must speak to the man herself. Irritation over that hardened her voice, and she made no effort to soften it. Kneeling instead of prostrate! "What communications? If I have been wakened for news of Aiel, I will not be pleased, Banner-General."

Her tone failed to intimidate the man. He even raised his eyes almost to meet hers. "Not Aiel, High Lady," he said calmly. "Captain-General Galgan wishes to tell you himself, so you can hear every detail correctly."

Suroth's breath caught for an instant. Whether Najirah was just reluctant to tell her the contents of these communications or had been ordered not to, this sounded ill. "Lead on," she commanded, then swept out of the room without waiting for him, ignoring as best she could the pair of Deathwatch Guards standing like statues in the hallway to either side of the door. The "honor" of being guarded by those men in red-and-green armor made her skin crawl. Since Tuon's disappearance, she tried not to see them at all.

The corridor, lined with gilded stand-lamps whose flames flickered in errant drafts that stirred tapestries of ships and the sea, was empty except for a few liveried palace servants, scurrying on early tasks, who thought deep bows and curtsies sufficient. And they always looked right at her! Perhaps a word with Beslan? No; the new King of Altara was her equal, now, in law at any rate, and she doubted that he would make his servants behave properly. She stared straight ahead as she walked. That way, she did not have to see the servants' insults.

Najirah caught up to her quickly, his boots ringing on the too-bright blue floor tiles, and fell in at her side. In truth, she needed no guide. She knew where Galgan must be.

The room had begun as a chamber for dancing, a square thirty paces on a side, its ceiling painted with fanciful fish and birds frolicking in often confusing fashion among clouds and waves. Only the ceiling remained to recall the room's beginnings. Now mirrored stand-lamps and shelves full of filed reports in leather folders lined the pale red walls. Brown-coated clerks scurried along the aisles between the long, map-strewn tables that covered the green-tiled dancing-floor. A young officer, an under-lieutenant with no plume on her red-and-yellow helmet, raced past Suroth without so much as a move to prostrate herself. Clerks merely squeezed themselves out of her path. Galgan gave his people too much leeway. He claimed that what he called excessive ceremony at "the wrong time" hindered efficiency; she called it effrontery.

Lunal Galgan, a tall man in a red robe richly worked with bright-feathered birds, the hair of his crest snow white and its tail plaited in a tight but untidy queue that hung to his shoulders, stood at a table near the center of the room with a knot of other high-ranking officers, some in breastplates, others in robes and nearly as disheveled as she. It seemed she was not the first to whom he had sent a messenger. She struggled to keep anger from her face. Galgan had come with Tuon and the Return, and thus she knew little of him beyond that his ancestors had been among the first to throw their support to Luthair Paendrag and that he owned a high reputation as a soldier and a general. Well, reputation and truth were sometimes the same. She disliked him entirely for himself.

He turned at her approach and formally laid his hands on her shoulders, kissing her on either cheek, so she was forced to return the greeting while trying not to wrinkle her nose at the strong, musky scent he favored. Galgan's face was as smooth as his creases would allow, but she thought she detected a hint of worry in his blue eyes. A number of the men and women behind him, mainly low Blood and commoners, wore open frowns.

The large map of Tarabon spread out on the table in front of her and held flat by four lamps gave reason enough for worry. Markers covered it, red wedges for Seanchan forces on the move and red stars for forces holding in place, each supporting a small paper banner inked with their numbers and composition. Scattered across the map, across the entire map, lay black discs marking engagements, and even more white discs for enemy forces, many of those without the banners. How could there be *any* enemies in Tarabon? It was as secure as. . . .

"What happened?" she demanded.

"*Raken* began arriving with reports from Lieutenant-General Turan about three hours ago," Galgan began in conversational tones. Pointedly *not* making a report himself. He studied the map as he talked, never glancing in her direction. "They aren't complete—each new one adds to the lists, and I expect that won't change for a while—but what I've seen runs this way. Since dawn yesterday, seven major supply camps overrun and burned, along with more than two dozen smaller camps. Twenty supply trains attacked, the wagons and their contents put to the torch. Seventeen small outposts have been wiped out, eleven patrols have failed to report in, and there have been an additional fifteen skirmishes. Also a few attacks against our settlers. Only a handful of fatalities, mostly men who tried to defend their belongings, but a good many wagons and stores burned along with some half-built houses, and the same message delivered everywhere. Leave Tarabon. All this was done by bands of between two and perhaps five hundred men. Estimates are a minimum of ten thousand and perhaps twice that, nearly all Taraboners. Oh, yes," he finished casually, "and most of them are wearing armor painted with stripes."

She wanted to grind her teeth. Galgan commanded the soldiers of the Return, yet she commanded the *Hailene*, the Forerunners, and as such, she possessed the higher rank in spite of his crest and red-lacquered fingernails. She suspected the only reason he did not claim that the Forerunners had been absorbed into the Return by its very arrival was that supplanting her meant assuming responsibility for Tuon's safety. And for that apology, should it become necessary. "Dislike" was too mild a word. She loathed Galgan.

"A mutiny?" she said, proud of the coolness of her voice. Inside, she had begun to burn.

Galgan's white queue swung slowly as he shook his head. "No. All reports say our Taraboners have fought well, and we've had a few successes, taken a few prisoners. Not one of them can be found on the rosters of loyal Taraboners. Several have been identified as Dragonsworn believed to be up in Arad Doman. And the name Rodel Ituralde has been mentioned a number of times as the brain behind it all, and the leader. A Domani. He's supposed to be one of the best generals this side of the ocean, and if he planned and carried out all this," he swept a hand over the map, "then I believe it." The fool sounded admiring! "Not a mutiny. A raid on a grand scale. But he won't get out with nearly as many men as he brought in."

Dragonsworn. The word was like a fist clutching Suroth's throat. "Are there Asha'man?"

"Those fellows who can channel?" Galgan grimaced and made a sign against evil, apparently unconscious of doing so. "There was no mention of them," he said drily, "and I rather think there would have been."

Red-hot anger needed to erupt at Galgan, but screaming at another of the High Blood would lower her eyes. And, as bad, gain nothing. Still, it had to be directed somewhere. It had to come out. She was proud of what she had done in Tarabon, and now the country appeared to be halfway back to the chaos she found when she first landed there. And one man was to blame. "This Ituralde." Her tone was ice. "I want his head!"

"Never fear," Galgan murmured, folding his hands behind his back and bending to examine some of the small banners. "It won't be long before Turan chases him back to Arad Doman with his tail between his legs, and with luck, he'll be with one of the bands we snap up."

"Luck?" she snapped. "I don't trust to luck!" Her anger was open, now, and she did not consider trying to suppress it again. Her eyes scanned the map as though she could find Ituralde that way. "If Turan is hunting a hundred bands, as you suggest, he'll need more scouts to run them down, and I want them run down. Every last one of them. Especially Ituralde. General Yulan, I want four in every five—no, nine in every ten *raken* in Altara and Amadicia moved to Tarabon. If Turan can't find them all with that, then he can see if his own head will appease me."

Yulan, a dark little man in a blue robe embroidered with black-crested eagles, must have dressed in too great a hurry to apply the gum that normally held his wig in place, because he was constantly touching the thing to make sure it was straight. He was Captain of the Air for the Forerunners, but the Return's Captain of the Air was only a banner-general, a more senior man having died on the voyage. Yulan would have no trouble with him.

"A wise move, High Lady," he said, frowning at the map, "but may

I suggest leaving the *raken* in Amadicia and those assigned to Banner-General Khirgan. *Raken* are the best way we have to locate Aiel, and in two days we still haven't found those Whitecloaks. That will still give General Turan—"

"The Aiel are less of a problem every day," she told him firmly, "and a few deserters are nothing." He inclined his head in assent, one hand keeping his wig in place. He was only low Blood, after all.

"I hardly call seven thousand men a few deserters," Galgan murmured dryly.

"It shall be as I command!" she snapped. Curse those so-called Children of the Light! She still had not decided whether to make Asunawa and the few thousand who had remained *da'covale*. They had remained, yet how long before they offered betrayal, too? And Asunawa seemed to hate *damane*, of all things. The man was unbalanced!

Galgan shrugged, utterly unperturbed. A red-lacquered fingernail traced lines on the map as though he were planning movements of soldiers. "So long as you don't want the *to'raken*, too, I raise no objections. That plan must go forward. Altara is falling into our hands with barely a struggle, I'm not ready to move on Illian yet, and we need to pacify Tarabon again quickly. The people will turn against us if we can't give them safety."

Suroth began to regret letting her anger show. He would raise no *objections*? *He* was not ready for Illian yet? He was all but saying that he did not have to follow her orders, only not openly, not so he had to take her responsibility along with her authority.

"I expect this message to be sent to Turan, General Galgan." Her voice was steady, kept so by will alone. "He is to send me Rodel Ituralde's head if he has to hound the man across Arad Doman and into the Blight. And if he fails to send me that head, I *will* take his."

Galgan's mouth tightened briefly, and he frowned down at the map. "Turan sometimes needs a fire lit under him," he muttered, "and Arad Doman has always been next for him. Very well. Your message will be sent, Suroth."

She could stay no longer in the same room with him. Without a word, she left. Had she spoken, she *would* have screamed. She stalked all the way back to her rooms without bothering to mask her fury. The Deathwatch Guards took no notice, of course; they might as well have been carved of stone. Which made her slam the anteroom door behind her with a crash. Perhaps they noticed that!

Padding toward her bed, she kicked off her slippers, let the robe and sash fall to the floor. She must find Tuon. She *had* to. If only she could puzzle out Tuon's target, puzzle out where she was. If only—

Suddenly the walls of her bedchamber, the ceiling, even the floor, began to glow with a silvery light. Those surfaces seemed to have *become* light. Gaping in shock, she turned slowly, staring at the box of light that surrounded her, and found herself looking at a woman made of roiling flames, clothed in roiling flames. Almandaragal was on his feet, awaiting his owner's command to attack.

"I am Semirhage," the woman of fire said in a voice like a tolling funeral gong.

"Belly, Almandaragal!" That command, taught as a child because it amused her to have the *lopar* prostrate himself before her, ended with a grunt because she obeyed it herself even as she gave it. Kissing the red-and-green-patterned carpet, she said, "I live to serve and obey, Great Mistress." There was no doubt in her mind that this woman was who she said. Who would dare claim *that* name falsely? Or could appear as living fire?

"I think you would also like to rule." The tolling gong sounded faintly amused, but then it hardened. "Look at me! I dislike the way you Seanchan avoid meeting my eyes. It makes me believe you are hiding something. You don't want to try hiding anything from me, Suroth."

"Of course not, Great Mistress," Suroth said, pushing herself up to sit on her heels. "Never, Great Mistress." She raised her gaze as far as the other woman's mouth, but she could not make herself raise it higher. Surely that would be enough.

"Better," Semirhage murmured. "Now. How would you like to rule in these lands? A handful of deaths—Galgan and a few others—and you could manage to name yourself Empress, with my help. It's hardly important, but circumstances provide the opportunity, and you would certainly be more amenable than the current Empress has been so far."

Suroth's stomach clenched. She feared she might vomit. "Great Mistress," she said dully, "the penalty for that is to be taken before the true Empress, may she live forever, and have your entire skin removed, great care being taken to keep you alive. After that—"

"Inventive, if primitive," Semirhage broke in wryly. "But of no account. The Empress Radhanan is dead. Remarkable how much blood there is in a human body. Enough to cover the whole Crystal Throne.

Take the offer, Suroth. I will not make it again. You will make certain matters slightly more convenient, but not enough for me to put myself out a second time."

Suroth had to make herself breathe. "Then Tuon is the Empress, may she live. . . ." Tuon would take a new name, rarely to be spoken outside the Imperial family. The Empress was the Empress, might she live forever. Wrapping her arms around herself, Suroth began to sob, shaking beyond her ability to stop. Almandaragal lifted his head and whined at her interrogatively.

Semirhage laughed, the music of deep gongs. "Grief for Radhanan, Suroth, or is your dislike of Tuon becoming Empress so deep?"

Haltingly, in spurts of three or four words broken by unmanageable weeping, Suroth explained. As the proclaimed heir, Tuon had become Empress the moment her mother died. Except, if her mother had been assassinated, then it must have been arranged by one of her sisters, which meant that Tuon herself was surely dead. And none of that made the slightest difference. The forms would be carried out. She would have to return to Seandar and apologize for Tuon's death, for the death of an Empress, now, to the very woman who had arranged it. Who would, of course, not take the throne until Tuon's death was announced. She could not bring herself to admit that she would kill herself first; it was too shaming to say aloud. Words died as howling sobs racked her. She did not want to die. She had been promised she would live forever!

This time, Semirhage's laughter was so shocking that it shut off Suroth's tears. That head of fire was thrown back, emitting great peals of mirth. At last she regained control, wiping away tears of flame with fiery fingers. "I see I didn't make myself clear. Radhanan is dead, and her daughters, and her sons, and half the Imperial Court, as well. There *is* no Imperial family except for Tuon. There is no Empire. Seandar is in the hands of rioters and looters, and so are a dozen other cities. At least fifty nobles are contending for the throne, with armies in the field. There is war from the Aldael Mountains to Salaking. Which is why you will be perfectly safe in disposing of Tuon and proclaiming yourself Empress. I've even arranged for a ship, which should arrive soon, to bring word of the disaster." She laughed again, and said something strange. "Let the lord of chaos rule."

Suroth gaped at the other woman in spite of herself. The Empire . . . destroyed? Semirhage had killed the . . . ? Assassination was not unknown among the Blood, High or low, nor within the Imperial family, yet for anyone else to reach inside the Imperial family in that way was horrifying, unthinkable. Even one of the *Da'concion*, the Chosen Ones. But to become Empress herself, even here. She felt dizzy, with a hysterical desire to laugh. She could complete the cycle, conquering these lands, and then send armies to reclaim Seanchan. With an effort, she managed to regain possession of herself.

"Great Mistress, if Tuon really is alive, then . . . then killing her will be difficult." She had to force those words out. To kill the Empress . . . Even thinking it was difficult. To become Empress. Her head felt as if it might float off her shoulders. "She will have her *sul'dam* and *damane* with her, and some of her Deathwatch Guards." Difficult? Killing her would be impossible in those circumstances. Unless Semirhage could be induced to do it herself. Six *damane* might well be dangerous even to her. Besides, there was a saying among commoners. The mighty tell the lesser to dig in the mud and keep their own hands clean. She had heard it by chance, and punished the man who spoke it, but it was true.

"Think, Suroth!" The gongs rang strong, imperative. "Captain Musenge and the others would have gone the same night Tuon and her maid left if they had had any inkling of what she was about. They are looking for her. You must put every effort into finding her first, but if that fails, her Deathwatch Guards will be less protection than they seem. Every soldier in your army has heard that at least some of the Guards are involved with an impostor. The general feeling seems to be that the impostor and anyone connected to her should be torn apart bodily and the pieces buried in a dungheap. Quietly." Lips of fire curled in a small, amused smile. "To avoid the shame to the Empire."

It might be possible. A party of Deathwatch Guards would be easy to locate. She would need to find out exactly how many Musenge had taken with him, and send Elbar with fifty for every one. No, a hundred, to account for the *damane*. And then . . . "Great Mistress, you understand I am reluctant to proclaim anything until I am certain Tuon is dead?"

"Of course," Semirhage said. The gongs were amused once more. "But remember, if Tuon manages to return safely, it will matter little to me, so don't dally."

"I will not, Great Mistress. I intend to become Empress, and for that I must kill the Empress." This time, saying it was not very hard at all.

In Pevara's estimation, Tsutama Rath's rooms were flamboyant beyond the point of extravagance, and her own beginnings as a butcher's daughter played no part in her opinion. The sitting room simply put her on edge. Beneath a cornice carved with swallows in flight and gilded, the walls held two large silk tapestries, one displaying bright red bloodroses, the other a calma bush covered in scarlet blossoms larger than her two hands together. The tables and chairs were delicate pieces, if you ignored sufficient carving and gilding for any throne. The stand-lamps were heavily gilded, too, and the mantel, worked with running horses, above the red-streaked marble fireplace. Several of the tables held red Sea Folk porcelain, the rarest, four vases and six bowls, a small fortune in themselves, as well as any number of jade or ivory carvings, none small, and one figure of a dancing woman, a hand tall, that appeared be carved from a *ruby*. A gratuitous display of wealth, and she knew for a fact that aside from the gilded barrel-clock on the mantel, there was another in Tsutama's bedroom and even one in her dressing room. Three clocks! That went far beyond flamboyant, never mind gilding or rubies.

And yet, the room suited the woman seated across from her and Javindhra. "Flamboyant" was exactly the word for her appearance. Tsutama was a strikingly beautiful woman, her hair caught in a fine golden net, with firedrops thick at her throat and ears and dressed as always in crimson silk that molded her full bosom, today with golden scrollwork embroidery to increase the emphasis. You might almost think she wanted to attract men, if you did not know her. Tsutama had made her dislike of men well known long before being sent into exile; she would have given mercy to a rabid dog before a man.

Back then, she had been hammer-hard, yet many had thought her a broken reed when she returned to the Tower. For a while, they had. Then everyone who spent any time near her realized that those shifting eyes were far from nervous. Exile *had* changed her, only not toward softness. Those eyes belonged on a hunting cat, searching for enemies or prey. The rest of Tsutama's face was not so much serene as it was still, an unreadable mask. Unless you pushed her to open anger, at least. Even then her voice would remain as calm as smooth ice, though. An unnerving combination.

"I heard disturbing rumors this morning about the battle at Dumai's Wells," she said abruptly. "Bloody disturbing." She had the habits now of long silences, no small talk, and sudden, unexpected statements. Exile had coarsened her language, too. The isolated farm she had been confined to must have been . . . vivid. "Including that three of the dead sisters were from our Ajah. Mother's milk in a cup!" All delivered in the most even tones. But her eyes stabbed at them accusingly.

Pevara took that gaze in stride. Any direct look from Tsutama seemed accusing, and on edge or not, Pevara knew better than to let the Highest see it. The woman swooped on weakness like a falcon. "I can't see why Katerine would disobey your orders to keep her knowledge to herself, and you cannot believe Tarna is likely to put discredit on Elaida." Not publicly, at any rate. Tarna guarded her feelings on Elaida as carefully as a cat guarded a mousehole. "But sisters do get reports from their eyes-and-ears. We can't stop them learning what happened. I'm surprised it's taken this long."

"That's so," Javindhra added, smoothing her skirts. The angular woman wore no jewelry aside from the Great Serpent ring, and her dress was unadorned, and a red deep enough to appear near black. "Sooner or later, the facts will all come out if we work till our fingers bleed." Her mouth was so tight she seemed to be biting something, yet she sounded almost satisfied. Odd, that. She was Elaida's lapdog.

Tsutama's stare focused on her, and after a moment a flush grew on Javindhra's cheeks. Perhaps as an excuse to break eye contact, she took a long drink of her tea. From a cup of beaten gold worked with leopards and deer, of course, Tsutama being as she now was. The Highest continued to stare silently, but whether at Javindhra or something beyond her, Pevara could no longer say.

When Katerine brought word that Galina was among the dead at Dumai's Wells, Tsutama had been raised to replace her by near acclamation. She had possessed a very good reputation as a Sitter, at least before her involvement in the disgusting events that led to her downfall, and many in the Red believed the times called for as hard a Highest as could be found. Galina's death had lifted a great weight from Pevara's shoulders—the Highest, a Darkfriend; oh, that had been agony!—yet she was uncertain about Tsutama. There was something . . . wild . . .

about her, now. Something unpredictable. Was she entirely sane? But then, the same question could be asked regarding the whole White Tower. How many of the sisters were entirely sane, now?

As if sensing her thoughts, Tsutama shifted that unblinking gaze to her. It did not make Pevara color or start, as it did so many besides Javindhra, but she did find herself wishing Duhara were there, just to give the Highest a third Sitter to stare at, just to share them out. She wished she knew where the woman had gone and why, with a rebel army camped outside Tar Valon. Over a week ago, Duhara had simply taken ship without a word to anyone, so far as Pevara was aware, and no one seemed to know whether she had gone north or south. These days, Pevara was suspicious of everyone and nearly everything.

"Did you call us here because of something in that letter, Highest?" she said at last. She met that unsettling stare levelly, yet she was beginning to want a long pull from her own ornate cup, and she wished it held wine rather than tea. Deliberately she rested the cup on the narrow arm of her chair. The other woman's gaze made her feel as though spiders were crawling on her skin.

After a very long moment, Tsutama's eyes dropped to the folded letter in her lap. Only her hand held it from rolling up into a little cylinder. It was on the very thin paper used for messages sent by pigeon, and the small inked letters clearly visible through the page appeared to cover it densely.

"This is from Sashalle Anderly," she said, bringing a wince of pity from Pevara and a grunt that might have been anything from Javindhra. Poor Sashalle. Tsutama continued without any outward sign of sympathy, though. "The bloody woman believes Galina escaped, because it is addressed to her. Much of what she writes merely confirms what we already know from other sources, including Toveine. But, without naming them, she bloody well says that she is 'in charge of most of the sisters in the city of Cairhien.'"

"How can Sashalle be in charge of *any* sisters?" Javindhra shook her head, her expression denying the possibility. "Could she have gone insane?"

Pevara held her silence. Tsutama gave answers when she wished, rarely when you asked. Toveine's earlier letter, also addressed to Galina, had not mentioned Sashalle at all, or the other two, but of course, she would have found the entire subject beyond distasteful.

Even thinking of it was like eating rotten plums. Most of her words had been devoted to laying the whole blame for events at Elaida's feet, however indirectly.

Tsutama's eyes flickered toward Javindhra like dagger thrusts, but she went on without pausing. "Sashalle recounts Toveine's bloody visit to Cairhien with the other sisters and the flaming Asha'man, though she clearly doesn't know about the bloody bonding. She found it all very strange, sisters mingling with Asha'man on 'tense yet often friendly' terms. Blood and bloody ashes! That is how she puts it, burn me." Tsutama's tone, suitable for discussing the price of lace, in strong contrast to the intensity of her eyes, and her language, gave no hint of what she felt on the subject. "Sashalle says that when they left, they took flaming Warders belonging to sisters she believes are with the boy, so it seems bloody certain they were looking for him and likely have found him by now. She has no idea why. But she confirms what Toveine claimed concerning Logain. Apparently, the bloody man is no longer gentled."

"Impossible," Javindhra muttered into her teacup, but softly. Tsutama disliked having her statements challenged. Pevara kept her opinions to herself and sipped from her own cup. So far, there seemed nothing in the letter worthy of discussion except how Sashalle could be "in charge" of anything, and she would rather think of anything other than Sashalle's fate. The tea tasted of blueberries. How had Tsutama obtained blueberries this early in the spring? Perhaps they had been dried.

"I will read the rest to you," Tsutama said, unfolding the page and scanning almost to the bottom before beginning. Apparently Sashalle had been very detailed. What was the Highest not sharing? So many suspicions.

> "I have been so long without communicating because I could not work out how to say what I must, but now I see that simply telling the facts is the only way. Along with a number of other sisters, who I will leave to decide for themselves whether to reveal what I am about to, I have sworn an oath of fealty to the Dragon Reborn which is to last until Tarmon Gai'don has been fought."

Javindhra gasped loudly, her eyes popping, but Pevara merely whispered, "*Ta'veren.*" It must be that. *Ta'veren* had always been her explanation for most of the disturbing rumors out of Cairhien.

Tsutama read on right over them.

"What I do, I do for the good of the Red Ajah and the good of the Tower. Should you disagree, I will surrender myself for your discipline. After Tarmon Gai'don. As you may have heard, Irgain Fatamed, Ronaille Vevanios and I were all stilled when the Dragon Reborn escaped at Dumai's Wells. We have been Healed, however, by a man named Damer Flinn, one of the Asha'man, and we all seem to be restored fully. Unlikely as this seems, I swear beneath the Light and by my hope of salvation and rebirth that it is true. I look forward to my eventual return to the Tower, where I will retake the Three Oaths to reaffirm my dedication to my Ajah and to the Tower."

Folding the letter again, she gave her head a small shake. "There's more, but it's all more bloody pleading that what she's doing is for the Ajah and the Tower." A glitter in her eyes suggested that Sashalle might come to regret surviving the Last Battle.

"If Sashalle truly has been Healed," Pevara began, and could not go on. She wet her lips with tea, then raised the cup again and took a mouthful. The possibility seemed too wonderful to hope for, a snowflake that might melt at a touch.

"This is impossible," Javindhra growled, though not very strongly. Even so, she directed the comment to Pevara lest the Highest think it meant for her. A deep scowl made her face harsher. "Gentling cannot be Healed. Stilling cannot be Healed. Sheep will fly first! Sashalle *must* be delusional."

"Toveine might be mistaken," Tsutama said, in a *very* strong voice, "though if she is, I can't see why these flaming Asha'man would let Logain be one of them, much less command, but I hardly think Sashalle could be bloody mistaken about herself. And she doesn't write like a woman having flaming delusions. Sometimes what is bloody impossible is only bloody impossible until the first woman does it. So. Stilling has been Healed. By a man. Those flaming Seanchan locusts are chaining every woman they find who can channel, apparently including a number of sisters. Twelve days past . . . Well, you know what happened as bloody well as I. The world has become a more dangerous place than at any time since the Trolloc Wars, perhaps since the Breaking itself. Therefore I've decided we will move forward with your scheme for these flaming Asha'man, Pevara. Distasteful and hazardous, yet burn me, there is no bloody choice. You and Javindhra will arrange it together."

Pevara winced. Not for the Seanchan. They were human, whatever strange *ter'angreal* they possessed, and they would be defeated eventually. Mention of what the Forsaken had done twelve days ago brought a grimace, though, despite her efforts at keeping a smooth face. So much of the Power wielded in one place could have been no one else. To the extent she could, she avoided thinking about that or what they might have been trying to accomplish. Or worse, what they might have accomplished. A second wince came at hearing the proposal to bond Asha'man named as hers. But that had been inevitable from the moment she presented Tarna's suggestion to Tsutama, while holding her breath against the eruption she was sure would come. She had even used the argument of increasing the size of linked circles by including men, against that monstrous display of the Power. Surprisingly, there had been no eruption, and small reaction of any kind. Tsutama merely said she would think on it, and insisted on having the relevant papers about men and circles delivered to her from the Library. The third wince, the largest, was for having to work with Javindhra, for being saddled with the job at all. She had more than enough on her plate at the moment, besides which, working with Javindhra was always painful. The woman argued against anything put forward by anyone save herself. Nearly anything.

Javindhra had been vehemently against bonding Asha'man, horrified at the notion of Red sisters bonding anyone almost as much as at bonding men who could channel, yet now that the Highest had commanded it, she was stymied. Still, she found a way to argue against. "Elaida will never allow it," she muttered.

Tsutama's glittering eyes caught her gaze and held it. The bony woman swallowed audibly.

"Elaida will not know until it is too late, Javindhra. I hide her secrets—the disaster against the Black Tower, Dumai's Wells—as best I can because she was raised from the Red, but she is the Amyrlin Seat, of all Ajahs and none. That means she is no longer Red, and this is Ajah business, not hers." A dangerous tone entered her voice. And she had not cursed once. That meant she was on the edge of open fury. "Do you disagree with me on this? Do you intend to inform Elaida despite my express wishes?"

"No, Highest," Javindhra replied quickly, then buried her face in her cup. Strangely, she seemed to be hiding a smile.

Pevara contented herself with shaking her head. If it had to be done, and she was certain it must, then clearly Elaida had to be kept in the dark. What did Javindhra have to smile about? Too many suspicions.

"I'm very glad that you both agree with me," Tsutama said dryly, leaning back in her chair. "Now, leave me."

They paused only to set down their cups and curtsy. In the Red, when the Highest spoke, everyone obeyed, including Sitters. The sole exception, by Ajah law, was voting in the Hall, though some women who held the title had managed to insure that any vote near to their hearts went as they wished. Pevara was certain Tsutama intended to be one such. The struggle was going to be distinctly unpleasant. She only hoped she could give as good as she got.

In the corridor outside, Javindhra muttered something about correspondence and rushed off down the white floor tiles marked with the red Flame of Tar Valon before Pevara could say a word. Not that she had intended to say anything, but surely as peaches were poison, the woman was going to drag her heels in this and leave the whole matter in her lap. Light, but this was the last thing she needed, at the worst possible time.

Pausing at her own rooms only long enough to gather her long-fringed shawl and check the hour—a quarter of an hour to noon; she was almost disappointed that her one clock agreed with Tsutama's; clocks frequently did not—she left the Red quarters and hurried deeper into the Tower, down into the common areas below the quarters. The wide hallways were well lighted with mirrored stand-lamps but almost empty of people, which made them seem cavernous and the frieze-banded white walls stark. The occasional rippling of a bright tapestry in a draft had an eerie feel, as though the silk or wool had taken on life. The few people she saw were serving men and women with the Flame of Tar Valon on their chests, scurrying along about their chores and barely pausing long enough to offer hurried courtesies. They kept their eyes lowered. With the Ajahs separated into all but warring camps, fetid tension and antagonism filled the Tower, and the mood had infected the servants. Frightened them, at least.

She could not be sure, but she thought fewer than two hundred sisters remained in the Tower, most keeping to their Ajah quarters except for necessity, so she really did not expect to see another sister strolling. When Adelorna Bastine glided up the short stairs from a crossing corridor almost right in front of her, she was so surprised she gave a start. Adelorna, who made slimness appear stately despite her lack of height, walked on without acknowledging Pevara in any way. The Saldaean woman wore her shawl, too—no sister was seen outside her Ajah quarters without her shawl, now—and was followed by her three Warders. Short and tall, wide and lean, they wore their swords, and their eyes never ceased moving. Warders wearing swords and plainly guarding their Aes Sedai's back, in the Tower. That was all too common, yet Pevara could have wept at it. Only, there were too many reasons for weeping to settle on one; instead she set about solving what she could.

Tsutama could command Reds to bond Asha'man, command them not to go running to Elaida, but it seemed best to begin with sisters who might be willing to entertain the notion without being ordered, especially with rumors spreading of three Red sisters dead at Asha'man hands. Tarna Feir had already entertained it, so a very private conversation with her was in order. She might know others of a like mind. The greatest difficulty would be approaching the Asha'man with the idea. They were very unlikely to agree just because they themselves had already bonded fifty-one sisters. Light of the world, fifty-one! Broaching the subject would require a sister who possessed diplomacy and a way with words. And iron nerve. She was still mulling over names when she saw the woman she had come to meet, already at the appointed place, apparently studying a tall tapestry.

Tiny and willowy, and regal in her pale silver silk with a slightly darker lace at her neck and wrists, Yukiri appeared throughly engrossed in the tapestry and quite at her ease. Pevara could only recall seeing her the slightest bit flustered on one occasion, and putting Talene to the question had been nerve-racking for everyone there. Yukiri was alone, of course, though of late she had been heard to say she was thinking of taking a Warder again. Doubtless that was equal parts the current times and their own present situation. Pevara could have done with a Warder or two herself.

"Is there any truth in this, or is it all the weaver's fancy?" she asked, joining the smaller woman. The tapestry showed a long-ago battle against Trollocs, or was purported to. Most such things were made

long after the fact, and the weavers usually went by hearsay. This one
was old enough to need the protection of a warding to keep it from
falling apart.

"I know as much about tapestries as a pig knows about black-
smithing, Pevara." For all her elegance, Yukiri seldom let long pass
without revealing her country origins. The silvery gray fringe of her
shawl swung as she gathered it around her. "You're late, so let's be brief.
I feel like a hen being watched by a fox. Marris broke this morning, and
I gave her the oath of obedience myself, but as with the others, her 'one
other' is out of the Tower. With the rebels, I think." She fell silent as a
pair of serving women approached up the hallway carrying a large
wicker laundry basket with neatly folded bed linens bulging from the
top.

Pevara sighed. It had seemed so encouraging, at the start. Terrifying and nearly overwhelming, too, yet they had appeared to be making
a good beginning. Talene had only known the name of one other Black
sister actually in the Tower at present, but once Atuan had been
kidnapped—Pevara would have liked to think of it as an arrest, yet she
could not when they seemed to be violating half of Tower Law and a
good many strong customs besides—once Atuan was safely in hand,
she had soon been induced to surrender the names of her heart: Karale
Sanghir, a Domani Gray, and Marris Thornhill, an Andoran Brown.
Only Karale among them had a Warder, though he had turned out to
be a Darkfriend, too. Luckily, soon after learning that his Aes Sedai had
betrayed him, he had managed to take poison in the basement room
where he had been confined while Karale was questioned. Strange to
think of that as lucky, but the Oath Rod only worked on those who
could channel, and they were too few to guard and tend prisoners.

It had been such a bright beginning, however fraught, and now
they were at an impasse unless one of the others returned to the Tower,
back to searching for discrepancies between what sisters claimed to
have done and what it could be proven they actually had, something
made harder by the inclination of most sisters to be oblique in nearly
everything. Of course, Talene and the other three would pass along
whatever they knew, whatever came into their hands—the oath of obedience took care of that—but any message very much more important
than "take this and put it in that place" would be in a cipher known
only to the woman who sent it and the woman it was directed to. Some
were protected by a weave that made the ink vanish if the wrong hand

broke the seal; that could be done with so little of the Power it might go unnoticed unless you were looking for it, and there appeared to be no way to circumvent the ward. If they were not at an impasse, then their flow of success was reduced to a creeping trickle. And always there was the danger that the hunted would learn of them and become the hunters. Invisible hunters, for all practical purposes, just as they now seemed invisible prey.

Still, they had four names plus four sisters in hand who would admit they were Darkfriends, though likely Marris would be as quick as the other three to claim she now rejected the Shadow, repented of her sins, and embraced the Light once more. Enough to convince anyone. Supposedly, the Black Ajah knew everything that passed in Elaida's study, yet it might be worth the risk. Pevara refused to believe Talene's claim that Elaida was a Darkfriend. After all, she had initiated the hunt. The Amyrlin Seat could rouse the entire Tower. Perhaps a revelation that the Black Ajah truly existed might do what the appearance of the rebels with an army had failed to, stop the Ajahs from hissing at one another like strange cats and bind them back together. The Tower's wounds called for desperate remedies.

The serving women passed beyond earshot, and Pevara was about to bring up the suggestion when Yukiri spoke again.

"Last night, Talene received an order to appear tonight before their 'Supreme Council'." Her mouth twisted around the words in distaste. "It seems that happens only if you're being honored or given a very, very important assignment. Or if you're to be put to the question." Her lips almost writhed. What they had learned about the Black Ajah's means of putting someone to the question was as nauseating as it was incredible. Forcing a woman into a circle against her will? Guiding a circle to inflict pain? Pevara felt her *stomach* writhing. "Talene doesn't think she's to be honored or given an assignment," Yukiri went on, "so she begged to be hidden away. Saerin put her in a room in the lowest basement. Talene may be wrong, but I agree with Saerin. Risking it would be letting a dog into the chicken yard and hoping for the best."

Pevara stared up at the tapestry stretching well above their heads. Armored men swung swords and axes, stabbed spears and halberds at huge, man-like shapes with boars' snouts and wolves' snouts, with goats' horns and rams' horns. The weaver had seen Trollocs. Or accurate drawings. Men fought alongside the Trollocs, too. Darkfriends.

Sometimes, fighting the Shadow required spilling blood. And desperate remedies.

"Let Talene go to this meeting," she said. "We'll all go. They won't expect us. We can kill or capture them and decapitate the Black at a stroke. This Supreme Council must know the names of all of them. We can destroy the whole Black Ajah."

Lifting an edge of the fringe on Pevara's shawl with a slim hand, Yukiri frowned at it ostentatiously. "Yes, red. I thought it might have turned green when I wasn't looking. There will be thirteen of them, you know. Even if some of this 'Council' are out of the Tower, the rest will bring in sisters to make up the number."

"I know," Pevara replied impatiently. Talene had been a fount of information, most of it useless and much of it horrifying, almost more than they could take in. "We take everyone. We can order Zerah and the others to fight alongside us, and even Talene and that lot. They'll do as they're told." In the beginning, she had been uneasy about that oath of obedience, but over time you could become accustomed to anything.

"So, nineteen of us against thirteen of them," Yukiri mused, sounding much *too* patient. Even the way she adjusted her shawl radiated patience. "Plus whoever they have watching to make sure their meeting isn't disturbed. Thieves are always the most careful of their purses." That had the irritating sound of an old saying. "Best to call the numbers even at best, and probably favoring them. How many of us die in return for killing or capturing how many of them? More importantly, how many of them escape? Remember, they meet hooded. If just one escapes, then we won't know who she is, but she'll know us, and soon enough, the whole Black Ajah will know, too. It sounds to me less like chopping off a chicken's head than like trying to wrestle a leopard in the dark."

Pevara opened her mouth, then closed it without speaking. Yukiri was right. She should have tallied the numbers and reached the same conclusion herself. But she wanted to strike out, at something, at anything, and small wonder. The head of her Ajah might be insane; she was tasked with arranging for Reds, who by ancient custom bonded no one, to bond not just any men, but Asha'man; and the hunt for Darkfriends in the Tower had reached a stone wall. Strike out? She wanted to bite holes through bricks.

She thought their meeting was at an end—she had come only to learn how matters progressed with Marris, and a bitter harvest that had turned out—but Yukiri touched her arm. "Walk with me awhile. We've been here too long, and I want to ask you something." Nowadays, Sitters of different Ajahs standing together too long made rumors of plots sprout like mushrooms after rain. For some reason, talking while walking seemed to cause many fewer. It made no sense, but there it was.

Yukiri took her time getting to her question. The floor tiles turned from green-and-blue to yellow-and-brown as they walked along one of the main corridors that spiraled gently through the Tower, down five floors without seeing anyone else, before she spoke. "Has the Red heard from anyone who went with Toveine?"

Pevara almost tripped over her own slippers. She should have expected it, though. Toveine would not have been the only one to write from Cairhien. "From Toveine herself," she said, and told almost everything that had been in Toveine's letter. Under the circumstances, there was nothing else she could do. She did hold back the accusations against Elaida, and also how long ago the letter had arrived. The one was still Ajah business, she hoped, while the other might require awkward explanations.

"We heard from Akoure Vayet." Yukiri walked a few paces in silence, then muttered, "Blood and bloody ashes!"

Pevara's eyebrows rose in shock. Yukiri was often earthy, but never vulgar before this. She noted that the other woman had not said when Akoure's letter arrived, either. Had the Gray received other letters from Cairhien, from sisters who had sworn to the Dragon Reborn? She could not ask. They trusted one another with their lives in this hunt, and still, Ajah business was Ajah business. "What do you intend doing with the information?"

"We will keep silent for the good of the Tower. Only the Sitters and the head of our Ajah know. Evanellein is for pulling Elaida down because of this, but that can't be allowed now. With the Tower to mend and the Seanchan and Asha'man to be dealt with, perhaps never." She did not sound happy over that.

Pevara stifled her irritation. She could not like Elaida, yet you did not have to like the Amyrlin Seat. Any number of very unlikable women had worn the stole and done well for the Tower. But could sending fifty-one sisters into captivity be called doing well? Could Dumai's Wells, with four sisters dead and more than twenty delivered into another sort of captivity, to a *ta'veren*? No matter. Elaida was Red—had been Red—and far too long had passed since a Red gained the stole and staff. All the rash actions and ill-considered decisions seemed things of the past since the rebels appeared, and saving the Tower from the Black Ajah would redeem her failures.

That was not how she put it, of course. "She began the hunt, Yukiri; she deserves to finish it. Light, everything we've uncovered so far has come by chance, and we are at a full stop. We need the authority of the Amyrlin Seat behind us if we're to get any further."

"I don't know," the other woman said, wavering. "All four of them say the Black knows everything that happens in Elaida's study." She bit at her lip and shrugged uncomfortably. "Perhaps if we can meet her alone, away from her study—"

"There you are. I've been looking everywhere."

Pevara turned calmly at the sudden voice behind them, but Yukiri gave a start and muttered something pungent almost under her breath. If she kept this up, she would be as bad as Doesine. Or Tsutama.

Seaine hurried down to them with the fringe of her shawl swinging and her thick black eyebrows rising in surprise at Yukiri's glare. How like a White, logical in everything and often blind to the world around them. Half the time, Seaine seemed unaware they were in any danger at all.

"You were looking for us?" Yukiri almost growled, planting her fists on her hips. Despite her diminutive size, she gave a good impression of fierce looming. Doubtless part of that was for being startled, but she still believed Seaine should be guarded closely for her own protection, no matter what Saerin had decided, and here the woman was, out and about alone.

"For you, for Saerin, for anyone," Seaine replied calmly. Her earlier fears, that the Black Ajah might know what work Elaida had assigned her, were quite gone. Her blue eyes held warmth, yet otherwise she was back to being the prototypical White, a woman of icy serenity. "I have urgent news," she said as though it were anything but. "The lesser is this. This morning I saw a letter from Ayako Norsoni that arrived several days ago. From Cairhien. She and Toveine and all the others have been captured by the Asha'man and. . . ." Tilting her head to one side, she studied them in turn. "You aren't surprised in the slightest. Of course. You've seen letters, too. Well, there's nothing to be done about it now, anyway."

Pevara exchanged looks with Yukiri, then said, "This is the *less* urgent, Seaine?"

The White Sitter's composure faded into worry, tightening her mouth and creasing the corners of her eyes. Her hands tightened into fists gripping her shawl. "For us, it is. I've just come from answering a summons to Elaida. She wanted to know how I was getting on." Seaine took a deep breath. "With discovering proof that Alviarin entered a treasonous correspondence with the Dragon Reborn. Really, she was so circumspect in the beginning, so indirect, it's no wonder I misunderstood what she wanted."

"I think that fox is walking on my grave," Yukiri murmured.

Pevara nodded. The notion of approaching Elaida had vanished like summer dew. Their one assurance that Elaida was not herself Black Ajah had been that she instigated the hunt for them, but since she had done no such thing. . . . At least the Black Ajah remained in ignorance of them. At least they had that, still. But for how much longer?

"On mine, too," she said softly.

Alviarin glided along the corridors of the lower Tower with an outward air of serenity that she held on to hard. Night seemed to cling to the walls despite the mirrored stand-lamps, the ghosts of shadows dancing where none should be. Imagination, surely, yet they danced on the edges of vision. The hallways were very nearly empty, though the second sitting of supper had just ended. Most sisters preferred to have food brought up to their rooms, these days, but the hardier and the more defiant ventured to the dining halls from time to time, and a handful still took many of their meals below. She would not risk sisters seeing her appear flustered or hurried; she refused to let them believe she was scuttling about furtively. In truth, she disliked anyone looking at her at all. Outwardly calm, she seethed inside.

Abruptly she realized that she was fingering the spot on her forehead where Shaidar Haran had touched her. Where the Great Lord himself had marked her as his. Hysteria bubbled almost to the surface with that thought, but she maintained a smooth face by sheer will and gathered her white silk skirts slightly. That should keep her hands occupied. The Great Lord had marked her. Best not to think on that. But how to avoid it? The Great Lord . . . On the outside she displayed absolute composure, but within was a swirling tangle of mortification and hatred and very near to gibbering terror. The external calm was what mattered, though. And there was a seed of hope. That mattered, too. An odd thing to think of as hopeful, yet she would hang on to anything that might keep her alive.

Stopping in front of a tapestry that showed a woman wearing an elaborate crown kneeling to some long-ago Amyrlin, she pretended to examine it while glancing quickly to left and right. Aside from her, the corridor remained as barren of life as an abandoned tomb. Her hand darted behind the edge of the tapestry, and in an instant she was walking on again, clutching a folded message. A miracle that it had reached her so quickly. The paper seemed to burn her palm, but she could not read it here. At a measured pace, she climbed reluctantly to the White Ajah quarters. Calm and unfazed by anything, on the outside. The Great Lord had marked her. Other sisters were going to look at her.

The White was the smallest of the Ajahs, and barely more than twenty of its sisters were in the Tower at present, yet it seemed that nearly all of them were out in the main hallway. The walk along the plain white floor tiles seemed like running a gauntlet.

Seaine and Ferane were heading out despite the hour, shawls draped along their arms, and Seaine gave her a small smile of commiseration, which made her want to kill the Sitter, always thrusting her sharp nose in where it was unwanted. Ferane held no sympathy. She scowled with more open fury than any sister should have allowed herself to show. All Alviarin could do was try to ignore the copper-skinned woman without being obvious. Short and stout, with her usually mild round face and an ink smudge on her nose, Ferane was no one's image of a Domani, but the First Reasoner possessed a fierce Domani temper. She was quite capable of handing down a penance for any slight, especially to a sister who had "disgraced" both herself and the White.

The Ajah felt keenly the shame of her having been stripped of the Keeper's stole. Most felt anger at the loss of influence, as well. There were far too many glares, some from sisters who stood far enough below her that they should leap to obey if she gave a command. Others deliberately turned their backs.

She made her way through those frowns and snubs at a steady pace, unhurried, yet she felt her cheeks beginning to heat. She tried to immerse herself in the soothing nature of the White quarters. The plain white walls, lined with silvered stand-mirrors, held only a few simple

tapestries, images of snowcapped mountains, shady forests, stands of
bamboo with sunlight slanting through them. Ever since attaining the
shawl she had used those images to help her find serenity in times of
stress. The Great Lord had marked her. She clutched her skirts in fists
to hold her hands at her sides. The message seemed to burn her hand.
A steady, measured pace.

Two of the sisters she passed ignored her simply because they did
not see her. Astrelle and Tesan were discussing food spoilage. Arguing,
rather, faces smooth but eyes heated and voices on the brink of heat.
They were arithmetists, of all things, as if logic could be reduced to
numbers, and they seemed to be disagreeing on how those numbers
were used.

"Calculating with Radun's Standard of Deviation, the rate is eleven
times what it should be," Astrelle said in tight tones. "Furthermore,
this must indicate the intervention of the Shadow—"

Tesan cut her off, beaded braids clicking as she shook her head.
"The Shadow, yes, but Radun's Standard, it is outdated. You must use
Covanen's First Rule of Medians, and calculate separately for rotting
meat or rotten. The correct answers, as I said, are thirteen and nine. I
have not yet applied it to the flour or the beans and the lentils, but it
seems intuitively obvious—"

Astrelle swelled up, and since she was a plump woman with a formidable bosom, she could swell impressively. "Covanen's First Rule?" she
practically spluttered, breaking in. "That hasn't been properly proven
yet. Correct and *proven* methods are always preferable to slipshod. . . ."

Alviarin very nearly smiled as she moved on. So someone had finally noticed that the Great Lord had laid his hand on the Tower. But
knowing would not help them change matters. Perhaps she had
smiled, but if so, she crushed it as someone spoke.

"You'd grimace too, Ramesa, if you were being strapped every
morning before breakfast," Norine said, much too loudly and plainly
meaning for Alviarin to hear. Ramesa, a tall slender woman with silver
bells sewn down the sleeves of her white-embroidered dress, looked
startled at being addressed, and likely she was. Norine had few friends,
perhaps none. She went on, cutting her eyes toward Alviarin to see
whether she had noticed. "It is irrational to call a penance private and
pretend nothing is happening when the Amyrlin Seat has imposed it.
But then, her rationality has always been overrated, in my opinion."

Fortunately, Alviarin had only a short way further to reach her rooms. Carefully she closed the outer door and latched the latch. Not that anyone would disturb her, but she had not survived by taking chances except where she had to. The lamps were lit, and a small fire burned on the white marble hearth against the cool of an early spring evening. At least the servants still performed their duties. But even the servants knew.

Silent tears of humiliation began to stream down her cheeks. She wanted to kill Silviana, yet that would only mean a new Mistress of Novices laying the strap across her every morning until Elaida relented. Except that Elaida would never relent. Killing *her* would be more to the point, yet such killings had to be carefully rationed. Too many unexpected deaths would cause questions, perhaps dangerous questions.

Still, she had done what she could against Elaida. Katerine's news of this battle was spreading through the Black Ajah, and beyond it already. She had overheard sisters who were not Black talking of Dumai's Wells in detail, and if the details had grown in the telling, so much the better. Soon, the news from the Black Tower would have diffused though the White Tower, too, likely expanding in the same way. A pity that neither would be sufficient to see Elaida disgraced and deposed, with those cursed rebels practically on the bridges, yet Dumai's Wells and the disaster in Andor hanging over her head would keep her from undoing what Alviarin had done. Break the White Tower from within, she had been ordered. Plant discord and chaos in every corner of the Tower. Part of her had felt pain at that command, a part of her still did, yet her greater loyalty was to the Great Lord. Elaida herself had made the first break in the Tower, but she had shattered half of it past mending.

Abruptly she realized that she was touching her forehead again and snatched her hand down. There was no mark there, nothing to feel or see. Every time she glanced into a mirror, she checked in spite of herself. And yet, sometimes she thought people were looking at her forehead, seeing something that escaped her own eyes. That was impossible, irrational, yet the thought crept in no matter how often she chased it away. Dashing tears from her face with the hand holding the message from the tapestry, she pulled the other two she had retrieved out of her belt pouch and went to the writing table, standing against the wall.

It was a plain table, and unadorned like all of her furnishings, some of which she suspected might be of indifferent workmanship. A trivial matter; so long as furniture did what it was supposed to do, nothing more mattered. Dropping the three messages on the table beside a small, beaten copper bowl, she produced a key from her pouch, unlocked a brass-banded chest sitting on the floor beside the table, and sorted through the small leather-bound books inside until she found the three she needed, each protected so that the ink on the pages would vanish if any hand but hers touched them. There were far too many ciphers in use for her to keep them in memory. Losing these books would be a painful trial, replacing them arduous, hence the stout chest and the lock. A very good lock. Good locks were not trivialities.

Quickly she stripped off the thin strips of paper wrapping the message recovered from behind the tapestry, held them to a lamp flame and dropped them into the bowl to burn. They were only directions as to where the message was to be left, one meant for each woman in the chain, the extra strips merely a way of disguising how many links the message had to go through to reach its recipient. Too many precautions were an impossibility. Even the sisters of her own heart believed her no more than they. Only three on the Supreme Council knew who she was, and she would have avoided that had it been possible. There could never be too many precautions, especially now.

The message, once she worked it out, bending to write on another sheet, was much as she had expected since the previous night when Talene failed to appear. The woman had left the Green quarters early yesterday carrying fat saddlebags and a small chest. Not having a servant carry them, she had performed the task herself. No one seemed to know where she had gone. The question was, had she panicked on receiving her summons to the Supreme Council, or was there something more? Something more, Alviarin decided. Talene *had* looked to Yukiri and Doesine as though seeking . . . guidance, perhaps. She was sure she had not imagined it. Could she have? A very small seed of hope. There must be something more. She *needed* a threat to the Black, or the Great Lord would withdraw his protection.

Angrily, she pulled her hand away from her forehead.

She never considered using the small *ter'angreal* she had hidden away to call Mesaana. For one thing, one very important thing, the woman surely intended to kill her, very likely despite the Great Lord's protection. On the instant, if that protection were lost. She had seen Mesaana's face, knew of her humiliation. No woman would let that pass, especially not one of the Chosen. Every night she dreamed of killing Mesaana, often daydreamed of how to manage it successfully, yet that must wait on finding her without the woman knowing herself found. In the meanwhile, she needed more proof. It was possible that neither Mesaana nor Shaidar Haran would see Talene as verification of anything. Sisters had panicked and run in the past, if rarely, and assuming Mesaana and the Great Lord were ignorant of that would be dangerous.

In turn she touched the ciphered message and the clear copy to the lamp flame and held each by a corner until they had burned nearly to her fingers before dropping them atop the ashes in the bowl. With a smooth black stone that she kept as a paperweight, she crushed the ashes and stirred them about. She doubted that anyone could reconstitute words from ash, but even so. . . .

Still standing, she deciphered the other two messages and learned that Yukiri and Doesine both slept in rooms warded against intrusion. That was unsurprising—hardly a sister in the Tower slept without warding these days—but it meant kidnapping either would be difficult. That was always easiest when carried out in the depths of the night by sisters of the woman's own Ajah. It might yet turn out those glances were happenstance, or imagination. She needed to consider the possibility.

With a sigh, she gathered more of the small books from the chest and gently eased herself onto the goose down cushion on the chair at the writing table. Not gently enough to stop a wince as her weight settled, though. She stifled a whimper. At first, she had thought the humiliation of Silviana's strap far worse than the pain, but the pain no longer really faded. Her bottom was a mass of bruises. And tomorrow, the Mistress of Novices would add to them. And the day after that, and the day after. . . . A bleak vision of endless days howling under Silviana's strap, of fighting to meet the eyes of sisters who knew all about the visits to Silviana's study.

Trying to chase those thoughts away, she dipped a good steel-nibbed pen and began to write out ciphered orders on thin sheets of paper. Talene must be found and brought back, of course. For punishment and execution, if she had simply panicked, and if she had not, if she had somehow found a way to betray her oaths. . . . Alviarin clung to that hope while she commanded a close watch put on Yukiri and Doesine. A way had to be found to take them. And if they were caught up in chance and imagination, something could still be manufactured from whatever they said. She would guide the flows in the circle. Something could be made.

She wrote furiously, unaware that her free hand had risen to her forehead, searching for the mark.

Afternoon sunlight slanted through the tall trees on the ridge above the vast Shaido encampment, dappling the air, and songbirds trilled on the branches overhead. Redbirds and bluejays flashed by, slashes of color, and Galina smiled. Heavy rain had fallen in the morning, and the air still held a touch of coolness beneath sparse, slowly drifting white clouds. Likely her gray mare, with its arched neck and lively step, had been the property of a noblewoman, or at the least a wealthy merchant. No one else but a sister could have afforded such a fine animal. She enjoyed these rides on the horse she had named Swift, because one day it would carry her swiftly to freedom; just as she enjoyed this time alone to dwell on what she would do once she had her freedom. She had plans for repaying those who had failed her, beginning with Elaida. Thinking about those plans, about their eventual fruition, was *most* enjoyable.

At least, she enjoyed her rides so long as she managed to forget that the privilege was as much a mark of how thoroughly Therava owned her, as were the thick white silk robe she wore and her firedrop-studded belt and collar. Her smile faded into a grimace. Adornments for a pet that was allowed to amuse itself when not required to amuse its owner. And she could not remove those jeweled markers, even out here. Someone might see. She rode here to get away from the Aiel, yet they could be encountered in the forest, too. Therava might learn of it. Difficult as it was to admit to herself, she feared the hawk-eyed Wise One to her bones. Therava filled her dreams, and they were never pleasant. Often she woke sweat-soaked and weeping. Waking from those nightmares was always a relief, whether or not she managed to get any sleep for the rest of the night.

There was never any order against escape on these rides, an order she would have had to obey, and that lack produced its own bitterness. Therava knew she would return, no matter how she was mistreated, in the hope that some day the Wise One might remove that cursed oath of obedience. She would be able to channel again, when and as *she* wished. Sevanna sometimes made her channel to perform menial tasks, or just to demonstrate that she could command it, but that occurred so seldom that she hungered for even that chance to embrace *saidar*. Therava refused to let her so much as touch the Power unless she begged and groveled, but then refused her permission to channel a thread. And she had groveled, abased herself completely, just to be granted that scrap. She realized that she was grinding her teeth, and forced herself to stop.

Perhaps the Oath Rod in the Tower could lift that oath from her as well as the nearly identical rod in Therava's possession, yet she could not be sure. The two were *not* identical. It was only a difference in marking, yet what if that indicated that an oath sworn on one was particular to that rod? She dared not leave without Therava's rod. The Wise One often left it lying in the open in her tent, but *you will never pick that up,* she had said.

Oh, Galina could touch that wrist-thick white rod, stroke its smooth surface, yet however hard she strained, she could not make her hand close on it. Not unless someone handed it to her. At least, she hoped that would not count as picking the thing up. It had to be so. Just the thought that it might not be filled her with bleakness. The yearning in her eyes when she gazed at the rod brought Therava's rare smiles.

Does my little Lina want to be free of her oath? she would say mockingly. *Then Lina must be a* very *good pet, because the only way I will consider freeing you is for you to convince me that you will remain my pet even then.*

A lifetime of being Therava's plaything and the target for her temper? A surrogate to be beaten whenever Therava raged against Sevanna? Bleakness was not strong enough to describe her feelings on that. Horror was more like it. She feared she might go mad if that happened. And equally, she feared there might be no escape into madness.

Mood thoroughly soured, she shaded her eyes to check the height of the sun. Therava had merely said that she would like her back before dark, and a good two hours of daylight remained, but she sighed with regret and immediately turned Swift downslope through the trees toward the camp. The Wise One enjoyed finding ways to enforce obedience without direct commands. A thousand ways to make her crawl. For safety, the woman's slightest suggestion must be taken as a command. Being a few minutes late brought punishments that made Galina cringe at the memories. Cringe and heel the mare to a faster pace through the trees. Therava accepted no excuses.

Abruptly an Aielman stepped out in front of her from behind a thick tree, a very tall man in *cadin'sor* with his spears thrust through the harness that held his bowcase on his back and his veil hanging on his chest. Without speaking, he seized her bridle.

For an instant, she gaped at him, then drew herself up indignantly. "Fool!" she snapped. "You must know me by now. Release my horse, or Sevanna and Therava will take turns removing your skin!"

These Aiel usually showed little on their faces, yet she thought his green eyes widened slightly. And then she screamed as he seized the front of her robe in a huge fist and jerked her from the saddle.

"Be silent, *gai'shain*," he said, but as though he cared nothing for whether she obeyed.

At one time she would have had to, but once they realized that she obeyed any order from anyone, there had been too many who enjoyed sending her on foolish errands that kept her occupied when Therava or Sevanna wanted her. Now, she need obey only certain Wise Ones and Sevanna, so she kicked and flailed and screamed in desperate hope of attracting someone who knew she belonged to Therava. If only she were allowed to carry a knife. Even that would have been a help. How could this man not recognize her, or at least know what her jeweled belt and collar meant? The encampment was immense, as filled with people as many large cities, yet it seemed that everyone could point out Therava's pet wetlander. The woman *would* have this fellow skinned, and Galina meant to enjoy every minute of watching.

All too quickly it became apparent that a knife would have been no use at all. Despite her struggles, the brute handled her easily, pulling her cowl down over her head, blinding her, then stuffing as much of it as he could into her mouth before binding it there. Then he flipped her face down and bound her wrists and ankles tightly. As easily as if she had been a child! She still thrashed, but it was wasted effort.

"He wanted some *gai'shain* that aren't Aiel, Gaul, but a *gai'shain* in silk and jewels, and out riding?" a man said, and Galina stiffened. That was no Aielman. Those were the accents of Murandy! "Sure and that's none of your ways, is it?"

"Shaido." The word was spat out like a curse.

"Well, we still need to find a few more if he's to learn anything useful. Maybe more than a few. There are tens of thousands of folks in white down there, and she could be anywhere among them."

"I think maybe this one can tell Perrin Aybara what he needs to know, Fager Neald."

If she had stiffened before, now she froze. Ice seemed to form in her stomach, and in her heart. Perrin Aybara had sent these men? If he attacked the Shaido trying to rescue his wife, he would be killed, destroying her leverage with Faile. The woman would not care what was revealed, with her man dead, and the others had no secrets they feared having known. In horror, Galina saw her hopes of obtaining the rod melting away. She had to stop him. But how?

"And why would be you thinking that, Gaul?"

"She is Aes Sedai. And a friend of Sevanna, it seems."

"Is she, now?" the Murandian said in a thoughtful tone. "Is she that?"

Strangely, neither man sounded the least uneasy over laying hands on an Aes Sedai. And the Aielman apparently had done so fully aware of what she was. Even if he was a renegade Shaido, he had to be ignorant of the fact that she could not channel without permission. Only Sevanna and a handful of the Wise Ones knew that. This was all growing more confusing by the moment.

Suddenly she was lifted into the air and laid on her belly. Across her own saddle, she realized, and the next moment she was bouncing on the hard leather, one of the men using a hand to keep her from falling as the mare began to trot.

"Let us go to where you can make us one of your holes, Fager Neald."

"Just the other side of the slope, Gaul. Why, I've been here so often, I can make a gateway nearly anywhere at all. Do you Aiel run everywhere?"

A gateway? What was the man blathering about? Dismissing his nonsense, she considered her options, and found none good. Bound like a lamb for market, gagged so she would not be heard ten paces away if she shrieked her lungs out, her chances of escape were nonexistent unless some of the Shaido sentries intercepted her captors. But did she want them to? Unless she reached Aybara, she had no way to stop him from ruining everything. On the other hand, how many days off did his camp lie? He could not be very near, or the Shaido would have found him by now. She knew scouts had been making sweeps as far as ten miles from the camp. However many days were required to reach him, it would take as many to return. Not merely minutes late, but days late.

Therava would not kill her for it. Just make her wish she were dead. She could explain. A tale of being captured by brigands. No, just a pair; it was hard enough to believe two men had gotten this near the encampment, much less a band of brigands. Unable to channel, she had needed time to escape. She could make the tale convincing. It might persuade Therava. If she said. . . . It was useless. The first time Therava had punished her for being late, it had been because her cinch broke and she had had to walk back leading her horse. The woman had not accepted that excuse, and she would not accept being kidnapped, either. Galina wanted to weep. In fact, she realized that she was weeping, hopeless tears she was helpless to stop.

The horse halted, and before she could think, she convulsed wildly, trying to fling herself off the saddle, screaming as loudly as her gag permitted. They had to be trying to avoid sentries. Surely Therava would understand if the sentries returned with her and her captors, even if she was late. Surely she could find a way to handle Faile even with her husband dead.

A hard hand smacked her rudely. "Be silent," the Aielman said, and they began to trot again.

Her tears began again, too, and the silk cowl covering her face grew damp. Therava was going to make her *howl*. But even while she wept, she began to work on what she would say to Aybara. At least she could salvage her chances of obtaining the rod. Therava was going to. . . . No. No! She needed to concentrate on what *she* could do. Images of the cruel-eyed Wise One holding a switch or a strap or binding cords reared in her mind, but every time she forced them down while she went over every question Aybara might ask and what answers she would give him. On what she would say to make him leave his wife's safety in her hands.

In none of her calculations had she expected to be lifted down and stood upright no more than an hour after being captured.

"Unsaddle her horse, Noren, and picket it with the others," the Murandian said.

"Right away, Master Neald," came a reply. In a Cairhienin accent.

The bonds around her ankles fell away, a knife blade slid between her wrists, severing those cords, and then whatever held her gag in place was untied. She spat out silk sodden with her own saliva and jerked the cowl back.

A short man in a dark coat was leading Swift away through a straggle of large, patched brown tents and small, crude huts that seemed made from tree branches, including pine boughs with brown needles. How long for pine to turn brown? Days, surely, perhaps weeks. The sixty or seventy men tending cook fires or sitting on wooden stools looked like farmers in their rough coats, but some were sharpening swords, and spears and halberds and other polearms stood stacked in a dozen places. Through the gaps between the tents and huts, she could see more men moving about to either side, a number of them in helmets and breastplates, mounted and carrying long, streamered lances. Soldiers, riding out on patrol. How many more lay beyond her sight? No matter. What was in front of her eyes was impossible! The Shaido had sentries farther from their camp than this. She was certain they did!

"If the face wasn't enough," Neald murmured, "that cool, calculating study would convince me. Like she's examining worms under a rock she's turned over." A weedy fellow in a black coat, he knuckled his waxed mustaches in an amused way, careful not to spoil the points. He wore a sword, but he certainly had no look of soldier or armsman about him. "Well, come along then, Aes Sedai," he said, clasping her upper arm. "Lord Perrin will be wanting to ask you some questions." She jerked free, and he calmly took a firmer grip. "None of that, now."

The huge Aielman, Gaul, took her other arm, and she could go with them or be dragged. She walked with her head high, pretending they were merely an escort, but anyone who saw how they held her arms would know differently. Staring straight ahead, she was still aware of armed farmboys—most were young—staring at her. Not gaping in astonishment, just watching, considering. How could they be so high-handed with an Aes Sedai? Some of the Wise Ones who were unaware of the oath holding her had begun expressing doubt that she was Aes Sedai because she obeyed so readily and truckled so for Therava, but these two knew what she was. And did not care. She suspected those farmers knew, too, and yet none displayed any surprise at how she was being treated. It made the back of her neck prickle.

As they approached a large red-and-white striped tent with the doorflaps tied back, she overheard voices from inside.

". . . . said he was ready to come right now," a man was saying.

"I can't afford to feed one more mouth when I don't know for how long," another man replied. "Blood and ashes! How long does it take to arrange a meeting with these people?"

Gaul had to duck into the tent, but Galina strode in as though entering her own rooms in the Tower. A prisoner she might be, yet she was Aes Sedai, and that simple fact was a powerful tool. And weapon. Who was he trying to arrange a meeting with? Not Sevanna, surely. Let it be anyone but Sevanna.

In stark contrast to the ramshackle camp outside, there was a good flowered carpet for a floor here, and two silk hangings embroidered with flowers and birds in a Cairhienin fashion hung from the roof poles. She focused on a tall, broad-shouldered man in his shirtsleeves with his back to her, leaning on his fists against a slender-legged table that was decorated with lines of gilding and covered with maps and sheets of paper. She had only glimpsed Aybara at a distance in Cairhien, yet she was sure this was the farmboy from Rand al'Thor's home village in spite of the silk shirt and well-polished boots. Even the turndowns were polished. If nothing else, everyone in the tent seemed to be looking to him.

As she walked into the tent, a tall woman in high-necked green silk with small touches of lace at her throat and wrists, black hair falling in waves to her shoulders, laid a hand on Aybara's arm in a familiar manner. Galina recognized her. "She seems cautious, Perrin," Berelain said.

"Wary of a trap, in my estimation, Lord Perrin," put in a graying, hard-bitten man in an ornate breastplate worn over a scarlet coat. A Ghealdanin, Galina thought. At least he and Berelain explained the presence of soldiers, if not how they could be where they could not possibly be.

Galina was very glad she had not encountered the woman in Cairhien. That would have made matters now more than merely awkward. She wished her hands were free to wipe the residue of tears from her face, but the two men held onto her arms firmly. There was nothing to be done about it. She was Aes Sedai. That was all that mattered. That was all she would allow to matter. She opened her mouth to take command of the situation. . . .

Aybara suddenly looked over his shoulder at her, as though he had sensed her presence in some way, and his golden eyes froze her tongue.

She had dismissed tales that the man had a wolf's eyes, but he did. A wolf's hard eyes in a stone-hard face. He made the Ghealdanin look almost soft. A sad face behind that close-cropped beard, as well. Over his wife, no doubt. She could make use of that.

"An Aes Sedai wearing *gai'shain* white," he said flatly, turning to face her. He was a large man, if not nearly so large as the Aielman, and he loomed just by standing there, those golden eyes taking in everything. "And a prisoner, it seems. She didn't want to come?"

"She thrashed like a trout on the riverbank while Gaul was tying her up, my Lord," Neald replied. "Myself, I had nothing to do but stand and watch."

A strange thing to say, and in such a significant tone. What could he have . . . ? Abruptly she became aware of another man in a black coat, a stocky, weathered fellow with a silver pin in the shape of a sword fastened to his high collar. And she remembered where she had last seen men in black coats. Leaping out of holes in the air just before everything turned to utter disaster at Dumai's Wells. Neald and his holes, his gateways. These men could channel.

It took everything she could summon not to try jerking free of the Murandian's clasp, not to edge away. Just being this close to him made her stomach writhe. Being touched by him. . . . She wanted to whimper, and that surprised her. Surely she was tougher than that! She concentrated on maintaining an appearance of calm while trying to work moisture back into her suddenly dry mouth.

"She claims friendship with Sevanna," Gaul added.

"A friend of Sevanna," Aybara said, frowning. "But wearing a *gai'shain* robe. A silk robe, and jewels, but still. . . . You didn't want to come, but you didn't channel to try stopping Gaul and Neald from bringing you. And you're terrified." He shook his head. How did he know she was afraid? "I'm surprised to see an Aes Sedai with the Shaido after Dumai's Wells. Or don't you know about that? Let her go, let her go. I doubt she'll take off running since she let you bring her this far."

"Dumai's Wells does not matter," she said coldly as the men's hands fell away. The pair remained on either side of her like guards, though, and she was proud of the steadiness of her voice. A man who could channel. Two of them, and she was alone. Alone, and unable to channel a thread. She stood straight, head erect. She was Aes Sedai, and they must see her every inch an Aes Sedai. How *could* he know she was afraid? Not a shred of fear tinged her words. Her face might as well have been carved of stone for all she let show. "The White Tower has purposes none but Aes Sedai can know or understand. I am about White Tower business, and you are interfering. An unwise choice for any man." The Ghealdanin nodded ruefully, as though he had learned that lesson personally; Aybara merely looked at her, expressionless.

"Hearing your name was the only reason I didn't do something drastic to these two," she continued. If the Murandian or the Aielmen brought up how long that had taken, she was ready to claim that she had been stunned at first, but they held silent, and she spoke quickly and forcefully. "Your wife Faile is under my protection, as well as Queen Alliandre, and when my business with Sevanna is done, I will take them to safety with me and help them reach wherever they wish to go. In the meanwhile, however, your presence here endangers my business, White Tower business, which I cannot allow. It also endangers you, and your wife, and Alliandre. There are tens of thousands of Aiel in that camp. Many tens of thousands. If they descend on you, and their scouts will find you soon if they haven't already, they will wipe all of you from the face of the earth. They may harm your wife and Alliandre for it, as well. I may not be able to stop Sevanna. She is a harsh woman, and many of her Wise Ones can channel, nearly four hundred of them, all willing to use the Power to do violence, while I am one Aes Sedai, and constrained by my oaths. If you wish to protect your wife and the Queen, turn away from their camp and ride as hard as you can. They may not attack you if you are obviously retreating. That is the only hope you or your wife have." There. If only a few of the seeds she had planted took root, they should be enough to turn him back.

"If Alliandre is in danger, Lord Perrin," the Ghealdanin began, but Aybara stopped him with a raised hand. That was all it took. The soldier's jaw tightened till she thought she might hear it creak, yet he remained silent.

"You've seen Faile?" the young man said, excitement touching his voice. "She's well? She hasn't been harmed?" The fool seemed not to have a word she said beyond mention of his wife.

"Well, and under my protection, Lord Perrin." If this jumped-up country boy wanted to call himself a lord, she would tolerate it for the moment. "She and Alliandre, both." The soldier glowered at Aybara, but he did not take the opportunity to speak. "You must listen to me. The Shaido will kill you—"

"Come here and look at this," Aybara broke in, turning to the table and drawing a large page toward him.

"You must forgive his lack of manners, Aes Sedai," Berelain murmured, handing her a worked silver cup of dark wine. "He is under considerable strain, as you might understand in the circumstances. I haven't introduced myself. I am Berelain, the First of Mayene."

"I know. You may call me Alyse."

The other woman smiled as though she knew that was a false name, yet accepting it. The First of Mayene was far from unsophisticated. A pity she had to deal with the boy instead; sophisticated people who thought they could dance with Aes Sedai were easily led. Country folk could prove stubborn out of ignorance. But the fellow should know *something* of Aes Sedai by now. Perhaps ignoring him would give him reason to think on who and what she was.

The wine tasted like flowers on her tongue. "This is very good," she said with genuine gratitude. She had not tasted decent wine for weeks. Therava would not permit her a pleasure the Wise One denied herself. If the woman learned that she had found several barrels in Malden, she would not even have mediocre wine. And surely would be beaten as well.

"There are other sisters in the camp, Alyse Sedai. Masuri Sokawa and Seonid Traighan, and my own advisor, Annoura Larisen. Would you like to speak to them after you finish with Perrin?"

With feigned casualness, Galina drew up her cowl till her face was shadowed and took another swallow of wine for time to think. Annoura's presence was understandable, given Berelain's, but what were the other two doing there? They had been among those who fled the Tower after Siuan was deposed and Elaida raised. True, none of them would know of her involvement in kidnapping the al'Thor boy for Elaida, but still. . . .

"I think not," she murmured. "Their business is theirs, and mine is mine." She would have given a great deal to know their business, but not at the cost of being recognized. Any friend of the Dragon Reborn might have . . . notions . . . about a Red. "Help me convince Aybara, Berelain. Your Winged Guards are no match for what the Shaido will send against them. Whatever Ghealdanin you have with you won't make a difference. An army will make no difference. The Shaido are too many, and they have hundreds of Wise Ones ready to use the One Power as a weapon. I have seen them do it. You may die, too, and even if you are captured, I can't promise I can make Sevanna release you when I leave."

Berelain laughed as though thousands of Shaido and hundreds of Wise Ones who could channel were of no account. "Oh, have no fear they will find us. Their camp lies a good three-day ride from here, perhaps four. The terrain turns rough not far from where we are."

Three days, perhaps four. Galina shivered. She should have put it together before this. Three or four days of ground covered in less than an hour. Through a hole in the air created with the male half of the Power. She had been near enough for *saidin* to touch her. She kept her voice steady, though. "Even so, you must help me convince him not to attack. It would be disastrous, for him, for his wife, for everyone involved. Beyond that, what I am doing is important to the Tower. You have always been a strong supporter of the Tower." Flattery, for the ruler of a single city and a few hides of land, but flattery oiled the insignificant as well as it did the mighty.

"Perrin is stubborn, Alyse Sedai. I doubt you'll change his mind. That isn't easy to do once he has it set." For some reason, the young woman smiled a smile mysterious enough to credit a sister.

"Berelain, could you have your talk later?" Aybara said impatiently, and it was not a suggestion. He tapped the sheet of paper with a thick finger. "Alyse, would you look at this?" That was not a suggestion, either. Who did the man think he was, ordering an Aes Sedai?

Still, moving to the table took her a little way from Neald. It brought her nearer the other one, who was studying her intently, but he was on the other side of the table. A feeble barrier, yet she could ignore him by looking at the sheet of paper under Aybara's finger. Keeping her eyebrows from rising was difficult. The town of Malden was outlined there, complete with the aqueduct that brought water from a lake five miles away, and also a rough outline of the Shaido camp surrounding the city. The real surprise was that markings seemed to indicate the arrival of septs since the Shaido reached Malden, and the number of those meant his men had been observing the camp for some time. Another map, roughly sketched, seemed to show the city itself in some detail.

"I see you have learned how large their camp is," she said. "You must know rescuing her is hopeless. Even if you have a hundred of those men," speaking of them was not easy, and she could not entirely keep the contempt from her voice, "it isn't enough. Those Wise Ones will fight back. Hundreds of them. It would be a slaughter, thousands dead, your wife perhaps among them. I have told you, she and Alliandre are under my protection. When my business is finished, I will take them to safety. You have heard me say it, so by the Three Oaths you know it is true. Don't make the mistake of thinking that your connection to Rand al'Thor will protect you if you interfere in what the White Tower is doing. Yes, I know who you are. Did you think your wife wouldn't tell me? She trusts me, and if you want to keep her safe, you must trust me, too."

The idiot looked at her as though her words had flown over his head without touching his ears. Those eyes were truly unsettling. "Where does she sleep? Her, and everyone else who was captured with her. Show me."

"I cannot," she replied levelly. "*Gai'shain* seldom sleep in the same place two nights running." With that lie vanished the last chance that she could leave Faile and the others alive. Oh, she had never intended to increase the risk of her own escape by aiding them, but that could always have been explained later by some change in circumstances. She could not hazard the possibility that they might actually escape one day and uncover her direct lie, however.

"I will get her free," he growled, almost too softly for her to hear. "Whatever it takes."

Her thoughts raced. There seemed no way to divert him from it, but perhaps she could delay him. She *had* to do at least that. "Will you at least hold off your attack? I may be able to conclude my affairs in a few more days, perhaps a week." A deadline should sharpen Faile's efforts. Before, it would have been dangerous; a threat not carried out lost all force, and the chance had been too great that the woman might be unable to get the rod in time. Now, the chance became necessary. "If I can do that, and bring your wife and others out, there will be no reason for you to die needlessly. One week."

Frustration painting his face, Aybara thumped his fist on the table hard enough to make it bounce. "You can have a few days," he growled, "maybe even a week or more, if—" He bit off whatever he had been about to say. Those strange eyes centered on her face. "But I can't promise how many days," he went on. "If I had my druthers, I'd be attacking now. I won't leave Faile a prisoner a day longer than I have to while I wait on Aes Sedai schemes for the Shaido to bear fruit. You say she's under your protection, but how great a protection can you really give, wearing that robe? There are signs of drunkenness in the camp. Even some of their sentries drink. Are the Wise Ones given to it as well?"

The sudden shift nearly made her blink. "The Wise Ones drink only water, so you needn't think you can find them all in a stupor," she told him dryly. And quite truthfully. It always amused her when the truth served her purposes. Not that the Wise Ones' example was bearing much fruit. Drunkenness was rife among the Shaido. Every raid brought back all the wine that could be found. Dozens and dozens of small stills produced vile brews from grains, and every time the Wise Ones destroyed a still, two sprang up in its place. Letting him know that would only encourage him, though. "As for the others, I have been with armies before this and seen more drinking than I have among the Shaido. If a hundred are drunk among tens of thousands, what gain is there for you? Really, it will be better if you promise me a week. Two would be better still."

His eyes flashed to the map, and his right hand made a fist again, but there was no anger in his voice. "Do the Shaido go inside the town walls very often?"

She set the winecup down on the table and drew herself up. Meeting that yellow-eyed gaze required effort, yet she managed without a falter. "I think it's past time you showed proper respect. I am an Aes Sedai, not a servant."

"Do the Shaido go inside the town walls very often?" he repeated in exactly the same even tone. She wanted to grind her teeth.

"No," she snapped. "They've looted everything worth stealing and some things that aren't." She regretted the words as soon as they left her tongue. They had seemed safe, until she remembered men who could leap through holes in the air. "That isn't to say they never enter. Most days, a few go in. There might be twenty or thirty at any time, more on occasion, in groups of two or three." Did he have the wit to see what that would mean? Best to make sure he saw. "You could not secure them all. Inevitably, some will escape to warn the camp."

Aybara only nodded. "When you see Faile, tell her that on the day she sees fog on the ridges and hears wolves howl by daylight, she and the others must go to Lady Cairen's fortress at the north end of the city and hide there. Tell her I love her. Tell her I'm coming for her."

Wolves? Was the man demented? How could he ensure that wolves would . . . ? Suddenly, with those wolf's eyes on her, she was not sure she wanted to know.

"I will tell her," she lied. Perhaps he only meant to use the men in black coats to grab his wife? But why wait at all, in that case? Those yellow eyes hid secrets she wished she knew. Who was he trying to meet? Clearly not Sevanna. She would have thanked the Light for that if she had not abandoned that foolishness long since. Who was ready to come to him right away? One man had been mentioned, but that might mean a king with an army. Or al'Thor himself? Him, she prayed never to see again.

Her promise seemed to release something in the young man. He exhaled slowly, and a tension she had not noticed left his face. "The trouble with a blacksmith's puzzle," he said softly, tapping the outline of Malden, "is always getting the key piece into place. Well, that's done. Or soon will be."

"Will you stay for supper?" Berelain asked. "The hour is near."

The light was dimming in the open doorway. A lean serving woman in dark wool, her white hair in a bun on the back of her head, entered and began lighting the lamps.

"Will you promise me at least a week?" Galina demanded, but Aybara shook his head. "In that case, every hour is important." She had never intended staying a moment longer than necessary, but she had to force her next words out. "Will you have one of your . . . men . . . take me back to as near the camp as possible?"

"Do it, Neald," Aybara commanded. "And at least try to be polite." *He* said that!

She drew a deep breath and pushed her cowl back. "I want you to hit me, here." She touched her cheek. "Hard enough to bruise."

Finally she had said something that got through to the man. Those yellow eyes widened, and he tucked his thumbs behind his belt as though securing his hands. "I will not," he said, sounding as though she were insane.

The Ghealdanin's mouth hung open, and the serving woman was staring at her, the burning taper in her hand hanging dangerously near her skirts.

"I require it," Galina said firmly. She would need every scrap of verisimilitude she could find with Therava. "Do it!"

"I don't believe he will," Berelain said, gliding forward with her skirts gathered. "He has very country ways. If you will permit me?"

Galina nodded impatiently. There was nothing for it, though the woman likely would not leave a very convincing. . . . Her vision went dark, and when she could see again, she was swaying slightly. She could taste blood. Her hand went to her cheek, and she winced.

"Too hard?" Berelain inquired anxiously.

"No," Galina mumbled, fighting to keep her face smooth. Had she been able to channel, she would have torn the woman's head off! Of course, if she could have channeled, none of this would be necessary. "Now, the other cheek. And have someone fetch my horse."

She rode into the forest with the Murandian, to a place where several of the huge trees lay toppled and oddly slashed, sure it would be difficult for her to use his hole in the air, but when the man produced a vertical silver-blue slash that widened into a view of steeply climbing land, she did not think of tainted *saidin* at all as she heeled Swift through the opening. Never a thought except of Therava.

She almost howled when she realized she was on the opposite side of the ridge from the encampment. Frantically she raced the sinking sun. And lost.

She had been right, unfortunately. Therava did not accept excuses. She was particularly upset over the bruises. She herself never marred Galina's face. What followed easily equaled her nightmares. And it lasted much longer. At times, when she was screaming her loudest, she almost forgot her desperate need to get the rod. But she clung to that. Obtain the rod, kill Faile and her friends, and she would be free.

Egwene regained awareness slowly, and muzzy as she was, barely had the presence of mind to keep her eyes closed. Pretending still to be unconscious was all too easy. Her head lay slumped on a woman's shoulder, and she could not have lifted it had she tried. An Aes Sedai's shoulder; she could sense the woman's ability. Her brain felt stuffed with wool, her thoughts were slow and veering, her limbs all but numb. Her wool riding dress and cloak were dry, she realized, despite the soaking she had received in the river. Well, that was easily managed with the Power. Small chance they had channeled the water from her garments for her comfort, though. She was seated, wedged in between two sisters, one of whom wore a flowery perfume, each using a hand to keep her more or less upright. They were in a coach by the way they all swayed and the clatter of a trotting team's horseshoes on paving stones. Carefully, she opened her eyes to narrow slits.

The coach's side curtains were tied back, though the stink of rotting garbage made her think it would have been better to pull them shut. Garbage, rotting! How *could* Tar Valon have come to that? Such neglect of the city was reason enough by itself for Elaida to be removed. The windows let in enough moonlight for her to dimly make out three Aes Sedai seated facing her, in the rear of the coach. Even had she not known they could channel, their fringed shawls would have made it certain. In Tar Valon, wearing a shawl with fringe could result in unpleasantness for a woman who was not Aes Sedai. Oddly, the sister on the left appeared to be huddling against the side of the coach, away from the other two, and if they were not exactly huddling, at least they were sitting very close together, as though avoiding contact with the third Aes Sedai. Very odd.

Abruptly it came to her that she was not shielded. Muddled she might be, but that made no sense at all. They could feel her strength, as she could theirs, and while none was weak, she thought she could overcome all five if she were quick enough. The True Source was a vast sun just beyond the edge of sight, calling to her. The first question was, did she dare try yet? In the state her head was, thought wading through knee-deep mud, whether she could actually embrace *saidar* was uncertain, and succeed or fail, they would know once she tried. Best to try recovering a little beforehand. The second question was, how long did she dare wait? They would not let her go unshielded forever. Experimentally, she tried wiggling her toes inside her stout leather shoes, and was delighted when they moved obediently. Life seemed to be returning slowly to her arms and legs. She thought she might be able to raise her head now, if unsteadily. Whatever they had given her was wearing off. How long?

Events were taken out of her hands by the dark-haired sister sitting in the middle of the rear seat, who leaned forward and slapped her so hard that she toppled onto the lap of the woman she had been leaning against. Her hand went to her stinging cheek on its own volition. So much for pretending unconsciousness.

"There was no need for that, Katerine," a raspy voice said above her as its owner lifted her upright again. She could hold her head up, just, it turned out. Katerine. That would be Katerine Alruddin, a Red. It seemed important to identify her captors for some reason, though she knew nothing of Katerine beyond her name and Ajah. The sister she had fallen onto was yellow-haired, but her moon-shadowed face belonged to a stranger. "I think you gave her too much of the forkroot," the woman went on.

A chill flashed through her. So that was what she had been fed! She racked her brain for everything Nynaeve had told her about that vile tea, but her thoughts were still slow. Better, though, it seemed. She was sure Nynaeve had said the effects took some time to go away completely.

"I gave her the exact dose, Felaana," the sister who had slapped her replied dryly, "and as you can see, it is leaving her precisely as it should. I want her able to walk by the time we reach the Tower. I certainly don't intend to help carry her again," she finished with a glare for the sister seated to Egwene's left, who gave a dismissive shake of her head. That was Pritalle Nerbaijan, a Yellow who had done her best to avoid teaching novices or Accepted and made little secret of her dislike for the task when forced to it.

"To have my Harril carry her would have been most improper," she said coldly. In fact, icily. "Myself, I will be glad if she can walk, but if not, so be it. In any case, I look forward to handing her over to others. If you do not want to carry her again, Katerine, I do not want to stand guard over her half the night in the cells." Katerine gave a dismissive toss of her head.

The cells. Of course; she was bound for one of those small, dark rooms on the first level of the Tower's basement. Elaida would charge her with falsely claiming to be the Amyrlin Seat. The penalty for that was death. Strangely, that brought no fear. Perhaps it was the herb working on her. Would Romanda or Lelaine give way, agreeing to be raised Amyrlin after she was dead? Or would they continue to struggle with one another until the entire rebellion faltered and failed, and the sisters straggled back to Elaida? A sad thought, that. Bone-deep sad. But if she could feel sorrow, the forkroot was not quenching her emotions, so why was she not afraid? She thumbed her Great Serpent ring. At least, she tried to, and discovered it gone. Anger flared, white-hot. They might kill her, but they would not deny she was Aes Sedai.

"Who betrayed me?" she asked, pleased that her tone was even and cool. "It can't hurt to tell me, since I'm your prisoner." The sisters stared at her as though surprised she had a voice.

Katerine leaned forward casually, raising her hand. The Red's eyes tightened when pale-haired Felaana lunged to catch the slap before it could land on Egwene.

"She will no doubt be executed," the raspy-voiced woman said firmly, "but she is an initiate of the Tower, and none of us has the right to beat her."

"Take your hand off me, Brown," Katerine snarled, and shockingly, the light of *saidar* enveloped her.

In an instant the glow surrounded every woman in the coach except Egwene. They eyed one another like strange cats on the brink of hissing, on the brink of lashing out with claws. No, not everyone; Katerine and the taller sister seated against her flank never glanced at one another. But they had glares aplenty for the rest. What under the Light was going on? The mutual hostility was so thick in the air, she could have sliced it like bread.

After a moment, Felaana released Katerine's wrist and leaned back, yet no one released the Source. Egwene suddenly suspected that no one was willing to be the first. Their faces were all serene in the pale moonlight, but the Brown's hands were knotted in her shawl, and the sister leaning away from Katerine was smoothing her skirts repeatedly.

"About time for this, I think," Katerine said, weaving a shield. "We wouldn't want you to try anything . . . futile." Her smile was vicious. Egwene merely sighed as the weave settled on her; she doubted she could have embraced *saidar* yet in any case, and against five already full of the Power, success would have lasted moments at most. Her mild reaction appeared to disappoint the Red. "This may be your last night in the world," she went on. "It wouldn't surprise me in the slightest if Elaida had you stilled and beheaded tomorrow."

"Or even tonight," her lanky companion added, nodding. "I think Elaida may be that eager to see the end of you." Unlike Katerine, she was merely stating a fact, but she was surely another Red. And watching the other sisters, as though she suspected one of *them* might try something. This was *very* strange!

Egwene held on to her composure, denying them the response they wanted. The response Katerine wanted, at least. She was determined to maintain her dignity right to the headsman's block. Whether or not she had managed to do well as Amyrlin, she would die in a manner fitting for the Amyrlin Seat.

The woman huddling away from the two Reds spoke, and her

voice, full of Arafel, allowed Egwene to put a name to the hard, narrow
face, dimly seen by moonlight. Berisha Terakuni, a Gray with a reputation for the strictest, and often harshest, interpretation of the law.
Always to the letter, of course, but never with any sense of mercy. "Not
tonight *or* tomorrow, Barasine, not unless Elaida is willing to summon
the Sitters in the middle of the night, and they're willing to answer.
This requires a High Court, no thing of minutes or even hours, and the
Hall seems less eager to please Elaida than she might wish, small wonder. The girl will be tried, but the Hall will sit in the matter when
they choose, I think."

"The Hall will come when Elaida calls or she'll hand them all
penances that will make them wish they had," Katerine sneered. "The
way Jala and Merym galloped off when we saw who we'd caught, she
knows by now, and I'll wager that for this one, Elaida will drag Sitters
from their beds with her own hands if she must." Her voice grew
smug, and cutting at the same time. "Perhaps she will name you to the
Chair of Pardon. Would you enjoy that?"

Berisha drew herself up indignantly, shifting her shawl on her
arms. In some instances, the Chair of Pardon faced the same penalty as
the one she defended. Perhaps this charge required it; despite Siuan's
best efforts to complete her education, Egwene did not know.

"What I want to hear," the Gray said after a moment, ostentatiously ignoring the women on the seat with her, "is what did you do
to the harbor chain? How can it be undone?"

"It can't be undone," Egwene replied. "You must know that it's
cuendillar, now. Even the Power won't break it, only strengthen it. I
suppose you could sell it if you tear down enough of the harbor wall to
remove it. If anyone can afford a piece of *cuendillar* that big. Or would
want such a thing."

This time, no one tried to stop Katerine from slapping her, and
very hard, too. "Hold your tongue!" the Red snapped.

That seemed good advice unless she wanted to be slapped silly. She
could taste blood in her mouth already. So Egwene held her tongue,
and silence descended on the rolling coach, the others all glowing with
saidar and watching each other suspiciously. It was incredible! Why
had Elaida ever chosen women who clearly detested one another for tonight's task? As a demonstration of her power, just because she could?
No matter. If Elaida allowed her to live through the night, at least she
could let Siuan know what had happened to her—and likely to Leane,

as well. She could let Siuan know they had been betrayed. And pray that Siuan could track down the betrayer. Pray that the rebellion would not collapse. She offered a small prayer for that on the spot. It was much more important than the other.

By the time the coachman reined in the team, she had recovered enough to follow Katerine and Pritalle from the coach unaided, though her head still felt a trifle thick. She could stand, but she doubted she had the strength to run far, not that trying would achieve anything beyond being halted after a few steps. So she stood calmly beside the dark-lacquered coach and waited as patiently as the four-horse team in their harness. After all, she was harnessed, too, in a manner of speaking. The White Tower loomed over them, a thick pale shaft rearing into the night. Few of its windows were alight, but some of those were near the very top, perhaps in the rooms Elaida occupied. It was very strange. She was a prisoner and unlikely to live much longer, yet she felt she had come home. The Tower seemed to renew her vigor.

Two Tower-liveried backriders, the Flame of Tar Valon on their chests, had dismounted from the rear of the coach to unfold the steps, and they stood offering a white-gloved hand to each woman who dismounted, but only Berisha availed herself, and only because it let her reach the paving stones quickly while eyeing the other sisters, Egwene suspected. Barasine gave the fellows such looks that one gulped audibly and the other's face grew pale. Felaana, busy trying to watch the others, merely waved the men away irritably. All five still held *saidar*, even here.

They were at the main rear entrance, stone-railed marble stairs descending from the second level beneath four massive bronze lanterns that cast a wide pool of flickering light, and to her surprise, a single novice stood alone at the foot of the stairs, clutching her white cloak against a slight chill in the air. She had more than half-expected Elaida to meet them in person, to gloat over her capture with a retinue of sycophants. That the novice was Nicola Treehill was a second surprise. The last place she would have thought to find the runaway was inside the White Tower itself.

By the way Nicola's eyes widened when Egwene emerged from the coach, the novice was more startled than herself, but she dropped a neat if hasty curtsy to the sisters. "The Amyrlin says she . . . she is to be handed over to the Mistress of Novices, Katerine Sedai. She says that Silviana Sedai has her instructions."

"So, it seems you'll be birched tonight, at least," Katerine murmured with a smile. Egwene wondered whether the woman hated her personally, or for what she represented, or simply hated everyone. Birched. She had never seen it done, but she had heard a description. It sounded extremely painful. She met Katerine's gaze levelly, and after a moment the smile faded. The woman looked about to strike her again. The Aiel had a way of dealing with pain. They embraced it, gave themselves over to it without fighting or even trying to hold back screams. Perhaps that would help. The Wise Ones said that way the pain could be cast off without keeping its hold on you.

"If Elaida means to drag this out unnecessarily, I'll have no more part in it tonight," Felaana announced, frowning at everyone in sight including Nicola. "If the girl is to be stilled and executed, that should be sufficient." Gathering her skirts, the yellow-haired sister darted past Nicola up the stairs. Actually running! The glow of *saidar* still surrounded her as she vanished inside.

"I agree," Pritalle said coolly. "Harril, I think I'll walk with you while you stable Bloodlance." A dark, stocky man, who had come out of the darkness leading a tall bay, bowed to her. Stone-faced, he wore a Warder's chameleon cloak that made most of him seem not to be there when he stood still and rippled with colors when he moved. Silently he followed Pritalle off into the night, but watching over his shoulder, guarding Pritalle's back. The light remained around her, too. There was something here that Egwene was missing.

Suddenly, Nicola spread her skirts in another curtsy, deeper this time, and words burst out of her in a rush. "I'm sorry I ran away, Mother. I thought they'd let me go faster here. Areina and I thought—"

"Don't call her that!" Katerine barked, and a switch of Air caught the novice across the bottom hard enough to make her squeal and jump. "If you're attending the Amyrlin Seat tonight, child, get back to her and tell her I said her orders will be carried out. Now, run!"

With one last, frantic glance at Egwene, Nicola gathered her cloak and her skirts and went scrambling up the stairs so fast that twice she stumbled and nearly fell. Poor Nicola. Her hopes had surely been disappointed, and if the Tower discovered her age. . . . She must have lied about that to be taken in; lying was one of her several bad habits. Egwene dismissed the girl from her mind. Nicola was no longer her concern.

"There was no need to frighten the child out of her wits," Berisha said, surprisingly. "Novices need to be guided, not bludgeoned." A far cry from her views on the law.

Katerine and Barasine rounded on the Gray together, staring at her intently. Only two cats, now, but rather than another cat, they saw a mouse.

"Do you mean to come with us to Silviana alone?" Katerine asked with a decidedly unpleasant smile twisting her lips.

"Aren't you afraid, Gray?" Barasine said, a touch of mockery in her voice. For some reason, she swung one arm a little so the long fringe of her shawl swayed. "Just the one of you, and two of us?"

The two backriders stood like statues, like men who desired heartily to be anywhere else and hoped to remain unnoticed if sufficiently still.

Berisha was no taller than Egwene, but she drew herself up and clutched her shawl around her "Threats are specifically prohibited by Tower—"

"Did Barasine threaten you?" Katerine cut in softly. Softly, yet with sharp steel wrapped in it. "She just asked whether you are afraid. Should you be?"

Berisha licked her lips uneasily. Her face was bloodless, and her eyes grew wider and wider, as though she saw things she had no wish to see. "I. . . . I think I will take a walk in the grounds," she said at last, in a strangled voice, and sidled away without ever taking her eyes from the two Reds. Katerine gave a small, satisfied laugh.

This was absolute madness! Even sisters who hated one another to the toenails did not behave in this fashion. No woman who gave in to fear as easily as Berisha had could ever have become Aes Sedai in the first place. Something was wrong in the Tower. Very wrong.

"Bring her," Katerine said, starting up the stairs.

At last releasing *saidar*, Barasine gripped Egwene's arm tightly and followed. There was no choice save to gather her divided skirts and go along without a struggle. Yet her spirits were oddly buoyant.

Entering the Tower truly did feel like returning home. The white walls with their friezes and tapestries, the brightly colored floor tiles, seemed as familiar as her mother's kitchen. More so, in a way; it had been far longer since she saw her mother's kitchen than these hallways. She took in the strength of home with every breath. But there was strangeness, too. The stand-lamps were all alight, and the hour could

not be all that late, yet she saw no one. There were *always* a few sisters
gliding along the corridors, even in the dead of night. She remembered
that vividly, catching sight of some sister while running on an errand
in the small hours and despairing that she would ever be so graceful, so
queenly. Aes Sedai kept their own hours, and some Browns hardly
liked being awake during daylight at all. Night held fewer distractions
from their studies, fewer interruptions to their reading. But there was
no one. Neither Katerine nor Barasine made any comment as they
walked along hallways lifeless except for the three of them. Apparently
this silent emptiness was a matter of course, now.

As they reached pale stone stairs set in an alcove, another sister finally appeared, climbing from below. A plump woman in a red-slashed
riding dress, with a mouth that looked ready to smile, she wore her
shawl, edged with long red silk fringe, draped along her arms. Katerine and the others might well have worn theirs to mark them out
clearly at the docks—no one in Tar Valon would bother a woman wearing a fringed shawl, and most kept clear, if they could, particularly
men—but why here?

The newcomer's thick black eyebrows raised over bright blue eyes
at the sight of Egwene, and she planted her fists on ample hips, letting
her shawl slide to her elbows. Egwene did not think she had ever seen
the woman before, but apparently, the reverse was not true. "Why,
that's the al'Vere girl. They sent *her* to Northharbor? Elaida will give
you a pretty for this night's work; yes, she will. But look at her. Look at
how she stands so. You'd think the pair of you were an honor guard for
escort. I'd have thought she'd be weeping and wailing for mercy."

"I believe the herb is still dulling her senses," Katerine muttered
with a sidelong scowl for Egwene. "She doesn't seem to realize her situation." Barasine, still holding Egwene's arm, gave her a vigorous
shake, but after a small stagger she managed to catch her balance and
kept her face smooth, ignoring the taller woman's glares.

"In shock," the plump Red said, nodding. She did not sound exactly sympathetic, but after Katerine, she was near enough. "I've seen
that before."

"How did matters go at Southharbor?" Barasine asked.

"Not so well as with you, it seems. With everyone else squealing to
themselves like shoats caught under a fence over there being two of us,
I was afraid we'd scare off who we were trying to catch. It's a good
thing there *were* two of us who would talk to one another. As it was, all

we caught was a wilder, and not before she turned half the harbor chain to *cuendillar*. We ended up near killing the coach horses by galloping back like, well, like we'd caught your prize. Zanica insisted. Even put her Warder up in place of the coachman."

"A wilder," Katerine said contemptuously.

"Only half?" Relief stood out clearly in Barasine's voice. "Then Southharbor isn't blocked."

Melare's eyebrows climbed again as the implications sank in. "We'll see how clear it is in the morning," she said slowly, "when they let down the half that's still iron. The rest of it stands out stiff like, well, like a bar of *cuendillar*. Myself, I doubt any but smaller vessels will be able to cross." She shook her head with a puzzled expression. "There was something strange, though. More than strange. We couldn't find the wilder, at first. We couldn't feel her channeling. There was no glow around her, and we couldn't see her weaves. The chain just started turning white. If Arebis's Warder hadn't spotted the boat, she might have finished and gotten away."

"Clever Leane," Egwene murmured. For an instant, she squeezed her eyes shut. Leane had prepared everything in advance, before coming in sight of the harbor, all inverted and her ability masked. If she herself had been as clever, she likely would have escaped cleanly. But then, hindsight always saw farthest.

"That's the name she gave," Melare said, frowning. The woman's eyebrows, like dark caterpillars, were *very* expressive. "Leane Sharif. Of the *Green* Ajah. Two *very* stupid lies. Desala is striping her from top to bottom down there, but she won't budge. I had to come up for a breath. I never liked flogging, even for one like that. Do you know this trick of hers, child? How to hide your weaves?"

Oh, Light! They thought Leane was a wilder pretending to be Aes Sedai. "She's telling the truth. Stilling cost her the ageless look and made her appear younger. She was Healed by Nynaeve al'Meara, and since she was no longer of the Blue, she chose a new Ajah. Ask her questions only Leane Sharif could know the answers—" Speech ended for her as a ball of Air filled her mouth, forcing her jaws wide till they creaked.

"We don't have to listen to this nonsense," Katerine growled.

Melare stared into Egwene's eyes, though. "It sounds senseless, to be sure," she said after a moment, "but I suppose it wouldn't hurt to ask a few questions besides 'What is your name?' At worse, it'll cut the tedium of the woman's answers. Shall we take her down to the cells, Katerine? I don't dare leave Desala alone with the other one for long. She despises wilders, and she purely hates women who claim to be Aes Sedai."

"She's not going to the cells, yet," Katerine replied. "Elaida wants her taken to Silviana."

"Well, as long as I learn that trick from this child or the other one." Hitching her shawl up onto her shoulders, Melare took a deep breath and headed back down the stairs, a woman with labor ahead of her she was not looking forward to. She gave Egwene hope for Leane, though. Leane was "the other one," now, no longer "the wilder."

Katerine set off down the corridor walking quickly, and in silence, but Barasine pushed Egwene ahead of her after the other Red, muttering half under her breath about how ridiculous it was to think that a sister could learn anything from a wilder, or from a jumped-up Accepted who told outlandish lies. Maintaining some shreds of dignity was difficult, to say the least, while being shoved down a hallway by a long-legged woman with your mouth gaping open as wide as it would go and drool leaking down your chin, but she managed as best she could. In truth, she hardly thought about it. Melare had given her too much to think on. Melare added to the sisters in the coach. It could hardly mean what it seemed to, but if it did. . . .

Soon the blue-and-white floor tiles became red-and-green, and they approached an unmarked wooden door between two tapestries of flowered trees and stout-beaked birds so colorful they seemed unlikely to be real. Unmarked, but bright with polish and known to every initiate of the Tower. Katerine rapped on the door with what might almost have been a display of diffidence, and when a strong voice inside called, "Come," she drew a deep breath before pushing the door open. Did she have bad memories of entering here as novice or Accepted, or was it the woman who awaited them who made her hesitant?

The study of the Mistress of Novices was exactly as Egwene recalled, a small, dark-paneled room with plain, sturdy furnishings. A narrow table by the doorway was lightly carved in a peculiar pattern, and bits of gilt clung to the carved frame of the mirror on one wall, but nothing else was decorated in any way. The stand-lamps and the pair of lamps on the writing table were unadorned brass, though of six different patterns. The woman who held the office usually changed when a new Amyrlin was raised, yet Egwene was ready to wager that a woman who had come to this room as a novice two hundred years ago would recognize nearly every stick and perhaps everything.

The current Mistress of Novices—in the Tower, at least—was on her feet when they entered, a stocky woman nearly as tall as Barasine, with a dark bun on the back of her head and a square, determined chin. There was an air of brooking no nonsense about Silviana Brehon. She was a Red, and her charcoal-colored skirts had discreet red slashes, but her shawl lay draped across the back of the chair behind the writing table. Her large eyes were unsettling, however. They seemed to take in everything about Egwene in a glance, as though the woman not only knew every thought in her head, but also what she would think tomorrow.

"Leave her with me and wait outside," Silviana said in a low, firm voice.

"Leave her?" Katerine said incredulously.

"Which words did you not understand, Katerine? Need I repeat myself?"

Apparently she did not. Katerine flushed, but she said no more. The glow of *saidar* surrounded Silviana, and she took over the shield smoothly, without giving any opening when Egwene might have embraced the Power herself. She was certain that she could, now. Except that Silviana was far from weak; there was no hope she could break the woman's shield. The gag of Air disappeared at the same time, and she contented herself with digging a handkerchief from her belt pouch and calmly wiping her chin. The pouch had been searched—she always kept the handkerchief on top, not beneath everything else—but learning whether anything besides her ring had been taken would have to wait. There had not been anything of much use to a prisoner in any case. A comb, a packet of needles, some small scissors, odds and ends. The Amyrlin's stole. What sort of dignity she could maintain while being birched was beyond her, but that was the future; this was now.

Silviana studied her, arms folded beneath her breasts, until the door closed behind the other two Reds. "You aren't hysterical, at least," she said then. "That makes matters easier, but why aren't you hysterical?"

"Would it do any good?" Egwene replied, returning the handkerchief to her pouch. "I can't see how."

Silviana strode to the writing table and stood reading from a sheet of paper there, occasionally glancing up. Her expression was a perfect mask of Aes Sedai serenity, unreadable. Egwene waited patiently, hands folded at her waist. Even upside down she could recognize Elaida's distinctive hand on that page, if not read what it said. The woman need not think she would grow nervous at waiting. Patience was one of the few weapons left to her, at present.

"It seems the Amyrlin has been mulling over what to do about you for some time," Silviana said finally. If she had expected Egwene to begin shifting her feet or wringing her hands, she gave no sign of disappointment. "She has a very complete plan ready. She doesn't want the Tower to lose you. Nor do I. Elaida has decided that you have been used as a dupe by others and should not be held accountable. So you will not be charged with claiming to be Amyrlin. She has stricken your name from the roll of the Accepted and entered it in the novice book again. I agree with that decision, frankly, though it's never been done before. Whatever your ability with the Power, you missed almost everything else you should have learned as a novice. You needn't fear that you'll have to take the test again, though. I wouldn't force anyone to go through *that* twice."

"I am Aes Sedai by virtue of having been raised to the Amyrlin Seat," Egwene replied calmly. There was no incongruity in fighting for a title when claiming it might still lead to her death. Acquiescence would be as sharp a blow to the rebellion as her execution. Maybe sharper. A novice again? That was laughable! "I can cite the relevant passages in the law, if you wish."

Silviana arched an eyebrow and sat down to open a large leatherbound book. The punishments book. Dipping her pen in the simple glass ink jar, she made a notation. "You've just earned your first visit to me. I'll give you the night to think about it rather than putting you over my knee now. Let's hope contemplation increases the salubrious effect."

"Do you think you can make me deny who I am with a spanking?" Egwene was hard put to keep incredulity from her voice. She was not sure she succeeded.

"There are spankings and spankings," the other woman replied. Wiping the nib clean on a scrap, she replaced the pen in its glass holder and considered Egwene. "You're accustomed to Sheriam Bayanar as Mistress of Novices." Silviana shook her head disparagingly. "I've browsed her punishments book. She let the girls get away with too much, and was far too lenient with her favorites. As a result, she was forced to deal out correction much more often than she should have had to. I record a third of the punishments in a month that Sheriam did, because I make sure that everyone I punish leaves here wishing above all things never to be sent to me again."

"Whatever you do, you'll never make me deny who I am," Egwene said firmly. "How can you possibly think you can make this work? Am I to be escorted to classes, shielded all the while?"

Silviana leaned back against her shawl, resting her hands on the edge of the table. "You mean to resist as long as you can, do you?"

"I will do what I must."

"And I will do what I must. During the day, you will not be shielded at all. But every hour you will be given a mild tincture of fork-root." Silviana's mouth twisted on the word. She picked up the sheet that contained Elaida's notes as if to read, then let it drop back onto the tabletop, rubbing her fingertips as though something noxious clung to them. "I cannot like the stuff. It seems aimed directly at Aes Sedai. Someone who cannot channel can drink five times the amount that makes a sister pass out and barely grow dizzy from it. A disgusting brew. Yet useful, it seems. Perhaps it can be used on those Asha'man. The tincture won't make you dizzy, but you won't be able to channel enough to cause any problems. Only trickles. Refuse to drink, and it will be poured down your throat anyway. You'll be closely watched as well, so you don't try to slip away afoot. At night, you will be shielded, since giving you enough forkroot to make you sleep through the night would leave you doubled up with stomach cramps the next day.

"You are a novice, Egwene, and you will *be* a novice. Many sisters still consider you a runaway, no matter what orders Siuan Sanche gave, and others doubtless will think Elaida wrong not to have you beheaded. They'll watch for every infraction, every fault. You may sneer at a spanking now, before you've received it, but when you're being sent to me for five, six, seven every day? We'll see how long it takes you to change your mind."

Egwene surprised herself by giving a small laugh, and Silviana's eyebrows shot up. Her hand twitched as though to reach for her pen.

"Did I say something funny, child?"

"Not at all," Egwene replied truthfully. It had occurred to her that she could deal with the pain by embracing it in the Aiel manner. She hoped it worked, but there went all hope for dignity. While she was being punished, at least. For the rest, she could only do what she could.

Silviana glanced at her pen, but finally stood without touching it. "Then I am done with you. For tonight. I will see you before breakfast, however. Come with me."

She started for the door, confident that Egwene would follow, and Egwene did. Attacking the other woman physically would achieve no more than another entry in the book. Forkroot. Well, she would find a way around that somehow. If not. . . . She refused to think about that.

Katerine and Barasine were startled to say the least at hearing Elaida's plans for Egwene, and not best pleased to learn that they would be watching her and shielding her while she slept, although Silviana told them she would arrange for other sisters to come after an hour or two.

"Why both of us?" Katerine wanted to know, which earned her a wry glance from Barasine. If only one were sent, it surely would not be Katerine, who stood higher.

"Firstly, because I said so." Silviana waited until the other two Reds nodded in acceptance. They did so with obvious reluctance, but not enough to make her wait long. She had not put on her shawl to come into the hallway, and in some odd fashion, she seemed the one out of place. "And secondly, because this child is tricky, I think. I want her watched carefully awake or asleep. Which of you has her ring?"

After a moment, Barasine produced the circle of gold from her belt pouch, muttering, "I only thought to keep it as a memento. Of the rebels being brought to heel. They're finished, now, for sure." A memento? It was stealing was what it was!

Egwene reached for the ring, but Silviana's hand got there first, and it was into her pouch that the ring went. "I'll keep this until you have the right to wear it again, child. Now take her to the novices' quarters and settle her in. A room should have been prepared by now."

Katerine resumed the shield, and Barasine reached for Egwene's arm again, but Egwene stretched out a hand toward Silviana. "Wait. There's something I must tell you." She had agonized over this. It would be all too easy to reveal far more than she wanted. But she had to do it. "I have the Talent of Dreaming. I've learned to tell the true dreams, and to interpret some of them. I dreamt of a glass lamp that burned with a white flame. Two ravens flew out of mist, struck the lamp, and flew on. The lamp wobbled, flinging off droplets of flaming oil. Some of those burned up in midair, others landed scattered about,

and the lamp still wobbled on the edge of falling. It means the Seanchan will attack the White Tower and do great harm."

Barasine sniffed. Katerine gave a derisive snort.

"A Dreamer," Silviana said flatly. "Is there anyone who can back up
your claim? And if there is, how can be sure your dream means the
Seanchan? Ravens would indicate the Shadow, to me."

"I'm a Dreamer, and when a Dreamer knows, she knows. Not the
Shadow. The Seanchan. As for who knows what I can do. . . ." Egwene
shrugged. "The only one you can reach is Leane Sharif, who's being
held in the cells below." She saw no way to bring the Wise Ones into
this, not without revealing entirely too much.

"That woman is a wilder, not—" Katerine began angrily, but her
mouth snapped shut when Silviana raised a peremptory hand.

The Mistress of Novices studied Egwene carefully, her face still an
unreadable mask of calmness. "You truly believe you are what you say,"
she said finally. "I do hope your Dreaming won't cause as many problems as young Nicola's Foretelling. If you truly can Dream. Well, I will
pass along your warning. I can't see how the Seanchan could strike at
us here in Tar Valon, but watchfulness never hurts. And I'll question
this woman being held below. Carefully. And if she fails to back up
your tale, then your visit to me in the morning will be even more
memorable for you." She waved her hand at Katerine. "Take her away
before she hands me another nugget and keeps me from getting any
sleep at all tonight."

This time, Katerine muttered as much as Barasine. But they both
waited until they were beyond earshot of Silviana. That woman was
going to be a formidable opponent. Egwene hoped embracing pain
worked as well as the Wise Ones claimed. Otherwise. . . . Otherwise
did not bear thinking about.

A lean, gray-haired serving woman gave them directions to the
room she had just finished making up, on the third gallery of the
novices' quarters, and hurried on after brief curtsies to the two Reds.
She never so much as glanced at Egwene. What was another novice to
her? It tightened Egwene's jaw. She was going to have to make people
not see her as just another novice.

"Look at her face," Barasine said. "I think it's finally settling in
on her."

"I am who I am," Egwene replied calmly. Barasine pushed her toward the stairs that rose through the hollow column of railed galleries, lit by the fat, waning moon. A breeze sighed through, the only sound. It all seemed so peaceful. There was no light showing around any door. The novices would be asleep by now, except for those who had late chores or tasks. It was peaceful for them. Not for Egwene, though.

The tiny, windowless room might almost have been the one she had occupied when she first came to the Tower, with its narrow bed built against the wall and a small fire burning on the little brick hearth. The lamp on the small table was lit, but it lighted little more than the tabletop, and the oil must have gone bad, because it gave off a faint, unpleasant stink. A washstand completed the furnishings, except for a three-legged stool, onto which Katerine promptly lowered herself, adjusting her skirts as though on a throne. Realizing there was nowhere for her to sit, Barasine crossed her arms beneath her breasts and frowned at Egwene.

The room was quite crowded with three women in it, but Egwene pretended the other two did not exist as she readied herself for bed, hanging her cloak and belt and dress on three of the pegs set along one rough-plastered white wall. She did not ask for help with her buttons. By the time she laid her neatly rolled stockings atop her shoes, Barasine had settled herself cross-legged on the floor and was immersed in a small, leather-bound book that she must have carried in her belt pouch. Katerine kept her eyes on Egwene as though she expected her to make a break for the door.

Crawling beneath the light woolen blanket in her shift, Egwene settled her head on the small pillow—not a goose down pillow, that was for sure!—and went through the exercises, relaxing her body one part at a time, that would put her to sleep. She had done that so often that it seemed no sooner had she begun, than she was asleep . . .

. . . and floating, formless, in a darkness that lay between the waking world and *Tel'aran'rhiod*, the narrow gap between dream and reality, a vast void filled with a myriad of twinkling specks of light that were all the dreams of all the sleepers in the world. They floated around her, in this place with no up or down, as far as the eye could see, flickering out as a dream ended, springing alight as one began. She could recognize some at sight, put a name to the dreamer, but she did not see the one she sought.

It was to Siuan she needed to speak, Siuan who likely knew by now that disaster had struck, who might be unable to sleep until exhaus-

tion took her under. She settled herself to wait. There was no sense of
time here; she would not grow bored with waiting. But she had to
work out what to say. So much had changed since she wakened. She
had learned so much. Then, she had been sure she would die soon, sure
the sisters inside the Tower were a solid army behind Elaida. Now. . . .
Elaida thought her safely imprisoned. No matter this talk of making
her a novice again; even if Elaida really believed it, Egwene al'Vere did
not. She did not consider herself a prisoner, either. She was carrying the
battle into the heart of the Tower itself. If she had had lips there, she
would have smiled.

CHAPTER 1

When Last Sounds

The Wheel of Time turns, and Ages come and pass, leaving memories that become legend. Legend fades to myth, and even myth is long forgotten when the Age that gave it birth comes again. In one Age, called the Third Age by some, an Age yet to come, an Age long past, a wind rose above the broken mountain named Dragonmount. The wind was not the beginning. There are neither beginnings nor endings to the turning of the Wheel of Time. But it was *a* beginning.

Born beneath the glow of a fat, sinking moon, at an altitude where men could not breathe, born among writhing currents heated by the fires inside the ragged peak, the wind was a zephyr in the beginning, yet it gained in strength as it rushed down the steep, rugged slope. Carrying ash and the stench of burning sulfur from the heights, the wind roared across the sudden, snowy hills that reared from the plain surrounding the impossible height of Dragonmount, roared and tossed trees in the night.

Eastward out of the hills the wind howled, across a large pasture encampment, a considerable village of tents and wooden walkways lining streets of frozen ruts. Soon enough the ruts would melt and the last of the snow vanish, replaced by spring rains and mud. If the encampment remained that long. Despite the hour, many among the Aes

Sedai were awake, gathered in small groups warded against eavesdropping, discussing what had transpired this night. No few of those discussions were quite animated, little short of argument, and some held undeniable heat. Fists might have been shaken or worse had they not belonged to Aes Sedai. What to do next was the question. Every sister knew the news from the riverbank by now, if the details remained sketchy. The Amyrlin herself had gone in secret to seal Northharbor, and her boat had been found overturned and caught in the reeds. Survival in the swift, icy currents of the Erinin was unlikely, and hour by hour it had become more so, until certainty hardened. The Amyrlin Seat was dead. Every sister in the camp knew that her future and perhaps her life hung by a thread, not to mention the future of the White Tower itself. What to do now? Yet voices fell silent and heads came up as the fierce blast struck the camp, fluttering tent canvas like flags, pelting it with clods of snow. The sudden stink of burning sulphur hung heavy in the air, announcing where that wind had come from, and more than one Aes Sedai offered a silent prayer against evil. In moments, though, the wind had passed, and the sisters bent back to their deliberations on a future bleak enough to fit the sharp, fading stench left behind.

On the wind roared toward Tar Valon, gaining strength as it went, shrieking over military camps near the river where soldiers and camp followers sleeping on the ground suddenly had their blankets stripped off and those in tents awoke to canvas jerking and sometimes whipping away into the darkness as tent pegs gave way or guy ropes snapped. Laden wagons rocked and toppled, and banners stood out stiff before they were uprooted, their hurtling staffs now spears that pierced whatever lay in their path. Leaning against the gale, men struggled to the horselines to calm animals that reared and screamed in fear. None knew what the Aes Sedai knew, yet the biting, sulphurous smell that filled the chill night air seemed an ill omen, and hardened men offered their prayers aloud as fervently as the beardless boys. Camp followers added their own, and loudly, armorers and farriers and fletchers, wives and laundresses and seamstresses, all clutched by the sudden fear that something darker than blackness stalked the night.

The fierce flutter of canvas overhead, near to ripping, the babble of voices and the screams of horses, loud enough to cut through the wailing wind, helped Siuan Sanche struggle awake for the second time.

The abrupt stink of burning sulphur made her eyes water, and she was grateful for it. Egwene might be able to don and doff sleep like a pair of stockings, but the same was not true for her. Sleep had been hard enough to come by after she finally made herself lie down. Once the news had reached her from the riverbank, she had been sure she never would sleep short of utter exhaustion. She had offered prayers for Leane, but all of their hopes rested on Egwene's shoulders, and all of their hopes seemed gutted and hung up to dry. Well, she had exhausted herself with nerves and worry and pacing. Now there was hope again, and she did not dare let her leaden eyelids close for fear she would sink back into slumber and not wake till midday, if then. The ferocious wind abated, but people's shouts and horses' cries did not.

Wearily, she tossed aside her blankets and stood up unsteadily. Her bedding was hardly comfortable, laid out on the canvas ground-cloth in a corner of the not-very-large square tent, yet she had come here, though it meant riding. Of course, she had been near falling down by then, and likely not in her right mind from grief. She touched the twisted ring *ter'angreal* hanging from a leather cord around her neck. Her first waking, every bit as hard as this one, had been to fetch that from her belt pouch. Well, the grief was vanquished now, and that was adequate to keep her moving. A sudden yawn made her jaws creak like rusty oarlocks. Barely adequate. You would have thought Egwene's message, the fact that Egwene was alive to send a message, would be enough to banish bone-weariness. Not so, it appeared.

Channeling a globe of light long enough to see the box-lantern on the main tent pole, she lit it with a thread of Fire. The single flame gave a very pale, flickering illumination. There were other lamps and lanterns, but Gareth went on so about how little lamp oil there was in stock. The brazier, she left unlit; Gareth was not so parsimonious with charcoal as oil—charcoal was easier to come by—but she was barely aware of the frigid air. She frowned at his bedding, still lying untouched on the other side of the tent. He surely was aware of the boat's discovery and who it had carried. The sisters did their best to keep secrets from him, but somehow, they succeeded less often than most believed. More than once he had startled her with what he knew. Was he out there in the night organizing his soldiers for whatever the Hall decided? Or had he already departed, leaving a lost cause? No longer lost, yet he must be unaware of that.

"No," she muttered, feeling an odd sense of . . . treachery . . . that she had cast doubt on the man, even in her own mind. He would still be there at sunrise, and for every sunrise until the Hall commanded him to leave. Maybe longer. She did not believe he would abandon Egwene whatever the Hall commanded. He was too stubborn, proud. No; it was not that. Gareth Bryne's word was his honor. Once given, he would not take it back unless released, whatever the cost to himself. And maybe, just maybe, he had other reasons to stay. She refused to think of that.

Putting Gareth out of her mind—why *had* she come to his tent? It would have been so much easier to lie down in her own in the sisters' camp, cramped as it was, or even to have kept the weeping Chesa company, though on second thought, that last might have been beyond her. She could not *abide* weeping, and Egwene's maid would not stop— putting Gareth *firmly* out of her head, she ran a hasty brush through her hair, changed her shift for a fresh one, and dressed as quickly as she could in the dim light. Her plain blue wool riding dress was rumpled, and spotted with mud on the hem besides—she had gone down to see the boat for herself—but she did not take the time to clean and press it with the Power. She had to hurry.

The tent was far from the spacious affair you would have expected of a general, so hurrying meant bumping her hip against a corner of the writing table hard enough that one of the legs almost folded before she could catch it, nearly tripping over the camp stool, the only thing approaching a chair, and barking her shins on the brass-bound chests that lay scattered about. That brought a curse that would have singed any listener's ears. The things served double duty, seats as well as storage, and one with a flat top did for a makeshift washstand with a white pitcher and bowl. In truth, they were arrayed in a neat enough fashion, but one peculiar to him. *He* could find his way through that maze in pitch dark. Anyone else would break a leg trying to reach his bedding. She supposed he must have a concern for assassins, though he had never voiced it.

Gathering her dark cloak from atop one of the chests and folding it over her arm, she paused on the point of snuffing the lantern with a flow of Air. For a moment she stared at Gareth's second pair of boots, standing at the foot of his bedding. Channeling another small sphere of light, she moved it close to the boots. As she had thought. Freshly blacked. The bloody man insisted she work off her debt, then sneaked in behind her back—or worse, under her nose while she slept—and blacked his own bloody boots! Gareth bloody Bryne treated her like a maidservant, never so much as tried to kiss her . . . !

She jerked upright, her mouth going taut as a mooring rope. Now where had *that* thought come from? No matter what Egwene claimed, she was *not* in love with Gareth bloody Bryne! She was *not*! She had too much work in front of her to get caught in *that* kind of foolishness. *That's why you stopped wearing embroidery, I suppose,* a small voice whispered in the back of her head. *All those pretty things, stuffed into chests because you're afraid.* Afraid? Burn her if she was afraid of him or any man!

Carefully channeling Earth, Fire and Air just so, she laid the weave on the boots. Every last bit of the blacking, and most of the dye as well, came away and formed into a neat, glistening sphere that floated in the air, leaving the leather decidedly gray. For a moment she contemplated depositing the ball among his blankets. That would be a suitable surprise for him when he finally lay down!

With a sigh, she pushed open the doorflap and took the ball outside into the darkness to let it splash onto the ground. The man had a short and extremely disrespectful way when she let her temper carry her too far, as she had discovered the first time she hit him over the head with the boots she was cleaning. And when he made her so angry she put salt in his tea. Quite a lot of salt, but it had not been her fault he was hurried enough to drain the cup in a gulp. To try to, at any rate. Oh, he never seemed to mind when she shouted, and sometimes he shouted back—sometimes he just smiled, which was purely infuriating!—yet he had his limits. She could have stopped him with a simple weave of Air, of course, but she had her honor as much as he had his, burn him! Anyway, she had to stay close to him. Min said so, and the girl seemed infallible. *That* was the only reason she had not stuffed a fistful of gold down Gareth Bryne's throat and told him he was paid and be burned. The *only* reason! Besides her own honor, of course.

Yawning, she left the dark puddle shining in the cold moonlight. If he stepped in it before it dried and tracked the mess inside, the blame would be his own and none of hers. At least the sulphur smell had faded a little. Her eyes had stopped overflowing, though what she could see was turmoil.

This sprawling, night-shrouded camp had never had much order. The rutted streets were straight enough, true, and wide for moving soldiers, but for the rest it had always seemed a haphazard array of tents and rough shelters and stone-lined pits for cook fires. Now, it looked much as if it had been under attack. Collapsed tents lay everywhere, some tossed atop others that still stood, though a good many of those stood askew, and dozens of wagons and carts lay on their sides or upside down. Voices on every side called for help with the injured, of whom there appeared to be a fair number. Men limped along the street in front of Gareth's tent supported by other men, while several small groups hurried by carrying blankets being used as stretchers. Farther away she could see four blanket-covered shapes on the ground, three attended by kneeling women who rocked back and forth as they keened.

She could do nothing for the dead, but she could offer her ability with Healing to the others. That was hardly her greatest skill, not very strong at all, though it seemed to have returned to her fully when Nynaeve Healed her, yet she doubted there was another sister anywhere in the camp. They did avoid the soldiers, most of them. Her ability would be better than none. She could, except for the news she carried. It was urgent that it reach the right people as soon as possible. So she closed her ears to the groans and the keens alike, ignored dangling arms and rags clutched to bleeding heads, and hurried to the horselines on the edge of the camp, where the oddly sweet smell of horse dung was beginning to win over the sulphur. A rawboned, unshaven fellow with a haggard glare on his dark face tried to rush past her, but she caught his rough coatsleeve.

"Saddle me the mildest horse you can find," she told him, "and do it right now." Bela would have done nicely, but she had no notion where among all those animals the stout mare was tied and no intention of waiting for her to be found.

"You want to go riding?" he said incredulously, jerking his sleeve free. "If you own a horse, then saddle it yourself, if you're fool enough to. Me, I've the rest of the night ahead of me in the cold tending the ones what's hurt themselves, and lucky if at least one don't die."

Siuan ground her teeth. The imbecile took her for one of the seamstresses. Or one of the *wives*! For some reason, that seemed worse. She stuck her right fist in front of his face so quickly that he stepped back with a curse, but she shoved her hand close enough to his nose that her Great Serpent ring had to be only thing he could see. His eyes crossed, staring at it. "The mildest mount you can find," she said in a flat voice. "But quickly."

The ring did the trick. He swallowed, then scratched his head and stared along the horselines, where every animal seemed be either stamping or shivering. "Mild," he muttered. "I'll see what I can do, Aes Sedai. Mild." Touching a knuckle to his forehead, he hurried off down the rows of horses still muttering to himself.

Siuan did a little muttering herself as she paced, three strides this way and three that. Snow trampled to slush and frozen again crunched under her stout shoes. From what she could see, it might take him hours to find anything that would not pitch her off if it heard a grunter jump. Swinging her cloak around her shoulders, she shoved the small silver circle pin in place with an impatient jab, nearly stabbing her own thumb. Afraid, was she? She would show Gareth bloody, *bloody* Bryne! Back and forth, back and forth. Perhaps she should walk the whole long way. It would be unpleasant, but better than being dumped from the saddle and maybe breaking bones in the bargain. She never mounted a horse, including Bela, without thinking of broken bones. But the fellow returned with a dark mare bearing a high-cantled saddle.

"She's mild?" Siuan demanded skeptically. The animal was stepping as though ready to dance, and looked sleek. That was supposed to indicate speed.

"Nightlily here's meek as milk-water, Aes Sedai. Belongs to my wife, and Nemaris is on the delicate side. She don't like a mount what gets frisky."

"If you say so," she replied, and sniffed. Horses were seldom meek in her experience. But there was nothing for it.

Taking the reins, she clambered awkwardly into the saddle, then had to shift so she was not sitting on her cloak and half-strangling herself every time she moved. The mare did dance, however she sawed the reins. She had been sure it would. Trying to break her bones already. A boat now—with one oar or two, a boat went where you wanted and stopped when you wanted, unless you were a complete fool about tides and currents and winds. But horses possessed brains, however small, and that meant they might take it into their minds to ignore bridle and reins and what the rider wanted. That had to be considered when you had to straddle a bloody horse.

"One thing, Aes Sedai," the man said as she was trying to find a comfortable seat. Why did saddles always seem harder than wood? "I'd keep her to a walk tonight, was I you. That wind, you know, and all that stink, well, she might be just a touch—"

"No time," Siuan said, and dug her heels in. Meek-as-milk-water Nightlily leaped ahead so fast that she nearly pitched backward over the cantle. Only a quick grab at the pommel kept her in the saddle. She thought the fellow shouted something after her, but she could not be certain. What in the Light did this Nemaris consider a *frisky* horse? The mare sped out of the camp as though trying to win a race, sped toward the falling moon and Dragonmount, a dark spike rising against the starry sky.

Cloak billowing behind, Siuan made no effort to slow her, rather digging in her heels again and slapping the mare's neck with the reins as she had seen others do to urge speed. She had to reach the sisters before anybody did something irretrievable. All too many possibilities came to mind. The mare galloped past small thickets and tiny hamlets and sprawling farms with their stone-walled pastures and fields. Snug beneath snow-covered slate roofs, behind walls of stone or brick, the inhabitants had not been roused by that fierce wind; every building lay dark and still. Even the bloody cows and sheep were probably enjoying a good night's sleep. Farmers always had cows and sheep. And pigs.

Bouncing around on the hard leather of the saddle, she tried leaning forward over the mare's neck. That was how it was done; she had seen it. Almost immediately she lost the left stirrup and nearly slid off on that side, barely clawing her way back to get her foot back in place. The only thing to do was sit bolt upright, one hand clutching the pommel in a deathgrip, the other tighter still on the reins. Her flailing cloak tugged uncomfortably against her throat, and she jounced up and down so hard that her teeth clicked if she opened her mouth at the wrong time, but she hung on, and even heeled the animal once more. Ah, Light, but she was going to be bruised within an inch of her life come sunrise. On through the night, smacking the saddle with the mare's every bounding stride. At least her clenched teeth kept her from yawning.

At last the horselines and rows of wagons that ringed the Aes Sedai camp appeared out of the darkness though a thin rim of trees, and with a sigh of relief, she hauled back on the reins as hard as she could. For a horse moving this fast, surely it required hard hauling to stop. Nightlily did stop, so abruptly that she would have hurdled over its head if the mare had not reared at the same time. Wide-eyed, she clung to the animal's neck until it finally settled all four hooves to the ground again. And for some little time after, as well.

Nightlily was breathing hard, too, she realized. Panting, really. She felt no sympathy. The fool animal had tried to kill her, just the way horses would! Recovering herself took a moment, but then she pulled her cloak straight, gathered the reins and rode past the wagons and the long lines of horses at a sedate walk. Shadowy men moved in the darkness along the horselines, doubtless grooms and farriers seeing to the visibly unsettled animals. The mare seemed more biddable, now. Really, this was not too bad at all.

As she entered the camp proper, she hesitated only a moment before embracing *saidar*. Strange to think of a camp full of Aes Sedai as dangerous, yet two sisters had been murdered here. Considering the circumstances of their deaths, it seemed unlikely that holding the Power would be enough to save her if she was the next target, but *saidar* at least gave an illusion of safety. So long as she remembered it was only illusion. After a moment, she wove the flows of Spirit that would hide her ability and the glow of the Power. There was no need to advertise, after all.

Even at this hour, with the moon low in the west, there were a few people out on the wooden walkways, serving women and workmen scurrying about late tasks. Or perhaps early would be a better word now. Most of the tents, in nearly every size and shape imaginable, were dark, but a number of the larger ones glowed with the light of lamps or candles. Unsurprising under the circumstances. Every lit tent had men around it, or gathered in front. Warders. No one else could stand so still they seemed to fade into the night, especially not in this icy night. With the Power filling her, she could make out others, their Warders' cloaks making them vanish in the shadows. Between the murdered sisters and what their bonds to their Aes Sedai must be carrying to them, not surprising at all. She suspected more than one sister was ready to tear her own hair, or someone else's. They took note of her, heads swiveling to follow her passage as she rode slowly along the frozen ruts, searching.

The Hall had to be informed, of course, but others needed to hear first. In her estimation, they were much more likely to do something . . . precipitate. And quite possibly disastrous. Oaths held them, but oaths given under duress, to a woman they now believed dead. For the Hall, for most of the Hall, they had nailed their flag to the mast in accepting a seat. None of *them* would be jumping until they were very, very sure where they would land.

Sheriam's tent was too small for what she was sure she would find, and dark besides, she noted in passing. She very much doubted the woman was asleep inside, though. Morvrin's, big enough to sleep four comfortably, would have done if there was room among all the books the Brown had managed to acquire on the march, but that was dark as well. Her third choice provided a catch, though, and she reined in Nightlily well short of it.

Myrelle had two peaked tents in the camp, one for herself and one for her three Warders—the three she dared acknowledge—and her own shone brightly, the shadows of women moving on the patched canvas walls. Three dissimilar men stood on the walkway in front of the tent—their stillness marked them Warders—but she ignored them for the moment. What exactly were they talking about inside? Certain that it was useless effort, she wove Air with just a hint of Fire; her weave touched the tent and struck a barrier against eavesdropping. Inverted, of course, and so invisible to her. She had only made the attempt on the chance they were being careless. Small possibility of that with the secrets they had to hide. The shadows against the canvas were still, now. So they knew someone had tried. She rode the rest of the way wondering what they had been talking about.

As she dismounted—well, at least she managed to turn half-falling off into something akin to jumping down—one of the Warders, Sheriam's Arinvar, a lean Cairhienin little taller than she, stepped forward to reach for the reins with a small bow, but she waved him away. Releasing *saidar*, she tied the mare to one of the wooden slats of the walkway using a knot that would have held a sizable boat against heavy wind and a strong current. None of those casual loops that others used, not for her. She might dislike riding, but when she tied a horse, she wanted it there when she came back. Arinvar's eyebrows climbed as he watched her finish the knot, but he would not be the one who had to pay for the bloody animal if it got loose and lost itself.

Only one of the other two Warders belonged to Myrelle, Avar Hachami, a Saldaean with a nose like an eagle's beak and thick, gray-streaked mustaches. After sparing her one glance and a slight inclination of his head, he returned to watching the night. Morvrin's Jori, short and bald and nearly as wide as he was tall, did not acknowledge her at all. His eyes studied the darkness, and his hand rested lightly on his long sword hilt. Supposedly he was among the best of the Warders with a blade. Where were the others? She could not ask, of course, any more than she could ask who was within. The men would have been shocked to their bones. None of them tried to stop her from entering. At least matters had not gotten that bad.

Inside, where two braziers gave off the scent of roses and made the air almost toasty compared to the night, she found almost everyone she had hoped for, and all watching to see who entered.

Myrelle herself, sitting on a sturdy straight-chair in a silk robe covered with red and yellow flowers, her arms folded beneath her breasts, wore such a perfect expression of calm on her olive face that it only pointed up the heat in her dark eyes. The light of the Power shone around her. It was her tent, after all; she would be the one to weave a ward here. Sheriam, seated on one end of Myrelle's cot with a straight back, pretended to be adjusting her blue-slashed skirts; her expression was as fiery as her hair, and it grew hotter when she saw Siuan. She was not wearing the Keeper's stole, a bad sign.

"I might have expected it would be you," Carlinya said coldly, fists on her hips. She was never a warm woman, but now the ringlets that stopped well short of her shoulders framed a face that seemed carved from ice nearly as pale as her dress. "I will not have you trying to listen in on my private conversations, Siuan." Oh, yes; they thought everything was at an end.

Round-faced Morvrin, for once not appearing at all absentminded or sleepy-eyed despite the creases in her brown wool skirt, walked around the small table where a tall silver pitcher and five silver cups sat on a lacquered tray. It seemed no one felt like tea; the cups were all dry. Dipping into her belt pouch, the graying sister thrust a carved horn comb into Siuan's hand. "You are all windblown, woman. Fix your hair before some lout takes you for a tavern trull instead of an Aes Sedai and tries to dandle you on his knee."

"Egwene and Leane are alive and prisoners inside the Tower," Siuan announced, more calmly than she felt. A tavern trull? Touching her hair, she discovered that the other woman was right and began working the comb through the tangles. If you wanted to be taken seriously, you could not look as though you had been tussling in an alley. She had enough difficulty with that as it was, now, and would have until some years after she could lay hands on the Oath Rod again. "Egwene spoke to me in my dreams. They succeeded in blocking the harbors, near enough, but they were captured. Where are Beonin and Nisao? One of you go fetch them. I don't want to scale the same fish twice."

There. If they thought themselves free of their oaths, and free of Egwene's orders to obey her, that should disabuse them. Except that no one moved to obey.

"Beonin wanted her bed," Morvrin said slowly, studying Siuan. A very intense study. A sharp mind hid behind that placid face. "She was too tired to talk any more. And why would we have asked Nisao to join us?" That earned a small frown from Myrelle, who was Nisao's friend, but the other two nodded agreement. They and Beonin thought of Nisao as apart from themselves in spite of the oaths of fealty they shared. In Siuan's opinion, these women had never stopped believing they might still guide events somehow, even after the rudder had long since been taken from their hands.

Sheriam rose from the cot as though about to rush off, even gathering her skirts, but that had nothing to do with Siuan's command. Anger had vanished, replaced by shining eagerness. "We don't need them for the moment in any case. 'Prisoners' means the deep cells until the Hall convenes for a trial. We can Travel there and free them before Elaida knows what is happening."

Myrelle gave a sharp nod and stood, reaching to undo the sash of her robe. "Best if we leave the Warders behind, I think. They won't be needed in this." She drew more deeply on the Source, already anticipating.

"No!" Siuan said sharply, and winced as the comb caught in her hair. Sometimes she thought of cutting it shorter than Carlinya's, for convenience, but Gareth had complimented her, saying how much he liked the way it brushed her shoulders. Light, could she not escape the man even here? "Egwene isn't to be tried, and she isn't in the deep cells. She wouldn't tell me where she *is* being held except to say that she is guarded constantly. And she orders that there be no attempt to rescue her that involves sisters."

The other women stared at her in shocked silence. In truth, she herself had argued the point with Egwene, to no avail. It *had* been an order, delivered by the Amyrlin Seat in full fig.

"What you're saying is irrational," Carlinya said finally. Her tone was still cool, her face serene, but her hands smoothed her embroidered white skirts unnecessarily. "If we capture Elaida, we will try her and very likely still her." If. Their doubts and fears were not put to rest yet. "Since she has Egwene, surely she will do the same. I don't need Beonin to tell me what the law says in that regard."

"We *must* rescue her, whatever she wants!" Sheriam's voice was hot as Carlinya's was chill, and her green eyes sparkled. Her hands had turned to fists gripping her skirts. "She cannot realize the danger she is in. She must be in shock. Did she give you any hints where she's held?"

"Don't try to hide things from us, Siuan," Myrelle said firmly. *Her* eyes seemed almost on fire, and she jerked the silk sash tighter for emphasis. "Why would she hide where she's being held?"

"For fear of what you and Sheriam suggest." Giving up on the wind-whipped tangles, Siuan tossed the comb down on the table. She could not stand there combing her hair and expect them to pay attention. Tousled would have to do. "She is *guarded*, Myrelle. By sisters. And they won't give her up easily. If we try a rescue, Aes Sedai will die at the hands of Aes Sedai, sure as silverpike spawn in the reeds. It's happened once, but it must not happen again, or all hope dies of reuniting the Tower peacefully. We cannot *allow* it to happen again. So there is to be *no* rescue. As to why Elaida has decided not to try her, I can't say." Egwene had been vague on that, as if she did not understand either. But she had been definite on the facts, and it was not a claim she would make unless she was sure.

"Peacefully," Sheriam muttered, sinking back onto the cot. She imbued the word with a world of bitterness. "Was there ever any chance of that, from the beginning? Elaida has *abolished* the Blue Ajah! What chance of peace is there?"

"Elaida cannot simply do away with an Ajah," Morvrin murmured, as though that had anything to do with anything. She patted Sheriam's shoulder, but the fire-haired woman sullenly shrugged off her plump hand.

"There is always a chance," Carlinya said. "The harbors are blocked, strengthening our position. The negotiators meet every morning . . ." Trailing off with a troubled look in her eyes, she poured a cup of tea and drank half of it down in one go without adding honey. Blocking the harbors likely would have put an end to the negotiations by itself, not that they had seemed to be going anywhere. Would Elaida let them continue with Egwene in her hands besides?

"I do not comprehend why Elaida would not have Egwene put on trial," Morvrin said, "since conviction would be sure and certain, but the fact remains that she is a prisoner." She displayed none of Sheriam or Myrelle's heat and none of Carlinya's coldness. She was simply presenting the facts, with only a slight tightness of her mouth. "If she is not to be tried, then without any doubt she is to be broken. She has proven to be a stronger woman than I took her for at first, but no one is strong enough to resist the White Tower when it decides to break her. We must consider the consequences if we don't get her out before it can."

Siuan shook her head. "She isn't even going to be birched, Morvrin. I don't understand why either, but she'd hardly tell us to leave her if she thought they were going to torture—"

She broke off as the tentflap was pushed open and Lelaine Akashi stepped in, blue-fringed shawl draped along her arms. Sheriam stood, though she need not have; Lelaine was a Sitter, but Sheriam was the Keeper. Then again, Lelaine was imposing in blue-slashed velvet despite her slenderness, dignity made flesh, with an air of authority that seemed greater than ever tonight. Every hair in place, she might have been entering the Hall after a sound night's sleep.

Smoothly Siuan turned to the table and picked up the pitcher as if in anticipation. That normally would have been her role in this company, to pour tea and speak when her opinion was sought. Perhaps if she remained quiet, Lelaine would be about her business with the others and leave quickly without giving her a second glance. The woman seldom did give her that much.

"I thought that horse outside was the same I saw you ride in on, Siuan." Lelaine's gaze ran over the other sisters, each of them absolutely smooth-faced now. "Am I interrupting?"

"Siuan says Egwene is alive," Sheriam said as though relating the price of delta perch on the dockhead. "And Leane. Egwene spoke to Siuan's dreams. She refuses any attempt at a rescue." Myrelle gave her a sidelong glance, unreadable, but Siuan could have boxed her ears! Likely Lelaine would have been the next she sought out, but to tell her in her own way, not spilled out on the wharf like this. Of late, Sheriam had become as flighty as a novice!

Pursing her lips, Lelaine directed a look like twin awls at Siuan. "Did she, now? You really should be wearing your stole, Sheriam. You *are* the Keeper. Will you walk with me, Siuan? It's been far too long since we had a conversation alone." With one hand, she drew back the doorflap, shifting that penetrating gaze to the other sisters. Sheriam blushed as only a redhead could, brilliantly, and fumbled the narrow blue stole from her belt pouch to lay it across her shoulders, but Myrelle and Carlinya met Lelaine's study with level eyes. Morvrin had begun tapping her round chin with a fingertip as though unaware of anyone else. She might well have been. Morvrin was like that.

Had Egwene's orders sunk in? Siuan had no chance even for a firm look while putting the pitcher down. A suggestion from a sister of Lelaine's standing, Sitter or not, was a command to one of Siuan's standing. Gathering her cloak and skirts, she went out, murmuring thanks to Lelaine for holding the flap for her. Light, she hoped those fools had *listened* to what she said.

Four Warders stood outside now, but one of them was Lelaine's Burin, a copper-skinned stump of a Domani wrapped in a Warder cloak that made most of him seem not there, and Avar had been replaced by another of Myrelle's, Nuhel Dromand, a tall, burly man with an Illianer beard that left his upper lip bare. The man was so still you might have thought him a statue if not for the wisps of mist in front of his nostrils. Arinvar bowed to Lelaine, a quick courtesy, though formal. Nuhel and Jori did not let their vigilance slacken. Nor did Burin, for that matter.

The knot that secured Nightlily took as long to undo as it had to tie, but Lelaine waited patiently until Siuan straightened with the reins in her hands, then set off at a slow pace along the wooden walkway past dark tents. Moonshadows masked her face. She did not embrace the Power, so Siuan could not either. Trailed by Burin, Siuan walked beside Lelaine leading the mare, holding her silence. It was the Sitter's place to begin, and not only because she was a Sitter. Siuan fought the urge to bend her neck and so lose the extra inch she had on the other woman. She seldom thought any longer of the time when she had been Amyrlin. She had been embraced as Aes Sedai once more, and part of being Aes Sedai meant fitting into your niche among the sisters instinctively. The bloody horse nuzzled at her hand as though it thought itself a pet, and she shifted the reins to her other hand long enough to wipe her fingers on her cloak. Filthy slobbering beast. Lelaine eyed her sideways, and she felt her cheeks heating. Instinct.

"Strange friends you have, Siuan. I believe some of them were in favor of sending you away when you first appeared in Salidar. Sheriam, I might comprehend, though I'd think the fact that she stands so much higher than you now would make for awkwardness. That was the major reason I avoided you myself, to avoid awkwardness."

Siuan nearly gaped in astonishment. That came very near to talking about what was never to be talked about, *very* near, a transgression she would never had expected from this woman. From herself, perhaps—she had fitted herself into her niche, yet she was who she was—but never from Lelaine!

"I hope you and I can become friends again, Siuan, though I can understand if that proves impossible. This meeting tonight confirms what Faolain told me." Lelaine gave a small laugh and folded her hands at her waist. "Oh, don't grimace so, Siuan. She didn't betray you, at least not intentionally. She made one slip too many, and I decided to press her, rather hard. Not the way to treat another sister, but then, she's really just an Accepted until she can be tested and passes. Faolain will make a fine Aes Sedai. She was very reluctant to surrender every-thing she gave. Just bits and pieces, really, and a few names, but put together with you in that gathering, it gives me a complete picture, I think. I suppose I can let her free of confinement now. She certainly won't think of spying on me again. You and your friends have been very faithful to Egwene, Siuan. Can you be as faithful to me?"

So that was why Faolain had seemed to go into hiding. How many "bits and pieces" had she revealed while being "pressed hard"? Faolain did not know everything, yet it would be best to assume that Lelaine did. But assume while revealing nothing unless she herself was pressed hard.

Siuan stopped dead, drawing herself up. Lelaine halted, too, clearly waiting for her to speak. Even with her face half in shadow that was clear. Siuan had to steel herself to confront this woman. Some instincts were buried in the bone for Aes Sedai. "I'm faithful to you as a Sitter for my Ajah, but Egwene al'Vere is the Amyrlin Seat."

"So she is." Lelaine's expression remained unruffled, as much as Siuan could make out. "She spoke in your dreams? Tell me what you know of her situation, Siuan." Siuan glanced over her shoulder at the stocky Warder. "Don't mind him," the Sitter said. "I haven't kept a se-cret from Burin in twenty years."

"In my dreams," Siuan agreed. She certainly did not intend to ad-mit that had been only to summon her to Salidar in *Tel'aran'rhiod*. She was not supposed to have that ring in her possession. The Hall would take it away if they learned of it. Calmly—outwardly calm, at least—she related what she had told Myrelle and the others, and more. But not everything. Not the certainty of betrayal. That had to have come from the Hall itself—no one else had known of the plan to block the harbor, except the women involved—though whoever was accountable could not have known they were betraying Egwene. Only helping Elaida, which was mystery enough. Why would any among them want to help Elaida? There had been talk of Elaida's secret adherents from the start, yet she herself had long since dismissed the notion. Most assuredly every Blue fervently wanted Elaida pulled down, but until she knew who was responsible, no Sitter, not even a Blue, would learn everything. "She's called a sitting of the Hall for tomorrow . . . no, it would be tonight, now, when Last sounds," she finished. "Inside the Tower, in the Hall of the Tower."

Lelaine laughed so hard that she had to brush a tear from her eye. "Oh, that is priceless. The Hall to sit right under Elaida's nose, as it were. I almost wish I could let her know just to see her face." Just as abruptly, she turned serious again. Lelaine had always had a ready laugh, when she chose to let it out, but the core of her was always serious. "So Egwene thinks the Ajahs may be turning on one another. That hardly seems possible. She's only seen a handful of sisters, you say. Still, it bears looking into the next time in *Tel'aran'rhiod*. Perhaps someone can see what they can find in the Ajah quarters instead of concentrating on Elaida's study."

Siuan barely suppressed a wince. She planned to do a little searching in *Tel'aran'rhiod* herself. Whenever she went to the Tower in the World of Dreams, she was a different woman in a different dress every time she turned a corner, but she would have to be even more cautious than usual.

"Refusing rescue is understandable, I suppose, even laudable—no one wants any more dead sisters—but very risky," Lelaine went on. "No trial, and not even a birching? What can Elaida be playing at? Can she think to make her take up as Accepted again? That hardly seems likely." But she gave a small nod, as though considering it.

This was heading in a dangerous direction. If sisters convinced themselves they knew where Egwene *might* be, the chance increased that someone would try to bring her out, Aes Sedai guards or no. Trying at the wrong place could be as risky as at the right one, if not more so. Worse, Lelaine was ignoring something.

"Egwene has called the Hall to sit," Siuan asked acidly. "Will you go?" Reproving silence answered her, and her cheeks grew hot again. Some things *were* buried in the bone.

"Of course, I will go," Lelaine said at last. A direct statement, yet there had been a pause. "The entire Hall will go. Egwene al'Vere *is* the

Amyrlin Seat, and we have more than sufficient dream *ter'angreal*. Perhaps she will explain how she believes she can hold out if Elaida orders her broken. I would very much like to hear that."

"Then what are you asking me to be faithful to you about?"

Instead of answering, Lelaine resumed her slow walk through the moonlight, carefully adjusting her shawl. Burin followed her, a half-invisible lion in the night. Siuan hurried to catch up, tugging Nightlily after her, fending off the fool mare's attempts to nuzzle her hand again.

"Egwene al'Vere is the lawful Amyrlin Seat," Lelaine said finally. "Until she dies. Or is stilled. Should either happen, we would be back to Romanda trying for the staff and the stole and me forestalling her." She snorted. "That woman would be a disaster as bad as Elaida. Unfortunately, she had enough support to forestall me, as well. We'd be back to that, except that if Egwene dies or is stilled, you and your friends will be as faithful to me as you've been to Egwene. And you will help *me* gain the Amyrlin Seat in spite of Romanda."

Siuan felt as though her stomach had turned to ice. No Blue would have been behind the first betrayal, but one Blue, at least, had reason to betray Egwene now.

CHAPTER
2

The Dark One's Touch

Beonin woke at first light, as was her habit, though little of the dawn trickled into her tent past the closed doorflap. Habits were good when they were the right habits. She had taught herself a number over the years. The air inside the tent held a touch of the night's chill, but she left the brazier unlit. She did not intend to remain long. Channeling briefly, she lit a brass lamp, then heated the water in the white-glazed pitcher and washed her face at the rickety washstand with its bubbled mirror. Nearly everything in the small round tent was unsteady, from the tiny table to her narrow camp cot, and the only sturdy piece, a low-backed chair, was rude enough to have come from the poorest farm kitchen. She was accustomed to making do, though. Not all of the judgments she had been called on to make had been given in palaces. The meanest hamlet also deserved justice. She had slept in barns and even hovels to make it so.

Moving deliberately, she put on the best riding dress she had with her, a plain gray silk that was very well cut, and snug boots that came to her knees, then began brushing her dark golden hair with an ivory-backed hairbrush that had belonged to her mother. Her reflection in the mirror was slightly distorted. For some reason, that irritated her this morning.

Someone scratched at the tentflap, and a man called cheerily in a

Murandian accent, "Breakfast, Aes Sedai, if it pleases you." She low-ered the brush and opened herself to the Source.

She had not acquired a personal serving woman, and it often seemed a new face brought every meal, yet she remembered the stout, graying man with a permanent smile who entered at her command carrying a tray covered with a white cloth.

"Leave it on the table, please, Ehvin," she said, releasing *saidar*, and was rewarded with a widening of his smile, a deep bow over the tray, and another before he left. Too many sisters forgot the small courtesies to those beneath them. Small courtesies were the lubricant of daily life.

Eyeing the tray without enthusiasm, she resumed her brushing, a twice-a-day ritual that she always found soothing. Rather than finding comfort in the brush sliding through her hair this morning, however, she had to make herself complete the full one hundred strokes before laying the brush on the washstand beside the matching comb and hand mirror. Once, she could have taught the hills patience, yet that had be-come harder and harder since Salidar. And nearly impossible since Mu-randy. So she schooled herself to it, as she had schooled herself to go to the White Tower against her mother's stern wishes, schooled herself to accept the Tower's discipline along with its teaching. As a girl, she had been headstrong, always aspiring to more. The Tower had taught her that you could achieve much if you could control yourself. She prided herself on that ability.

Self-control or no self-control, lingering over her breakfast of stewed prunes and bread proved as difficult as completing her ritual with the hairbrush. The prunes had been dried, and perhaps too old to begin with; they had been stewed to mush, and she was sure she had missed a few of the black flecks that decorated the crusty bread. She tried to convince herself that anything that crunched between her teeth was a barley grain or a rye seed. This was not the first time she had eaten bread containing weevils, yet it was hardly a thing to enjoy. The tea had a strange aftertaste, too, as though that also was beginning to spoil.

When she finally replaced the linen cloth over the carved wooden tray, she very nearly sighed. How long before nothing edible remained in the camp? Was the same happening inside Tar Valon? It must be so. The Dark One was touching the world, a thought as bleak as a field of jagged stones. But victory would come. She refused to entertain any other possibility. Young al'Thor had a great deal to answer for, a very great deal, yet he would—must!—achieve that somehow. Somehow. But the Dragon Reborn lay beyond her purview; all she could do was watch events unfold from afar. She had never liked sitting to one side and watching.

All this bitter musing was useless. It was time to be moving. She stood up so quickly that her chair toppled over backward, but she left it lying there on the canvas ground-cloth.

Putting her head out at the doorflap, she found Tervail on a stool on the walkway, his dark cloak thrown back, leaning on the scabbarded sword propped between his boots. The sun stood on the horizon, two-thirds of a bright golden ball, yet dark clouds in the other direction, massing around Dragonmount, suggested more snow before long. Or perhaps rain. The sun felt close to warm after the previous night. Either way, with luck she could be snug indoors soon.

Tervail gave a small nod to acknowledge her without stopping what appeared to be an idle study of everyone who moved in his sight. There were none but laborers at the moment, men in rough woolens carrying baskets on their backs, men and women just as roughly clad driving high-wheeled carts, laden with bound firewood and sacks of charcoal and water barrels, that clattered along the rutted street. At least, his scrutiny would have seemed idle to someone lacking the Warder bond with him. Her Tervail, he was focused as a drawn arrow. It was only the men he studied, and his gaze lingered on those he did not know personally. With two sisters and a Warder dead at the hands of a man who could channel—it seemed beyond possibility there could be two murderers of that sort—everyone was leery of strange men. Everyone who knew, at least. The news had hardly been shouted abroad.

How he thought he might recognize the killer was beyond her unless the man carried a banner, but she would not upbraid or belittle him for trying to perform his duty. Whipcord lean, with a strong nose and a thick scar along his jaw earned in her service, he had been little more than a boy when she found him, cat-quick and already one of the finest swordsmen in her native Tarabon, and for all the years since there had never been a moment when he did less. At least twenty times he had saved her life. Quite aside from brigands and footpads too ignorant to recognize an Aes Sedai, the law could be dangerous when one side or the other became desperate not to have the judgment go against them, and often he had spotted the peril before she herself.

"Saddle Winterfinch for me and bring your own horse," she told him. "We are going for the little ride."

Tervail raised one eyebrow slightly, half-glancing in her direction, then attached the scabbard to the right side of his belt and set off down the wooden walkway toward the horselines, walking very quickly. He never asked unnecessary questions. Perhaps she was more agitated within than she believed.

Ducking back inside, she carefully wrapped the hand mirror in a silk scarf woven in a black-and-white Tairen maze and tucked it into one of the two large pockets sewn inside her good gray cloak, along with the hairbrush and comb. Her neatly folded shawl and a small box of intricately carved blackwood went into the other. The box contained a few pieces of jewelry, some that had come down from her mother and the rest from her maternal grandmother. She herself seldom wore jewelry aside from her Great Serpent ring, yet she always took the box and the brush, comb and mirror with her when she journeyed, reminders of the women whose memories she loved and honored, and of what they had taught her. Her grandmother, a noted advocate in Tanchico, had infused her with a love for the intricacies of the law, while her mother had demonstrated that it was always possible to better yourself. Advocates rarely became wealthy, though Collaris certainly had been more than comfortable, yet despite her disapproval, her daughter Aeldrine had become a merchant and amassed a tidy fortune buying and selling dyes. Yes, it was always possible to better yourself, if you seized the moment when it appeared, as she had when Elaida a'Roihan deposed Siuan Sanche. Matters since had not gone anywhere near as she had foreseen, of course. Matters seldom did. That was why a wise woman always planned alternative paths.

She considered waiting inside for Tervail to return—he could not fetch two horses in mere minutes—but now that the time had actually arrived, her last stores of patience seemed to flee. Settling the cloak around her shoulders, she snuffed the lamp with an air of finality. Outside, however, she forced herself to stand in one place rather than pacing along the walkway's rough planks. Pacing would attract eyes, and perhaps some sister who thought she was fearful of being alone. In all truth, she was afraid, a little. When a man could kill you, unseen, undetected, it was most reasonable to be afraid. She did not want company, though. She pulled up her cowl, signaling a desire for privacy, and drew the cloak around her.

A gray cat, notch-eared and lean, began stropping himself against her ankles. There were cats all over the camp; they appeared anywhere that Aes Sedai gathered, tame as house pets however feral they had been before. After a few moments without having his ears scratched, the cat strolled away, as proud as a king, in search of someone who would see to them. He had plenty of candidates.

Just moments earlier there had been only roughly garbed laborers and cart drivers in view, but now the camp began to bustle. Clusters of white-clad novices, the so-called "families," scurried along the walkways to reach their classes, held in any tent large enough to accommodate them, or even in the open. Those who hurried by her ceased their childish prattle to offer perfect curtsies in passing. The sight never ceased to amaze her. Or to produce anger. A fair number of those "children" were well into their middle years or older—no few had at least some gray in their hair, and some were grandmothers!—yet they were bending to the ancient routines as well as any girl she had ever seen come to the Tower. And so many. A seemingly endless flood pouring down the streets. How much had the Tower lost through its focus on bringing in girls born with the spark and those already on the brink of channeling through their own fumbling while leaving the rest to find their way to Tar Valon as they would or could? How much lost through insisting no girl above eighteen could submit to the discipline? Change was nothing she had ever sought—law and custom ruled an Aes Sedai's life, a bedrock of stability—and some changes, such as these novice families, seemed too radical to go on, but how much had the Tower lost?

Sisters glided along the walkways, too, usually in pairs or even threes, usually trailed by their Warders. The flow of novices parted around them in ripples of curtsies, ripples made jagged by the stares directed at the sisters, who pretended not to notice. Very few of the Aes Sedai lacked the glow of the Power around them. Beonin came close to clicking her tongue in irritation. The novices knew that Anaiya and Kairen were dead—there had been no thought of hiding the funeral pyres—but telling them how the two sisters had died would simply have frightened them. The newest, added to the novice book in Murandy, had worn white long enough to be aware that sisters walking about filled with *saidar* was beyond unusual, though. Eventually that alone would frighten them, and to no purpose. The killer seemed unlikely to strike in public, with dozens of sisters about.

Five mounted sisters riding slowly eastward, none carrying the light of *saidar*, caught her eye. Each was followed by a small entourage, generally a secretary, a serving woman, perhaps a serving man as well in case of heavy lifting, and some Warders. All rode with their hoods up, but she had no difficulty making out who was who. Varilin, of her own Gray, would have been tall as a man, while Takima, the Brown, was a tiny thing. Saroiya's cloak was flamboyant with white embroidery—she must use *saidar* to keep it so sparkling bright—and a pair of Warders trailing Faiselle marked her as clearly as her brilliant green cloak. Which made the last, wrapped in dark gray, Magla, the Yellow. What would they find when they reached Darein? Surely not negotiators from the Tower, not now. Perhaps they thought they must go through the motions anyway. People frequently continued to go on as they had been after all purpose in it had been lost. That seldom lasted long with Aes Sedai, however.

"They hardly seem to be together at all, do they, Beonin? You might think they just happened to be riding in the same direction."

So much for the cowl providing a modicum of privacy. Luckily, she was practiced at suppressing sighs, or anything else that might give away more than she wished. The two sisters who had stopped beside her were much of a height, both small-boned, dark-haired and brown-eyed, but there resemblance ended. Ashmanaille's narrow face, with its pointed nose, seldom displayed any emotion at all. Her silk dress, slashed with silver, might have come from a tirewoman's hands only moments before, and silver scrollwork decorated the edges of her fur-lined cloak and cowl. Phaedrine's dark wool bore a number of creases, not to mention several stains, her woolen cloak was unadorned and needed darning, and she frowned much too often, as she was doing right then. She might have been pretty without that. An odd pair of friends, the usually unkempt Brown and the Gray who paid as much attention to her clothes as to anything else.

Beonin glanced at the departing Sitters. They did appear to be riding in the same direction by chance more than riding together. It was a measure of her upset this morning that she had failed to note that. "Perhaps," she said turning to face her unwanted visitors, "they are contemplating the consequences of last night, yes, Ashmanaille?" Unwelcome or not, courtesy must be observed.

"At least the Amyrlin is alive," the other Gray replied, "and by what I've been told, she will remain alive and . . . healthy. Her and

Leane both." Not even Nynaeve's Healing of Siuan and Leane could make anyone speak of stilling with ease.

"Alive and a captive, it is better than being beheaded, I suppose. But not a great deal better." When Morvrin woke her to tell her the news, it had been hard to share the Brown's excitement. Excitement for Morvrin, at least. The woman had worn a small grin. Beonin had never considered altering her plans, though. Facts, they must be faced. Egwene was a prisoner, and that was that. "Do you not agree, Phaedrine?"

"Of course," the Brown replied curtly. Curtly! But that was Phaedrine, always so immersed in whatever had caught her attention that she forgot how she should behave. And she was not done. "But that is not why we sought you. Ashmanaille says you have considerable acquaintance with murders." A sudden gust of wind snatched at their cloaks, but Beonin and Ashmanaille caught theirs smoothly. Phaedrine let hers swirl behind her, eyes intent on Beonin.

"Perhaps you have had some thoughts on our murders, Beonin," Ashmanaille said smoothly. "Will you share them with us? Phaedrine and I have been putting our heads together, but we are getting nowhere. My own experience is more with civil matters. I know that you have gotten to the bottom of a number of unnatural deaths."

Of course she had thought on the murders. Was there a sister in the camp who had not? She herself could not have avoided it had she tried. Finding a murderer was a joy, far more satisfying than settling a boundary dispute. It was the most heinous of crimes, the theft of what could never be recovered, all the years that would never be lived, all that might have been done in them. And these were the deaths of Aes Sedai, which surely made it personal for every sister in the camp. She waited for a last covey of white-clad women, two with gray hair, to make their curtsies and hurry on. The number of novices on the walkways was finally beginning to thin out. The cats seemed to be following them. Novices were more free with petting than most sisters.

"The man who stabs from greed," she said once the novices were beyond hearing, "the woman who poisons from jealousy, they are one thing. This is quite another altogether. There are two killings, surely by the same man, but well over a week apart. That implies both the patience and the planning. The motive is unclear, yet it seems very unlikely that he chose his victims by chance. Knowing no more of him than the fact that he can channel, you must begin by looking at what ties the victims together. In this case, Anaiya and Kairen, they were both Blue Ajah. So I ask myself, what connection has the Blue Ajah with a man who can channel? The answer comes back, Moiraine Damodred and Rand al'Thor. And Kairen, she also had contact with him, yes?"

Phaedrine's frown deepened to near a scowl. "You cannot be suggesting *he* is the killer." Really, she was getting much too far above herself.

"No," Beonin said coolly. "I am saying you must follow the connection. Which leads to the Asha'man. Men who can channel. Men who can channel, who know how to Travel. Men who have some reason to fear Aes Sedai, perhaps particular Aes Sedai more than others. A connection is not the proof," she admitted reluctantly, "but it is suggestive, yes?"

"Why would an Asha'man come here twice and each time kill one sister? That sounds as though the killer wanted those two and no others." Ashmanaille shook her head. "How could he know when Anaiya and Kairen would be alone? You cannot think he is lurking about disguised as a workman. From all I hear, these Asha'man are far too arrogant for that. To me, it seems more likely we have an actual workman who can channel and bears a grudge of some sort."

Beonin sniffed dismissively. She could feel Tervail approaching. He must have run to be back so soon. "And why would he have waited until now? The last workmen, they were taken on in Murandy, more than a month ago."

Ashmanaille opened her mouth, but Phaedrine darted in, quick as a sparrow snatching a crumb. "He might have only just learned how. A male wilder, as it were. I've overheard workmen talking. As many admire the Asha'man as fear them. I've even heard some say they wish they had the nerve to go to the Black Tower themselves."

The other Gray's left eyebrow twitched, as much as both shooting to her hairline in another woman. The two were friends, yet she could not be pleased with Phaedrine plucking the words from her mouth in that way. All she said, though, was "An Asha'man could find him, I'm sure."

Beonin let herself feel Tervail, waiting only a few paces behind her, now. The bond carried a steady flow of unwavering calm and patience as strong as the mountains. How she wished she could draw on that as she could on his physical strength. "That is most unlikely to happen,

I'm sure you will agree." she said thinly. Romanda and the others might have stood in favor of this nonsensical "alliance" with the Black Tower, but from that moment on they had fought like drunken cart drivers over how to implement it, how to word the agreement, how to present it, every single detail torn apart, put back together and torn apart again. The thing was doomed, thank the Light.

"I must go," she told them, and turned to take Winterfinch's reins from Tervail. His tall bay gelding was sleek and powerful and fast, a trained warhorse. Her brown mare was stocky, and not fast, yet she had always preferred endurance to speed. Winterfinch could keep going long after taller, supposedly more powerful animals gave up. Putting a foot in the stirrup, she paused with her hands on tall pommel and cantle. "Two sisters dead, Ashmanaille, and both Blues. Find sisters who knew them and learn what else they had in common. To locate the murderer, you must follow the connections."

"I doubt very much they will lead to Asha'man, Beonin."

"The important thing is that the killer is found," she replied, pulling herself into the saddle, and turned Winterfinch away before the other woman could go on. An abrupt ending, and discourteous, but she had no more wisdom to offer, and time seemed to press down on her, now. The sun was clear of the horizon and climbing. After so long, time pressed very hard indeed.

The ride to the Traveling ground used for departures was short, but near a dozen Aes Sedai were waiting in a line outside the tall canvas wall, some leading horses, some cloakless as if they expected to be indoors before long, and one or two wearing their shawls for some reason. About half were accompanied by Warders, several of whom wore their color-shifting cloaks. The one thing the sisters shared was that each shone with the glow of the Power. Tervail expressed no surprise at their destination, of course, but more than that, the Warder bond continued to carry steady calm. He trusted her. A silvery flash appeared inside the walls, and after sufficient time to count slowly to thirty, a pair of Greens who could not make a gateway alone entered together with four Warders leading horses. The custom of privacy already had attached itself to Traveling. Unless someone allowed you to see her weave a gateway, trying to learn where she was going was accounted akin to asking direct questions about her business. Beonin waited patiently on Winterfinch, with Tervail towering over her on Hammer. At

least the sisters here respected her raised cowl. Or perhaps they had their own reasons for silence. Either way, she did not have to talk with anyone. At this moment, that would have been insupportable.

The line in front of her dwindled quickly, and soon enough she and Tervail were dismounting at the head of a much shorter line, only three sisters. He held aside the heavy canvas flap for her to enter first. Hung between tall poles, the wall enclosed a space of nearly twenty paces by twenty where frozen slush covered the ground, an uneven surface marked by footprints and hoofprints atop one another and scored in the middle by a razor-straight line. Everyone used the middle. The ground glistened faintly, perhaps the beginning of another thaw that would turn it all to slush that might well freeze again. Spring came later here than in Tarabon, but it was on the brink.

As soon as Tervail let the canvas fall, she embraced *saidar* and wove Spirit almost caressingly. This weave fascinated her, a rediscovery of something thought lost forever and surely the greatest of Egwene al'-Vere's discoveries. Every time she wove it she felt a sense of wonder, so familiar as novice and even Accepted, that had not come to her since she attained the shawl. Something new and marvelous. The vertical silvery line appeared in front of her, right atop the scoring on the ground, and suddenly became a gap that widened, the view through appearing to rotate until she was faced by a square hole in the air, more than two paces by two, that showed snow-draped oaks with heavy spreading limbs. A light breeze blew through the gateway, rippling her cloak. She had often enjoyed walking in that grove, or sitting on one of the low branches for hours reading, though never in snow.

Tervail did not recognize it, and darted through, sword in hand, tugging Hammer behind him, the warhorse's hooves kicking up puffs of snow on the other side. She followed a little more slowly and let the weave dissipate almost reluctantly. It truly was wondrous.

She found Tervail looking at what rose above the treetops in the near distance, a thick pale shaft rearing against the sky. The White Tower. His face was very still, and the bond seemed filled with stillness, too. "I think me you are planning something dangerous, Beonin." He still held his blade bared, though lowered now.

She laid a hand on his left arm. That should be enough to reassure him; she would never have impeded his sword arm if there was any real danger. "No more dangerous than is ne. . . ."

The words trailed off as she saw a woman some thirty paces away, walking slowly toward her through the grove of massive trees. She must have been behind a tree before. An Aes Sedai in a dress of old-fashioned cut, with straight white hair held back by a pearl-studded cap of silver wire and falling to her waist. It could not be. That strong face with its dark, tilted eyes and hooked nose was unmistakable, though. Unmistakable, but Turanine Merdagon had died when Beonin was Accepted. In midstep, the woman vanished.

"What is it?" Tervail spun, his sword coming up, to stare in the direction she had been looking. "What frightened you?"

"The Dark One, he is touching the world," she said softly. It was impossible! Impossible, but she was not given to delusions or fancies. She had seen what she had seen. Her shiver had nothing to with standing ankle-deep in snow. Silently, she prayed. *May the Light illumine me all of my days, and may I shelter in the Creator's hand in the sure and certain hope of salvation and rebirth.*

When she told him about seeing a sister more than forty years dead, he did not try to dismiss it as hallucination, merely muttered his own prayer half under his breath. She felt no fear in him, though. Plenty in herself, but none in him. The dead could not frighten a man who took each day as his last. He was not so sanguine when she revealed what she intended. Part of it, anyway. She did so looking into the hand mirror and weaving very carefully. She was not as adept with Illusion as she would have liked. The face in the mirror changed as the weave settled on her. It was not a great change, but the face was no longer an Aes Sedai's face, no longer Beonin Marinye's face, just that of a woman who looked vaguely like her, though with much paler hair.

"Why do you want to reach Elaida?" he demanded suspiciously. Abruptly the bond carried an edge. "You mean to get close to her then lower the Illusion, yes? She will attack you, and— No, Beonin. If it must be done, let me go. There are too many Warders in the Tower for her to know them all, and she will never expect a Warder to attack her. I can put a dagger in her heart before she knows what is happening." He demonstrated, a short blade appearing in his right hand quick as lightning.

"What I do, I must do myself, Tervail." Inverting the Illusion and tying it off, she prepared several other weaves just in case matters went too far awry, inverting them also, then began another, a very complex weave that she laid on herself. That would hide her ability to channel. She had always wondered why some weaves, such as Illusion, could be placed on yourself while it was impossible to make others, such as Healing, touch your own body. When she had asked that question as Accepted, Turanine had said in that memorable deep voice, "As well ask why water is wet and sand dry, child. Put your mind on what is possible rather than why some things are not." Good advice, yet she never had been able to accept the second part. The dead were walking. *May the Light illumine me all the days of.* . . . She tied off the last weave and removed her Great Serpent ring, tucking it into her belt pouch. Now she could stand beside any Aes Sedai unrecognized for what she was. "You have always trusted me to know what is best," she went on. "Do you still?"

His face remained as smooth as a sister's, yet the bond brought an instant of shock. "But of course, Beonin."

"Then take Winterfinch and go into the city. Hire a room at an inn until I come for you." He opened his mouth, but she raised an admonitory hand. "Go, Tervail."

She watched him disappear through the trees, leading both horses, then turned to face the Tower. The dead were walking. But all that mattered was that she reach Elaida. Only that.

Gusts of wind rattled the casements set in the windows. The fire on the white marble hearth had warmed the air to the point that moisture condensed on the glass panes and trickled down like raindrops. Seated behind her gilded writing table with her hands calmly folded on the tabletop, Elaida do Avriny a'Roihan, the Watcher of the Seals, the Flame of Tar Valon, the Amyrlin Seat, kept a smooth face while she listened to the man in front of her rant, shoulders hunched and shaking his fist.

". . . did be kept bound and gagged for most of the voyage, confined day and night to a cabin better called a cupboard! For that, I demand the captain of that vessel be punished, Elaida. More, I do demand an apology from you and from the White Tower. Fortune stab me, the Amyrlin Seat does no have the right to kidnap kings any longer! The White Tower does no have that right! I do demand. . . ."

He was repeating himself again. The man barely paused for breath. It was difficult to keep her attention on him. Her eyes wandered to the bright tapestries on the walls, the neatly arrayed red roses on white plinths in the corners. Tiresome, maintaining outward calm while enduring this tirade. She wanted to stand up and slap him. The audacity of the man! To speak so to the Amyrlin Seat! But enduring calmly served her purpose better. She would let him exhaust himself.

Mattin Stepaneos den Balgar was muscular, and he might have been good-looking when young, but the years had proven unkind. The white beard that left his upper lip bare was neatly trimmed, but the hair had retreated from most of his scalp, his nose had been broken more than once, and his scowl deepened creases on his flushed face that needed no deepening. His green silk coat, embroidered on the sleeves with the Golden Bees of Illian, had been brushed and cleaned well, short of a sister channeling to do the work, yet it had been his only coat for the voyage, and not all the stains had come out. The ship carrying him had been slow, arriving late the day before, but for once, she was not displeased with someone else's slowness. The Light only knew what a mess Alviarin would have made of matters had he arrived in a timely fashion. The woman deserved to go to the headsman for the mire she had driven the Tower into, a mire Elaida now had to dig out of, much less for *daring* to blackmail the Amyrlin Seat.

Mattin Stepaneos cut off abruptly, taking half a step back on the patterned Taraboner carpet. Elaida wiped the frown from her face. Thinking of Alviarin always made her glare unless she was careful.

"Your rooms are comfortable enough for you?" she said into the silence. "The serving men are suitable?"

He blinked at the sudden change of direction. "The rooms do be comfortable and the serving men suitable," he replied in a much milder tone, perhaps remembering her frown. "Even so, I—"

"You should be grateful to the Tower, Mattin Stepaneos, and to me. Rand al'Thor took Illian only days after you departed the city. He took the Laurel Crown, as well. The Crown of Swords, he named it. Can you believe he would have faltered in cutting off your head to take it? I knew you would not leave voluntarily. I saved your life." There. He should believe it had been done with his best interests at heart, now.

The fool had the temerity to snort and fold his arms across his chest. "I am no a toothless old hound yet, Mother. I did face death defending Illian many times. Do you believe I fear dying so much I would rather be your 'guest' for the rest of my life?" Still, that was the first time he had given her her proper title since entering the room.

The ornate gilded case clock standing against the wall chimed, small figures of gold and silver and enamel moving on three levels. On the highest, above the clockface, a king and queen knelt to an Amyrlin Seat. Unlike the wide stole resting on Elaida's shoulders, that Amyrlin's stole still had seven stripes. She had not yet gotten around to bringing in an enameler. There was so much to be done that was so much more important.

Adjusting her stole on the bright red silk of her dress, she leaned back so the Flame of Tar Valon, picked out in moonstones on the tall gilded chairback, would stand directly above her head. She intended to make the man take in every symbol of who she was and what she represented. Had the Flame-topped staff been at hand, she would have held it under his crooked nose. "A dead man can reclaim nothing, my son. From here, with my help, it may be that you can reclaim your crown and your nation."

Mattin Stepaneos' mouth opened a crack and he inhaled deeply, like a man scenting a home he had never thought to see again. "And how would you arrange that, Mother? I understand the City do be held by these . . . Asha'man," he fumbled the cursed name slightly, "and Aiel who follow the Dragon Reborn." Someone had been talking to him, telling him too much. His news of events was to be strictly rationed. It seemed his serving man would have to be replaced. But hope had washed the anger from his voice, and that was to the good.

"Regaining your crown will require planning, and time," she told him, since at the moment she had no idea of how it could be accomplished. She certainly intended to find a way, however. Kidnapping the King of Illian had been meant to demonstrate her power, but restoring him to a stolen throne would demonstrate it even further. She would rebuild the full glory of the White Tower at its highest, the days when thrones trembled if the Amyrlin Seat frowned.

"I am sure you are still weary from your journey," she said, standing. Just as if he had undertaken it of his own free will. She hoped he was intelligent enough to make that pretense, too. It would serve them both far better than the truth in the days to come. "We will dine together at midday and discuss what might be done. Cariandre, escort His Majesty to his rooms and see to fetching a tailor. He will need new clothes made. A gift from me." The plump Ghealdanin Red who had been standing still as a mouse beside the door to the anteroom glided forward to touch his arm. He hesitated, reluctant to go, but Elaida continued as though he were already leaving. "Tell Tarna to come in to me, Cariandre. I have a great deal of work today," she added for his benefit.

At last Mattin Stepaneos let himself be turned, and she sat down again before he reached the door. Three lacquered boxes were arranged just so on the tabletop, one her correspondence box, where she kept recently received letters and reports from the Ajahs. The Red shared whatever their eyes-and-ears learned—she thought they did—but the other Ajahs still provided only dribbles, though they had produced a number of unwelcome pieces of information in the last week or so. Unwelcome in part because they indicated contact with the rebels that must go beyond those farcical negotiations. It was the fat, gold-embossed leather folder in front of her that she opened, however. The Tower itself generated enough reports to have buried the table had she tried to read them all herself, and Tar Valon produced ten times as many. Clerks handled the vast majority, selecting only the most important for her to read. They still made a thick stack.

"You wanted me, Mother?" Tarna said coolly, shutting the door behind her. There was no disrespect in it; the yellow-haired woman was cold by nature, her blue eyes icy. Elaida did not mind that. What irritated her was that the bright red Keeper's stole around Tarna's neck was little more than a wide ribbon. Her pale gray dress was slashed with enough red to display her pride in her Ajah, so why was her stole so narrow? But Elaida had a great deal of trust in the woman, and of late that was a rare commodity.

"What news from the harbor, Tarna?" There was no need to say which. Southharbor alone had any hope of remaining functional without massive repairs.

"Only riverships of the shallowest draft can enter," Tarna said, crossing the carpet to stand in front of the writing table. She might have been discussing the possibility of rain. Nothing fazed her. "But the rest are taking turns tying up to the part of the chain that's *cuendillar* so they can off-load into barges. The ship captains complain, and it takes considerably longer, yet for the time being, we can make do."

Elaida's mouth compressed, and she drummed her fingers on the tabletop. For the time being. She could not begin to repair the harbors until the rebels finally collapsed. So far, they had not launched an assault, thank the Light. That might begin with soldiers only, yet sisters certainly would be drawn into it, something they must want to evade

as much as she did. But razing the harbor towers, as repairs would require, laying the harbors open and defenseless, might lead them to desperate acts. Light! Fighting *must* be avoided, if at all possible. She
intended to fold their army into the Tower Guard once they realized
they were finished and returned to the Tower. Part of her already
thought as if Gareth Bryne were commanding the Tower Guard for
her. An infinitely better man for High Captain than Jimar Chubain.
The world would know the White Tower's influence then! She did not
want her soldiers killing one another, any more than she wanted the
Tower weakened by her Aes Sedai killing one another. The rebels *were*
hers as much as those inside the Tower, and she meant to make them
acknowledge it.

Picking up the top sheet from the stack of reports, she scanned it
rapidly. "Apparently, despite my express order, the streets are still not
being cleaned. Why?"

An uneasy light appeared in Tarna's eyes, the first time Elaida had
ever seen her look troubled. "People are frightened, Mother. They
don't leave their homes except at need, and with great reluctance even
then. They say they have seen the dead walking in the streets."

"This has been confirmed?" Elaida asked quietly. Her blood suddenly seemed chill. "Have any sisters seen them?"

"None in the Red, that I know of." The others would speak with
her as Keeper, yet not freely, not to share confidences. *How* under the
Light was that to be mended? "But people in the city are adamant.
They have seen what they've seen."

Slowly, Elaida set the page down to one side. She wanted to shiver.
So. She had read everything she could find concerning the Last Battle,
even studies and Foretellings so old they had never been translated out
of the Old Tongue and had lain covered in dust in the darkest corners
of the library. The al'Thor boy had been a harbinger, but now it seemed
that Tarmon Gai'don would come sooner than anyone had thought.
Several of those ancient Foretellings, from the earliest days of the
Tower, said the dead appearing was the first sign, a thinning of reality
as the Dark One gathered himself. There would be worse before long.

"Have the Tower Guards drag able-bodied men out of their houses,
if need be," she said calmly. "I want those streets clean, and I want to
hear that a start was made today. Today!"

The other woman's pale eyebrows lifted in surprise—she *had* lost her usual frigid self-control!—but all she said, of course, was, "As you command, Mother."

Elaida projected serenity, but it was a charade. What would come, would come. And she still had secured no hold on the al'Thor boy. To think she had once had him right under her hand! If only she had known then. Curse Alviarin and that triply cursed proclamation calling anathema on anyone who approached him save through the Tower. She would have recalled it, except that would seem weakness, and in any case, the damage had been done beyond simple mending. Still, soon she would have Elayne back in hand, and the Royal House of Andor was the key to winning Tarmon Gai'don. *That*, she had Foretold long ago. And news of rebellion against the Seanchan sweeping across Tarabon had been very pleasant reading. Not everything was a tangle of briars stabbing her from every side.

Scanning the second report, she grimaced. No one liked sewers, yet they were one-third of the life's blood of a city, the other two being trade and clean water. Without the sewers, Tar Valon would become prey to a dozen diseases, overwhelming anything the sisters could do, not to mention even more malodorous than the rotting garbage must have made the streets already. Though trade was cut to a trickle for the moment, the water still came in at the upriver end of the island and was distributed to watertowers throughout the city, then to fountains, ornamental and plain, that anyone was free to use, but now it seemed the sewer outlets on the downriver end of the island were nearly clogged. Dipping her pen in the ink jar, she scrawled I WANT THESE CLEARED BY TOMORROW across the top of the page and signed her name below. If the clerks had any sense, the work was already underway, but she never accused clerks of having much sense.

The next report made her own eyebrows rise. "Rats inside the Tower?" That was beyond serious! This should have been on top! "Have someone check the Wards, Tarna." Those Wardings had held since the Tower was built, but perhaps they could have weakened after three thousand years. How many of those rats were the Dark One's spies?

A rap came at the door, followed an instant later by a plump Accepted named Anemara, who spread her striped skirts in a deep curtsy. "If it pleases you, Mother, Felaana Sedai and Negaine Sedai have brought a woman to you they found wandering in the Tower. They say she wants to present a petition to the Amyrlin Seat."

"Tell her to wait and offer her tea, Anemara," Tarna said briskly. "The Mother is busy—"

"No, no," Elaida broke in. "Send them in, child. Send them in." It had been too long since anyone had come to present her with a petition. She was of a mind to grant whatever it was, if it was not too ridiculous. Perhaps that would restart the flow. It was far too long since any sisters had come to her without being summoned, too. Perhaps the two Browns would end that drought, as well.

But only one woman entered the room, carefully closing the door behind her. By her silk riding dress and good cloak, she appeared to be a noblewoman or a prosperous merchant, a supposition supported by her confident manner. Elaida was sure she had never met the woman before, yet there seemed something vaguely familiar about that face framed by hair even fairer than Tarna's.

Elaida stood and started around the table, hands outstretched and an unaccustomed smile on her face. She tried to make it seem welcoming. "I understand that you have a petition for me, my daughter. Tarna, pour her some tea." The silver pot sitting on a silver tray atop the side table must still be at least warm.

"The petition, it was something I let them believe in order to reach you unbruised, Mother," the woman replied in Taraboner accents, curtsying, and halfway through that, her face was suddenly that of Beonin Marinye.

Embracing *saidar*, Tarna wove a shield on the woman, but Elaida contented herself with planting her fists on her hips.

"To say that I'm surprised you dare show me your face would be an understatement, Beonin."

"I managed to become part of what you might call the ruling council in Salidar," the Gray said calmly. "I made sure they sat there and did nothing, and I put the rumors about that many among them were in truth your secret adherents. The sisters, they were looking at one another with so much suspicion, I think me most might have returned to the Tower soon at that point, but then other Sitters beside the Blues appeared. The next I knew, they had chosen their own Hall of the Tower, and the ruling council, it was done. Still, I continued to do what I could. I know that you commanded me to remain with them until they were all ready to return, but that must happen within days, now. If I may say, Mother, it was the most excellent decision not to try Egwene. For one thing, she has the genius for discovering new weaves, even better than Elayne Trakand or Nynaeve al'Meara. For another, before they raised her, Lelaine and Romanda struggled with one another to be named Amyrlin. With Egwene alive, they will struggle again, but neither can succeed, yes? Me, I think very soon now sisters will begin following behind me. In a week or two, Lelaine and Romanda will find themselves alone with the remainder of their so-called Hall."

"How did you know the al'Vere girl wasn't to be tried?" Elaida demanded. "How did you know she's even alive? Unshield her, Tarna!"

Tarna complied, and Beonin gave her a nod as if in gratitude. A small gratitude. Those large blue-gray eyes might make Beonin appear constantly startled, but she was a very composed woman. Combine composure with a wholehearted dedication to the law and also ambition, which she possessed in as great a measure, and Elaida had known immediately that Beonin was the one to send off after the sisters fleeing the Tower. And the woman had failed utterly! Oh, she had apparently sowed a little dissension, but really, she had achieved *nothing* of what Elaida had expected from her. Nothing! She would find her rewards commensurate with her failure.

"Egwene, she can enter *Tel'aran'rhiod* simply by going to sleep, Mother. I myself have been there and seen her, but I must use a *ter'angreal*. I could not acquire any of those the rebels have to bring with me. In any event, she spoke to Siuan Sanche, in her dreams, it is claimed, though I think more likely in the World of Dreams. Apparently, she said that she is a prisoner, but she would not tell where, and she forbade any rescue attempt. May I pour myself that tea?"

Elaida was so stunned she could not speak. She motioned Beonin to the side table, and the Gray curtsied again before going over to feel the silver pitcher cautiously with the back of her hand. The girl could *enter Tel'aran'rhiod*? And there were *ter'angreal* that allowed the same thing? The World of Dreams was almost a legend. And according to those troubling scraps the Ajahs had deigned to share with her, the girl had rediscovered the weave for Traveling and made any number of other discoveries as well. They had been the determining factor in her decision to preserve the girl for the Tower, but this on top of it?

"If Egwene can do this, Mother, perhaps she really is a Dreamer," Tarna said. "The warning she gave Silviana—"

"Is useless, Tarna. The Seanchan are still deep in Altara and barely touching Illian." At least the Ajahs were willing to pass on everything they learned of the Seanchan. Or rather, she hoped they passed on everything. The thought roughened her voice. "Unless *they* learn to Travel, can you think of any precaution I need to take beyond what is already in place?" She could not, of course. The girl had *forbidden* a rescue. That was good on the face of it, but it indicated she still thought of herself as Amyrlin. Well, Silviana would remove that nonsense from her head soon enough if the sisters teaching her classes failed. "Can she be fed enough of that potion to keep her out of *Tel'aran'rhiod*?"

Tarna grimaced slightly—no one liked that vile brew, even the Browns who had brought themselves to test it—and shook her head. "We can make her sleep through the night, but she would be useless for anything the next day, and who can say whether it would affect this ability of hers."

"May I pour for you, Mother?" Beonin said, balancing a thin white teacup on her fingertips. "Tarna? The most important news I have—"

"I don't care for any tea," Elaida said harshly. "Did you bring back anything to save your skin from your miserable failure? Do you know the weave for Traveling, or this Skimming, or. . . ." There were so many. Perhaps they were all Talents and skills that had been lost, but apparently most had not been named yet.

The Gray peered at her across the teacup, her face very still. "Yes," she said at last. "I cannot make *cuendillar*, but I can make the new Healing weaves work as well as most sisters, and I know them all." An edge of excitement crept into her voice. "The most marvelous is Traveling." Without asking permission, she embraced the Source and wove Spirit. A vertical line of silver appeared against one wall and widened into a view of snow-covered oaks. A cold breeze blew into the room, making the flames dance in the fireplace. "That is called a gateway. It can only be used to reach a place you know well, but you learn a place by making a gateway there, and to go somewhere you do not know well, you use Skimming." She altered the weave, and the opening dwindled into that silvery line once more then widened again. The oaks were replaced by blackness, and a gray-painted barge, railed and gated, that floated on nothing against the opening.

"Release the weave," Elaida said. She had the feeling that if she walked over to that barge, the darkness would extend as far as she could see in any direction. That she could fall in it forever. It made her queasy. The opening—the gateway—vanished. The memory remained, however.

Resuming her seat behind the table, she opened the largest of the lacquered boxes, decorated with red roses and golden scrollwork. From the top tray, she picked up a small ivory carving, a fork-tailed swallow dark yellow with years, and stroked her thumb along the curved wings. "You will not teach these things to anyone without receiving my permission."

"But . . . why ever not, Mother?"

"Some of the Ajahs oppose the Mother almost as strongly as those sisters beyond the river," Tarna said.

Elaida shot a dark look at her Keeper, but that cool visage absorbed it without changing a hair. "*I* will decide who is . . . reliable enough . . . to be taught, Beonin. I want your promise. No, I want your oath."

"On my way here, I saw sisters of different Ajahs glaring at one another. Glaring. What has happened in the Tower, Mother?"

"Your oath, Beonin."

The woman stood peering into her teacup long enough that Elaida was beginning to think she would refuse. But ambition won out. She had tied herself to Elaida's skirts in the hope of preferment, and she would not abandon that now. "Under the Light and by my hope of salvation and rebirth, I swear that I will teach the weaves I learned among the rebels to no one without the permission of the Amyrlin Seat." She paused, taking a sip from the cup. "Some sisters in the Tower, they are perhaps less reliable than you think. I tried to stop it, but that 'ruling council' sent ten sisters to return to the Tower and spread the tale of the Red Ajah and Logain." Elaida recognized few of the names she reeled off, until the last. That one made her sit bolt upright.

"Shall I have them arrested, Mother?" Tarna asked, still as chill as ice.

"No. Have them watched. Watch whoever they associate with." So there *was* a conduit between the Ajahs inside the Tower and the rebels. How deeply had the rot spread? However deep, she would clean it out!

"That may be difficult as matters stand, Mother."

Elaida slapped the table with her free hand, a sharp crack. "I didn't ask whether it would be difficult. I said do it! And inform Meidani that I invite her to dinner this evening." The woman had been persistent in trying to resume a friendship that had ended many years before. Now she knew why. "Go and do that now." A shadow crossed Tarna's face as she curtsied. "Don't worry," Elaida said. "Beonin can feel free to teach you every weave she knows." She did trust Tarna, after all, and it certainly made her expression brighter, if not warmer.

As the door closed behind her Keeper, Elaida pushed the leather folder to one side and leaned her elbows on the table, focusing on Beonin. "Now. Show me everything."

CHAPTER

3

At the Gardens

A ran'gar arrived in answer to Moridin's summons, spoken into
her furious dreams, to find him not yet there. That was hardly
surprising; he liked to make an entrance. Eleven tall armchairs,
carved and gilded, sat in a circle in the middle of the striped wooden
floor, but they were empty. Semirhage, all in black as usual, looked
around to see who had entered, then returned to her huddled conversation with Demandred and Mesaana in one corner of the room. Demandred's hook-nosed face carried an expression of anger that only made
him more striking. Not enough to attract her, of course. He was far too
dangerous for that. That well-fitted coat of bronze silk, with falls of
snowy lace at neck and wrists, suited him, however. Mesaana also wore
the style of this Age, a darker, pattern-embroidered bronze. She appeared wan and subdued, for some reason, almost as if she had taken
ill. Well, that was possible. This Age had a number of nasty diseases,
and it seemed unlikely even she would trust Semirhage for Healing.
Graendal, the only other human present, stood in the corner opposite
cradling a delicate crystal goblet filled with dark wine, but watching
the trio rather than drinking. Only idiots ignored being studied by
Graendal, yet the three went on with their fierce murmurs.

The chairs jarred with the rest of their surroundings. The room appeared to have view-walls, though the stone arch of a doorway de-

stroyed the illusion. The chairs could have been anything, here in
Tel'aran'rhiod, so why not something to suit the room, and why eleven
when that was surely two more than needed? Asmodean and Sammael
must be as dead as Be'lal and Rahvin. Why not the usual dilating door
of a view-room? The display made the floor seem to be surrounded by
the Ansaline Gardens, with Cormalinde Masoon's immense sculptures
of stylized humans and animals towering over low buildings themselves like delicate sculptures in spinglass. At the Gardens only the
finest wines had been served, the finest dishes, and it almost always
had been possible to impress a beautiful woman with large winnings at
the *chinje* wheels, though cheating enough to win consistently had
been difficult. Difficult, but necessary for a scholar who lacked wealth.
All gone, in ruins by the third year of the war.

A golden-haired, ever-smiling *zomara* in a flowing white blouse
and tight breeches bowed fluidly and offered Aran'gar a crystal goblet
of wine on a silver tray. Graceful and beautifully androgynous, apparently human despite those dead black eyes, the creatures had been one
of Aginor's less inspired creations. Still, even in their own Age, when
Moridin had been called Ishamael—there was no longer any doubt in
her mind of who he was—he had trusted the creatures above any human servant, despite their uselessness for every other task. Somewhere
he must have found a stasis box stuffed with the things. He had
dozens, although he seldom brought them out. Yet ten more stood
waiting, graceful while standing still. He must consider this meeting
more important than most.

Taking the goblet, she waved the *zomara* away, though it was already turning before she gestured. She hated the creatures' ability to
know what was in her head. At least it could not communicate what it
learned to anyone. Memories of anything but commands faded in minutes. Even Aginor possessed sense enough to see the need for that.
Would he appear today? Osan'gar had missed every meeting since the
failure at Shadar Logoth. The true question was, was he among the
dead or was he moving in secret, perhaps at the Great Lord's direction?
Either way, his absences presented delicious opportunities, but the latter presented as many dangers. Dangers had been much on her mind
lately.

Casually, she strolled over to Graendal. "Who do you think arrived
first, Graendal? The Shadow take me, whoever it was chose a depress-

ing setting." Lanfear had preferred meetings that floated in endless night, yet this was worse in its own way, like meeting in a cemetery.

Graendal smiled thinly. At least, she attempted a thin smile, but no amount of effort would make those lips thin. Lush was the word for all of Graendal, lush and ripe and beautiful, and barely concealed by the gray mist of her streith gown. Though perhaps she should not have worn quite so many rings, all but one adorned with gems. The coronet encrusted with rubies clashed with her sun-gold hair, too. The emerald necklace Delana had provided went much better with her own green satin silks. Of course, while the emeralds were real, her silks were a product of the World of Dreams. She would have attracted too much notice in the waking world with a dress cut so low, if it would even stay up, there. And there was the slit that bared her left leg to the hip. Her legs were better than Graendal's. She had considered two slits. Her abilities here were not as large as some—she could not find Egwene's dreams without the girl right beside her—but she could manage the clothes she wanted. She enjoyed having her body admired, and the more she flaunted it, the more the others took her for inconsequential.

"I arrived first," Graendal said, frowning slightly into her wine. "I have fond memories of the Gardens."

Aran'gar managed a laugh. "So do I, so do I." The woman was a fool like the rest, living in the past among the tatters of what was lost. "We'll never see the Gardens again, but we'll see their like." She herself was the only one of them suited to rule in this Age. She was the only one who understood primitive cultures. They had been her specialty before the war. Still, Graendal had useful skills, and a wider range of contacts among the Friends of the Dark than she herself had, though the other woman would certainly disapprove of how Aran'gar meant to use them should she learn. "Has it occurred to you that all of the others have alliances, while you and I stand alone?" And Osan'gar, if he was alive, but there was no need to bring him into this.

Graendal's gown turned a darker gray, regrettably obscuring the view. It was real streith. Aran'gar had found a pair of stasis-boxes herself, but filled with the most appalling rubbish for the most part. "Has it occurred to *you* that this room must have ears? The *zomaran* were here when I arrived."

"Graendal." She purred the name. "If Moridin is listening, he'll assume I'm trying to get into your bed. He knows I never made alliances with anyone." In truth, she had made several, but her allies always seemed to suffer fatal misfortunes once their usefulness ended, and they took all knowledge of the affiliations to their graves. Those who found graves.

The streith went black as midnight in Larcheen, and spots of color appeared on Graendal's creamy cheeks. Her eyes became blue ice. But her words were at odds with her face, and her gown faded to near transparency as she spoke, slowly, sounding thoughtful. "An intriguing notion. One I've never before considered. I might do so now. Perhaps. You will have to . . . convince me, though." Good. The other woman was as quick-witted as ever. It was a reminder that she must be careful. She meant to use Graendal and dispose of her, not be caught in one of her traps.

"I am very good at convincing beautiful women." She stretched out a hand to caress Graendal's cheek. Now was not too soon to begin convincing the others. Besides, something more than an alliance might come of it. She had always fancied Graendal. She no longer really remembered having been a man. In her memories, she wore the body she did now, which did make for a few oddities, yet that body's influence had not changed everything. Her appetites had not altered, only broadened. She would like very much to have that streith gown. And anything else useful that Graendal might possess, of course, but she dreamed of wearing that dress sometimes. The only reason she was not wearing one now was that she would not have the other woman thinking she had imitated her.

The streith remained barely opaque, but Graendal stepped away from the caress looking past Aran'gar, who turned to find Mesaana approaching, flanked by Demandred and Semirhage. He still appeared angry, and Semirhage coolly amused. Mesaana was still pale, but no longer subdued. No, not subdued at all. She was a hissing *coreer*, spitting venom.

"Why did you let her go, Aran'gar? You were supposed to be controlling her! Were you so busy playing your little dream-games with her that you forgot to learn what she was thinking? The rebellion will fall apart without her for a figurehead. All my careful planning ruined because you couldn't keep a grasp on one ignorant girl!"

Aran'gar held on to her temper firmly. She could hold it, when she was willing to make the effort. Instead of snarling, she smiled. Could Mesaana actually have based herself inside the White Tower? How wonderful it would be if she could find a way to split that threesome apart. "I listened in on a sitting of the rebels' Hall last night. In the World of Dreams, so they could meet inside the White Tower, with Egwene leading it. She's not the figurehead you believe. I've tried telling you before, but you never listened." That came out too hard. With an effort, and it required effort, she moderated her tone. "Egwene told them all about the situation inside the Tower, the Ajahs at one another's throats. She convinced them it's the Tower that is about to fall apart, and that she might be able to help it along from where she is. Were I you, I'd worry whether the Tower can hold together long enough to keep this conflict going."

"They're determined to hold on?" Mesaana murmured, half under her breath. She nodded. "Good. Good. Then everything is proceeding according to plan. I had been thinking I would need to stage some sort of 'rescue,' but perhaps I can wait until Elaida has broken her. Her return should create even more confusion, then. You need to sow more dissension, Aran'gar. Before I'm done, I want these so-called Aes Sedai hating each other in their blood."

A *zomara* appeared, bowing gracefully as it offered a tray with three goblets. Mesaana and her companions took the wine without a glance at the creature, and it bowed again before flowing away.

"Dissension was always something she was good at," Semirhage said. Demandred laughed.

Aran'gar forced her anger down. Sipping her own wine—it was quite good, with a heady aroma, if nowhere near the vintages served at the Gardens—she laid her free hand on Graendal's shoulder and toyed with one of those sun-colored curls. The other woman never flinched, and the streith remained a bare mist. Either she was enjoying this, or she had better control of herself than seemed possible. Semirhage's smile grew more amused. She, too, took her pleasures where she found them, though Semirhage's pleasures had never attracted Aran'gar.

"If you're going to fondle one another," Demandred growled, "do it in private."

"Jealous?" Aran'gar murmured, and laughed lightly at his scowl. "Where is the girl kept, Mesaana? She didn't say."

Mesaana's big blue eyes narrowed. They were her best feature, yet only ordinary when she frowned. "Why do you want to know? So you can 'rescue' her yourself? I won't tell you."

Graendal hissed, and Aran'gar realized that her hand had become a fist in that golden hair, bending Graendal's head back. The other woman's face remained tranquil, but her gown was a red mist and rapidly growing darker, more opaque. Aran'gar loosened her grip, holding on lightly. One of the first steps was making your quarry accustomed to your touch. She did nothing to keep the anger from her voice this time, however. Her bared teeth were an undisguised snarl. "I want the girl, Mesaana. Without her, I have much weaker tools to work with."

Mesaana sipped wine calmly before responding. Calmly! "By your own account, you don't need her at all. It has been *my* plan from the start, Aran'gar. I will adapt it according to need, but it is mine. And *I* will decide when and where the girl is set free."

"No, Mesaana, *I* will decide when and where, or whether, she is freed," Moridin announced, striding through the stone arch. So he *had* set ears in place. He was in unrelieved black this time, a black somehow darker than what Semirhage wore. As usual, Moghedien and Cyndane followed him, both attired in identical red-and-black that suited neither. What hold did he have on them? Moghedien, at least, had never willingly followed anyone. As for that beautiful, bosomy little pale-haired doll Cyndane. . . . Aran'gar had approached her, just to see what might be learned, and the girl had coldly threatened to rip her heart out if Aran'gar touched her again. Hardly the words of someone who submitted easily.

"Sammael appears to have resurfaced," Moridin announced, crossing the floor to take a seat. He was a big man, and he made the ornate high-backed chair seem a throne. Moghedien and Cyndane sat down to either side of him, but interestingly, not until he had. *Zomaran* in snowy white were there instantly with wine, yet Moridin received his first. Whatever was at work there, the *zomaran* sensed it.

"That hardly seems possible," Graendal said as they all moved to take chairs. Her gown was dark gray now, concealing everything. "He must be dead." No one moved quickly, though. Moridin was Nae'blis, yet no one except Moghedien and Cyndane was willing to display any hint of subservience. Aran'gar certainly was not.

She took a seat across from Moridin, where she could watch him without seeming to. And Moghedien and Cyndane. Moghedien was so still she would have faded into the chair except for her bright dress. Cyndane was a queen, her face chiseled from ice. Trying to pull down the Nae'blis was dangerous, yet those two might hold the key. If she could figure out how to turn it. Graendal sat down beside her, and the chair was suddenly closer. Aran'gar could have laid her hand on the other woman's wrist but refrained from anything more than a slow smile. It was best to keep her mind centered right then.

"He could never have borne staying hidden this long," Demandred put in, lounging into his chair between Semirhage and Mesaana, legs crossed as though perfectly at ease. That seemed doubtful. He was another who was unreconciled, she was sure. "Sammael needed to have every eye directed at him."

"Nevertheless, Sammael, or someone disguised as him, gave orders to Myrddraal, and they obeyed, so it was one of the Chosen." Moridin scanned around the chairs as though he could detect who it had been. Black *saa* trickled across his blue eyes in a continuous stream. She had no regrets that the True Power was limited to his use alone, now. The price was much too high. Ishamael had certainly been at least half insane, and he still was as Moridin. How long before she could remove him?

"Are you going to tell us what these orders were?" Semirhage's tone was cool, and she sipped her wine calmly, watching Moridin over the goblet's rim. She sat very erect, but she always did. She too appeared completely at ease, yet that was unlikely.

Moridin's jaw tightened. "I don't know," he said at last, reluctantly. He never liked saying that. "But they sent a hundred Myrddraal and thousands of Trollocs into the Ways."

"That sounds like Sammael," Demandred said thoughtfully, twisting his goblet and studying the swirling wine. "Perhaps I was mistaken." A remarkable admission, coming from him. Or an attempt to hide being the one who had worn Sammael as a disguise. She would like very much to know who had begun playing her own game. Or whether Sammael really was alive.

Moridin grunted sourly. "Pass orders to your Friends of the Dark. Any report of Trollocs or Myrddraal outside the Blight is to be handed to me as soon as you receive it. The Time of Return is coming soon. No one is allowed to go adventuring on their own any longer." He studied them again, each in turn save for Moghedien and Cyndane. With a smile even more languorous than Graendal's, Aran'gar met his gaze. Mesaana shrank back from it.

"As you learned to your sorrow," he told Mesaana, and impossible as it seemed, her face went paler still. She took a long drink from her goblet, her teeth clicking on the crystal. Semirhage and Demandred avoided looking at her.

Aran'gar exchanged looks with Graendal. Something had been done to punish Mesaana's failure to appear at Shadar Logoth, but what? Once, dereliction on that scale would have meant death. They were too few for that, now. Cyndane and Moghedien appeared as curious as she was, so they did not know either.

"We can see the signs as clearly as you, Moridin," Demandred said irritably. "The Time *is* near. We need to find the rest of the seals on the Great Lord's prison. I've had my followers searching everywhere, but they've found nothing."

"Ah, yes. The seals. Indeed, they must be found." Moridin's smile was almost complacent. "Only three remain, all in al'Thor's possession, though I doubt he has them with him. They're too susceptible to breaking, now. He will have hidden them. Direct your people to places he has been. Search them yourselves."

"The easiest way is to kidnap Lews Therin." In strong contrast to her ice-maiden appearance, Cyndane's voice was breathy and sultry, a voice made for lying on soft pillows wearing very little. There was considerable heat in those big blue eyes, now. A searing heat. "I can make him tell where the seals are."

"No!" Moridin snapped, fixing her with a steady stare. "You would 'accidentally' kill him. The time and manner of al'Thor's death will be at my choosing. No one else." Strangely, he put his free hand to the breast of his coat, and Cyndane flinched. Moghedien shivered. "No one else," he repeated, in a hard voice.

"No one else," Cyndane said. When he lowered his hand, she exhaled softly then took a swallow of wine. Sweat glistened on her forehead.

Aran'gar found the exchange illuminating. It seemed that once she had disposed of Moridin, she would have Moghedien and the girl on leashes. Very good, indeed.

Moridin straightened himself in his chair, directing that stare at the rest of them. "That goes for all of you. Al'Thor is mine. You will not harm him in any way!" Cyndane bent her head over her goblet, sipping, but the hatred in her eyes was plain. Graendal had said she was not Lanfear, that she was weaker in the One Power, but she surely was fixated on al'Thor, and she called him by the same name Lanfear had always used.

"If you want to kill someone," he went on, "kill these two!" Suddenly the semblances of two young men in rough country clothes stood in the center of the circle, turning so that everyone could get a good look at their faces. One was tall and wide, with yellow eyes, of all things, while the other was not quite slender and wore a cheeky grin. Creations of *Tel'aran'rhiod*, they moved stiffly and their expressions never altered. "Perrin Aybara and Mat Cauthon are *ta'veren*, easily found. Find them, and kill them."

Graendal laughed, a mirthless sound. "Finding *ta'veren* was never as simple as you made out, and now it's harder than ever. The whole Pattern is in flux, full of shifts and spikes."

"Perrin Aybara and Mat Cauthon," Semirhage murmured, inspecting the two shapes. "So that is what they look like. Who knows, Moridin. If you had shared this with us before now, they might already have been dead."

Moridin's fist came down hard on the arm of his chair. "Find them! Make doubly sure that your followers know their faces. Find Aybara and Cauthon and kill them! The Time is coming, and they must be dead!"

Aran'gar took a sip of her wine. She had no objections to killing these two if she happened to come across them, but Moridin was going to be terribly disappointed over Rand al'Thor.

CHAPTER
4

A Deal

P errin sat Stepper's saddle a little back from the edge of the trees and watched the large meadow where red and blue wildflowers were beginning to poke through the winter-brown grass that the now vanished snows had flattened into a mat. This stand was mainly leatherleaf that kept its broad dark foliage through the winter, but only a few small pale leaves decorated the branches of the sweetgums among them. The dun stallion stamped a hoof with an impatience Perrin shared, though he let none of it show. The sun stood almost overhead; he had been waiting there nearly an hour. A stiff, steady breeze blew out of the west, down the meadow toward him. That was good.

Every so often his gauntleted hand stroked a nearly straight branch hacked from an oak, thicker than his forearm and more than twice as long, that lay across the saddle in front of him. For half its length he had shaved two sides flat and smooth. The meadow, ringed by huge oaks and leatherleaf, towering pine and shorter sweetgum, was less than six hundred paces wide, though longer than that. The branch should be broad enough. He had planned for every possibility he could imagine. The branch fit more than one.

"My Lady First, you should return to the camp," Gallenne said, not for the first time, rubbing irritably at his red eyepatch. His crimson-plumed helmet hung from the pommel of his saddle, leaving his shoulder-length gray hair uncovered. He had been heard to say, in Berelain's hearing, that most of those gray hairs were presents from her. His black warhorse tried to take a nip at Stepper, and he reined the heavy-chested gelding sharply without taking his attention from Berelain. He had counseled against her coming in the first place. "Grady can take you back and return while the rest of us wait a while longer to see whether the Seanchan are going to show up."

"I will remain, Captain. I *will* remain." Berelain's tone was firm and calm, yet beneath her usual smell of patience lay an edge of concern. She was not so certain as she made herself sound. She had taken to wearing a light perfume that smelled of flowers. Perrin sometimes found himself trying to puzzle out which flowers, but he was too focused for idle thoughts today.

Vexation spiked in Annoura's scent, though her ageless Aes Sedai face, framed by dozens of thin braids, remained as smooth as ever. But then, the beak-nosed Gray sister had smelled vexed ever since the rift between her and Berelain. It was her own fault, visiting Masema behind Berelain's back. She also had counseled Berelain to stay behind. Annoura edged her brown mare closer to the First of Mayene, and Berelain moved her white mare just that far away without so much as a glance in her advisor's direction. Vexation spiked again.

Berelain's red silk dress, heavily embroidered in golden scrollwork, displayed more bosom than she had in some time, though a wide necklace of firedrops and opals provided a degree of modesty. A wide matching belt, supporting a jeweled dagger, cinched her waist. The narrow crown of Mayene resting on her black hair, holding a golden hawk in flight above her brows, appeared ordinary beside the belt and necklace. She was a beautiful woman, the more so, it seemed to him, since she had stopped chasing him, though still not a patch on Faile, of course.

Annoura wore an unadorned gray riding dress, but most of them were in their best. For Perrin, that was a dark green silk coat with silver embroidery covering the sleeves and shoulders. He was not much for fancy clothes—Faile had chivvied him into buying what little he had; well, she had chivvied him gently—but today he needed to impress. If the wide, plain leather belt fastened over the coat spoiled the impression a little, so be it.

"She must come," Arganda muttered. A short stocky man, Alliandre's

First Captain had not removed his silvered helmet with its three short white plumes, and he sat his saddle, easing his sword in its scabbard, as though awaiting a charge. His breastplate was silver-plated, too. He would be visible for miles out in the sunlight. "She must!"

"The Prophet says they won't," Aram put in, and not softly, heeling his leggy gray up beside Stepper. The brass wolfhead pommel of his sword stuck up over the shoulder of his green-striped coat. Once, he had seemed too good looking for a man, but now his face grew grimmer every day. There was a haggardness about him, his eyes sunken and his mouth tight. "The Prophet says either that, or it's a trap. He says we shouldn't trust the Seanchan."

Perrin held his silence, but felt his own spike of irritation, as much with himself as with the onetime Tinker. Balwer had informed him that Aram had begun spending time with Masema, yet it had seemed unnecessary to tell the man not to let Masema know everything Perrin was doing. There was no putting the egg back into the shell, but he would know better in the future. A workman should know his tools, and not use them to breaking. The same went for people. As for Masema, no doubt he was afraid they would meet someone who knew he himself was dealing with the Seanchan.

They were a large party, though most would remain right there among the trees. Fifty of Berelain's Winged Guards in rimmed red helmets and red breastplates, scarlet streamers floating from their slender steel-tipped lances, were mounted behind the golden hawk on blue of Mayene, rippling on the breeze. Beside them fifty Ghealdanin in burnished breastplates and dark green conical helmets sat their horses behind Ghealdan's three silver stars on red. The streamers on their lances were green. They made a brave show, yet all of them together were far less deadly than Jur Grady, with his weathered farmer's face, even if they made him appear drab in his plain black coat with a silver sword pin on the high collar. He knew it, whether or not they did, and he stood beside his bay gelding with the ease of a man resting before the day's labor.

In contrast, Leof Torfinn and Tod al'Caar, the only other Two Rivers men present, were still all but bouncing in their saddles with excitement despite the long wait. It might have taken some of their pleasure away had they known they had been chosen in large part because they came nearest fitting their borrowed coats of dark, finely woven green wool. Leof carried Perrin's own Red Wolfhead banner, Tod the Red Eagle of Manetheren, both rippling on staffs a little longer than the lances. They had almost come to blows over who was to carry which. Perrin hoped it was not because neither wanted to carry the red-bordered Wolfhead. Leof looked happy enough. Tod looked ecstatic. Of course, he did not know why Perrin had brought the thing along. In any trade, you needed to make the other fellow think he was getting something extra, as Mat's father often said. Colors swirled in Perrin's head, and for a brief instant he thought he saw Mat talking to a small dark woman. He shook off the image. Here and now, today, were all that mattered. Faile was all that mattered.

"They will come," Arganda snapped in answer to Aram, though he glared through the face-bars of his helmet as if expecting a challenge.

"What if they don't?" Gallenne demanded, his one eye scowling as fiercely as Arganda's pair. His red-lacquered breastplate was not much better than Arganda's silvered one. Small chance they could be talked into painting them something dull. "What if it *is* a trap?" Arganda growled, almost a wolf's guttural growl. The man was near the end of his tether.

The breeze brought the scent of horses only moments before Perrin's ears caught the first bluetits' trills, too distant for anyone else to hear. They came from the trees flanking the meadow. Large parties of men, perhaps unfriendly, were entering the woods. More trills sounded, closer.

"They're here," he said, which earned him looks from Arganda and Gallenne. He tried to avoid revealing the acuteness of his hearing, or his sense of smell, yet that pair had been on the point of coming to blows. The relayed trills grew nearer, and everyone could hear them. The two men's looks grew odd.

"I can't risk the Lady First if there's any chance of a trap," Gallenne said, buckling on his helmet. They all knew what the signal meant.

"The choice is mine, Captain," Berelain replied before Perrin could open his mouth.

"And your safety is my responsibility, my Lady First."

Berelain drew breath, her face darkening, but Perrin got there first. "I told you how we're going to spring that trap, if that's what it is. You know how suspicious the Seanchan are. Likely they're worried about us ambushing them." Gallenne harrumphed loudly. The patience in Berelain's smell flickered, then settled in again rock steady.

"You should listen to him, Captain," she said with a smile for Perrin. "He knows what he is doing."

A party of riders appeared at the far end of the meadow and drew rein. Tallanvor was easy to pick out. In a dark coat and mounted on a good dappled gray, he was the only man not wearing armor vividly striped in red and yellow and blue. The other pair unarmored were women, one in blue with red on her skirts and breast, the other in gray. The sun reflected off something connecting them. So. A *sul'dam* and *damane*. There had been no mention of that in all the negotiations carried out through Tallanvor, but Perrin had counted on it.

"It's time," he said, gathering Stepper's reins one-handed. "Before she decides *we're* not coming."

Annoura managed to get close enough to lay a hand on Berelain's arm for a moment before the other woman could move her mare away. "You should let me come with you, Berelain. You may need my counsel, yes? This sort of negotiation, it is my specialty."

"I suspect the Seanchan know an Aes Sedai face by now, don't you, Annoura? I hardly think they'd negotiate with you. Besides," Berelain added, in a too sweet voice, "you must remain here to assist Master Grady."

Spots of color appeared briefly on the Aes Sedai's cheeks, and her wide mouth tightened. It had taken the Wise Ones to make her agree to take orders from Grady today, though Perrin was just as glad he did not know how they had done it, and she had been trying to wiggle out ever since leaving the camp.

"You stay, too," Perrin said when Aram made to ride forward. "You've been hotheaded lately, and I won't risk you saying or doing the wrong thing out there. I won't risk Faile on it." That was true. No need to say he would not risk the man carrying what was said out there back to Masema. "You understand?"

Bubbles of disappointment filled Aram's scent, but he nodded, however reluctantly, and rested his hands on the pommel of his saddle. He might come close to worshiping Masema, but he would give his life a hundred times over rather than risk Faile's. On purpose, anyway. What he did without thinking was another matter.

Perrin rode out of the trees flanked by Arganda on one side and Berelain and Gallenne on the other. The banners followed behind, and ten Mayeners and ten Ghealdanin in a column of twos. As they walked their mounts forward, the Seanchan started toward them, also in column, with Tallanvor riding beside the leaders, one on a roan, the other a bay. The horses' hooves made no sound on the thick mat of dead grass. The forest had gone silent, even to Perrin's ears.

While the Mayeners and Ghealdanin spread out in a line, and most of the Seanchan in their brightly painted armor did the same, Perrin and Berelain advanced toward Tallanvor and two of the armored Seanchan, one with three thin blue plumes on that lacquered helmet that was so like an insect's head, the other with two. The *sul'dam* and *damane* came, too. They met in the middle of the meadow, surrounded by wildflowers and silence, with six paces between them.

As Tallanvor positioned himself to one side between the two groups, the armored Seanchan removed their helmets with hands in steel-backed gauntlets that were striped like the rest of their armor. The two-plumed helmet revealed a yellow-haired man with half a dozen scars seaming his square face. He was a hard-bitten man who smelled of amusement, strangely, but it was the other who interested Perrin. Mounted on the bay, a trained warhorse if he had ever seen one, she was tall and broad-shouldered for a woman, though lean otherwise, and not young. Gray marked the temples of her close-cut, tightly curled black hair. As dark as good topsoil, she displayed only two scars, one slanting across her left cheek. The other, on her forehead, had taken part of her right eyebrow. Some people thought scars a sign of toughness. It seemed to Perrin that fewer scars meant that you knew what you were doing. Confidence filled the scent of her in the breeze.

Her gaze flickered across the fluttering banners. He thought she paused slightly on Manetheren's Red Eagle, and again on Mayene's Golden Hawk, yet she quickly settled to studying him. Her expression never altered a whit, but when she noticed his yellow eyes, something unidentifiable entered her scent, something sharp and hard. When she saw the heavy blacksmith's hammer in its loop on his belt, the strange scent grew.

"I give you Perrin t'Bashere Aybara, Lord of the Two Rivers, Liege Lord to Queen Alliandre of Ghealdan," Tallanvor announced, raising a hand toward Perrin. He claimed the Seanchan were sticklers for formality, but Perrin had no idea whether this was a Seanchan ceremony or something from Andor. Tallanvor could have made it up for all of him. "I give you Berelain sur Paendrag Paeron, First of Mayene, Blessed of the Light, Defender of the Waves, High Seat of House Paeron." With a bow to the pair of them, he shifted his reins and raised the other hand toward the Seanchan. "I give you Banner-General Tylee Khirgan of the Ever Victorious Army, in service to the Empress of Seanchan. I give you Captain Bakayar Mishima of the Ever Victorious Army, in service to the Empress of Seanchan." Another bow, and Tallanvor turned his gray to ride back to a place beside the banners. His face was as grim as Aram's, but he smelled of hope.

"I'm glad he didn't name you the Wolf King, my Lord," the Banner-General drawled. The way she slurred her words, Perrin had to listen hard to make out what she was saying. "Otherwise, I'd think Tarmon Gai'don was on us. You know the Prophecies of the Dragon? 'When the Wolf King carries the hammer, thus are the final days known. When the fox marries the raven, and the trumpets of battle are blown.' I never understood that second line, myself. And you, my Lady. Sur Paendrag. That would mean from Paendrag?"

"My family is descended from Artur Paendrag Tanreall," Berelain replied, holding her head high. An eddy in the breeze brought a whiff of pride among the patience and perfume. They had agreed that Perrin was to do all of the talking—she was there to dazzle the Seanchan with a beautiful young ruler, or at least to lend weight to Perrin with it—but he supposed she had to answer a direct question.

Tylee nodded as though that were exactly the answer she expected. "That makes you a distant cousin of the Imperial family, my Lady. No doubt the Empress, may she live forever, will honor you. So long as you make no claims to Hawkwing's empire yourself, anyway."

"The only claim I make is to Mayene," Berelain said proudly. "And that I will defend to my last breath."

"I didn't come here to talk about the Prophecies or Hawkwing or your Empress," Perrin said irritably. For the second time in a matter of moments those colors tried to coalesce in his head only to be dispelled. He had no time. The Wolf King? Hopper would come as near to laughing as a wolf could over that. Any wolf would. Still, he felt a chill. He had not realized that he was mentioned in the Prophecies. And his hammer was a harbinger of the Last Battle? But nothing mattered except Faile. Only her. And whatever it took to free her. "The agreement for this meeting was no more than thirty in either party, but you have men in the woods on both sides of us. A lot of men."

"So do you," Mishima said with grin distorted by a white scar that met the corner of his mouth, "or you wouldn't know about ours." His drawl was worse than hers.

Perrin kept his eyes on the Banner-General. "As long as they both remain, there's the chance of accidents. I don't want any accidents. I want my wife back from the Shaido."

"And how do you propose we avoid accidents?" Mishima said, idly flipping his reins. He sounded as though the question was not urgent. It seemed Tylee was content to let him do the talking while she observed Perrin's reactions. "Are we supposed to trust you if we send our men out first, or you to trust us if we ask you to withdraw first? 'On the heights, the paths are paved with daggers.' There isn't much room for trust. I suppose we could both order our men to pull back at the same time, but one side might cheat."

Perrin shook his head. "You're going to have to trust me, Banner-General. I have no reason to want to attack you or capture you, and every reason not to. I can't be sure of the same about you. You might think capturing the First of Mayene worth a little betrayal." Berelain laughed softly. It was time for the branch. Not just to force the Seanchan out of the woods first, but to convince them that they needed what he could offer. He stood the branch upright on the saddle in front of him. "I expect your men are probably good soldiers. My men aren't soldiers, though they've fought Trollocs and Shaido and done well against both." Gripping the branch at its base, he held it high overhead, the shaved sides uppermost and facing either side. "But they're used to hunting lions and leopards and ridgecats come down out of the mountains after our flocks, and wild boar and bear, animals that hunt back, in forests not much different from this."

The branch tried to twist violently in his gauntleted fist as twin impacts not a heartbeat apart shivered down his arm. He lowered the branch to display two pile arrows, their chisel-shaped heads driven clear of the tough wood on either side. Three hundred paces was a long range for that target, but he had chosen Jondyn Barran and Jori Congar to makes the shots. They were the best he had. "If it comes down to it, your men won't even see who's killing them, and that armor won't do much good against a Two Rivers longbow. I hope it doesn't come to that." With all of his strength, he heaved the branch up into the air.

"My eyes!" Mishima growled, a hand going to his sword even as he tried to rein the roan back and watch Perrin and the branch all at the same time. His helmet toppled from his saddle to the grass.

The Banner-General made no move toward her sword, though she also tried watching Perrin and the branch. At first she did. Then her gaze followed only the branch as it continued to climb until it hung centered between them a hundred feet in the air. Abruptly a ball of flame enveloped the branch, so fierce that Perrin felt the heat as from an open furnace. Berelain put up a hand to shield her face. Tylee merely watched thoughtfully.

The fire lasted just moments, yet that was enough to leave only ash drifting on the breeze when it vanished. Ash and two plummeting specks that fell into the dry grass. Small flames shot up immediately and began growing, spreading. Even the warhorses snorted in fear. Berelain's mare danced in an attempt to fight her reins and flee.

Perrin muttered a curse—he should have thought of the arrowheads—and started to dismount to stamp out the fire, but before he could swing his leg over the saddle, the flames vanished, leaving only thin tendrils of smoke rising from a patch of blackened grass.

"Good Norie," the *sul'dam* murmured, patting the *damane*. "Norie is a wonderful *damane*." The gray-clad woman smiled shyly at the praise. Despite her words, the *sul'dam* looked worried.

"So," Tylee said, "you have a *marath*—" She paused, pursing her lips. "You have an Aes Sedai with you. More than one? No matter. I can't say the Aes Sedai I've seen have impressed me very much."

"Not *marath'damane*, my general," the *sul'dam* said quietly.

Tylee sat very still, studying Perrin intently. "Asha'man," she said at last, not a question. "You begin to interest me, my Lord."

"Then maybe one last thing will convince you," Perrin said. "Tod, roll that banner around the staff and bring it here." Hearing nothing behind him, he looked over his shoulder. Tod was staring at him with a stricken look. "Tod."

Giving himself a shake, Tod began winding the Red Eagle around its staff. He still looked unhappy when he rode forward and handed it to Perrin, though. He sat there with his hand still stretched out as though hoping the staff might be returned to him.

Heeling Stepper toward the Seanchan, Perrin held the banner in front of him in his fist, parallel to the ground. "The Two Rivers was the heart of Manetheren, Banner-General. The last King of Manetheren died in a battle right where Emond's Field, the village I was born in, grew up. Manetheren is in our blood. But the Shaido have my wife prisoner. To free her, I'll give up any claim to reviving Manetheren, sign any sort of oath on it you want. That claim would be a field of brambles for you Seanchan. You could be the one who cleared that field without a drop of blood shed." Behind him, someone groaned miserably. He thought it was Tod.

Suddenly, the breeze was a gale howling in the opposite direction, pelting them with grit, blowing so hard that he had to cling to his saddle to kept from being knocked out of it. His coat seemed on the point of being ripped from his body. Where had the grit come from? The forest was carpeted inches deep with dead leaves. The tempest stank of burned sulphur, too, sharp enough to burn Perrin's nose. The horses tossed their heads, mouths open, but the roar of the wind buried their frightened whinnies.

Only moments the ferocious wind lasted, and then as suddenly as it came, it was gone, leaving only the breeze blowing the other way The horses stood shivering, snorting and tossing their heads and rolling their eyes. Perrin patted Stepper's neck and murmured soothing sounds, yet it had little effect.

The Banner-General made a strange gesture and muttered, "Avert the Shadow. Where under the Light did that come from? I've heard tales of strange things happening. Or was it more 'convincing' on your part, my Lord?"

"No," Perrin said truthfully. Neald possessed abilities with weather, it had turned out, but not Grady. "What does it matter where it came from?"

Tylee looked at him thoughtfully, then nodded. "What does it matter?" she said, sounding as if she did not necessarily agree with him. "We have stories about Manetheren. That *would* be brambles underfoot and no boots. Half of Amadicia is buzzing with talk of you and that banner, come to bring Manetheren alive again and 'save' Amadicia from us. Mishima, sound withdrawal." Without hesitation, the yellow-haired man raised a small, straight horn that was hanging by a red cord around his neck. Blowing four shrill notes, he repeated the sequence twice before letting the horn fall to swing against his chest. "My part is done," Tylee said.

Perrin put back his head and shouted as loudly and distinctly as he could. "Dannil! Tell! When the last Seanchan moves below the end of the meadow, gather everyone and join Grady!"

The Banner-General stuck her little finger into her ear and wiggled it about in spite of her gauntlet. "You have a strong voice," she said dryly. Only then did she reach out to take the banner-staff, laying it carefully across the saddle in front of her. She did not look at it again, but one hand stroked the banner itself, perhaps unconsciously. "Now what do you have that can aid my plan, my Lord?" Mishima hooked an ankle behind the tall pommel of his saddle and lowered himself to catch up his helmet. The wind had rolled it across the beaten-down grass halfway back to the line of Seanchan soldiers. From the trees came a brief snatch of larksong, then another, another. The Seanchan were withdrawing. Had they felt the wind, too? No matter.

"Not near as many men as you already have," Perrin admitted, "not that are trained soldiers, at least, but I have Asha'man and Aes Sedai and Wise Ones who can channel, and you'll need every one of them." She opened her mouth, and he raised a hand. "I'll want your word that you won't try putting collars on them." He glanced pointedly at the *sul'dam* and *damane*. The *sul'dam* was keeping her eyes on Tylee, awaiting orders, but at the same time she was idly stroking the other woman's hair the way you might stroke a cat to soothe it. And Norie looked to be almost purring! Light! "Your word that they're safe from you, them and anyone in the camp wearing a white robe. Most of those aren't Shaido anyway, and the only Aiel among them I know about are friends of mine."

Tylee shook her head. "You have strange friends, my Lord. In any case, we've found people from Cairhien and Amadicia with bands of Shaido and let them go, though most of the Cairhienin seem too disoriented to know what to do with themselves. The only ones in white we keep are the Aiel. These *gai'shain* make marvelous *da'covale*, unlike the rest. Still, I'll agree to letting your friends go free. And your Aes Sedai and Asha'man. Putting an end to this gathering is very important. Tell me where they are, and I can start incorporating you into my plans."

Perrin rubbed the side of his nose with a finger. It seemed unlikely many of those *gai'shain* were Shaido, but he was not about to tell her that. Let them have their chance at freedom when their year and a day was up. "It'll have to be my plan, I'm afraid. Sevanna will be a tough nut to crack, but I've worked out how. For one thing, she has maybe a hundred thousand Shaido with her, and she's gathering in more. Not every one is *algai'd'siswai*, but any adult will pick up a spear if they need to."

"Sevanna." Tylee gave a pleased smile. "We've heard that name. I would dearly love to present Sevanna of the Jumai Shaido to the Captain-General." Her smile faded. "A hundred thousand is many

more than I expected, but not more than I can handle. We've fought
these Aiel before, in Amadicia. Eh, Mishima?"

Riding back to join them, Mishima laughed, but it was a harsh
sound, no amusement in it. "That we have, Banner-General. They're
fierce fighters, disciplined and crafty, but they can be handled. You surround one of their bands, their septs, with three or four *damane* and
pound them till they give up. It's a nasty business. They have their
families with them. But they surrender the sooner for it."

"I understand you have a dozen or so *damane*," Perrin said, "but is
that enough to face three or four hundred Wise Ones channeling?"

The Banner-General frowned. "You mentioned that before, Wise
Ones channeling. Every band we've caught had its Wise Ones, but not
one of them could channel."

"That's because all the Shaido have are with Sevanna," Perrin
replied. "At least three hundred and maybe four. The Wise Ones with
me are sure of it."

Tylee and Mishima exchanged a look, and the Banner-General
sighed. Mishima looked glum. "Well," she said, "orders or no orders,
that puts an end to finishing this quietly. The Daughter of the Nine
Moons will have to be disturbed if I must apologize for it to the Empress, may she live forever. Likely I will." The Daughter of the Nine
Moons? Some high-ranking Seanchan, apparently. But how was she
supposed to be disturbed by any of this?

Mishima grimaced, a fearsome sight with all those scars crisscross-
ing his face. "I read there were four hundred *damane* on each side at
Semalaren, and that was a slaughterhouse. Half the Imperial army on
the field dead and better than three out of four among the rebels."

"Nevertheless, Mishima, we have it to do. Or rather, someone else
does. You might escape an apology, but I won't." What under the
Light was so upsetting about an apology? The woman smelled . . . resigned. "Unfortunately, it will take weeks if not months to gather
enough soldiers and *damane* to prick this boil. I thank you for your offer of help, my Lord. It will be remembered." Tylee held out the banner. "You'll want this back since I can't deliver my side of the bargain,
but a piece of advice. The Ever Victorious Army may have other tasks
in front of it for the nonce, but we won't let anyone take momentary
advantage of the situation to set himself up as a king. We mean to reclaim this land, not divide it into parcels."

"And we mean to keep our lands," Berelain said fiercely, making her mare lunge across the few paces of dead grass between her and the Seanchan. The mare was eager to lunge, eager to run, away from that wind, and she had trouble reining the animal in. Even her scent was fierce. No patience now. She smelled like a she-wolf defending her injured mate. "I've heard that your Ever Victorious Army is misnamed. I've heard the Dragon Reborn defeated you soundly to the south. Don't you ever think that Perrin Aybara can't do the same." Light, and he had been worried over Aram's hotheadedness!

"I don't want to defeat anybody except the Shaido," Perrin said firmly, fighting off the image that tried to form in his mind. He folded his hands on the pommel of his saddle. Stepper seemed to be settling down, at least. The stallion still gave small shivers now and then, but he had stopped rolling his eyes. "There's a way to do that and still keep everything quiet so you don't need to apologize." If that was important to her, he was ready to use it. "The Daughter of the Nine Moons can rest easy. I told you I had this planned out. Tallanvor told me you have some kind of tea that makes a woman who can channel go wobbly in the knees."

After a moment, Tylee lowered the banner back to her saddle and sat studying him. "A woman or a man," she drawled at last. "I've heard of several men being caught that way. But just how do you propose feeding it to these four hundred women when they're surrounded by a hundred thousand Aiel?"

"By feeding it to all of them without letting them know they're drinking it. I'll need as much as I can get, though. Wagonloads, probably. There's no way to heat the water, you see, so it'll be thin tea."

Tylee laughed softly. "A bold plan, my Lord. I suppose they might have cartloads at the manufactory where the tea's made, but that's a long way from here, in Amadicia almost to Tarabon, and the only way I could get more than a few pounds at once would be to tell someone of higher rank why I wanted it. And there's the end of keeping it quiet all over again."

"The Asha'man know a thing called Traveling," Perrin told her, "a way to cross hundred of miles in a step. And as for getting the tea, maybe this will help." From his left gauntlet he pulled a folded, grease-stained piece of paper.

Tylee's eyebrows rose as she read it. Perrin had the short text by heart. THE BEARER OF THIS STANDS UNDER MY PERSONAL PROTECTION. IN THE NAME OF THE EMPRESS, MAY SHE LIVE FOREVER, GIVE HIM WHAT-

EVER AID HE REQUIRES IN SERVICE TO THE EMPIRE AND SPEAK OF IT TO NONE BUT ME. He had no idea who Suroth Sabelle Meldarath was, but if she signed her name to something like that, she had to be important. Maybe she was this Daughter of the Nine Moons.

Handing the paper to Mishima, the Banner-General stared at Perrin. That sharp, hard scent was back, stronger than ever. "Aes Sedai, Asha'man, Aiel, your eyes, that hammer, now this! Who *are* you?"

Mishima whistled through his teeth. "Suroth herself," he murmured.

"I'm a man who wants his wife back," Perrin said, "and I'll deal with the Dark One to get her." He avoided looking at the *sul'dam* and *damane*. He was not far short of making a deal with the Dark One. "Do we have a bargain?"

Tylee looked at his outstretched hand, then took it. She had a firm grip. A deal with the Dark One. But he would do whatever it took to get Faile free.

CHAPTER
5

Something . . . Strange

T he drumbeat of rain on the tent roof that had lasted through
most of the night faded to something softer as Faile approached
Sevanna's chair, a heavily carved and gilded throne placed in the
center of the bright, layered carpets that made up the tent's floor, with
her eyes carefully lowered, to avoid offense. Spring had arrived in a
rush, but the braziers were unlit, and the morning air held a touch of
chill. Curtsying deeply, she presented the ropework silver tray. The
Aiel woman took the golden goblet of wine and drank without so
much as a glance in her direction, but she gave another deep curtsy before backing away and setting the tray down on the brass-bound blue
chest that already held a tall-necked silver wine pitcher and three more
goblets, then returned to her place with the other eleven *gai'shain* present, standing between the mirrored stand-lamps along the red silk tent
wall. It was a spacious tent, and tall. No low Aiel tent for Sevanna.

Often it was hard to see her as Aiel at all. This morning, she
lounged in a red brocaded silk robe, tied so it gaped nearly to her waist
and exposed half her considerable bosom, though she wore enough
jeweled necklaces, emeralds and firedrops and opals, ropes of fat pearls,
that she came near to being decent. The Aiel did not wear rings, yet
Sevanna had at least one be-gemmed ring on every finger. The thick
band of gold and firedrops worn over the folded blue silk scarf that

held back her waist-long yellow hair had taken on the aspect of a coronet if not a crown. There was nothing Aiel in that.

Faile and the others, six women and five men, had been wakened in the night to stand beside Sevanna's bed—a pair of feather mattresses laid one atop the other—in case the woman woke and wanted something. Was any ruler in the world attended by a dozen servants while she slept? She fought the urge to yawn. Many things *might* earn punishment, but yawning surely would. *Gai'shain* were supposed to be meek and eager to please, and it seemed that that meant obsequious to the point of groveling. Bain and Chiad, fierce as they were otherwise, seemed to find it easy. Faile did not. In the near month since she was stripped and tied up like a blacksmith's puzzle for hiding a knife, she had been switched nine times for trivial offenses that were serious in Sevanna's eyes. Her last set of welts had not faded completely yet, and she had no intention of earning another set through carelessness.

She hoped that Sevanna thought her tamed by that night trussed up in the cold. Only Rolan and his braziers had saved her life. She hoped that she was not being tamed. Pretend something too long, and it could become truth. She had been a prisoner less than two months, yet she could no longer recall exactly how many days ago she was captured. At times it seemed she had been in white robes for a year or more. Sometimes the wide belt and collar of flat golden links felt natural. That frightened her. She clung hard to hope. She would escape soon. She *had* to. Before Perrin caught up and tried to rescue her. Why had he not caught up yet? The Shaido had been camped at Malden for a long time, now. He would not have abandoned her. Her wolf would be coming to rescue her. She had to escape before he got himself killed in the attempt. Before she was no longer pretending.

"How long are you going to keep punishing Galina Sedai, Therava?" Sevanna demanded, frowning at the Aes Sedai. Therava was seated cross-legged in front of her on a tasseled blue cushion, straight-backed and stern. "Last night, she made my bath water too hot, and she is so welted, I had to order the soles of her feet beaten. That is not very effective when she must be left able to walk."

Faile had been avoiding looking at Galina ever since Therava brought her into the tent, but her eyes went to the woman of their own accord at mention of her name. Galina was kneeling erect halfway between the two Aiel women and slightly to one side, mottled brown bruises on her cheeks, her skin damp and slick from the heavy rain she had been walked through to get there, her feet and ankles muddy. She wore only her firedrop-studded golden collar and belt, and seemed more naked than naked. Just a stubble remained of her hair and eyebrows. Every hair from head to toe had been singed from her with the One Power. Faile had heard it described, along with how the Aes Sedai had been hung from her ankles for her first beating. That had been half the talk among the *gai'shain* for days. Only the handful who recognized her ageless face for what it was still believed that she was Aes Sedai, and some of those had the same doubts that had plagued Faile on finding an Aes Sedai among the *gai'shain*. After all, she possessed the face, and the ring, but why would an Aes Sedai let Therava treat her so? Faile asked herself that question often without arriving at any answer. She kept telling herself that Aes Sedai often did what they did for reasons no one else could understand, but that was not very satisfying.

Whatever her reasons for tolerating such abuse, Galina's eyes were wide and frightened, now, and fixed on Therava. She was panting so hard that her breasts heaved. She had reason for fear. Anyone passing Therava's tent was likely to hear Galina howling for mercy inside. For more than half a week Faile had gotten glimpses of the Aes Sedai on some errand, hairless and garbed as she was now and running as hard as she could with panic painting her face, and every day Therava added to the bands of welts that striped Galina from her shoulders to the backs of her knees. Whenever one band began to heal, Therava refreshed it. Faile had heard Shaido mutter that Galina was being treated too harshly, but no one was about to interfere with a Wise One.

Therava, nearly as tall as most Aiel men, adjusted her dark shawl in a rattle of gold and ivory bracelets and regarded Galina like a blue-eyed eagle regarding a mouse. Her necklaces, also gold and ivory, seemed plain compared to Sevanna's opulence, her dark woolen skirts and white *algode* blouse drab, yet of the two women, Faile feared Therava far more than she did Sevanna. Sevanna might have her punished for a stumble, but Therava could kill her or crush her for a whim. She surely would if Faile attempted escape and failed. "So long as the faintest bruise remains on her face, the rest of her will be bruised as well. I have left the front of her unmarked so she *can* be punished for other misdeeds." Galina began trembling. Silent tears leaked down her cheeks.

Faile averted her gaze. It was painful to watch. Even if she managed to get the rod from Therava's tent, could the Aes Sedai still be of help in escape? She gave every sign of being completely broken. That was a harsh thought, but a prisoner needed to be practical above all else. Would Galina betray her to try buying her way out of the beatings? She had threatened to betray her, if Faile failed to obtain the rod. It was Sevanna who would be interested in Perrin Aybara's wife, yet Galina looked desperate enough to try anything. Faile prayed for the woman to find strength to hold out. Of course she was planning an escape on her own, in case Galina could not keep her promise to take them with her when she left, but it would be so much easier, so much safer for everyone, if she could do it. Oh, Light, why had Perrin not caught up yet? No! She had to keep her focus.

"She is not very impressive like that," Sevanna muttered, frowning into her goblet, now. "Even that ring cannot make her look like an Aes Sedai." She shook her head irritably. For some reason Faile did not understand, it was very important to Sevanna that everyone know that Galina was a sister. She had even taken to giving her the honorific. "Why are you here so early, Therava? I have not even eaten, yet. Will you take some wine?"

"Water," Therava said firmly. "As for it being early, the sun is almost over the horizon. I broke fast before it rose. You grow as indolent as a wetlander, Sevanna."

Lusara, a buxom Domani *gai'shain*, quickly filled a goblet from the silver water pitcher. Sevanna seemed amused by the Wise Ones' insistence on drinking only water, yet she provided it for them. Anything else would have been an insult even she would want to avoid. The copper-skinned Domani had been a merchant, and well into her middle years, but a few white hairs among the black falling below her shoulders had not been enough to save her. She was stunningly beautiful, and Sevanna gathered the rich, the powerful and the beautiful, simply taking them if they were *gai'shain* to someone else. There were so many *gai'shain* that few complained at having one taken. Lusara curtsied gracefully and bowed to present her tray to Therava on her cushion, all very proper, but on the way back to her place against the wall, she smiled at Faile. Worse, it was a conspiratorial smile.

Faile suppressed a sigh. Her last switching had been for a sigh at the wrong moment. Lusara was one of those who had sworn fealty to her in the past two weeks. After Aravine, Faile had tried to choose carefully, but rejecting someone who asked to swear was creating a possible betrayer, so she had far too many adherents, a good number of whom she was unsure of. She was beginning to believe that Lusara was trustworthy, or at least that she would not intentionally betray her, but the woman treated their escape plans like a child's game, without cost if they lost. It seemed she had treated merchanting in the same way, making and losing several fortunes, but Faile would have no chance to start over if they lost. Nor would Alliandre or Maighdin. Or Lusara. Among Sevanna's *gai'shain*, those who actually attempted escape were kept chained when not serving her or performing tasks.

Therava took a swallow of water, then set the goblet down on the flowered carpet beside her and fixed Sevanna with a steely gaze. "The Wise Ones believe it is past time for us to move north and east. We can find easily defended valleys in the mountains there, and we can reach them in less than two weeks even slowed as we are by the *gai'shain*. This place is open on every side, and our raids to find food must go further and further."

Sevanna's green eyes met that stare without blinking, which Faile doubted she herself could have done. It nettled Sevanna when the other Wise Ones met without her, and frequently she took it out on her *gai'shain*, but she smiled and took a sip of wine before replying in patient tones, as though explaining to someone not quite bright enough to understand. "Here, there is good soil for planting, and we have their seed to add to our own. Who knows what the soil is like in the mountains? Our raids bring in cattle and sheep and goats, too. Here, there are good pastures. What pasturage do you know of in these mountains, Therava? Here, we have more water than any clan has ever had. Do you know where the water is in the mountains? As to defending ourselves, who will come against us? These wetlanders run from our spears."

"Not all run," Therava said drily. "Some are even good at dancing the spears. And what if Rand al'Thor sends one of the other clans against us? We would never know until the horns closed in on us." Suddenly she smiled, too, a smile that never reached her eyes. "Some say your plan is to be captured and made *gai'shain* to Rand al'Thor so you can induce him to marry you. An amusing idea, you agree?"

Despite herself, Faile flinched. Sevanna's mad intention to marry al'Thor—she *had* to be mad to think she could!—was what put Faile in danger from Galina. If the Aiel woman did not know that Perrin was linked to al'Thor, Galina could tell her. Would tell her if she could not get her hands on that cursed rod. Sevanna would take no chances on losing her then. She would be chained as certainly as if caught trying to escape.

Sevanna looked anything except amused. Eyes glittering, she leaned forward, her robe gaping to expose her bosom completely. "Who says this? Who?" Therava picked up her goblet and took another swallow of water. Realizing she would get no answer, Sevanna leaned back, and rearranged her robe. Her eyes still glittered like polished emeralds, though, and there was nothing casual in her words. They came out as hard as her eyes. "I *will* marry Rand al'Thor, Therava. I almost had him, until you and the other Wise Ones failed me. I will marry him, unite the clans, and conquer all of the wetlands!"

Therava sneered over her goblet. "*Couladin* was the *Car'a'carn*, Sevanna. I have not found the Wise Ones who gave him permission to go to Rhuidean, but I will. Rand al'Thor is a creature of the Aes Sedai. They told him what to say at Alcair Dal, and a black day it was when he revealed secrets few are strong enough to know. Be grateful that most believe he lied. But I forget. You have never gone to Rhuidean. You believed his secrets lies yourself."

Gai'shain began entering past the tentflap, their white robes raindamp, holding their hems knee-high until they were inside. Each wore the golden collar and belt. Their soft white laced boots left muddy marks on the carpets. Later, when those had dried, they would have to clean them away, but getting visible mud on your robes was a sure path to the switch. Sevanna wanted her *gai'shain* spotless when they were around her. Neither Aiel woman paid the slightest attention to the arrivals.

Sevanna seemed taken aback by what Therava had said. "Why do you care who gave Couladin permission? No matter," she said, waving a hand as though brushing away a fly, when she got no reply. "Couladin is dead. Rand al'Thor has the markings, however he got them. I will marry him, and I will make use of him. If the Aes Sedai could control him, and I saw them handling him like a babe, then I can. With a little help from you. And you will help. You agree that uniting the clans is worth doing no matter how it is done? You did once." Somehow, there was more than a hint of threat in that. "We Shaido will become the most powerful of the clans in one leap."

Lowering their cowls, the new *gai'shain* filed wordlessly along the tent walls, nine men and three women, one of them Maighdin. The sun-haired woman wore a grim expression that had been on her face since the day Therava had discovered her in the Wise One's tent. Whatever Therava had done, all Maighdin would say of it was that she wanted to kill the other woman. Sometimes she whimpered in her sleep, though.

Therava kept whatever she thought about uniting the clans to herself. "There is much feeling against staying here. Many of the sept chiefs press the red disc on their *nar'baha* every morning. I advise you to heed the Wise Ones."

Nar'baha? That would mean 'box of fools,' or something very near. But what could this be? Bain and Chiad were still teaching her about Aiel ways, when they could find time, and they had never mentioned any such thing. Maighdin stopped beside Lusara. A slender Cairhienin nobleman named Doirmanes stopped beside Faile. He was young and very pretty, but he bit his lip nervously. If he learned about the oaths of fealty, he would have to be killed. She was certain he would run to Sevanna in a heartbeat.

"We remain here," Sevanna said angrily, flinging her goblet to the carpets in a spray of wine. "I speak for the clan chief, and I have spoken!"

"You have spoken," Therava agreed calmly. "Bendhuin, sept chief of the Green Salts, has received permission to go to Rhuidean. He left five days ago with twenty of his *algai'd'siswai* and four Wise Ones to stand witness."

Not until one of the new *gai'shain* stood beside each of those already there did Faile and the others raise their cowls and begin filing along the walls toward the doorflap, already gathering their robes to the knee. She had become quite sanguine about exposing her legs so.

"He seeks to replace me, and I was not even informed?"

"Not you, Sevanna. Couladin. As his widow, you speak for the clan chief until a new chief returns from Rhuidean, but you are not the clan chief."

Faile stepped out into the cold, gray morning drizzle, and the tentflap cut off whatever Sevanna said to that. What *was* going on between the two women? Sometimes, as this morning, they seemed antagonists, but at others they seemed reluctant conspirators bound together by something that gave neither any comfort. Or perhaps it was the being bound together itself that made them uncomfortable. Well, she could not see how knowing would help her escape, so it did not really matter. But the puzzle nagged at her.

Six Maidens stood clustered in front of the tent, veils hanging down onto their chests, spears thrust up through the harness of the bow cases on their backs. Bain and Chiad were contemptuous of Sevanna for using Maidens of the Spear for her guard of honor though she herself had never been a Maiden, and for having her tent always guarded, but there were never fewer than six, night or day. Those two were contemptuous of the Shaido Maidens for allowing it, too. Neither being a clan chief nor speaking for one gave you as much power as most nobles possessed. These Maidens' hands were flashing in a rapid conversation. She caught the sign for *Car'a'carn* several times, but not sufficient else to make out what they were saying, or whether about al'Thor or Couladin.

Standing there long enough to find out, if she could find out, was beyond the question. With the others already hurrying away down the muddy street, the Maidens would become suspicious, for one thing, and then they might switch her themselves, or worse, use her own bootlaces. She had had a hard dose of that from some Maidens, for having "insolent eyes," and she did not want another. Especially when it meant baring herself in public. Being Sevanna's *gai'shain* gave no protection. Any Shaido could discipline any *gai'shain* they thought was behaving improperly. Even a child could, if the child was set to watch you carry out a chore. For another thing, the cold rain, light as it was, was going to soak through her woolen robes soon enough. She had only a short walk back to her tent, no more than a quarter of a mile, but she would not complete it without being stopped for a time.

A yawn cracked her jaw as she turned from the large red tent. She very much wanted her blankets and a few more hours sleep. There would be more chores come afternoon. What they might be, she did not know. Matters would be much simpler if Sevanna settled on who she wanted to do what when, but she seemed to choose names at random, and always at the last minute. It made planning anything, much less the escape, very difficult.

All sorts of tents surrounded Sevanna's, low, dark Aiel tents, peaked tents, walled tents, tents of every sort and size in every color imaginable, separated by a tangle of dirt streets that were now rivers of mud. Lacking enough of their own, the Shaido snatched up every tent they could find. Fourteen septs were camped in a sprawl around Malden now, a hundred thousand Shaido and as many *gai'shain*, and rumor said two more septs, the Morai and the White Cliff, would arrive within days. Aside from small children splashing through the mud with romping dogs, most of the people she could see as she walked wore mud-stained white and were carrying baskets or bulging sacks.

Most of the women did not hurry; they ran. Except for the black-smiths, the Shaido seldom did any work themselves, and generally only out of boredom, she suspected. With so many *gai'shain*, finding chores for them all was itself a chore. Sevanna was no longer the only Shaido to actually sit in a bathtub with a *gai'shain* scrubbing her back. None of the Wise Ones had gone that far yet, but some of the others would not stir themselves two paces to pick something up when they could tell a *gai'shain* to fetch it.

She was almost to the *gai'shain* portion of the camp, hard against the gray stone walls of Malden, when she saw a Wise One striding toward her with her dark shawl wrapped around her head against the rain. Faile did not stop, but she bent her knees a little. Meira was not so frighten-ing as Therava, but the grim-faced woman was hard enough, and shorter than Faile. Her narrow mouth always grew even tighter when she was confronted with a woman taller than she. Faile would have thought that learning her own sept, the White Cliff, would be there soon, would brighten the woman's mood, but the news had had no dis-cernable effect at all.

"So you were just lagging," Meira said as she came close. Her eyes were as hard as the sapphires they resembled. "I left Rhiale listening to the others because I feared some drunken fool had pulled you into a tent." She glared around her as though looking for a drunken fool about to do just that.

"No one accosted me, Wise One," Faile said quickly. Several had in the last few weeks, some drunk and some not, but Rolan always ap-peared in the nick of time. Twice the big *Mera'din* had had to fight to save her, and once he had killed the other man. She had expected nine kinds of uproar and trouble, but the Wise Ones judged it a fair fight, and Rolan said her name had never been mentioned. For all that Bain and Chiad insisted it went against all custom, assault was a constant danger for *gai'shain* women here. She was sure that Alliandre had been assaulted once, before she and Maighdin also acquired *Mera'din* shad-ows. Rolan denied having asked them to help her people. He said they were just bored and looking for something to do. "I'm very sorry I was slow."

"Do not cringe. I am not Therava. I will not beat you for the plea-sure of it." Words said in tones hard enough for a headsman. Meira might not beat people for pleasure, but Faile knew for a fact that she had a strong arm swinging a switch. "Now tell me what Sevanna said and did. This water falling from the sky may be a wondrous thing, but it is miserable to walk around in."

Obeying the command was easy. Sevanna had not wakened during the night, and once she did rise, all her talk had been of what clothes and jewels she would wear, especially the jewels. Her jewelry chest had been made to hold clothing, and it was filled to the top with more gems than most queens possessed. Before putting on any garment at all, Sevanna had spent time trying on different combinations of neck-laces and rings and studying herself in the gilt-framed stand-mirror. It had been very embarrassing. For Faile.

She had just reached Therava's arrival with Galina when every-thing in front of her eyes rippled. *She* rippled! It was not imagina-tion. Meira's blue eyes widened as far as they could go; she had felt it, too. Again everything rippled, including herself, harder than be-fore. In shock, Faile stood up straight and let go of her robe. A third time the world rippled, harder still, and as it passed through her, she felt as if she might blow away in a breeze, or simply dissipate in a mist.

Breathing hard, she waited for the fourth ripple, the one she knew would destroy her and everything else. When it did not come, she ex-pelled every bit of air in her lungs from relief. "What just happened, Wise One? What was that?"

Meira touched her own arm and looked faintly surprised that her hand did not pass through flesh and bone. "I . . . do not know," she said slowly. Giving herself a shake, she added, "Go on about your busi-ness, girl." She gathered her skirts and strode past Faile at little short of a trot, splashing mud as she went.

The children had vanished from the street, but Faile could hear them wailing inside the tents. Abandoned dogs shivered and whined, tails tucked between their legs. People in the street were touching themselves, touching each other, Shaido and *gai'shain* alike. Faile clasped her hands together. Of course she was solid. She had only *felt* as though she were turning to mist. Of course. Hoisting her robes to avoid any more washing than she absolutely had to do, she began to walk. And then to run, careless of how much mud she splashed onto herself or any-one else. She knew there could be no running from another of those rip-ples. But she ran anyway, as fast as her legs could carry her.

The *gai'shain* tents made a broad ring around Malden's high gran-ite walls, and they were as varied as the tents in the outer part of the encampment, though most were small. Her own peaked tent could have slept two uncomfortably; it housed herself and three others, Alliandre, Maighdin and a former Cairhienin noblewoman named Dairaine, one of those who curried favor with Sevanna by carrying tales about the other *gai'shain*. That complicated matters, but there was no mending it short of killing the woman, and Faile would not countenance that. Not unless Dairaine became a real threat. They slept huddled together like puppies of necessity, glad of the shared body warmth on cold nights.

The interior of the low tent was dim when she ducked inside. Lamp oil and candles were in short supply, and not wasted on *gai'shain*. Only Alliandre was there, lying facedown on her blankets in her collar with a damp cloth, dipped in an herbal infusion, over her bruised bottom. At least the Wise Ones were as willing to give their healing herbs to *gai'shain* as to Shaido. Alliandre had done nothing wrong, but had been named as one of the five who had pleased Sevanna least yesterday. Unlike some, she had done quite well while being punished—Doirmanes had begun weeping even before he was bent over the chest—but she seemed to be among those chosen out every three or four days. Being a queen did not teach you how to serve a queen. But then, Maighdin was picked nearly as often, and she was a lady's maid, if not a very skilled one. Faile herself had only been chosen once.

It was a measure of how Alliandre's spirits had fallen that she made no move to cover herself, only raised up on her elbows. Still, she had combed her long hair. If she failed to do that, Faile would know the woman had reached bottom. "Did anything . . . strange . . . happen to you just now, my Lady?" she asked, fear strong in her unsteady voice.

"It did," Faile said, standing crouched under the ridgepole. "I don't know what it was. Meira doesn't know what it was. I doubt any of the Wise Ones do. But it didn't harm us." Of course it had not harmed them. Of course not. "And it changes nothing in our plans." Yawning, she unfastened the wide golden belt and dropped it on her blankets, then grasped her outer robe to pull it over her head.

Alliandre put her head down on her hands and began weeping quietly. "We'll never escape. I'm going to be beaten again tonight. I know it. I'm going to be beaten every day for the rest of my life."

With a sigh, Faile left her outer robe where it was and knelt to stroke her liege woman's hair. There were as many responsibilities down as up. "I have those same fears now and then," she admitted softly. "But I refuse to let them take control. I *will* escape. *We* will escape. You have to keep your courage, Alliandre. I know you're brave. I know you've dealt with Masema and kept your nerve. You can keep it now, if you try."

Aravine put her head in at the tentflap. She was a plain, plump woman, a noble Faile was sure, though she never claimed it, and despite the dimness Faile could see that she was beaming. She wore Sevanna's belt and collar, too. "My Lady, Alvon and his son have something for you."

"It will have to wait a few minutes," Faile said. Alliandre had stopped crying, but she was just lying there, silent and still.

"My Lady, you won't want to wait for this."

Faile's breath caught. Could it be possible? It seemed too much to hope for.

"I can keep my nerve," Alliandre said, raising her head to gaze at Aravine. "If what Alvon has is what I hope it is, I'll keep my nerve if Sevanna has me put to the question."

Snatching up her belt—being seen outside without belt and collar both meant punishment almost as severe as for trying to run away— Faile hurried out of the tent. The drizzle had slackened to a misting rain, but she pulled up her cowl anyway. The rain was still cold.

Alvon was a stocky man, overtopped by his son Theril, a lanky boy. Both wore mud-stained, almost-white robes made of tentcloth. Theril, Alvon's eldest, was only fourteen, but the Shaido had not believed it because of his height, as much as most men in Amadicia. Faile had been ready to trust Alvon from the start. He and his son were something of legends among the *gai'shain*. Three times they had run away, and each time it had taken the Shaido longer to bring them back. And despite increasingly fierce punishment, on the day they swore fealty they had been planning a fourth attempt to return to the rest of their family. Neither ever smiled that Faile had seen, but today, smiles wreathed Alvon's weathered face and Theril's skinny one alike.

"What do you have for me?" Faile asked, hastily fastening her belt around her waist. She thought her heart was going to pound its way out of her chest.

"It was my Theril, my Lady," Alvon said. A woodcutter, he spoke with a coarse accent that made him barely intelligible. "He was just walking by, see, and there was nobody around, nobody at all, so he ducked in quick like, and . . . Show the Lady, Theril."

Shyly, Theril reached into his wide sleeve—the robes usually had pockets sewn in there—and drew out a smooth white rod that looked like ivory, about a foot long and as slim as her wrist.

Looking around to see if anyone was watching—the street was empty save for them, for the moment at least—Faile took it quickly and pushed it up her own sleeve to tuck into the pocket there. The pocket was just deep enough to keep it from falling out, but now that she had the thing in hand, she did not want to let go of it. It felt like glass, and was distinctly cool to the touch, cooler than the morning air. Perhaps it was an *angreal* or a *ter'angreal*. That would explain why Galina wanted it, if not why she had not taken it herself. Hand buried in her sleeve, Faile gripped the rod hard. Galina was no longer a threat. Now she was salvation.

"You understand, Alvon, that Galina may be unable to take you and your son with her when she leaves," she said. "She has only promised that to me and those captured with me. But I promise you that I will find a way to free you and everyone who has sworn to me. All the rest, too, if I can, but those above all. Under the Light and by my hope of salvation and rebirth, I swear it." How, she had no idea short of calling on her father for an army, but she would do it.

The woodcutter made as if to spit then glanced at her, and his face colored. He swallowed, instead. "That Galina ain't going to help nobody, my Lady. Says she's Aes Sedai and all, but she's that Therava's plaything if you ask me, and that Therava ain't never going to let her go. Anyways, I know if we can get you free, you'll come back for the rest of us. No need for you to swear and all that. You said you wanted the rod if anybody could lay hands on it without getting caught, and Theril got it for you, that's all."

"I want to be free," Theril said suddenly, "but if we get anybody free, then we've beaten them." He looked surprised that he had spoken, and blushed deep red. His father frowned at him, then nodded thoughtfully.

"Very well said," Faile told the boy gently, "but I made my oath, and I stand by it. You and your father—" She cut off as Aravine, looking past her shoulder, laid a hand on her arm. The woman's smile had been replaced by fright.

Turning her head, Faile saw Rolan standing beside her tent. A good two hands taller than Perrin, he wore his *shoufa* coiled around his neck with the black veil hanging down his broad chest. Rain slicked his face and made his short red hair cling to his scalp in curls. How long had he been there? Not long, or Aravine would have noticed him before. The tiny tent offered little concealment. Alvon and his son had their shoulders hunched, as if they were thinking about attacking the tall *Mera'din*. That was a very bad idea. Mice attacking a cat was not in it, as Perrin would have said.

"Go on about your duties, Alvon," she said quickly. "You, too, Aravine. Go on, now."

Aravine and Alvon had sense enough not to offer courtesies before leaving with final worried glances at Rolan, but Theril half raised a hand toward knuckling his forehead before catching himself. Blushing, he scurried away after his father.

Rolan came out from beside the tent to stand in front of her. Oddly, he had a small bunch of blue and yellow wildflowers in one hand. She was very conscious of the rod she was holding in her sleeve. Where was she to hide it? Once Therava discovered it missing, she likely would turn the camp upside down.

"You must be careful, Faile Bashere," Rolan said, smiling down at her. Alliandre called him not quite pretty, but Faile had decided she was wrong. Those blue eyes and that smile made him very nearly beautiful. "What you are about is dangerous, and I may not be here to protect you much longer."

"Dangerous?" She felt a chill in her middle. "What do you mean? Where are you going?" The thought of losing his protection made her stomach lurch. Few of the wetlander women had escaped the attentions of Shaido men. Without him. . . .

"Some of us are thinking of returning to the Three-fold Land." His smile faded. "We cannot follow a false *Car'a'carn*, and a wetlander at that, but perhaps we will be allowed to live out our lives in our own holds. We think on it. We have been a long time from home, and these Shaido sicken us."

She would find a way to deal with it once he was gone. She would have to. Somehow. "And what am I doing that is dangerous?" She tried to make her voice light, but it was difficult. Light, what would happen to her without him?

"These Shaido are blind even when they are not drunk, Faile Bashere," he replied calmly. Pushing her cowl back, he tucked one of the wildflowers into her hair above her left ear. "We *Mera'din* use our eyes." Another wildflower went into her hair, on the other side. "You have made many new friends lately, and you are planning to escape with them. A bold plan, but dangerous."

"And will you tell the Wise Ones, or Sevanna?" She was startled when that came out in an even tone. Her stomach was trying to tie itself into knots.

"Why would I do that?" he asked, adding another flower to her decorations. "Jhoradin thinks he will take Lacile Aldorwin back to the Three-fold Land with him even if she is a Treekiller. He believes he may convince her to make a bridal wreath to lay at his feet." Lacile had found her own protector by climbing into the blankets of the *Mera'din* who had made her *gai'shain*, and Arrela had done the same with one of the Maidens who had captured her, but Faile doubted that Jhoradin would attain his wish. Both women were focused on escape like arrows aimed at a target. "And now that I think on it, I may take you with me if we go."

Faile stared up at him. The rain was beginning to soak through her hair. "To the Waste? Rolan, I love my husband. I've told you that, and it is true."

"I know," he said, continuing to add flowers. "But for the moment, you still wear white, and what happens while you wear white is forgotten when you put it off. Your husband cannot hold it against you. Besides, if we go, when we come near to a wetlander town, I will let you go. I should never have made you *gai'shain* in the first place. That collar and belt hold enough gold to get you safely back to your husband."

Her mouth fell open in shock. It surprised her when her fist struck his wide chest. *Gai'shain* were *never* allowed to offer violence, but the man just grinned at her. "You—!" She struck him again, harder. She beat at him. "You—! I can't think of a word bad enough. You let me think you were going to abandon me to these Shaido while all along you were meaning to help me escape?"

Finally he caught her fist and held it easily with a hand that enveloped hers completely. "If we go, Faile Bashere," he laughed. The man laughed! "It is not decided. Anyway, a man cannot let a woman think he is too eager."

Again she surprised herself, this time by beginning to laugh and cry at the same time, so hard that she had to lean against him or fall down. That *bloody* Aiel sense of humor!

"You are very beautiful with flowers in your hair, Faile Bashere," he murmured, tucking in another blossom. "Or without them. And for the moment, you still wear white."

Light! She had the rod, leaning against her arm so coolly, but there was no way to give it to Galina until Therava let her walk around freely again, no way to be sure that the woman would not betray her before then out of desperation. Rolan offered her escape, *if* the *Mera'din* decided to leave, but he would continue to try to inveigle her into his blankets so long as she wore white. And if the *Mera'din* decided not to go, would one of them betray her escape plans? If Rolan could be believed, they all knew! Hope and danger, all tied together inextricably. What a tangle.

She turned out to have been exactly right about Therava's reaction. Just before midday all of the *gai'shain* were herded into the open and made to strip to their skins. Covering herself as best she could with her hands, Faile huddled together with other women wearing Sevanna's belt and collar—they had been made to put those on again straightaway—huddled for a scrap of decency while Shaido rummaged through the *gai'shain* tents, tossing everything out into the mud. All Faile could do was think about her hiding place inside the town and pray. Hope and danger, and no way to untangle them.

CHAPTER
6

A Stave and a Razor

Mat had never really expected Luca to leave Jurador after only one day—the stone-walled salt town was wealthy, and Luca did like to see coin stick to his hands—so he was not exactly disappointed when the man told him that Valan Luca's Grand Traveling Show and Magnificent Display of Marvels and Wonders would remain there at least two more days. Not *exactly* disappointed, yet he had hoped that his luck might hold good, or his being *ta'veren*. But then, being *ta'veren* had never brought anything other than bad that he could see.

"The lines at the entrance are already as long as they were at their best, yesterday," Luca said, gesturing expansively. They were inside Luca's huge gaudy wagon, early in the morning after Renna's death, and the tall man sat in the gilded chair at the narrow table—a real table, with stools tucked under for guests; most other wagons had an affair rigged on ropes from the ceiling, and people sat on the beds to eat. Luca had not yet donned one of his flamboyant coats, but he made up for it with gestures. Latelle, his wife, was cooking the breakfast porridge on a small, iron-topped brick stove built into a corner of the windowless wagon, and the air was sharp with spices. The harsh-faced woman put so many spices into everything she prepared that it was all inedible, in Mat's estimation, yet Luca always gobbled down whatever she set in front of him as if it were a feast. He must have a leather tongue. "I expect twice as many visitors today, maybe three times as many, and tomorrow as well. People can't see everything in one visit, and here they can afford to come twice. Word of mouth, Cauthon. Word of mouth. That brings as many as Aludra's nightflowers. I feel almost like a *ta'veren*, the way things are falling out. Large audiences and the prospect of more. A warrant of protection from the High Lady." Luca cut off abruptly, looking faintly embarrassed, as if he had just remembered that Mat's name was on that warrant as being excluded from protection.

"You might not like it if you really were *ta'veren*," Mat muttered, which made the other man give him an odd look. He put a finger behind the black silk scarf that hid his hanging scar and tugged at it. For a moment, the thing had felt too tight. He had spent a night of bleak dreams about corpses floating downstream and woken to the dice spinning in his head, always a bad sign, and now they seemed to be bouncing off the inside of his skull harder than before. "I can pay you as much as you'll make for every show you give between here and Lugard, no matter how many people attend. That's on top of what I promised for carrying us to Lugard." If the show was not stopping all the time, they could cut the time to reach Lugard by three quarters at the least. More, if he could convince Luca to spend whole days on the road instead of half days, the way they did now.

Luca seemed taken with the idea, nodding thoughtfully, but then he shook his head with a sadness that was plainly feigned and spread his hands. "And what will that look like, a traveling show that never stops to give shows? It will look suspicious, that's what. I have the warrant, and the High Lady will speak up for me besides, but you certainly don't want to pull the Seanchan down on us. No, it's safer for you this way." The man was not thinking of Mat Cauthon's bloody safety, he was thinking that his bloody shows might earn him more than Mat paid. That, plus making himself as much the center of attention as any of the performers was nearly as important to him as gold. Some of the showfolk talked of what they would do when they retired. Not Luca. He intended to keep on until he fell over dead in the middle of a show. And he would arrange it so he had the largest audience possible when he did.

"It's ready, Valan," Latelle said affectionately as she lifted the iron pot from the stove with a cloth protecting her hands and set it down on a thick woven mat on the table. Two places had already been set, with white-glazed plates and silver spoons. Luca would have silver spoons when everyone else settled for tin or pot metal or even horn or wood. Stern-eyed, with a hard set to her mouth, the bear trainer looked quite odd wearing a long white apron over her spangled blue dress. Her bears probably wished they had trees to climb when she frowned at them. Strangely, though, she jumped to ensure her husband's comforts. "Will you be eating with us, Master Cauthon?" There was no welcome in that; in fact, just the opposite, and she showed no sign of turning to the cupboard where the plates were stored.

Mat gave her a bow that soured her face further. He had never been less than civil to the woman, but she refused to like him. "I thank you for the kind invitation, Mistress Luca, but no." She grunted. So much for being courteous. He put on his flat-brimmed hat and left, the dice rattling away.

Luca's big wagon, glittering in red and blue and covered with golden stars and comets, not to mention the phases of the moon in silver, stood in the middle of the show, as far as possible from the animals' smelly cages and the horselines. It was surrounded by smaller wagons, little houses on wheels, most windowless and most painted just a single color with none of Luca's extra decorations, and by wall-tents the size of small houses in blue or green or red, sometimes striped. The sun stood nearly its own height above the horizon in a sky where a sprinkling of white clouds drifted slowly, and children ran playing with hoops and balls while the showfolk were limbering up for their morning performances, men and women twisting and stretching, many with glittering, colorful spangles on their coats or dresses. Four contortionists, in filmy trousers tied at the ankle and blouses thin enough to leave little to the imagination, made him wince. Two were sitting on their own heads atop blankets spread on the ground beside their red tent, while the others had twisted themselves into a pair of knots that looked beyond untying. Their backbones must have been made of spring-wire! Petra, the strongman, stood bare-chested beside the green wagon he shared with his wife, warming up by lifting weights with either hand that Mat was not sure he could have lifted with both. The man had arms thicker than Mat's legs, and he was not sweating at all. Clarine's small dogs stood in a line at the steps of the wagon wagging their tails and eagerly waiting on their trainer. Unlike Latelle's bears,

Mat figured the plump woman's dogs performed so they could make her smile.

He was always tempted to just sit quietly somewhere when the dice were clicking in his head, some place nothing seemed likely to happen, waiting for the dice to stop, and though he would have enjoyed watching some of the female acrobats, a number of whom wore as little as the contortionists, he set out to walk the half mile to Jurador, eyeing everyone on the wide, hard-packed clay road closely. There was a purchase he hoped to make.

People were coming to join the long line waiting behind a stout rope stretched along the show's tall canvas wall, only a handful with more than a touch of embroidery on the women's dresses or the men's short coats, and a few farmers' high-wheeled carts lumbering behind a horse or an ox. Figures moved among the small forest of windmills that pumped the salt wells on the low hills behind the town, and around the long evaporation pans. A merchant's train of canvas-covered wagons, twenty of them behind six-horse teams, rumbled out of the town gates as he approached, the merchant herself in a bright green cloak seated beside the driver of the first wagon. A flock of crows cawed past overhead, giving him a chill, but no one vanished before his eyes, and everybody cast a long shadow so far as he could make out. There were no dead people's shades walking the road today, although he was convinced that was what he had seen the day before.

The dead walking surely could mean nothing good. Very likely it had something to with Tarmon Gai'don and Rand. Colors whirled in his brain, and for an instant, in his head, he saw Rand and Min standing beside a large bed, kissing. He stumbled and nearly tripped over his own boots. They had not been wearing any clothes! He would have to be careful thinking about Rand. . . . The colors swirled and resolved for a moment, and he stumbled again. There were worse things to spy on than kissing. *Very* careful what he thought. Light!

The pair of guards leaning on their halberds at the iron-studded gates, hard-faced men in white breastplates and conical white helmets with horsetail crests, eyed him suspiciously. They probably thought he was drunk. A reassuring nod failed to change their expressions by a hair. He could have used a stiff drink right then. The guards did not try to stop him entering, though, just watched him pass. Drunks caused trouble, especially a man who was drunk this early in the day, but a drunk in a good coat—plain, but well-cut and good silk—a man with a little lace at his wrists was an altogether different matter.

The stone-paved streets of Jurador were noisy even at this hour, with hawkers carrying trays or standing behind barrows crying their wares, and shopkeepers beside narrow tables in front of their shops bellowing the fineness of their goods, and coopers hammering hoops onto barrels for shipping salt. The clatter of rugmakers' looms nearly drowned out the ringing of the occasional blacksmith's hammer, not to mention the music of flutes and drums and dulcimers drifting from inns and taverns. It was a jumble of a town, with shops and houses and inns cheek by jowl with taverns and stables, all of stone and roofed with reddish tiles. A solid town, Jurador. And one accustomed to thievery. Most windows on the lower floors were covered with stout screens of wrought iron. The upper windows as well on the homes of the wealthy, most of whom were no doubt salt merchants. The music of the inns and taverns pulled at him. Likely there would be dice games going on in most of them. He could almost feel those dice spinning across a table. It had been too long since he had rattled a set of dice in his hands instead of inside his head, but he was not there for gambling this morning.

He had had no breakfast yet, so he approached a wrinkled woman with a tray hung from a strap around her neck who shouted "meat pies, made from the finest beef to be found in Altara." He took her word for it and handed over the coppers she demanded. He had seen no cattle at any farms near Jurador, only sheep and goats, but it was best not to inquire too closely what was in a pie bought in the streets of any town. There could be cows on nearby farms. There could be. In any case, the meat pie was tasty, and still hot for a wonder, and he walked on along the crowded street juggling the pie and wiping greasy juice from his chin.

He was careful not to bump into anyone in the throng. Altarans were a touchy lot, by and large. In this town, you could tell somebody's station to within a whisker by the amount of embroidery on coat or dress or cloak, the more the higher, long before you were close enough to tell wool from silk, though the richer women covered their olive-skinned faces with transparent veils hung from ornate combs stuck into their tightly coiled braids, but men and women alike, whether salt merchants or ribbon hawkers, wore long belt knives with curved blades and sometimes fondled the hilts as though looking for a fight. He always tried to avoid fighting, though his luck seldom did him much good there. *Ta'veren* took over with that, it seemed. The dice had never before signaled a fight—battles, yes, but never a dust-up in the street—yet he walked very carefully indeed. Not that that would help, of course. When the dice stopped, they stopped, and that was that. But he saw no reason to take chances. He hated taking chances. Except with gambling, of course, and that was hardly taking a chance for him.

He spotted a barrel full of thick quarterstaffs and walking staffs in front of a shop displaying swords and daggers under the watchful eye of a bulky fellow with sunken knuckles, a nose that had been broken more than once, and a thick truncheon hanging at his belt beside the inevitable dagger. The man announced in a rough voice that all the blades on display were Andoran made, but anybody who did not make his own blades always claimed they were Andoran or else from the Borderlands. Or Tairen, sometimes. Tear made good steel.

To Mat's surprise and delight, a slim stave of what appeared to be black yew, more than a foot taller than he was, stood upright in the barrel. Pulling the stave out, he checked the fine, almost braided grain. It was black yew, all right. That braided grain was what gave bows made from it such power, twice what any other wood could give. You could never be sure until you started slicing away the excess, but the stave looked perfect. How in the Light had black yew come to be in southern Altara? He was sure it only grew in the Two Rivers.

When the proprietor, a sleek woman with bright-feathered birds embroidered to below her bosom, came out and began extolling the virtues of her blades, he said, "How much for this black stick, Mistress?"

She blinked, startled that a man in silk and lace wanted a quarterstaff—slim as it was, she bloody well thought the bloody thing was a quarterstaff!—and named a price that he paid without bargaining. Which made her blink again, and frown as if she thought she should have asked for more. He would have paid more for the makings of a Two Rivers bow. With the raw bowstave over his shoulder, he walked on, wolfing down the last of the meat pie and wiping his hand on his coat. But he had not come for breakfast or a bowstave any more than for gambling. It was the stables that interested him.

Livery stables always had a horse or three for sale, and if the price was right, they would usually sell one that had not been for sale. At least, they did when the Seanchan had not snapped them up already. Luckily, the Seanchan presence in Jurador had been fleeting so far. He wandered from stable to stable examining bays and roans, blue roans and piebalds, duns, sorrels, blacks, whites, grays and dapples, all mares or geldings. A stallion would not serve his purposes. Not every animal he looked at had a shallow girth or long cannons, yet none matched what he had in mind. Until he entered a narrow stable jammed between a large stone inn called The Twelve Salt Wells and a rugmaker's shop.

He would have thought the racketing looms would have bothered the horses, but they were all quiet, apparently accustomed to the noise. Stalls stretched farther into the block than he had expected, but lanterns hanging from the stall posts gave a fair light away from the doors. The air, speckled with dust from the loft above, smelled of hay and oats and horse dung, but not old dung. Three men with shovels were mucking out stalls. The owner kept his place clean. That meant less chance of disease. Some stables he had walked out of after getting one whiff.

The black-and-white mare was out of her stall on a rope halter while a groom put down fresh straw, and she stood squarely, and with her ears perked forward, showing alertness. About fifteen hands tall, she was long in front, with a deep girth that promised endurance, and her legs were perfectly proportioned, with short cannons and a good angle to her fetlocks. Her shoulders were well sloped, and her croup dead level with her whithers. She had lines as good as Pips', or even better. More than that, she was a breed he had heard tell of but never thought to see, a razor, from Arad Doman. No other breed would have that distinctive coloring. In her coat, black met white in straight lines that could have been sliced by a razor, hence the name. Her presence here was as mystifying as the black yew. He had always heard no Domani would sell a razor to any outlander. He let his eyes sweep past her without lingering, studying the other animals in their stalls. Had the dice inside his skull slowed? No, it was his imagination. He was sure they were spinning as hard as they had in Luca's wagon.

A wiry man with only a fringe of gray hair remaining came forward, ducking his head over folded hands. "Toke Fearnim, my Lord," he introduced himself in rough accents, eyeing the bowstave on Mat's shoulder dubiously. Men who wore silk coats and gold signet rings rarely carried such things. "How can I be of service? My Lord wishes to

rent a horse? Or to buy?" Embroidery, small bright flowers, covered
the shoulders of the vest he wore over a shirt that might have been
white once. Mat avoided looking at the flowers at all. The fellow had
one of those curved knives at his belt and two long white scars on his
leathery face. Old scars. Any fighting he had done lately had not
marked him where it showed.

"Buy, Master Fearnim, if you have anything for sale. If I can find
one that's halfway decent. I've had more spavined gluebaits offered to
me as six-year-olds when they were eighteen if a day than I can shake
a stick at." He hefted the bowstave slightly with a grin. His Da
claimed bargaining went better if you could make the other fellow
start grinning.

"I have three for sale, my Lord, none of them spavined," the wiry
man replied with another bow, and no hint of a grin. Fearnim gestured. "One is out of her stall there. Five years old and prime horseflesh, my Lord. And a steal at ten crowns. Gold," he added blandly.

Mat let his jaw drop. "For a *piebald*? I know the Seanchan have
driven prices up, but that's ridiculous!"

"Oh, she's not your common piebald, my Lord. A razor is what she
is. Domani bloodborn ride razors."

Blood and bloody ashes! So much for catching a bargain. "So you
say, so you say," Mat muttered, lowering one end of the bowstave to the
stone floor so he could lean on it. His hip seldom bothered him any
longer except when he did a lot of walking, but he had done so this
morning, and he felt twinges. Well, bargain or no, he had to play out
the game. There were rules to horse trading. Break them, and you were
asking to have your purse emptied out. "I've never heard of any horse
called a razor myself. What else do you have? Only geldings or mares,
mind."

"Geldings are all I have for sale except the razor, my Lord," Fearnim
said, emphasizing the word razor a little. Turning toward the back of
the stable, he shouted, "Adela, bring out that big bay what's for sale."

A lanky young woman with a pimply face, in breeches and a plain
dark vest, came darting out of the back of the stable to obey. Fearnim
had Adela walk the bay and then a dappled gray on rope leads in the
good light near the doors. Mat had to hand him that. Their conforma-
tion was not bad at all, but the bay was too big, better than seventeen
hands, and the gray kept his ears half laid back and tried to bite Adela's
hand twice. She was deft with the animals, though, easily evading the

bad-tempered gray's lunges. Rejecting the pair of them would have been easy even if he had not had his mind set on the razor.

A lean, gray-striped tomcat, like a ridgecat in miniature, appeared and sat at Fearnim's feet to lick a bloody gash on his shoulder. "Rats are worse this year than I ever recall," the stablekeeper muttered, frowning down at the cat. "They fight back more, too. I'm going to have to get another cat, or maybe two." He brought himself back to the business at hand. "Will my Lord take a look at my prize, since the others don't suit?"

"I suppose I could look at the piebald, Master Fearnim," Mat said doubtfully. "But not for any ten crowns."

"In gold," Fearnim said. "Hurd, walk the razor for the Lord here." He emphasized the breed again. Working the man down would be difficult. Unless he got some help for a change from being *ta'veren*. His luck never helped with anything as straightforward as dickering.

Hurd was the fellow refreshing the straw in the razor's stall, a squat man who had about three white hairs left on his head and no teeth in his mouth at all. That was evident when he grinned, which he did while he led the mare in a circle. He clearly liked the animal, and well he should.

She walked well, but Mat still inspected her closely. Her teeth said Fearnim had been honest enough about her age—only a fool lied very far about a horse's age unless the buyer was a fool himself, though it was surprising how many sellers thought buyers were all just that— and her ears pricked toward him when he stroked her nose while checking her eyes. They were clear and bright, free of rheum. He felt along her legs without finding any heat or swelling. There was never a hint of a lesion or sore, or of ringworm, anywhere on her. He could get his fist easily between her rib cage and her elbow—she would have a long stride—and was barely able to fit his flat hand between her last rib and the point of her hip. She would be hardy, unlikely to strain a tendon if run fast.

"My Lord knows his horseflesh, I see."

"That I do, Master Faernim. And ten crowns gold is too much, especially for a piebald. Some say they're bad luck, you know. Not that I believe it, not as such, or I wouldn't offer at all."

"Bad luck? I never heard that, my Lord. What do you offer?"

"I could get Tairen bloodstock for ten crowns gold. Not the best, true, but still Tairen. I'll give you ten crowns. In silver."

Fearnim threw back his head, laughing uproariously, and when he stopped, they settled down to the dickering. In the end, Mat handed over five crowns in gold along with four marks gold and three crowns silver, all stamped in Ebou Dar. There were coins from many countries in the chest under his bed, but foreign coin usually meant finding a banker or money changer to weigh them and work out what they were worth locally. Aside from attracting more notice than he wanted, he would have ended paying more for the animal, maybe even the full ten crowns gold. Money changers' scales always seemed to work that way. He had not expected to get the man down that far, but from Fearnim's expression, grinning at last, he had never expected to receive so much. It was the best way for horse trading to end, with both sides thinking they had come out ahead. All in all, the day had begun very well, dice or no bloody dice. He should have known it would not last.

When he got back to the show at midday, riding the razor bareback because of his aching hip and with the dice rattling in his head, the line of people was longer than when he had left, waiting to pass beneath the big blue banner, stretched between two tall poles, that carried the show's name in big red letters. As people dropped their coins into the clear glass pitcher held by a heavy-set horse handler in a rough woolen coat, to be poured from there into an iron-bound chest under the watchful eyes of another horse handler who was even larger, more people joined the line, so it never seemed to grow shorter. The thing stretched beyond the end of the rope and around the corner. For a small wonder, no one was pushing or shoving. There were obvious farmers in the line, wearing rough woolens and with dirt ingrained in their hands, though the children's faces and those of the farmwives at least had been scrubbed clean. Luca was getting his hoped-for crowd, unfortunately. No chance of convincing him to leave tomorrow now. The dice said something was going to happen, something fateful to Mat bloody Cauthon, but what? There had been times when the dice stopped and he still had no idea what happened.

Just inside the canvas wall, with people streaming past to enjoy the performers lining both sides of the main street, Aludra was taking delivery of two wagonloads of barrels in various sizes. Of more than the barrels, it seemed. "I will show you where to park the wagons," the slender woman told the driver of the lead wagon, a lean man with a jutting jaw. Aludra's waist-long beaded braids swung as her eyes followed Mat for a moment, but she quickly turned back to the wagon driver. "The horses, you will take to the horselines afterward, yes?"

Now, what had she bought in such quantity? Something for her fireworks, certainly. Every night, soon after dark so she would catch everyone before they went to bed, she launched her nightflowers, two or three for a town the size of Jurador or if there were several villages close together. He had had some thoughts on why she wanted a bellfounder, but the only one that seemed to make any sense actually made no sense at all that he could see.

He hid the mare on the horselines. Well, you could not really hide a razor, but a horse was noticed less among other horses, and the time was not right, yet. The bowstave he left in the wagon he shared with Egeanin and Domon, neither of whom was there, then headed for Tuon's faded purple wagon. That was parked not far from Luca's wagon, now, though Mat wished it had been left near the storage wagons. Only Luca and his wife knew that Tuon was a High Lady rather than a servant who had been about to expose Mat and Egeanin to her supposed husband as lovers, but many among the showfolk were already wondering why Mat spent more time with Tuon than with Egeanin. Wondering and disapproving. They were an oddly prim lot for the most part, even the contortionists. Running off with the wife of a cruel lord was romantic. Canoodling with the lady's maid was sordid. Giving Tuon's wagon this favored spot, among the people who had been with Luca for years and were his most prized performers, was going to cause more talk.

In truth, he hesitated about going to Tuon at all with the dice drumming in his head. They had stopped too often in her presence, and he still did not know the why for a single one of those times. Not for certain. Maybe the first time, it had just been meeting her. Thinking of it made the hair on the back of his neck want to stand up. Still, with women, you always had to take chances. With a woman like Tuon, ten chances a day, and never knowing the odds until it was too late. Sometimes he wondered why his luck failed to help him more with women. Women were certainly as unpredictable as any honest dice ever made.

None of the Redarms was on guard outside the wagon—they were beyond that, now—so he trotted up the short flight of steps at the back of the wagon and rapped once before pulling the door open and entering. After all, he paid the rent for the thing, and they were hardly likely to be lying around unclothed at this time of day. Anyway, the door had a latch if they needed to keep people out.

Mistress Anan was off somewhere, but the interior was still crowded. The narrow table had been let down on ropes from the ceiling, with mismatched plates of bread and olives and cheese laid out on it along with one of Luca's tall silver wine pitchers, a squat red-striped pitcher and flower-painted cups. Tuon, a month's growth of tightly curled black hair on her head, sat on the wagon's sole stool at the far end of the table, with Selucia sitting on one of the beds at her side, and Noal and Olver on the other bed, elbows on the table. Today, Selucia was in the dark blue Ebou Dari dress that displayed her memorable bosom so well, with a flowered scarf tied around her head, but Tuon wore a red dress that seemed to be made entirely of tiny pleats. Light, he had only bought her the silk yesterday! How had she convinced the show's seamstresses to complete a dress already? He was pretty certain that usually took longer than a day. With liberal promises of his gold, he suspected. Well, if you bought a woman silk, you had to expect to pay to have it sewn. He had heard that saying as a boy, when he never expected to be able to afford silk, but it was the Light's own truth.

". . . . only the women are ever seen outside their villages," Noal was saying, but the gnarled, white-haired old man cut off when Mat entered the wagon, pulling the door shut behind him. The scraps of lace at Noal's wrists had seen better days, as had his well-cut coat of fine gray wool, but both were clean and neat, though in truth they looked odd with his crooked fingers and battered face. Those belonged on an aging tavern tough, one who had gone on fighting long past his prime. Olver, in the good blue coat Mat had had made for him, grinned as widely as an Ogier. Light, he was a good boy, but he would never be handsome with those big ears and that wide mouth. His manner with women needed vast improvement if he was ever to have any luck there at all. Mat had been trying to spend more time with Olver, to get him away from the influence of his "uncles," Vanin and Harnan and the other Redarms, and the boy seemed to enjoy that. Just not as much as he enjoyed playing Snakes and Foxes or stones with Tuon and staring at Selucia's bosom. It was all very well for those fellows to teach Olver how to shoot a bow and use a sword and the like, but if Mat ever learned who was teaching him to leer . . .

"Manners, Toy," Tuon drawled like honey sliding out of a dish. Hard honey. Around him, unless they were playing stones, her expression was usually severe enough for a judge handing down a death sentence, and her tone matched it. "You knock, then wait for permission to enter. Unless you are property or a servant. Then you do not knock. You also have grease on your coat. I expect you to keep yourself clean." Olver's grin faded at hearing Mat admonished. Noal raked bent fingers through his long hair and sighed, then began studying the green plate in front of him as if he might find an emerald among the olives.

Grim tone or no grim tone, Mat enjoyed looking at the dark little woman who was to be his wife. Who was halfway his wife already. Light, all she had to do was say three sentences and the thing was done! Burn him but she was beautiful. Once, he had mistaken her for a child, but that had been because of her size, and her face had been obscured by a transparent veil. Without that veil, it was plain that that heart-shaped face belonged to a woman. Her big eyes were dark pools a man could spend a lifetime swimming in. Her rare smiles could be mysterious or mischievous, and he prized them. He enjoyed making her laugh, too. At least, when she was not laughing at him. True, she was a little slimmer than he had always preferred, but if he could ever get an arm around her without Selucia there, he believed she would feel just right. And he might convince her to give him a few kisses with those full lips. Light, he dreamed about that sometimes! Never mind that she called him down as if they were already married. Well, almost never mind. Burn him if he could see what a little grease mattered. Lopin and Nerim, the two serving men he was saddled with, would fight over which one got to clean the coat. They had little enough to do that they really would if he did not name who received the task. He did not say that to her. Women liked nothing better than making you defend yourself, and once you started, she had won.

"I'll try to remember that, Precious," he said with his best smile, sliding in beside Selucia and putting his hat down on the other side from her. The blanket scrunched up between them, and they were a foot apart to boot, yet you would have thought he had pressed himself against her hip. Her eyes were blue, but the furious look she gave him was hot enough his coat should have been singed. "I hope there's more water than wine in that cup in front of Olver."

"It's goat's milk," the boy said indignantly. Ah. Well, maybe Olver was still a little too young even for well-watered wine.

Tuon sat up very straight, though she was still shorter than Selucia, who was a short woman herself. "What did you call me?" she said, as close to crisply as her accent allowed.

"Precious. You have a pet name for me, so I thought I should have one for you, Precious." He thought Selucia's eyes were going to pop right out of her head.

"I see," Tuon murmured, pursing her lips in thought. The fingers of her right hand waggled, as though idly, and Selucia immediately slid off the bed and went to one of the cupboards. She still took time to glare at him over Tuon's head. "Very well," Tuon said after a moment. "It will be interesting to see who wins *this* game. Toy."

Mat's smile slipped. Game? He was just trying to regain a little balance. But she saw a game, and that meant he could lose. Was likely to, since he had no idea what the game was. Why did women always make things so . . . complicated?

Selucia resumed her place and slid a chipped cup in front of him, and a blue-glazed plate that held half a loaf of crusty bread, six varieties of pickled olives mounded up, and three sorts of cheese. That perked his spirits again. He had hoped for this, if not expected it. Once you got a woman feeding you, she had a hard time finding it in herself to stop you from putting your feet under her table again.

"The thing of it is," Noal said, resuming his tale, "in those Ayyad villages, you can see woman of any age, but no men much above twenty if that. Not a one." Olver's eyes grew even wider. The boy practically inhaled Noal's tales, about the countries he had seen, even the lands beyond the Aiel Waste, swallowed them whole without butter.

"Are you any relation to Jain Charin, Noal?" Mat chewed an olive and discreetly spat the pit into his palm. The thing tasted not far from spoiling. So did the next one. But he was hungry, so he gobbled them down and followed with some crumbly white goat cheese while ignoring the frowns Tuon directed at him.

The old man's face went still as stone, and Mat had torn off a piece of bread and eaten that as well before Noal answered. "A cousin," he said at last, grudgingly. "He was my cousin."

"You're related to Jain Farstrider?" Olver said excitedly. His favorite book was *The Travels of Jain Farstrider*, which he would have sat up reading by lamplight long past his bedtime had Juilin and Thera allowed. He said he intended to see everything Farstrider had, when he grew up, all that and more.

"Who is this man with two names?" Tuon asked. "Only great men are spoken of so, and you speak as if everyone should know him."

"He was a fool," Noal said grimly before Mat could open his mouth, though Olver did get his open, and left it gaping while the old man continued. "He went gallivanting about the world and left a good and loving wife to die of a fever without him there to hold her hand while she died. He let himself be made into a tool by—" Abruptly Noal's face went blank. Staring through Mat, he rubbed at his forehead as though attempting to recall something.

"Jain Farstrider *was* a great man," Olver said fiercely. His hands curled into small fists, as though he was ready to fight for his hero. "He fought Trollocs and Myrddraal, and he had more adventures than anyone else in the whole world! Even Mat! He captured Cowin Gemallan after Gemallan betrayed Malkier to the Shadow!"

Noal came to himself with a start and patted Olver's shoulder. "He did that, boy. That much is to his credit. But what adventure is worth leaving your wife to die alone?" He sounded sad enough to die on the spot himself.

Olver had no answer to that, and his face fell. If Noal had put the boy off his favorite book, Mat was going to have words with the old man. Reading was important—he read himself; sometimes, he did—and he had made sure Olver had books he enjoyed.

Standing, Tuon leaned across the table to rest a hand on Noal's arm. The stern look had vanished from her face, replaced by tenderness. A wide belt of dark yellow tooled leather cinched her waist, emphasizing her slim curves. More of his coin spent. Well, coin was always easy to come by for him, and if she did not spend it, likely he would throw it away on some other woman. "You have a good heart, Master Charin." She gave everybody their bloody names except for Mat Cauthon!

"Do I, my Lady?" Noal said, sounding as though he really wanted to hear an answer. "Sometimes I think—" Whatever he thought sometimes, they were not to learn it now.

The door swung open and Juilin put his head into the wagon. The

Tairen thief-catcher's conical red cap was at its usual jaunty angle, but his dark face was worried. "Seanchan soldiers are setting up across the road. I'm going to Thera. She'll take a fright if she hears it from anybody else." And as quickly as that he was gone again, leaving the door swinging.

CHAPTER
7

A Cold Medallion

Seanchan soldiers. Blood and bloody ashes! That was all Mat needed, with the dice spinning his head. "Noal, find Egeanin and warn her. Olver, you warn the Aes Sedai, and Bethamin and Seta." Those five would all be together or at least close by one another. The two former *sul'dam* shadowed the sisters whenever they left the wagon they all shared. Light, he hoped none of them had gone into the town again. That could put a weasel in the chicken yard for sure! "I'll go down to the entrance and try to see whether we're in any trouble."

"She won't answer to that name," Noal muttered, sliding out from the table. He moved spryly for a fellow who looked to have had half the bones in his body broken one time or another. "You know she won't."

"You know who I mean," Mat told him sharply, frowning at Tuon and Selucia. This name foolishness was their fault. Selucia had told Egeanin that her name was now Leilwin Shipless, and that was the name Egeanin was using. Well, he was not about to put up with that sort of thing, not for himself and not for her. She had to come to her senses, soon or late.

"I'm just saying," Noal said. "Come on, Olver."

Mat slid out after them, but before he reached the door, Tuon spoke.

"No warnings for us to remain inside, Toy? No one left to guard us?"

The dice said he should find Harnan or one of the other Redarms and plant him outside just to guard against accidents, but he did not hesitate. "You gave your word," he said, settling his hat on his head. The smile he got in reply was worth the risk. Burn him, but it lit up her face. Women were always a gamble, but sometimes a smile could be win enough.

He saw from the entrance that Jurador's days without a Seanchan presence had come to an end. Directly across the road from the show, several hundred men were taking off armor, unloading wagons, setting up tents in ordered rows, establishing horselines. All very efficiently done. He saw Taraboners with mail veils hanging from their helmets and bars of blue, yellow and green painted across their breastplates, and men who were clearly infantry, stacking long pikes and racking bows much shorter than a Two Rivers bow, in armor painted the same. He thought those must be Amadicians. Neither Tarabon nor Altara ran much to foot, and Altarans in service to the Seanchan had their armor marked differently for some reason. There were actual Seanchan, of course, perhaps twenty or thirty that he could see. There was no mistaking that painted armor of over-lapping plates or those strange, insectile helmets.

Three of the soldiers came ambling across the road, lean, hard-bitten men. Their blue coats, with the collars striped green-and-yellow, were plain enough despite the colors and showed the wear of armor use, but no signs of rank. Not officers, then, but still maybe as dangerous as red adders. Two of the fellows could have been from Andor or Murandy or even the Two Rivers, but the third had eyes tilted like a Saldaean's, and his skin was the color of honey. Without slowing, they started into the show.

One of the horse handlers at the entrance gave a shrill three-note whistle that began to echo through the show while the other, a squint-eyed fellow named Bollin, pushed the glass pitcher in front of the three. "Price is a silver penny each, Captain," he said with deceptive mildness. Mat had heard the big man speak in the same tone a heartbeat before he thumped another horse handler over the head with a stool. "Children is five coppers if they's more than waist-high on me, and three if they's shorter, but only children as has to be carried gets in free."

The honey-skinned Seanchan raised a hand as if to push Bollin out of his way, then hesitated, his face growing harder, if that was possible.

The other two squared up beside him, fists clenched, as pounding boots announced the arrival of every man in the show, it seemed, performers in their flashy garb and horse handlers in coarse wool. Every man had a club of some sort in his hand, including Luca, in a brilliant red coat embroidered with golden stars to his turned-down boot-tops, and even the bare-chested Petra, who possessed the mildest nature of any man Mat had ever met. Petra's face was a thunderhead now, though.

Light, this had the makings of a massacre, with these fellows' companions not a hundred paces away and all their weapons to hand. It was a good place for Mat Cauthon to take himself out of. Surreptitiously he touched the throwing knives hidden up his sleeves and shrugged just to feel the one hanging down behind the back of his neck. No way to check those under his coat or in his boots without being noticed, though. The dice seemed like continuous thunder. He began to plan how to get Tuon and the others away. He had to hang onto her a while longer, yet.

Before disaster could open the door, another Seanchan appeared, in blue-green-and-yellow striped armor but carrying her helmet on her right hip. She had the tilted eyes and honey-colored skin, and there was a scattering of white in her close-cropped black hair. She was near a foot shorter than any of the other three, and there were no plumes on her helmet, just a small crest like a bronze arrowhead at the front, but the three soldiers stood up very straight when they saw her. "Now why am I not surprised to find you here at what looks to be the fine beginnings of a riot, Murel?" Her slurred accent had a twang in it. "What's this all about then?"

"We paid our money, Standardbearer," the honey-skinned man replied in the same twangy accents, "then they said we had to pay more on account of us being soldiers of the Empire."

Bollin opened his mouth, but she silenced him with a raised hand. She had that kind of presence. Running her eyes over the men gathered in a thick semicircle with their clubs, and pausing a moment to shake her head over Luca, she settled on Mat. "Did you see what happened?"

"I did," Mat replied, "and they tried to walk in without paying."

"That's good for you, Murel," she said, getting a surprised blink from the man. "Good for all three of you. Means you won't be out your coin. Because you're all confined to camp for ten days, and I doubt this show will be here that long. You're all docked ten days' pay, as well.

You're supposed to be unloading wagons so the homefolks don't get the idea we think we're better than they are. Or do you want a charge of causing dissension in the ranks?" The three men paled visibly. Apparently that was a serious charge. "I didn't think so. Now get out of my sight and get to work before I make it a full month instead of a week."

"Yes, Standardbearer," they snapped out as one, then ran back across the road as hard as they could go while tugging off their coats. Hard men, yet the Standardbearer was harder.

She was not finished, however. Luca stepped forward, bowing with a grand flourish, but she cut off whatever thanks he was about to offer. "I don't much like fellows threatening my men with cudgels," she drawled, resting her free hand on her sword hilt, "not even Murel, not at these odds. Still, shows you have backbone. Any of you fine fellows want a life of glory and adventure? Step across the road with me, and I'll sign you up. You there in that fancy red coat. You have the look of a born lancer, to me. I'll wager I can whip you into a proper hero in no time." A ripple of head-shaking ran through the assembled men, and some, seeing that no trouble was likely now, began slipping away. Petra was one of those. Luca looked as though he had been poleaxed. A number of others appeared almost as stunned by the offer. Performing paid better than soldiering, and you avoided the risk of people sticking swords into you. "Well, as long as you're standing here, maybe I can convince you. Not likely you'll get rich, but the pay is usually on time, and there always the chance of loot if the order is given. Happens now and then. The food varies, but it's usually hot, and there's usually enough to fill your belly. The days are long, but that just means you're tired enough to get a good night's sleep. When you don't have to work the night, too. Anyone interested yet?"

Luca gave himself a shake. "Thank you, Captain, but no," he said, sounding half-strangled. Some fools thought soldiers were flattered by someone thinking they had a higher rank than they did. Some fool soldiers were. "Excuse me, if you please. We have a show to put on. And people who aren't going to be pleased if they have to wait much longer to see it." With a last, wary look at the woman, as if he feared she might try to drag him off by his collar, he rounded on the men behind him. "All of you get back to your stands. What are you doing lounging around here? I have everything well in hand. Get back to your stands before people start demanding their money back." That would have been a disaster in his book. Given the choice between handing back coin and having a riot, Luca would have been unable to decide which was worse.

With the showfolk dispersing and Luca hurrying away while shooting glances at her over his shoulder, the woman turned to Mat, the only man remaining aside from the two horse handlers. "And what about you? From the look of you, you might be made an officer and get to give me orders." She sounded amused by the notion.

He knew what she was doing. The people in the line had seen three Seanchan soldiers sent running, and who could say for sure why they had run, but now they had seen her disperse a much larger crowd by herself. He would have given her a place in the Band as a Bannerman in a breath. "I'd make a terrible soldier, Standardbearer," he said, tipping his hat, and she laughed.

As he turned away, he heard Bollin saying, mildly, "You didn't hear what I told that man? It's a silver penny for you and another for your goodwife." Coins clinked into the pitcher. "Thank you." Things were back to normal. And the dice were still racketing in his head.

Making his way through the show, where acrobats were again tumbling for the crowds on their wooden platforms and jugglers juggling and Clarine's dogs running atop large wooden balls and Miyora's leopards standing on their hind legs inside a cage that looked barely strong enough to hold them, he decided to check on the Aes Sedai. The leopards brought them to mind. The common soldiers might spend the day working, yet he would have laid coin on at least some of the officers coming for a look before long. He trusted Tuon, strangely enough, and Egeanin had enough sense to stay out of sight when there might be other Seanchan around, but common sense seemed in short supply among Aes Sedai. Even Teslyn and Edesina, who had spent time as *damane*, took foolish chances. Joline, who had not, seemed to think herself invulnerable.

Everybody in the show knew the three women were Aes Sedai now, but their large wagon, covered with rain-streaked whitewash, still stood near the canvas-topped storage wagons, not far from the horselines. Luca had been willing to rearrange his show for a High Lady who gave him a warrant of protection, but not for Aes Sedai who put him at risk with their presence and were practically penniless besides. The women among the showfolk were sympathetic to the sisters for the most part, the men wary to one degree or another—it was almost always so with Aes Sedai—but Luca likely would have turned them out to make their own way without Mat's gold. Aes Sedai were more threat than anything else so long as they were in lands controlled by the Seanchan. Mat Cauthon got no thanks for it, not that he was looking for any. He would have settled for a touch of respect, unlikely as that was. Aes Sedai were Aes Sedai, after all.

Joline's Warders, Blaeric and Fen, were nowhere to be seen, so there was no need to talk his way past them to get inside, but as he approached the dirt-streaked steps at the back of the wagon, the foxhead medallion hanging beneath his shirt went icy cold against his chest, then colder still. For a moment, he froze like a statue. Those fool women were *channeling* in there! Coming to himself, he pounded up the steps and banged the door open.

The women he expected to see were all present, Joline, a Green sister, slender and pretty and big-eyed, and Teslyn, a narrow-shouldered Red who looked as though she chewed rocks, and Edesina, a Yellow, handsome rather than pretty, with waves of black hair spilling to her waist. He had saved all three from the Seanchan, had gotten Teslyn and Edesina out of the *damane* kennels themselves, yet their gratitude was variable to say the best. Bethamin, as dark as Tuon but tall and nicely rounded, and yellow-haired Seta had been *sul'dam* before they were forced into helping rescue the three Aes Sedai. The five of them shared this wagon, the Aes Sedai to keep an eye on the former *sul'dam*, the former *sul'dam* to keep an eye on the Aes Sedai. None realized their task, but mutual distrust made them carry it out assiduously. The one woman he had not expected to see was Setalle Anan, who had kept the Wandering Woman in Ebou Dar before she decided to make herself part of that rescue for some reason. But then, Setalle had a way of pushing herself in. Of meddling, in fact. She meddled between him and Tuon incessantly. What they were doing was completely unexpected, though.

In the middle of the wagon, Bethamin and Seta were standing rigid as fence posts, jammed shoulder-to-shoulder between the two beds that could not be raised against the walls, and Joline was slapping Bethamin's face again and again, first with one hand then the other. Silent tears trickled down the tall woman's cheeks, and Seta looked afraid that she would be next. Edesina and Teslyn, arms folded beneath their breasts, were watching with no expression whatsoever while Mistress Anan frowned her disapproval over Teslyn's shoulder. Whether disapproval of the slapping or of what Bethamin had done to earn it, he could not have said and did not care.

Crossing the floor in one stride, he seized Joline's upraised arm and spun her around. "What in the Light are you—?" That was as far as he got before she used her other hand to catch him a buffet so hard that his ears rang.

"Now, that killed the goat," he said, and, spots still floating in his vision, he dropped down onto the nearest bed and pulled a surprised Joline across his lap. His right hand landed on her bottom with a loud smack that pulled a startled squawk from her. The medallion went colder still, and Edesina gasped when nothing happened, but he tried to keep one eye on the other two sisters and one on the open door for Joline's Warders while he held her in place and whacked as fast and as hard as he could. With no idea how many shifts or petticoats she was wearing under that worn blue wool, he wanted to make sure he left an impression. It seemed his hand was beating time for the dice spinning in his head. Struggling and kicking, Joline began cursing like a wagon driver as the medallion seemed to turn to ice, and then to grow so cold he wondered if it would give him frostbite, but he soon added wordless yelps to her pungent vocabulary. His arm might not match Petra's, but he was far from weak. Practice with bow and quarterstaff gave you strong arms.

Edesina and Teslyn seemed as frozen in place as the two wide-eyed former *sul'dam*—well, Bethamin was grinning, yet she appeared as amazed as Seta—but just as he began to think Joline's yelps were out-numbering her curses, Mistress Anan tried to push past the two Aes Sedai. Astonishingly, Teslyn made a peremptory gesture for her to re-main where she was! Very few women, or men, argued with an Aes Sedai's commands, but Mistress Anan gave the Red sister a frosty look and squeezed between the two Aes Sedai muttering something that made both of them eye her curiously. She still had to force her way be-tween Bethamin and Seta, and he took advantage of that to land a final flurry of hard smacks, then rolled the Green sister off his lap. His hand had begun to sting anyway. Joline landed with a thump and let out a gasped "Oh!"

Planting herself in front of him, close enough that she interfered with Joline's hasty scramble to her feet, Mistress Anan studied him with her arms folded beneath her breasts in a way that increased the generous cleavage displayed by her plunging neckline. Despite the dress, she was not Ebou Dari, not with those hazel eyes, but she had large golden hoops in her ears, a marriage knife, the hilt marked with red and white stones for her sons and daughters, dangling from a wide silver collar around her neck, and a curved dagger thrust behind her belt. Her dark green skirts were sewn up on the left side to show red petticoats. With touches of gray in her hair, she was every inch the stately Ebou Dari innkeeper, sure of herself and accustomed to giving orders. He expected her to upbraid him—she was as good as an Aes Sedai when it came to upbraiding!—so he was surprised when she spoke, sounding very thoughtful.

"Joline must have tried to stop you, and Teslyn and Edesina as well, but whatever they did failed. I think that means you possess a *ter'angreal* that can disrupt flows of the Power. I've heard of such things—Cadsuane Melaidhrin supposedly had one, or so rumor said— but I've never seen the like. I would very much like to. I won't try to take it away from you, but I would appreciate seeing it."

"How do you know Cadsuane?" Joline demanded, attempting to brush off the seat of her skirt. The first brush of her hand brought a wince, and she gave over with a glare for Mat just to show him she still had him in mind. Tears glistened in her big brown eyes and on her cheeks, but if he had to pay for them, it was worth the price.

"She said something about the test for the shawl," Edesina said.

"She did say, 'How could you have passed the test for the shawl if you freeze at moments like this?'" Teslyn added.

Mistress Anan's mouth tightened for a moment, but if she was dis-composed, she regained her poise in a breath. "You may recall that I owned an inn," she said dryly. "Many people visited The Wandering Woman, and many of them talked, perhaps more than they should have."

"No Aes Sedai would," Joline began, then turned hurriedly. Blaeric and Fen were starting up the steps. Borderlanders both, they were big men, and Mat quickly got to his feet, ready to use his knives if necessary. They might drub him, but not without bleeding for it.

Surprisingly, Joline darted to the door and shut it right in Fen's face, then fastened the latch. The Saldaean made no effort to open the door, but Mat had no doubt the pair of them would be waiting when he left. When she turned around, her eyes were blazing hot, tears and all, and she seemed to have forgotten Mistress Anan for the moment. "If you ever even *think* of . . ." she began, shaking a finger at him.

He stepped forward and stuck a finger of his own to her nose, so fast that she jumped back and bumped into the door. From which she rebounded with a squeak, spots of red blooming in her cheeks. He cared not a whisker whether that was anger or embarrassment. She opened her mouth, but he refused to let her get a word in edgewise.

"Except for me, you'd be wearing a *damane* collar around your neck, and so would Edesina and Teslyn," he said, as much heat in his voice as there was in her eyes. "In return, you all try to bully me. You go your own way and endanger all of us. You bloody well *channeled* when you *know* there are Seanchan right across the road! They could have a *damane* with them, or a dozen, for all you know." He doubted there was even one, but doubt was not certainty, and in any case, he was not about to share his doubts with her, not now. "Well, I might have to put up with some of that, though you'd better know I'm getting close to my edge, but I won't put up with you hitting me. You do that again, and I vow I'll pepper your hide twice as hard and twice as hot. My word on it!"

"And I won't try to stop him next time if you do," Mistress Anan said.

"Nor I," Teslyn added, echoed after a long moment by Edesina.

Joline looked as though she had been hit between the eyes with a hammer. Very satisfactory. As long as he could figure out how to avoid having his bones broken by Blaeric and Fen.

"Now would someone like to tell me why you bloody decided to start channeling like it was the Last Battle? Do you have to keep holding them like that, Edesina?" He nodded at Seta and Bethamin. It was only an educated guess, but Edesina's eyes widened for a moment as if she thought his *ter'angreal* let him see flows of the Power as well as stop them. In any case, an instant later both women were standing normally. Bethamin calmly began drying her tears with a white linen handkerchief. Seta sat down on the nearest bed, hugging herself and shivering; she looked more shaken than Bethamin.

None of the Aes Sedai seemed to want to answer, so Mistress Anan did it for them. "There was an argument. Joline wanted to go see these Seanchan for herself, and she wouldn't be argued out of it. Bethamin decided to discipline her, just as if she had no clue what would happen." The innkeeper shook her head in disgust. "She tried to pull Joline across her lap, with Seta helping her, and Edesina wrapped them up in flows of air. I'm assuming," she said when the Aes Sedai all looked at her sharply. "I may not be able to channel, but I do use my eyes."

"That doesn't account for what I felt," Mat said. "There was a *lot* of channeling going on in here."

Mistress Anan and the three Aes Sedai studied him speculatively, long stares that seemed to probe for the medallion. They were not going to forget about his *ter'angreal*, that was for sure.

Joline took up the story. "Bethamin channeled. I've never before seen the weave she used, but for a few moments, until she lost the Source, she had sparks dancing all over the three of us. I think she may have used as much of the Power as she could draw."

Sobs suddenly racked Bethamin. She sagged, halfway to falling to the floor. "I didn't mean to," she wept, shoulders shaking, face contorted. "I thought you were going to kill me, but I didn't mean to. I didn't." Seta began rocking back and forth, staring at her friend in horror. Or perhaps her former friend. They both knew *a'dam* could hold them, and maybe any *sul'dam*, but they might well have denied the full import. Any woman who could use an *a'dam* could learn to channel. Likely they had tried as hard as they could to deny that hard fact, to forget it. Actually channeling altered everything, however.

Burn him, this was all he needed on top of everything else. "What are you going to do about it?" Only an Aes Sedai could handle this. "Now she's started, she can't just stop. I know that much."

"Let her die," Teslyn said harshly. "We can keep her shielded until we can be rid of her, then she can die."

"We can't do that," Edesina said, sounding shocked. Though not, apparently, at the thought of Bethamin dying. "Once we let her go, she'll be a danger to everyone around her."

"I won't do it again," Bethamin wept, almost pleading. "I won't!"

Pushing past Mat as if he were a coatrack, Joline confronted Bethamin, staring up at the taller woman with her fists on her hips. "You won't stop. You can't, once you begin. Oh, you may be able to go months between attempts to channel, but you will try again, and again, and every time, your danger will increase." With a sigh, she lowered her hands. "You are much too old for the novice book, but there's nothing for it. We will have to teach you. Enough to make you safe, at least."

"Teach her?" Teslyn screeched, planting *her* fists on her hips. "I do say let her die! Do you have any idea how these *sul'dam* did treat me when they did have me prisoner?"

"No, since you've never gone into detail beyond moaning over how horrible it was," Joline replied dryly, then added in very firm tones, "But I will not leave any woman to die when I can stop it."

That did not end things, of course. When a woman wanted to argue, she could keep it going if she was by herself, and they *all* wanted to argue. Edesina joined in on Joline's side, and so did Mistress Anan, just as if she had as much right to speak as the Aes Sedai. Of all things, Bethamin and Seta took Teslyn's part, denying any wish to learn to channel, waving their hands and arguing as loudly as anyone. Wisely, Mat took the opportunity to slip out of the wagon and pull the door shut behind him softly. No need to remind them of him. The Aes Sedai, at least, would remember soon enough. At least he could stop worrying about where the bloody *a'dam* were and whether the *sul'dam* would try using them again. That was well and truly finished, now.

He had been right about Blaeric and Fen. They were waiting at the foot of the steps, and stormclouds were not in it for their faces. Without any doubt, they knew exactly what had happened to Joline. But not who was to blame, it turned out.

"What went on in there, Cauthon?" Blaeric demanded, his blue eyes sharp enough to poke holes. Slightly the taller of the two, he had shaved his Shienaran topknot and was not best pleased by the growth of short hair covering his scalp.

"Were you involved?" Fen asked coldly.

"How could I have been?" Mat replied, trotting down the steps as if he had not a care in the world. "She's Aes Sedai, in case you hadn't noticed. If you want to know what happened, I suggest you ask her. I'm not woolheaded enough to talk about it, I'll tell you that. Only, I wouldn't ask her right now. They're all still arguing in there. I took the chance to slip out while my hide was still intact."

Not the best choice of words, perhaps. The two Warders' faces grew darker still, impossible as that seemed. But they let him go on his way without having to resort to his knives. There was that. Neither seemed very eager to enter the wagon, either. Instead, they settled on the wagon's steps to wait, more fools they. He doubted Joline would be very forthcoming with them, but she might well take out some of her temper on them because they knew. Had he been them, he would have found tasks to keep him clear of that wagon for . . . oh, say, a month or two. That might help. Some. Women had long memories for some things. He was going to need to watch over his shoulder for Joline himself from now on. But it had still been worth it.

With Seanchan camped across the road and Aes Sedai arguing and women channeling as if they had never heard of the Seanchan and the dice spinning in his head, not even winning two games of stones from Tuon that night could make him feel anything but wary. He went to sleep—on the floor, since it was Domon's turn to use the second bed; Egeanin always got the other—with the dice bouncing off the insides of his skull, but he was sure that tomorrow had to be better than today. Well, he had never claimed to always be right. He just wished he was not quite so wrong so often.

CHAPTER
8

Dragons' Eggs

Luca had the showfolk breaking camp, taking down the big canvas wall and packing everything into the wagons, while the sky was still dark the next morning. It was the clatter and banging of it, the shouting, that woke Mat, groggy and stiff from sleeping on the floor. As much as he could sleep, for the bloody dice. Those things gave a man dreams that slaughtered sleep. Luca was rushing about in his shirtsleeves with a lantern, giving orders and likely impeding matters as much as speeding them, but Petra, wide enough to seem squat though he was not all that much shorter than Mat, paused in hitching the four-horse team to his and Clarine's wagon to explain. With the waning moon low on the horizon and half-hidden by trees, a lantern on the driver's seat gave all the light they had, a flickering pool of yellow that was repeated a hundred times and more through the camp. Clarine was off walking the dogs, since they would be spending most of the day inside the wagon.

"Yesterday. . . ." The strongman shook his head and patted the nearest animal, patiently waiting for the last straps to be buckled, as if the horse had showed signs of nerves. Maybe he felt edgy himself. The night was only cool, not really cold, yet he was bundled up in a dark coat and had on a knitted cap. His wife worried about him falling sick from drafts or the cold, and took care that he would not. "Well, we're strangers everywhere, you see, and a lot of people think they can take advantage of strangers. But if we let one man get away with it, ten more will try, if not a hundred. Sometimes the local magistrate, or what passes for one, will uphold the law for us, too, but only sometimes. Because we're strangers, and tomorrow or the next day, we'll be gone, and anyway, everybody knows strangers are usually up to no good. So we have to stand up for ourselves, fight for what's ours if need be. Once you do that, though, it's time to move along. Same now as when there were only a few dozen of us with Luca, counting the horse handlers, though in those days, we'd have been gone as soon as those soldiers left. In those days, there weren't so many coins to be lost by leaving in a hurry," he said dryly, and shook his head, perhaps for Luca's greed or perhaps for how large the show had grown, before going on.

"Those three Seanchan have friends, or at least companions who won't like their own being faced down. That Standardbearer did it, but you can be sure they'll lay it to us, because they think they can hit at us, and they can't at her. Maybe their officers will uphold the law, or their rules or whatever, like she did, but we can't be sure of that. What is certain sure, though, is that those fellows will cause trouble if we stay another day. No point to staying when it means fights with soldiers, and maybe people hurt so they can't perform, and sure trouble with the law one way or another." It was the longest speech Mat had ever heard from Petra, and the man cleared his throat as though embarrassed by saying so much. "Well," he muttered, bending back to the harness, "Luca will want to be on the road soon. You'll want to be seeing to your own horses."

Mat wanted no such thing. The most wonderful thing about having coin was not what you could buy, but that you could pay others to do the work. As soon as he realized the show was preparing to move, he had rousted the four Redarms from the tent they shared with Chel Vanin to hitch the teams for his wagon and Tuon's, do as he instructed with the razor and saddle Pips. The stout horsethief—he had not stolen a horse since Mat had known him, but that was what he was— had roused himself long enough to say that he would get up when the others returned, then rolled over in his blankets and was snoring again before Harnan and the others had their boots half on. Vanin's skills were such that no one voiced any complaint beyond the usual grumbling about the hour, and all but Harnan would have grumbled if al-

lowed to sleep till noon. When those skills were needed, he would repay them tenfold, and they knew it, even Fergin. The skinny Redarm
was none too bright except when it came to soldiering, but he was
plenty smart enough there. Well, smart enough.

The show left Jurador before the sun broke the horizon, a long
snake of wagons rolling along the wide road through the darkness with
Luca's lurid monstrosity pulled by six horses at its head. Tuon's wagon
came just behind with Gorderan driving, almost wide-shouldered
enough to seem a strongman himself, and Tuon and Selucia, well-
cloaked and hooded, squeezed in on either side of him. The storage
wagons and animal cages and spare horses brought up the tail. Sentries
at the Seanchan camp watched them depart, silent armored figures in
the night marching the camp's perimeter. Not that the camp itself was
quiet. Shadowy forms stood in rigid lines among the tents while loud
voices bellowed the rollcall at a steady pace and others answered. Mat
all but held his breath until those regular shouts faded away behind
him. Discipline was a wonderful thing. For other men, anyway.

He rode Pips alongside the Aes Sedai wagon, near the middle of
the long line, flinching a little every time the foxhead went cool
against his chest, which it began to do before they had gone much
more than a mile. It seemed that Joline was wasting no time. Fergin,
handling the reins, chattered away about horses and women with
Metwyn. Both were as happy as pigs in clover, but then, neither had
any idea what was going on inside the wagon. At least the medallion
only turned cool, and barely that. They were using small amounts of
the Power. Still, he disliked being so near any channeling at all. In his
experience, Aes Sedai carried trouble in their belt pouches and seldom
were shy about scattering it, never mind who might be in the way. No,
with the dice bouncing inside his head, he could have done without
Aes Sedai within ten miles.

He would have ridden up beside Tuon, for the chance to talk with
her, no matter that Selucia and Gorderan would hear every word, but
you never wanted a woman thinking you were too eager. Do that, and
she either took advantage or else skittered away like a water drop on a
hot greased griddle. Tuon found enough ways to take advantage already, and he had too little time for very much in the way of chasing.
Sooner or later she would speak the words that completed the marriage
ceremony, sure as water was wet, but that only made it more urgent for
him to find out what she was like, which had hardly been easy so far.

That little woman made a blacksmith's puzzle seem simple. But how could a man be married to a woman if he did not know her? Worse, he had to make her see him as something more than Toy. Marriage to a woman with no respect for him would be like wearing a shirt of black-wasp nettles day and night. Worse still, he had to make her care for him, or he would find himself forced to hide from his own wife to keep her from making him *da'covale*! And to cap it off, he had to do all of that in whatever time remained before he had to send her back to Ebou Dar. A fine stew, and doubtless a tasty meal for some hero out of legend, a little something to occupy his idle time before he rushed off to perform some great deed, only Mat bloody Cauthon was no bloody hero. He still had it to do, though, and no time or room for missteps.

It was the earliest start they had made yet, but his hopes that the Seanchan had frightened Luca into moving faster were soon dashed. As the sun climbed, they passed stone farm buildings clinging to hillsides and occasionally a tiny tile- or thatch-roofed village nestled beside the road in a surround of stone-walled fields carved out of the forest, where men and women stood gaping as the show streamed past and children ran alongside until their parents called them back, but in the mid-afternoon, the show reached something larger. Runnien Crossing, near a so-called river that could have been waded in fewer than twenty paces without going more than waist-deep despite the stone bridge across it, was never a patch on Jurador, but it possessed four inns, each three stories of stone roofed in green or blue tiles, and near half a mile of hard-packed dirt between the village and the river where merchants could park their wagons for the night. Farms with their walled fields and orchards and pastures made a quilt of the countryside for a good league along the road and maybe more beyond the hills to either side of it. They certainly covered the hillsides Mat could see. That was enough for Luca.

Ordering the canvas wall erected in the clearing, near to the river to make watering the animals easier, the man strutted into the village wearing coat and cloak red enough to make Mat's eyes hurt and so embroidered with golden stars and comets that a Tinker would have wept for the shame of donning the garments. The huge blue-and-red banner was stretched across the entrance, each wagon in its place, the performing platforms unloaded and the wall nearly all up by the time he returned escorting three men and three women. The village was not all that far from Ebou Dar, yet their clothing might have come from another country altogether. The men wore short wool coats in bright colors embroidered with angular scrollwork along the shoulders and sleeves, and dark, baggy trousers stuffed into knee boots. The women, their hair in a sort of coiled bun atop their heads, wore dresses nearly as colorful as Luca's garments, their narrow skirts resplendent with flowers from hem to hips. They did all carry long belt knives, though with straight blades for the most part, and caressed the hilts whenever anybody looked at them; that much was the same. Altara was Altara when it came to touchiness. These were the village Mayor, the four innkeepers, and a lean, leathery, white-haired woman in red; the others addressed her respectfully as Mother. Since the round-bellied Mayor was as white-haired as she, not to mention mostly bald, and none of the innkeepers lacked at least a little gray hair, Mat decided she must be the village Wisdom. He smiled and tipped his hat to her as she passed, and she gave him a sharp look and sniffed in near perfect imitation of Nynaeve. Oh, yes, a Wisdom all right.

Luca showed them around with wide smiles and expansive gestures, elaborate bows and flourishes of his cloak, stopping here and there to make a juggler or a team of acrobats perform a little for his guests, but his smile turned to a sour grimace once they were safely back on their way and out of sight. "Free admission for them and their husbands and wives and *all* the children," he growled to Mat, "and I'm supposed to pack up if a merchant comes down the road. They weren't that blunt, but they were clear enough, especially that Mother Darvale. As if this flyspeck ever attracted enough merchants to fill this field. Thieves and scoundrels, Cauthon. Country folk are all thieves and scoundrels, and an honest man like me is at their mercy."

Soon enough he was toting up what he might earn there despite the complimentary admissions, but he never did give over complaining entirely, even when the line at the entrance stretched nearly as far as it had in Jurador. He just added complaining about how much he would have taken in with another three or four days at the salt town. It was three or four more days, now, and likely he would have lingered until the crowds had dwindled to nothing. Maybe those three Seanchan had been *ta'veren* work. Not likely, but it was a pleasant way to think of it. Now that it was all in the past, it was.

That was how they progressed. At best a mere two leagues or perhaps three at an unhurried pace, and usually Luca would find a small town or a cluster of villages that he felt called for a halt. Or better to say that he felt their silver calling to him. Even if they passed nothing but flyspecks not worth the labor of erecting the wall, they never made as much as four leagues before Luca called a halt. He was not about to risk having to camp strung out along the road. If there was not to be a show, Luca liked to find a clearing where the wagons could be parked without too much crowding, though if driven to it, he would dicker with a farmer for the right to stop in an unused pasture. And mutter over the expense the whole next day if it cost no more than a silver penny. He was tight with his purse strings, Luca was.

Trains of merchants' wagons passed them in both directions, making good speed and managing to raise small clouds of dust from the hard-packed road. Merchants wanted to get their goods to market as quickly as possible. Now and then they saw a caravan of Tinkers, too, their boxy wagons as bright as anything in the show except for Luca's wagon. All of them were headed toward Ebou Dar, oddly enough, but then, they moved as slowly as Luca. Not likely any coming the other way would overtake the show. Two or three leagues a day, and the dice rattled away so that Mat was always wondering what lay beyond the next bend in the road or what was catching him up from behind. It was enough to give a man hives.

The very first night, outside Runnien Crossing, he approached Aludra. Near her bright blue wagon she had set up a small canvas enclosure, eight feet tall, for launching her nightflowers, and she straightened with a glare when he pulled back a flap and ducked in. A closed lantern sitting on the ground near the wall gave enough light for him to see that she was holding a dark ball the size of a large melon. Runnien Crossing was only big enough to merit a single nightflower. She opened her mouth, all set to chivvy him out. Not even Luca was allowed in here.

"Lofting tubes," he said quickly, gesturing to the metal-bound wooden tube, as tall as he was and near enough a foot across, sitting upright in front of her on a broad wooden base. "That's why you want a bellfounder. To make lofting tubes from bronze. It's the why I can't puzzle out." It seemed a ridiculous idea—with a little effort, two men could lift one of her wooden lofting tubes into the wagon that carried them and her other supplies; a bronze lofting tube would require a derrick—but it was the only thing that had occurred to him.

With the lantern behind her, shadows hid her expression, but she was silent for a long moment. "Such a clever young man," she said

finally. Her beaded braids clicked softly as she shook her head. Her
laugh was low and throaty. "Me, I should watch my tongue. I always
get into the trouble when I make promises to clever young men. Never
think I will tell you the secrets that would make you blush, though,
not now. You are already juggling two women, it seems, and me, I will
not be juggled."

"Then I'm right?" He was barely able to keep the incredulity from
his voice.

"You are," she said. And casually tossed the nightflower at him!

He caught it with a startled oath, and only dared to breathe when
he was sure he had a good grip. The covering seemed to be stiff leather,
with a tiny stub of fuse sticking out of one side. He had a little famil-
iarity with smaller fireworks, and supposedly those only exploded from
fire or if you let air touch what was inside—though he had cut one
open once without it going off—yet who could say what might make a
nightflower erupt? The firework he had opened had been small enough
to hold in one hand. Something the size of this nightflower would
likely blow him and Aludra to scraps.

Abruptly he felt foolish. She was not very likely to go throwing the
thing if dropping it was dangerous. He began tossing the ball from
hand to hand. Not to make up for gasping and all that. Just for something to do.

"How will casting lofting tubes from bronze make them a better
weapon?" That was what she wanted, weapons to use against the Seanchan, to repay them for destroying the Guild of Illuminators. "They
seem fearsome enough to me already."

Aludra snatched the nightflower back muttering about clumsy oafs
and turning the ball over in her hands to examine the leather surface.
Maybe it was not so safe as he had assumed. "A proper lofting tube,"
she said once she was sure he had not damaged the thing, "it will send
this close to three hundred paces straight up into the sky with the
right charge, and a longer distance across the ground if the tube is
tilted at an angle. But not far enough for what I have in mind. A lofting charge big enough to send it further would burst the tube. With a
bronze tube, I could use a charge that would send something a little
smaller close to two miles. Making the slow-match slower, to let it
travel that far, is easy enough. Smaller but heavier, made of iron, and
there would be nothing for pretty colors, only the bursting charge."

Mat whistled through his teeth, seeing it in his head, explosions erupting among the enemy before they were near enough to see you clearly. A nasty thing to be receiving. Now that would be as good as having Aes Sedai on your side, or some of those Asha'man. Better. Aes Sedai had to be in danger to use the Power as a weapon, and while he had heard rumors about hundreds of Asha'man, rumors grew with every telling. Besides, if Asha'man were anything like Aes Sedai, they would start deciding where they were needed and then take over the whole fight. He began envisioning how to use Aludra's bronze tubes, and right away he spotted a glaring problem. All your advantage was gone if the enemy came from the wrong direction, or got behind you, and if you needed derricks to move these things. . . . "These bronze lofting tubes—"

"Dragons," she broke in. "Lofting tubes are for making the night-flowers bloom. For delighting the eye. I will call them dragons, and the Seanchan will howl when my dragons bite." Her tone was grim as sharp stone.

"These dragons, then. Whatever you call them, they'll be heavy and hard to move. Can you mount them on wheels? Like a wagon or cart? Would they be too heavy for horses to pull?"

She laughed again. "It's good to see you are more than the pretty face." Climbing a three-step folding ladder that put her waist nearly level with the top of the lofting tube, she set the nightflower into the tube with the fuse down. It slid in a little way and stopped, a dome above the top of the tube. "Hand me that," she told him, gesturing to a pole as long and thick as a quarterstaff. When he handed it up to her, she held it upright and used a leather cap on one end to push the nightflower deeper. That appeared to take little effort. "I have already drawn plans for the dragoncarts. Four horses could draw one easily, along with a second cart to hold the eggs. Not nightflowers. Dragons' eggs. You see, I have thought long and hard about how to use my dragons, not just how to make them." Pulling the capped rod from the tube, she climbed down and picked up the lantern. "Come. I must make the sky bloom a little, then I want my supper and my bed."

Just outside the canvas enclosure stood a wooden rack filled with more peculiar implements, a forked stick, tongs as long as Mat was tall, other things just as odd and all made of wood. Setting the lantern on the ground, she placed the capped pole in the rack and took a square wooden box from a shelf. "I suppose now you want to learn how to make the secret powders, yes? Well, I did promise. I am the Guild, now," she added bitterly, removing the box's lid. It was an odd box, a solid piece of wood drilled with holes, each of which held a thin stick. She plucked out one and replaced the lid. "I can decide what is secret."

"Better than that, I want you to come with me. I know somebody who'll be happy to pay for making as many of your dragons as you want. He can make every bellfounder from Andor to Tear stop casting bells and start casting dragons." Avoiding Rand's name did not stop the colors from whirling inside his head and resolving for an instant into Rand—fully clothed, thank the Light—talking with Loial by lamplight in a wood-paneled room. There were other people, but the image focused on Rand, and it vanished too quickly for Mat to make out who they were. He was pretty sure that what he saw was what was actually happening right that moment, impossible as that seemed. It would be good to see Loial again, but burn him, there had to be some way to keep those things out of his head! "And if he isn't interested," again the colors came, but he resisted, and they melted away, "I can pay to have hundreds cast myself. A lot of them, anyway."

The Band was going to end up fighting Seanchan, and most likely Trollocs as well. And he would be there when it happened. There was no getting around the fact. Try to avoid it how he would, that bloody *ta'veren* twisting would put him right in the bloody middle. So he was ready to pour out gold like water if it gave him a way to kill his enemies before they got close enough to poke holes in his hide.

Aludra tilted her head to one side, pursing her rosebud lips. "Who is this man with such power?"

"It'll have to be a secret between us. Thom and Juilin know, and Egeanin and Domon, and the Aes Sedai, Teslyn and Joline at least, and Vanin and the Redarms, but nobody else, and I want to keep it that way." Blood and bloody ashes, far too many people knew already. He waited for her curt nod before saying, "The Dragon Reborn." The colors swirled and despite his fighting them again became Rand and Loial for a moment. This was not going to be as easy as it had seemed.

"You know the Dragon Reborn," she said doubtfully.

"We grew up in the same village," he growled, already fighting the colors. This time, they nearly coalesced before vanishing. "If you don't believe me, ask Teslyn and Joline. Ask Thom. But don't do it around anyone else. A secret, remember."

"The Guild has been my life since I was a girl." She scraped one of the sticks quickly down the side of the box, and the thing sputtered into flame! It smelled of sulphur. "The dragons, they are my life now. The dragons, and revenge on the Seanchan." Bending, she touched the flame to a dark length of fuse that ran under the canvas. As soon as the fuse caught, she shook the stick until the fire went out, then dropped it. With a crackling hiss the flame sped along the fuse. "I think me I believe you." She held out her free hand. "When you leave, I will go with you. And you will help me make many dragons."

For a moment, as he shook her hand, he was sure the dice had stopped, but a heartbeat later they were rattling again. It must have been imagination. After all, this agreement with Aludra might help the Band, and incidentally Mat Cauthon, stay alive, yet it could hardly be called fateful. He would still have to fight those battles, and however you planned, however well-trained your men were, luck played its part, too, bad as well as good, even for him. These dragons would not change that. But were the dice bouncing as loudly? He thought not, yet how could he be sure? Never before had they slowed without stopping. It had to be his imagination.

A hollow thump came from inside the enclosure, and acrid smoke billowed over the canvas wall. Moments later the nightflower bloomed in the darkness above Runnien Crossing, a great ball of red and green streaks. It bloomed again and again in his dreams that night and for many nights after, but there it bloomed among charging horsemen and massed pikes, rending flesh as he had once seen stone rent by fireworks. In his dreams, he tried to catch the things with his hands, tried to stop them, yet they rained down in unending streams on a hundred battlefields. In his dreams, he wept for the death and destruction. And somehow it seemed that the rattling of the dice in his head sounded like laughter. Not his laughter. The Dark One's laughter.

The next morning, with the sun just rising toward a cloudless sky, he was sitting on the steps of his green wagon, carefully scraping at the bowstave with a sharp knife—you had to be careful, almost delicate; a careless slice could ruin all your work—when Egeanin and Domon came out. Strangely, they seemed to have dressed with special care, in their best, such as it was. He was not the only one to have bought cloth in Jurador, but without promises of Mat's gold to speed them, the seamstresses were still sewing for Domon and Egeanin. The blue-eyed Seanchan woman wore a bright green dress heavily embroidered with tiny white and yellow flowers on the high neck and all down the sleeves. A flowered scarf held her long black wig in place. Domon, looking decidedly odd with a head of very short hair and that Illianer beard that left his upper lip bare, had brushed his worn brown coat till it actually had some semblance of neatness. They squeezed past Mat and hurried off without a word, and he thought no more of it until they returned an hour or so later to announce that they had been into the village and gotten Mother Darvale to marry them.

He could not stop himself from gaping. Egeanin's stern face and sharp eyes gave good indications of her character. What could have brought Domon to *marry* the woman? As soon marry a bear. Realizing the Illianer was beginning to glare at him, he hastily got to his feet and made a presentable bow over the bowstave. "Congratulations, Master Domon. Congratulations, Mistress Domon. The Light shine on you both." What else was he to say?

Domon kept glaring as if he had heard Mat's thoughts, though, and Egeanin snorted. "My name is Leilwin Shipless, Cauthon," she drawled. "That's the name I was given and the name I'll die with. And a good name it is, since it helped me reach a decision I should have made weeks ago." Frowning, she looked sideways at Domon. "You do understand why I could not take your name, don't you, Bayle?"

"No, lass," Domon replied gently, resting a thick hand on her shoulder, "but I will take you with any name you do care to use so long as you be my wife. I told you that." She smiled and laid her hand atop his, and he began smiling, too. Light, but the pair of them were sickening. If marriage made a man start smiling like dreamy syrup. . . . Well, not Mat Cauthon. He might be as good as wed, but Mat Cauthon was never going to start carrying on like a loon.

And that was how he ended up in a green-striped wall-tent, not very large, that belonged to a pair of lean Domani brothers who ate fire and swallowed swords. Even Thom admitted that Balat and Abar were good, and they were popular with the other performers, so finding them places to stay was easy, but that tent cost as much as the wagon had! Everybody knew he had gold to fling about, and that pair just sighed over giving up their snug home when he tried to bargain them down. Well, a new bride and groom needed privacy, and he was more than glad to give it to them if it meant he did not have to watch them go moon-eyed at each other. Besides, he was tired of taking his turn sleeping on the floor. In the tent, at least he had his own cot every night—narrow and hard it might be, yet it was softer than floorboards—and with only him, he had more room than in the wagon even after the rest of his clothes were moved in and stowed in a pair of brass-bound chests. He had a washstand of his very own, a ladder-back chair that was not too unsteady, a sturdy stool, and a table big enough to hold a plate and cup and a pair of decent brass lamps. The chest of gold he left in the green wagon. Only a blind fool would try robbing Domon. Only a madman would try robbing Egeanin. Leilwin, if she insisted, though he was still certain she would regain her senses eventually. After the first night, spent close by the Aes Sedai wagon, with the foxhead cool for half the night, he had the tent set up facing Tuon's wagon by dint of making sure that the Redarms started raising it before anyone else could claim the space.

"Are you placing yourself as my guard now?" Tuon said coolly when she saw the tent for the first time.

"No," he replied. "I'm just hoping for more glimpses of you." That was the Light's own truth—well, getting away from the Aes Sedai was part of it, but the other was true, too—yet the woman waggled her fingers at Selucia, and the pair of them launched into gales of giggles before recovering themselves and reentering the faded purple wagon with all the dignity of a royal procession. Women!

He was not often alone in the tent. He had taken on Lopin as his bodyservant after Nalesean's death, and the stout Tairen, with his blocky face and a beard that nearly reached his chest, was always popping in to bow his balding head and ask what "my Lord" would enjoy for his next meal or inquire whether "my Lord" had any need of wine or tea or would care for a plate of candied dried figs he had vaguely acquired somewhere. Lopin was vain over his ability to find delicacies where it seemed there could be none. That, or he was rifling through the clothes chests to see whether anything needed repair or cleaning or ironing. Something always did, in his estimation, though it all looked fine to Mat. Nerim, Talmanes' melancholy bodyservant, frequently accompanied him, largely because the skinny, gray-haired Cairhienin was bored. Mat could not understand how anyone could get bored with not having any work to do, but Nerim was full of dolorous comments on how poorly Talmanes must be faring without him, mournfully sighing about five times a day that Talmanes must have given his place to another by now, and he was ready to wrestle Lopin if need be for a share of the cleaning and mending. He even wanted his turn blacking Mat's boots!

Noal dropped by to spin his tall tales, and Olver to play stones or

Snakes and Foxes, when he was not playing with Tuon instead. Thom
came to play stones, too, and to share rumors he picked up in the
towns and villages, knuckling his long white mustache over the
choicer bits. Juilin brought his own reports, but he always brought
Amathera, as well. The former Panarch of Tarabon was pretty enough
for Mat to understand why the thief-catcher was interested, with a
rosebud mouth just made for kissing, and she clung to Juilin's arm as
if she might return some of his feelings, but her big eyes always gazed
fearfully toward Tuon's wagon, even when they were all inside Mat's
tent, and it was still all Juilin could do to keep her from dropping to
her knees and putting her face to the ground whenever she glimpsed
Tuon or Selucia. She did the same with Egeanin, and with Bethamin
and Seta, besides. Considering that Amathera had been *da'covale* for
just a matter of months, it fair made Mat's skin crawl. Tuon could not
really mean to make him *da'covale* when she was going to marry him.
Could she?

He soon told them to stop bringing him rumors about Rand.
Fighting the colors in his head was too much effort, and he lost that
fight as often as he won. Sometimes it was all right, but sometimes he
caught glimpses of Rand and Min, and it seemed those two were carrying on something awful. Anyway, the rumors were all the same, really.
The Dragon Reborn was dead, killed by Aes Sedai, by Asha'man, by
the Seanchan, by a dozen other assassins. No, he was in hiding, he was
massing a secret army, he was doing some fool thing or other that varied village by village and usually inn by inn. The one thing that was
clear was that Rand was no longer in Cairhien, and nobody had any
idea where he was. The Dragon Reborn had vanished.

It was odd how many of these Altaran farmers and villagers and
townsfolk seemed worried by that, as worried as the merchants passing
through and the men and women who worked for them. Not one of
those people knew any more of the Dragon Reborn than the tales they
carried, yet his disappearance frightened them. Thom and Juilin were
clear on that, until he made them stop. If the Dragon Reborn was
dead, what was the world to do? That was the question that people
asked over breakfast in the morning and ale in the evening and likely
on going to bed. Mat could have told them Rand was alive—those
bloody visions made him sure of that—but explaining how he knew
was another matter. Even Thom and Juilin seemed uncertain about the
colors. The merchants and the others would have thought him a mad-

man. And if they believed, that would only scatter rumors about him, not to mention likely setting the Seanchan to hunting for him. All he wanted was the bloody colors out of his head.

Moving into the tent made the showfolk eye him very oddly, and small wonder. First he had been running off with Egeanin—Leilwin, if she insisted on it—and Domon supposedly was her servant, but now she was married to Domon, and Mat was out of the wagon entirely. Some of the showfolk seemed to think it no more than he deserved for trailing after Tuon, yet a surprising number offered him sympathy. Several men commiserated over the fickleness of women—at least they did when they there were no women around—and some of the unmarried women, contortionists and acrobats and seamstresses, began eyeing him much too warmly. He might have enjoyed that if they had not been so willing to give him smoky looks right in front of Tuon. The first time that happened, he was so startled that his eyes nearly popped. Tuon seemed to find it amusing, of all things! She *seemed* to. But only a fool thought he knew what was in a woman's head just because she had a smile on her face.

He continued to dine with her every midday, if they were halted, and began arriving for his nightly games of stones early, so she had to feed him then, too. Light's truth, if you got a woman to feed you on a regular basis, she was halfway won. At least, he dined with her when she would let him into the wagon. One night he found the latch down, and no amount of talking would make her or Selucia open the door. It seemed a bird had managed to get inside during the day, an extremely bad omen apparently, and the pair of them had to spend the night in prayer and contemplation to avert some evil or other. They seemed to run half their lives according to strange superstitions. Tuon or Selucia either one would make odd signs with their hands if they saw a torn spiderweb with the spider in it, and Tuon explained to him, just as serious as if she were making sense, that the sure result of clearing away a spiderweb before shooing the spider out of it was the death of someone close to you within the month. They would see a flight of birds circle more than once and predict a storm, or draw a finger through a line of marching ants, count how long it took for the ants to rejoin their line, and predict how many days of fair weather lay ahead, and never mind that it did not work out that way. Oh, there was rain three days after the birds—crows, disturbingly enough—but it was nowhere near a storm, just a gray, drizzling day.

"Obviously, Selucia miscounted with the ants," Tuon said, placing a white stone on the board with that oddly graceful arching of her fingers. Selucia, watching over her shoulder in a white blouse and divided brown skirts, nodded. As usual, she wore a head scarf over her short golden hair even indoors, a length of red-and-gold silk that day. Tuon was all in brocaded blue silk, a coat of odd cut that covered her hips and divided skirts so narrow they seemed to be wide trousers. She spent considerable time giving the seamstresses detailed instructions on what she wanted sewn, and little of it was much like anything he had ever seen before. It was all in Seanchan styles, he suspected, though she had had a few riding dresses sewn that would not draw comment, for when she went outside. Rain pattered softly on the roof of the wagon. "Obviously, what the birds told us was modified by the ants. It is never simple, Toy. You must learn these things. I will not have you ignorant."

Mat nodded as if that made sense and placed his black stone. And she called his uneasiness about crows and ravens superstition! Knowing when to keep your mouth shut was a useful skill around women. Around men, too, but more so around women. You could be pretty certain what would set a man's eyes on fire.

Talking with her could be dangerous in other ways, too. "What do you know of the Dragon Reborn?" she asked him another evening.

He choked on a mouthful of wine, and the whirling colors in his brain dissipated in a fit of coughing. The wine was near enough vinegar; but even Nerim had a hard time finding good wine these days. "Well, he's the Dragon Reborn," he said when he could speak, wiping wine from his chin with one hand. For a moment, he saw Rand eating at a large dark table. "What else is there to know?" Selucia refilled his cup smoothly.

"A great deal, Toy. For one thing, he must kneel to the Crystal Throne before Tarmon Gai'don. The Prophecies are clear on that, but I haven't even been able to learn where he is. It becomes still more urgent if he is the one who sounded the Horn of Valere, as I suspect."

"The Horn of Valere?" he said weakly. The Prophecies said *what*? "It's been found, then?"

"It must have been, mustn't it, if it was sounded?" she drawled dryly. "The reports I've seen from the place where it was blown, a place called Falme, are very disturbing. Very disturbing. Securing whoever blew the Horn, man or woman, may be as important as securing the Dragon Reborn himself. Are you going to play a stone or not, Toy?"

He played his stone, but he was so shaken that the colors whirled and faded without forming any image. In fact, he was barely able to eke out a draw from what had seemed a clear winning position.

"You played very poorly toward the end," Tuon murmured, frowning thoughtfully at the board, now divided evenly between the control of black stones and white. He could all but *see* her start trying to work out what they had been talking about when his poor play began. Talking with her was like walking a crumbling ledge across the face of a cliff. One misstep, and Mat Cauthon would be as dead as last year's mutton. Only, he had to walk that ledge. He had no bloody choice. Oh, he enjoyed it. In a way. The longer he spent with her, the more opportunity to memorize that heart-shaped face, to get it down so he could see her just by closing his eyes. But there was always that misstep waiting ahead. He could almost see that, too.

For several days after giving her the little bunch of silk flowers, he brought her no presents, and he thought he was beginning to detect hints of disappointment when he appeared empty-handed. Then, four days out of Jurador, just as the sun was peeking over the horizon into a nearly cloudless sky, he got her and Selucia out of the purple wagon. Well, he just wanted Tuon, but Selucia might as well have been her shadow when it came to trying to separate them. He had commented on that once, making a joke, and both women went on talking as if he had not spoken. It was a good thing he knew Tuon could laugh at a joke, because sometimes she seemed to have no sense of humor at all. Selucia, wrapped in a green wool cloak with the cowl all but hiding her red headscarf, eyed him suspiciously, but then, she nearly always did. Tuon never bothered with a scarf, yet the shortness of her black hair was not so apparent with the hood of her blue cloak up.

"Cover your eyes, Precious," he said. "I have a surprise for you."

"I like surprises," she replied, placing her hands over her big eyes. For an instant, she smiled in anticipation, but only for an instant. "Some surprises, Toy." That had the sound of a warning. Selucia stood hard by her shoulder, and though the bosomy woman appeared completely at her ease, something told him she was as tense as a cat ready to leap. He suspected she did *not* like surprises.

"Wait right there," he said, and ducked around the side of the purple

wagon. When he returned, he was leading Pips and the razor, both saddled and bridled. The mare stepped lively, frisking at the prospect of an
outing. "You can look now. I thought you might like a ride." They had
hours; the show might as well have been deserted for all the evidence of
life among the wagons. Only a handful had smoke rising from their
metal chimneys. "She's yours," he added, and stiffened as the words
nearly froze in his throat.

There was no doubt this time. He had said the horse was hers, and
suddenly the dice were not beating so loudly in his head. It was not
that they had slowed; he was sure of that. There had been more than
one set rattling away. One *had* stopped when he made his agreement
with Aludra, and another when he told Tuon the horse was hers. That
was odd in itself—how could giving her a horse be fateful for him?—
but Light, it had been bad enough when he had to worry about one set
of dice giving warning at a time. How many sets were still bouncing
off the inside of his skull? How many more fateful moments were waiting to crash down on him?

Tuon went immediately to the razor, all smiles as she examined the
animal as thoroughly as he had himself. She did train horses for fun, after all. Horses and *damane*, the Light help him. Selucia was studying
him, he realized, her face an expressionless mask. Because of the horse,
or because he had gone stiff as a post?

"She's a razor," he said, patting Pips' blunt nose. The gelding had
been getting plenty of exercise, but the razor's eagerness seemed to
have infected him. "Domani bloodborn favor razors, and it's not likely
you'll ever see another one outside of Arad Doman. What will you
name her?"

"It is bad luck to name a horse before riding it," Tuon replied, taking the reins. She was still beaming. Her big eyes shone. "She's a very
fine animal, Toy. A wonderful gift. Either you have a good eye, or you
were very lucky."

"I have a good eye, Precious," he said warily. She seemed more delighted than even the razor called for.

"If you say so. Where is Selucia's mount?"

Oh, well. It had been worth a try. A smart man hedged his bets,
though, so a sharp whistle brought Metwyn at a trot leading a saddled dapple. Mat ignored the wide grin that split the man's pale face.
The Cairhienin Redarm had been sure he would not get away with
leaving Selucia behind, but there was no need to smirk over it. Mat

judged the dapple gelding, ten years old, to be gentle enough for
Selucia—in his memory, ladies's maids seldom were more than tolera-
ble riders—but the woman gave the animal a going over as complete
as Tuon's. And when she was done, she directed a look at Mat that
said she would ride the horse so as not to make a bother, but she
found it decidedly lacking. Women could compress a great deal into
one look.

Once clear of the field where the show was camped, Tuon walked
the razor along the road for a time, then took her to a trot, and then a
canter. The surface was hard-packed yellow clay here, studded with
edges of old paving stones. No trouble for a well-shod horse, though,
and he had made sure of the razor's shoes. Mat kept Pips even with
Tuon as much for the pleasure of watching her smile as anything else.
When Tuon was enjoying herself, the stern judge was forgotten and
pure delight shone on her face. Not that watching her was easy, since
Selucia held the dapple between them. The yellow-haired woman was
a formidable chaperone, and by the sidelong glances she gave him, her
small smiles, she very much enjoyed the job of frustrating him.

At the start they had the road to themselves except for a few farm
carts, but after a while a Tinker caravan appeared ahead of them, a line
of garishly painted and lacquered wagons rolling slowly southward
down the other side of the road with massive dogs trotting alongside.
Those dogs were the only real protection Tinkers had. The driver of the
lead wagon, a thing as red as Luca's coats, trimmed in yellow and with
violent green-and-yellow wheels to boot, half-stood to peer toward
Mat, then sat back down and said something to the woman beside him,
doubtless reassured by the presence of the two women with Mat. Tinkers were a cautious lot, of necessity. That whole caravan would whip
up their horses and flee a single man they thought meant harm.

Mat nodded to the fellow as the wagons began to pass. The lean,
gray-haired man's high-collared coat was as green as his wagon's
wheels, and his wife's dress was striped in shades of blue, most bright
enough to suit any of the show's performers. The gray-haired man
raised his hand in a wave . . .

And Tuon suddenly turned the razor and galloped into the trees,
cloak streaming out behind her. In a flash, Selucia had the dapple darting after her. Snatching his hat off so as not to lose it, Mat wheeled
Pips and followed. Shouts rose from the wagons, but he paid them no
mind. His attention was all on Tuon. He wished he knew what she was

up to. Not escape, he was sure. Likely she was just trying to make him tear out his hair. If so, she was in a fair way for succeeding.

Pips quickly reeled in the dapple and left a scowling Selucia behind flailing her mount with the reins, but Tuon and the razor kept their lead as the rolling land climbed toward hills. Startled flights of birds sprang up from beneath both animals' hooves, coveys of gray dove and of brown-speckled quail, sometimes ruffed brown grouse. All disaster needed was for the mare to be frightened by one of those. The best-trained mount could rear and fall when a bird burst up under hoof. Worse, Tuon rode like a madwoman, never slowing, only swerving from her line where the underbrush lay dense, leaping trees toppled by old storms as if she had a clue what lay on the other side. Well, he had to ride like a madman himself to keep up, though he winced every time he set Pips to jump a tree trunk. Some were near as thick as he was tall. He dug his bootheels into the gelding's flanks, urging more speed though he knew Pips was running as hard as he ever had. He had chosen too well in that bloody razor. Up and up they raced through the forest.

As abruptly as she had begun her mad dash, Tuon reined in, well over a mile from the road. The trees were old here and widely spaced, black pines forty paces tall and wide-spreading oaks with branches that arched down to touch the ground before rising again and could have been sliced crosswise into tables to seat a dozen in comfort. Thick creepers shrouded half-buried boulders and stone outcrops, but aside from that only a few weeds pushed through the mulch. Oaks that size killed off any lesser undergrowth beneath them.

"Your animal is better than he looks," the fool woman said, patting her mount's neck, when he reached her. Oh, she was all innocence, just out for a pleasant ride. "Maybe you do have a good eye." With the cowl of her cloak fallen down her back, her cap of short hair was visible, glistening like black silk. He suppressed a desire to stroke it.

"Burn how good my eye is," he growled, clapping his hat on. He knew he should speak smoothly, but he could not have taken the roughness from his voice with a file. "Do you always ride like a moon-blinded idiot? You could have broken that mare's neck before she even got a name. Worse, you could have broken your own. I promised to get you home safely, and I mean to do just that. If you're going to risk killing yourself every time you go riding, then I won't let you ride." He wished he had those last words back as soon as they left his tongue.

A man might laugh off a threat like that as a joke, maybe, if you were lucky, but a woman. . . . Now all he could do was wait for the explosion. He expected Aludra's nightflowers to pale by comparison.

She raised the hood of her cloak, settling it just so. She studied him, tilting her head first one way then the other. Finally, she nodded to herself. "I name her Akein. That means 'swallow.' "

Mat blinked. That was it? No eruption? "I know. A good name. It suits her." What was she about now? The woman almost never did or said what he expected.

"What is this place, Toy?" she said, frowning at the trees. "Or should I say, what was it? Do you know?"

What did she mean, what was this place? It was a bloody forest was what it was. But suddenly what had seemed a large boulder right in front of him, nearly obscured by thick vines, resolved into a huge stone head, slightly tilted to one side. A woman's head, he thought; those smooth roundels were probably meant for jewels in her hair. The statue it sat on must have been immense. A full span of the thing showed, yet only her eyes and the top of her head were out of the ground. And that long white stone outcrop with an oak tree's roots growing over it was piece of a spiral column. All around them now he could make out bits of columns and large worked stones that plainly had been part of some grand structure and what had to be a stone sword two spans long, all half buried. Still, ruins of cities and monuments could be found in many places, and few even among Aes Sedai had any idea what they had been. Opening his mouth to say that he did not know, he caught sight through the trees of three tall hills in a row, perhaps another mile on. The middle hill had a cleft top, like a wedge cut cleanly out, while the hill on the left had two. And he knew. There could hardly be three hills exactly like that anywhere else.

Those hills had been called The Dancers when this place had been Londaren Cor, the capital city of Eharon. The road behind them had been paved then and ran through the heart of the city, which had sprawled for miles. People had said that the artistry in stone that the Ogier had practiced in Tar Valon, they had perfected in Londaren Cor. Of course, the people of every Ogier-built city had claimed their own outdid Tar Valon, confirming Tar Valon as the touchstone. He had a number of memories of the city—dancing at a ball in the Palace of the Moon, carousing in soldiers' taverns where veiled dancers writhed, watching the Procession of Flutes during the Blessing of the Swords—but oddly, he had another memory of those hills, from near enough five hundred years after the Trollocs left no stone standing in Londaren Cor and Eharon died in blood and fire. Why it had been necessary for Nerevan and Esandara to invade Shiota, as the land was then, he did not know. Those old memories were fragments however long a time any one covered, and full of gaps. He had no idea why those hills had been called The Dancers, either, or what the Blessing of the Swords was. But he remembered being an Esandaran lord in a battle fought among these ruins, and he remembered having those hills in view when he took an arrow through his throat. He must have fallen no more than half a mile from the very spot where he sat Pips, drowning in his own blood.

Light, I hate *to remember dying*, he thought, and the thought turned to a coal burning in his brain. A coal that burned hotter and hotter. He *remembered* those men's deaths, not just one but dozens of them. He—remembered—dying.

"Toy, are you ill?" Tuon brought the mare close and peered up into his face. Concern filled her big eyes. "You've gone pale as the moon."

"I'm right as spring water," he muttered. She was close enough for him to kiss if he bent his head, but he did not move. He could not. He was thinking so furiously he had nothing left for motion. Somehow only the Light knew, the Eelfinn had gathered the memories they had planted in his head, but how could they harvest memory from a corpse? A corpse in the world of men, at that. He was certain they never came to this side of that twisted doorframe *ter'angreal* for longer than minutes at a time. A way occurred to him, one he did not like, not a scrap. Maybe they created some sort of link to any human who visited them, a link that allowed them to copy all of a man's memories after that right up to the moment he died. In some of those memories from other men he was white-haired, in some only a few years older than he really was, and everything in between, but there were none of childhood or growing up. What were the odds of that, if they had just stuffed him with random bits and pieces, likely things they considered rubbish or had done with? What *did* they do with memories, anyway? They had to have some reason for gathering them beyond giving them away again. No, he was just trying to avoid where this led. Burn him, the bloody foxes were inside his head right then! They had to be. It was the only explanation that made sense.

"Well, you look as if you're about to vomit," Tuon said, backing the razor away with a grimace. "Who in the show would have herbs? I have some knowledge there."

"I'm all right, I tell you." In truth, he did want to sick up. Having those foxes in his head was a thousand times worse than the dice however hard the dice rattled. Could the Eelfinn see through his eyes? Light, what was he going to do? He doubted any Aes Sedai could Heal him of this, not that he would trust them to, not when it meant leaving off the foxhead. There *was* nothing to be done. He would just have to live with it. He groaned at the thought.

Cantering up to them, Selucia gave him and Tuon each a quick look, as if considering what they might have been up to in their time alone. But then, she had taken her time in catching up, giving them that time. That was hopeful. "Next time, you can ride this gentle creature and I will ride your gelding," she told Mat. "High Lady, people from those wagons are following us with dogs. They're afoot, but they will be here soon. The dogs don't bark."

"Trained guard dogs, then," Tuon said, gathering her reins. "Mounted, we can avoid them easily enough."

"No need to try, and no use," Mat told her. He should have expected this. "Those people are Tinkers, Tuatha'an, and they're no danger to anybody. They couldn't be violent if their lives depended on it. That's no exaggeration, just simple truth. But they saw you two go haring off, trying to get away from me as it must have seemed, and me chasing after. Now that those dogs have a scent trail, the Tinkers will follow us all the way back to the show if need be to make sure you two haven't been kidnapped or harmed. We'll go meet them to save the time and trouble." It was not the Tinkers' time he cared about. Luca probably would not care one way or the other if a bunch of Tinkers getting in the way delayed the show setting out, but Mat certainly would.

Selucia scowled at him indignantly, and her fingers flew, but Tuon laughed. "Toy wishes to be commanding today, Selucia. I will let him command and see how he does." Bloody kind of her.

They trotted back the way they had come—riding around the fallen trees this time, though now and then Tuon would gather her reins as if she meant to jump one, then give Mat a mischievous grin— and it was not long before the Tinkers came into sight running through the trees behind their huge mastiffs like a flight of butterflies, fifty or so men and women in bright colors, often in jarring combinations. A man might be wearing a red-and-blue striped coat and baggy yellow trousers tucked into knee boots, or a violet-colored coat above red trousers, or worse. Some women wore dresses striped in as many colors as there were colors and even colors Mat had no name for, while others wore skirts and blouses as varied in hue and as clashing as the men's coats and trousers. A fair number had shawls, as well, to add more colors to the eye-scrambling blend. Except for the gray-haired man who had been driving the lead wagon, they all appeared to be short of their middle years. He must be the Seeker, the leader of the caravan. Mat dismounted, and after a moment, Tuon and Selucia did, too.

The Tinkers stopped at that, calling their dogs to heel. The big animals slumped to the ground, tongues lolling out, and the people came on more slowly. None carried so much as a stick, and though Mat wore no weapons that showed, they eyed him warily. The men clustered in front of him, while the women gathered around Tuon and Selucia. There was no threat in it, but as easily as that, Tuon and Selucia were separated from him, off where the Tinker women could make inquiries. Suddenly it occurred to him that Tuon might think it a fine game to claim he was trying to bother her. She and Selucia could ride off while he was trying to contend with Tinkers crowding around him and Pips so he could not climb into the saddle. That was all they would do, but unless he was willing to fight his way clear, they might keep him here for hours, maybe, to give that pair time to "escape."

The gray-haired man bowed with his hands pressed to his chest. "Peace be on you and yours, my Lord. Forgiveness if we intrude, but we feared our dogs had frightened the ladies' horses."

Mat responded with a bow in the same fashion. "Peace be on you always, Seeker, and on all the People. The ladies' horses weren't frightened. The ladies are . . . impetuous at times." What were the women saying? He tried to eavesdrop, but their voices were low murmurs.

"You know something of the People, my Lord?" The Seeker sounded surprised and had a right to. The Tuatha'an kept away from anywhere larger than a moderate-sized village. They would seldom encounter anyone in a silk coat.

"Only a little," Mat replied. A very little. He had memories of meeting Tinkers, but he himself had never spoken to one before. What were those bloody women saying? "Will you answer me a question? I've seen a number of your caravans the past few days, more than I'd have expected to, and all heading toward Ebou Dar. Is there a reason?"

The man hesitated, darting a glance toward the women. They were still murmuring away, and he had to be wondering why their conversation was lasting so long. After all, it only needed a moment to say yes, I need help, or the opposite. "It is the people called Seanchan, my Lord," he said finally. "Word is spreading among the People that there is safety where the Seanchan rule, and equal justice for all. Elsewhere. . . . You understand, my Lord?"

Mat did. Like the showfolk, Tinkers were strangers wherever they went, and worse, strangers with an undeserved reputation for thievery—well, they stole no more often than anyone else—and a deserved one for trying to entice young people into joining them. And on top of it, for Tinkers there was no question of fighting back if anybody tried to rob them or chase them away. "Take a care, Seeker. Their safety comes at a price, and some of their laws are harsh. You know what they do with women who can channel?"

"Thank you for your concern, my Lord," the man said calmly, "but few of our women ever begin channeling, and if one does, we will do as we always do and take her to Tar Valon."

Abruptly, the women began laughing, great gales and peals. The Seeker relaxed visibly. If the women were laughing, Mat was not the kind of man who would strike them down or kill them for getting in his way. For Mat's part, he scowled. There was nothing in that laughter that he liked.

The Tinkers made their departure with more apologies from the Seeker for having bothered them, but the women kept looking back and laughing behind cupped hands. Some of the men leaned close as they walked, plainly asking questions, but the women just shook their heads. And looked back again, laughing.

"What did you tell them?" Mat asked sourly.

"Oh, that's none of your business, now is it, Toy?" Tuon replied, and Selucia laughed. Oh, she bloody cackled, she did. He decided he was better off not knowing. Women just purely enjoyed planting needles in a man.

CHAPTER
9

A Short Path

T uon and Selucia were not the only women who caused Mat trouble, of course. Sometimes it seemed that most of the trouble
in his life came from women, which he could not understand at
all since he always tried to treat them well. Even Egeanin gave her
share of grief, though it was the smallest share.

"I was right. You do think you can marry her," she drawled when
he asked her for help with Tuon. She and Domon were seated on the
steps of their wagon, with their arms around each other. A trickle of
smoke rose from Domon's pipe. It was midmorning on a fine day,
though gathering clouds threatened rain for later, and the performers
were putting on their acts for the inhabitants of four small villages
that, combined, perhaps equaled Runnien Crossing in size. Mat had no
desire to go watch. Oh, he still enjoyed watching the contortionists,
and better still the female acrobats and tumblers, but when you saw
jugglers and fire-eaters and the like every day just about, even Miyora
and her leopards became, well, less interesting if not exactly ordinary.

"Never you mind what I think, Egeanin. Will you tell me what
you know of her? Trying to find out from her is like fishing blindfolded
and bare-handed in a briar patch trying to catch a rabbit."

"My name is Leilwin, Cauthon. Don't forget it again," she said in
tones suitable for giving orders on a ship's deck. Her eyes tried to drive

the command home like blue hammers. "Why should I help you? You aim too high above yourself, a mole yearning for the sun. You could face execution for simply saying you want to marry her. It's disgusting. Besides, I've left all that behind me. Or it's left me," she added bitterly. Domon gave her a one-armed hug.

"If you've left all that behind you, what do you care how disgusting my wanting to marry her is?" There. It was out in the open. Partly, at least.

Domon removed the pipe from his mouth long enough to blow a smoke-ring aimed at Mat's face. "If she does no want to help you, then give over." He gave it that same ship's deck voice of command.

Egeanin muttered under her breath. She appeared to be arguing with herself. Finally, she shook her head. "No, Bayle. He's right. If I'm cast adrift, then I have to find a new ship and a new course. I can never return to Seanchan, so I might as well cut the cable and be done with it."

What she knew of Tuon was mainly rumor—it seemed the Imperial family lived their lives behind walls even when in plain sight, and only whispers of what went on behind those walls escaped—yet those were sufficient to make the hair on the back of Mat's neck stand up. His wife-to-be had had a brother and a sister *assassinated*? After they tried to have *her* killed, true, but still! What kind of family went around killing one another? The Seanchan Blood and the Imperial family, for starters. Half of her siblings were dead, assassinated, most of them, and maybe the others, too. Some of what Egeanin—Leilwin— had to tell was generally known among Seanchan, and hardly more comforting. Tuon would have been schooled in intrigue from infancy, schooled in weapons and fighting with her bare hands, heavily guarded yet expected to be her own last line of defense. All of those born to the Blood were taught to dissemble, to disguise their intentions and ambitions. Power shifted constantly among the Blood, some climbing higher, others slipping down, and the dance was only faster and more dangerous in the Imperial family. The Empress—she started to add, "May she live forever," and half-choked in swallowing the words, then closed her eyes for a long moment before continuing—the Empress had borne many children, as every Empress did, so that among those who survived there would be one fit to rule after her. It would not do to have someone who was stupid or a fool ascend the Crystal Throne. Tuon was accounted very far from either. Light! The woman he was to marry was as bad as Warder and Aes Sedai wrapped into one. And maybe as dangerous.

He had several conversations with Egeanin—he was careful to name her Leilwin to her face lest she go for him with her dagger, yet he thought of her as Egeanin—trying to learn more, but her knowledge of the Blood was largely from the outside looking in, and her knowledge of the Imperial Court, by her own admission, little better than that of a street urchin in Seandar. The day he gave Tuon the mare, he had ridden alongside Egeanin's wagon having one of those fruitless conversations. He had accompanied Tuon and Selucia for a time, but they kept looking at him sideways, then exchanging glances and giggling. Over what they had told the Tinker women, without a sliver of doubt. A man could only take so much of that sort of thing.

"A clever gift, that mare," Egeanin said, leaning out from the driver's seat to look up the line of wagons. Domon was handling the reins. She took her turn sometimes, but handling a team was not among the skills she had learned on ships. "How did you know?"

"Know what?" he asked.

She straightened and adjusted her wig. He did not know why she continued to wear the thing. Her own black hair was short, but no shorter than Selucia's. "About courting gifts. Among the Blood, when you are courting someone higher than you, a traditional gift is something exotic or rare. Best of all is if you can connect the gift somehow to one of the recipient's pleasures, and it's well known the High Lady loves horses. It's good you've acknowledged that you don't expect to be her equal, too. Not that this is going to work, you understand. I don't have a clue why she's still here, now you've stopped guarding her, but you can't believe she'll actually say the words. When she marries, it will be for the good of the Empire, not because some layabout like you gave her a horse or made her smile."

Mat ground his teeth to keep from shouting a curse. He had acknowledged *what*? No wonder a set of bloody dice had stopped. Tuon would let him forget this when it snowed on Sunday. He was certain sure of that.

If Leilwin bloody Shipless gave him small griefs, the Aes Sedai managed larger. Aes Sedai liked nothing better. He was resigned to them traipsing about every village and town they stopped at, asking questions and doing the Light knew what else. He had no choice but resignation, with no way to stop them. They claimed to be taking care—at least, Teslyn and Edesina did; Joline snapped that he was a fool for worrying—yet an Aes Sedai taking care was still clearly a woman of consequence whether or not anybody recognized what she was. Lacking the coin for silks, they had purchased bolts of fine wool in Jurador, and the seamstresses worked as hard for Aes Sedai as they did for Mat's gold, so they strolled about dressed like wealthy merchants and as sure of themselves as any noble ever born. Nobody saw one of them walk five strides without knowing that she expected the world to conform itself to her. Three women like that, with a traveling show at that, were sure to cause talk. At least Joline left her Great Serpent ring in her belt pouch. The other two had lost theirs to the Seanchan. If Mat had seen Joline with the thing actually on her finger, he thought he would have wept.

He got no more reports on their activities from the former *sul'dam*. Joline had Bethamin firmly in hand; the tall dark woman ran when Joline said run and jumped when she said toad. Edesina was giving her lessons, too, but Joline considered Bethamin a personal project for some reason. She was never harsh that Mat saw, not after the face slapping, but you might have thought she was getting Bethamin ready to go to the Tower, and Bethamin returned a sort of gratitude that made it clear her loyalties had shifted. As for Seta, the yellow-haired woman was so frightened of the sisters that she did not dare follow them any longer. She actually shivered when he suggested it. Strange as it seemed, Seta and Bethamin had been so accustomed to how Seanchan women who could channel saw themselves that they had really believed Aes Sedai could not be much different. They were dangerous when off the leash, yet dangerous dogs could be handled by someone who knew how, and they were experts with that particular sort of dangerous dog. Now they knew that Aes Sedai were not dogs of any kind. They were wolves. Seta would have found another place to sleep had that been possible, and he learned from Mistress Anan that the Seanchan woman put her hands over her eyes whenever Joline or Edesina was teaching Bethamin in the wagon.

"I'm certain she can see the weaves," Setalle said. He would have said she sounded envious except that he doubted she envied anyone. "She's halfway to admitting it, or she wouldn't hide her eyes. Soon or late, she'll come around and want to learn, too." Maybe she did sound envious at that.

He could have wished for Seta to come around soon rather than late. Another student would have left the Aes Sedai less time to trouble him. If the show was halted, he could hardly turn around without seeing Joline or Edesina peering around the corner of a tent or wagon at him. Usually, the foxhead cooled on his chest. He could not prove they were actually channeling at him, yet he was certain of it. He was unsure which of them found the loophole in his protection that Adeleas and Vandene had, that something thrown with the Power would hit him, but after that, he could barely leave his tent without getting hit by a rock, and later, by other things, burning sparks like a shower from a forge fire, stinging sparks that made him leap and his hair try to stand on end. He was positive that Joline was behind it. If for no other reason, he never saw her without Blaeric or Fen or both nearby for protection. And she smiled at him like a cat smiling at a mouse.

He was planning how to get her alone—it was that or spend his time hiding from her—when she and Teslyn got into a shouting match that cleared Edesina out of the whitewashed wagon almost as quickly as Bethamin and Seta, and those two ran out and stood gaping at the wagon. The Yellow sister calmly went back to brushing her long black hair, lifting it up with one hand and sweeping the wooden hairbrush down it with the other. Seeing Mat, she smiled at him without ceasing the motions of her brush. The medallion went cold, and the shouting vanished as though cut off by a knife.

He never learned what was said behind that Power-woven shield. Teslyn favored him somewhat, yet when he asked her, she gave him one of those looks and silence. It was Aes Sedai business and none of his. Whatever had gone on in there, though, the rocks stopped, and the sparks. He tried thanking Teslyn, but she was having none of it.

"When something be no to be spoken of, it be no to be spoken of," she told him firmly. "It would be well for you to learn that lesson if you are to be around sisters, and I think your life be tied to Aes Sedai, now if it was no before." Bloody thing for her to say.

She never cracked her teeth about his *ter'angreal*, but the same could not be said of Joline and Edesina, even after the argument. They tried to bully him into handing it over every single day, Edesina cornering him by herself, Joline with her Warders glowering over her shoulders at him. *Ter'angreal* were rightfully the property of the White Tower. *Ter'angreal* needed proper study, particularly one with the odd properties this one possessed. *Ter'angreal* were potentially dangerous, too much so to be left in the hands of the uninitiated. Neither said especially a man's hands, but Joline came close. He began to worry that the Green would have Blaeric and Fen simply take it from him. That pair still suspected he had been involved in what had happened to her, and the dark looks they gave him said they wanted any excuse to beat him like a drum.

"That would be stealing," Mistress Anan told him in a lecturing tone, gathering her cloak around her. The sunlight was beginning to fade, and coolness already setting in. They were standing outside Tuon's wagon, and he was hoping to get inside in time to be fed. Noal and Olver were already inside. Setalle was apparently off to visit the Aes Sedai, something she did frequently. "Tower law is quite clear on that. There might be considerable . . . discussion . . . over whether it had to be given back to you—I rather think it would not be, in the end—but Joline would face a fairly harsh penance for theft all the same."

"Maybe she'd think it worth a penance," he muttered. His stomach rumbled. The potted finches and creamed onions that Lopin had presented proudly for his midday meal had both turned out to be spoiling, to the Tairen's extreme mortification, which meant Mat had had a heel of bread since breakfast and no more. "You know an awful lot about the White Tower."

"What I know, Lord Mat, is that you've made just about every misstep a man can make with Aes Sedai, short of trying to kill one. The reason I came with you in the first place instead of going with my husband, half the reason I'm still here, is to try to keep you from making too many missteps. Truth to tell, I don't know why I should care, but I do, and that's that. If you had let yourself be guided by me, you'd not be in trouble with them now. I can't say how much I can recover for you, not now, but I am still willing to try."

Mat shook his head. There were only two ways to deal with Aes Sedai without getting burned, let them walk all over you or stay away from them. He would not do the first and could not do the second, so he had to find a third way, and he doubted it could come from following Setalle's advice. Women's advice about Aes Sedai generally was to follow the first path, though they never worded it that way. They talked of accommodation, but it was never the Aes Sedai who was expected to do any accommodating. "Half the reason? What's the other . . . ?" He grunted as though he had been punched in the stomach. "Tuon? You think I can't be trusted with Tuon?"

Mistress Anan laughed at him, a fine rich laugh. "You are a rogue, my Lord. Now, some rouges make fine husbands, once they've been tamed a little around the edges—my Jasfer was a rogue when I met him—but you still think you can nibble a pastry here, nibble a pastry there, then dance off to the next."

"There's no dancing away from this one," Mat said frowning up at the wagon door. The dice clicked away in his head. "Not for me." He was not sure he really wanted to dance away anymore, but want and wish as he might, he was well and truly caught.

"Like that, is it?" she murmured. "Oh, you've chosen a fine one to break your heart."

"That's as may be, Mistress Anan, but I have my reasons. I'd better get inside before they eat everything." He turned toward the steps at the back of the wagon, and she laid a hand on his arm.

"Could I see it? Just to see?"

There was no doubt what she meant. He hesitated, then fished in the neck of his shirt for the leather cord that held the medallion. He could not have said why. He had refused Joline and Edesina even a glimpse. It was a fine piece of work, a silver foxhead nearly as big as his palm. Only one eye showed, and enough daylight remained to see, if you looked close, that the pupil was half shaded to form the ancient symbol of Aes Sedai. Her hand trembled slightly as she traced a finger around that eye. She had said she only wanted to see it, but he allowed the touching. She breathed out a long sigh.

"You were Aes Sedai, once," he said quietly, and her hand froze.

She recovered herself so quickly that he might have imagined it. She was stately Setalle Anan, the innkeeper from Ebou Dar with the big golden hoops in her ears and the marriage knife dangling hilt-down into her round cleavage, about as far from an Aes Sedai as could be. "The sisters think I'm lying about never having been to the Tower. They think I was a servant there as a young woman and listened where I shouldn't have."

"They haven't seen you looking at this." He bounced the foxhead once on his hand before tucking it safely back under his shirt. She pretended not to care, and he pretended not to know she was pretending.

Her lips twitched into a brief, rueful smile, as if she knew what he was thinking. "The sisters would see it if they could let themselves," she said, as simply as if she were discussing the chances of rain, "but Aes Sedai expect that when . . . certain things . . . happen, the woman will go away decently and die soon after. I went away, but Jasfer found me half starved and sick on the streets of Ebou Dar and took me to his mother." She chuckled, just a woman telling how she met her husband. "He used to take in stray kittens, too. Now, you know some of my secrets, and I know some of yours. Shall we keep them to ourselves?"

"What secrets of mine do you know?" he demanded, instantly wary. Some of his secrets were dangerous to have known, and if too many knew of them, they were not really secrets anymore.

Mistress Anan glanced at the wagon, frowning. "That girl is playing a game with you as surely as you are playing one with her. Not the same game that you are. She's more like a general plotting a battle than a woman being courted. If she learns you're moonstruck with her, though, she'll still gain the advantage. I am willing to let you have an even chance. Or as near to one as any man has with a woman of any brains. Do we have an agreement?"

"We do," he replied fervently. "That we do." He would not have been surprised if the dice stopped then, but they went on bouncing.

Had the sisters' fixation on his medallion been the only problem they gave him, had they contented themselves with creating rumors everywhere the show stopped, he could have said those days were no more than tolerably bad for traveling with Aes Sedai. Unfortunately, by the time the show departed Jurador they had learned who Tuon was. Not that she was the Daughter of the Nine Moons, but that she was a Seanchan High Lady, someone of rank and influence.

"Do you take me for a fool?" Luca protested when Mat accused him of telling them. He squared up beside his wagon, fists on his hips, a tall man full of indignation and ready to fight over it by his glare. "That's a secret I want buried deep until . . . well . . . until she says I can use that warrant of protection. That won't be much use if she revokes it because I told something she wants hidden." But his voice was a shade too earnest, and his eyes shifted a hair from meeting Mat's directly. The truth of it was, Luca liked to boast nearly as much as he liked gold. He must have thought it was safe—safe!—to tell the sisters and only realized the snarl he had created after the words were out of his mouth.

A snarl it was, as tangled as a pit full of snakes. The High Lady Tuon, readily at hand, presented an opportunity no Aes Sedai could have resisted. Teslyn was every bit as bad as Joline and Edesina. The three of them visited Tuon in her wagon daily, and descended on her when she went out for a walk. They talked of truces and treaties and negotiations, tried to learn what connection she had to the leaders of the invasion, attempted to convince her to help arrange talks to end the fighting. They even offered to help her leave the show and return home!

Unfortunately for them, Tuon did not see three Aes Sedai, representatives of the White Tower, perhaps the greatest power on earth, not even after the seamstresses began delivering their riding dresses and they could change out of the ragbag leavings Mat had been able to find for them. She saw two escaped *damane* and a *marath'damane*, and she had no use for either until they were decently collared. Her phrase, that. When they came to her wagon, she latched the door, and if they managed to get inside before she could, she left. When they cornered her, or tried to, she walked around them the same as walking around a stump. They all but talked themselves hoarse. And she refused to listen.

Any Aes Sedai could teach a stone patience if she had reason, yet they were unaccustomed to flat being ignored. Mat could see the frustration growing, the tight eyes and tighter mouths that took longer and longer to relax, the hands gripping skirts in fists to keep them from grabbing Tuon and shaking her. It all came to a head sooner than he expected, and not at all in the way he had imagined.

The night after he gave Tuon the mare, he ate his supper with her and Selucia. And with Noal and Olver, of course. That pair managed as much time with Tuon as he did. Lopin and Nerim, as formal as if they were in a palace instead of squeezed for room to move, served a typical early-spring meal, stringy mutton with peas that had been dried and turnips that had sat too long in somebody's cellar. It was too early yet for anything to be near harvesting. Still, Lopin had made a pepper sauce for the mutton, Nerim had found pine nuts for the peas, there was plenty to go around, and nothing tasted off, so it was as fine a meal as could be managed. Olver left once supper was done, having already had his games with Tuon, and Mat changed places with Selucia to play stones. Noal remained too, despite any number of telling looks, rambling on about the Seven Towers in dead Malkier, which apparently had overtopped anything in Cairhien, and Shol Arbela, the City of Ten Thousand Bells, in Arafel, and all manner of Borderland wonders, strange spires made of crystal harder than steel and a metal bowl a hundred paces across set into a hillside and the like. Sometimes he interjected comments on Mat's play, that he was exposing himself on the left, that he was setting a fine trap on the right, and just when Tuon looked ready to fall into it. That sort of thing. Mat kept his mouth shut except for chatting with Tuon, though it took gritting his teeth more than once to accomplish. Tuon found Noal's natter entertaining.

He was studying the board, wondering whether he might have a small chance of gaining a draw, when Joline led Teslyn and Edesina into the wagon like haughty on a pedestal, smooth-faced Aes Sedai to their toenails. Joline was wearing her Great Serpent ring. Squeezing by Selucia, giving her very cold looks when she was slow to move aside, they arrayed themselves at the foot of the narrow table. Noal went very still, eyeing the sisters sideways, one hand beneath his coat as if the fool thought his knives would do any good here.

"There must be an end to this, High Lady," Joline said, very pointedly ignoring Mat. She was telling, not pleading, announcing what would be because it had to be. "Your people have brought a war to these lands such as we have not seen since the War of the Hundred Years, perhaps not since the Trolloc Wars. Tarmon Gai'don is approaching, and this war must end before it comes lest it bring disaster to the whole world. It threatens no less than that. So there will be an end to your petulance. You will carry our offer to whoever commands among you. There can be peace until you return to your own lands across the sea, or you can face the full might of the White Tower followed by every throne from the Borderlands to the Sea of Storms. The Amyrlin Seat has likely summoned them against you already. I have heard of vast Borderland armies already in the south, and other armies moving. Better to end this without more bloodshed, though. So avert your people's destruction and help bring peace."

Mat could not see Edesina's reaction, but Teslyn simply blinked. For an Aes Sedai, that was as good as a gasp. Maybe this was not exactly what she had expected Joline to say. For his part, he groaned under his breath. Joline was no Gray, as deft as a skilled juggler in negotiations, that was for sure, but neither was he, and he still figured she had found a short path to putting Tuon's back up.

But Tuon folded her hands in her lap beneath the table and sat very straight, looking right through the Aes Sedai. Her face was as stern as it had ever been for him. "Selucia," she said quietly.

Moving up behind Teslyn, the yellow-haired woman bent long enough to take something from beneath the blanket Mat was sitting on. As she straightened, everything seem to happen all at once. There was a click, and Teslyn screamed, clapping her hands to her throat. The foxhead turned to ice against Mat's chest, and Joline's head whipped around with an incredulous stare for the Red. Edesina turned and ran for the door, which swung half open, then slammed shut. Slammed against Blaeric or Fen, by the sound of men falling down the wagon's steps. Edesina jerked to a halt and stood very stiffly, arms at her sides and divided skirts pressed against her legs by invisible cords. All that in moments, and Selucia had not stayed still. She bent briefly to the bed Noal was sitting on, then snapped the silver collar of another *a'dam* around Joline's neck. Mat could see that was what Teslyn was gripping with both hands. She was not trying to take it off, just holding on to it, but her knuckles were white. The Red's narrow face was an image of despair, her eyes staring and haunted. Joline had regained the utter calm of an Aes Sedai, but she did touch the segmented collar encircling her neck.

"If you think that you can," she began, then cut off abruptly, her mouth going tight. An angry light shone in her eyes.

"You see, the *a'dam* can be used to punish, though that is seldom done." Tuon stood, and she had the bracelet of an *a'dam* on each wrist, the gleaming leashes snaking away under the blankets on the beds. How in the Light had she managed to get her hands on those?

"No," Mat said. "Your promised not to harm my followers, Precious." Maybe not the wisest thing to use that name now, but it was too late to call it back. "You've kept your promises so far. Don't go back on one now."

"I promised not to cause dissension among your followers, Toy," she said snippily, "and in any case, it is very clear that these three are not your followers." The small sliding door used to talk to whoever was driving or pass out food slid open with a loud bang. She glanced over her shoulder, and it slid shut with a louder. A man cursed outside and began beating at the door.

"The *a'dam* can also be used to give pleasure, as a great reward," Tuon told Joline, ignoring the hammering fist behind her.

Joline's lips parted, and her eyes grew very wide. She swayed, and the rope-suspended table swung as she caught herself with both hands to keep from falling. If she was impressed, though, she hid it well. She did smooth her dark gray skirts once after she was upright again, but that might have meant nothing. Her face was all Aes Sedai composure. Edesina, looking over her shoulder, matched that calm gaze, although she now wore the third *a'dam* around her neck—and come to it, her face was paler than usual—but Teslyn had begun weeping silently, shoulders shaking, tears leaking down her cheeks.

Noal was tensed, a man ready to do something stupid. Mat kicked him under the table and, when the man glared at him, shook his head. Noal's scowl deepened, but he took his hand out of his coat and leaned back against the wall. Still glaring. Well, let him. Knives were no use here, but maybe words could be. Much better if this could be ended with words.

"Listen," Mat said to Tuon. "If you think, you'll see a hundred reasons this won't work. Light, you can learn to channel yourself. Doesn't knowing that change anything? You're not far different from them." He might as well have turned to smoke and blown away for all the attention she paid.

"Try to embrace *saidar*," she drawled, stern eyes steady on Joline. Her voice was quite mild in comparison to her gaze, yet plainly she expected obedience. Obedience? She looked a bloody leopard staring at three tethered goats. And strangely, more beautiful than ever. A beautiful leopard who might rake him with her claws as soon as the goats. Well, he had faced a leopard a few times before this, and those were his own memories. There was an odd sort of exhilaration that came with confronting a leopard. "Go ahead," she went on. "You know the shield is gone." Joline gave a small grunt of surprise, and Tuon nodded. "Good. You've obeyed for the first time. And learned that you cannot touch the Power while you wear the *a'dam* unless I wish it. But now, I wish you to hold the Power, and you do, though you didn't try to embrace it." Joline's eyes widened slightly, a small crack in her calm. "And now," Tuon went on, "I wish you not to be holding the Power, and it is gone from you. Your first lessons." Joline drew a deep breath. She was beginning to look . . . not afraid, but uneasy.

"Blood and bloody ashes, woman," Mat growled, "do you think you can parade them around on those leashes without anyone noticing?" A heavy thump came from the door. A second produced the sound of cracking wood. Whoever was beating at the wooden window was still at it, too. Somehow, that caused no sense of urgency. If the Warders got in, what could they do?

"I will house them in the wagon they are using and exercise them at night," she snapped irritably. "I am nothing like these women, Toy. *Nothing* like them. Perhaps I could learn, but I choose not to, just as I choose not to steal or commit murder. That makes all the difference."

Recovering herself with visible effort, she sat down with her hands on the table, focused on the Aes Sedai once again. "I've had considerable success with one woman like you." Edesina gasped, murmured a name too low to be caught. "Yes," Tuon said. "You must have met my Mylen in the kennels or at exercise. I will train you all as well as she is. You have been cursed with a dark taint, but I will teach you to have pride in the service you give the Empire."

"I didn't bring these three out of Ebou Dar so you could take them back," Mat said firmly, sliding himself along the bed. The foxhead grew colder still, and Tuon made a startled sound.

"How did you . . . do that, Toy? The weave . . . melted . . . when it touched you."

"It's a gift, Precious."

As he stood up, Selucia started toward him, crouching, her hands outstretched in pleading. Fear painted her face. "You must not," she began.

"No!" Tuon said sharply.

Selucia straightened and backed away, though she kept her eyes on him. Strangely, the fear vanished from her expression. He shook his head in wonder. He knew the bosomy woman obeyed Tuon instantly— she was *so'jhin*, after all, as much owned as Tuon's horse, and she actually thought that right and good—but how obedient did you need to be to lose your fear at an order?

"They have annoyed me, Toy," Tuon said as he put his hands on Teslyn's collar. Still trembling, tears still streaming down her cheeks, the Red looked as though she could not believe he would actually remove the thing.

"They annoy me, too." Placing his fingers just so, he pressed, and the collar clicked open.

Teslyn seized his hands and began kissing them. "Thank you," she wept over and over. "Thank you. Thank you."

Mat cleared his throat. "You're welcome, but there's' no need for. . . . Would you stop that? Teslyn?" Reclaiming his hands took some effort.

"I want them to stop annoying me, Toy," Tuon said as he turned to Joline. From anyone else, that might have been petulant. The dark little woman made it a demand.

"I think they'll agree to that after this," he said dryly. But Joline was looking up at him with a stubborn set to her jaw. "You will agree, won't you?" The Green said nothing.

"I do agree," Teslyn said quickly. "We do all agree."

"Yes, we all agree," Edesina added.

Joline stared at him silently, stubbornly, and Mat sighed.

"I could let Precious keep you for a few days, until you change your mind." Joline's collar clicked open in his hands. "But I won't."

Still staring into his eyes, she touched her throat as though to confirm the collar was gone. "Would you like to be one of my Warders?" she asked, then laughed softly. "No need to look like that. Even if I would bond you against your will, I couldn't so long as you have that *ter'angreal*. I agree, Master Cauthon. It may cost our best chance to stop the Seanchan, but I will no longer bother . . . Precious."

Tuon hissed like a doused cat, and he sighed again. What you gained on the swings, you lost on the roundabouts.

He spent part of that night doing what he liked least in the world. Working. Digging a deep hole to bury the three *a'dam*. He did the job himself because, surprisingly, Joline wanted them. They were *ter'angreal*, after all, and the White Tower needed to study them. That might well have been so, but the Tower would just have to find their *a'dam* elsewhere. He was fairly certain that none of the Redarms would have handed them over if he told them to bury the things, yet he was taking no chances that they would reappear to cause more trouble. It started raining before the hole was knee-deep, a cold driving rain, and by the time he was done, he was soaked to the skin and mud to his waist. A fine end to a fine night, with the dice bouncing around his skull.

CHAPTER 10

A Village in Shiota

The following day brought a respite, or so it seemed. Tuon, in a blue silk riding dress and her wide tooled-leather belt, not only rode beside him as the show rolled slowly north, she waggled her fingers at Selucia when the woman tried to put her dun between them. Selucia had acquired her own mount, somehow, a compact gelding that could not match Pips or Akein but still surpassed the dapple by a fair margin. The blue-eyed woman, with a green head scarf beneath her cowl today, fell in on Tuon's other side, and her face would have done an Aes Sedai proud when it came to giving nothing away. Mat could not help grinning. Let *her* hide frustration for a change. Lacking horses, the real Aes Sedai were confined to their wagon; Metwyn was too far away, on the driver's seat of the purple wagon, to overhear what he said to Tuon; only a few thin clouds remained in the sky from the night's rain; and all seemed right in the world. Even the dice bouncing in his head could steal nothing from that. Well, there were bad moments, but only moments.

Early on, a flight of ravens winged overhead, a dozen or more big black birds. They flew swiftly, never deviating from their line, but he eyed them anyway until they dwindled to specks and vanished. Nothing to spoil the day there. Not for him, at least. Maybe for someone farther north.

"Did you see some omen in them, Toy?" Tuon asked. She was as graceful in the saddle as she was in everything else she did. He could not recall seeing her be awkward about anything. "Most omens I know concerning ravens specifically have to do with them perching on someone's rooftop or cawing at dawn or dusk."

"They can be spies for the Dark One," he told her. "Sometimes. Crows, too. And rats. But they didn't stop to look at us, so we don't need to worry."

Running a green-gloved hand across the top of her head, she sighed. "Toy, Toy," she murmured, resettling the cowl of her cloak. "How many children's tales do you believe? Do you believe that if you sleep on Old Hob's Hill under a full moon, the snakes will give you true answers to three questions, or that foxes steal people's skins and take the nourishment from food so you can starve to death while eating your fill?"

Putting on a smile took effort. "I don't think I ever heard either one of those." Making his voice amused required effort, too. What were the odds of her mentioning snakes giving true answers, which the Aelfinn did after a fashion, in the same breath with foxes stealing skins? He was pretty sure that the Eelfinn did, and made leather from it. But it was Old Hob that nearly made him flinch. The other was likely just *ta'veren* twisting at the world. She certainly knew nothing about him and the snakes or the foxes. In Shandalle, the land where Artur Hawkwing had been born, though, Old Hob, *Caisen Hob*, had been another name for the Dark One. The Aelfinn and the Eelfinn both surely deserved to be connected to the Dark One, yet that was hardly anything he wanted to think on when he had his own connection to the bloody foxes. And to the snakes, too? That possibility was enough to sour his stomach.

Still, it was a pleasant ride, with the day warming as the sun rose, though it never could be called warm. He juggled six colored wooden balls, and Tuon laughed and clapped her hands, as well she should. That feat had impressed the juggler he bought the balls from, and it was harder while riding. He told several jokes that made her laugh, and one that made her roll her eyes and exchange finger-twitchings with Selucia. Maybe she did not like jokes about common room serving maids. It had not been the least off-color. He was no fool. He did wish she had laughed, though. She had a marvelous laugh, rich and warm and free. They talked of horses and argued over training methods

with stubborn animals. That pretty head held a few odd notions, such
as that you could calm a fractious horse by biting its ear! That sounded
more likely to send it up like a haystack fire. And she had never heard
of humming under your breath to soothe a horse, and would not believe his father had taught him such a skill shy of demonstration.

"Well, I can hardly do that without a horse that needs soothing,
can I?" he said. She rolled her eyes again. Selucia rolled hers, too.

There was no heat in the argument, though, no anger, just spirit.
Tuon had so much spirit it seemed impossible it could fit into such a
tiny woman. It was her silences that put a small damper on the day,
more so than snakes or foxes. They were far away, and there was nothing to be done. She was right there beside him, and he had a great deal
to do concerning her. She never alluded to what had happened with the
three Aes Sedai, or to the sisters themselves either. She never mentioned his *ter'angreal*, or the fact that whatever she had made Teslyn or
Joline weave against him had failed. The night before might as well
have been a dream.

She was like a general planning a battle, Setalle had said. Trained
at intrigue and dissembling from infancy, according to Egeanin. And it
was all aimed straight at him. But to what end? Surely it could not be
some Seanchan Blood form of courting. Egeanin knew little of that,
but surely not. He had known Tuon a matter of weeks and kidnapped
her, she called him Toy, had tried to buy him, and only a vain fool
could twist that into a woman falling in love. Which left anything
from some elaborate scheme for revenge to . . . to the Light alone knew
what. She had threatened to make him a cupbearer. That meant *da'covale*, according to Egeanin, though she had scoffed at the notion. Cupbearers were chosen for their beauty, and in Egeanin's estimation, he
fell far short. Well, in his own as well, truth to tell, not that he was
likely to admit it to anybody. Any number of women had admired his
face. Nothing said Tuon could not complete the marriage ceremony
just to make him think himself home free and safe, then have him executed. Women were never simple, but Tuon made the rest look like
children's games.

For a long while they saw not so much as a farm, but perhaps two
hours after the sun passed its zenith, they came on a sizable village.
The ring of a blacksmith's hammer on an anvil sounded dimly. The
buildings, some of three stories, were all heavy timber framing with
whitish plaster between and had high-peaked roofs of thatch and tall

stone chimneys. Something about them tugged at Mat's memory, but he could not say what. There was not a farm to be seen anywhere in the unbroken forest. But villages were always tied to farms, supporting them and living off them. They must all be further in from the road, back in the trees.

Oddly, the people he could see ignored the approaching train of show wagons. A fellow in his shirtsleeves, right beside the road, glanced up from the hatchet he was sharpening on a grindstone worked by a footpedal, then bent to his work again as though he had seen nothing. A cluster of children came hurtling around a corner and darted into another street without more than a glance in the show's direction. Very odd. Most village children would stop to stare at a passing merchant's train, speculating on the strange places the merchant had been, and the show had more wagons than any number of merchants' trains. A peddler was coming from the north behind six horses, his wagon's high canvas cover almost hidden by clusters of pots and pans and kettles. That should have caused interest, too. Even a large village on a well-traveled road depended on peddlers for most things the people bought. But no one pointed or shouted that a peddler had come. They just went on about their business.

Perhaps three hundred paces short of the village, Luca stood up on his driver's seat and looked back over the roof of his wagon. "We'll turn in here," he bellowed, gesturing toward a large meadow where wildflowers, cat daisies and jumpups and something that might have been loversknots, dotted spring grasses already a foot high. Sitting back down, he suited his own words, and the other wagons began following, their wheels rutting the rain-sodden ground.

As Mat turned Pips toward the meadow, he heard the shoes of the peddler's horses ringing on paving stones. The sound jerked him upright. That road had not been paved since . . . He pulled the gelding back around. The canvas-topped wagon was rolling over level gray paving stones that stretched just the width of the village. The peddler himself, a rotund fellow in a wide hat, was peering at the pavement and shaking his head, peering at the village and shaking his head. Peddlers followed fixed routes. He must have been this way a hundred times. He had to know. The peddler halted his team and tied the reins to the brake handle.

Mat cupped both hands around his mouth. "Keep going, man!" he shouted at the top of his lungs. "As fast as you can! Keep going!"

The peddler glanced in his direction, then hopped up on his seat quite spryly for such a stout man. Gesturing as grandly as Luca, he began to declaim. Mat could not make out the words, but he knew what they would be. News of the world that he had picked up along the way interspersed with lists of his goods and claims for their vast superiority. Nobody in the village stopped to listen or even paused.

"Keep going!" Mat bellowed. "They're dead! Keep going!" Behind him, somebody gasped, Tuon or Selucia. Maybe both.

Suddenly the peddler's horses screamed, tossing their heads madly. They screamed like animals beyond the ragged edge of terror and kept screaming.

Pips jerked in fear, and Mat had his hands full; the gelding danced in circles, wanting to run, in any direction so long as it was away from here. Every horse belonging to the show heard those screams and began whinnying fearfully. The lions and bears began roaring, and the leopards joined in. That set some of the show's horses to screaming, too, and rearing in their harnesses. The tumult built on itself in moments. As Mat swung round, struggling to control Pips, every one he could see handling reins was fighting to keep a wild-eyed team from racing off or injuring themselves. Tuon's mare was dancing, too, and Selucia's dun. He had a moment of fear for Tuon, but she seemed to be handling Akein as well as she had in her race into the forest. Even Selucia seemed sure of her seat, if not of her mount. He caught glimpses of the peddler, as well, pulling off his hat, peering toward the show. At last, Mat got Pips under control. Blowing hard, as if he had been run too hard for too long, but no longer trying to race away. It was too late. Likely, it had always been too late. Hat in hand, the round peddler leaped down to see what was the matter with his horses.

Landing, he lurched awkwardly and looked down toward his feet. His hat fell from his hand, landing on the hardpacked road. That was when he began screaming. The paving stones were gone, and he was ankle-deep in the road, just like his shrieking horses. Ankle-deep and sinking into rock-hard clay as if into a bog, just like his horses and his wagon. And the village, houses and people melting slowly into the ground. The people never stopped what they were doing. Women walked along carrying baskets, a line of men carried a large timber on their shoulders, children darted about, the fellow at the grindstone continued sharpening his hatchet, all of them nearly knee-deep in the ground by this time.

Tuon caught Mat's coat from one side, Selucia from the other. That was the first he realized he had moved Pips. Toward the peddler. Light!

"What do you think you can do?" Tuon demanded fiercely.

"Nothing," he replied. His bow was done, the horn nocks fitted, the linen bowstrings braided and waxed, but he had not fitted one arrowhead to its ash shaft yet, and with all the rain they had been having, the glue holding the goose-feather fletchings was still tacky. That was all he could think of, the mercy of an arrow in the peddler's heart before he was pulled under completely. Would the man die, or was he being carried to wherever those dead Shiotans were going? That was what had caught him about those buildings. That was how country people had built in Shiota for near enough three hundred years.

He could not tear his eyes away. The sinking peddler shrieked loudly enough to be heard over the screaming of his team.

"Help meeee!" he cried, waving his arms. He seemed to be looking straight at Mat. "Help meeee!" Over and over.

Mat kept waiting for him to die, hoping for him to die—surely that was better than the other—but the man kept on screaming as he sank to his waist, to his chest. Desperately, he tipped back his head like a man being pulled under water, sucking for one last breath. Then his head vanished, and just his arms remained, frantically waving until they, too, were gone. Only his hat lying on the road said there had ever been a man there.

When the last of the thatched rooftops and tall chimneys melted away, Mat let out a long breath. Where the village had been was another meadow decked out in cat daisies and jumpups where red and yellow butterflies fluttered from blossom to blossom. So peaceful. He wished he could believe the peddler was dead.

Except for the few that had followed Luca into the meadow, the show's wagons stood strung out along the road, and everybody was down on the ground, women comforting crying children, men trying to quiet trembling horses, everyone talking fearfully, and loudly, to be heard over the bears and the lions and the leopards. Well, everyone except the three Aes Sedai. They glided hurriedly up the road, Joline heeled by Blaeric and Fen. By their expressions, Aes Sedai and Warders alike, you might have thought villages sinking into the ground were as common as house cats. Pausing beside the peddler's wide hat, the three of them stared down it. Teslyn picked it up and turned over in her hands, then let it drop. Moving into the meadow where the village had

stood, the sisters walked about talking, peering at this and that as if
they could learn something from wildflowers and grasses. None had
taken the time to don a cloak, but for once Mat could not find it in him
to upbraid them. They might have channeled, but if so they did not
use enough of the Power to make the foxhead turn chilly. He would not
have taken them to task if they had. Not today, not after what he had
just seen.

The arguing started right away. No one wanted to cross that patch
of hard-packed clay that seemingly had been paved with stone. They
shouted over one another, including the horse handlers and the seamstresses, all telling Luca what had to be done, and right now. Some
wanted to turn back far enough to find a country road and use those
narrower ways to find their way to Lugard. Others were for forgetting
Lugard altogether, for striking out for Illian by those country roads, or
even going all the way back to Ebou Dar and beyond. There was always
Amadicia, and Tarabon. Ghealdan, too, for that matter. Plenty of
towns and cities there, and far from this Shadow-cursed spot.

Mat sat Pips' saddle, idly playing with his reins, and held his peace
through all the shouting and arm-waving. The gelding gave a shiver
now and then, but he was no longer attempting to bolt. Thom came
striding through the crowd and laid a hand on Pips' neck. Juilin and
Amathera were close behind, she clinging to him and eyeing the showfolk fearfully, and then Noal and Olver. The boy looked as though he
would have liked to cling to someone for comfort, to anyone, but he
was old enough not to want it seen if he did. Noal appeared troubled,
too, shaking his head and muttering under his breath. He kept peering
up the road toward the Aes Sedai. Doubtless by that night he would be
claiming to have seen something very like this before, only on a much
grander scale.

"I think we'll be going on alone from here," Thom said quietly.
Juilin nodded grimly.

"If we must," Mat replied. Small parties would stand out for those
who were hunting for Tuon, for the kidnapped heir to the Seanchan
Empire, else he would have left the show long since. Making their way
to safety without the show to hide in would be much more dangerous,
but it could be done. What he could not do was turn these people's
minds. One glance into any of those frightened faces told him he did
not have enough gold for that. There might not have been enough gold
in the world.

Luca listened in silence, a bright red cloak wrapped around him, until most of the showfolk's energy was spent. When their shouts began to trickle away, he flung back the cloak and walked among them. There were no grand gestures, now. Here he clapped a man on the shoulder, there peered earnestly into a woman's eyes. The country roads? They would be half mud, more streams than roads, from the spring rains. It would take twice as long to reach Lugard that way, three times, maybe longer. Mat almost choked to hear Luca invoke speed, but the man was hardly warming up. He talked of the labor of freeing wagons that bogged down, made his listeners all but see themselves straining to help the teams pull them through mud nearly hub-deep on the wagon wheels. Not even a country road would get that bad, but he made them see it. At least, he made Mat see it. Towns of any size would be few and far between along those back roads, the villages tiny for the most part. Few places to perform, and food for so many hard to come by. He said that while smiling sadly at a little girl of six or so who was peering up at him from the shelter of her mother's skirts, and you just knew he was envisioning her hungry and crying for food. More than one woman pulled her children close around her.

As for Amadicia and Tarabon, and yes, Ghealdan, they would be fine places to perform. Valan Luca's Grand Traveling Show and Magnificent Display of Marvels and Wonders would visit those lands and draw immense crowds. One day. To reach any of them now, they must first return to Ebou Dar, covering the same ground they had crossed these past weeks, passing the same towns, where people were unlikely to lay out coin to see again what they had seen so short a time before. A long way, with everyone's purses growing lighter and their bellies tighter by the day. Or, they could press on to Lugard.

Here his voice began to take on energy. He gestured, but simply. He still moved among them, but stepping more quickly. Lugard was a grand city. Ebou Dar was a shadow beside Lugard. Lugard *truly* was one of the great cities, so populous they might perform there all spring and always have new crowds. Mat had never been to Lugard, but he had heard it was half a ruin, with a king who could not afford to keep the streets clean, yet Luca made it sound akin to Caemlyn. Surely some of these people had seen the place, but they listened with rapt faces as he described palaces that made the Tarasin Palace in Ebou Dar seem a hovel, talked of the silk-clad nobles by the score who would come to see them perform or even commission private performances. Surely

King Roedran would want such. Had any of them ever performed before a king before? They would. They would. From Lugard, to Caemlyn, a city that made Lugard look an imitation of a city. Caemlyn, one of the largest and wealthiest cities in the world, where they might perform the whole summer to never-ending throngs.

"I should like to see these cities," Tuon said, moving Akein nearer to Pips. "Will you show them to me, Toy?" Selucia kept the dun at Tuon's hip. The woman looked composed enough, but doubtless she was shaken by what she had seen.

"Lugard, maybe. From there I can find a way to send you back to Ebou Dar." With a well-guarded merchant's train and as many reliable bodyguards as he could hire. Tuon might be as capable and dangerous as Egeanin made out, but two women alone would be seen as easy prey by too many, and not just brigands. "Maybe Caemlyn." He might need more time than from here to Lugard, after all.

"We shall see what we shall see," Tuon replied cryptically, then began exchanging finger-wriggles with Selucia.

Talking about me behind my back, only doing it right under my nose. He hated it when they did that. "Luca's as good as a gleeman, Thom, but I don't think he's going to sway them."

Thom snorted derisively and knuckled his long white mustaches. "He's not bad, I'll grant him that, but he's no gleeman. Still, he's caught them, I'd say. A wager on it, my boy? Say one gold crown?"

Mat surprised himself by laughing. He had been sure he would not be able to laugh again until he could rid his head of the image of that peddler sinking into the road. And the horses. He could almost hear them screaming still, loudly enough that it came near to drowning out the dice. "You want to wager with *me*? Very well. Done."

"I wouldn't play at dice with you," Thom said dryly, "but I know a man turning a crowd's head with words when I see it. I've done as much myself."

Finishing with Caemlyn, Luca gathered himself with a spark of his usual grandiosity. The man strutted. "And from there," he announced, "to Tar Valon itself. I will hire ships to carry us all." Mat did choke at that. Luca would hire *ships*? *Luca*, who was tight enough to render mice for tallow? "Such crowds will come in Tar Valon that we could spend the rest of our lives in that vast city's splendor, where Ogier-built shops seem like palaces and palaces are beyond description. Rulers seeing Tar Valon for the first time weep that their cities are villages and their own palaces no more than peasant's huts. The White Tower itself is in Tar Valon, remember, the greatest structure in the world. The Amyrlin Seat herself will ask us to perform before her. We have given shelter to three Aes Sedai in need. Who can believe they will do other than speak for us with the Amyrlin Seat?"

Mat looked over his shoulder, and found the three sisters no longer wandering about the meadow where the village had vanished. Instead, they stood side by side in the road watching him, perfect images of Aes Sedai serenity. No, they were not watching him, he realized. They were studying Tuon. The three had agreed not to bother her anymore, and being Aes Sedai, were bound by that, but how far did an Aes Sedai's word ever go? They found ways around the Oath against lying all the time. So Tuon would not get to see Caemlyn, and perhaps not Lugard. Chances were, there would be Aes Sedai in both cities. What easier for Joline and the others than to inform those Aes Sedai that Tuon was a Seanchan High Lady? In all likelihood, Tuon would be on her way to Tar Valon before he could blink. As a "guest," of course, to help stop the fighting. No doubt many would say that would be for the good, that he should hand her over himself and tell them who she really was, but he had given his word. He began to calculate how near to Lugard he dared wait before finding her passage back to Ebou Dar.

Luca had had a difficult time making Tar Valon sound greater than Caemlyn after his spiel on that city, and if they ever reached Tar Valon, some might actually be disappointed comparing his mad descriptions— the White Tower a thousand paces high? Ogier-built palaces the size of small mountains? he claimed there was an Ogier *stedding* actually inside the city!—but finally he called for a show of hands in favor of pressing on. Every hand shot up, even the children's hands, and they had no vote.

Mat pulled a purse from his coat pocket and handed over an Ebou Dari crown. "I never enjoyed losing more, Thom." Well, he *never* enjoyed losing, but in this instance it was better than winning.

Thom accepted with a small bow. "I think I'll keep this as a memento," he said, rolling the fat gold coin across the back of his fingers. "To remind me that even the luckiest man in the world can lose."

For all of the show of hands, there was a shadow of reluctance to cross that patch of road ahead. After Luca got his wagon back onto the road, he sat staring, with Latelle clinging to his arm as hard as Amathera ever clung to Juilin. Finally, he muttered something that might have been an oath and whipped his team up with the reins. By the time they reached the fatal stretch, they were at a gallop, and Luca kept them there until well beyond where the paving stones had been. It was the same with every wagon. A pause, waiting until the wagon ahead was clear, then a flailing of reins and a hard gallop. Mat himself drew a deep breath before heeling Pips forward. At a walk, not a gallop, but it was hard not to dig his heels in, especially when passing the peddler's hat. Tuon's dark face and Selucia's pale displayed no more emotion than Aes Sedai's faces did.

"I will see Tar Valon one day," Tuon said calmly in the middle of that. "I shall probably make it my capital. I shall have you show me the city, Toy. You *have* been there?"

Light! She was a tough little woman. Gorgeous, but definitely tough as nails.

After slowing from his gallop, Luca set the pace at a fast walk rather than the show's usual amble. The sun slid lower, and they passed several roadside meadows sufficiently large to hold the show, but Luca pressed on until their shadows stretched long ahead of them and the sun was a fat red ball on the horizon. Even then he sat holding the reins and peering at a grassy expanse beside the road.

"It's just a field," he said at last, too loudly, and turned his team toward it.

Mat accompanied Tuon and Selucia to the purple wagon once the horses had been handed over to Metwyn, but there was to be no meal or games of stones with her that night.

"This is a night for prayer," she told him before going in with her maid. "Do you know nothing, Toy? The dead walking is a sign that Tarmon Gai'don is near." He did not take this for one of her superstitions; after all, he had thought something very like that himself. He was not much for praying, yet he offered a small one then and there. Sometimes there was nothing else to do.

No one wanted to sleep, so lamps burned late throughout the camp. No one wanted to be alone, either. Mat ate by himself in his tent, with little appetite and the dice in his head sounding louder than ever, but Thom came to play stones just as he finished, and Noal soon after. Lopin and Nerim popped in every few minutes, bowing and inquiring whether Mat or the others wanted anything, but once they fetched wine and cups—Lopin carried the tall pottery jar and broke the wax seal; Nerim carried the cups on a wooden tray—Mat told them to find Harnan and the other soldiers.

"I don't doubt they're getting drunk, which seems a good notion to me," he said. "That's an order. You tell them I said to share."

Lopin bowed gravely over his round belly. "I have assisted the file leader now and again by procuring a few items for him, my Lord. I expect he will be generous with the brandy. Come along, Nerim. Lord Mat wants us to get drunk, and you are getting drunk with me if I have to sit on you and pour brandy down your throat." The abstemious Cairhienin's narrow face grew pinched with disapproval, but he bowed and followed the Tairen out with alacrity. Mat did not think Lopin would need to sit on the man, not tonight.

Juilin came with Amathera and Olver, so games of Snakes and Foxes, played sprawled on the ground-cloth, were added to stones played at the small table. Amathera proved an adequate player at stones, unsurprising given that she had been a ruler once, but her mouth became even more pouty when she and Olver lost at Snakes and Foxes, although nobody ever won that game. Then again, Mat suspected she had not been a very good ruler. Whoever was not playing sat on the cot. Mat watched the games when it was his turn there, as did Juilin if Amathera was playing. He seldom took his eyes from her except when it was his turn at a game. Noal nattered on with his stories—but then, he spun those tales even while playing, and talking seemed to have no effect on his skill at stones—and Thom sat reading the letter Mat had brought him what seemed a very long time ago. The page was heavily creased from being carried in Thom's coat pocket and much smudged from being read and re-read. He had said it was from a dead woman.

It was a surprise when Domon and Egeanin ducked through the entry flaps. They had not precisely been avoiding Mat since he moved out of the green wagon, but neither had they gone out of their way to seek him out. Like everyone else, they were in better clothes than they had worn for disguises in the beginning. Egeanin's divided skirts and high-collared coat, both of blue wool and embroidered in a yellow near to gold on the hem and cuffs, had something of a uniform about them, while Domon, in a well-cut brown coat and baggy trousers stuffed into turned-down boots just below his knees, looked every inch the prosperous, if not exactly wealthy, Illianer merchant.

As soon as Egeanin entered, Amathera, who was on the ground-cloth with Olver, curled herself into a ball on her knees. Juilin sighed and got up from the stool across the table from Mat, but Egeanin reached the other woman first.

"There's no need for that, with me or anyone else," she drawled, bending to take Amathera by the shoulders and draw her to her feet. Amathera rose slowly, hesitantly, and kept her eyes down until Egeanin put a hand beneath her chin and raised her head gently. "You look me in the eyes. You look everyone in the eyes." The Taraboner woman touched her tongue to her lips nervously, but she did keep looking straight at Egeanin's face when the hand was removed from her chin. On the other hand, her eyes were very wide.

"This is a change," Juilin said suspiciously. And with a touch of anger. He stood stiff as a statue carved from dark wood. He disliked any Seanchan, for what they had done to Amathera. "You've called me a thief for freeing her." There was more than a touch of anger in that. He hated thieves. And smugglers, which Domon was.

"All things change given time," Domon said jovially, smiling to head off more heated words. "Why, you do be looking at an honest man, Master Thief-catcher. Leilwin did make me promise to give up smuggling before she would agree to marry me. Fortune prick me, who did ever hear of a woman refusing to marry a man unless he did give up a lucrative trade?" He laughed as though that were the funniest joke in the world.

Egeanin fisted him in the ribs hard enough to change his laughter to a grunt. Married to her, his ribs must be a mass of bruises. "I expect you to keep that promise, Bayle. I am changing, and so must you." Eyeing Amathera briefly—perhaps to make sure she was still obeying; Egeanin was big on others doing as she told them—she stuck out a hand toward Juilin. "I am changing, Master Sandar. Will you?"

Juilin hesitated, then clasped her hand. "I'll make a try at it." He sounded doubtful.

"An honest try is all I ask." Frowning around the tent, she shook her head. "I've seen orlop decks less crowded than this. We have some decent wine in our wagon, Master Sandar. Will you and your lady join us in a cup or two?"

Again Juilin hesitated. "He has this game all but won," he said finally. "No point in playing it out." Clapping his conical red hat on his head, he adjusted his dark, flaring Tairen coat unnecessarily, and offered his arm to Amathera formally. She clasped it tightly, and though her eyes were still on Egeanin's face, she trembled visibly. "I expect Olver will want to stay here and play his game, but my lady and I will be pleased to share wine with you and your husband, Mistress Shipless." There was a hint of challenge in his gaze. It was clear that to him, Egeanin had further to go to prove she no longer saw Amathera as stolen property.

Egeanin nodded as if she understood perfectly. "The Light shine on you tonight, and for as many days and nights as we have remaining," she said by way of farewell to those staying. Cheerful of her.

No sooner had the four departed than thunder boomed overhead. Another loud peal, and rain began pattering on the tent roof, quickly growing to a downpour that drummed the green-striped canvas. Unless Juilin and the others had run, they would do their drinking wet.

Noal settled on the other side of the red cloth from Olver and took up Amathera's part of the game, rolling the dice for the snakes and the foxes. The black discs that now represented Olver and him were nearly to the edge of the web-marked cloth, but it was evident to any eye that they would not make it. To any eye but Olver's, at least. He groaned loudly when a pale disc inked with a wavy line, a snake, touched his piece, and again when a disc marked with a triangle touched Noal's.

Noal took up the tale he had left off when Egeanin and Domon appeared, as well, a story of some supposed voyage on a Sea Folk raker. "Atha'an Miere women are the most graceful in the world," he said, moving the black discs back to the circle in the center of the board, "even more so than Domani, and you know that's saying something. And when they're out of sight of land——" He cut off abruptly and cleared his throat, eyeing Olver, who was stacking the snakes and foxes on the board's corners.

"What do they do then?" Olver asked.

"Why. . . ." Noal rubbed his nose with a gnarled finger. "Why, they scramble about the rigging so nimbly you'd think they had hands where their feet should be. That's what they do." Olver oohed, and Noal gave a soft sigh of relief.

Mat began removing the black and white stones from the board on the table, placing them in two carved wooden boxes. The dice in his head bounced and rattled even when the thunder was loudest. "Another game, Thom?"

The white-haired man looked up from his letter. "I think not, Mat. My mind's in a maze, tonight."

"If you don't mind my asking, Thom, why do you read that letter the way you do? I mean, sometimes your face looks like you're trying to puzzle out what it means." Olver yelped with glee at a good toss of the dice.

"That's because I am. In a way. Here." He held out the letter, but Mat shook his head.

"It's no business of mine, Thom. It's your letter, and I'm no good with puzzles."

"Oh, it's your business, too. Moiraine wrote it just before. . . . Well, anyway, she wrote it."

Mat stared at him for a long moment before taking the creased page, and when his eyes fell on the smudged ink, he blinked. Small, precise writing covered the sheet, but it began, "My dearest Thom." Who would have thought Moiraine, of all people, would address old Thom Merrilin so? "Thom, this is personal. I don't think I should—"

"Read," Thom cut in. "You'll see."

Mat drew a deep breath. A letter from a dead Aes Sedai that was a puzzle and concerned him in some way? Suddenly, he wanted nothing less than to read the thing. But he began anyway. It was near enough to make his hair stand on end.

My dearest Thom,

There are many words I would like to write to you, words from my heart, but I have put this off because I knew that I must, and now there is little time. There are many things I cannot tell you lest I bring disaster, but what I can, I will. Heed carefully what I say. In a short while I will go down to the docks, and there I will confront Lanfear. How can I know that? That secret belongs to others. Suffice it that I know, and let that foreknowledge stand as proof for the rest of what I say.

When you receive this, you will be told that I am dead. All will believe that. I am not dead, and it may be that I shall live to my appointed years. It also may be that you and Mat Cauthon and another, a man I do not know, will try to rescue me. May, I say because it may be that you will not or cannot, or because Mat may refuse. He does not hold me in the affection you seem to, and he has his reasons which he no doubt thinks are good. If you try, it must be only you and Mat and one other. More will mean death for all. Fewer will mean death for all. Even if you come only with Mat and one other, death also may come. I have seen you try and die, one or two or all three. I have seen myself die in the attempt. I have seen all of us live and die as captives.

Should you decide to make the attempt anyway, young Mat knows the way to find me, yet you must not show him this letter until he asks about it. That is of the utmost importance. He must know nothing that is in this letter until he asks. Events must play out in certain ways, whatever the costs.

If you see Lan again, tell him that all of this is for the best. His destiny follows a different path from mine. I wish him all happiness with Nynaeve.

A final point. Remember what you know about the game of Snakes and Foxes. Remember, and heed.

It is time, and I must do what must be done.

May the Light illumine you and give you joy, my dearest Thom, whether or not we ever see one another again.

Moiraine

Thunder boomed as he finished. Fitting, that. Shaking his head, he handed the letter back. "Thom," he said gently, "Lan's bond to her was broken. It takes death to do that. He *said* she was dead."

"And her letter says everyone would believe that. She knew, Mat. She knew it all in advance."

"That's as may be, but Moiraine and Lanfear went into that doorframe *ter'angreal*, and it melted. The thing was redstone, or looked to be, *stone*, Thom, yet it melted like wax. I *saw* it. She went to wherever the Eelfinn are, and even if she is alive, there's no way for us to get there anymore."

"The Tower of Ghenjei," Olver piped up, and all three adults turned their heads to stare at him. "Birgitte told me," he said defensively. "The Tower of Ghenjei is the way to the lands of the Aelfinn and the Eelfinn." He made the gesture that began a game of Snakes and Foxes, a triangle drawn in the air and then a wavy line through it. "She knows even more stories than you, Master Charin."

"That wouldn't be Birgitte Silverbow, would it?" Noal said wryly.

The boy gave him a level look. "I'm not an infant, Master Charin. But she is very good with a bow, so maybe she is. Birgitte born again, I mean."

"I don't think there's any chance of that," Mat said. "I've talked with her, too, you know, and the last thing she wants is to be any kind of hero." He kept his promises, and Birgitte's secrets were safe with him. "In any case, knowing about this tower doesn't help much unless she told you where it is." Olver shook his head sadly, and Mat bent to ruffle his hair. "Not your fault, boy. Without you, we wouldn't even know it exists." That did not seem to help much. Olver stared at the red cloth game board dejectedly.

"The Tower of Ghenjei," Noal said, sitting up cross-legged and tugging his coat straight. "Not many know that tale anymore. Jain always said he'd go looking for it one day. Somewhere along the Shadow Coast, he said."

"That's still a lot of ground to search." Mat fitted the lid on one of the boxes. "It could take years." Years they did not have if Tuon was right, and he was sure that she was.

Thom shook his head. "She says you know, Mat. 'Mat knows the way to find me.' I doubt very much she'd have written that on a whim."

"Well, I can't help what she says, now can I? I never heard of any Tower of Ghenjei until tonight."

"A pity," Noal sighed. "I'd like to have seen it, something Jain bloody Farstrider never did. You might as well give over," he added when Thom opened his mouth. "He wouldn't forget seeing it, and even if he never heard the name, he'd have to think of it when he heard of a strange tower that lets people into other lands. The thing gleams like burnished steel, I'm told, two hundred feet high and forty thick, and there's not an opening to be found in it. Who could forget seeing that?"

Mat went very still. His black scarf felt too tight against his hanging scar. The scar itself suddenly felt fresh and hot. It was hard for him to draw breath.

"If there's no opening, how do we get in?" Thom wanted to know.

Noal shrugged, but Olver spoke up once more. "Birgitte says you make the sign on the side of it anywhere with a bronze knife." He made the sign that started the game. "She says it has to be a bronze knife. Make the sign, and a door opens."

"What else did she tell you about—" Thom began, then cut off with a frown. "What ails you, Mat? You look about to sick up."

What ailed him was his memory, and not the other men's memories for once. Those had been stuffed into him to fill holes in his own memories, which they did and more, or so it seemed. He certainly remembered many more days than he had lived. But whole stretches of his own life were lost to him, and others were like moth-riddled blankets or shadowy and dim. He had only spotty memories of fleeing Shadar Logoth, and very vague recollections of escaping on Domon's rivership, but one thing seen on that voyage stood out. A tower shining like burnished steel. Sick up? His stomach wanted to empty itself.

"I think I know where that tower is, Thom. Rather, Domon knows. But I can't go with you. The Eelfinn will know I'm coming, maybe the Aelfinn, too. Burn me, they might already know about this letter, because I read it. They might know every word we've said. You can't trust them. They'll take advantage if they can, and if they know you're coming, they'll be planning to do just that. They'll skin you and make harnesses for themselves from your hide." His memories of them were all his own, but they were more than enough to support the judgment.

They stared at him as if he were mad, even Olver. There was nothing for it but to tell them about his encounters with the Aelfinn and the Eelfinn. As much as was needful, at least. Not about his answers from the Eelfinn, certainly, or his two gifts from the Aelfinn. But the other men's memories were necessary to explain what he had reasoned out about the Eelfinn and Aelfinn having links to him, now. And the pale leather harnesses the Eelfinn wore; those seemed important. And how they had tried to kill him. That was very important. He had said he wanted to leave and failed to say alive, so they took him outside and hanged him. He even removed the scarf to show his scar for extra weight, and he seldom let anybody see that. The three of them listened in silence, Thom and Noal intently, Olver's mouth slowly dropping open in wonder. The rain beating on the tent roof was the only sound aside from his voice.

"That all has to stay inside this tent," he finished. "Aes Sedai have enough reasons already to want to put their hands on me. If they find out about those memories, I'll never be free of them." *Would* he ever be entirely free of them? He was beginning to think not, yet there was no reason to give them fresh reasons to meddle in his life.

"Are *you* any relation to Jain?" Noal raised his hands in a placating gesture. "Peace, man. I believe you. It's just, that tops anything I ever did. Anything Jain ever did, too. Would you mind if I made the third? I can be handy in tight spots, you know."

"Burn me, did everything I said pass in one ear and out the other? They'll know I'm coming. They may already know everything!"

"And it doesn't matter," Thom put in, "not to me. I'll go by myself, if necessary. But if I read this correctly," he began folding the letter up,

almost tenderly, "the only hope of success is if you are one of the three."
He sat there on the cot, silent now, looking Mat in the eye.

Mat wanted to look away, and could not. Bloody Aes Sedai! The
woman almost certainly was dead, and yet she still tried coercing him
into being a hero. Well, heroes got patted on the head and pushed out
of the way until the next time a hero was needed, if they survived being a hero in the first place. Very often heroes did not. He had never really trusted Moiraine, or liked her either. Only fools trusted Aes Sedai.
But then, if not for her, he would be back in the Two Rivers mucking
out the barn and tending his da's cows. Or he would be dead. And
there old Thom sat, saying nothing, just staring at him. That was the
rub. He liked Thom. *Oh, blood and bloody ashes.*

"Burn me for a fool," he muttered. "I'll go."

Thunder crashed deafeningly right atop a flash of lightning so
bright it shone through the tent canvas. When the rumbling booms
faded, there was dead silence in his head. The last set of dice had
stopped. He could have wept.

CHAPTER
11

A Hell in Maderin

Despite the late hours kept by everyone that night, the show made a very early start the next morning. Grainy-eyed and groggy, Mat trudged out of his tent while the sky was still dark to find men and women with lanterns trotting to get ready when they were not running, and nearly everyone shouting for somebody or other to move faster. Many had the unsteady step of people who had not slept. Everyone seemed to feel that the farther they could get from where that village had vanished in front of their eyes, the better. Luca's great gaudy wagon took to the road before the sun had cleared the horizon, and once again he set a goodly pace. Two merchants' trains of twenty or so wagons each passed them heading south, and a slow caravan of Tinkers, but nothing going the other way. The farther, the better.

Mat rode with Tuon, and Selucia made no attempt to put the dun between them, yet there was no conversation however much he tried to start one. Save for an occasional unreadable glance when he made a sally or told a joke, Tuon rode looking straight ahead, the cowl of her blue cloak hiding her face. Even juggling failed to catch her attention. There was something broody about her silence, and it worried him. When a woman went silent on you, there usually was trouble in the offing. When she brooded, you could forget about usually. He doubted

it was the village of the dead that had her fretting. She was too tough
for that. No, there was trouble ahead.

Little more than an hour after they set out, a farm on rolling
ground hove into sight, with dozens of black-faced goats cropping
grass in a wide pasture and a large olive grove. Boys weeding among
the rows of dark-leaved olive trees dropped their hoes and rushed down
to the stone fences to watch the show pass, shouting with excitement
to know who they were and where they were going and where coming
from. Men and women came out of the sprawling tile-roofed farmhouse and two big thatch-roofed barns, shading their eyes to watch.
Mat was relieved to see it. The dead paid no mind to the living.

As the show rolled onward, farms and olive groves grew thicker on
the ground until they ran side by side, pushing the forest back a mile
or more on either side of the road, and well short of midmorning they
reached a prosperous town somewhat larger than Jurador. A merchant's
long train of canvas-topped wagons was turning in at the main gates,
where half a dozen men in polished conical helmets and leather coats
sewn with steel discs stood guard with halberds. More men, cradling
crossbows, kept watch atop the two gate towers. But if the Lord of
Maderin, one Nathin Sarmain Vendare, expected trouble, the guards
were the only sign of it. Farms and olive groves reached right to the
stone walls of Maderin, an unsound practice, and right costly should
the town ever need to be defended. Luca had to bargain with a farmer
for the right to set up the show in an unused pasture and came back
muttering that he had just bought the scoundrel a new flock of goats or
maybe two. But the canvas wall was soon rising, with Luca chivvying
everyone for speed. They were to perform today and leave early in the
morning. Very early. Nobody complained, or much said an unneeded
word. The farther, the better.

"And tell no one what you saw," Luca cautioned more than once.
"We saw nothing out of the ordinary. We wouldn't want to frighten the
patrons away." People looked at him as if he were insane. No one wanted
to think of that melting village or the peddler, much less speak of them.

Mat was sitting in his tent in his shirtsleeves, waiting for Thom
and Juilin to return from their trip into the town to learn whether
there was a Seanchan presence. He was idly tossing a set of dice on his
small table. After an early run of mostly high numbers, five single pips
stared up at him ten times in a row; most men thought the Dark One's
eyes an unlucky toss.

Selucia pulled back the entry flap and strode in. Despite her plain brown divided skirts and white blouse, she managed to seem a queen entering a stable. A filthy stable, by the expression on her face, though Lopin and Nerim could have satisfied his mother when it came to cleaning.

"She wants you," she drawled peremptorily, touching her flowered scarf to make sure her short yellow hair was covered. "Come."

"What's she want with me, then?" he said, and leaned his elbows on the table. He even stretched out his legs and crossed his ankles. Once you let a woman think you would jump whenever she called, you never got out from under again.

"She'll tell you. You are wasting time, Toy. She won't be pleased."

"If Precious expects me to come running when she crooks a finger, she better learn to like being displeased."

Grimacing—if her mistress tolerated the name, Selucia took it for a personal affront—she folded her arms beneath that impressive bosom. It was clear as good glass that she intended to wait there until he went with her, and he was of a mind to make it a long wait. He tossed the dice. The Dark One's Eyes. Expecting him to jump when Tuon said toad. Hah! Another toss, spinning across the table, one die nearly going over the edge. The Dark One's Eyes. Still, he had nothing else to do at the moment.

Even so, he took his time donning his coat, a good bronze-colored silk. By the time he picked up his hat, he could hear her foot tapping impatiently. "Well, what are you waiting for?" he asked. She hissed at him. She held the entry flap open, but she purely hissed like a cat.

Setalle and Tuon were sitting on one of the beds talking when he entered the purple wagon, but they cut off the instant he stepped through the door and gave him brief but appraising looks. Which told him the subject of their talk had been Mat Cauthon. It made his hackles rise. Plainly, whatever Tuon wanted was something they thought he would disapprove of. And just as plainly, she meant to have it anyway. The table was snug against the ceiling, and Selucia brushed past him to take a place behind Tuon as the tiny woman sat down on the stool, her face stern and those beautiful big eyes steady. Hang all the prisoners immediately.

"I wish to visit the common room of an inn," she announced. "Or a tavern. I have never seen the inside of either. You will take me to one in this town, Toy."

He let himself breathe again. "That's easy enough. Just as soon as Thom or Juilin lets me know it's safe."

"It must be a low place. What is called a hell."

His mouth fell open. Low? Hells were the lowest of the low, dirty and dimly lit, where the ale and wine were cheap and still not worth half what you paid, the food was worse, and any woman who sat on your lap was trying to pick your pocket or cut your purse or else had two men waiting upstairs to crack you over the head as soon as you walked into her room. At any hour of the day or night you would find dice rolling in a dozen games, sometimes for surprising stakes given the surroundings. Not gold—only a stone fool displayed gold in a hell—but silver often crossed the tables. Few of the gamblers would have come by their coin by any means even halfway honest, and those few would be as hard-eyed as the headcrackers and knife-men who preyed on drunks in the night. Hells always had two or three strong-arms with cudgels about to break up fights, and most days they worked hard for their pay. They usually stopped the patrons from killing one another, but when they failed, the corpse was dragged out the back and left in an alley somewhere or on a rubbish heap. And while they were dragging, the drinking never slowed, or the gambling either. That was a hell. How had she even heard of such places?

"Did you plant this fool notion in her head?" he demanded of Setalle.

"Why, what in the Light makes you think that?" she replied, going all wide-eyed the way women did when pretending to be innocent. Or when they wanted you to think they were pretending, just to confuse you. He could not see why they bothered. Women confused him all the time without trying.

"It's out of the question, Precious. I walk into a hell with a woman like you, and I'll be in six knife fights inside the hour, if I survive that long."

Tuon gave a pleased smile. Just a flicker, but definitely pleased. "Do you really think so?"

"I know so for a fact." Which produced another brief smile of delight. Delight! The bloody woman *wanted* to see him in a knife fight!

"Even so, Toy, you promised."

They were arguing over whether he had made a promise—well, he was calmly presenting the logic that saying something was easy was no promise; Tuon just stubbornly insisted he had promised, while Setalle took up her embroidery hoop and Selucia watched him with the amused air of someone watching a man try to defend the indefensible; and he did not shout, no matter what Tuon said—when a knock came at the door.

Tuon paused. "You see, Toy," she said after a moment, "that is how it is done. You knock and then wait." She made a simple gesture over one shoulder at her maid.

"You may enter the presence," Selucia called, drawing herself up regally. She probably expected whoever came in to prostrate themselves!

It was Thom, in a dark blue coat and dark gray cloak that would make him unremarked in any common room or tavern, neither well-to-do nor poor. A man who could afford to pay for his own drink while listening to the gossip, or buy another man a cup of wine to pay for hearing his news and the latest rumors. He did not prostrate himself, but he did make an elegant bow despite his bad right leg. "My Lady," he murmured to Tuon before turning his attention to Mat. "Harnan said he saw you strolling this way. I trust I'm not interrupting? I heard . . . voices."

Mat scowled. He had *not* been shouting. "You're not interrupting. What did you find out?"

"That there may be Seanchan in the town from time to time. No soldiers, but it seems they're building two farm villages a few miles to the north of the road and three more a few miles south. The villagers come to town to buy things now and then."

Mat managed to keep from smiling as he spoke over his shoulder. He even got a smattering of regret into his voice. "I'm afraid there's no jaunt into Maderin for you, Precious. Too dangerous."

Tuon folded her arms, emphasizing her bosom. There were more curves to her than he once had thought. Not like Selucia, certainly, but nice curves. "Farmers, Toy," she drawled dismissively. "No farmer has ever seen my face. You promised me a tavern or a common room, and you won't escape on this puny excuse."

"A common room should present no difficulties," Thom said. "It's a pair of scissors or a new pot these farmers are after, not drink. They make their own ale, it seems, and don't much like the local brew."

"Thank you, Thom," Mat said through gritted teeth. "She wants to see a hell."

The white-haired man gave a wheezing cough and knuckled his mustache vigorously. "A hell," he muttered.

"A hell. Do *you* know a hell in this town where I might take her without starting a riot?" He intended the question for sarcasm, but Thom surprised him by nodding.

"I might just know a place at that," the man said slowly. "The White Ring. I intend to go there anyway, to see what news I can pick up."

Mat blinked. However unremarked Thom might be elsewhere, he would be looked at askance in a hell wearing that coat. More than askance. The usual garb there was coarse dirty wool and stained linen. Besides, asking questions in a hell was a good way to have a knife planted in your back. But maybe Thom meant that this White Ring was not a hell at all. Tuon might not know the difference if the place were only a little rougher than the usual. "Should I get Harnan and the others?" he asked, testing.

"Oh, I think you and I should be protection enough for the Lady," Thom said with what might have been the ghost of a smile, and knots loosened in Mat's shoulders.

He still cautioned the two women—there was no question of Selucia staying behind, of course; Mistress Anan refused Tuon's invitation to accompany them, saying she had already seen as many hells as she had any wish to—about keeping their hoods well up. Tuon might believe no farmer had ever seen her face, but if a cat could gaze on a king, as the old saying said, then a farmer might have gazed on Tuon some time or other, and it would be just their luck to have one or two of them turn up in Maderin. Being *ta'veren* usually seemed to twist the Pattern for the worst in his experience.

"Toy," Tuon said gently as Selucia settled the blue cloak on her slim shoulders, "I have met many farmers while visiting the country, but they very properly kept their eyes on the ground even if I allowed them to stand. Believe me, they never saw my face."

Oh. He went to fetch his own cloak. White clouds nearly obscured the sun, still short of its midday peak, and it was a brisk day for spring, with a strong breeze to boot.

People from the town crowded the main street of the show, men in rough woolens or sober coats of finer stuff with just a touch of embroidery on the cuffs; women, many wearing lace caps, in somber, collared dresses beneath long white aprons or dark, high-necked dresses with embroidery curling across the bosom; children darting everywhere, escaping their parents and being chased down, all of them oohing and aahing at Miyora's leopards or Latelle's bears, at the jugglers or Balat and Abar eating fire, the lean brothers moving in unison. Not pausing for so much as a glimpse of the female acrobats, Mat threaded through the throng with Tuon on his arm, which he assured by placing her hand on his left wrist. She hesitated a moment, then nodded slightly, a queen giving assent to a peasant. Thom had offered his arm to Selucia, but she stayed at her mistress's left shoulder. At least she did not try to crowd between.

Luca, in scarlet coat and cloak, was beneath the big banner at the entrance watching coins clink into the glass pitcher, clink again as they were dropped into the strongbox. He wore a smile on his face. The line waiting to get in stretched near a hundred paces along the canvas wall, and more people were trickling out of the town and heading toward the show. "I could take in a fine bit here over two or three days," he told Mat. "After all, this place is solid, and we're far enough from. . . ." His smile flickered out like a snuffed candle. "You think we're far enough, don't you?"

Mat sighed. Gold would defeat fear every time in Valan Luca.

He could not hold his cloak closed with Tuon on his arm, so it flared behind him in the stiff breeze, yet that was to the good. The gate guards, slouching in a ragged line, eyed them curiously, and one made a sketchy bow. Silk and lace had that effect, with country armsmen, at least, and that was what these men were no matter how brightly they had burnished their helmets and coin-armor coats. Most leaned on their halberds like farmers leaning on shovels. But Thom stopped, and Mat was forced to halt too, a few paces into the town. After all, he had no idea where The White Ring lay.

"A heavy guard, Captain," Thom said, worry touching his voice. "Are there brigands in the area?"

"No outlaws around here," a grizzled guard said gruffly. A puckered white scar slanting across his square face combined with a squint to give him a villainous appearance. He was not one of the leaners, and he held his halberd as if he might know how to use it. "The Seanchan cleaned out the few we hadn't caught. Move along, now, old fellow. You're blocking the way." There was not a wagon or cart in sight, and the few people leaving the town afoot had plenty of room. The gate arch was wide enough for two wagons abreast, though it might be a squeeze.

"The Seanchan said we didn't set enough guards," a stocky fellow about Mat's age put in cheerfully, "and Lord Nathin listens close when the Seanchan talk."

The grizzled man clouted him with a gauntleted hand on the back of his helmet hard enough to stagger him. "You watch your mouth with people from off, Keilar," the older man growled, "else you'll be back behind a plow before you can blink. My Lord," he added to Mat, raising his voice, "you want to call your servant before he gets himself in trouble."

"My apologies, Captain," Thom said humbly, ducking his white head, the very image of a chastened serving man. "No offense meant. My apologies."

"He would have thumped you, too, if I hadn't been here," Mat told him when he caught up. Thom was limping noticeably. He must have been tired for it to show that much. "He almost did anyway. And what did you learn that was worth risking that?"

"I wouldn't have asked without you, in that coat." Thom chuckled as they walked deeper into the town. "The first lesson is what questions to ask. The second, and just as important, is when and how to ask. I learned there aren't any brigands, which is always good to know, though I've heard of very few bands big enough to attack something as large as the show. I learned Nathin is under the Seanchan thumb. Either he's obeying a command with those extra guards, or he takes their suggestions as commands. And most important, I learned that Nathin's armsmen don't resent the Seanchan."

Mat quirked an eyebrow at him.

"They didn't spit when they said the name, Mat. They didn't grimace or growl. They won't fight the Seanchan, not unless Nathin tells them to, and he won't." Thom exhaled heavily. "It's very strange. I've found the same everywhere from Ebou Dar to here. These outlanders come, take charge, impose their laws, snatch up women who can channel, and if the nobles resent them, very few among the common people seem to. Unless they've had wife or relation collared, anyway. Very strange, and it bodes ill for getting them out again. But then, Altara is Altara. I'll wager they're finding a colder reception in Amadicia and Tarabon." He shook his head. "We had best hope they are, else. . . ." He did not say what else, but it was easy to imagine.

Mat glanced at Tuon. How did she feel hearing Thom talk about her people so? She said nothing, only walked at his side peering curiously at everything from the shelter of her cowl.

Tile-roofed buildings three and four stories tall, most of brick, lined the wide, stone-paved main street of Maderin, shops and inns with signs that swung in the stiff breeze crowded in beside stables and rich people's homes with large lamps above the arched doorways and humbler structures that housed poorer folk, by the laundry hanging from nearly every window. Horse carts and hand-barrows laden with bales or crates or barrels slowly made their way through a moderately thick throng, men and women with brisk strides, full of that storied southern industry, children dashing about in games of catch. Tuon studied it all with equal interest. A fellow pushing a wheeled grind-stone and crying that he sharpened scissors or knives till they could cut wishes caught her attention as much as a lean, hard-faced woman in leather trousers with two swords strapped to her back. Doubtless a merchant's guard or perhaps a Hunter for the Horn, but a rarity either way. A buxom Domani in a clinging red dress that fell just short of transparent with a pair of bulky bodyguards in scale-armor jerkins at her back got neither more nor less study than a lanky one-eyed fellow in frayed wool hawking pins, needles and ribbons from a tray. He had not noticed this sort of curiosity from her in Jurador, but she had been intent on finding silk in Jurador. Here, she seemed to be trying to memorize all she saw.

Thom soon led them off into a maze of twisting streets, most of which deserved the name only because they were paved with rough stone blocks the size of a man's two fists. Buildings as big as those on the main street, some housing shops on the ground floor, loomed over them, almost shutting out the sky. Many of those ways were too narrow for horse carts—in some Mat would not have had to extend his arms fully to touch the walls on either side—and more than once he had to press Tuon against the front of a building to let a heavy-loaded hand-barrow rumble past over the uneven paving stones, the barrow-man calling apologies for the inconvenience without slowing. Porters trudged through that cramped warren, too, men walking bent nearly parallel to the ground, each with a bale or crate on his back held level by a padded leather roll strapped to his hips. Just the sight of them made Mat's own back ache. They reminded him how much he hated work.

He was on the point of asking Thom how far they had to go— Maderin was not that big a town—when they reached The White Ring, on one of those winding streets where his arms could more than compass the width of the pavement, a brick building of three floors across from a cutler's shop. The painted sign hanging over the inn's red door, a frilly white circle of lace, made the knots return to his shoulders. Ring, it might be called, but that was a woman's garter if ever he had seen one. It might not be a hell, but inns with signs like that usually were rowdy enough in their own right. He eased the knives up his coatsleeves, and those in his boot tops, as well, felt the blades under his coat, shrugged just to get the feel of the one hanging behind his neck. Though if it went that far. . . . Tuon nodded approvingly. The bloody woman was *dying* to see him get into a knife fight! Selucia had the sense to frown.

"Ah, yes," Thom said. "A wise precaution." And he checked his own knives, tightening those knots in Mat's shoulders a little more. Thom carried almost as many blades as he did, up his sleeves, beneath his coat.

Selucia writhed her fingers at Tuon, and suddenly they were in a silent argument, fingers flashing. Of course, it could not be that— Tuon bloody well owned Selucia the same as owning a dog, and you did not argue with your dog—but an argument it seemed, both women with their jaws set stubbornly. Finally, Selucia folded her hands and bowed her head in acquiescence. A reluctant submission.

"It will be well," Tuon told her in a jollying tone. "You will see. It will be well."

Mat wished he was sure of that. Taking a deep breath, he extended his wrist for her hand again and followed Thom.

The spacious, wood-paneled common room of The White Ring held better than two dozen men and women, nearly half obvious out-landers, at square tables beneath a thick-beamed ceiling. All neatly dressed in finely woven wool with little by way of ornamentation, most were talking quietly over their wine in pairs, cloaks draped over their low-backed chairs, though three men and a woman with long beaded braids were tossing bright red dice from a winecup at one table. Pleas-ant smells drifted from the kitchen, including meat roasting. Goat, most likely. Beside the wide stone fireplace, where a parsimonious fire burned and a polished brass barrel-clock sat on the mantel, a saucy-eyed young woman who rivaled Selucia—and with her blouse unlaced nearly to her waist to prove it—swayed her hips and sang, accompa-nied by a hammered dulcimer and a flute, a song about a woman jug-gling all of her lovers. She sang in a suitably bawdy voice. None of the patrons appeared to be listening.

"As I walked out one fine spring day,
I met young Jac who was pitching hay,

his hair so fair, and his eyes were, too.
Well, I gave him a kiss; oh, what could I do?
We snuggled and we tickled while the sun rose high,
and I won't say how often he made me sigh."

Lowering her hood, Tuon stopped just inside the door and frowned around the room. "Are you certain this is a hell, Master Merrilin?" she asked. In a low voice, thank the Light. Some places, a question of that sort could get you thrown out and roughly, silk coat or no. In others, the prices just doubled.

"I assure you, you won't find a bigger collection of thieves and rascals anywhere in Maderin at this hour," Thom murmured, stroking his mustaches.

"Now Jac gets an hour when the sky is clear,
and Willi gets an hour when my father's not near.
It's the hayloft with Moril, for he shows no fear,
and Keilin comes at midday; he's oh so bold!
Lord Brelan gets an evening when the night is cold.
Master Andril gets a morning, but he's very old.
Oh, what, oh, what is a poor girl to do?
My loves are so many and the hours so few."

Tuon looked doubtful, but with Selucia at her shoulder, she walked over to stand in front of the singer, who faltered a moment at Tuon's intense scrutiny before catching the song up again. She sang over the top of Tuon's head, plainly attempting to ignore her. It seemed that with every other verse, the woman in the song added a new lover to her list. The male musician, playing the dulcimer, smiled at Selucia and got a frosty stare back. The two women got other looks as well, the one so small and with very short black hair, the other rivaling the singer and with her head wrapped in a scarf, but no more than glances. The patrons were intent on their own business.

"It isn't a hell," Mat said softly, "but what is it? Why would so many people be here in the middle of the day?" It was mornings and evenings when common rooms filled up like this.

"The locals are selling olive oil, lacquerware or lace," Thom replied just as quietly, "and the outlanders are buying. It seems local custom is to begin with a few hours of drink and conversation. And if you have no head for it," he added dryly, "you sober up to find you've made much less of a bargain than you thought in your wine."

"Light, Thom, she'll never believe this place is a hell. I thought you were taking us somewhere merchants' guards drink, or apprentices. At least she might believe that."

"Trust me, Mat. I think you'll find she has lived a very sheltered life in some ways."

Sheltered? When her own brothers and sisters tried to kill her? "You wouldn't care to wager a crown on it, would you?"

Thom chuckled. "Always glad to take your coin."

Tuon and Selucia came gliding back, faces expressionless. "I expected rougher garb on the patrons," Tuon said quietly, "and perhaps a fight or two, but the song is too salacious for a respectable inn. Though she is much too covered to sing it properly, in my opinion. What is that for?" she added in tones of suspicion as Mat handed Thom a coin.

"Oh," Thom said, slipping the crown into his coat pocket, "I thought you might be disappointed that only the more successful blackguards were present—they aren't always so colorful as the poorer sort—but Mat said you'd never notice."

She leveled a look at Mat, who opened his mouth indignantly. And closed it again. What was there to say? He was already in the pickling kettle. No need to stoke the fire.

As the innkeeper approached, a round woman with suspiciously black hair beneath a white lace cap and stuffed into a gray dress embroidered in red and green across her more than ample bosom, Thom slipped away with a bow and a murmured, "By your leave, my Lord, my Lady." Murmured, but loud enough for Mistress Heilin to hear.

The innkeeper had a flinty smile, yet she exercised it for a lord and lady, curtsying so deeply that she grunted straightening back up, and she seemed only a little disappointed that Mat wanted wine and perhaps food, not rooms. Her best wine. Even so, when he paid, he let her see that he had gold in his purse as well as silver. A silk coat was all very well, but gold wearing rags got better service than copper wearing silk.

"Ale," Tuon drawled. "I've never tasted ale. Tell me, good mistress, is it likely any of these people will start a fight any time soon?" Mat nearly swallowed his tongue.

Mistress Heilin blinked and gave her head a small shake, as if uncertain she really had heard what she thought she had. "No need to worry, my Lady," she said. "It happens time to time, if they get too far in their cups, but I'll settle them down hard if it does."

"Not on my account," Tuon told her. "They should have their sport."

The innkeeper's smile went crooked and barely held, but she managed another curtsy then scurried away clutching Mat's coin and calling, "Jera, wine for the lord and lady, a pitcher of the Kiranaille. And a mug of ale."

"You mustn't ask questions like that, Precious," Mat said quietly as he escorted Tuon and Selucia to an empty table. Selucia refused a chair, taking Tuon's cloak and draping it over the chair she held for Tuon, then standing behind it. "It isn't polite. Besides, it lowers your eyes." Thank the Light for those talks with Egeanin, whatever name she wanted to go by. Seanchan would do any fool thing or refuse to do what was sensible to avoid having their eyes lowered.

Tuon nodded thoughtfully. "Your customs are often very peculiar, Toy. You will have to teach me about them. I have learned some, but I must know the customs of the people I will rule in the name of the Empress, may she live forever."

"I'll be glad to teach you what I can," Mat said, unpinning his cloak and letting it fall carelessly over the low back of his chair. "It will be good for you to know our ways even if you end up ruling a sight less than you expect to." He set his hat on the table.

Tuon and Selucia gasped as one, hands darting for the hat. Tuon's reached it first, and she quickly put it on the chair next to her. "That is *very* bad luck, Toy. *Never* put a hat on a table." She made one of those odd gestures for warding off evil, folding under the middle two fingers and extending the other two stiffly. Selucia did the same.

"I'll remember that," he said dryly. Perhaps too dryly. Tuon gave him a level look. Very level.

"I have decided you will not do for a cupbearer, Toy. Not until you learn meekness, which I almost despair of teaching you. Perhaps I will make you a running groom, instead. You are good with horses. Would you like trotting at my stirrup when I ride? The robes are much the same as for a cupbearer, but I will have yours decorated with ribbons. Pink ribbons."

He managed to maintain a smooth face, but he felt his cheeks growing hot. There was only one way she could know pink ribbons had any special significance to him. Tylin had told her. It had to be. Burn him, women would talk about *anything*!

The arrival of the serving maid with their drink saved him from having to make any response. Jera was a smiling young woman with nearly as many curves as the singer, not so well displayed yet not really concealed by the white apron she wore tied snugly. Her dark woolen dress fit quite snugly, too. Not that he gave her more than a glance, of course. He was with his wife-to-be. Anyway, only a complete woolhead looked at a woman while with another.

Jera placed a tall pewter wine pitcher and two polished pewter cups on the table and handed a thick mug of ale to Selucia, then blinked in confusion when Selucia transferred the mug to Tuon and took a cup of wine in return. He handed her a silver penny to settle her discomposure, and she gave him a beaming smile with her curtsy before darting off to another call from the innkeeper. It was unlikely she received much in the way of silver.

"You could have smiled back at her, Toy," Tuon said, holding the mug up for a sniff and wrinkling her nose. "She is very pretty. You were so stone-faced, you probably frightened her." She took a sip, and her eyes widened in surprise. "This actually is quite good."

Mat sighed and took a long swallow of dark wine that smelled faintly of flowers. In none of his memories, his own or those other men's, could he recall having understood women. Oh, one or two things here and there, but never anywhere near completely.

Sipping her ale steadily—he was not about to tell her ale was taken in swallows, not sips; she might get herself drunk deliberately, just to experience a hell fully; he was not ready to put anything past her today. Or any day—taking sips between every sentence, the maddening little woman questioned him on customs. Telling her how to behave in a hell was easy enough. Keep to yourself, ask no questions, and sit with your back to a wall if you could and near to a door in case of a need to leave suddenly. Better not to go at all, but if you had to. . . . Yet she quickly passed on to courts and palaces, and got few answers there. He could have told her more of customs in the courts of Eharon or Shiota or a dozen other dead nations than in those of any nation that still lived. Scraps of how things were done in Caemlyn and Tear were all he really knew, and bits from Fal Dara, in Shienar. Well, that and Ebou Dar, but she already knew those ways.

"So you have traveled widely and been in other palaces than the

Tarasin," she said finally, and took the last bit of ale in her mug. He had not finished half his wine yet; he thought Selucia had not taken above two small swallows of hers. "But you are not nobly born, it seems. I thought you must not be."

"That I am not," he told her firmly. "Nobles. . . ." He trailed off, clearing his throat. He could hardly tell her nobles were fools with their noses so high in the air they could not see where they were stepping. She was who and what she was, after all.

Expressionless, Tuon studied him while pushing her empty mug to one side. Still studying, she flickered the fingers of her left hand over her shoulder, and Selucia clapped her own hands together loudly. Several of the other patrons looked at them in surprise. "You called yourself a gambler," Tuon said, "and Master Merrilin named you the luckiest man in the world."

Jera came running, and Selucia handed her the mug. "Another, quickly," she commanded, though not in an unkindly way. Still, she had a regal manner to her. Jera dropped a hasty curtsy and scurried off again as though she had been shouted at.

"I have luck sometimes," Mat said cautiously.

"Let's see whether you have any today, Toy." Tuon looked toward the table where the dice were rattling on the tabletop.

He could see no harm in it. It was a certainty he would win more than he lost, yet he thought it unlikely one of the merchants would pull a knife however much his luck was in. He had not noticed anyone carrying one of those long belt knives that everybody wore farther south. Standing, he offered Tuon his arm, and she rested her hand lightly on his wrist. Selucia left her wine on the table and stayed close to her mistress.

Two of the Altaran men, one lean and bald except for a dark fringe, the other round-faced above three chins, scowled when he asked whether a stranger might join the game, and the third, a graying, stocky fellow with a pendulous lower lip, went stiff as a fence post. The Taraboner woman was not so unfriendly.

"Of course, of course. Why not?" she said, her speech slightly slurred. Her face was flushed, and the smile she directed at him had a slackness about it. Apparently she was one of those with no head for wine. It seemed the locals wanted to keep her happy because the scowls vanished, though the graying man remained wooden-faced. Mat fetched chairs from a nearby table for himself and Tuon. Selucia chose to remain standing behind Tuon, which was just as well. Six people crowded the table.

Jera arrived to curtsy and proffer a refilled mug to Tuon with both hands and a murmured "My Lady," and another serving woman, graying and nearly as stout as Mistress Heilin, replaced the wine pitcher on the gambler's table. Smiling, the bald man filled the Taraboner's cup to the brim. They wanted her happy and drunk. She drained half the cup and with a laugh wiped her lips delicately with a lace-edged handkerchief. Getting it back up her sleeve required two tries. She would come away with no good bargains this day.

Mat watched a little play and soon recognized the game. It used four dice rather than two, but without a doubt it was a version of *Piri*, Match, a game that had been popular for a thousand years before Artur Hawkwing began his rise. Small piles of silver admixed with a few gold coins lay in front of each of the players, and it was a silver mark that he laid in the middle of the table to buy the dice while the stout man was gathering his winnings from the last toss. He expected no trouble from merchants, but trouble was less likely if they lost silver rather than gold.

The lean man matched the wager, and Mat rattled the crimson dice in the pewter cup, then spun them out onto the table. They came to rest showing four fives.

"Is that a winning toss?" Tuon asked.

"Not unless I match it," Mat replied, scooping the dice back into the cup, "without tossing a fourteen or the Dark One's eyes first." The dice clattered in the cup, clattered across the table. Four fives. His luck was in, for sure. He slid one coin over in front of himself and left the other.

Abruptly, the graying fellow scraped back his chair and stood up. "I've had enough," he muttered, and began fumbling the coins in front of him into his coat pockets. The other two Altarans stared at him incredulously.

"You're *leaving*, Vane?" the lean man said. "*Now?*"

"I said I've had enough, Camrin," the graying man growled and went stumping out into the street pursued by Camrin's scowl at his back.

The Taraboner woman leaned over unsteadily, her beaded braids clicking on the tabletop, to pat the fat man's wrist. "Just means I'll buy my lacquerware from you, Master Kostelle," she said fuzzily. "You and Master Camrin."

Kostelle's triple chins wobbled as he chuckled. "So it does, Mistress Alstaing. So it does. Doesn't it, Camrin?"

"I suppose," the bald man replied grumpily. "I suppose." He shoved a mark out to match Mat's.

Once again the dice spun across the table. This time, they came up totaling fourteen.

"Oh," Tuon said, sounding disappointed. "You lost."

"I won, Precious. That's a winning toss if it's your first." He left his original bet in the middle of the table. "Another?" he said with a grin.

His luck was in, all right, as strong as it had ever been. The bright red dice rolled across the table, bounced across the table, ricocheted off the wagered coins sometimes, and toss after toss they came to rest showing fourteen white pips. He made fourteen every way it could be made. Even at one coin to a wager, the silver in front of him grew to a tidy sum. Half the people in the common room came to stand around the table and watch. He grinned at Tuon, who gave him a slight nod. He had missed this, dice in a common room or tavern, coin on the table, wondering how long his luck would hold. And a pretty woman at his side while he gambled. He wanted to laugh with pleasure.

As he was shaking the dice in the cup again, the Taraboner merchant glanced at him, and for an instant, she did not look drunk at all. Suddenly, he no longer felt like laughing. Her face slackened immediately, and her eyes became a tad unfocused once more, but for that instant they had been awls. She had a much better head for wine than he had supposed. It seemed Camrin and Kostelle would not get away with fobbing off shoddy work at top prices or whatever their scheme had been. What concerned him, though, was that the woman was suspicious of him. Come to think, she herself had not risked a coin against him. The two Altarans were frowning at him, but just the way men who were losing frowned over their bad luck. She thought he had found some way to cheat. Never mind that he was using their dice, or more likely the inn's dice; an accusation of cheating could get a man a drubbing even in a merchants' inn. Men seldom waited on proof of that charge.

"One last toss," he said, "and I think I'll call it done. Mistress Heilin?" The innkeeper was among the onlookers. He handed her a

small handful of his new-won silver coins. "To celebrate my good fortune, serve everybody what they want to drink until those run out."
That brought appreciative murmurs, and someone behind him clapped
him on the back. A man drinking your wine was less likely to believe
you had bought it with cheated coin. Or at least they might hesitate
long enough to give him a chance to get Tuon out.

"He can't keep this run going forever," Camrin muttered, scrubbing a hand through the hair he no longer possessed. "What say you,
Kostelle? Halves?" Fingering a gold crown free of the coins piled in
front of him, he slid it over beside Mat's silver mark. "If there's only to
be one more toss, let's make a real wager on it. Bad luck has to follow
this much good." Kostelle hesitated, rubbing his chins in thought,
then nodded and added a gold crown of his own.

Mat sighed. He could refuse the bet, but walking away now might
well trigger Mistress Alstaing's charge. So could winning this toss. Reluctantly he pushed out silver marks to match their gold. That left
only two in front of him. He gave the cup an extra heavy shake before
spilling the dice onto the table. He did not expect that to alter anything. He was just venting his feelings.

The red dice tumbled across the tabletop, hit the piled coins and
bounced back, spinning before they fell to a stop. Each showing a single pip. The Dark One's Eyes.

Laughing just as if it were not just their own coin won back, Camrin and Kostelle began dividing their winnings. The watchers started
drifting away, calling congratulations to the two merchants, murmuring words of commiseration to Mat, some lifting the cup he was paying for in his direction. Mistress Alstaing took a long pull at her
winecup, studying him over the rim, to all outward appearance as
drunk as a goose. He doubted she thought he had been cheating any
longer, not when he was walking away with only one mark more than
he sat down with. Sometimes bad luck could turn out to be good.

"So your luck is not endless, Toy," Tuon said as he escorted her back
to their table. "Or is it that you are lucky only in small things?"

"Nobody has endless luck, Precious. Myself, I think that last toss
was one of the luckiest I've ever made." He explained about the
Taraboner woman's suspicions, and why he had bought wine for the
whole common room.

At the table, he held her chair for her, but she remained standing, looking at him. "You may do very well in Seandar," she said finally, thrusting her nearly empty mug at him. "Guard this until I return."

He straightened in alarm. "Where are you going?" He trusted her not to run away, but not to stay out of trouble without him there to pull her out of it.

She put on a long-suffering face. Even that was beautiful. "If you must know, I am going to the necessary, Toy."

"Oh. The innkeeper can tell you where it is. Or one of the serving women."

"Thank you, Toy," she said sweetly. "I'd never have thought to *ask*." She waggled her fingers at Selucia, and the two of them walked toward the back of the common room having one of their silent talks and giggling.

Sitting down, he scowled into his winecup. Women seemed to enjoy finding ways to make you feel a fool. And he was half-married to this one.

"Where are the women?" Thom asked, dropping down into the chair beside Mat and setting a nearly full winecup on the table. He grunted when Mat explained, and went on in a low voice, leaning his elbows on the table to put his head close. "We have trouble behind and ahead. Far enough ahead that it may not bother us here, but best we leave as soon as they return."

Mat sat up straight. "What kind of trouble?"

"Some of those merchant trains that passed us the last few days brought news of a murder in Jurador about the time we left. Maybe a day or two later; it's hard to be sure. A man was found in his own bed with his throat ripped, only there wasn't enough blood." He had no need to say more.

Mat took a long pull at his wine. The bloody gholam was still following him. How had it found out he was with Luca's show? But if it was still a day or two behind at the pace the show was making, likely it would not catch up to him soon. He fingered the silver foxhead through his coat. At least he had a way to fight it if it did appear. The thing carried a scar he had given it. "And the trouble ahead?"

"There's a Seanchan army on the border of Murandy. How they assembled it without my learning about it before this. . . ." He puffed out his mustaches, offended by his failure. "Well, no matter. Everybody who passes through they make drink a cup of some herbal tea."

"*Tea?*" Mat said in disbelief. "Where's the trouble in tea?"

"Every so often, this tea makes a woman go unsteady in her legs, and then the *sul'dam* come and collar her. But that's not the worst. They're looking very hard for a slight, dark young Seanchan woman."

"Well, of course they are. Did you expect they wouldn't be? This solves my biggest problem, Thom. When we get closer, we can leave the show, take to the forest. Tuon and Selucia can travel on with Luca. Luca will like being the hero who returned their Daughter of the Nine Moons to them."

Thom shook his head gravely. "They're looking for an impostor, Mat. Somebody *claiming* to be the Daughter of the Nine Moons. Except the description fits her too closely. They don't talk about it openly, but there are always men who drink too much, and some always talk too much as well when they do. They mean to kill her when they find her. Something about blotting out the shame she caused."

"Light!" Mat breathed. "How could that be, Thom? Whatever general commands that army must know her face, wouldn't he? And other officers, too, I'd think. There must be nobles who know her."

"Won't do her much good if they do. Even the lowest soldier will slit her throat or bash in her head as soon as she's found. I had that from three different merchants, Mat. Even if they're all wrong, are you willing to take the chance?"

Mat was not, and over their wine they began planning. Not that they did much drinking. Thom seldom did anymore for all his visits to common rooms and taverns, and Mat wanted a clear head.

"Luca will scream over letting us have enough horses to mount everyone whatever you pay him," Thom said at one point. "And there are packhorses for supplies if we're taking to the forest."

"Then I'll start buying, Thom. By the time we have to go, we'll have as many as we need. I'll wager I can find a few good animals right here. Vanin has a good eye, too. Don't worry. I'll make sure he pays for them." Thom nodded doubtfully. He was not so certain how reformed Vanin was.

"Aludra's coming with us?" the white-haired man said in surprise a little later. "She'll want to take all of her paraphernalia. That'll mean more packhorses."

"We have time, Thom. The border of Murandy is a long way, yet. I mean to head north into Andor, or east if Vanin knows a way through the mountains. Better east." Any way Vanin knew would be a smug-

gler's path, a horsethief's escape route. There would be much less
chance of unfortunate encounters along something like that. The Seanchan could be almost anywhere in Altara, and the way north took him
nearer that army than he liked.

Tuon and Selucia appeared from the back of the common room,
and he stood, taking up Tuon's cloak from her chair. Thom rose, too,
lifting Selucia's cloak. "We're leaving," Mat said, trying to place the
cloak around Tuon. Selucia snatched it out of his hands.

"I haven't seen even one fight yet," Tuon protested, too loudly. Any
number of people turned to stare, merchants and serving women.

"I'll explain outside," he told her quietly. "Away from prying ears."

Tuon stared up at him, expressionless. He knew she was tough,
but she was so tiny, like a pretty doll, that it was easy to believe she
would break if handled roughly. He was going to do whatever was
necessary to make sure she was not put in danger of being broken.
Whatever it took. Finally she nodded and let Selucia place the blue
cloak on her shoulders. Thom attempted to do the same for the
yellow-haired woman, but she took it away from him and donned it
herself. Mat could not recall ever seeing her let anyone help her with
her cloak.

The crooked street outside was empty of human life. A slat-ribbed
brown dog eyed them warily, then trotted away around the nearest
bend. Mat moved nearly as quickly in the other direction, explaining
as they went. If he had expected shock or dismay, he would have been
disappointed.

"It could be Ravashi or Chimal," the little woman said thoughtfully, as if having an entire Seanchan army out to kill her were no
more than an idle distraction. "My two nearest sisters in age. Aurana
is too young, I think, only eight. Fourteen, you would say. Chimal is
quiet in her ambition, but Ravashi has always believed she should
have been named just because she is older. She might well have sent
someone to plant rumors should I disappear for a time. It is really
quite clever of her. If she is the one." Just as coolly as talking about
whether it might rain.

"This plot could be dealt with easily if the High Lady were in the
Tarasin Palace where she belongs," Selucia said, and coolness vanished
from Tuon.

Oh, her face became as chill as that of an executioner, but she
rounded on her maid, fingers flashing so furiously they should have

been striking sparks. Selucia's face went pale, and she sank to her knees, head down and huddling. Her fingers gestured briefly, and Tuon let her own hands fall, stood looking down at the scarf-covered top of Selucia's head, breathing heavily. After a moment, she bent and lifted the other woman to her feet. Standing very close, she said something very short in that finger-talk. Selucia replied silently, Tuon made the same gestures again, and they exchanged tremulous smiles. Tears glistened in their eyes. Tears!

"Will you tell me what *that* was all about?" Mat demanded. They turned their heads to study him.

"What are your plans, Toy?" Tuon asked at last.

"Not Ebou Dar, if that's what you're thinking, Precious. If one army is out to kill you, then they probably all are, and there are too many soldiers between here and Ebou Dar. But don't worry; I'll find some way to get you back safely."

"So you always. . . ." Her eyes went past him, widening, and he looked over his shoulder to see seven or eight men round the last bend in the street. Every man had an unsheathed sword in his hand. Their steps quickened at sight of him.

"Run, Tuon!" he shouted, spinning to face their attackers. "Thom, get her away from here!" A knife came into either hand from his sleeves, and he threw them almost as one. The left-hand blade took a graying man in the eye, the right-hand a skinny fellow in the throat. They dropped as if their bones had melted, but before their swords clattered on the paving stones, he had already snatched another pair of knives from his boot tops and was sprinting toward them.

It took them by surprise, losing two of their number so quickly, and him closing the distance instead of trying to flee. But with him so close so quickly, and them jamming against one another on that narrow street, they lost most of the advantage that swords gave them over his knives. Not all, unfortunately. His blades could deflect a sword, but he only bothered when someone drew back for a thrust. In short order he had a fine collection of gashes, across his ribs, on his left thigh, along the right side of his jaw, a cut that would have laid open his throat had he not jerked aside in time. But had he tried to flee, they would have run him through from behind. Alive and bleeding was better than dead.

His hands moved as fast as ever they had, short moves, almost delicate. Flamboyance would have killed him. One knife slipped into a fat man's heart and out again before the fellow's knees began to crumple. He sliced inside the elbow of a man built like a blacksmith, who dropped his sword and awkwardly drew his belt knife with his left hand. Mat ignored him; the fellow was already staggering from blood loss before his blade cleared the scabbard. A square-faced man gasped as Mat sliced open the side of his neck. He clapped a hand to the wound, but he only managed to totter back two steps before he fell. As men died, the others gained room, but Mat moved faster still, dancing so that a falling man shielded him from another's sword while he closed inside the sword-arc of a third. To him, the world consisted of his two knives and the men crowding each other to get at him, and his knives sought the places where men bleed most heavily. Some of those ancient memories came from men who had not been very nice at all.

And then, miracle of miracles, bleeding profusely, but his blood too hot to let him feel the full pain yet, he was facing the last, one he had not noticed before. She was young and slim in a ragged dress, and she might have been pretty had her face been clean, had her teeth not been showing in a rictus snarl. The dagger she was tossing from hand to hand had a double-edged blade twice the length of his hand.

"You can't hope to finish alone what the others failed in together," he told her. "Run. I'll let you go unharmed."

With a cry like a feral cat, she rushed at him slashing and stabbing wildly. All he could do was dance backwards awkwardly, trying to fend her off. His boot slid in a patch of blood, and as he staggered, he knew he was about to die.

Abruptly Tuon was there, left hand seizing the young woman's wrist—not the wrist of her knife hand, worse luck—twisting so the arm went stiff and the girl was forced to double over. And then it mattered not at all which hand held her knife, because Tuon's right hand swept across, bladed like an axe, and struck her throat so hard that he heard the cartilage cracking. Choking, she clutched her ruined throat and sagged to her knees, then fell over still sucking hoarsely for breath.

"I told you to run," Mat said, not sure which of the two he was addressing.

"You very nearly let her kill you, Toy," Tuon said severely. "Why?"

"I promised myself I'd never kill another woman," he said wearily. His blood was beginning to cool, and Light, he hurt! "Looks like I've ruined this coat," he muttered, fingering one of the blood-soaked slashes. The motion brought a wince. When had he been gashed on the left arm?

Her gaze seemed to bore into his skull, and she nodded as if she had come to some conclusion.

Thom and Selucia were standing a little down the street, in front of the reason Tuon was still there, better than half a dozen bodies sprawled on the paving stones. Thom had a knife in either hand and was allowing Selucia to examine a wound on his ribs through the rent in his coat. Oddly, by evidence of the dark glistening patches on his coat, he seemed to have fewer injuries than Mat. Mat wondered whether Tuon had taken part there, too, but he could not see a spot of blood on her anywhere. Selucia had a bloody gash down her left arm, though it appeared not to hinder her.

"I'm an old man," Thom said suddenly, "and sometimes I imagine I see things that can't be, but luckily, I always forget them."

Selucia paused to look up at him coolly. Lady's maid she might be, but blood seemed not to faze her at all. "And what might you be trying to forget?"

"I can't recall," Thom replied. Selucia nodded and went back to examining his wounds.

Mat shook his head. Sometimes he was not entirely sure Thom still had all his wits. For that matter, Selucia seemed a shovel shy of a full load now and then, too.

"This one can't live to be put to the question," Tuon drawled, frowning at the woman choking and twitching at her feet, "and she can't talk if she somehow managed to." Bending fluidly, she scooped up the woman's knife and drove it hard beneath the woman's breastbone. That rasping fight for air went silent; glazing eyes stared up at the narrow strip of sky overhead. "A mercy she did not deserve, but I see no point to needless suffering. I won, Toy."

"You won? What are you talking about?"

"You used my name before I used yours, so I won."

Mat whistled faintly through his teeth. Whenever he thought he knew how tough she was, she found a way to show him he did not know the half. If anybody happened to be looking out a window, that stabbing might raise questions with the local magistrate, probably Lord Nathin himself. But there were no faces at any window he could see. People avoided getting embroiled in this sort of thing if they could. For all he knew, any number of porters or barrow-men might have come along during the fight. For a certainty, they would have turned right around again as quickly as they could. Whether any might have gone for Lord Nathin's guards was another question. Still, he had no fear of Nathin or his magistrate. A pair of men escorting two women did not decide to attack more than a dozen carrying swords. Likely these fellows, and the unfortunate young woman, were well known to the guards.

Limping to retrieve his thrown knives, he paused in the act of pulling the blade from the graying man's eye. He had not really taken in that face, before. Everything had happened too quickly for more than general impressions. Carefully wiping the knife on the man's coat, he tucked it away up his sleeve as he straightened. "Our plans have changed, Thom. We're leaving Maderin as fast as we can, and we're leaving the show as fast as we can. Luca will want to be rid of us so much that he'll let us have all the horses we need."

"This must be reported, Toy," Tuon said severely. "Failure to do so is as lawless as what they did."

"You know that fellow?" Thom said.

Mat nodded. "His name is Vane, and I don't think anybody in this town will believe a respectable merchant attacked us in the street. Luca will *give* us horses to be rid of this." It was very strange. The man had not lost a coin to him, had not *wagered* a coin. So, why? Very strange indeed. And reason enough to be gone quickly.

CHAPTER
12

A Manufactory

The midday Amadician sun was warm on Perrin's head as he rode Stayer toward the roofs of Almizar beneath high, scudding white clouds, a hundred miles southwest of Amador. Impatient, he kept the bay at a trot. Farms stretched as far as he could see in any direction on both sides of the road, thatch-roofed stone houses with gray smoke rising from the chimneys and chickens scratching in front of the barns. Fat-tailed sheep and spotted black cattle grazed in stone-walled pastures, and men and boys were plowing the fields or sowing those already plowed. It seemed to be laundry day; he could see large kettles sitting over fires behind houses, and women and girls hanging shirts and blouses and bed linens on long lines to dry. There was little of wildness, only scattered thickets, and most of those neatly coppiced to provide firewood.

He reached out with his mind to find wolves, and found nothing. Unsurprising. Wolves stayed clear of this many people, this much tameness. The breeze stiffened, and he gathered his cloak around him. Despite the need to make a show, it was plain brown wool. The only silk cloak he had was lined with fur, and too hot for the day. His green silk coat worked in silver would have to do. That and his cloak pin, two wolves' heads in silver-and-gold. A gift from Faile, it had always seemed too ornate to wear, but he had dug it out of the bottom of a chest that morning. A little something to make up for the plain cloak.

What was surprising were the Tinker caravans camped in fields scattered around the town, five of them within his sight. According to Elyas, there was always feasting when two caravans encountered one another, and a meeting of three caused days of celebration, but larger gatherings seldom occurred except in the summer, at Sunday, when they had their meeting places. He almost wished he had brought Aram, despite the risk of Masema learning too much. Maybe if the man could spend a little time among his own people, he might decide to put down his sword. That was the best solution Perrin could think of to a thorny problem, although not likely to work. Aram liked the sword, perhaps too well. But he could not send the man away. He had as good as put that sword in Aram's hand, and now Aram and the sword were his responsibility. The Light only knew what would become of the man if he truly went over to Masema.

"You study the Tuatha'an and frown, my Lord," General Khirgan drawled. He could understand her speech a little better, now that they had spent time together. "You've had problems with them in your lands? We have nothing like them at home, but the only trouble connected to them I know of has been locals trying to drive them away. Apparently, they're supposed to be great thieves."

She and Mishima were ornate today in blue cloaks trimmed with red and yellow, and red coats with blue cuffs and lapels edged in yellow. Three small vertical blue bars, shaped like the thin plumes of a Seanchan helmet, on the left breast of her coat indicated her rank, as two did for Mishima. The dozen soldiers riding behind wore their striped armor and painted helmets, however, and carried steel-tipped lances held at precisely the same angle. The cluster of Faile's hangers-on following the Seanchan, also twelve in number, made a brave display in Tairen coats with puffy satin-striped sleeves and dark Cairhienin coats with stripes of House colors across the chests, yet in spite of their swords they looked much less dangerous than the soldiers and seemed to know it. Whenever the breeze gusted from behind, it carried traces of irritation that Perrin doubted came from the Seanchan. The soldiers' scent was of stillness, waiting, like wolves who knew teeth might be needed soon, but not now. Not yet.

"Ah, they steal a chicken now and then, General," Neald said with a laugh, giving one of his thin waxed mustaches a twist, "but I'd not be calling them great thieves." He had enjoyed the Seanchan astonishment at the gateway that had brought them all here, and he was still posing over it, somehow managing to strut while sitting his saddle. It was difficult to remember that had he not earned that black coat, he would still be working his father's farm and perhaps wondering about marriage to a neighbor girl in a year or two. "Great theft requires courage, and Tinkers have not a bit of it."

Huddled in his dark cloak, Balwer grimaced, or perhaps smiled. Sometimes it was hard to tell the difference with the desiccated little man unless Perrin could catch his scent. The pair of them accompanied Perrin in much the same way as a gray-haired *sul'dam* linked to a cool-eyed *damane* with touches of gray in her own dark hair accompanied Khirgan and Mishima, supposedly to balance the numbers. To the Seanchan, *sul'dam* and *damane* counted as one when connected by the segmented metal leash. He would have been satisfied to come with Neald alone, or Neald and Balwer at least, but Tallanvor had been right about Seanchan and protocol. The talks had dragged on for three days, and while some time had been spent on whether to follow Perrin's plan or make it a part of something Tylee would come up with—with her yielding at the end only because she could find nothing better—a good part had been wasted on how many each side was to bring here. It had to be the same number for each, and the Banner-General had wanted to bring a hundred of her soldiers and a pair of *damane*. For honor's sake. She had been astounded that he was willing to come with less, and was only willing to accept it after he pointed out that everyone among Faile's people was noble in his or her own lands. He had the feeling she thought she had been cheated because she could not match his escorts' rank with her own. Strange folk, these Seanchan. Oh, there were sides, to be sure. This alliance was purely temporary, not to mention delicate, and the Banner-General was just as aware of that as he.

"Twice they offered me shelter when I needed it, me and my friends, and asked nothing in return," Perrin said quietly. "Yet what I remember best about them was when Trollocs surrounded Emond's Field. The Tuatha'an stood on the green with children strapped to their backs, the few of their own that survived and ours. They would not fight—it isn't their way—but if the Trollocs overran us, they were ready to try to carry the children to safety. Carrying our children would have hampered them, made escape even less likely than it already was, but they asked for the task." Neald gave an embarrassed cough and looked away. A flush tinged his cheek. For all he had seen and done, he was young yet, just seventeen. This time, there was no doubt about Balwer's thin smile.

"I think your life might make a story," the general said, her expression inviting him to tell as much of it as he would.

"I'd rather my life were ordinary," he told her. Stories were no place for a man who wanted peace.

"One day, I'd very much like to see some of these Trollocs I keep hearing about," Mishima said when the silence began to stretch. Amusement tinged his smell, yet he stroked his sword hilt, perhaps without knowing it.

"No you wouldn't," Perrin told him. "You'll get your chance soon or late, but you won't like it." After a moment, the scarred man nodded solemnly in understanding, amusement melting. At last he must be beginning to believe that Trollocs and Myrddraal were more than travelers' fanciful tales. If any doubts remained to him, the time was coming that would erase doubt forever.

Heading into Almizar, as they turned their horses toward the north end of the town along a narrow cart lane, Balwer slipped away. Medore went with him, a tall woman nearly as dark as Tylee but with deep blue eyes, in dark breeches and a man's coat with puffy red-striped sleeves, a sword at her hip. Balwer rode with his shoulders hunched, a bird perched precariously on his saddle, Medore straight-backed and proud, every inch a High Lord's daughter and leader of Faile's people, though she followed Balwer rather than riding beside. Surprisingly, Faile's hangers-on seemed to have accepted taking direction from the fussy little man. It made them much less bother than they once had been; it actually made them useful in some ways, which Perrin would have thought impossible. The Banner-General offered no objection to them leaving, though she gazed after them thoughtfully.

"Kind of the Lady to visit a servant's friend," she mused. That was the tale Balwer had given, that he used to know a woman who lived in Almizar and Medore wanted to meet her if she was still alive.

"Medore's a kind woman," Perrin replied. "It's our way, being kind to servants." Tylee gave him one glance, only that, yet he reminded himself not to take her for a fool. It was too bad he knew nothing of Seanchan ways to speak of, or they might have come up with a better

story. But then, Balwer had been in a frenzy—a dry, dusty frenzy, yet
still a frenzy—to seize this chance to gather information on what was
happening in Amadicia under the Seanchan. For himself, Perrin could
barely make himself care. Only Faile mattered, now. Later he could
worry about other matters.

Just north of Almizar, the stone walls dividing seven or eight fields
had been removed to make a long stretch of bare earth that appeared
thoroughly turned by the harrow, the dirt all scored and scuffed. A
large odd creature with a pair of hooded people crouched on its back
was running awkwardly along that stretch on two legs that seemed
spindly for its size. In fact, "odd" barely began to encompass it. Leathery and gray, the thing was larger than a horse without counting a
long, snake-like neck and a thin, even longer tail that it held stretched
out stiffly behind. As it ran, it beat wings ribbed like those of a bat,
stretching as long as most riverships. He had seen animals like this before, but in the air, and at a distance. Tylee had told him they were
called *raken*. Slowly the creature lumbered into the air, barely clearing
the treetops of a coppiced thicket at the end of the field. His head
swiveled to follow as the *raken* climbed slowly toward the sky, awkwardness vanishing in flight. Now, that would be a thing, to fly on one
of those. He crushed the thought, ashamed and angered that he could
let himself be diverted.

The Banner-General slowed her bay and frowned at the field. At
the far end, men were feeding four more of the peculiar animals, holding up large baskets for them to eat from, horned snouts darting and
horny mouths gulping. Perrin hated to think what a creature that
looked like that might eat. "They should have more *raken* than this
here," she muttered. "If this is all there are. . . ."

"We take what we can get and go on," he said. "None, if it comes
to that. We already know where the Shaido are."

"I like to know if anything is coming up behind me," she told him
dryly, picking up the pace again.

At a nearby farm that appeared to have been taken over by the
Seanchan, a dozen or so soldiers were dicing at tables set up haphaz-
ardly in front of the thatch-roofed house. More were passing in and out
of the stone barn, though he saw no sign of horses except for a team
hitched to a wagon that was being unloaded of its crates and barrels
and jute sacks by a pair of men in rough woolens. At least, Perrin assumed the others were soldiers. Nearly half were women, the men as

short as the women for the most part and thin if taller, and none carried a sword, but they all wore close-fitting coats of sky-blue and each had a pair of knives in scabbards sewn to their snug boots. Uniforms implied soldiers.

Mat would be right at home with this lot, he thought, watching them laugh over good tosses and groan over bad. Those colors spun in his head, and for an instant he glimpsed Mat riding off a road into forest followed by a line of mounted folk and packhorses. An instant only, because he dashed the image aside without so much as a thought to why Mat was going into the woods or who was with him. Only Faile mattered. That morning he had tied a fifty-first knot in the leather cord he carried in his pocket. Fifty-one days she had been a prisoner. He hoped she had been a prisoner that long. It would mean she was still alive to be rescued. If she was dead. . . . His hand tightened on the head of the hammer hanging at his belt, tightened until his knuckles hurt.

The Banner-General and Mishima were watching him, he realized, Mishima warily, with a hand hovering near his sword hilt, Tylee thoughtfully. A delicate alliance, and little trust on either side. "For a moment, I thought you might be ready to kill the fliers," she said quietly. "You have my word. We will free your wife. Or avenge her."

Perrin drew a shuddering breath and released his hold on the hammer. Faile had to be alive. Alyse had said she was under her protection. But how much protection could the Aes Sedai give when she wore *gai'shain* white herself? "Let's be done here. Time is wasting." How many more knots would he need to tie in that cord? The Light send not many.

Dismounting, he handed Stayer's reins to Carlon Belcelona, a clean-shaven Tairen with a long nose and an unfortunately narrow chin. Carlon had a habit of fingering that chin as if wondering where his beard had gone, or running a hand over his hair as though wondering why it was tied with a ribbon at the nape of his neck, making a tail that just reached his shoulders. But he gave no more sign of giving up his fool pretense that he was following Aiel ways than the others did. Balwer had given them their instructions, and at least they obeyed those. Most of them were already drifting over to the tables, leaving their mounts in the care of the rest, some producing coin, others offering leather flasks of wine. Which the soldiers were rejecting, strangely, though it seemed anyone with silver was welcome in their games.

Without more than glancing in their direction, Perrin tucked his gauntlets behind his thick belt and followed the two Seanchan inside, tossing back his cloak so his silk coat showed. By the time he came out, Faile's people—his people, he supposed—would have learned a great deal of what those men and women knew. One thing he had learned from Balwer. Knowledge could be very useful, and you never knew which scrap would turn out worth more than gold. For the moment, though, the only knowledge he was interested in would not come from this place.

The front room of the farmhouse was filled with tables facing the door, where clerks sat poring over papers or writing. The only sound was the scritching of pen on paper and a man's dry persistent cough. The men wore coats and breeches of dark brown, the women dresses in the exact same shade. Some wore pins, in silver or brass, in the shape of a quill pen. The Seanchan had uniforms for everything, it seemed. A round-cheeked fellow at the back of the room who wore two silver pens on his chest stood and bowed deeply, belly straining his coat, as soon as Tylee entered. Their boots were loud on the wooden floor as they walked back to him between the tables. He did not straighten until they reached his table.

"Tylee Khirgan," she said curtly. "I would speak with whoever is in command here."

"As the Banner-General commands," the fellow replied obsequiously, made another deep bow, and hurried through a door behind him.

The clerk who was coughing, a smooth-faced fellow younger than Perrin who, by his face, might have come from the Two Rivers, began hacking more roughly, and covered his mouth with a hand. He cleared his throat loudly, but the harsh cough returned.

Mishima frowned at him. "Fellow shouldn't be here if he's ill," he muttered. "What if it's catching? You hear about all sorts of strange sicknesses these days. Man's hale at sunrise, and by sunfall, he's a corpse and swollen to half again his size, with no one knowing what he died of. I heard of a woman who went mad in the space of an hour, and everybody who touched her went mad, too. In three days, she and her whole village were dead, those who hadn't fled." He made a peculiar gesture, forming an arc with thumb and forefinger, the others curled tightly.

"You know better than to believe rumors, or repeat them," the

Banner-General said sharply, making the same gesture. She seemed unaware she had done so.

The stout clerk reappeared, holding the door for a graying, lean-
faced man with a black leather patch hiding the spot where his right
eye had been. A puckered white scar ran down his forehead, behind the
patch and onto his cheek. As short as the men outside, he wore a coat
of darker blue, with two small white bars on his chest, though he had
the same sheaths sewn to his boots. "Blasic Faloun, Banner-General,"
he said with a bow as the clerk hurried back to his table. "How may I
serve you?"

"Captain Faloun, we need to speak in—" Tylee cut off when the
man who was coughing surged to his feet, his stool toppling with a
clatter.

Clutching his middle, the young man doubled over and vomited a
dark stream that hit the floor and broke up into tiny black beetles that
went scurrying in every direction. Someone cursed, shockingly loud in
what was otherwise dead silence. The young man stared at the beetles
in horror, shaking his head to deny them. Wild-eyed, he looked around
the room still shaking his head and opened his mouth as if to speak.
Instead, he bent over and spewed another black stream, longer, that
broke into beetles darting across the floor. The skin of his face began
writhing, as though more beetles were crawling on the outside of his
skull. A woman screamed, a long shriek of dread, and suddenly clerks
were shouting and leaping up, knocking over stools and even tables in
their haste, frantically dodging the flitting black shapes. Again and
again the man vomited, sinking to his knees, then falling over, twitching disjointedly as he spewed out more and more beetles in a steady
stream. He seemed somehow to be getting . . . flatter. Deflating. His
jerking ceased, but black beetles continued to pour from his gaping
mouth and spread across the floor. At last—it seemed to have gone on
for an hour, but could not have been more than a minute or two—at
last, the torrent of insects dwindled and died. What remained of the
fellow was a pale flat thing inside his clothes, like a wineskin that had
been emptied. The shouting went on, of course. Half the clerks were
up on the tables that remained upright, men as well as women, cursing
or praying or sometimes alternating both at the tops of their lungs.
The other half had fled outside. Small black beetles scuttled all across
the floor. The room stank of terror.

"I heard a rumor," Faloun said hoarsely. Sweat beaded on his forehead. He smelled of fear. Not terror, but definitely fear. "From east of here. Only that was centipedes. Little black centipedes." Some of the beetles scurried toward him, and he backed away with a curse, making the same odd gesture that Tylee and Mishima had.

Perrin crushed the beetles under his boot. They made the hair on the back of his neck want to stand, but nothing mattered except Faile. Nothing! "They're just borer beetles. You can find them almost anywhere there's old fallen timber."

The man jerked, lifted his gaze and jerked again when he saw Perrin's eyes. Catching sight of the hammer at Perrin's belt, he darted a quick, startled glance at the Banner-General. "These beetles came from no log. They're Soulblinder's work!"

"That's as may be," Perrin replied calmly. He supposed Soulblinder was a name for the Dark One. "It makes no difference." He moved his foot, revealing the crushed carcasses of seven or eight of the insects. "They can be killed. And I have no time to waste on beetles I can crush underfoot."

"We do need to talk in private, Captain," Tylee added. Her scent was full of fear, too, yet tightly controlled. Mishima's hand was locked in that same strange gesture. His fear was almost as well controlled as hers.

Faloun gathered himself visibly, the fear smell fading. It did not go away, yet he had mastery of himself, now. He avoided looking at the beetles, however. "As you say, Banner-General. Atal, get down off that table and have these . . . these things swept out of here. And see that Mehtan is laid out properly for the rites. However he died, he died in service." The stout clerk bowed before climbing down, gingerly, and again when he was on the floor, but the captain was already turning away. "Will you follow me, Banner-General?"

His study might have been a bedroom originally, but now it held a writing table with flat boxes full of papers and another table, larger, that was covered with maps weighted down by inkwells, stones and small brass figures. A wooden rack against one wall held rolls that appeared to be more maps. The gray stone fireplace was cold. Faloun gestured them to half a dozen mismatched chairs that stood on the bare floor in front of the writing table and offered to send for wine. He seemed disappointed when Tylee refused both. Perhaps he wanted a drink to steady his nerves. A small scent of fright still clung to him.

Tylee began. "I need to replace six *raken*, Captain, and eighteen *morat'raken*. And a full company of groundlings. The one I had is somewhere in Amadicia heading west, and beyond finding."

Faloun winced. "Banner-General, if you lost *raken*, you know everything has been stripped to the bone because of. . . ." His one eye flickered to Perrin, and he cleared his throat before going on. "You ask for three-quarters of the animals I have left. If you can possibly do with fewer, perhaps only one or two?"

"Four," Tylee said firmly, "and twelve fliers. I'll settle for that." She could make that slurred Seanchan accent sound crisp when she wanted to. "This region is as stable as Seandar by all I hear, but I'll leave you four."

"As you say, Banner-General," Faloun sighed. "May I see the order, please? Everything has to be recorded. Since I lost the ability to fly myself, I spend all my time pushing a pen like a clerk."

"Lord Perrin?" Tylee said, and he produced the document signed by Suroth from his coat pocket.

That made Faloun's eyebrows climb higher and higher as he read, and he fingered the wax seal lightly, but he did not question it any more than the Banner-General had. It appeared the Seanchan were accustomed to such things. He appeared relieved to hand it back, though, and wiped his hands on his coat unconsciously. Accustomed to them, but not comfortably so. He studied Perrin, trying to be surreptitious, and Perrin could all but see on his face the question the Banner-General had asked. Who was he, to have such a thing?

"I need a map of Altara, Captain, if you have such a thing," Tylee said. "I can manage if you don't, but better if you do. The northwestern quarter of the country is what I'm interested in."

"You're favored by the Light, Banner-General," the man said, bending to pull a roll from the lowest level of the rack. "I have the very thing you want. By accident, it was in with the Amadician maps I was issued. I'd forgotten I had the thing until you mentioned it. Uncommon luck for you, I'd say." Perrin shook his head slightly. Accident, not *ta'veren* work. Even Rand was not *ta'veren* enough to make this happen. The colors whirled, and he splintered them unformed.

Once Faloun had the map spread out on the map table, the corners held down by brass weights in the form of *raken*, the Banner-General studied it until she had her landmarks fixed. It was large enough to cover the table and showed exactly what she had asked for, along with narrow strips of Amadicia and Ghealdan, the terrain rendered in great detail, with the names of towns and villages, rivers and streams, in very small letters. Perrin knew he was looking at a fine example of the map-maker's art, far better than most maps. Could it be *ta'veren* work? No. No, that was impossible.

"They'll find my soldiers here," she drawled, marking a point with her finger. "They're to leave immediately. One flier to a *raken*, and no personal items. They fly light, and as fast as possible. I want them there before tomorrow night. The other *morat'raken* will travel with the groundlings. I hope to be leaving in a few hours. Have them assembled and ready."

"Carts," Perrin said. Neald could not make a gateway large enough to accommodate a wagon. "Whatever they bring has to be in carts, not wagons." Faloun mouthed the word incredulously.

"Carts," Tylee agreed. "See to it, Captain."

Perrin could smell an eagerness in the man that he interpreted as a desire to ask questions, but all Faloun said, bowing, was, "As you command, Banner-General, so shall it be done."

The outer room was in a different sort of turmoil when they left the captain. Clerks darted everywhere, sweeping frantically or beating at the remaining beetles with their brooms. Some of the women wept as they wielded their brooms, some of the men looked as though they wanted to, and the room was still rank with terror. There was no sign of the dead man, but Perrin noticed that the clerks moved around the place where he had lain, refusing to let a foot touch it. They tried not to step on any beetles, either, which made for considerable dancing about on their toes. When Perrin crunched his way toward the outer door, they stopped to stare at him.

Outside, the mood was calmer, but not by much. Tylee's soldiers still stood by their horses in a row, and Neald was affecting an air of casual indifference, even to yawning and patting his mouth, but the *sul'-dam* was petting the trembling *damane* and murmuring soothingly, and the blue-coated soldiers, many more than had been there before, stood in a large cluster talking worriedly. The Cairhienin and Tairens rushed to surround Perrin, leading their horses and all talking at once.

"Is it true, my Lord?" Camaille asked, her pale face twisted with worry, and her brother Barmanes said uneasily, "Four men carried out something in a blanket, but they averted their eyes from whatever it was."

All of them atop one another, all smelling of near panic. "They said he spewed beetles," and "They said the beetles chewed their way out of him," and "The Light help us, they're sweeping beetles out of the door; we'll be killed," and "Burn my soul, it's the Dark One breaking free," and more that made less sense.

"Be quiet," Perrin said, and for a wonder, they fell silent. Usually, they were very prickly with him, insisting that they served Faile, not him. Now they stood staring at him, waiting for him to put their fears to rest. "A man did spew up beetles and die, but they're ordinary beetles you can find in dead timber anywhere. Give you a nasty pinch if you sit on one, but nothing worse. Likely it was the Dark One's work somehow, true enough, but it has nothing to do with freeing the Lady Faile, and that means it has nothing to do with us. So calm yourselves, and let's get on about our business."

Strangely, it worked. More than one cheek reddened, and the smell of fear was replaced—or at least suppressed—by the scent of shame at letting themselves come so near to panic. They looked abashed. As they began mounting, their own natures reasserted themselves, though. First one then another offered boasts of the deeds they would do in rescuing Faile, each wilder than the next. They knew them for wild, because each boast brought laughter from the others, yet the next always tried to make his more outrageous still.

The Banner-General was watching him again, he realized as he took Stayer's reins from Carlon. What did she see? What did she think she might learn? "What sent all the *raken* away?" he asked.

"We should have come here second or third," she replied, swinging up into her saddle. "I still have to acquire *a'dam*. I wanted to keep believing I had a chance as long as I could, but we might as well get to the heart. That piece of paper faces a real test now, and if it fails, there's no point to going after *a'dam*." A frail alliance, and small trust.

"Why should it fail? It worked here."

"Faloun's a soldier, my Lord. Now we must talk with an Imperial functionary." She imbued that last word with a wealth of scorn. She turned her bay, and he had no choice but to mount and follow.

Almizar was a considerable town, and prosperous, with six tall watchtowers around its edge but no wall. Elyas said Amadician law forbade walls anywhere save Amador, a law made at the behest of the Whitecloaks and enforced by them as much as by whoever held the throne. Balwer would no doubt learn who that might be now, with

Ailron dead. The streets were paved with granite blocks, and lined with solid buildings of brick or stone, some gray, some black, many three or four stories high and most roofed in dark slate, the rest in thatch. People filled the streets, dodging between wagons and horse carts and handcarts, hawkers crying their wares, women in deep bonnets that hid their faces carrying shopping baskets, men in knee-length coats striding along self-importantly, apprentices in aprons or vests running errands. As many soldiers walked the streets as locals, men and women, with skin as dark as any Tairen, skin the color of honey, men as pale as Cairhienin but fair-haired and tall, all in brightly colored Seanchan uniforms. Most wore no more than a belt knife or dagger, but he saw some with swords. They walked in pairs, watchful of everyone around them, and had truncheons at their belts, too. A town Watch, he supposed, but a lot of them for a place the size of Almizar. He never had fewer than two of those pairs in his sight.

Two men and a woman came out of a tall, slate-roofed inn and mounted horses held by grooms. He knew her for a woman only by the way her long, split-tailed coat fit over her bosom because her hair was cut shorter than the men's and she wore men's clothing and a sword, just like the other two. Her face was certainly as hard as theirs. As the three cantered off west down the street, Mishima grunted sourly.

"Hunters for the Horn," he muttered. "My eyes if they're not. Those fine fellows cause trouble everywhere they go, getting in fights, sticking their noses where they don't belong. I've heard the Horn of Valere has already been found. What do you think, my Lord?"

"I've heard it's been found, too," Perrin replied cautiously. "There are all sorts of rumors floating about."

Neither one so much as glanced at him, and in the middle of a crowded street, catching their scents was well-nigh impossible, yet for some reason he thought they were mulling over his answer as if it had hidden depths. Light, could they think *he* was tied up with the Horn? He knew where it was. Moiraine had carried it off to the White Tower. He was not about to tell them, though. Small trust worked both ways.

The local people gave the soldiers no more heed than they did each other, nor the Banner-General and her armored followers, but Perrin was another matter. At least, when they noticed his golden eyes. He could tell instantly when someone did. The quick jerk of a woman's head, her mouth falling open as she stared. The man who froze, gaping at him. One fellow actually tripped over his own boots and stumbled to his knees. That one stared, then scrambled to his feet and ran, pushing people from his path, as though fearful Perrin might pursue him.

"I suppose he never saw yellow eyes on a man before," Perrin said wryly.

"Are they common where you come from?" the Banner-General asked.

"Not common, I wouldn't say that, but I'll introduce you to another man who has them."

She and Mishima exchanged glances. Light, he hoped there was nothing in the Prophecies about *two* men with yellow eyes. Those colors whirled, and he dashed them.

The Banner-General knew exactly where she was going, a stone stable on the southern edge of the town, but when she dismounted in the empty stableyard, no groom came rushing out. A stone-fenced paddock stood next to the stable, but it held no horses. She handed her reins to one of her soldiers and stood staring at the stable doors, only one of which was open. By her scent, Perrin thought she was steeling herself.

"Follow my lead, my Lord," she said finally, "and don't say anything you don't have to. It might be the wrong thing. If you must speak, speak to me. Make it clear you're speaking to me."

That sounded ominous, but he nodded. And began planning how to steal the forkroot if things went wrong. He would need to learn whether the place was guarded at night. Balwer might already know. The little man seemed to pick up information like that without trying. When he followed her inside, Mishima remained with the horses, and looking relieved not to accompany them. What did that mean? Or did it mean anything? Seanchan. In just a few days they had him seeing hidden meanings in everything.

The place had been a stable once, obviously, but now it was something else. The stone floor had been swept clean enough to satisfy any farmwife, there were no horses, and a thick smell like mint would have overwhelmed the remaining scent of horse and hay to any nose but his or Elyas'. The stalls at the front were filled with stacked wooden crates, and in the back, the stalls had been removed except for the uprights that supported the loft. Now men and women were working back there, some using mortars and pestles or sieves at tables, others carefully tending flat pans sitting on metal legs above charcoal braziers, using tongs to turn what appeared to be roots.

A lean young man in his shirtsleeves put a plump jute bag into one of the crates, then bowed to Tylee as deeply as the clerk had, body parallel to the floor. He did not straighten until she spoke.

"Banner-General Khirgan. I wish to speak with whoever is in charge, if I may." Her tone was much different than it had been with the clerk, not peremptory at all.

"As you command," the lean fellow replied in what sounded an Amadician accent. At least, if he was Seanchan, he spoke at a proper speed and without chewing his words.

Bowing again, just as deeply, he hurried to where six stalls had been walled in, halfway down the left-hand row, and tapped diffidently at a door, then awaited permission before going in. When he came out, he went to the back of the building without so much as a glance toward Perrin and Tylee. After a few minutes, Perrin opened his mouth, but Tylee grimaced and shook her head, so he closed it again and waited. A good quarter of an hour he waited, growing more impatient by the heartbeat. The Banner-General smelled solidly of patience.

At last a sleekly plump woman in a deep yellow dress of odd cut came out of the small room, but she paused to study the work going on in the back of the building, ignoring Tylee and him. Half of her scalp had been shaved bald! Her remaining hair was in a thick, graying braid that hung to her shoulder. Finally she nodded in satisfaction and made her unhurried way to them. An oval blue panel on her bosom was embroidered with three golden hands. Tylee bowed as deeply as Faloun had for her, and remembering her admonition, Perrin did the same. The sleek woman inclined her head. Slightly. She smelled of pride.

"You wish to speak with me, Banner-General?" She had a smooth voice, as sleek as she herself. And not welcoming. She was a busy woman being bothered. A busy woman well aware of her own importance.

"Yes, Honorable," Tylee said respectfully. A spike of irritation appeared among her smell of patience, then was swallowed again. Her face remained expressionless. "Will you tell me how much prepared forkroot you have on hand?"

"An odd request," the other woman said as though considering whether to grant it. She tilted her head in thought. "Very well," she said after a moment. "As of the midmorning accounting, I have four thousand eight hundred seventy-three pounds nine ounces. A remarkable achievement, if I do say it myself, considering how much I have shipped off and how hard it is getting to find the plant in the wild without sending diggers unreasonable distances." Impossible as it seemed, the pride in her scent deepened. "I've solved that problem, however, by inducing the local farmers to plant some of their fields in forkroot. By this summer I will need to build something bigger to house this manufactory. I'll confide in you, I will not be surprised if I am offered a new name for this. Though of course, I may not accept." Smiling a small, sleek smile, she touched the oval panel lightly, but it was near a caress.

"The Light will surely favor you, Honorable," Tylee murmured. "My Lord, will you do me the favor of showing your document to the Honorable?" That with a bow to Perrin markedly lower than the one she had offered the Honorable. The sleek woman's eyebrows twitched.

Reaching out to take the paper from his hand, she froze, staring at his face. She had finally noticed his eyes. Giving herself a small shake, she read without any outward expression of surprise, then folded the paper up again and stood tapping it against her free hand. "It seems you walk the heights, Banner-General. And with a very strange companion. What aid do you—or he—ask of me?"

"Forkroot, Honorable," Tylee said mildly. "All that you have. Loaded into carts as soon as possible. And you must provide the carts and drivers as well, I fear."

"Impossible!" the sleek woman snapped, drawing herself up haughtily. "I have established strict schedules as to how many pounds of prepared forkroot are shipped every week, which I have adhered to rigidly, and I'll not see that record sullied. The harm to the Empire would be immense. The *sul'dam* are snapping up *marath'damane* on every hand."

"Forgiveness, Honorable," Tylee said, bowing again. "If you could see your way clear to let us have—"

"Banner-General," Perrin cut in. Plainly this was a touchy encounter, and he tried to keep his face smooth, but he could not avoid a frown. He could not be certain that even near five tons of the stuff would be sufficient, and she was trying to negotiate some lesser weight! His mind raced, trying to find a way. Fast thought was shoddy thought, in his estimation—it led to mistakes and accidents—but he had no choice. "This may not interest the Honorable, of course, but Suroth promised death and worse if there was any hindrance to her plans. I don't suppose her anger will go beyond you and me, but she did say to take it all."

"Of course, the Honorable will not be touched by the High Lady's anger." Tylee sounded as though she was not so sure of that.

The sleek woman was breathing hard, the blue oval with the golden hands heaving. She bowed to Perrin as deeply as Tylee had. "I'll need most of the day to gather enough carts and load them. Will that suffice, my Lord?"

"It will have to, won't it," Perrin said, plucking the note from her hand. She let go reluctantly and watched hungrily as he tucked it into his coat pocket.

Outside, the Banner-General shook her head as she swung into the saddle. "Dealing with the Lesser Hands is always difficult. None of them see anything lesser in themselves. I thought this would be in the charge of someone of the Fourth or Fifth Rank, and that would have been hard enough. When I saw that she was of the Third Rank—only two steps below a Hand to the Empress herself, may she live forever—I was sure we wouldn't get away with more than a few hundred pounds if that. But you handled it beautifully. A risk taken, but still, beautifully masked."

"Well, nobody wants to chance death," Perrin said as they started out of the stableyard into the town with everyone strung out behind them. Now they had to wait for the carts, perhaps find an inn. Impatience burned in him. The Light send they did not need to spend the night.

"You didn't know," the dark woman breathed. "That woman knew she stood in the shadow of death as soon as she read Suroth's words, but she was ready to risk it to do her duty to the Empire. A Lesser Hand of the Third Rank has standing enough that she might well escape death on the plea of duty done. But you used Suroth's name. That's all right most of the time, except when addressing the High Lady herself, of course, but with a Lesser Hand, using her name without her title meant you were either an ignorant local or an intimate of Suroth herself. The Light favored you, and she decided you were an intimate."

Perrin barked a mirthless laugh. Seanchan. And maybe *ta'veren*, too.

"Tell me, if the question does not offend, did your Lady bring powerful connections, or perhaps great lands?"

That surprised him so much that he twisted in his saddle to stare at her. Something hit his chest hard, sliced a line of fire across his chest, punched his arm. Behind him, a horse squealed in pain. Stunned, he stared down at the arrow sticking through his left arm.

"Mishima," the Banner-General snapped, pointing, "that four-story building with the thatched roof, between two slate roofs. I saw movement on the rooftop."

Shouting a command to follow, Mishima galloped off down the crowded street with six of the Seanchan lancers, horseshoes ringing on the paving stones. People leapt out of their way. Others stared. No one in the street seemed to realize what had happened. Two of the other lancers were out of their saddles, tending the trembling mount of one that had an arrow jutting from its shoulder. Perrin fingered a broken button hanging by a thread. The silk of his coat was slashed from the button across his chest. Blood oozed, dampening his shirt, trickled down his arm. Had he not twisted just at that moment, that arrow would have been through his heart instead of his arm. Maybe the other would have hit him as well, but the one would have done the job. A Two Rivers shaft would not have been deflected so easily.

Cairhienin and Tairens crowded around him as he dismounted, all of them trying to help him, which he did not need. He drew his belt knife, but Camaille took it from him and deftly scored the shaft so she could break it cleanly just above his arm. That sent a jolt of pain down his arm. She did not seem to mind getting blood on her fingers, just plucking a lace-edge handkerchief from her sleeve, a paler green than usual for Cairhienin, and wiping them, then examined the end of the shaft sticking out of his arm to make sure there were no splinters.

The Banner-General was down off her bay, too, and frowning. "My eyes are lowered that you have been injured, my Lord. I'd heard that there has been an increase in crime of late, arsons, robbers killing when there was no need, murders done for no reason anyone knows. I should have protected you better."

"Grit your teeth, my Lord," Barmanes said, tying a length of leather cord just above the arrowhead. "Are you ready, my Lord?" Perrin tightened his jaw and nodded, and Barmanes jerked the blood-stained shaft free. Perrin stifled a groan.

"Your eyes aren't lowered," he said hoarsely. Whatever that meant. It did not sound good, the way she said it. "Nobody asked you to wrap me in swaddling. I certainly never did." Neald pushed through the crowd surrounding Perrin, his hands already raised, but Perrin waved him away. "Not here, man. People can see." Folk in the street had finally noticed and were gathering to watch, murmuring excitedly to one another. "He can Heal this so you'd never know I was hurt," he explained, flexing his arm experimentally. He winced. That had been a bad idea.

"You'd let him use the One Power on you?" Tylee said disbelievingly.

"To be rid of a hole in my arm and a slice across my chest? As soon as we're somewhere half the town isn't staring at us. Wouldn't you?"

She shivered and made that peculiar gesture again. He was going to have to ask her what that meant.

Mishima joined them, leading his horse and looking grave. "Two men fell from that roof with bows and quivers," he said quietly, "but it wasn't that fall that killed them. They hit the pavement hard, yet there was hardly any blood. I think they took poison when they saw they'd failed to kill you."

"That doesn't make any sense," Perrin muttered.

"If men will kill themselves rather than report failure," Tylee said gravely, "it means you have a powerful enemy."

A powerful enemy? Very likely Masema would like to see him dead, but there was no way Masema's reach could extend this far. "Any enemies I have are far away and don't know where I am." Tylee and Mishima agreed that he must know about that, but they looked doubtful. Then again, there were always the Forsaken. Some of them had tried to kill him before. Others had tried to use him. He did not think he was going to bring the Forsaken into the discussion. His arm was throbbing. The cut on his chest, too. "Let's find an inn where I can hire a room." Fifty-one knots. How many more? Light, how many more?

CHAPTER
13

Siege

P ush them!" Elayne shouted. Fireheart tried to dance, impatient at being crowded in a narrow cobblestone street with other horses and women afoot, but she steadied the black gelding with a firm hand. Birgitte had insisted she remain well back. Insisted! As if she were a brainless fool! "Push them, burn you!"

None of the hundreds of men on the wide guardwalk atop the city wall, white-streaked gray stone rearing fifty feet, paid her any heed, of course. It was doubtful they heard her. Amid shouts of their own, curses and screams, the clash of steel rang over the broad street that ran alongside the wall beneath the noonday sun suspended in a rare cloudless sky as those men sweated and killed one another with sword or spear or halberd. The melee spanned two hundred paces of the wall, enveloping three of the high round towers where the White Lion of Andor flew and threatening two more, though all still seemed secure, thank the Light. Men stabbed and hacked and thrust, no one giving ground or quarter that she could see. Red-coated crossbowmen atop the towers did their share of killing, but once fired, a crossbow required time to ready for another shot, and they were too few to turn the tide in any case. They were the only Guardsmen up there. The rest were mercenaries. Save Birgitte.

This near, the bond let Elayne's eye find her Warder easily, intricate golden braid swaying as she shouted encouragement to her soldiers, pointing her bow to where reinforcement was needed. In her short white-collared red coat and wide sky-blue trousers tucked into her boots, she alone atop the wall wore no armor of any sort. She had insisted Elayne don plain gray in the hope of avoiding notice, and any effort to capture or kill her—some of the men up there had crossbows or shortbows slung on their backs, and for those not in the forefront and engaged, fifty paces made an easy shot—but the four golden knots of rank on her own shoulder would make Birgitte the target of any of Arymilla's men with eyes. At least she was not actually mingling in the press. At least she. . . .

Elayne's breath caught as a wiry fellow in breastplate and conical steel cap lunged at Birgitte with a sword, but the golden-haired woman dodged the thrust calmly—the bond said she might have been out for a hard ride, no more!—and a backhand blow with her bow caught the fellow on the side of his head, knocking him from the rampart. He had time to scream before he hit the paving stones with a sickening splat. His was not the only corpse decorating the street. Birgitte said men would not follow you unless they knew you were ready to face the same dangers and hardships they did, but if she got herself killed with this man-foolishness. . . .

Elayne did not realize she had heeled Fireheart forward until Caseille seized her bridle. "I am not an idiot, Guardswoman Lieutenant," she said frigidly. "I have no intention of going closer until it is . . . *safe.*"

The Arafellin woman jerked her hand back, her face becoming very still behind the face-bars of her burnished conical helmet. Instantly, Elayne felt sorry for the outburst—Caseille was just doing her job—but she still felt coldly angry, too. She would *not* apologize. Shame surged as she recognized the sulkiness of her own thoughts. Blood and bloody ashes, but there were times she wanted to slap Rand for planting these babes in her. These days, she could not be certain from one moment to the next which way her emotions would leap. Leap they did, however.

"If this is what happens to you when you get with child," Aviendha said, adjusting the dark shawl looped over her arms, "I think I will never have any." The high-cantled saddle of her dun pushed her bulky Aiel skirts high enough to bare her stockinged legs to the knee, but she showed no discomfort at the display. With the mare standing still, she looked quite at home on a horse. But then, Mageen, Daisy in the Old Tongue, was a gentle, placid animal tending to stoutness. Luckily, Aviendha was too ignorant of horses to realize that.

Muffled laughter pulled Elayne's head around. The women of her bodyguard, all twenty-one of them assigned this morning counting Caseille, in polished helmets and breastplates, wore smooth faces—much too smooth, in fact; without doubt they were laughing inside—but the four Kinswomen standing behind them had hands over their mouths and their heads together. Alise, a pleasant-faced woman normally, with touches of gray in her hair, saw her looking—well, glaring—and rolled her eyes ostentatiously, which set the others off in another round of laughter. Caiden, a plumply pretty Domani, laughed so hard she had to hold on to Kumiko, though the stout graying woman seemed to be having her own difficulties. Irritation stabbed at Elayne. Not at the laughter—all right, a little at the laughter—and certainly not at the Kinswomen. Not very much, at least. They were invaluable.

This fight on the wall was not Arymilla's first assault in recent weeks by far. In truth, the frequency was increasing, with three or four attacks coming some days, now. She knew very well that Elayne had insufficient soldiers to hold six leagues of wall. Burn her, Elayne was all too aware that she could not even spare trained hands to fit hoardings to all those miles of wall and towers. Untrained hands would only bungle the work. All Arymilla needed was to get enough men across to seize a gate. Then she could bring the battle into the city, where Elayne would be badly outnumbered. The population might rise in her favor, no certain thing, yet that only meant adding to the slaughter, apprentices and grooms and shopkeepers fighting trained armsmen and mercenaries. Whoever sat on the Lion Throne then—and very likely that would not be Elayne Trakand—it would be stained red with the blood of Caemlyn. So apart from holding the gates and leaving watchmen on the towers, she had pulled all of her soldiers back into the Inner City, close to the Royal Palace, and stationed men with looking glasses in the tallest spires of the palace. Whenever a watchman signaled an attack forming, linked Kinswomen made gateways to carry soldiers to the spot. They took no part in the fighting, of course. She would not have allowed them to use the Power as a weapon even had they been willing.

So far it had worked, though often by a hair. Low Caemlyn, outside
the walls, was a warren of houses, shops, inns and warehouses that allowed men to close before they were seen. Three times her soldiers had
been forced to fight on the ground inside the wall and to retake at least
one wall tower. Bloody work, that. She would have burned Low Caemlyn to the ground to deny Arymilla's people cover, except that the fire
might easily spread inside the walls and spawn a conflagration, spring
rains or no spring rains. As it was, every night saw arsons inside the
city, and containing those was difficult enough. Besides, people lived
in those houses despite the siege, and she did not want to be remembered as the one who had destroyed their homes and livelihoods. No,
what nettled her was that she had not thought of using the Kin that
way earlier. If she had, she would not be saddled with Sea Folk still,
not to mention a bargain that gave up a square mile of Andor. Light, a
square mile! Her mother had never given up one inch of Andor. Burn
her, this siege hardly gave her time to mourn her mother. Or Lini, her
old nursemaid. Rahvin had murdered her mother, and likely Lini had
died trying to protect her. White-haired and thin with age, Lini would
not have backed down even for one of the Forsaken. But thinking of
Lini made her hear the woman's reedy voice. *You can't put honey back in
the comb, child.* What was done, was done, and she had to live with it.

"That's it, then," Caseille said. "They're making for the ladders." It
was true. All along the wall Elayne's soldiers were pushing forward,
Arymilla's falling back, climbing through the crenels where their ladders were propped. Men still died on the rampart, but the fight was
ending.

Elayne surprised herself by digging her heels into Fireheart's
flanks. No one was quick enough to catch her this time. Pursued by
shouts, she galloped across the street and flung herself out of the saddle
at the base of the nearest tower before the gelding was fully halted.
Pushing open the heavy door, she gathered her divided skirts and raced
up the widdershins spiraling stairs, past large niches where clusters of
armored men stared in amazement as she darted by. These towers were
made to be defended against attackers trying to make their way down
and into the city. At last the stairs opened into a large room where
stairs on the other side spiraled upward in the opposite direction.
Twenty men in mismatched helmets and breastplates were taking their
ease, tossing dice, sitting against the wall, talking and laughing as if
there were no dead men beyond the room's two iron-strapped doors.

Whatever they were doing, they stopped to gape when she appeared.

"Uh, my Lady, I wouldn't do that," a rough voice said as she laid hands on the iron bar across one of the doors. Ignoring the man, she turned the bar on its pivot pin and pushed the door open. A hand caught at her skirt, but she pulled free.

None of Arymilla's men remained on the wall. None standing, at least. Dozens of men lay on the blood-streaked guardwalk, some still, others groaning. Any number of those might belong to Arymilla, but the ringing of steel had vanished. Most of the mercenaries were tending the wounded, or just squatting on their heels to catch their breath.

"Shake them off and pull up the bloody ladders!" Birgitte shouted. Loosing an arrow into the mass of men trying to flee down the dirt-paved Low Caemlyn street below the wall, she nocked another and fired again. "Make them build more if they want to come again!" Some of the mercenaries leaned through crenels to obey, but only a handful. "I knew I shouldn't have let you come along today," she went on, still loosing shafts as fast as she could nock and draw. Crossbow bolts from the towertops struck down men below as well, but tile-roofed warehouses offered shelter here for any who could get inside.

It took a moment for Elayne to realize that last comment had been directed at her, and her face heated. "And how would you have stopped me?" she demanded, drawing herself up.

Quiver empty, Birgitte lowered her bow and turned with a scowl. "By tying you up and having her sit on you," she said, nodding toward Aviendha, who was striding out of the tower. The glow of *saidar* surrounded her, yet her horn-hilted belt knife was in her fist. Caseille and the rest of the Guardswomen spilled out behind her, swords in hand and faces grim. Seeing Elayne unharmed changed their expressions not a whit. Those bloody women were insufferable when it came to treating her like a blown glass vase that might break at the rap of a knuckle. They would be worse than ever after this. And she would have to suffer it.

"I would have caught you," Aviendha muttered, rubbing her hip, "except that fool horse tossed me off." That was highly unlikely with such a placid mare. Aviendha had simply managed to fall off. Seeing the situation, she slipped her knife back into its sheath quickly, trying to pretend she had never had it out. The light of *saidar* vanished, too.

"I was quite safe." Elayne tried to remove the acerbic touch from her voice, without much success. "Min said I will bear my babes, sister.

Until they're born, no harm can come to me."

Aviendha nodded slowly, thoughtfully, but Birgitte growled, "I'd just as soon you didn't put her visions to the test. Take too many chances, and you might prove her wrong." That was foolish. Min was *never* wrong. Surely not.

"That was Aldin Miheres' company," a tall mercenary said in a lilting if rough Murandian accent as he removed his helmet to reveal a lean, sweaty face with gray-streaked mustaches waxed to spikes. Rhys a'Balaman, as he called himself, had eyes like stones and a thin-lipped smile that always seemed a leer. He had been listening to their conversation, and he kept darting sideways glances at Elayne while he talked to Birgitte. "I recognized him, I did. Good man, Miheres. I fought alongside him more times than I can number, I have. He'd almost made it to that warehouse door when your arrow took him in the neck, Captain-General. A shame, that."

Elayne frowned. "He made his choice as you did, Captain. You may regret the death of a friend, but I hope you aren't regretting your choice." Most of the mercenaries she had put out of the city, maybe all, had signed on with Arymilla. Her greatest fear at present was that the woman would succeed in bribing companies still inside the walls. None of the mercenary captains had reported anything, but Mistress Harfor said approaches had been made. Including an approach to a'Balaman.

The Murandian favored her with his leer and a formal bow, flourishing a cloak he was not wearing. "Oh, I fought against him as often as with, my Lady. I'd have killed him, or he'd have killed me, had we come face to face this fine day. More acquaintance than friend, you see. And I'd much rather take gold to defend a wall like this than to attack it."

"I notice some of your men have crossbows on their backs, Captain, but I didn't see any using them."

"Not the mercenary way," Birgitte said dryly. Irritation floated in the bond, though whether with a'Balaman or Elayne there was no way to know. The sensation vanished quickly. Birgitte had learned to master her emotions once they discovered how she and Elayne mirrored one another through the bond. Very likely she wished Elayne could do the same, but then, so did Elayne.

A'Balaman rested his helmet on his hip. "You see, my Lady, the way of it is, if you press a man too hard when he's trying to get off the field, attempting to ride him down and the like, well, the next time it's you trying to get off the field, he might return the favor. After all, if a man's leaving the field, then he's out of the fight, now isn't he?"

"Until he comes back tomorrow," Elayne snapped. "The next time, I want to see those crossbows put to work!"

"As you say, my Lady," a'Balaman said stiffly, making an equally stiff bow. "If you'll pardon me, I must be seeing to my men." He stalked off without waiting on her pardon, shouting to his men to stir their lazy stumps.

"How far can he be trusted?" Elayne asked softly.

"As far as any mercenary," Birgitte replied, just as quietly. "If someone offers him enough gold, it becomes a toss of the dice, and not even Mat Cauthon could say how they'll land."

That was a very odd remark. She wished she knew how Mat was. And dear Thom. And poor little Olver. Every night she offered prayers that they had escaped the Seanchan safely. There was nothing she could do to help them, though. She had enough on her plate trying to help herself at the moment. "Will he obey me? About the crossbows?"

Birgitte shook her head, and Elayne sighed. It was bad to give orders that would not be obeyed. It put people in the habit of disobeying.

Moving close, she spoke in a near whisper. "You look tired, Birgitte." This was nothing for anyone else's ears. Birgitte's face was tight, her eyes haggard. Anyone could see that, but the bond said she was bone-weary, as it had for days now. But then, Elayne felt that same dragging tiredness, as though her limbs were made of lead. Their bond mirrored more than emotions. "You don't have to lead every counter-attack yourself."

"And who else is there?" For a moment weariness larded Birgitte's voice, too, and her shoulders actually slumped, but she straightened quickly and strengthened her tone. It was pure willpower. Elayne could feel it, stone hard in the bond, so hard she wanted to weep. "My officers are inexperienced boys," Birgitte went on, "or else men who came out of retirement and should still be warming their bones in front of their grandchildren's fireplace. Except for the mercenary captains, anyway, and there isn't one I'd trust without someone looking over his shoulder. Which brings us back to: Who else but me?"

Elayne opened her mouth to argue. Not about the mercenaries. Birgitte had explained about them, bitterly and at great length. At times, mercenaries would fight as hard as any Guardsman, but other times, they pulled back rather than take too many casualties. Fewer men meant less gold for their next hire unless they could be replaced with men as good. Battles that could have been won had been lost instead because mercenaries left the field to preserve their numbers. They disliked doing it if anybody except their own kind was watching, though. That spoiled their reputation and lowered their hire price. But there had to be someone else. She could not afford Birgitte falling over from exhaustion. Light, she wished Gareth Bryne were there. Egwene needed him, but so did she. She opened her mouth, and suddenly rumbling booms crashed from the city behind her. She turned, and her mouth stayed open, gaping in astonishment, now.

Where moments before there had been clear sky over the Inner City, a huge mass of black clouds loomed like sheer-sided mountains, forked lightning slashing down through a gray wall of rain that seemed as solid as the city walls. The gilded domes of the Royal Palace that should have been glittering in the sun were invisible behind that wall. That torrent fell only over the Inner City. Everywhere else the sky remained bright and cloudless. There was nothing natural in that. Amazement lasted only moments, though. That silver-blue lightning, three-tined, five-tined, was striking inside Caemlyn, causing damage and maybe deaths. How had those clouds come to be? She reached to embrace *saidar*, to disperse them. The True Source slipped away from her, and then again. It was like trying to grasp a bead buried in a pot of grease. Just when she thought she had it, it squirted away. It was like this far too often, now.

"Aviendha, will you deal with that, please?"

"Of course," Aviendha replied, embracing *saidar* easily. Elayne stifled a surge of jealousy. Her difficulty was Rand's bloody fault, not her sister's. "And thank you. I need the practice."

That was untrue, an attempt to spare her feelings. Aviendha began weaving Air, Fire, Water and Earth in complex patterns, and doing so nearly as smoothly as she herself could have, if much more slowly. Her sister lacked her skill with weather, but then, she had not had the advantage of Sea Folk teaching. The clouds did not simply vanish, of course. First the lightnings became single bolts, dwindled in number, then ceased. That was the hardest part. Calling lightning was twirling a feather between your fingers compared to stopping it. That was more like picking up a blacksmith's anvil in your hands. Then the clouds began to spread out, to thin and grow paler. That was slow, too. Doing too much too fast with weather could cause effects that rippled across the countryside for leagues, and you never knew what the effects might be. Raging storms and flash floods were as likely as balmy days and gentle breezes. By the time the clouds had spread far enough to reach the outer walls of Caemlyn, they were gray and dropping a steady, soaking downpour that quickly slicked Elayne's curls to her scalp.

"Is that enough?" Smiling, Aviendha turned her face up to let the rain run down her cheeks. "I love to watch water falling from the sky." Light, you would think she had had enough of rain. It had rained nearly every bloody day since spring came!

"It's time to be getting back to the palace, Elayne," Birgitte said, tucking her bowstring into her coat pocket. She had begun unstringing her bow as soon as the clouds began moving toward them. "Some of these men need a sister's attention. And my breakfast seems two days past."

Elayne scowled. The bond carried a wariness that told her all she needed to know. They must return to the palace to get Elayne, in her delicate condition, out of the rain. As if she might melt! Abruptly she became aware of the groans from the wounded, and her face grew hot. Those men *did* need a sister's attention. Even if she could hold on to *saidar*, the least of their injuries were beyond her modest abilities, and Aviendha was no better at Healing.

"Yes, it *is* time," she said. If only she could get her emotions back under control! Birgitte would be pleased at that, too. Spots of color decorated her cheeks, too, echoes of Elayne's shame. They looked very odd with the frown she wore as she hurried Elayne into the tower.

Fireheart and Mageen and the other horses were all standing patiently where their reins had been dropped, as Elayne expected. Even Mageen was well trained. They had the wall street utterly to themselves until Alise and the other Kin walked out of the narrower way. There was not a cart or wagon to be seen. Every door in sight was tightly shut, every window curtained, though there might well be no one behind any of them. Most people had had sense enough to leave as soon they caught a glimmering that hundreds of men were about to start swinging swords in their vicinity. One curtain twitched; a woman's face showed for a moment, then vanished. Some others took ghoulish delight in watching.

Talking quietly among themselves, the four Kinswomen took their places where they had opened their gateway some hours earlier. They eyed the corpses in the street and shook their heads, but these were not the first dead men they had seen. Not one would have been allowed to test for Accepted, yet they were calm, sure of themselves, as dignified as sisters despite the rain soaking their hair and dresses. Learning Egwene's plans for the Kin, to be associated with the Tower and a place for Aes Sedai to retire, had lessened their fears over their future, especially once they found out that their Rule would remain in place and the former Aes Sedai would have to follow it, too. Not all believed—over the last month, seven of their number had run away without leaving so much as a note—yet most did, and took strength from belief. Having work to do had restored their pride. Elayne had not realized that had been dented until they stopped seeing themselves as refugees wholly dependent on her. They held themselves straighter, now. Worry had vanished from their faces. And they were not so quick to bend their necks for a sister, unfortunately. Though that part of it really had begun earlier. They once had considered Aes Sedai superior to mortal flesh, but had learned to their dismay that the shawl did not make a woman more than she was without it.

Alise eyed Elayne, compressing her lips for a moment and adjusting her brown skirts unnecessarily. She had argued against Elayne being allowed—allowed!—to come here. And Birgitte had almost given way! Alise was a forceful woman. "Are you ready for us, Captain-General?" she said.

"We are," Elayne said, but Alise waited until Birgitte nodded before linking with the other three Kinswomen. She ignored Elayne after that one glance. Really, Nynaeve should never have begun trying to "put some backbone into them," as she had put it. When she could lay hands on Nynaeve again, she was going to have words with the woman.

The familiar vertical slash appeared and seemed to rotate into a view of the main stableyard in the palace, a hole in the air nearly four paces by four, but the view through the opening, of the tall arched doors of one of the white marble stables, was a little off-center from what she expected. When she rode onto the rain-drenched flagstones of the stableyard, she saw why. There was another gateway, slightly smaller, open. If you tried to open a gateway where one already existed, yours was displaced just enough that the two did not touch, though the gap between was thinner than a razor's edge. From that other gateway a twinned column of men seemed to be riding out of the stable-yard's outer wall, curving away to exit the stableyard through the open iron-strapped gates. Some wore burnished helmets and breastplates or plate-and-mail, but every man had on the white-collared red coat of the Queen's Guard. A tall, broad-shouldered man with two golden knots on the left shoulder of his red coat stood in the rain watching them, helmet balanced on his hip.

"That's a sight to soothe sore eyes," Birgitte murmured. Small groups of Kinswomen were scouring the countryside for anyone trying to come to Elayne's support, but it was a chancy business. Thus far, the Kinswomen had brought word of dozens and dozens of groups trying to find a way into the city, yet they had only managed to locate five bands totaling fewer than a thousand. Word had spread of how many men Arymilla had around the city, and men supporting Trakand were skittish about being found. About who might do the finding.

As soon as Elayne and the others appeared, red-clad grooms with the White Lion on their left shoulders came running. A scrawny, gap-toothed fellow with a fringe of white hair took Fireheart's bridle while a lean, graying woman held Elayne's stirrup for her to dismount. Ignoring the downpour, she strode toward the tall man, splashing water with every step. His hair hung every which way over his face, clinging wetly, but she could see he was young, well short of his middle years.

"The Light shine on you, Lieutenant," she said. "Your name? How many did you bring? And from where?" Through that smaller opening she could see a line of horsemen extending out of sight among tall trees. Whenever a pair rode through, another appeared at the far end of the column. She would not have believed that many of the Guards remained anywhere.

"Charlz Guybon, my Queen," he replied, sinking to one knee and pressing a gauntleted fist to the flagstones. "Captain Kindlin in Aringill gave me permission to try reaching Caemlyn. That was after we learned Lady Naean and the others had escaped."

Elayne laughed. "Stand, man. Stand. I'm not Queen yet." Aringill? There had never been so many of the Guards there.

"As you say, my Lady," he said as he regained his feet and made a bow that was more proper for the Daughter-Heir.

"Can we continue this inside?" Birgitte put in irritably. Guybon took in her coat with its gold stripes on the cuffs and knots of rank, and offered a salute that she returned with a quick arm across her chest. If he was surprised to see a woman as Captain-General, he was wise enough not to show it. "I'm soaked to the skin, and so are you, Elayne." Aviendha was right behind her, shawl wrapped around her head and not looking so pleased with rain now that her white blouse clung wetly and her dark skirts hung with water. The Guardswomen were leading their horses toward one of the stables, except for the eight who would remain with Elayne until their replacements arrived. Guybon made no comment on them, either. A very wise man.

Elayne allowed herself to be hustled as far as the simple colonnade that offered entrance to the palace itself. Even here the Guardswomen surrounded her, four ahead and four behind, so she felt a prisoner. Once out of the rain, though, she balked. She wanted to *know*. She tried again to embrace *saidar*—removing the moisture from her clothes would be a simple matter with the Power—but the Source skittered away once more. Aviendha did not know the weave, so they had to stand there dripping. The plain iron stand-lamps along the wall were still unlit, and with the rain, the space was dim. Guybon raked his hair into a semblance of order with his fingers. Light, he was little short of beautiful! His greenish hazel eyes were tired, but his face seemed suited to smiling. He looked as if he had not smiled in too long.

"Captain Kindlin said I could try to find men who'd been discharged by Gaebril, my Lady, and they started flocking in as soon as I put out the call. You'd be surprised how many tucked their uniforms into a chest against the day they might be wanted again. A good many carried off their armor, too, which they shouldn't have done, strictly speaking, but I'm glad they did. I feared I'd waited too long when I heard of the siege. I was considering trying to fight my way to one of the city gates when Mistress Zigane and the others found me." A puzzled look came over his face. "She became very upset when I called her Aes Sedai, but that has to be the One Power that brought us here."

"It was, and she isn't," Elayne said impatiently. "How many, man?"

"Four thousand seven hundred and sixty-two of the Guards, my Lady. And I encountered a number of lords and ladies who were trying to reach Caemlyn with their armsmen. Be content. I made sure they were loyal to you before I let them join me. There are none from the great Houses, but they bring the total near to ten thousand, my Lady." He said that as if it were of no moment at all. There are forty horses fit for riding in the stable. I have brought you ten thousand soldiers.

Elayne laughed and clapped her hands in delight. "Wonderful, Captain Guybon! Wonderful!" Arymilla still had her outnumbered, but not so badly as before.

"Guardsman Lieutenant, my Lady. I am a Lieutenant."

"From this moment, you are Captain Guybon."

"And my second," Birgitte added, "at least for the present. You've shown resourcefulness, you're old enough to have experience, and I need both."

Guybon seemed overwhelmed, bowing and murmuring stammered thanks. Well, a man of his age would normally expect to serve at least ten or fifteen more years before being considered for captain, much less second to the Captain-General, however temporary.

"And now it's past time for us to be getting into dry clothes," Birgitte continued. "Especially you, Elayne." The Warder bond carried an implacable firmness that suggested she might try dragging Elayne if she dallied.

Temper flared, hot and sharp, but Elayne fought it down. She had nearly doubled the number of her soldiers, and she would not let anything spoil this day. Besides, she wanted dry clothes, too.

CHAPTER
14

Wet Things

I nside, the gilded stand-lamps were lit, since daylight never penetrated far into the palace, flames flickering on the lamps that lacked
glass mantles. The lamps' mirrors provided a good light in the
bustling corridor, though, and bustling it was, with liveried servants
scurrying in every direction, or sweeping or mopping. Serving men
with the White Lion on the left breast of their red coats were up on tall
ladders taking down the winter tapestries, mainly flowers and scenes of
summer, and putting up the spring tapestries, many displaying the
colorful foliage of fall. Always two seasons ahead for the majority of the
hangings was the custom, to provide a touch of relief from winter's
cold or summer's heat, to remind while spring's new growth was on all
the trees that the branches would grow bare and the snows come again,
to remind when dead leaves were falling and the first snows, too, and
days grew ever colder, that there would be a spring. There were a few
battles among them, showing days of particular glory for Andor, but
Elayne did not enjoy looking at those as much as she had as a girl. Still,
they had their place now, as well, tokens of what battle actually was.
The difference between how a child looked at things and a woman did.
Glory was always bought with blood. Glory aside, necessary things
were often paid for with battle and blood.

There were too few servants to carry out such tasks in a timely manner, and a fair number were white-haired pensioners with bent backs who seldom moved quickly in any case. However slow they were, she was glad they had willingly come out of retirement, to train those newly hired and take up the slack left by those who had fled while Gaebril reigned or after Rand took Caemlyn, else the palace would have taken on the aspect of a barn by this time. A dirty barn. At least all of the winter runners were up off the floors. She left a damp trail behind her on the red-and-white floor tiles, and with all the spring rains, wet runners would have been sprouting mildew before nightfall.

Servants in red-and-white hurrying about their duties looked aghast as they bowed or curtsied, which did nothing for her temper. They did not appear upset to see Aviendha or Birgitte drenched and dripping, or the Guardswomen either. Burn her, if everyone did not stop expecting her to be mollycoddled all the day long. . . ! Her scowl was such that the servants began making their courtesies quickly and scurrying on. Her temper was becoming the stuff of evening stories in front of the fireplace, though she tried not to unleash it on servants. On anyone, really, but more so with servants. They lacked the luxury of shouting back.

She intended to go straight to her apartments and change, but intentions or no, she turned aside when she saw Reanne Corly walking in a crossing corridor where the floor tiles were all red. The servants' reactions had nothing to do with it. She was *not* being stubborn. She was wet, and she wanted dry clothing and a warm towel in the worst way, but seeing the Kinswoman was a surprise, and the two women with Reanne also caught her eye. Birgitte muttered a curse before following her, swishing her bowstave sideways through the air as though thinking of striking someone. The bond carried a blend of long-suffering and irritability, soon stifled. Aviendha never left Elayne's side, though busily trying to wring water out of her shawl. Despite all the rain she had seen, all the rivers since crossing the Spine of the World and the great cisterns beneath the city, Aviendha winced at the waste, the water splashing uselessly on the floor. The eight Guardswomen, left behind by her sudden swerve, hurried to catch up, stolid and silent except for the stamp of their boots on the floor tiles. Give anyone a sword and boots, and they began stamping.

One of the women with Reanne was Kara Defane, who had been the wise woman, or Healer, of a fishing village on Toman Head before the Seanchan collared her. Plump and merry-eyed in brown wool with embroidered blue and white flowers at her cuffs, Kara appeared little older than Elayne, though she was nearly fifty. The other was named Jillari, a former *damane* from Seanchan. Despite everything, the sight of her made Elayne's flesh feel cold. Whatever else could be said of her, the woman was Seanchan, after all.

Not even Jillari herself knew how old she was, though she appeared just into her middle years. Slight of build, with long, fiery red hair and eyes as green as Aviendha's, she and Marille, the other Seanchan-born *damane* who remained in the palace, persisted in maintaining that they still were *damane*, that they needed to be collared because of what they could do. Daily walks were one way the Kin were trying to accustom them to freedom. Carefully supervised walks, of course. They were always closely watched, day and night. Either might try to free the *sul'dam*, otherwise. For that matter, Kara herself was not trusted alone with any of the *sul'dam*, nor was Lemore, a young Taraboner noble collared when Tanchico fell. The notion would not come to them on its own, yet there was no saying what either would do if a *sul'dam* ordered her to help the woman escape. The habit of obedience remained strong in Kara and Lemore both.

Jillari's eyes widened at the sight of Elayne, and she immediately fell to her knees with a thud. She tried to fold herself into a bundle on the floor, but Kara caught her shoulders and gently urged her back to her feet. Elayne tried not to let her distaste show. And hoped that if it did, everyone would take it for the kneeling and crouching. Some of it was. How could anyone *want* to be collared? She heard Lini's voice again, and shivered. *You can't know another woman's reasons until you've worn her dress for a year.* Burn her if she had any desire to do that!

"No need for all that," Kara said. "This is what we do." She curtsied, not very gracefully. She had never seen a town larger than a few hundred people before the Seanchan took her. After a moment, the red-haired woman spread her own dark blue skirts more awkwardly still. She almost fell over, in fact, and blushed a bright crimson.

"Jillari is sorry," she almost whispered, folding her hands at her waist. Her eyes, she kept meekly directed at the floor. "Jillari will try to remember."

" 'I,' " Kara said. "Remember what I told you? I call you Jillari, but you call yourself 'I' or 'me.' Try it. And look at me. You can do it." She sounded as though she were encouraging a child.

The Seanchan woman wet her lips, giving Kara a sidelong look.

"I," she said softly. And promptly began weeping, tears rolling down her cheeks faster than she could wipe them away with her fingers. Kara enveloped her in a hug and made soothing noises. She seemed about to cry, too. Aviendha shifted uncomfortably. It was not the tears—men or women, Aiel wept unashamed when they felt the need—but for them, touching hands was a great display in public.

"Why don't you two walk on alone for a while," Reanne told the pair with a comforting smile that deepened the fine lines at the corners of her blue eyes. Her voice was high and lovely, suitable for singing. "I'll catch you up, and we can eat together." They offered her curtsies, too, Jillari still weeping, and turned away with Kara's arm around the smaller woman's shoulders. "If you care to, my Lady," Reanne said before they had gone two steps, "we could talk on the way to your apartments."

The woman's face was calm, and her tone put no special freight on the words, yet Elayne's jaw tightened. She forced it to relax. There was no point in being stubborn stupid. She *was* wet. And beginning to shiver, though the day could hardly be called cold. "An excellent suggestion," she said, gathering her sodden gray skirts. "Come."

"We could walk a little faster," Birgitte muttered, not quite far enough under her breath.

"We could run," Aviendha said, without trying to keep her voice low at all. "We might get dry from the exertion."

Elayne ignored them and glided at a suitable pace. In her mother, it would have been called regal. She was not sure she managed that, but she was not about to run through the palace. Or even hurry. The sight of her rushing would start a dozen rumors if not a hundred, each one of some dire event worse than the one before. Too many rumors floated on every breath of air as it was. The worst was that the city was about to fall, that she planned to flee before it did. No, she would be seen to be utterly unruffled. Everyone had to believe her completely confident. Even if that was a false facade. Anything else, and she might as well yield to Arymilla. Fear of defeat had lost as many battles as weakness had, and she could not afford to lose a single one. "I thought the Captain-General had you out scouting, Reanne."

Birgitte had been using two of the Kin for scouts, women who could not make a gateway large enough to admit a horse cart, but with circles of Kinswomen available to make gateways, for trade as well as moving soldiers, she had coopted the remaining six who could Travel on their own. An encircling army was no impediment to them. Yet Reanne's well-cut, fine blue wool, though unadorned save for a red-enameled circle pin on the high neck, was decidedly unsuited for skulking about the countryside.

"The Captain-General believes her scouts need rest. Unlike herself," Reanne added blandly, raising an eyebrow at Birgitte. The bond carried a brief flash of annoyance. Aviendha laughed for some reason; Elayne still did not understand Aiel humor. "Tomorrow, I go out again. It takes me back to the days long ago when I was a pack-peddler with one mule." The Kin all followed many crafts during their long lives, always changing location and craft before anyone took note of how slowly they aged. The oldest among them had mastered half a dozen crafts or more, shifting from one to another easily. "I decided to use my freeday helping Jillari settle on a surname." Reanne grimaced. "It's custom in Seanchan to strike a girl's name from her family's rolls when she's collared, and the poor woman feels she has no right to the name she was born with. Jillari was given with the collar, but she wants to keep that."

"There are more reasons to hate the Seanchan than I can count," Elayne said heatedly. Then, belatedly, she caught up to the import of it all. Learning to curtsy. Choosing a new surname. Burn her, if pregnancy was making her slow-witted on top of everything else. . . ! "When did Jillari change her mind about the collar?" There was no reason to let everyone know she was being dense today.

The other woman's expression did not alter a whit, but she hesitated just long enough to let Elayne know her deception had failed. "Just this morning, after you and the Captain-General left, or you'd have been informed." Reanne hurried on so the point had no time to fester. "And there's other news as good. At least, it's somewhat good. One of the *sul'dam*, Marli Noichin—you recall her?—has admitted seeing the weaves."

"Oh, that *is* good news," Elayne murmured. "Very good. Twenty-eight more to go, but they might be easier now that one of them has broken." She had watched an attempt to convince Marli that she could learn to channel, that she could already see weaves of the Power. The plump Seanchan woman had been stubbornly defiant even after she began crying.

"Somewhat good, I said." Reanne sighed. "In Marli's opinion, she might as well have admitted she kills children. Now she insists that she must be collared. She *begs* for the *a'dam*. It makes my skin creep. I don't know what to do with her."

"Send her back to the Seanchan as soon as we can," Elayne replied.

Reanne stopped dead in shock, her eyebrows climbing. Birgitte cleared her throat loudly—impatience filled the bond before being stifled—and the Kinswoman gave a start, then began walking again, at a faster pace than before. "But they'll make her a *damane*. I can't condemn any woman to that."

Elayne gave her Warder a look that slid off like a dagger sliding off good armor. Birgitte's expression was . . . bland. To the golden-haired woman, being a Warder contained strong elements of older sister. And worse, sometimes mother.

"*I* can," she said emphatically, lengthening her own stride. Well, it would not hurt to get dry a little sooner rather than later. "She helped hold enough others prisoner that she deserves a taste of it herself, Reanne. But that's not why I mean to send her back. If any of the others wants to stay and learn, and make up for what she's done, I certainly won't hand her to the Seanchan, but Light's truth, I hope they all feel like Marli. They'll put an *a'dam* on her, Reanne, but they won't be able to keep secret who she was. Every one-time *sul'dam* I can send the Seanchan to collar will be a mattock digging at their roots."

"A harsh decision," Reanne said sadly. She plucked at her skirts in an agitated manner, smoothed them, then plucked at them again. "Perhaps you might consider thinking on it for a few days? Surely it isn't anything that has to be done immediately."

Elayne gritted her teeth. The woman had as much as implied that she had reached this decision in one of her swinging moods! But had she? It seemed reasonable and logical. They could not keep the *sul'dam* imprisoned forever. Sending those who did not *want* to be free back to the Seanchan was a way to be rid of them and strike a blow at the Seanchan at the same time. It *was* more than hatred of any Seanchan. Of course, it was. Burn her, but she bloody well hated being unsure whether her own decisions were sound! She could not afford to make unsound decisions. Still, there was no hurry. Better to send back a group, if possible, in any event. There was less chance of someone arranging an "accident," that way. She did not put that sort of thing past the Seanchan. "I will think on it, Reanne, but I doubt I'll change my mind."

Reanne sighed again, deeply. Eager for her promised return to the

White Tower and novice white—she had been heard to say she envied Kirstian and Zarya—she wanted very much to enter the Green Ajah, but Elayne had her doubts. Reanne was kindhearted, softhearted in fact, and Elayne had never met any Green who could be called soft. Even those who seemed frilly or frail on the surface were cold steel inside.

Ahead of them, Vandene glided from a crossing corridor, slender, white-haired and graceful in dark gray wool with deep brown trim, and turned in the same direction they were going, apparently without noticing them. She was Green, and as hard as a hammerhead. Jaem, her Warder, walked beside her, head bent in close conversation, now and then raking a hand through his thinning gray hair. Gnarled and lean, his dark green coat hanging loose on him, he was old, but every scrap as hard as she, an old root that could dull axes. Kirstian and Zarya, both in plain novice white, followed meekly with their hands folded at their waists, the one pale as a Cairhienin, the other short and slim-hipped. For runaways who had succeeded in what so few did, remaining free of the White Tower for years, over three hundred years in Kirstian's case, they had resettled into their places as novices with remarkable ease. But then, the Kin's Rule was a blending of the rules that governed novices and those that Accepted lived by. Perhaps, to them, the white woolen dresses and the loss of freedom to come and go as they chose were the only real change, though the Kin regulated that last to some extent.

"I'm very glad she has those two to occupy her," Reanne murmured in tones of sympathy. Pained caring shone in her eyes. "It's good that she mourns her sister, but I fear she'd be obsessed with Adeleas' death without Kirstian and Zarya. She may be anyway. I believe that dress she's wearing belonged to Adeleas. I've tried offering solace—I have experience helping people overcome grief; I've been a village Wise Woman as well as wearing the red belt in Ebou Dar many years ago—but she won't give me two words."

In fact, Vandene wore *only* her dead sister's clothing, now, and Adeleas' flowery perfume, as well. At times, Elayne thought Vandene was trying to become Adeleas, to offer up herself in order to bring her sister back to life. But could you fault someone for being obsessed with finding who had murdered her sister? Not that more than a handful of people knew that was what she was doing. Everyone else believed as Reanne did, that she was absorbed with teaching Kirstian and Zarya, that and beginning their punishment for running away. Vandene was doing both, of course, and with a will, yet it was really just a cover for her true purpose.

Elayne reached out without looking, and found Aviendha's hand waiting to take hers, a comforting grip. She squeezed back, unable to imagine the grief of losing Aviendha. They shared a quick glance, and Aviendha's eyes mirrored her own feelings. Had she really once thought Aiel faces impassive and unreadable?

"As you say, Reanne, she has Kirstian and Zarya to occupy her." Reanne was not among the handful who knew the truth. "We all mourn in our own way. Vandene will find solace along her own path."

When she found Adeleas' murderer, it was to be hoped. If that failed to at least begin assuaging the pain. . . . Well, that was to be faced when it must be. For now, she must allow Vandene her head. Especially since she had no doubt the Green would ignore any attempt to rein her in. That was more than irritating; it was infuriating. She had to watch Vandene perhaps destroying herself, and worse, make use of it. Having no alternative made that no less unpalatable.

As Vandene and her companions turned aside down another hallway, Reene Harfor appeared out of a side corridor right in front of Elayne, a stout, quiet woman with a graying bun atop her head and an air of regal dignity, her formal scarlet tabard with the White Lion of Andor as always looking freshly ironed. Elayne had never seen her with a hair out of place or looking even slightly the worse for a long day spent overseeing the workings of the palace. And more besides. Her round face appeared puzzled for some reason, but it took on a look of concern at the sight of Elayne. "Why, my Lady, you're drenched," she said, sounding shocked, as she made her curtsy. "You need to get out of those wet things right away."

"Thank you, Mistress Harfor," Elayne said through her teeth. "I hadn't noticed."

She regretted the outburst instantly—the First Maid had been as faithful to her as to her mother—but what made matters worse was that Mistress Harfor took her flare-up in stride, never so much as blinking. Elayne Trakand's moods were no longer anything to be surprised at.

"I will walk with you if I may, my Lady," she said calmly, falling in at Elayne's side. A freckled young serving woman carrying a basket of folded bed linens began to offer her courtesies, only a hair more directed at Elayne than the First Maid, but Reene made a quick gesture that sent the girl scurrying before she completed bending her knees. Perhaps it was just to keep her from overhearing. Reene did not stop talking. "Three of the mercenary captains are demanding to meet with you. I put them in the Blue Reception Room, and told the servants to keep watch so no small valuables accidentally fall into their pockets. Not that I had to, as it turned out. Careane Sedai and Sareitha Sedai appeared soon after and settled in to keep the captains company. Captain Mellar is with them, too."

Elayne frowned. Mellar. She was trying to keep him too busy for mischief, yet he had a way of turning up where and when she least wanted him. For that matter, so did Careane and Sareitha. One of them had to be the Black Ajah killer. Unless it was Merilille, and she was beyond reach, it seemed. Reene knew about that. Keeping her in the dark would have been criminal. She had eyes everywhere, and they might notice a vital clue. "What do the mercenaries want, Mistress Harfor?"

"More money, is my guess," Birgitte growled, and swung her unstrung bow like a club.

"Most likely," Reene agreed, "but they refused to tell me." Her mouth tightened slightly. No more than that, yet it seemed these mercenaries had managed to offend her. If they were stupid enough not to see that she was more than a superior serving woman, then they were very dense indeed.

"Has Dyelin returned?" Elayne asked, and when the First Maid said not, added, "Then I will see these mercenaries as soon as I've changed clothes." She might as well get them out of the way.

Rounding a corner, she found herself face-to-face with two of the Windfinders and barely suppressed a sigh. The Sea Folk were the last people on earth she wanted to confront right then. Lean and dark and barefoot in red brocaded silk trousers and a blue brocaded silk blouse with a green sash tied in an elaborate knot, Chanelle din Seran White Shark was aptly named. Elayne had no idea what a white shark looked like—it might well have been a little thing—but Chanelle's big eyes were hard enough to belong on a fierce predator, especially when she took in Aviendha. There was bad blood, there. A tattooed hand raised the gold piercework scent box hanging on a chain about Chanelle's neck, and she inhaled the sharp, spicy scent deeply, as though covering some foul odor. Aviendha laughed out loud, which made Chanelle's full lips grow thin. Thinner, at least. Thin was beyond them.

The other was Renaile din Calon, once Windfinder to the Mistress of the Ships, in blue linen trousers and a red blouse sashed with blue, tied in a much less intricate knot. Both women wore the long white mourning stoles for Nesta din Reas, yet Renaile must have felt Nesta's death most keenly. She was carrying a carved wooden writing box with a capped ink jar set in one corner and a sheet of paper with a few scrawled lines clipped to its top. Wings of white in her black hair hid the six gold earrings in her ears, much thinner rings than the eight she had worn before learning of Nesta's fate, and the gold honor chain crossing her dark left cheek looked stark supporting only the medallion that named her clan. After Sea Folk custom, Nesta's death had meant starting over for Renaile, with no more rank than a woman raised from apprentice on the day she herself had put off her honors. Her face still held dignity, though much subdued now that she was acting as Chanelle's secretary.

"I am on my way—" Elayne began, but Chanelle cut her off imperiously.

"What news do you have of Talaan? And of Merilille. Are you even trying to find them?"

Elayne took a deep breath. Shouting at Chanelle never did any good. The woman was more than willing to shout back and seldom willing to listen to reason. She would *not* engage in another screaming match. Servants slipping by to either side did not pause to offer bows or curtsies—they could sense the mood here—but they shot grim looks at the Sea Folk women. That was pleasing, though it should not have been. However upsetting they were, the Windfinders were guests. In a way, they were, bargain or no bargain. Chanelle had complained more than once of slow-footed servants and tepid bathwater. And that was pleasing, too. Still, she would maintain her dignity, and civility.

"The news is the same as yesterday," she replied in tones of moderation. Well, she attempted tones of moderation. If traces of sharpness remained, the Windfinder would have to live with them. "The same as last week, and the week before that. Inquiries have been made at every inn in Caemlyn. Your apprentice is not to be found. Merilille is not to be found. It seems they must have managed to leave the city." The gate guards had been warned to watch for a Sea Folk woman with tattooed hands, but they would not have tried to stop an Aes Sedai leaving, or taking anyone with her that she wanted. For that matter, the mercenaries would let anyone at all pass who offered a few coins. "And now, if you will excuse me, I am on my way—"

"That is not good enough." Chanelle's voice was hot enough to singe leather. "You Aes Sedai stick together as tightly as oysters. Merilille kidnapped Talaan, and I think you are hiding her. We will search for them, and I assure you, when we find them, Merilille will be punished sharply before she is sent to the ships to fulfill her part of the bargain."

"You seem to be forgetting yourself," Birgitte said. Her voice was mild, her face calm, but the bond quivered with anger. She held her bowstave propped in front of her with both hands as if to keep them from making fists. "You'll withdraw your accusations, or you'll suffer for it." Perhaps she was not as self-controlled as she seemed. This was no way to go on with Windfinders. They were women of power among their own people, and accustomed to wielding it. But Birgitte did not hesitate. "By the bargain Zaida made, you're under the Lady Elayne's authority. You're under *my* authority. Any searching you do will be when you aren't needed. And unless I misremember badly, you're supposed to be in Tear right now to bring back wagonloads of grain and salt beef. I strongly suggest you Travel there immediately, or you might learn a little about punishment yourself." Oh, that was entirely the wrong way with Windfinders.

"No," Elayne said as hotly as Chanelle, surprising herself. "Search if you wish, Chanelle, you and all of the Windfinders. Search Caemlyn from end to end. And when you can't find Talaan or Merilille, you *will* apologize for calling me a liar." Well, the woman *had*. As good as, anyway. She felt a strong desire to slap Chanelle. She wanted to. . . . Light, her anger and Birgitte's were feeding each other! Frantically she tried to soothe her fury before it burst into open rage, but the only result was a sudden longing to weep that she had to fight just as wildly.

Chanelle drew herself up, scowling. "You would claim we had reneged on the bargain. We have labored like bilge girls this past month and more. You will not cast us off without meeting your side of the bargain. Renaile, the Aes Sedai at The Silver Swan are to be told—told, mind!—that they must produce Merilille and Talaan or else pay what the White Tower owes themselves. They cannot pay all, but they can make a start."

Renaile began unscrewing the silver cap of the ink jar.

"Not a note," Chanelle snapped. "Go yourself and tell them. Now."

Tightening the cap, Renaile bowed almost parallel to the floor, quickly touching fingertips to her heart. "As you command," she mur-

mured, her face a dark mask. She did not delay in obeying, setting out
at a trot the way she had come with the writing box tucked under her
arm.

Still fighting the desire to strike Chanelle and weep at the same
time, Elayne winced. This was not the first time the Sea Folk had gone
to The Silver Swan, nor even the second or third, but always before
they had gone asking, not demanding. There were nine sisters resident
at the inn at present—the number kept changing as sisters entered the
city or left, and rumor said there were other Aes Sedai in the city,
too—and it worried her that none had appeared at the palace. She had
stayed clear of the Swan—she knew how much Elaida wanted to lay
hands on her, but not who the sisters at the Swan supported, or
whether they supported anyone; they had been closemouthed as mus-
sels with Sareitha and Careane—yet she had expected some of them to
come to the palace if only to learn what was behind the Sea Folk's
claim. Why were so many Aes Sedai in Caemlyn when Tar Valon itself
was under siege? She herself was the first answer that came to mind,
and that made her more determined to avoid any sister she did not personally know to be a supporter of Egwene. But that would not stop
word of the bargain made for aid in using the Bowl of the Winds from
spreading, and of the price the Tower had been committed to pay for
that help. Burn her, but that news would be a bloody wagonload of
fireworks going off at once when it became general knowledge among
Aes Sedai. Worse. Ten wagonloads.

Watching Renaile trot away, she fought to steady her emotions.
And tried to bring the tone back to something approaching civility.
"She handles her change in circumstances very well, I think."

Chanelle gave a dismissive puff. "And well she should. Every
Windfinder knows she will rise and fall many times before her body is
given back to the salt." She twisted to gaze after the other Sea Folk
woman, and a touch of malice entered her voice. She seemed to be
speaking to herself. "She fell from a greater height than most, and she
should not have been surprised to find her landing hard after so many
fingers she trod on while she was—" Her mouth snapped shut, and she
jerked her head around to glare at Elayne, at Birgitte, at Aviendha and
Reene, even at the Guardswomen, daring them to comment.

Elayne prudently kept her mouth closed, and, the Light be
thanked, so did everyone else. For her part, she thought she almost had
her temper smoothed, the desire to cry suppressed, and she did not

want to say anything that might start Chanelle shouting and undo all her work. For that matter, she could not think of anything to say after hearing that. She doubted it was part of Atha'an Miere custom to take revenge on someone you believed had misused their position above you. It was very human, though.

The Windfinder stared her up and down, frowning. "You're wet," she said as though just noticing. "It is very bad to be wet for long in your condition. You should change your clothes right away."

Elayne threw back her head and screamed as loudly as she could, a howl of pure outrage and fury. She screamed until her lungs were empty, leaving her panting.

In the silence that followed, everyone stared at her in amazement. Almost everyone. Aviendha began laughing so hard she had to lean against a tapestry of mounted hunters confronting a leopard that had turned. She had one arm pressed across the middle as if her ribs hurt. The bond carried amusement, too—amusement!—though Birgitte's face remained as smooth as a sister's.

"I must Travel to Tear," Chanelle said breathily after a moment, and she turned away without another word or any gesture toward a courtesy. Reene and Reanne offered curtsies, neither quite meeting Elayne's eye, and pled duties before hurrying off.

Elayne stared at Birgitte and Aviendha in turn. "If one of you says a single word," she said warningly.

Birgitte put on such an expression of innocence that it was palpably false, and the bond carried such mirth that Elayne found herself fighting the urge to laugh. Aviendha only laughed the harder.

Gathering her skirts and such dignity as she could summon, Elayne set out for her apartments. If she walked faster than before, well, she *did* want to get out of these damp clothes. That was the only reason. The *only* reason.

CHAPTER

15

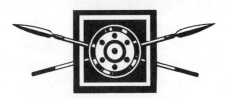

A Different Skill

To Elayne's fury, a quiet, simmering fury that clenched her jaw, she got lost on the way to her apartments. Those rooms had been hers since she left the nursery, yet twice she took a turn only to find that it did not lead where she expected. And a sweeping flight of marble-railed stairs took her in entirely the wrong direction. Burn her, now being with child was fuzzing her wits completely! She could feel puzzlement, and increasing concern, through the bond as she retraced her way, climbed a different set of stairs. Some of the Guardswomen murmured uneasily, not quite loudly enough for her to make out the words, until the Bannerwoman in charge, a slim, cool-eyed Saldaean named Devore Zarbayan, silenced them with a sharp word. Even Aviendha began looking at her doubtfully. Well, she was not *about* to have getting lost—in the palace!—flung in her face.

"Not a word from anybody," she said grimly. "Not one!" she added when Birgitte opened her mouth anyway.

The golden-haired woman snapped her jaws shut and gave a tug at her thick braid, almost the way Nynaeve did. She did not bother to keep disapproval from her face, and the bond still carried puzzlement, and worry. Enough that Elayne began to feel worried herself. She struggled to fight that off before she found herself wringing her hands and apologizing. It was that strong.

"I think I'll try to find *my* rooms, if I can have just a *few* words," Birgitte said in a tight voice. "I want to get dry before I wear out my boots. We need to talk of this later. I fear there's nothing to be done, but. . . ." With a stiff nod, barely bending her neck, she stalked off slashing her unstrung bow from side to side.

Elayne almost called her back. She wanted to. But Birgitte had as much need of dry clothing as she. Besides, her mood had swung to grumpy and stubborn. She was *not* going to talk about losing her way in the very halls where she had grown up, not now or later. Nothing to be done? What did *that* mean? If Birgitte was suggesting that her wits were too befuddled to be set straight. . . ! Her jaw tightened all over again.

At last, after yet another unexpected turn, she found the tall, lion-carved doors of her apartments and heaved a small sigh of relief. She had begun to think her memories of the palace really were completely jumbled. A pair of Guardswomen, resplendent in broad-brimmed hats with white plumes and lace-edged sashes embroidered with the White Lion slanting across their burnished breastplates and more pale lace at their cuffs and necks, stiffened on either side of the doors at her approach. She intended them to have red-lacquered breastplates to match their silk coats and breeches when she had time to spend on that sort of thing. If they were to be so pretty that any assailant would discount them until it was too late, she would make them positively gaudy. None of the Guardswomen seemed to mind. In fact, they were eagerly looking forward to the lacquered breastplates.

She had overheard some who were unaware she was near disparage the Guardswomen—mostly women, but including Doilin Mellar, their own commander—yet she had full confidence in their ability to protect her. They were brave and determined, or they would not have been there. Yurith Azeri and others who had been merchants' guards, a rare trade for women, gave daily lessons in the sword, and one or another of the Warders gave a second lesson every day, too. Sareitha's Ned Yarman and Vandene's Jaem were quite laudatory about how quickly they learned. Jaem said it was because they did not think they already knew something of how to use a blade, which seemed silly. How could you believe you already knew something if you needed lessons in it?

Despite the guards already there, Devore told off two of those who accompanied her, and they drew their swords and went inside while Elayne waited in the corridor with Aviendha and the rest, tapping her foot impatiently. Everyone avoided looking at her. The search was not a slur on the women guarding the doors—she supposed it was possible for someone to scale the side of the palace; there certainly was carving enough to provide handholds—yet she felt irritation at being made to wait on it. Only when they came out and reported to Devore that there were no assassins waiting within, no Aes Sedai waiting to whisk Elayne back to Elaida and the Tower, were she and Aviendha allowed to enter, with the Guardswomen forming up on either side of the doors with the others. She was not sure they would have physically prevented her from entering sooner, but so far she had been unwilling to put it to the test. Being restrained by her own bodyguards would have been beyond insufferable, no matter that they were just doing their jobs. Better to avoid the possibility altogether.

A small fire burned on the white marble hearth of the anteroom, but it seemed to give little warmth. The carpets had been taken up for spring, and the floor tiles felt cold beneath the soles of her shoes, stout as they were. Essande, her maid, spread red-trimmed gray skirts with still surprising grace, though the slim, white-haired woman suffered from painful joints, which she denied and refused Healing for. She would have refused any suggestion that she return to her retirement as vehemently. Elayne's Golden Lily was embroidered large on her breast, and proudly worn. Two younger women flanked her a pace back in similar livery but with smaller lilies, stocky square-faced sisters named Sephanie and Naris. Shy-eyed yet quite well trained by Essande, they made deep curtsies, settling nearly to the floor.

Slow-moving and frail Essande might be, but she never wasted time in idle chitchat or stating the obvious. There were no exclamations over how wet Elayne and Aviendha were, though doubtless the Guardswomen had alerted her. "We'll get you both warm and dry, my Lady, and right into something suitable for meeting mercenaries. The red silk with firedrops on the neck should impress them suitably. It's past time you ate, too. Don't bother telling me you have, my Lady. Naris, go fetch meals from the kitchens for the Lady Elayne and the Lady Aviendha." Aviendha gave a snort of laughter, yet she had long since ceased objecting to being called Lady. And a good thing, since she would never stop Essande. With servants, there were things you commanded and things you simply had to tolerate.

Naris grimaced and took a deep breath for some reason, but dropped another deep curtsy, this to Essande, and one only slightly deeper to Elayne—she and her sister were every bit as much in awe of the elderly woman as they were of the Daughter-Heir of Andor—before gathering her skirts and darting into the corridor.

Elayne grimaced, too. The Guardswomen also had told Essande about the mercenaries, apparently. And that she had not eaten. She hated people talking about her behind her back. But how much of that was her shifting moods? She could not recall being upset before because a maid knew what dress to lay out in advance, or because someone knew she was hungry and sent for a meal without being asked. Servants talked among themselves—gossiped constantly, in truth; that was a given—and passed along anything that might help their mistress be served better, if they were good at their jobs. Essande was very good at hers. Still, it rankled, and rankled the worse for her knowing that it was irrational.

She let Essande lead her and Aviendha into the dressing room, with Sephanie bringing up the rear. She was feeling very miserable by this time, damp and shivering, not to mention angry with Birgitte for stalking off, frightened by losing her way in the place where she had grown up, and sullen over her bodyguards gossiping about her. In truth, she felt absolutely wretched.

Soon enough, though, Essande had her out of her wet things and wrapped in a large white towel that had been hanging on a warming rack in front of the wide marble fireplace at the end of the room. That had a soothing effect. This fire was not at all small, and the room seemed not far short of hot, a welcome heat that soaked into the flesh and banished shivers. Essande toweled Elayne's hair dry while Sephanie performed the same office for Aviendha, which chagrined Aviendha still, though this was hardly the first time. She and Elayne frequently brushed each other's hair at night, yet accepting this simple service from a lady's maid put spots of color in Aviendha's sun-dark cheeks.

When Sephanie opened one of the wardrobes lining one wall, Aviendha sighed deeply. She held one towel loosely draped around her—another woman drying her hair might be embarrassing, but near nudity presented no difficulties—and a second, smaller, was wrapped around her hair. "Do you think I should wear wetlander clothes, Elayne, since we are going to meet these mercenaries?" she asked in tones of great reluctance. Essande smiled. She enjoyed dressing Aviendha in silks.

Elayne hid a smile of her own, no easy task since she wanted to laugh. Her sister pretended to disdain silks, but she seldom missed an opportunity to wear them. "If you can bear it, Aviendha," she said gravely, adjusting her own robing towel carefully. Essande saw her in her skin every day, and Sephanie, too, but it was nothing to let happen without reason. "For best effect, we should both over-awe them. You won't mind too much, will you?"

But Aviendha was already at the wardrobe, her towel gaping carelessly as she fingered dresses. Several sets of Aiel garb hung in another of the wardrobes, but Tylin had given her chests of finely cut silks and woolens before they left Ebou Dar, enough to fill nearly a quarter of the carved cabinets.

That brief burst of amusement left Elayne no longer feeling as if she had to argue over everything, so without demurral she let Essande get her into the red silk with firedrops the size of a finger joint sewn in a band around the high neck. The garment would impress, for sure, with no need for other jewels, though in truth the Great Serpent ring on her right hand was jewel enough for anyone. The white-haired woman had a delicate touch, but Elayne still winced as she began doing up the rows of tiny buttons down her back, tightening the bodice across her tender bosom. Opinions varied on how long that would last, yet all agreed that she could expect more swelling.

Oh, how she wished Rand were near enough to share the full effect of her bond with him. That would teach him to get her with child so carelessly. Of course, she could have drunk the heartleaf tea before lying with him—she pushed that thought away firmly. This was all Rand's fault, and that was that.

Aviendha chose blue, which she often did, with rows of tiny pearls edging the bodice. The silk was not so deeply cut as Ebou Dari fashions, yet still would display a little cleavage; few dresses sewn in Ebou Dar failed to do that. As Sephanie began fastening her buttons, Aviendha fondled something she had retrieved from her belt pouch, a small dagger with a rough hilt of deerhorn wrapped in gold wire. It was also a *ter'angreal*, though Elayne had not been able to puzzle out what it did before pregnancy forced a halt to such studies. She had not known her sister was carrying the thing. Aviendha's eyes were almost dreamy as she stared at it.

"Why does that fascinate you so?" Elayne asked. This was not the first time she had seen the other woman absorbed in that knife.

Aviendha gave a start and blinked at the dagger in her hands. The

iron blade—it looked like iron, at least, and felt almost like iron—had
never been sharpened so far as Elayne could tell and was little longer
than her palm, though wide in proportion. Even the point was too
blunt for stabbing. "I thought to give it to you, but you never said anything about it, so I thought I might be wrong, and then we would believe you were safe, from some dangers at least, when you were not. So
I decided to keep it. That way, if I am right, at least I could protect
you, and if I am wrong, it does no harm."

Elayne shook her towel-wrapped head in confusion. "Right about
what? What are you talking about?"

"This," Aviendha said, holding up the dagger. "I think that if you
have this in your possession, the Shadow cannot see you. Not the Eyeless or the Shadowtwisted, maybe not even Leafblighter. Except that I
must be wrong if you did not see it."

Sephanie gasped, her hands going still until Essande murmured a
soft admonition. Essande had lived too long to be shaken by mere
mention of the Shadow. Or much else, for that matter.

Elayne stared. She had tried teaching Aviendha to make ter'angreal,
but her sister possessed not a scrap of facility there. Yet perhaps she had
a different skill, maybe even one that could be called a Talent. "Come
with me," she said, and taking Aviendha's arm, she almost pulled her
out of the dressing room. Essande followed with a torrent of protest,
and Sephanie, attempting to continue buttoning up Aviendha's dress
on the fly.

In the larger of the apartment's two sitting rooms, goodly fires
blazed in both of the fireplaces, and if the air was not so warm as in the
dressing room, it was still comfortable. The scroll-edged table bor-
dered with low-backed chairs in the middle of the white-tiled floor was
where she and Aviendha took most of their meals. Several leather-
bound books from the palace library sat in a stack on one end of the
table, histories of Andor and books of tales. The mirrored stand-lamps
gave a good light, and they often read here of an evening.

More important, a long side table against one dark-paneled wall
was covered with ter'angreal from the cache the Kin had kept hidden in
Ebou Dar, cups and bowls, statuettes and figurines, jewelry, all manner
of things. Most looked commonplace, aside from perhaps a strangeness
of design, yet even the most fragile-seeming could not be broken, and
some were much lighter or heavier than they appeared. She could no
longer safely study them in any meaningful way—she had Min's assur-

ance her babes could not be harmed, but with her control of the Power so slippery, damaging herself was more a possibility than ever—yet she changed what was on the table every day, picking out pieces at random from the panniers kept in the apartment's boxroom, just so she could look at them and speculate on what she had learned before getting with child. Not that she had learned very much—well, nothing, really—but she could think on them. There was no worry of anything being stolen. Reene had rooted out most, if not all, of the dishonest among the servants, and the constant guard at the entrance saw to the rest.

Mouth tight with disapproval—dressing was done in the dressing room, decently, not out where anyone at all might walk in—Essande resumed her task with Elayne's buttons. Sephanie, likely as agitated by the older woman's displeasure as anything else, breathed hard as she worked on Aviendha's.

"Pick out something and tell me what you think it does," Elayne said. Looking and speculating had done no good, and she had not expected it to. Yet if Aviendha could somehow tell what a *ter'angreal* did just by holding it. . . . Jealousy surged up in her, hot and bitter, but she knocked it down, then for good measure jumped up and down on it until it vanished. She would *not* be jealous of Aviendha!

"I am not sure that I can, Elayne. I only think this knife makes a kind of warding. And I must be wrong or you would know it. You know more of these things than anyone."

Elayne's cheeks heated with embarrassment. "I don't know nearly as much as you seem to think. Try, Aviendha. I've never heard of anyone being able to . . . to 'read' *ter'angreal*, but if you can, even a little, don't you see how wonderful that would be?"

Aviendha nodded, but her face held doubt. Hesitantly, she touched a slim black rod, a pace long and so flexible it could be bent into a circle and spring back, lying in the middle of the table. Touched it and jerked her hand back swiftly, wiping her fingers unconsciously on her skirt. "This causes pain."

"Nynaeve told us that," Elayne said impatiently, and Aviendha gave her a level look.

"Nynaeve al'Meara did not say you can change how much pain each blow gives." Uncertainty overcame her again at once, though, and her voice became tentative. "At least, I think that can be done. I think one blow can feel like one, or a hundred. But I am only guessing, Elayne. It is only what I think."

"Keep going," Elayne told her encouragingly. "Maybe we'll find something that makes it certain. What about this?" She picked up an oddly shaped metal cap. Covered with strange, angular patterns of what seemed to be the most minute engraving, it was much too thin to be of use as a helmet, though it was twice as heavy as it appeared. The metal felt slick, too, not simply smooth, as if it were oiled.

Aviendha put down the dagger reluctantly and turned the cap over once in her hands before setting it back on the table and taking up the dagger again. "I think that allows you to direct a . . . a device of some sort. A machine." She shook her towel-wrapped head. "But I do not know how, or what kind of machine. You see? I am only guessing again."

Elayne would not let her stop, though. *Ter'angreal* after *ter'angreal* Aviendha touched or sometimes held for a moment, and every time she had an answer. Delivered hesitantly and with cautions that it was only a surmise, but always an answer. She thought a small hinged box, apparently ivory and covered with rippling red and green stripes, held music, hundreds of tunes, perhaps thousands. With a *ter'angreal*, that might be possible. After all, a fine music box might have cylinders for as many as a hundred tunes and some could play quite long pieces on one cylinder after another without changing them. A flattish white bowl almost a pace across was for looking at things that were far away, she thought, and a tall vase worked with vines in green and blue—blue vines!—would gather water out of the air. That sounded useless, but Aviendha almost caressed it, and after consideration, Elayne realized it would be very useful indeed in the Waste. If it worked as Aviendha believed. And someone figured out how to make it work. A black-and-white figurine of a bird with long wings spread in flight was for talking to people a long way off, she said. So was a blue figure of a woman, small enough to fit in the palm of her hand, in an oddly cut skirt and coat. And five earrings, six finger-rings and three bracelets.

Elayne began to think that Aviendha was giving up, offering the same answer every time in hopes that she would stop asking, but then she realized that her sister's voice was becoming more confident rather than less, that the protests that she was only guessing had dwindled. And her "guesses" were growing in detail. A bent, featureless rod of dull black, as wide as her wrist—it seemed metal, yet one end accommodated itself to any hand that gripped it—made her think of cutting, either metal or stone if they were not too thick. Nothing that could catch fire, though. The apparently glass figure of a man, a foot tall, with his hand raised as if to signal stop, would chase away vermin, which would certainly have been useful, given Caemlyn's plague of rats and flies. A stone carving the size of her hand, all deep blue curves—it felt like stone, at least, though somehow it did not really look carved— was for growing something. Not plants. It made her think of holes, only they were not exactly holes. And she did not believe anyone had to channel to make it work. Only sing the right song! Some *ter'angreal* did not require channeling, but really! Singing?

Done with Aviendha's dress, Sephanie had grown enthralled with the recitation, her eyes getting wider and wider. Essande listened with interest too, her head tilted to one side, murmuring small exclamations at each new revelation, but she was not bouncing on her toes the way Sephanie was. "What about that one, my Lady?" the younger woman blurted when Aviendha paused. She pointed to the statuette of a stout, bearded man with a merry smile, holding a book. Two feet tall, it appeared to be age-darkened bronze and was certainly heavy enough to be. "Looking at him always makes me want to smile, too, my Lady."

"Me as well, Sephanie Pelden," Aviendha said, stroking the bronze man's head. "He holds more than the book you see. He holds thousands and thousands of books." Abruptly the light of *saidar* enveloped her, and she touched thin flows of Fire and Earth to the bronze figure.

Sephanie squeaked as two words in the Old Tongue appeared in the air above the statuette, as black as if printed with good ink. Some of the letters were shaped a little oddly, but the words were quite clear. *Ansoen* and *Imsoen*, floating on nothing. Aviendha looked nearly as startled as the maid.

"I think we have proof at last," Elayne said more calmly than she felt. Her heart was in her throat, and pounding. Lies and Truth, the two words might be translated. Or in context, perhaps Fiction and Not Fiction would be better. It was proof enough for her. She marked where the flows touched the figure, for when she could return to her studies. "But you shouldn't have done that. It isn't safe."

The glow around Aviendha vanished. "Oh, Light," she exclaimed, flinging her arms around Elayne, "I never thought! I have great *toh* to you! I never meant to endanger you or your babes! Never!"

"My babes and I are safe." Elayne laughed, hugging back. "Min's viewing?" Her babes were safe, at least. Until they were born. So many babies died in their first year. Min had said nothing beyond them being born healthy. Min had said nothing about her not being burned out, either, but she had no intention of bringing that up with her sister already feeling guilty. "You have no *toh* to me. It was you I was thinking of. You could have died, or burned yourself out."

Aviendha pulled back enough to look into Elayne's eyes. What she saw there reassured her, for a small smile curved her lips. "I did make it work, though. Perhaps I can take over the study of them. With you to guide me, it should be perfectly safe. We have months before you can do it yourself."

"You have no time at all, Aviendha," a woman's voice said from the doorway. "We are leaving. I hope you have not grown too used to wearing silk. I see you, Elayne."

Aviendha leaped away from the embrace, flushing furiously, as two Aiel women entered the room, and not just any two Aiel. Pale-haired Nadere, as tall as most men and wide with it, was a Wise One of considerable authority among the Goshien, and Dorindha, her long red hair touched with white, was the wife of Bael, clan chief of the Goshien, though her true prominence came from being Roofmistress of Smoke Springs Hold, the clan's largest hold. It was she who had spoken.

"I see you, Dorindha," Elayne said. "I see you, Nadere. Why are you taking Aviendha away?"

"You said I could stay with Elayne, to help guard her back," Aviendha protested.

"You did, Dorindha." Elayne took her sister's hand in a firm grip, and Aviendha squeezed back. "You and the Wise Ones, too."

Gold and ivory bracelets clattered as Dorindha shifted her dark shawl. "How many do you need to guard your back, Elayne?" she asked dryly. "You have perhaps a hundred or more dedicated to nothing else, and as hard as *Far Dareis Mai*." A smile deepened the creases at the corners of her eyes. "I think those women outside wanted us to give up our belt knives before letting us in."

Nadere touched the horn hilt of her knife, her green eyes holding a fierce light, though it was unlikely the guards had shown any such desire. Even Birgitte, suspicious of everyone when it came to Elayne's safety, could see no danger from the Aiel, and Elayne had accepted certain obligations when she and Aviendha adopted each other. Wise Ones who had taken part in that ceremony, as Nadere had, could go wherever they wished in the palace whenever they wished; that was one of the obligations. As for Dorindha, her presence was so commanding, if in a quiet way, that it seemed inconceivable anyone would attempt to bar her way.

"Your training has been in abeyance too long, Aviendha," Nadere said firmly. "Go and change into proper clothing."

"But I am learning so much from Elayne, Nadere. Weaves even you do not know. I think I can make it rain in the Three-fold Land! And just now we learned that I can—"

"Whatever you may have learned," Nadere cut in sharply, "it seems you have forgotten as much. Such as the fact that you are an apprentice still. The Power is the least of what a Wise One must know, else only those who can channel would be Wise Ones. Now go and change, and count your luck that I do not make you return in your skin to face a strapping. The tents are being struck as we speak, and if the clan's departure is delayed, you *will* face the strap."

Without another word, Aviendha dropped Elayne's hand and ran from the room, bumping into Naris, who staggered and almost dropped the large, cloth-covered tray she was carrying. At a quick gesture from Essande, Sephanie hurried after Aviendha. Naris' eyes went wide at the sight of the Aiel women, but Essande admonished her for taking so long and directed her to lay out the meal on the table, setting the young maid into hurried motion while muttering apologies under her breath.

Elayne wanted to run after Aviendha, too, to grasp every moment with her, but Nadere's words held her. "You're leaving Caemlyn, Dorindha? Where are you going?" As much as Elayne liked the Aiel, she did not want them wandering about the countryside. With the situation as unstable as it was, they were problem enough simply venturing out of their camp to hunt or trade.

"We are leaving Andor, Elayne. In a few hours, we will be far beyond your borders. As to where, you must ask the *Car'a'carn*."

Nadere had walked over to study what Naris was laying out, and Naris began to tremble so that she nearly dropped more than one dish. "This looks good, but I do not recognize some of these herbs," the Wise One said. "Your midwife has approved all of this, Elayne?"

"I'll summon a midwife when my time is near, Nadere. Dorindha, you can't think Rand would want your destination kept from me. What did he say?"

Dorindha gave a small shrug. "He sent a messenger, one of the black coats, with a letter for Bael. Bael let me read it, of course"—her tone said there had never been any question of her not reading it— "but the *Car'a'carn* asked Bael not to tell anyone, so I cannot tell you."

"No midwife?" Nadere said incredulously. "Who tells you what to eat and drink? Who gives you the proper herbs? Stop looking daggers at me, woman. Melaine's temper is worse than yours could ever be, but she has sense enough to let Monaelle govern her in these things."

"Every woman in the palace governs what I eat," Elayne replied bitterly. "Sometimes I think every woman in Caemlyn does. Dorindha, can't you at least—"

"My Lady, your food is getting cold," Essande said mildly, but with just the touch of firmness that an elderly retainer was allowed.

Gritting her teeth, Elayne glided to the chair Essande stood behind. She did *not* flounce, much as she wanted to. She glided. Essande produced an ivory-backed hairbrush and, removing the towel from Elayne's head, began brushing her hair while she ate. She ate largely because not eating only meant someone would be told to fetch more hot food, because Essande and her own bodyguards between them might well keep her there until she did, but except for some dried apple that had not gone bad, the meal was decidedly unappetizing. The bread was crusty but flecked with weevils, and the soaked dried beans, since all of the preserved beans had spoiled, were tough and tasteless. The apple was mixed in a bowl of herbs—sliced burdock root, black haw, cramp bark, dandelion, nettle leaf—with a touch of oil, and for meat she had a piece of kid simmered in bland broth. With next to no salt, as far as she could tell. She would have killed for salty beef dripping with fat! *Aviendha's* plate had sliced beef, though it looked tough. *She* could as well ask for wine. To drink, she had her choice of water or goat's milk. She wanted tea almost as much as she did fatty meat, but even the weakest tea sent her running to make water, and she had quite enough difficulties with that as it was. So she ate methodically, mechanically, trying to think of anything but the tastes in her mouth. Except for the apple, at least.

She tried to pry some news of Rand out of the two Aiel women, but it seemed they knew less than she. As far as they would admit, anyway. They could be closemouthed when they wanted to be. She at least knew that he was somewhere far to the southeast. Somewhere in Tear, she suspected, though he could as easily have been on the Plains of Maredo or in the Spine of the World. Beyond that, she knew he was alive and not a whit more. She tried keeping the conversation on Rand in the hope they might let something slip, yet she might as well have tried dressing bricks with her fingers. Dorindha and Nadere had their own goal, convincing her to acquire a midwife right away. They went on and on about how she might be endangering herself and her babes, and not even Min's viewing would dissuade them.

"Very well," she said at last, slapping down her knife and fork. "I will start looking for one today." And if she failed to find one, well, they would never know.

"I have a niece who's a midwife, my Lady," Essande said. "Melfane dispenses herbs and ointments from a shop on Candle Street in the New City, and I believe she is quite knowledgeable." She patted a few last curls into place and stepped back with a pleased smile. "You do so remind me of your mother, my Lady."

Elayne sighed. It seemed she was to have a midwife whether she wanted one or not. Someone *else* to see that her meals were wretched. Well, perhaps the midwife could suggest a remedy for those backaches at night, and the tender bosom. Thank the Light she had been spared the desire to sick up. Women who could channel never suffered that part of pregnancy.

When Aviendha returned, she was in Aiel garb again, with her still-damp shawl draped over her arms, a dark scarf tied around her temples to hold back her hair, and a bundle on her back. Unlike the multitudes of bracelets and necklaces Dorindha and Nadere wore, she had a single silver necklace, intricately worked discs in a complex pattern, and one ivory bracelet densely carved with roses and thorns. She handed Elayne the blunt dagger. "You must keep this, so you will be safe. I will try to visit you as often as I can."

"There may be time for an occasional visit," Nadere said severely, "but you have fallen behind and must work hard to catch up. Strange," she mused, shaking her head, "to speak casually of visiting from so far. To cover leagues, hundreds of leagues, in a step. Strange things we have learned in the wetlands."

"Come, Aviendha, we must go," Dorindha said.

"Wait," Elayne told them. "Please wait, just a moment." Clutching the dagger, she raced to her dressing room. Sephanie paused in hanging up Aviendha's blue dress to curtsy, but Elayne ignored her and opened the carved lid of her ivory jewelry chest. Sitting atop the necklaces and bracelets and pins in their compartments were a brooch in the shape of a turtle that appeared to be amber and a seated woman, wrapped in her own hair, apparently carved from age-darkened ivory. Both were *angreal*. Placing the antler-hilted dagger in the chest, she picked up the turtle, and then, impulsively, snatched up the twisted stone dream ring, all red and blue and brown. It seemed to be useless to her since she became pregnant, and if she could manage to weave Spirit, she still had the silver ring, worked in braided spirals, that had been recovered from Ispan.

Hurrying back to the sitting room, she found Dorindha and Nadere arguing, or at least having an animated discussion, while Essande pretended to be checking for dust, running her fingers under the edge of the table. From the angle of her head, she was listening avidly, though. Naris, putting Elayne's dishes back on the tray, was gaping at the Aiel women openly.

"I told her she would feel the strap if we delayed the departure," Nadere was saying with some heat as Elayne entered the room. "It is hardly fair if she is not the cause, but I said what I said."

"You will do as you must," Dorindha replied calmly, but with a tightness to her eyes that suggested these were not the first words they had exchanged. "Perhaps we will not delay anything. And perhaps Aviendha will pay the price gladly to say farewell to her sister."

Elayne did not bother with trying to argue for Aviendha. It would have done no good. Aviendha herself displayed an equanimity that would have credited an Aes Sedai, as if whether she was to be beaten for another's fault were of no matter at all.

"These are for you," Elayne said, pressing the ring and the brooch into her sister's hand. "Not as gifts, I'm afraid. The White Tower will want them back. But to use as you need."

Aviendha looked at the things and gasped. "Even the loan of these is a great gift. You shame me, sister. I have no farewell gift to give in return."

"You give me your friendship. You gave me a sister." Elayne felt a tear slide down her cheek. She essayed a laugh, but it was a weak, tremulous thing. "How can you say you have nothing to give? You've given me everything."

Tears glistened in Aviendha's eyes, too. Despite the others watching, she put her arms around Elayne and hugged her hard. "I will miss you, sister," she whispered. "My heart is as cold as night."

"And mine, sister," Elayne whispered, hugging back equally hard.

"I will miss you, too. But you will be allowed to visit me sometimes. This isn't forever."

"No, not forever. But I will still miss you."

They might have begun weeping next, only Dorindha laid her hands on their shoulders. "It is time, Aviendha. We must go if you are to have any hope of avoiding the strap."

Aviendha straightened with a sigh, scrubbing at her eyes. "May you always find water and shade, sister."

"May you always find water and shade, sister," Elayne replied. The Aiel way had a finality about it, so she added, "Until I see your face again."

And as quickly as that, they were gone. As quickly as that, she felt very alone. Aviendha's presence had become a certainty, a sister to talk to, laugh with, share her hopes and fears with, but that comfort was gone.

Essande had slipped from the room while she and Aviendha were hugging, and now she returned to set the coronet of the Daughter-Heir on Elayne's head, a simple circlet of gold supporting a single golden rose on her forehead. "So these mercenaries won't forget who they're talking to, my Lady."

Elayne did not realize her shoulders had slumped until she straightened them. Her sister was gone, yet she had a city to defend and a throne to gain. Duty would have to sustain her, now.

CHAPTER
16

The New Follower

The Blue Reception Room, named for its arched ceiling, painted to display the sky and white clouds, and its blue floor tiles, was the smallest reception room in the palace, less than ten paces square. The arched windows that made up the far wall, overlooking a courtyard and still filled with glassed casements against the spring weather, gave a fair light even with the rain falling outside, but despite two large fireplaces with carved marble mantels, a cornice of plaster lions and a pair of tapestries bearing the White Lion that flanked the doors, a delegation of Caemlyn's merchants would have been insulted to be received in the Blue Room, a delegation of bankers livid. Likely that was why Mistress Harfor had put the mercenaries there, although they would not know they were being insulted. She herself was present, "overseeing" the pair of liveried young maids who were keeping the winecups full from tall silver pitchers standing on a tray atop a plainly carved sideboard, but she had the embossed leather folder used to carry her reports pressed to her bosom, as if in anticipation of the mercenaries being dealt with quickly. Halwin Norry, the wisps of white hair behind his ears as always looking like feathers, was standing in a corner, also with his leather folder clutched to his narrow chest. Their reports were a daily fixture, and seldom much in them to cheer the heart of late. Quite the opposite.

Warned by the pair of Guardswomen who had checked the room ahead of her, everyone was on their feet when Elayne entered with another pair at her back. Deni Colford, in charge of the Guardswomen who had replaced Devore and the others, had simply ignored her order for them all to remain outside. Ignored her! She supposed they made a good show, swaggering proudly as they did, yet she could not stop grinding her teeth.

Careane and Sareitha, formal in their fringed shawls, bowed their heads slightly in respect, but Mellar swept off his plumed hat in a flourishing bow, one hand laid over the lace-edged sash slanting across his burnished breastplate. The six golden knots brazed to that breastplate, three on each shoulder, rankled her, yet she had let them pass so far. His hatchet face offered her a smile that was much too warm, too, but then, however cold she was to him, he thought he had some chance with her because she had not denied the rumor her babes were his. Her reasons for not countering that filthy tale had changed—she no longer had need to protect her babes, Rand's babes—yet she let it stand. Give the man time, and he would braid a rope for his own neck. And if he failed to, she would braid one for him.

The mercenaries, all well into their middle years, were only a heartbeat behind Mellar, though not so elaborate in their courtesies. Evard Cordwyn, a tall, square-jawed Andoran, wore a large ruby in his left ear, and Aldred Gomaisen, short and slender, the front of his head shaved, had horizontal stripes of red and green and blue covering half his chest, far more than it seemed at all likely he was entitled to in his native Cairhien. Hafeen Bakuvun, graying, was ornamented with a thick gold hoop in his left ear and a jeweled ring on every finger. The Domani was very stout, but the way he moved spoke of solid muscle beneath the fat.

"Don't you have duties, Captain Mellar?" Elayne said coolly, taking one of the room's few chairs. There were only five, arms and high backs simply carved with vines and leaves and lacking even a hint of gilt. Standing in a widely spaced row in front of the windows, the chairs put the light behind whoever sat in them. On a bright day, those given audience here squinted in the glare. Unfortunately, that advantage was lost today. The two Guardswomen took up positions behind her and to either side, each with a hand resting on her sword hilt, watching the mercenaries with fierce expressions that made Bakuvun smile and Gomaisen rub his chin to half-hide a sly grin. The women

gave no sign of being offended; they knew the point of their uniforms.
Elayne knew they would wipe away any smiles very quickly if they
needed to draw their blades.

"My first duty above all is to protect you, my Lady." Easing his
sword, Mellar eyed the mercenaries as though he expected them to attack her, or perhaps him. Gomaisen looked bitterly amused, and Bakuvun laughed aloud. All three men had empty scabbards, Cordwyn a
pair on his back; no mercenary was allowed to enter the palace carrying
so much as a dagger.

"I know you have other duties," she said levelly, "because I assigned them to you, Captain. Training the men I brought in from the
countryside. You are not spending as much time with them as I expect. You have a company of men to train, Captain." A company of old
men and boys, and surely enough to occupy his hours. He spent few
enough with her bodyguards in spite of commanding them. That was
just as well, really. He liked to pinch bottoms. "I suggest you see to
them. Now."

Rage flashed across Mellar's narrow face—he actually quivered!—
but he mastered himself instantly. It was all gone so fast that she might
have imagined it. But she knew she had not. "As you command, my
Lady," he said smoothly. His smile had an oily smoothness, too. "My
honor is to serve you well." With another flamboyant bow, he started
for the door, as near to strutting as made no difference. Little could
dent Doilin Mellar's demeanor for long.

Bakuvun laughed again, throwing his head back. "Man wears so
much lace now, I vow, I keep expecting him to offer to teach us to
dance, and now he does dance." The Cairhienin laughed, too, a nasty,
guttural sound.

Mellar's back stiffened and his step hesitated, then quickened, so
much so that he bumped into Birgitte at the doorway. He hurried on
without stopping to ask pardon, and she frowned after him—the bond
carried anger, quickly suppressed, and impatience, which was not—
before shutting the door behind her and moving to stand beside
Elayne's chair with one hand resting on the chairback. Her thick braid
was not so neatly done as usual after having been undone for drying,
but the uniform of the Captain-General suited her. Taller than Gomaisen in her heeled boots, Birgitte had a commanding presence when
she wanted to. The mercenaries offered her small bows, respectful
though not deferential. Whatever misgivings of her they might have

entertained in the beginning, few who had seen her use her bow, or expose herself to the enemy, had any remaining.

"You speak as if you know Captain Mellar, Captain Bakuvun." Elayne put just a hint of question in that, but kept her tone casual. Birgitte was attempting to project confidence along the bond to equal her expression, yet wariness and worry kept intruding. And the ever-present weariness. Elayne tightened her jaw to fight a yawn. Birgitte *had* to get some rest.

"I've seen him once or twice before, my Lady," the Domani replied cautiously. "Not above thrice at most, I'd say. Yes, no more than that." He tilted his head, eyeing her almost sideways. "You know he's followed my trade in the past?"

"He did not try to hide the fact, Captain," she said, as if tired of the subject. Had he let anything interesting slip, she might have arranged to question him alone, but pressing was not worth the risk of Mellar discovering that questions were being asked. He might run then, before she could learn what she wanted to know.

"Do we really have need of the Aes Sedai, my Lady?" Bakuvun asked. "The other Aes Sedai," he added, glancing at her Great Serpent ring. He held out his silver cup, and one of the maids darted to fill it. They were both pretty women, perhaps not the best choices, but Reene had not much to choose from; most of the maids were either young or else aged and not so spry as they once had been. "All they've done the whole time we've been here is try to put us in awe of the White Tower's might and reach. I respect Aes Sedai as much as any man, yes, I do indeed, but if you'll forgive me, it gets tiresome when they turn to trying to browbeat a man. I vow it does, my Lady."

"A wise man always stands in awe of the Tower," Sareitha said calmly, shifting her brown-fringed shawl, perhaps to draw attention to it. Her dark, square face lacked the ageless look as yet, and she admitted yearning for it.

"Only fools fail to stand in awe of the Tower," Careane said on Sareitha's heels. A bulky woman, as wide in the shoulders as most men, the Green had no need for gestures. Her coppery face proclaimed what she was to anyone who knew what to look for as loudly as did the ring on her right forefinger.

"The word I hear," Gomaisen said darkly, "is that Tar Valon is besieged. I hear the White Tower is split, with two Amyrlins. I even hear the Tower itself is held by the Black Ajah." A brave man, to mention that rumor to Aes Sedai, but he still flinched saying it. Flinched and went right on. "Who is it you want us to be in awe of?"

"Do not believe everything you hear, Captain Gomaisen." Sareitha's voice was serene, a woman stating indisputable fact. "Truth has more shadings than you might think, and distance often distorts truth into something very different from the facts. Lies about Darkfriend sisters are dangerous to repeat, however."

"What you had best believe," Careane added, just as calmly, "is that the White Tower is the White Tower, now and always. And you stand before three Aes Sedai. You should have a care with your words, Captain."

Gomaisen scrubbed the back of a hand across his mouth, but his dark eyes held defiance. A hunted defiance. "I am just saying what can be heard on any street," he muttered.

"Are we here to talk about the White Tower?" Cordwyn said, scowling. He emptied his winecup before going on, as if this talk made him uneasy. How much had he already consumed? He seemed a trifle unsteady on his feet, and there was a touch of slur in his words. "The Tower is hundreds of leagues from here, and what happens there is no business of ours."

"True, friend," Bakuvun said. "True. Our business is swords, swords and blood. Which, my Lady, brings us to the sordid matter of . . ."—he waggled thick, be-gemmed fingers—"gold. Every day, we lose men, day after day with no end in sight, and there are very few suitable replacements to be found in the city."

"None at all that I've found," Cordwyn muttered, eyeing the young maid filling his cup. She blushed at his scrutiny and finished her task quickly, spilling wine on the floor tiles and making Mistress Harfor frown. "Those that might have been are all signing up for the Queen's Guards." That was true enough; enlistments seemed to increase by the day. The Queen's Guards would be a formidable force. Eventually. Unfortunately, the vast majority of those men were months from being able to handle a sword without stabbing themselves in the foot, and further from being of any use in battle.

"As you say, friend," Bakuvun murmured. "As you say." He directed a wide smile at Elayne. Perhaps he meant to seem friendly, or maybe reasonable, but it minded her of a man trying to sell her a pig in a sack. "Even after we're done here, finding new men won't be easy, my Lady. Suitable men aren't found under cabbage leaves, no they're not.

Fewer men means fewer coins for our next hires. An inescapable fact of the world. We think it's only just that we receive compensation."

Anger surged in Elayne. They thought she was desperate to hold on to them was what they thought! Worse, they were right. These three men represented better than a thousand more between them. Even with what Guybon had brought her, that would be a grievous loss. Especially if it started other mercenaries thinking her cause was lost. Mercenaries disliked being on the losing side. They would run like rats fleeing fire to avoid that. Her anger surged, but she held it in rein. By a hair's breadth. She could not keep the scorn from her voice, though. "Did you think you would take no casualties? Did you expect to mount guard and take gold for it without baring your swords?"

"You signed for so much gold each day," Birgitte put in. She did not say how much because every company had bargained for its own agreement. The last thing they needed was for the mercenary companies to grow jealous of one another. As it was, it seemed that half the common room fights the Guards broke up were between men of different companies. "A fixed amount. To put it cruelly, the more men you lose, the greater your profit."

"Ah, Captain-General," the stout man said blandly, "but you forget the death-money that has to be paid to the widows and orphans." Gomaisen made a choking noise, and Cordwyn stared at Bakuvun incredulously then tried to cover it by draining his winecup again.

Elayne trembled, her hands tightening to fists on the arms of her chair. She would not give way to anger. She would *not*! "I intend to hold you to your agreements," she said coldly. Well, at least she was not raging. "You'll be paid what you signed for, including the usual victory gold after I gain the throne, but not a penny more. If you try to back out, I'll assume you are turning coat and going over to Arymilla, in which case, I'll have you and your companies arrested and put outside the gates without swords or horses." The maid refilling Cordwyn's winecup yet again suddenly squealed and danced away from him rubbing her hip. The anger Elayne had been holding down fountained white hot. "And if one of you ever again dares fondle one of my women, he and his company will be put out without swords, horses, or *boots*! Do I make myself clear?"

"Very clear, my Lady." Bakuvun's voice held a distinct chill, and his wide mouth was tight. "Very clear indeed. And now, since our . . . discussion . . . seems concluded, may we withdraw?"

"Think carefully," Sareitha said suddenly. "Will the White Tower choose to see an Aes Sedai on the Lion Throne, or a fool like Arymilla Marne?"

"Count the Aes Sedai in this palace," Careane added. "Count the Aes Sedai inside Caemlyn. There are none in Arymilla's camps. Count and decide where the White Tower's favor lies."

"Count," Sareitha said, "and remember that the White Tower's displeasure can be fatal."

It was very hard to believe that one of them must be Black Ajah, yet it must be so. Unless it was Merilille, of course. Elayne hoped that was not so. She liked Merilille. But then, she liked Careane and Sareitha, too. Not as much as she did Merilille, yet still a liking. Any way she looked at it, a woman she liked was a Darkfriend, and already under penalty of death.

When the mercenaries had departed, making their courtesies hurriedly, and Mistress Harfor had sent the maids away with the remnants of the wine, Elayne leaned back in her chair and sighed. "I handled that very badly, didn't I?"

"Mercenaries require a strong hand on the reins," Birgitte replied, but there was doubt in the bond. Doubt and worry.

"If I may say, my Lady," Norry said in his dry voice, "I cannot see anything else you could have done. Mildness would only have emboldened them to make further demands." He had been so still that Elayne had almost forgotten he was there. Blinking at the world, he seemed a wading bird wondering where the water had gone. In contrast to Mistress Harfor's neatness, ink stains marked his tabard, and his fingers. She eyed the leather folder in his hands with distinct distaste.

"Will you leave us, please, Sareitha, Careane?" she said. They hesitated slightly, but there was nothing they could do save bow their heads and glide from the room like swans. "And you two as well," she added over her shoulder to the Guardswomen. *They* did not so much as twitch!

"Outside!" Birgitte snapped with a jerk of her head that set her braid swaying. "Now!" Oh, the pair jumped for her, they did! They headed for the doors so fast they might as well have trotted!

Elayne scowled as the door closed behind them. "Burn me, I don't want to hear any bloody bad news, not today. I don't want to hear how much of the food brought in from Illian and Tear is already spoiled when it arrives. I don't want to hear about arson, or flour black with weevils, or sewers breeding rats faster than they can be killed, or flies so thick you'd think Caemlyn was a filthy stable. I want to hear some bloody good news for a change." Burn her, she sounded *petulant*! Truth be told, she *felt* petulant. Oh, how that grated! She was trying to gain a throne, and behaving like a child in the nursery!

Master Norry and Mistress Harfor exchanged glances, which only made matters worse. He fondled his folder with a sigh of regret. The man *enjoyed* droning his numbers, even when they were dire. At least they no longer balked at giving their reports in company. Well, not very far. Jealous of their own responsibilities, each was wary of the other straying and quick to point out where some imagined boundary had been crossed. Still, they managed to run the palace and the city efficiently, with few barked knuckles.

"Are we private, my Lady?" Reene asked.

Elayne drew a deep breath and performed novice exercises that seemed to have no calming effect whatsoever, then attempted to embrace the Source. To her surprise, *saidar* came to her easily, filling her with the sweetness of life and joy. And soothing her moods, too. It was always that way. Anger or sorrow or just being with child might interfere with embracing the Power in the first place, yet once it filled her, her emotions stopped jumping about. Deftly she wove Fire and Air, just so, with traces of Water, but when she was done, she did not release the Source. The feel of being filled with the Power was wondrous, yet not that much more so than knowing she would not be wanting to weep for no reason or shout for as little in the next moment. After all, she was not foolish enough to draw too deeply.

"We are private," she said. *Saidar* touched her ward and was gone. Someone had tried to listen in, not the first time that had happened. With so many women who could channel gathered in the palace, it would have been surprising if no one attempted to snoop, but she wished she knew how to trace whoever was making those attempts. As it was, she hardly dared say anything of substance without a ward in place.

"Then I have a little good news," Mistress Harfor said, shifting her folder but not opening it, "from Jon Skellit." The barber had been most assiduous about carrying his reports, approved beforehand by Reene, out to Arymilla and bringing back what he could learn in the camps outside the city. He was in the employ of Naean Arawn, but Naean, supporting Arymilla's claim, would surely share Skellit's reports with Arymilla. Unfortunately, what he had been able to learn so far had not been much of use. "He says that Arymilla and the High Seats supporting her intend to be in the first party to ride into Caemlyn. She boasts of it constantly, it seems."

Elayne sighed. Arymilla and the others stayed together, moving from camp to camp according to no pattern she could see, and for some time great effort had gone into trying to learn where they would be ahead of time. A simple matter then to send soldiers through a gateway to seize all of them at once and decapitate her opposition. As simple as such things could be, anyway. Men would die under the best of circumstances, some of the High Seats might well escape, yet if only Arymilla herself could be taken, there would be an end to it. Elenia and Naean had made public renunciation of their own claims, which was irreversible. That pair might go on supporting Arymilla if they remained free—they had tied themselves to her tightly—but with Arymilla in hand, all Elayne really would have to contend with was gaining the support of at least four more of the great Houses. As if it were easy. So far, efforts in that direction had proven futile. Perhaps today would bring good news on that front, though. But this news was useless. If Arymilla and the others were riding into Caemlyn it would mean the city was beyond the brink of falling. Worse, if Arymilla was boasting, she must believe it would happen soon. The woman was a fool in many ways, but it would be a mistake to underestimate her completely. She had not carried her claim this far by being an absolute fool.

"This is your good news?" Birgitte said. She saw the implications, too. "A hint of when might help."

Reene spread her hands. "Arymilla gave Skellit a gold crown with her own hands once, my Lady. He turned it over to me as proof that he's reformed." Her lips compressed for a moment; Skellit had saved himself from hanging, yet he would never regain trust. "That's the only time the man's been within ten paces of her. He has to go by what he can pick up gossiping with the other men." She hesitated. "He's very afraid, my Lady. The men in those camps are certain they'll take the city in a matter of days."

"Afraid enough to turn his coat a third time?" Elayne asked quietly. There was nothing to say to the other matter.

"No, my Lady. If Naean, or Arymilla, learns what he's done, he's a dead man, and he knows it. But he's afraid if the city falls, they will learn. I think he may bolt soon."

Elayne nodded grimly. Mercenaries were not the only rats to flee fire. "Do *you* have any good news, Master Norry?"

The First Clerk had been standing quietly, fingering his embossed leather folder and trying to appear as if he were not listening to Reene. "I think I can better Mistress Harfor, my Lady." There might have been a touch of triumph in his smile. Of late, it was rare for him to have better news than she. "I have a man I believe can follow Mellar successfully. May I have him brought in?"

Now, that *was* excellent news. Five men had died trying to follow Doilin Mellar when he went out into the city at night, and the "coincidence" seemed strained. The first time, it had appeared the fellow fell afoul of a footpad, and she thought nothing of it beyond settling a pension on the man's widow. The Guards managed to keep crime under some control—except for arson, at least—yet robbers used darkness as a cloak to hide in. The other four had seemed the same, killed with a single knife thrust, their purses emptied, but however dangerous the streets at night, coincidence hardly seemed credible.

When she nodded, the spindly old man hurried to the doors and opened one to put his head out. She could not hear what he said—the ward worked both ways—but in a few minutes a burly Guardsman entered pushing ahead of him a shuffling man with fetters on his wrists and ankles. Everything about the prisoner seemed . . . average. He was neither fat nor thin, tall nor short. His hair was brown, of no particular shade she could name, and his eyes as well. His face was so ordinary she doubted she could describe him. No feature stood out at all. His clothing was just as unremarkable, a plain brown coat and breeches of neither the best wool nor the worst, somewhat rumpled and beginning to show dirt, a lightly embossed belt with a simple metal buckle that might have ten thousand twins in Caemlyn. In short, he was eminently forgettable. Birgitte motioned the Guardsman to stop the fellow well short of the chairs and told him to wait outside.

"A reliable man," Norry said, watching the Guardsman leave. "Afrim Hansard. He served your mother faithfully, and knows how to keep his mouth shut."

"Chains?" Elayne said.

"This is Samwil Hark, my Lady," Norry said, eyeing the man with the sort of curiosity he might have shown toward an unfamiliar and oddly shaped animal, "a remarkably successful cutpurse. The Guards only caught him because another ruffian . . . um . . . 'turned the cat on him,' as they say in the streets, hoping to lessen his own sentence for a third offense of strongarm robbery." A thief would be eager for that. Not only was the flogging longer, the thief-mark branded on his forehead would be much harder to disguise or hide than the mark on his thumb for his second offense. "Anyone who has managed to keep from being caught for as long as Master Hark should be able to carry out the task I have in mind for him."

"I'm innocent, I am, my Lady." Hark knuckled his forehead, the iron chains of his fetters clinking, and put on an ingratiating smile. He talked very quickly. "It's all lies and happenstances, it is. I'm a good Queen's man, I am. I wore your mother's colors in the riots, my Lady. Not that I took part in the rioting, you understand. I'm a clerk when I have work, which I'm out of at the moment. But I wore her colors on my cap for all to see, I did." The bond was full of Birgitte's skepticism.

"Master Hark's rooms contained chests full of neatly cut purses," the First Clerk went on. "There are thousands of them, my Lady. Quite literally thousands. I suppose he may regret keeping . . . um . . . trophies. Most cutpurses have sense enough to get rid of the purse as soon as possible."

"I picks them up when I sees one, I does, my Lady." Hark spread his hands as far as his chains allowed and shrugged, the very image of injured innocence. "Maybe it were foolish, but I never saw no harm. Just a harmless sort of amusement, my Lady."

Mistress Harfor sniffed loudly, disapproval clear on her face. Hark managed to look even more hurt.

"His rooms also contained coins to the value of over one hundred twenty gold crowns, secreted under the floorboards, in cubbyholes in the walls, in the rafters, everywhere. His excuse for that," Norry raised his voice as Hark opened his mouth again, "is that he distrusts bankers. He claims the money is an inheritance from an aged aunt in Four Kings. I myself very much doubt the magistrates in Four Kings will have registered such an inheritance, though. The magistrate judging his case says he seemed surprised to learn that inheritances are registered." Indeed, Hark's smile faded somewhat at being reminded. "He says that he worked for Wilbin Saems, a merchant, until Saems' death four months ago, but Master Saems' daughter maintains the business, and neither she nor any of the other clerks recall any Samwil Hark."

"They hates me, they does, my Lady," Hark said in a sullen voice. His hands gripped the chain between them in fists. "I was gathering evidence of how they was stealing from the good master—his own daughter, mind!—only he died afore I could give it to him, and I was turned out in the streets without a reference or a penny, I was. They burned what I'd gathered, gave me a drubbing and threw me out."

Elayne tapped her chin thoughtfully. "A clerk, you say. Most clerks are better spoken than you, Master Hark, but I'll offer you a chance to give evidence for your claim. Would you send for a lapdesk, Master Norry?"

Norry gave a thin smile. How *could* the man make a smile seem dry? "No need, my Lady. The magistrate in the case had the same idea." For the first time that she had ever seen, he took a sheet of paper from the folder clutched to his chest. She thought trumpets should sound! Hark's smile faded away completely as his eyes followed that page from Norry's hand to hers.

One glance was all that was needed. A few uneven lines covered less than half the sheet, the letters cramped and awkward. No more than half a dozen words were actually legible, and those barely.

"Hardly the hand of a clerk," she murmured. Returning the page to Norry, she tried to make her face stern. She had seen her mother passing judgment. Morgase had been able to make herself appear implacable. "I fear, Master Hark, that you will sit in a cell until the magistrates in Four Kings can be queried, and soon after that you will hang." Hark's lips writhed, and he put a hand to his throat as if he could already feel the noose. "Unless, of course, you agree to follow a man for me. A dangerous man who doesn't like to be followed. If you can tell me where he goes at night, instead of hanging, you will be exiled to Baerlon. Where you would be well advised to find a new line of work. The governor *will* be informed of you."

Suddenly Hark's smile was back. "Of course, my Lady. I'm innocent, but I can see how things look dark against me, I can. I'll follow any man you want me to. I was your mother's man, I was, and I'm your man, too. Loyal is what I am, my Lady, loyal if I suffers for it."

Birgitte snorted derisively.

"Arrange for Master Hark to see Mellar's face without being seen, Birgitte." The man was unmemorable, but there was no point in taking chances. "Then turn him loose." Hark looked ready to dance, iron chains or no iron chains. "But first. . . . You see this, Master Hark?" She held up her right hand so he could not miss the Great Serpent ring. "You may have heard that I am Aes Sedai." With the Power already in her, it was a simple matter to weave Spirit. "It is true." The weave she laid on Hark's belt buckle, his boots, his coat and breeches, was somewhat akin to that for the Warder bond, though much less complex. It would fade from the clothing and boots in a few weeks, or months at best, but metal would hold a Finder forever. "I've laid a weave on you, Master Hark. Now you can be found wherever you are." In truth, only she would be able to find him—a Finder was attuned to the one who wove it—but there was no reason to tell him that. "Just to be sure that you are indeed loyal."

Hark's smile seemed frozen in place. Sweat beaded on his forehead. When Birgitte went to the door and called in Hansard, giving him instructions to take Hark away and keep him safe from prying eyes, Hark staggered and would have fallen if the husky Guardsman had not held him up on the way out of the room.

"I fear I may just have given Mellar a sixth victim," Elayne muttered. "He hardly seems capable of following his own shadow without tripping over his boots." It was not so much Hark's death she regretted. The man would have hanged for sure. "I want whoever put that bloody man in my palace. I want them so badly my teeth ache!" The palace was riddled with spies—Reene had uncovered above a dozen beyond Skellit, though she believed that was all of them—but whether Mellar had been set to spy or to facilitate kidnapping her, he was worse than the others. He had arranged for men to die, or he had killed them, in order to gain his place. That those men had thought they were to kill *her* made no difference. Murder was murder.

"Trust me, my Lady," Norry said, laying a finger alongside his long nose. "Cutpurses are . . . um . . . stealthy by nature, yet they seldom last long. Sooner or later they cut the purse of someone faster afoot than they, someone who doesn't wait for the Guards." He made a quick gesture as if stabbing someone. "Hark has lasted at least twenty years. A number of the purses in his . . . um . . . collection were embroidered with prayers of thanks for the end of the Aiel War. Those went out of fashion very quickly, as I recall."

Birgitte sat down on the arm of the next chair and folded her arms beneath her breasts. "I could arrest Mellar," she said quietly, "and have him put to the question. You'd have no need of Hark then."

"A poor joke, my Lady, if I may say so," Mistress Harfor said stiffly, at the same time that Master Norry said, "That would be . . . um . . . against the law, my Lady."

Birgitte bounded to her feet, outrage flooding the bond. "Blood and bloody ashes! We know the man's as rotten as last month's fish."

"No." Elayne sighed, fighting not to feel outraged as well. "We have suspicions, not proof. Those five men *might* have fallen afoul of footpads. The law is quite clear on when someone may be put to the question, and suspicions are not reason enough. Solid evidence is needed. My mother often said, 'The Queen must obey the law she makes, or there is no law.' I will not begin by breaking the law." The bond carried something . . . stubborn. She fixed Birgitte with a steady look. "Neither will you. Do you understand me, Birgitte Trahelion? Neither will you."

To her surprise, the stubbornness lasted only moments longer before dwindling away to be replaced by chagrin. "It was only a suggestion," Birgitte muttered weakly.

Elayne was wondering how she had done that and how to do it again—sometimes there seemed doubt in Birgitte's mind over which of them was in charge—when Deni Colford slipped into the room and cleared her throat to draw attention to herself. A long, brass-studded cudgel balanced the sword hanging at the heavyset woman's waist, looking out of place. Deni was getting better with the sword but still preferred the cudgel she had used keeping order in a wagon drivers' tavern. "A servant came to say that the Lady Dyelin has arrived, my Lady, and will be at your service as soon as she's freshened herself."

"Send the Lady Dyelin word that she's to meet me in the Map Room." Elayne felt a surge of hope. At last, perhaps, she might hear some good news.

CHAPTER
17

A Bronze Bear

Leaving Mistress Harfor and Master Norry, Elayne started eagerly toward the Map Room still holding *saidar*. Eagerly, but not hurriedly. Deni and three Guardswomen strode ahead of her, heads swiveling in constant search of threats, and the other four stamped along behind. She doubted that Dyelin would take long over her ablutions, good news or bad. The Light send that it was good. Birgitte, hands clasped behind her back and wearing a frown, seemed sunk in silence as they walked, though she studied every crossing corridor as if expecting an attack from it. The bond still carried worry. And tiredness. A yawn cracked Elayne's jaws before she could stop herself.

An unwillingness to start rumors was not the only reason she maintained a stately pace. There were more than servants in the hallways, now. Courtesy had required her to offer rooms in the palace to the nobles who managed to reach the city with armsmen—counting armsmen loosely; some were well-trained and carried a sword every day, others had been guiding a plow before being called to follow their lord or lady—and a fair number had accepted. Mainly those who had no dwelling in Caemlyn or, she suspected, felt pinched for coin. Farmers or laborers might think all nobles wealthy, and certainly most were, if only in comparison, but the expenses required by their positions and duties left many counting coins as carefully as any farmwife. What she was to do for the newest arrivals she did not know. Nobles already were sleeping three and four to a bed wherever the beds were large enough; all but the narrowest could take at least two, and did. Many Kinswomen had been reduced to pallets on the floor in the servants' quarters, and thank the Light spring had made that possible.

It seemed the whole lot of her noble guests were out strolling, and when they offered her courtesies, she had to stop and pass at least a few words. Sergase Gilbearn, small and slim in a green riding dress, her dark hair lightly touched with white, who had brought all twenty of the armsmen in her service, and vinegary old Kelwin Janevor, wiry in his discreetly darned blue wool coat, who had brought ten, received as gracious an exchange as did lanky Barel Layden and stout Anthelle Sharplyn, though they were High Seats, if of minor Houses. All had ridden to her support with whatever they could gather, and none had turned back on learning the odds. Many looked uneasy today, though. No one said anything of it—they were all full of good wishes and hopes for a speedy coronation and how honored they were to follow her—but worry was written on their faces. Arilinde Branstrom, normally so ebullient you might think she believed her fifty armsmen could turn the tide for Elayne by themselves, was not the only woman chewing her lip, and Laerid Traehand, stocky and taciturn and usually as stolid as stone, was not the only man with a furrowed brow. Even news of Guybon and the aid he had brought caused only brief smiles, quickly swallowed in ill ease.

"Do you think they've heard of Arymilla's confidence?" she asked in one of the brief intervals when she was not responding to bows and curtsies. "No, that wouldn't be enough to upset Arilinde or Laerid." Arymilla inside the walls with thirty thousand men likely would fail to upset that pair.

"It wouldn't," Birgitte agreed. She glanced around as if to see who besides the Guardswomen might hear before going on. "Maybe they're worried over what's been worrying me. You didn't get lost when we got back. Or rather, you had help."

Elayne paused to offer a few hurried words to a gray-haired couple in woolens that would have suited prosperous farmers. Brannin and Elvaine Martan's manor house was much like a large farmhouse, sprawling and housing generations. A third of their armsmen were their sons and grandsons, nephews and great-nephews. Only those too young or too old to ride had been left behind to see to planting. She hoped the smiling pair did not feel they were getting short shrift, but she was walking on almost as soon as she stopped. "What do you mean, I had help?" she demanded.

"The palace is . . . changed." For a moment, there was confusion in the bond. Birgitte grimaced. "It sounds mad, I know, but it's as if the whole thing had been built to a slightly different plan." One of the Guardswomen ahead missed a step, caught herself. "I have a good memory. . . ." Birgitte hesitated, the bond filled with a jumble of emotions hastily pushed down. Most of her memories of past lives had vanished as surely as the winter's snow. Nothing remained before the founding of the White Tower, and the four lives she had lived between then and the end of the Trolloc Wars were beginning to fragment. Little seemed to frighten her, yet she feared losing the rest, especially her memories of Gaidal Cain. "I don't forget a path once I've followed it," she went on, "and some of these hallways aren't the same as they were. Some of the corridors have been . . . shifted. Others aren't there anymore, and there are some new. Nobody is talking about it that I could find out, but I think the old people are keeping quiet because they're afraid their wits are going, and the younger are afraid they'll lose their positions."

"That's—" Elayne shut her mouth. Clearly it was not impossible. Birgitte did not suffer from sudden fancies. Naris' reluctance to leave her apartments suddenly made sense, and perhaps Reene's earlier puzzlement, too. She almost wished being with child really had befuddled her. But how? "Not the Forsaken," she said firmly. "If they could do something like this, they'd have done it long since, and worse than. . . . A good day to you, too, Lord Aubrem."

Lean and craggy and bald save for a thin white fringe, Aubrem Pensenor should have been dandling his grandchildren's children on his knee, but his back was straight, his eyes clear. He had been among the first to reach Caemlyn, with near to a hundred men and the first news that it was Arymilla Marne marching against the city, with Naean and Elenia supporting her. He began reminiscing about riding for her mother in the Succession, until Birgitte murmured that Lady Dyelin would be waiting for her.

"Oh, in that case, don't let me delay you, my Lady," the old man said heartily. "Please give my regards to Lady Dyelin. She's been so busy, I've not exchanged two words with her since reaching Caemlyn.

My very best regards, if you will." House Pensenor had been allied to Dyelin's Taravin since time out of mind.

"Not the Forsaken," Birgitte said once Aubrem was out of earshot. "But what caused it is only the first question. Will it happen again? If it does, will the changes always be benign? Or might you wake up and find yourself in a room without doors or windows? What happens if you're sleeping in a room that disappears? If a corridor can go, so can a room. And what if it's more than the palace? We need to find out if all the streets still lead where they did. What if the next time, part of the city wall isn't there anymore?"

"You *do* think dark thoughts," Elayne said bleakly. Even with the Power in her, the possibilities were enough to give her a sour stomach.

Birgitte fingered the four golden knots on the shoulder of her white-collared red coat. "They came with these." Strangely, the worry carried by the bond was less now that she had shared her concerns. Elayne hoped the woman did not think *she* had answers. No, that really was impossible. Birgitte knew her too well for that.

"Does this frighten you, Deni?" she asked. "I'll admit it does me."

"No more than needful, my Lady," the blocky woman answered without stopping her careful scan of what lay ahead. Where the others walked with a hand on their sword hilts, her hand rested on her long cudgel. Her voice was as placid, and as matter-of-fact, as her face. "One time a big wagon man named Eldrin Hackly came near breaking my neck. Not usually a rough man, but he was drunk beyond drunk that night. I couldn't get the angle right, and my cudgel seemed to bounce off his skull without making a dent. That frightened me more, because I knew certain sure I was about to die. This is just maybe, and any day you wake up, maybe you die."

Any day you wake up, maybe you die. There were worse ways to look at life, Elayne supposed. Still, she shivered. She was safe, at least till her babes were born, but no one else was.

The two guards at the wide, lion-carved doors to the Map Room were experienced Guardsmen, one short and the next thing to scrawny, the other wide enough to appear squat though he was of average height. Nothing visible picked them out from any other men in the Guards, but only good swordsmen, trusted men, got this duty. The short man nodded to Deni, then straightened his back stiffly at a disapproving frown from Birgitte. Deni smiled at him shyly—Deni!

shyly!—while a pair of Guardswomen went through the inevitable routine. Birgitte opened her mouth, but Elayne laid a hand on her arm, and the other woman looked at her, then shook her head, thick golden braid swaying slowly.

"It's not good when they're on duty, Elayne. They should be seeing to their duties, not mooning over each other." She did not raise her voice, yet color appeared in Deni's round cheeks, and she stopped smiling and started watching the corridor again. It was better that way, perhaps, yet still a pity. *Somebody* ought to have a little pleasure in their lives.

The Map Room was the second-largest ballroom in the palace, and spacious, with four red-streaked marble fireplaces where small fires burned beneath the carved mantels, a domed ceiling worked with gilt and supported by widely spaced columns two spans from white marble walls that had been stripped of tapestries, and sufficient mirrored stand-lamps to light the room as well as if it had windows. The greatest part of its tile floor was a detailed mosaic map of Caemlyn, originally laid down more than a thousand years ago, after the New City had been completed though before Low Caemlyn began growing. Long before there was an Andor, before even Artur Hawkwing. It had been redone several times since, as tiles faded or became worn, so every street was exact—at least, they had been until today; the Light send they still were—and despite many buildings replaced over the years, even some of the alleys were unchanged from what the huge map showed.

There would be no dancing in the Map Room for the foreseeable future, however. Long tables between the columns held more maps, some large enough to spill over the edges, and shelves along the walls held stacks of reports, those not so sensitive they needed to be locked away or else committed to memory and burned. Birgitte's wide writing table, nearly covered with baskets, most full of papers, stood at the far end of the room. As Captain-General, she had her own study, but as soon as she discovered the Map Room, she had decided the map in the floor made it too good not to use.

A small wooden disc, painted red, marked the spot on the outer wall where the assault had just been beaten back. Birgitte scooped it up in passing and tossed it into a round basket full of the things on her writing table. Elayne shook her head. It was a small basket, but if there were enough attacks at once to need that many markers. . . .

"My Lady Birgitte, I have that report on available fodder you asked for," a graying woman said, holding out a page covered with neat lines. The White Lion was worked small on the breast of her neat brown dress. Five other clerks went on with their work, pens skritching. They were among Master Norry's most trusted, and Mistress Harfor had personally screened the half dozen messengers in red-and-white livery, swift young men—boys really—who stood against the wall behind the clerks' small writing tables. One, a pretty youth, began a bow before cutting it short with a blush. Birgitte had settled the question of courtesies, to her or other nobles, with very few words. Work came first, and any noble who disliked that could just avoid the Map Room.

"Thank you, Mistress Anford. I'll look at it later. If you and the others will wait outside, please?"

Mistress Anford quickly gathered up the messengers and the other clerks, giving them only time to stopper their ink jars and blot their work. No one showed a glimmer of surprise. They were accustomed to the need for privacy at times. Elayne had heard people call the Map Room the Secrets Room, though nothing very secret was kept there. All of that was locked away in her apartments.

While the clerks and messengers were filing out, Elayne strode to one of the long tables where a map showed Caemlyn and its surroundings for at least fifty miles in each direction. Even the Black Tower had been inked in, a square sitting less than two leagues south of the city. A growth on Andor, and no way to be rid of it. She still sent parties of Guardsman to inspect some days, via gateways, but the place was large enough that the Asha'man could have been up to anything without her learning of it. Pins with enameled heads marked Arymilla's eight camps around the city, and small metal figures various other camps. A falcon, finely wrought in gold and no taller than her little finger, showed where the Goshien were. Or had been. Were they gone yet? She slipped the falcon into her belt pouch. Aviendha was very much a falcon. On the other side of the table, Birgitte raised a questioning eyebrow.

"They're gone, or going," Elayne told her. There would be visits. Aviendha was not gone forever. "Sent somewhere by Rand. Where, I don't know, burn him."

"I wondered why Aviendha wasn't with you."

Elayne laid one finger atop a bronze horseman less than a hand tall, standing a few leagues west of the city. "Someone needs to take a look at Davram Bashere's camp. Find out whether the Saldaeans are leaving, too. And the Legion of the Dragon." It did not matter if they were, really. They had not interfered in matters, thank the Light, and the time when fear that they might restrained Arymilla was long past. But she disliked things happening in Andor without her knowledge. "Send Guardsmen to the Black Tower tomorrow, as well. Tell them to count how many Asha'man they see."

"So he's planning a big battle. Another big battle. Against the Seanchan, I suppose." Folding her arms beneath her breasts, Birgitte frowned at the map. "I'd wonder where and when, except we have enough in front of us to be going on with."

The map displayed the reasons Arymilla was pressing so hard. For one, to the northeast of Caemlyn, almost off the map, lay the bronze image of a sleeping bear, curled up with its paws over its nose. Two hundred thousand men, near enough, almost as many trained men as all of Andor could field. Four Borderland rulers, accompanied by perhaps a dozen Aes Sedai they tried to keep hidden, searching for Rand, their reasons unstated. Borderlanders had no cause to turn against Rand that she could see—though the simple fact was, he had not bound them to him as he had other lands—but Aes Sedai were another matter, especially with their allegiance uncertain, and twelve approached a dangerous number even for him. Well, the four rulers had in part deciphered her motives for asking them into Andor, yet she had managed to mislead them concerning Rand's whereabouts. Unfortunately, the Borderlanders had belied every tale of how swiftly they could move as they crept south, and now they sat in place, trying to find a way to avoid coming near a city under siege. That was understandable, even laudable. Outland armies in close proximity to Andoran armsmen, on Andoran soil, would make for a touchy situation. There were always at least a few hotheads. Bloodshed, and maybe war, could start all too easily under those circumstances. Even so, bypassing Caemlyn was going to be difficult; the narrow country roads had been turned to bogs by the rains, giving hard passage to an army that large. Elayne could have wished they had marched another twenty or thirty miles toward Caemlyn, though. She had hoped their presence would have had a different effect by now. It might still.

More important, certainly to Arymilla and possibly to herself, a few leagues below the Black Tower stood a tiny silver swordsman with his blade upright in front of him and a silver halberdier, plainly by the same silversmith's hand, one to the west of the black square, the other to the east. Luan, Ellorien and Abelle, Aemlyn, Arathelle and Pelivar had close to sixty thousand men between them in those two camps. Their estates and those of the nobles tied to them must have been stripped near the bone. Those two camps were where Dyelin had been these past three days, trying to learn their intentions.

The spindly Guardsman opened one of the doors and held it for an elderly serving woman carrying a rope-work silver tray with two tall golden wine pitchers and a circle of goblets made of blue Sea Folk porcelain. Reene must have been uncertain how many would be present. The frail woman moved slowly, careful not to tilt the heavy tray and drop anything. Elayne channeled flows of Air to take the tray, then let them dissipate unused. Implying that the woman could not do her job would only be hurtful. She was effusive in her thanks, though. The old woman smiled broadly, clearly delighted, and offered her a deep curtsy once unburdened of the tray.

Dyelin arrived almost right behind the maid, an image of vigor, and shooed her out before grimacing over the contents of one pitcher—Elayne sighed; doubtless it held goat's milk—and filling a goblet from the other. Plainly Dyelin had confined her freshening to washing her face and brushing her hair, golden flecked with gray, because her dark gray riding dress, with a large round silver pin worked with Taravin's Owl and Oak on the high neck, had spots of half-dried mud on the skirts.

"There's something seriously amiss," she said, swirling the wine in her goblet without drinking. A frown deepened the fine lines at the corners of her eyes. "I've been in this palace more times than I can remember, and today I got lost twice."

"We know about that," Elayne told her, and quickly explained what little they had puzzled out, what she intended to do. Belatedly, she wove a ward against eavesdropping and was unsurprised to feel it slice through *saidar*. At least whoever had been listening in would get a jolt from that. A small jolt, since so little of the power was involved that she had not sensed it. Maybe there was a way to make it a *hard* jolt next time, though. Maybe that would begin to discourage eavesdroppers.

"So it might happen again," Dyelin said when Elayne was done. Her tone was calm, but she licked her lips and took a swallow of wine, as if her mouth was suddenly dry. "Well. Well, then. If you don't know what caused it, and you don't know whether it will happen again, what are we to do?"

Elayne stared. Again someone seemed to think she had answers she did not. But then, that was what it meant to be queen. You were always expected to have an answer, to find one. That was what it meant to be Aes Sedai. "We can't stop it, so we'll live with it, Dyelin, and try to keep people from growing too afraid. I'll announce what happened, as much as we know, and have the other sisters do the same. That way, people will know that Aes Sedai are aware, and that should provide some comfort. A little. They'll still be frightened, of course, but not as much as they'll be if we say nothing and it does happen again."

That seemed a feeble effort to her, but surprisingly Dyelin agreed without hesitation. "I myself can suggest nothing else to be done. Most people think you Aes Sedai can handle anything. It should suffice, in the circumstances."

And when they realized that Aes Sedai could not handle anything, that *she* could not? Well, that was a river that she would cross when she reached it. "Is the news good, or bad?"

Before Dyelin could answer, the door opened again.

"I heard that Lady Dyelin had returned. You should have sent for us, Elayne. You aren't queen yet, and I dislike you keeping secrets from me. Where is Aviendha?" Catalyn Haevin, a cool-eyed, ungovernable young woman—a girl in truth, still long months short of her majority, though her guardian had abandoned her to go her own way—was pride to her toenails, her plump chin held high. Of course, that might have been because of the large enameled pin of Haevin's Blue Bear that decorated the high neck of her blue riding dress. She had begun showing Dyelin respect, and a certain wariness, shortly after she started sharing a bed with her and Sergase, but with Elayne she insisted on every perquisite of a High Seat.

"We all heard," Conail Northan said. Lean and tall in a red silk coat, with laughing eyes and an eagle's beak of a nose, he was of age, just, a few months past his sixteenth name day. He swaggered and caressed the hilt of his sword much too fondly, but there seemed no harm in him. Only boyishness, an unfortunate trait in a High Seat. "And none of us could wait to hear when Luan and the others will join us. This pair would have run the whole way." He ruffled the hair of the two younger boys with him, Perival Mantear and Branlet Gilyard, who gave him a dark look and raked fingers through his hair to straighten it. Perival blushed. Quite short but already pretty, he was the youngest at twelve, yet Branlet had only a year on him.

Elayne sighed, but she could not ask them to leave. Children most of them might be—perhaps all, considering Conail's behavior—yet they were the High Seats of their Houses, and along with Dyelin, her most important allies. She did wish she knew how they had learned the purpose of Dyelin's journey. That had been intended to be a secret until she knew what news Dyelin brought. Another task for Reene. Gossip unchecked, the wrong gossip, could be as dangerous as spies.

"Where is Aviendha?" Catalyn demanded. Strangely, she had become quite taken with Aviendha. Fascinated might have been a better word. Of all things, she had persisted in trying to make Aviendha teach her to use a spear!

"So, my Lady," Conail said, strolling over to fill a blue goblet with wine, "when are they joining us?"

"The bad news is that they aren't," Dyelin said calmly. "The good news is that they've each rejected an invitation to join Arymilla." She cleared her throat loudly as Branlet reached for the wine pitcher. His cheeks reddened, and he picked up the other pitcher as if he had really meant to all along. The High Seat of House Gilyard, yet still a boy for all of the sword on his hip. Perival also wore a sword, one that dragged on the floor tiles and looked too big for him, but he had already taken goat's milk. Pouring her own wine, Catalyn smirked at the younger boys, a superior smile that vanished when she noticed Dyelin looking at her.

"That's small turnips to call good news," Birgitte said. "Burn me, if it isn't. You bring back a bloody half-starved squirrel and call it a side of beef."

"Pungent as always," Dyelin said dryly. The two women glared at each other, Birgitte's hands balling into fists, Dyelin fingering the dagger at her belt.

"No arguing," Elayne said, making her voice sharp. The anger in the bond helped. At times she feared the pair might come to blows. "I won't put up with your bickering today."

"Where is Aviendha?"

"Gone, Catalyn. What else did you learn, Dyelin?"

"Gone where?"

"Gone away," Elayne said calmly. *Saidar* or no *saidar*, she wanted to slap the girl's face. "Dyelin?"

The older woman took a sip of wine to cover breaking off her staring match with Birgitte. Coming to stand beside Elayne, she picked up the silver swordsman, turned him over, set him down again. "Aemlyn, Arathelle and Pelivar tried to convince me to announce a claim to the throne, but they were less adamant than when I spoke with them last. I believe I've almost convinced them I won't do it."

"Almost?" Birgitte put a hundredweight of derision in the word. Dyelin ignored her pointedly. Elayne frowned at Birgitte, who shifted uncomfortably and stalked off long enough to get herself a goblet of wine. Very satisfying. Whatever she was doing right, she hoped it continued to work.

"My Lady," Perival said with a bow, extending one of two goblets he held to Elayne. She managed a smile and a curtsy before taking the offering. Goat's milk. Light, but she was beginning to revile the stuff!

"Luan and Abelle were . . . noncommittal," Dyelin continued, frowning at the halberdier. "They may be swaying toward you." She hardly sounded as though she believed it, however. "I reminded Luan that he helped me arrest Naean and Elenia, back in the beginning, but that may have done no more good than it did with Pelivar."

"So they may all be waiting for Arymilla to win," Birgitte said grimly. "If you survive, they'll declare for you against her. If you don't, one of them will make her own claim. Ellorien has the next best right after you, doesn't she?" Dyelin scowled, but she offered no denials.

"And Ellorien?" Elayne asked quietly. She was sure she knew the answer there already. Her mother had had Ellorien flogged. That had been under Rahvin's influence, but few seemed to believe that. Few seemed to believe Gaebril had even been Rahvin.

Dyelin grimaced. "The woman's head is stone! She'd announce a claim in my name if she thought it would do any good. At least she has enough sense to see it won't." Elayne noted that she made no mention of any claims in Ellorien's own name. "In any case, I left Keraille Surtovni and Julanya Fote to watch them. I doubt they'll move, but if they do, we'll know straightaway." Three Kinswomen who needed to form a circle to Travel were watching the Borderlanders for the same reason.

No good news at all, then, no matter what face Dyelin tried to put on it. Elayne had hoped the threat of the Borderlanders would drive some of the Houses to support her. *At least one reason I let them cross Andor still holds,* she thought grimly. Even if she failed to gain the throne, she had done that service for Andor. Unless whoever did take the throne bungled matters completely. She could see Arymilla doing just that. Well, Arymilla was not going to wear the Rose Crown, and that was that. One way or another, she had to be stopped.

"So it's six, six and six," Catalyn said, frowning and thumbing the long signet ring on her left hand. She looked thoughtful, unusual for her. Her usual style was to speak her mind with no consideration whatsoever. "Even if Candraed joins us, we are short of ten." Was she wondering whether she had tied Haevin to a hopeless cause? Unfortunately, she had not tied her House so tightly the knots could not be undone.

"I was certain Luan would join us," Conail muttered. "And Abelle and Pelivar." He took a deep swallow of wine. "Once we beat Arymilla, they'll come. You mark me on it."

"But what are they thinking?" Branlet demanded. "Are they trying to start a war with *three* sides?" His voice went from treble to bass halfway through that, and his face flooded with red. He buried his face in his goblet, but grimaced. Apparently he liked goat's milk as little as she did.

"It's the Borderlanders." Perival's voice was a boy's piping, but he sounded sure of himself. "They're holding back because whoever wins here, the Borderlanders still have to be dealt with." He picked up the bear, hefting it as if its weight would give him answers. "What I don't understand is why they're invading us in the first place. We're so far from the Borderlands. And why haven't they marched on and attacked Caemlyn? They could sweep Arymilla aside, and I doubt we could keep them out as easily as we do her. So why are they here?"

Smiling, Conail clapped him on the shoulder. "Now that will be a battle to see, when we face the Borderlanders. Northan's Eagles and Mantear's Anvil will do Andor proud that day, eh?" Perival nodded, but he did not look happy at the prospect. Conail certainly did.

Elayne exchanged glances with Dyelin and Birgitte, both of whom looked amazed. Elayne felt astonished herself. The other two women knew, of course, but little Perival had come near touching a secret that had to be kept. Others might puzzle out eventually that the Borderlanders had been meant to push Houses into joining her, but it *must* not be confirmed.

"Luan and the others sent to Arymilla asking for a truce until the Borderlanders were turned back," Dyelin said after a moment. "She asked time to consider. As near as I can calculate, it was then that she began increasing her efforts at the walls. She tells them she's still considering."

"Aside from anything else," Catalyn said heatedly, "that shows why Arymilla doesn't deserve the throne. She puts her own ambition above Andor's safety. Luan and the others must be fools not to see it."

"Not fools," Dyelin replied. "Just men and women who think they see the future better than they do."

What if she and Dyelin were the ones who were not seeing the future clearly, Elayne wondered. To save Andor, she would have thrown her support to Dyelin. Not gladly, but to save Andor's blood, she would have. Dyelin would have the support of ten Houses, more than ten. Even Danine Candraed might finally decide to stir herself in support of Dyelin. Except that Dyelin did not want to be queen. She believed that Elayne was the one to wear the Rose Crown. So did Elayne. But what if they were wrong? Not the first time that question had come to her, but now, staring at the map with all of its ill tidings, she could not shake free of it.

That evening, after a dinner memorable only for the surprise of tiny strawberries, she sat in the large sitting room of her apartments, reading. Trying to read. The leather-bound book was a history of Andor, as was most of her reading of late. It was necessary to read as many as possible to gain any real version of truth, cross-checking one against another. For one thing, a book first published during any monarch's reign never mentioned any of her missteps, or those of her immediate predecessors if they were of her own House. You had to read books written while Trakand held the throne to learn of Mantear's mistakes, and books written under Mantear to learn of Norwelyn's errors. Others' mistakes could teach her how not to make the same herself. Her mother had made that almost her first lesson.

She could not concentrate, however. She often found herself staring at a page without seeing a word, thinking of her sister, or starting to say something to Aviendha before remembering that she was not there. She felt very lonely, which was ridiculous. Sephanie stood in a corner against the possibility she wanted anything. Eight Guardswomen were standing outside the door to the apartments, and one of them, Yurith Azeri, was an excellent conversationalist, an educated woman though silent on her past. But none of them was Aviendha.

When Vandene glided into the room followed by Kirstian and Zarya, it seemed a relief. The two white-clad women stopped by the doorway, expressions meek. Untouched by the Oath Rod, pale Kirstian, hands folded at her waist, appeared just into her middle years; Zarya, with her tilted eyes and hooked nose, well short of them. She held something wrapped in white toweling.

"Forgive me if I'm interrupting," Vandene began, then frowned. The white-haired Green's face somehow gave an impression of age despite her Aes Sedai features. Those could have been twenty, or forty, or anything in between; that seemed to change at every blink. Perhaps it was her dark eyes, luminous and deep and pained, which had seen so much. There was an air of tiredness about her, too. Her back was straight, but she still looked weary. "It is none of my business, of course," she said delicately, "but is there a reason you are holding so much of the Power? I thought you must be weaving something very complex when I felt you in the corridor."

With a start, Elayne realized that she held nearly as much of *saidar* as she could contain safely. How had that happened? She did not recall drawing any deeper. Hastily, she released the Source, regret filling her as the Power drained away and the world became . . . ordinary again. On the instant, her mood bounced sideways.

"You aren't interrupting anything," she said peevishly, setting her book down on the table in front of her. She had not finished three pages of the thing anyway.

"May I make us private, then?"

Elayne gave a curt nod—it *was* none of the woman's bloody business how much of the Power she held; she knew the protocols as well as Elayne, or better—and told Sephanie to wait in the anteroom while Vandene wove a ward against eavesdropping.

Ward or no ward, Vandene waited until the door closed behind the maid before speaking. "Reanne Corly is dead, Elayne."

"Oh, Light, no." Temper vanished into sobs, and she hastily snatched a lace-edged handkerchief from her sleeve to blot the tears suddenly streaming down her cheeks. Her cursed shifting moods at work, yet Reanne surely deserved tears. She had so wanted to become a Green. "How?" Burn her, she wished she could stop blubbering!

There were no tears from Vandene. Perhaps there were no more tears in her. "She was smothered with the Power. Whoever did it used much more than was needed. The residues of *saidar* were thick on her and in the room where she was found. The murderer wanted to be sure no one would miss seeing how she died."

"That makes no sense, Vandene."

"Perhaps it does. Zarya?"

The Saldaean woman laid her small bundle on the table and un-wrapped it to reveal an articulated wooden doll. It was very old, the simple dress threadbare, the painted face flaking and missing an eye, half of its long dark hair gone.

"This belonged to Mirane Larinen," Zarya said. "Derys Nermala found it behind a cupboard."

"I don't see what Mirane leaving a doll behind has to do with Re-anne's death," Elayne said, wiping her eyes. Mirane was one of the Kinswomen who had run away.

"Only this," Vandene answered. "When Mirane went to the Tower, she hid this doll outside because she had heard that everything she owned would be burned. After she was put out, she retrieved it and al-ways carried it with her. Always. She had a quirk, though. Wherever she stopped for a time, she hid the doll again. Do not ask me why. But she would not have run away and abandoned it."

Still dabbing at her eyes, Elayne leaned back in her chair. Her weeping had dwindled to sniffles, but her eyes still leaked tears. "So Mirane didn't run away. She was murdered and . . . disposed of." A grisly way to put it. "The others, too, you think? All of them?"

Vandene nodded, and for a moment her slender shoulders slumped. "I very much fear so," she said, straightening. "I expect clues were left among the things they left behind, treasured keepsakes like this doll, a favorite piece of jewelry. The murderer wanted us to think she was being clever at hiding her crimes but not clever enough, only *we* weren't clever enough to find those clues, so she decided to become more blatant."

"To frighten the Kinswomen into fleeing," Elayne muttered. That would not cripple her, but it would throw her back on the mercies of the Windfinders, and those seemed to be growing mingy. "How many of them know of this?"

"All, by now, I should think," Vandene said dryly. "Zarya told Derys to keep quiet, but that woman likes the sound of her own voice."

"This seems aimed at me, at helping Arymilla gain the throne, but why would a Black sister have any interest in that? I can't think we have *two* murderers among us. At least this settles the question of Merilille. Speak with Sumeko and Alise, Vandene. They can make sure the rest don't panic." Sumeko ranked next after Reanne, as the Kin ordered their hierarchy, and while Alise stood much lower, she was a woman of great influence. "From now on, none of them is to be alone, not ever. Always at least two together, and three or four would be better. And warn them to be careful of Careane and Sareitha."

"I'd advise against that," Vandene said quickly. "They should be safe in groups, and word would reach Careane and Sareitha. Warned against Aes Sedai? The Kin would give themselves away in a minute." Kirstian and Zarya nodded solemnly.

After a moment, Elayne reluctantly agreed to the continued secrecy. The Kin *should* be safe in groups. "Let Chanelle know about Reanne and the others. I can't imagine the Windfinders are in any danger—losing them wouldn't hurt me the way losing the Kin would—but wouldn't it be wonderful if they did decide to leave?"

She did not expect that they would—Chanelle feared returning to the Sea Folk with the bargain unfulfilled—yet it would be a bright spot in an otherwise miserable day if they did. At least it seemed unlikely anything could darken the day further. The thought sent a chill through her. The Light send nothing would darken it more.

Arymilla pushed her plate of stew away with a grimace. She had been offered her choice of beds for the night—Arlene, her maid, was making the choice now; the woman knew what she liked—and the least she had expected was a decent meal, but the mutton was fatty, and definitely beginning to go rancid besides. There had been too much of that lately. This time the cook was going to be flogged! She was unsure which of the nobles in this camp employed him, just that he was supposed to be the best at hand—the best!—but that did not matter. He would be flogged to make an example. And then sent away, of course. You could never trust a cook after he had been punished.

The mood in the tent was far from lively. Several of the nobles in the camp had hoped for invitations to dine with her, but none stood high enough. She was beginning to regret not asking one or two, even some of Naean's or Elenia's people. They might have been entertaining. Her closest allies at table together, and you might have thought they sat over funeral meats. Oh, scrawny old Nasin, his thinning white hair uncombed, was eating away heartily, apparently not noticing that the meat was nearly rotten, and giving her fatherly pats on the hand. She met his smiles like a dutiful daughter. The fool was wearing one of his flower-embroidered coats tonight. The thing could have passed for a woman's dressing robe! Happily, his leers were all directed down the table at Elenia; the honey-haired woman flinched, her foxlike face paling whenever she glanced at him. She controlled House Sarand as if she were the High Seat instead of her husband, yet she feared that Arymilla would still let Nasin have his way with her. That threat was unneeded, now, but it was well to have it to hand just in case. Yes, Nasin was happy enough in his futile pursuit of Elenia, but the others were sunk in gloom. Their plates were abandoned barely touched, and they kept her two serving men trotting to refill wine cups. She never liked trusting others' servants. At least the wine had not turned.

"I still say we should make a heavier push," Lir grumbled drunkenly into his cup. A whip of a man, his red coat showing the wear of armor straps, the High Seat of Baryn was ever eager to strike. Subtlety was simply beyond him. "My eyes-and-ears report more armsmen entering the city every day through these 'gateways.'" He shook his head and muttered something under his breath. The man actually believed those rumors of dozens of Aes Sedai in the Royal Palace. "All these pinprick attacks do is lose men."

"I agree," Karind said, fiddling with a large golden pin, enameled with the running Red Fox of Anshar, that was fastened to her bosom. She was not much less intoxicated than Lir. Her square face had a slackness about it. "We need to press home instead of throwing men away. Once we're over the walls, our advantage in numbers will pay off."

Arymilla's mouth tightened. They might at least show her the respect due a woman who was soon to be Queen of Andor, rather than disagreeing with her all the time. Unfortunately, Baryn and Anshar were not bound to her so tightly as Sarand and Arawn. Unlike Jarid and Naean, Lir and Karind had announced their support of her without publishing it in writing. Neither had Nasin, but she had no fear of losing him. Him, she had wound around her wrist for a bracelet.

Forcing a smile, she made her voice jovial. "We lose mercenaries. What else are mercenaries good for if not dying in place of our armsmen?" She held up her winecup and a lean man in her silver-trimmed blue hastened to fill it. In fact, he was so hasty that he spilled a drop on her hand. Her scowl made him snatch a handkerchief from his pocket to blot up the drop before she could pull her hand away. His handkerchief! The Light only knew where that filthy thing had been, and he had *touched* her with it! His mouth writhed with fear as he retreated, bowing and mumbling apologies. Let him serve out the meal. He could be dismissed after. "We will need all of our armsmen when I ride against the Borderlanders. Don't you agree, Naean?"

Naean twitched as though stuck with a pin. Slim and pale in yellow silk worked with silver patterns of Arawn's Triple Keys on the breast, she had begun looking haggard in recent weeks, her blue eyes drawn and tired. All of her supercilious airs were quite gone. "Of course, Arymilla," she said meekly and drained her cup. Good. She and Elenia were definitely tamed, but Arymilla liked to check now and then to make sure neither was growing a new backbone.

"If Luan and the others will not support you, what good will taking Caemlyn do?" Sylvase, Nasin's granddaughter and heir, spoke so seldom that the question came as a shock. Sturdy and not quite pretty, she usually had a vapid gaze, but her blue eyes appeared quite sharp at the moment. Everyone stared at her. That seemed not to faze her a bit. She toyed with a winecup, but Arymilla thought it no more than her second. "If we must fight the Borderlanders, why not accept Luan's truce so Andor can field its full strength unhindered by divisions?"

Arymilla smiled. She wanted to slap the silly woman. Nasin would be angered by that, however. He wanted her kept as Arymilla's "guest" to prevent his removal as High Seat—part of him seemed aware that his wits were gone; all of him intended holding on as High Seat until he died—but he did love her. "Ellorien and some of the others will come to me yet, child," she said smoothly. Smoothness required some effort. Who did the chit think she was? "Aemlyn, Arathelle, Pelivar. They have grievances against Trakand." Surely they would come once Elayne and Dyelin were out of the way. Those two would not survive Caemlyn's fall. "Once I have the city, they will be mine in any event. Three of Elayne's supporters are children, and Conail Northan is little more than a child. I trust I can convince them to publish their support of me easily enough." And if she could not, Master Lounalt surely could. A pity if children had to be handed over to him and his cords. "I will be queen by sunset of the day Caemlyn falls to me. Isn't that right, father?"

Nasin laughed, spraying gobbets of half-chewed stew across the table. "Yes, yes," he said, patting Arymilla's hand. "You listen to your aunt, Sylvase. Do as she tells you. She'll be Queen of Andor soon." His smile faded, and an odd note entered his voice. It might almost have been . . . pleading. "Remember, you will be High Seat of Caeren after I'm gone. After I'm gone. You will be High Seat."

"As you say, Grandfather," Sylvase murmured, inclining her head briefly. When she straightened, her gaze was as insipid as ever. The sharpness must have been a trick of the light. Of course.

Nasin grunted and went happily back to wolfing down the stew. "Best I've had in days. I think I'll have another plate. More wine here, man. Can't you see my cup's dry?"

The silence around the table stretched in discomfort. Nasin's more open displays of senility had a way of causing that.

"I still say," Lir began finally, only to cut off as a stocky armsman with Marne's four Silver Moons on his chest entered the tent.

Bowing respectfully, the fellow made his way around the table and bent to whisper in Arymilla's ear. "Master Hernvil asks a word in private, my Lady."

Everyone but Nasin and his granddaughter pretended to concentrate on their wine, certainly not attempting to eavesdrop. He went on eating. She watched Arymilla, bland-faced. That sharpness *must* have been a trick of the light.

"I'll be but a few moments," Arymilla said, rising. She waved a hand, indicating the food and wine. "Enjoy yourselves until I return. Enjoy." Lir called for more wine.

Outside, she did not bother raising her skirts to keep them clear of the mud. Arlene would already have to clean them, so what did a little more mud matter? Light showed in some tents, but by and large the camp was dark beneath a half moon. Jakob Hernvil, her secretary, waited a little away from the tent in a plain coat, holding a lantern that made a yellow pool around him. He was a little man, and lean, as if all the fat had been boiled from him. Discretion was bred in his bones, and she ensured his loyalty by paying him enough that only the largest bribes could be of interest, far more than anyone would offer a scrivener.

"Forgive me for interrupting your meal, my Lady," he said with a bow, "but I was sure you would want to hear right away." It was always a surprise, hearing such a deep voice from such a tiny man. "They have agreed. But they want the whole amount of gold first."

Her lips compressed of their own accord. The whole amount. She had hoped to get off with paying only the first half. After all, who would dare dun her once she was queen? "Draw up a letter to Mistress Andscale. I'll sign and seal it first thing in the morning." Transferring that much gold would require days. And how long to have the armsmen ready? She had never really paid attention to that sort of thing. Lir could tell her, but she hated showing weakness. "Tell them a week from tomorrow, to the day." That should be enough. In a week, Caemlyn would be hers. The throne would be hers. Arymilla, by the Grace of the Light, Queen of Andor, Defender of the Realm, Protector of the People, High Seat of House Marne. Smiling, she went back inside to tell the others the wonderful news.

CHAPTER
18

News for the Dragon

E nough, Loial," Rand said firmly, thumbing tabac into his short-
stemmed pipe from a goatskin pouch. It was Tairen leaf, with a
slightly oily taste from the curing, but that was all that was to be
had. Thunder rolled overhead, slow and ponderous. "You'll talk me
hoarse with all these questions."

They were seated at a long table in one of the larger rooms in Lord
Algarin's manor house, the remains of the midday meal pushed down
to one end. The servants were old, for the most part, and slower moving than ever since Algarin left for the Black Tower. The rain pouring
down outside seemed to be slackening, though strong gusts of wind
still pelted the windows with raindrops hard enough to rattle the glass
in the six yellow-painted casements. Many of those panes held bubbles;
some distorted what lay outside almost beyond recognition. The table
and chairs were simply carved, no more elaborate than might be found
in many farmhouses, and the yellow cornices beneath the high, beamed
ceiling little more so. The two fireplaces, at either end of the room,
were broad and tall but of plain stone, the andirons and firetools sturdy
wrought iron and simple. Lord or no, Algarin was far from wealthy.

Tucking the tabac pouch into his pocket, Rand strolled to one of
the fireplaces and used small brass tongs from the mantel to lift a burning sliver of oak for lighting his pipe. He hoped no one thought that

strange. He avoided channeling any more than absolutely necessary, especially if anyone else was present—the dizziness that hit him when he did was difficult to conceal—but no one had mentioned it so far. A gust of wind brought a squeaking as though tree branches had scraped across the windowpanes. Imagination. The nearest trees were beyond the fields, more than half a mile away.

Loial had brought down a vine-carved chair from the Ogier rooms that put his knees level with the tabletop, so he had to lean forward sharply to write in his leather-bound notebook. The volume was small for him, little enough to fit neatly into one of his capacious coat pockets, but still as large as most human books Rand had seen. Fine hair decorated Loial's upper lip and a patch beneath his chin; he was attempting a beard and mustaches, though with only a few weeks' growth, it did not seem a very successful attempt so far.

"But you've told me almost nothing really useful," the Ogier rumbled, a drum booming its disappointment. His tufted ears drooped. Even so, he began wiping the steel nib of his polished wooden pen. Fatter than Rand's thumb and long enough to seem slender, it fitted Loial's thick fingers perfectly. "You never mention heroics, except by somebody else. You make it all sound so everyday. To hear you tell it, the fall of Illian was as exciting as watching a weaver repair her loom. And cleansing the True Source? You and Nynaeve linked, then you sat and channeled while everybody else was off fighting Forsaken. Even Nynaeve told me more than that, and she claims to remember almost nothing."

Nynaeve, wearing all of her jeweled *ter'angreal* and her strange bracelet-and-rings *angreal*, shifted in her chair in front of the other fireplace, then went back to watching Alivia. Every so often she glanced toward the windows and tugged at her thick braid, but for the most part she focused on the yellow-haired Seanchan woman. Standing beside the doorway like a guard, Alivia gave a small, brief smile of amusement. The former *damane* knew Nynaeve's display was meant for her. The intensity never left her hawkish blue eyes, though. It seldom had, ever since her collar had been removed in Caemlyn. The two Maidens squatting on their heels near her playing cat's cradle, Harilin of the Iron Mountain Taardad and Enaila of the Jarra Chareen, were making their own display. *Shoufa* wrapped around their heads and black veils hanging down their chests, each had three or four spears stuck through the harness holding her bow case on her back and a bullhide buckler lying on the floor. There were fifty Maidens in the manor house, several of them Shaido, and they all went about ready to dance the spears in a heartbeat. Perhaps with him. They seemed torn between delight at providing a guard for him again and displeasure over how long he had avoided them.

As for himself, he could not look at any of them without the litany of women who had died for him, women he had killed, starting up in his head. *Moiraine Damodred.* Her above all. Her name was written inside his skull in fire. *Liah of the Cosaida Chareen, Sendara of the Iron Mountain Taardad, Lamelle of the Smoke Water Miagoma, Andhilin of the Red Salt Goshien, Desora of the Musara Reyn.* . . . So many names. Sometimes he woke in the middle of the night muttering that list, with Min holding him and murmuring to him as if soothing a child. He always told her he was all right and wanted to go back to sleep, yet after he closed his eyes, he did not sleep until the list had been completed. Sometimes Lews Therin chanted it with him.

Min looked up from the volume she had open on the table, one of Herid Fel's books. She devoured those, and used the note he had sent Rand before his murder, the one where he said she was a distraction because she was so pretty, as a bookmark. Her short blue coat, embroidered with white flowers on the sleeves and lapels, was cut to fit snugly over her bosom, where her creamy silk blouse showed a touch of cleavage, and her big dark eyes, framed by dark ringlets to her shoulders, held a pleased light. He could feel her pleasure through the bond. She liked him looking at her. Without a doubt the bond told her how much he liked looking. Oddly enough, it said she liked looking at him, too. Pretty? He hummed, thumbing his earlobe. She was beautiful. And tied to him tighter than ever. She and Elayne and Aviendha. How was he to keep them safe now? He forced himself to smile back at her around his pipestem, unsure how well the deception was working. A touch of irritation had entered the bond from her end, though why she should become irritable whenever she thought he was worrying about her was beyond him. Light, *she* wanted to protect *him*!

"Rand isn't very talkative, Loial," she said, no longer smiling. Her low, almost musical voice held no anger, but the bond told another story. "In fact, sometimes he's about as talkative as a mussel." The look she directed at Rand made him sigh. It seemed there would be a great deal of talking once they were alone together. "I can't tell you much, myself, but I'm sure Cadsuane and Verin will tell you anything you want to know. Others will, too. Ask them if you want more than yes and no and two words besides."

Stout little Verin, knitting in a chair beside Nynaeve, appeared startled to hear her name mentioned. She blinked vaguely, as though wondering why it had been. Cadsuane, at the far end of the table with her sewing basket open beside her, only took her attention away from her embroidery hoop long enough to glance at Loial. Golden ornaments swayed, dangling from the iron-gray bun atop her head. It was only that, a glance, not a frown, yet Loial's ears twitched. Aes Sedai always impressed him, and Cadsuane more than any other.

"Oh, I will, Min, I will," he said. "But Rand is central to my book." With no sand jar at hand, he began blowing gently on the page of his notebook to dry the ink, but Loial being Loial, he still talked between puffs. "You never give enough detail, Rand. You make me drag everything out of you. Why, you never even mentioned being imprisoned in Far Madding until Min did. Never mentioned it! What did the Council of Nine say when they offered you the Laurel Crown? And when you renamed it? I can't think they liked that. What was the coronation like? Was there feasting, a festival, parades? How many Forsaken came against you at Shadar Logoth? Which ones? What did it *look* like at the end? What did it *feel* like? My book won't be very good without the details. I hope Mat and Perrin give me better answers." He frowned, long eyebrows grazing his cheeks. "I hope they're all right."

Colors spun in Rand's head, twin rainbows swirled in water. He knew how to suppress them, now, but this time he did not try. One resolved into a brief image of Mat riding through forest at the head of a line of mounted folk. He seemed to be arguing with a small, dark woman who rode beside him, taking his hat off and peering into it, then cramming it back onto his head. That lasted only moments, then was replaced by Perrin sitting over winecups in a common room or tavern with a man and a woman who wore identical red coats ornately trimmed with blue and yellow. Odd garments. Perrin looked grim as death, his companions wary. Of him?

"They're well," he said, calmly ignoring a piercing look from Cadsuane. She did not know everything, and he intended to keep it that way. Calm on the surface, content, blowing smoke rings. Inside was another matter. *Where are they?* he thought angrily, pushing down another appearance of the colors. That was as easy as breathing, now. *I need them, and they're off for a day at the Ansaline Gardens!*

Abruptly another image was floating his head, a man's face, and his breath caught. For the first time, it came without any dizziness. For the first time, he could see it clearly in the moments before it vanished. A blue-eyed man with a square chin, perhaps a few years older than himself. Or rather, he saw it clearly for the first time in a long while. It was the face of the stranger who had saved his life in Shadar Logoth when he fought Sammael. Worse. . . .

He was aware of me, Lews Therin said. He sounded sane for a change. Sometimes he did, but the madness always returned eventually. *How can a face appearing in my mind be* aware *of me?*

If you don't know, how do you expect me to? Rand thought. *But I was aware of him, as well.* It had been a strange sensation, as if he were . . . touching . . . the other man somehow. Only not physically. A residue hung on. It seemed he only had to move a hair's breadth, in any direction, to touch him again. *I think he saw my face, too.*

Talking to a voice in his head no longer seemed peculiar. In truth, it had not for quite a long time. And now . . . ? Now, he could see Mat and Perrin by thinking of them or hearing their names, and he had this other face coming to him unbidden. More than a face, apparently. What was holding conversations inside his own skull alongside that? But the man *had* been aware, and Rand of him.

When our streams of balefire touched in Shadar Logoth, it must have created some sort of link between us. I can't think of any other explanation. That was the only time we ever met. He was using their so-called True Power. It had to be that. I felt nothing, saw nothing except his stream of balefire. Having bits of knowledge seem his when he knew they came from Lews Therin no longer seemed odd, either. He could *remember* the Ansaline Gardens, destroyed in the War of the Shadow, as well as he did his father's farm. Knowledge drifted the other way, too. Lews Therin sometimes spoke of Emond's Field as if he had grown up there. *Does that make any sense to you?*

Oh, Light, why do I have this voice in my head? Lews Therin moaned. *Why can I not die? Oh, Ilyena, my precious Ilyena, I want to join you.* He trailed off into weeping. He often did when he spoke of the wife he had murdered in his madness.

It did not matter. Rand suppressed the sound of the man crying, pushed it down to a faint noise on the edge of hearing. He was certain that he was right. But who was the fellow? A Darkfriend, for sure, but not one of the Forsaken. Lews Therin knew their faces as well as he knew his own, and now Rand did, too. A sudden thought made him grimace. *How* aware of him was the other man? *Ta'veren* could be found by their effect on the Pattern, though only the Forsaken knew how. Lews Therin certainly had never mentioned knowing—their "conversations" were always brief, and the man seldom gave information willingly—and nothing had drifted across from him on the subject. At least, Lanfear and Ishamael had known how, but no one had found him that way since they had died. Could this link be used in the same fashion? They could all be in danger. More danger than usual, as if the usual were not enough.

"Are you well, Rand?" Loial asked worriedly, screwing the leaf-engraved silver cap onto his ink jar. The glass of that was so thick it could have survived anything short of being hurled against stone, but Loial handled it as though it were fragile. In his huge hands, it looked fragile. "I thought the cheese tasted off, but you ate a good bit of it."

"I'm fine," Rand said, but of course, Nynaeve paid him no heed. She was out of her chair and gliding down the room in a flash, blue skirts swirling. Goose bumps popped out on his skin as she embraced *saidar* and stretched to lay her hands on his head. An instant later, a chill rippled through him. The woman never *asked*! Sometimes she behaved as if she were still the Wisdom in Emond's Field and he would be heading back to the farm come morning.

"You're not ill," she said in tones of relief. Spoiled food was causing all sorts of sickness among the servants, some of it serious. People would have died except for the presence of Asha'man and Aes Sedai to give Healing. Reluctant to cost their lord scarce money by throwing food out, despite all the admonitions Cadsuane and Nynaeve and the other Aes Sedai gave them, they fed themselves things that should have been tossed on the midden heap. A different tingling centered briefly around the double wound in his left side.

"That wound is no better," she said with a frown. She had tried Healing it, succeeding no better than Flinn had. That did not sit well with her. Nynaeve took failure as a personal insult. "How can you even stand up? You must be in agony."

"He ignores it," Min said flatly. Oh, yes, there would be words.

"It hurts no worse standing than sitting," he told Nynaeve, gently

taking her hands from his head. Simple truth. So was what Min had
said. He could not afford to let pain make him a prisoner.

One of the twinned doors creaked open to admit a white-haired
man in a worn yellow coat trimmed with red and blue that hung
loosely on his bony frame. His bow was halting, a fault of his joints
rather than disrespect. "My Lord Dragon," he said in a voice nearly as
creaky as the hinges, "Lord Logain has returned."

Logain did not wait on invitations, entering practically on the serving man's heels. A tall man with dark hair curling to his shoulders, and
dark for a Ghealdanin, women likely thought him handsome, yet there
was a streak of darkness inside him as well. He wore his black coat with
the Sword and the Dragon on the high collar, and a long-hilted sword
on his hip, but he had made an addition, a round enameled pin on his
shoulder showing three golden crowns in a field of blue. Had the man
adopted a sigil? The old man's hairy eyebrows shot up in surprise, and
he looked to Rand as if inquiring whether he wanted Logain removed.

"The news from Andor is fair enough, I suppose," Logain said,
tucking black gauntlets behind his sword belt. He offered Rand a minimal bow, the slightest bending of his back. "Elayne still holds Caemlyn, and Arymilla still holds her siege, but Elayne has the advantage
since Arymilla can't even stop food getting in, much less reinforce-
ments. No need to scowl. I kept out of the city. Black coats aren't exactly welcome there, in any case. The Borderlanders are still in the
same place. You were wise to stay clear of them, it seems. Rumor says
there are thirteen Aes Sedai with them. Rumor says they're looking for
you. Has Bashere gotten back yet?" Nynaeve gave him a scowl and
moved away from Rand gripping her braid tightly. Aes Sedai bonding
Asha'man was all very well in her book, but not the reverse.

Thirteen and looking for him? He had stayed clear of the Borderlanders because Elayne did not welcome his help—interference, she
called it, and he had begun to see that she had the right of it; the Lion
Throne was hers to gain, not his to give—but perhaps it was as well
that he had. The Borderland rulers all had ties to the White Tower, and
no doubt Elaida was still eager to get her hands on him. Her and that
mad proclamation about no one approaching him except through her.
If she believed that would force him to come to her, she was a fool.

"Thank you, that will be all, Ethin. *Lord* Logain?" he asked as the
serving man bowed himself out with a last disgruntled glance at Lo-

gain. Rand thought the man would have tried had he told him to haul Logain out.

"The title is his by birth," Cadsuane said without looking up from her embroidery. She would know; she had helped capture him back when he was calling himself the Dragon Reborn, him and Taim both. Her hair ornaments bobbed as she nodded to herself. "Phaw! A minor lordling with a scrap of land in the mountains, most of it all but straight up and down. But King Johanin and the Crown High Council stripped him of his lands and title after he became a false Dragon."

Small spots of color appeared in Logain's cheeks, yet his voice was cool and composed. "They could take my estate, but they could not take away who I am."

Still seemingly intent on her embroidery needle, Cadsuane laughed softly. Verin's knitting needles had stopped. She was studying Logain, a plump sparrow studying an insect. Alivia had shifted her intense gaze to the man, too, and Harilin and Enaila seemed to be just going through the motions of their game. Min appeared to be reading still, but each hand rested near the opposite cuff of her coatsleeves. She kept some of her knives hidden there. None of them trusted him.

Rand frowned. The man could call himself whatever he wanted so long as he did what he was supposed to, but Cadsuane prodded him and anyone else in a black coat nearly as much as she did Rand himself. He was unsure how far to trust Logain either, yet he had to work with the tools he had to hand. "Is it done?" With Logain here, Loial was uncapping his ink jar again.

"More than half the Black Tower is in Arad Doman and Illian. I sent all the men with bonded Aes Sedai except those here, as you ordered." Logain walked to the table while he talked, found a blue-glazed pitcher that still held wine among the plates and scraps, and filled a green-glazed cup. There was very little silver in the house. "You should have let me bring more men here. The numbers tilt too much to Aes Sedai for my liking."

Rand grunted. "Since part of that is your doing, you can live with it. Others will have to, as well. Go on."

"Dobraine and Rhuarc will send a Soldier with a message as soon as they find anyone in charge of more than a village. The Council of Merchants claim King Alsalam still reigns, but they wouldn't or couldn't produce him or say where he is, they seem to be at one another's throats themselves, and Bandar Eban is more than half deserted and given over to the mob." Logain grimaced into his winecup. "Gangs of strongarms provide what little order there is, and they extort food and coin from the people they claim to protect and take whatever else they want, including women." The bond suddenly held white-hot rage, and Nynaeve growled in her throat. "Rhuarc has set about putting an end to that, but it was already turning into a battle when I left," Logain finished.

"Strongarms won't hold out long against Aiel. If Dobraine can't find anyone in charge, then he will have to be, for the time being." If Alsalam was dead, as seemed likely, he would have to appoint a Steward for the Lord Dragon in Arad Doman. But who? It would have to be someone the Domani would accept.

The other man took a long swallow of wine. "Taim wasn't pleased at me taking so many men out of the Tower and not telling him where they were going. I thought he was going to rip up your order. He tried every trick to learn where you are. Oh, he burns to know that. His eyes were practically on fire. I wouldn't put it past him to have had me put to the question if I'd been fool enough to meet him without company. One thing pleased him, though: that I didn't take any of his cronies. That was plain on his face." He smiled, a dark smile, not amused. "There are forty-one of those now, by the way. He's given over a dozen men the Dragon pin in the past few days, and he has above fifty more in his 'special' classes, most of them men recruited just lately. He's planning something, and I doubt you'll like it."

I told you to kill him when you had the chance, Lews Therin cackled in mad mirth. *I told you. And now it's too late. Too late.*

Rand angrily expelled a stream of blue-gray smoke. "Give over," he said, meaning it for both Logain and Lews Therin. "Taim built the Black Tower till it nearly matches the White Tower for numbers, and it grows every day. If he's a Darkfriend the way you claim, why would he do that?"

Logain met his stare levelly. "Because he couldn't stop it. From what I've heard, even in the beginning there were men who could Travel who weren't his toad-eaters, and he had no excuse to do *all* the recruiting himself. But he's made a Tower of his own hidden inside the Black Tower, and the men in it are loyal to him, not you. He amended the deserters' list and sends his apologies for an 'honest mistake,' but you can wager all you own it was no mistake."

And how loyal was Logain? If one false Dragon chafed at following the Dragon Reborn, why not another? He might think he had cause. He had been far more famous as a false Dragon than Taim, more successful, gathering an army that swept out of Ghealdan and nearly reached Lugard on its way to Tear. Half the known world had trembled at the name Logain. Yet Mazrim Taim commanded the Black Tower while Logain Ablar was only another Asha'man. Min still saw an aura of glory around him. Just how that glory was to be achieved was beyond her viewing, however.

He took the pipe from his mouth, and the bowl was hot against the heron branded into his palm. He must have been puffing away furiously without being aware of it. The trouble was, Taim and Logain were lesser problems. They had to wait. The tools at hand. He made an effort to keep his voice even. "Taim took their names off the list. That's the important thing. If he's showing favoritism, I'll put an end to it when I have time. But the Seanchan have to come first. And maybe Tarmon Gai'don, too."

"If?" Logain growled, slamming his cup down on the table so hard that it broke. Wine spread across the tabletop and dripped over the edge. Scowling, he wiped his damp hand on his coat. "Do you think I'm imagining things?" His tone grew more heated by the word. "Or making them up? Do you think this is *jealousy*, al'Thor? Is that what you think?"

"You listen to me," Rand began, raising his voice against a peal of thunder.

"I told you I espected you and your friends in black coats to be civil to me, my friends and my guests," Cadsuane said sternly, "but I've decided that must be expanded to include each other." Her head was still bent over her embroidery hoop, but she spoke as if she were shaking a finger under their noses. "At least when I am present. That means if you continue squabbling, I may have to spank both of you." Harilin and Enaila began laughing so hard they got the string of their game in a snarl. Nynaeve laughed, too, though she tried to hide it behind her hand. Light, even *Min* smiled!

Logain bristled, jaw tightening until Rand thought he should hear the man's teeth grating. He was trying hard not to bristle himself. Cadsuane and her bloody rules. Her *conditions* for becoming his advisor. She pretended that he had *asked* for them, and every so often she added another to her list. The rules were not precisely onerous, though their existence was, but her way of presenting them was always like a poke with a sharp stick. He opened his mouth to tell her he was finished with her rules, and with her, too, if need be.

"Taim very likely will have to wait on the Last Battle, whatever he's about," Verin said suddenly. Her knitting, a shapeless lump that might have been anything, sat in her lap. "It will come soon. According to everything I've read on the subject, the signs are quite clear. Half the servants have recognized dead people in the halls, people they knew alive. It's happened often enough that they aren't frightened by it any longer. And a dozen men moving the cattle to spring pasture watched a considerable town melt into mist just a few miles to the north."

Cadsuane had raised her head and was staring at the stout Brown sister. "Thank you for repeating what you told us yesterday, Verin," she said dryly. Verin blinked, then took up her knitting again, frowning at it as though she, too, were unsure what it was going to be.

Min caught Rand's eyes, shaking her head slowly, and he sighed. The bond held irritation and wariness, the last a deliberate warning to him, he suspected. At times, she seemed able to read his mind. Well, if he needed Cadsuane, and Min said he did, then he needed her. He just wished he knew what she was supposed to teach him aside from how to grind his teeth.

"Advise me, Cadsuane. What do you think of my plan?"

"At last the boy asks," she murmured, setting her embroidery down beside her sewing basket. "All his schemes in motion, some I've not been made privy to, and *now* he asks. Very well. Your peace with the Seanchan will be unpopular."

"A truce," he broke in. "And a truce with the Dragon Reborn will last only as long as the Dragon Reborn. When I die, everyone will be free to go to war with the Seanchan again if they wish."

Min slammed her book shut and folded her arms beneath her breasts. "Don't you talk that way!" she said, red-faced with anger. The bond also carried fear.

"The Prophecies, Min," he said sadly. Not sad for himself, but for her. He wanted to protect her, her and Elayne and Aviendha, but he would hurt them in the end.

"I said don't you talk that way! The Prophecies *don't* say you have to die! I'm not going to let you die, Rand al'Thor! Elayne and Aviendha and I won't let you!" She glared at Alivia, who her viewing had said would help Rand die, and her hands slid down her arms toward her cuffs.

"Behave, Min," he said. Her hands shot away from her cuffs, but she set her jaw, and the bond suddenly was flooded with stubbornness. Light, was he going to have to worry about Min trying to kill Alivia? Not that she was likely to succeed—as well try throwing a knife at an Aes Sedai as at the Seanchan woman—but she might get herself injured. He was not sure Alivia *knew* any weaves but those for weapons.

"Unpopular, as I say," Cadsuane said firmly, raising her voice. She favored Min with a brief frown before turning her attention back to Rand. Her face was smooth, composed, an Aes Sedai's face. Her dark eyes were hard, like polished black stones. "Especially in Tarabon, Amadicia and Altara, but also elsewhere. If you agree to allow the Seanchan to keep what they've already taken, what lands will you give away next? That is how most rulers will see matters."

Rand dropped back into his chair, stretching his legs in front of him and crossing his ankles. "It doesn't matter how unpopular it is. I went through that doorframe *ter'angreal* in Tear, Cadsuane. You know about that?" Golden ornaments bobbled as she nodded impatiently. "One of my questions for the Aelfinn was 'How can I win the Last Battle?'"

"A dangerous question to pose," she said quietly, "touching on the Shadow as it does. Supposedly, the results can be quite unpleasant. What was the answer?"

"'The north and the east must be as one. The west and the south must be as one. The two must be as one.'" He blew a smoke ring, put another in the middle of it as it expanded. That was not the whole of it. He had asked how to win and survive. The last part of his answer had been 'To live, you must die.' Not something he was going to bring up in front of Min anytime soon. In front of anyone except Alivia, for that matter. Now he just had to figure out how to live by dying. "At first, I thought it meant I had to conquer everywhere, but that wasn't what they said. What if it means the Seanchan hold the west and south, as you could say they already do, and there's an alliance to fight the Last Battle, the Seanchan with everybody else?"

"It's possible," she allowed. "But if you're going to make this . . . truce . . . why are you moving what seems to be a considerable army to Arad Doman and reinforcing what is already in Illian?"

"Because Tarmon Gai'don *is* coming, Cadsuane, and I can't fight the Shadow and the Seanchan at the same time. I'll have a truce, or I'll crush them whatever the cost. The Prophecies say I have to bind the nine moons to me. I only understood what that meant a few days ago. As soon as Bashere returns, I'll know when and where I'm to meet the Daughter of the Nine Moons. The only question now is how do I bind her, and she'll have to answer that."

He spoke matter-of-factly, now and then blowing a smoke ring for punctuation. Reactions varied. Loial just wrote very fast, trying to capture every word, while Harilin and Enaila went on with their game. If the spears had to be danced, they were ready. Alivia nodded fiercely, doubtless hoping it would come to crushing those who had kept her wearing an *a'dam* for five hundred years. Logain had found another winecup and filled it with the last of what was in the pitcher, but he merely held the cup rather than drinking, his expression unreadable. Now it was Rand whom Verin studied intently. But then, she had always been curious about him. But why in the Light would Min feel bone-deep sadness? And Cadsuane. . . .

"Stone cracks from a hard enough blow," she said, her face an Aes Sedai mask of calm. "Steel shatters. The oak fights the wind and breaks. The willow bends where it must and survives."

"A willow won't win Tarmon Gai'don," he told her.

The door creaked open again, and Ethin tottered in. "My Lord Dragon, three Ogier have arrived. They were most pleased to learn that Master Loial is here. One of them is his mother."

"My mother?" Loial squeaked, and even that sounded like a hollow wind gusting in caverns. He leaped up so fast that his chair fell over backward, wringing his hands, ears wilting. His head swung from side to side as if he were hunting for a way out besides the door. "What am I going to do, Rand? The other two must be Elder Haman and Erith. What am I going to do?"

"Mistress Covril said she was most anxious to speak with you, Master Loial," Ethin said in that creaky voice. "Most anxious. They are all damp from the rain, but she said they will wait for you in the Ogier sitting room upstairs."

"What am I going to do, Rand?"

"You said you want to marry Erith," Rand said as gently as he could. Gentleness was difficult except with Min.

"But my book! My notes aren't complete, and I'll never find out what happens next. Erith will take me back to Stedding Tsofu with her."

"Phaw!" Cadsuane picked up her embroidery again and began working the needle delicately. She was making the ancient symbol of Aes Sedai, the Dragon's Fang and the Flame of Tar Valon melded into a disc, black and white separated by a sinuous line. "Go to your mother, Loial. If she's Covril, daughter of Ella daughter of Soong, you don't want to keep her waiting. As I expect you know."

Loial seemed to take Cadsuane's words as a command. He began wiping his pen nib again, capping his ink jar. But he did everything very slowly, with his ears drooping. Every so often he moaned sadly, half under his breath, "My book!"

"Well," Verin said, holding up her knitting for inspection, "I believe I have done all that I can here. I think I'll go find Tomas. The rain makes his knee ache, though he denies it even to me." She glanced at the window. "It does seem to be slowing."

"And I think I'll go find Lan," Nynaeve said, gathering her skirts. "The company is better where he is." That with a sharp tug on her braid and a glare divided between Alivia and Logain. "The wind tells me a storm is coming, Rand. And you know I don't mean rain."

"The Last Battle?" Rand asked. "How soon?" When it came to weather, listening to the wind could sometimes tell her when the rains would come to the hour.

"It may be, and I don't know. Just remember. A storm is coming. A terrible storm." Overhead, thunder rolled.

CHAPTER
19

Vows

Uneasy, Loial watched Nynaeve glide off down the lamp-lit corridor in one direction and Verin in the other. Neither was much taller than his waist, but they were Aes Sedai. The fact knotted his tongue sufficiently that by the time he had worked up his nerve to ask one of them to accompany him, both were out of sight around sharp corners. The manor house was a rambling place, added to over many years with no real overall plan that he could discern, and hallways frequently met at odd angles. He really wished he had an Aes Sedai for company when he faced his mother. Even Cadsuane, although she made him very nervous with how she was always pinching at Rand. Sooner or later, Rand was going to explode. He was not the same man Loial first met in Caemlyn, or even the man he had left in Cairhien. The mood around Rand was dark and stony now, a dense patch of lion's claw and treacherous ground underfoot. The whole house felt that way with Rand in it.

A lean, gray-haired serving woman carrying a basket of folded towels gave a start, then shook her head and muttered something under her breath before offering him a brief curtsy and walking on. She made a small side-step as though she was moving around something. Or someone. He stared at the spot and scratched behind his ear. Maybe he could only see Ogier dead. Not that he actually wanted to. It was sad enough just knowing that human dead could no longer rest. Having the same confirmed for Ogier would be enough to break his heart. Most likely they would appear only inside *stedding*, in any case. He would very much like to see a town vanish, though. Not a real town, but a town that was as dead as those spirits the humans claimed to see. You might be able to walk its streets before it melted and see what people were like before the War of the Hundred Years, or even the Trolloc Wars. So Verin said, and she seemed to know a very great deal about it. That would certainly be worth a mention in his book. It was going to be a fine book. Scratching his beard with two fingers—the thing itched!—he sighed. It would have been a fine book.

Standing there in the corridor was only putting off the inevitable. Put off clearing the brush and you always find chokevine in it, so the old saying went. Only he felt as though the chokevine was tight around him instead of a tree. Breathing hard, he followed the serving woman all the way to the wide stairs that led up to the Ogier rooms. The staircase had two sturdy bannisters, shoulder-high on the gray-haired woman and stout enough to give a decent handhold. He was often afraid just to brush against stair rails made for humans for fear he might break them. One ran down the middle, with the steps along the wood-paneled wall pitched for human feet, those on the outside for Ogier.

The woman was old as humans counted years, yet she climbed more quickly than he and was scurrying down the corridor by the time he reached the top. Doubtless she was taking the towels to his mother's room, and to Elder Haman's and Erith's. Surely they would prefer to get dry before talking. He would suggest that. It would gain him time to think. His thoughts seemed as sluggish as his feet, and his feet felt like millstones.

There were six bedrooms built for Ogier along the corridor, which itself was properly scaled for them—his up-stretched hands would have come a pace short of touching the ceiling beams—along with a storeroom, a bathing room with a large copper tub, and the sitting room. This was the oldest part of the house, dating back nearly five hundred years. A lifetime for a very old Ogier, but many lifetimes for humans. They lived such brief lives, except for Aes Sedai; that had to be why they flitted about like hummingbirds. But even Aes Sedai could be nearly as precipitous as the rest. That was a puzzlement.

The sitting room door was carved with a Great Tree, not Ogier

work, yet finely detailed and instantly recognizable. He stopped, tugging his coat straight, combing his hair with his fingers, wishing he
had time to black his boots. There was an ink stain on his cuff. No
time to do anything about that, either. Cadsuane was right. His
mother was not a woman to be kept waiting. Strange that Cadsuane
knew of her. Perhaps knew her, by the way she had spoken. Covril,
daughter of Ella daughter of Soong, was a famous Speaker, but he had
not realized she was known Outside. Light, he was all but panting
with anxiety.

Trying to control his breathing, he went in. Even here the hinges
creaked. The servants had been aghast when he asked after some oil to
put on them—that was their task; he was a guest—but they still had
not gotten around to it themselves.

The high-ceilinged room was quite spacious, with dark polished
wallpapers and vine-carved chairs and small vine-carved tables and
wrought-iron stand-lamps of a proper size, their mirrored flames dancing above his head. Except for a shelf of books, all old enough that the
leather bindings were flaking and all of which he had read before, only
a small bowl of sung wood was Ogier made. A nice piece; he wished he
knew who had sung it, but it was aged enough that singing to it had
failed to raise so much as an echo. Yet everything had been made by
someone who at least had been to a *stedding*. The pieces would have
looked at home in any dwelling. Of course, the room looked nothing
like a room in a *stedding*, but Lord Algarin's ancestor had made an effort to have his visitors feel comfortable.

His mother was standing in front of one of the brick fireplaces, a
strong-faced woman with her vine-embroidered skirts spread to let the
flames dry them. He heaved a sigh of relief at seeing she was not as wet
as he had expected, although it put paid to suggesting they take the
time to get dry. Their raincloaks must have developed leaks. They did
that after a time, as the anseed oil wore off. Maybe her temper would
not be as bad as he feared, either. White-haired Elder Haman, his flaring coat dark with damp in several large patches, was examining one of
the axes from the wall, shaking his head over it. Its haft was as long as
he was tall. Made during the Trolloc Wars or even before, there were a
pair of those, the long axe heads inlaid with gold and silver, and a pair
of ornate pointed pruning knives with long shafts, as well. Of course,
pruning knives, sharp on one side and sawtoothed on the other, always
had long handles, but the inlays and long red tassels indicated that

these had been made for weapons, too. Not the most felicitous choices for hanging in a room meant for reading or conversation or the quiet contemplation of stillness.

But Loial's eyes swept past his mother and Elder Haman to the other fireplace, where Erith, small and almost fragile appearing, was drying her own skirts. Her mouth was straight, her nose short and well-rounded, her eyes the exact color of a silverbell's ripe seedpod. In short, she was beautiful! And her ears, sticking up through the glossy black hair that hung down her back. . . . Curving and plump, tipped with fine tufts that looked as soft as dandelion down, they were the most gorgeous ears he had ever seen. Not that he would be crude enough to say so. She smiled at him, a very mysterious smile, and his own ears quivered with embarrassment. Surely she could not know what he had been thinking. Could she? Rand said women could sometimes, but that was human women.

"So, here you are," his mother said, planting her fists on her hips. There were no smiles from her. Her brows were drawn down, her jaw set. If this was her better temper, she might as well have been drenched. "I must say, you've led me a merry chase, but I have you in hand now, and I do not mean to let you run— What is that on your lip? And your chin! Well, you can shave those right off again. Don't you grimace at me, Son Loial."

Fingering the growth on his upper lip uneasily, he tried to smooth his face—when your mother named you Son, she was in no mood to trifle with—but it was hard. He *wanted* his beard and mustaches. Some might think it pretentious, as young as he was, but just the same. . . .

"A merry chase indeed," Elder Haman said dryly, hanging the axe back on its hooks. *He* had long white mustaches that fell past his chin and a long narrow beard that hung to his chest. True, he was well above three hundred years old, but it still seemed unfair. "A very merry chase. First we walked to Cairhien, having heard you were there, only you had gone. After a stop at Stedding Tsofu, we walked to Caemlyn, where young al'Thor informed us you were in the Two Rivers and took us there. But you were gone again. To Caemlyn, it seemed!" His eyebrows rose almost to his hairline. "I began to think we were playing ring-in-the-dell."

"The people in Emond's Field told us how heroic you were," Erith said, her high voice like music. Clutching her skirts with both hands, ears fluttering with excitement, she seemed about to bounce up and down. "They told us all about you fighting Trollocs and Myrddraal, and going out among them by yourself to seal the Manetheren Waygate so no more could come."

"I wasn't by myself," Loial protested, waving his hands. He thought his ears might fly from his head, they were twitching so with embarrassment. "Gaul was with me. We did it together. I'd never have reached the Waygate without Gaul." She wrinkled her delicate nose at him, dismissing Gaul's participation.

His mother sniffed. *Her* ears were rigid with distaste. "Foolishness. Fighting in battles. Putting yourself in danger. *Gambling.* All of it. Pure foolishness, and there will be no more of it."

Elder Haman harrumphed, ears twitching irritably, and folded his hands behind his back. He disliked being interrupted. "So we returned to Caemlyn, to find you gone, and then to Cairhien once more, to find you gone yet again."

"And you put yourself in danger again in Cairhien," Loial's mother broke in, shaking a finger at him. "Have you no sense at all?"

"The Aiel said you were very brave at Dumai's Wells," Erith murmured, looking at him through her long eyelashes. He swallowed hard. Her gaze made his throat feel tight. He knew he should look away, but how could he be demure when she was looking at him?

"In Cairhien your mother decided she couldn't stay away from the Great Stump any longer, though why I cannot say, since they aren't likely to reach any sort of decision for another year or two, so we set out to return to Stedding Shangtai in the hope we could find you later." Elder Haman said all of that very fast, glaring at the two women as if he thought they might break in on him again. His beard and mustaches seemed to bristle.

Loial's mother gave another sniff, sharper. "I expect to bring a decision very quickly, in a month or two, or I'd never have given over the search for Loial even temporarily. Now that I've found him, we can finish matters and be on our way without any more delay." She took in Elder Haman, who was frowning, his ears slanted back, and amended her tone. He was an Elder, after all. "Forgive me, Elder Haman. I meant to say, if it pleases you, will you perform the ceremony?"

"I believe that it does please me, Covril," he said mildly. Much too mildly. When Loial heard that tone from his teacher, with ears back, he had always known that he had put a foot very badly wrong. Elder Haman had been known to throw a piece of chalk at a pupil when he used that tone. "Since I abandoned my students, not to mention speaking to the Great Stump, to follow you on this wild chase for that very reason, I believe it does please me indeed. Erith, you are very young."

"She's past eighty, old enough to marry," Loial's mother said sharply, folding her arms across her chest. Her ears twitched with impatience. "Her mother and I reached agreement. You yourself witnessed us signing the betrothal and Loial's dowry."

Elder Haman's ears tilted back a little further, and his shoulders hunched as if he was gripping his hands together very hard behind his back. His eyes never left Erith. "I know you want to marry Loial, but are you sure you are ready? Taking a husband is a grave responsibility."

Loial wished someone would ask *him* that question, but that was not the way. His mother and Erith's had reached their agreement, and only Erith could stop it now. If she wanted to. Did he want her to? He could not stop thinking of his book. He could not stop thinking of Erith.

She certainly looked grave. "My weaving sells well, and I am ready to buy another loom and take an apprentice. But that may not be what you mean. I am ready to tend a husband." Suddenly, she grinned, a lovely grin that divided her face in two. "Especially one with such beautiful long eyebrows."

Loial's ears quivered, and so did Elder Haman's, if not so much. Women were very free in their talk among themselves, so he had heard, but usually they tried not to embarrass men with it. Usually. His mother's ears actually trembled with amusement!

The older man cleared his throat. "This is serious, Erith. Come now. If you are sure, take his hands."

Without hesitation, she came to stand in front of Loial, smiling up at him as she took his hands in hers. Her small hands felt very warm. His felt numb and cold. He swallowed. It really was going to happen.

"Erith, daughter of Iva daughter of Alar," Elder Haman said, holding one hand palm down over each of their heads, "will you take Loial, son of Arent son of Halan, as husband and vow under the Light and by the Tree to treasure, esteem and love him so long as he lives, to care for him and tend him, and to guide his feet on the path they should follow?"

"Under the Light and by the Tree, I so vow." Erith's voice was firm and clear, and her smile seemed to have grown wider than her face

"Loial, son of Arent son of Halan, will you accept Erith, daughter of Iva daughter of Alar, as wife and vow under the Light and by the Tree to treasure, esteem and love her so long as she lives, to care for her and to heed her guidance?"

Loial took a deep breath. His ears trembled. He wanted to marry her. He did. Just not yet. "Under the Light and by the Tree, I so vow," he said hoarsely.

"Then under the Light and by the Tree, I declare you wed. May the blessings of the Light and the Tree be upon you always."

Loial looked down at his wife. His wife. She raised a hand and stroked slender fingers along his mustaches. The beginnings of mustaches, anyway.

"You are very handsome, and I think mustaches will be beautiful on you. A beard, too."

"Nonsense," his mother said. Surprisingly, she was dabbing at her eyes with a small lace handkerchief. She was never emotional. "He's much too young for that sort of thing."

For a moment, he thought Erith's ears began to slant back. That had to be his imagination. He had had a number of long talks with her—she was a wonderful conversationalist; though come to think of it, for the most part she listened, but what little she did say was always very cogent—and he was sure she possessed no sort of temper at all. He had no time to think on it, in any event. Resting her hands on his arms, she rose on tiptoes, and he bent to rub his nose against hers. In truth, they nosed for longer than they should have with Elder Haman and his mother present, but others faded from his thoughts as he inhaled his wife's scent and she his. And the *feel* of her nose on his! Pure bliss! He cupped the back of her head and barely had the presence of mind not to finger her ear. She tugged the tuft on one of his! After a while, a very long while it seemed, voices intruded.

"It is still raining, Covril. You cannot seriously be suggesting we set out again when we have a sound roof over our heads and proper beds to sleep in for a change. No, I say. No! I will not sleep on the ground tonight, or in a barn, or worst of all, in a house where my feet and knees hang over the end of the largest bed available. There have been times I've seriously thought of refusing hospitality, and to the Pit with rudeness."

"If you insist," his mother said grudgingly, "but I want an early start come morning. I refuse to waste an hour more than I must. The Book of Translation *must* be opened as soon as possible."

Loial jerked erect, aghast. "*That's* what the Great Stump is discussing? They can't do that, not now!"

"We must leave this world eventually, so we can come to it when the Wheel turns," his mother said, striding to the nearest fireplace to spread her skirts again. "That is written. Now is exactly the right time, and the sooner the better."

"Is that what you think, Elder Haman?" Loial asked worriedly.

"No, my boy, not at all. Before we left, I gave a speech of three hours that I think swayed a few minds in the right direction." Elder Haman picked up a tall yellow pitcher and filled a blue cup, but rather than drink, he frowned into the tea. "Your mother has swayed more, I fear. She may even get her decision in months, as she says."

Erith filled a cup for his mother, then two more, bringing one to him. His ears quivered with embarrassment yet again. He should have done that. He had a great deal to learn about being a husband, but he knew that much.

"I wish *I* could address the Stump," he said bitterly.

"You sound eager, Husband." Husband. That meant Erith was very serious. It was almost as bad as being called Son Loial. "What would you say to the Stump?"

"I won't have him embarrassed, Erith," his mother said before he could open his mouth. "Loial writes well, and Elder Haman says he may have the makings of a scholar about him, but he gets tongue-tied before even a hundred. Besides, he is only a boy."

Elder *Haman* had said that? Loial wondered when his ears would stop quivering.

"Any married man may address the Stump," Erith said firmly. There was no doubt this time. Her ears definitely slanted back. "Will you allow me to tend my own husband, Mother Covril?" His mother's mouth moved, but no sound came out, and her eyebrows were halfway up her forehead. He did not think he had ever seen her so taken aback, though she must have expected this. A wife always took precedence with her husband over his mother. "Well, Husband, what would you say?"

He was not eager, he was desperate. He took a long swallow of the spice-scented tea, but his mouth felt just as dry afterward. His mother was right; the more people were listening, the more he tended to forget what he intended to say and go off on tangents. In truth, he had to admit that sometimes he rambled a bit with only a few listeners. Just a bit. Now and then. He knew the forms—a child of fifty knew the forms—yet he could not make the words come. The few listening to him now were not just any few. His mother was a famous Speaker, Elder Haman a noted one, not to mention being an Elder. And there was Erith. A man wanted to stand well in his wife's eyes.

Turning his back on them, he strode to the nearest window and stood rolling the teacup between his palms. The window was sized decently, though the panes set in the carved casement were no larger than those in the rooms below. The rain had dwindled to a drizzle falling from a gray sky, and despite bubbles in the glass he could make out the trees beyond the fields, pine and sourgum and the occasional oak, all full of new growth. Algarin's people tended their forest well, clearing out the deadfall to rob wildfire of its tinder. Fire had to be used carefully.

The words came more easily now that he could not see the others watching him. Should he begin with the Longing? Could they dare leave if they would begin dying in a handful of years? No, that question would have been addressed first thing and suitable answers found, else the Stump would have finished inside a year. Light, if he did address the Stump. . . . For a moment, he saw the crowds standing all around him, hundreds and hundreds of men and women waiting to hear his words, perhaps several thousand. His tongue tried to cling to the roof of his mouth. He blinked, and there was only the bubbled glass before him, and the trees. He had to do it. He was not particularly brave, whatever Erith thought, but he had learned about bravery watching humans, watching them hang on no matter how strong the winds grew, fight when they had no hope, fight and win because they fought with desperate courage. Suddenly, he knew what to say.

"In the War of the Shadow, we did not huddle in our *stedding*, hoping no Trollocs or Myrddraal would be driven to enter. We did not open the Book of Translation and flee. We marched alongside the humans and fought the Shadow. In the Trolloc Wars, we neither hid in the *stedding* nor opened the Book of Translation. We marched with the humans and fought the Shadow. In the darkest years, when hope seemed gone, we fought the Shadow."

"And by the War of the Hundred Years we had learned not to get ourselves tangled in human affairs," his mother put in. That was allowed. Speaking could turn into a debate unless the pure beauty of your words held the listeners. She had once spoken from sunrise to sunset in favor of a very unpopular position without a single interruption, and the next day, no one had risen to Speak against her. He could not form beautiful sentences. He could only say what he believed. He did not turn from the window.

"The War of the Hundred Years was a human affair, and none of ours. The Shadow *is* our affair. When it is the Shadow that must be fought, our axes have always grown long handles. Perhaps in a year, or five, or ten, we will open the Book of Translation, but if we do it now, we cannot run away with any real hope of safety. Tarmon Gai'don is coming, and on that hangs the fate not only of this world, but of any world we might flee to. When fire threatens the trees, we do not run away and hope that the flames will not follow us. We fight. Now the Shadow is coming like wildfire, and we dare not run from it." Something was moving among the trees, all along the line he could see. A herd of cattle? A very big herd, if so.

"That isn't bad," his mother said. "Much too plainspoken to carry any weight at a *stedding* Stump much less the Great Stump, of course, but not bad. Go on."

"Trollocs," he breathed. That was what it was, thousands of Trollocs in black, spiked mail spilling out of the trees at a run with scythe-curved swords raised, shaking their spiked spears, some carrying torches. Trollocs as far as he could see to left and right. Not thousands. Tens of thousands.

Erith pushed in beside him at the window and gasped. "So many! Are we going to die, Loial?" She did not sound afraid. She sounded . . . excited!

"Not if I can warn Rand and the others." He was already starting for the door. Only Aes Sedai and Asha'man could save them now.

"Here, my boy, I think we may need these."

He turned just in time to catch the long-handled axe that Elder Haman tossed him. The other man's ears were back all the way, laid flat against his skull. Loial realized his own were, too.

"Here, Erith," his mother said calmly, lifting down one of the pruning knives. "If they get inside, we will try to hold them at the stairs."

"You are my hero, Husband," Erith said as she took the knife's shaft in hand, "but if you get yourself killed, I will be very angry with you." She sounded as if she meant it.

And then he and Elder Haman were running down the corridor together, pounding down the stairs, bellowing at the tops of their lungs a warning, and a battle cry that had not been heard in over two thousand years. "Trollocs coming! Up axes and clear the field! Trollocs coming!"

". . . so I will take care of Tear, Logain, while you—" Abruptly Rand wrinkled his nose. It was not that he actually smelled a rotting midden heap suddenly, but he felt as if he did, and the feeling was getting stronger.

"Shadowspawn," Cadsuane said quietly, putting down her embroidery and rising. His skin tingled as she embraced the Source. Or maybe it was Alivia, walking briskly toward the windows after the Green sister. Min stood, drawing a pair of throwing knives from her coatsleeves.

At the same instant, through the thick walls, he faintly heard Ogier shouting. There was no mistaking those deep, drumlike voices. "Trollocs coming! Up axes and clear the field!"

With an oath, he leaped to his feet and ran to a window. Trollocs in the thousands came running through the light rain across the newly planted fields, Trollocs as tall as Ogier and taller, Trollocs with rams' horns and goats' horns, wolves' snouts, boars' snouts, Trollocs with eagles' beaks and crests of feathers, muddy earth splashing beneath boots and hooves and paws. Silent as death they ran. Black-clad Myrddraal galloped behind them, cloaks hanging as if they were standing still. He could see thirty or forty. How many more on other sides of the house?

Others had heard the Ogier's cries, or maybe just looked out a window. Lightning began to fall among the charging Trollocs, silvery bolts that struck with a roar and hurled huge bodies in every direction. In other places, the ground erupted in flames, fountaining dirt and parts of Trollocs, heads, arms, legs wheeling through the air. Balls of fire struck them and exploded, each killing dozens. But on they ran, as fast as horses if not faster. Rand could not see the weaves that drew some of those lightning bolts. Now that they were discovered, the Trollocs began to shout, a wordless roar of rage. In the thatch-roofed outbuildings, large sturdy barns and stables, some of Bashere's Saldaeans stuck their heads out and quickly pulled them back again, drawing the doors shut behind them.

"You told your Aes Sedai they could channel to defend them-selves?" he said calmly.

"Do I look fool enough not to?" Logain snarled. At another win-dow, he already held *saidin*, nearly as much as Rand could draw. He was weaving as fast as he could. "Do you intend to help or just watch, my Lord Dragon?" There was entirely too much sarcasm in that, but now was not the time to bring it up.

Drawing a deep breath, Rand gripped the casement on either side of the window against the dizziness that would come—the Dragons' golden-maned heads on the backs of his hands seemed to writhe—and reached out to seize the Power. His head spun as *saidin* flooded into him, icy flames and crumbling mountains, a chaos trying to pull him under. But blessedly clean. He still felt the wonder of that. His head spun and his stomach wanted to empty itself, the odd illness that should have gone with the taint, yet that was not why he clung to the casement even harder. The One Power filled him—but in that moment of dizziness, Lews Therin had seized it away from him. Numb with horror, he stared at the Trollocs and Myrddraal racing toward the out-buildings. With the Power in him, he could make out the pins fas-tened to massive mailed shoulders. The silver whirlwind of the Ahf'frait band and the blood-red trident of the Ko'bal. The forked lightning of the Ghraem'lan and the hooked axe of the Al'ghol. The iron fist of the Dhai'mon and the red, bloodstained fist of the Kno'-mon. And there were skulls. The horned skull of the Dha'vol and the piled human skulls of the Ghar'ghael and the skull cloven by a scythe-curved sword of the Dhjin'nen and the dagger-pierced skull of the Bhan'sheen. Trollocs liked skulls, if they could be said to like any-thing. It seemed the twelve principal bands might all be involved, and some of the lesser. He saw pins he did not recognize. What seemed a staring eye, a dagger-pierced hand, a man-shape wrapped in flames. They neared the outbuildings, where swords were beginning to thrust through the thatch as the Saldaeans tried to cut ways onto the roofs. Thatch was tough. They would need to work desperately hard. Odd, the thoughts that came when a madman who wanted to die might well kill you in the next heartbeat.

Flows of Air pushed the casement in front of him out in a shower of shattered glass and fragmented wood. *My hands,* Lews Therin panted. *Why can't I move my hands? I need to raise my hands!* Earth, Air and Fire went into a weave Rand did not know, six of them at once. Except that

as soon as he saw the spinning, he did know. Blossom of Fire. Six vertical red shafts appeared among the Trollocs, ten feet tall and thinner
than Rand's forearm. The nearest Trollocs would be hearing their shrill
whine, but unless memories had been passed down from the War of the
Shadow, they would not realize they were hearing death. Lews Therin
spun the last thread of Air, and fire blossomed. With a roar that shook
the manor house, each red shaft expanded in a heartbeat to a disc of
flame thirty feet across. Horned heads and snouted heads flew into the
air, and pinwheeling arms, booted legs and legs that ended in paws or
hooves. Trollocs a hundred paces and more away from the explosions
went down, and only some got up again. Even as he was spinning those
webs, Lews Therin spun six others, Spirit touched with Fire, the weave
for a gateway, but then he added touches of Earth, so, and so. The familiar silvery-blue vertical streaks appeared, spaced out not far from
the manor house, ground Rand knew well, rotating into—not openings, but the misty back of a gateway, four paces by four. Rather than
remaining open, they rotated shut again, opening and shutting continuously. And rather than remaining fixed, they sped toward the Trollocs. Gateways and yet not. Deathgates. As soon as the Deathgates
began to move, Lews Therin knotted the webs, a loose knotting that
would hold only for minutes before allowing the whole weave to dissipate, and began spinning again. More Deathgates, more Blossoms of
Fire, rattling the walls of the house, blowing Trollocs apart, flinging
them down. The first of the speeding Deathgates struck the Trollocs
and carved through them. It was not just the slicing edge of the constantly opening and closing gateways. Where a Deathgate passed,
there simply were no Trollocs remaining. *My hands!* the madman
howled. *My hands!*

Slowly Rand raised his hands, stuck them through the opening.
Immediately Lews Therin wove Fire and Earth in intricate combination, and red filaments flashed from Rand's fingertips, ten from each,
fanning out. Arrows of Fire, this. He knew. As soon as those vanished,
more appeared, so fast that they seemed to flicker rather than actually
go away. Trollocs struck by the filaments jerked as flesh and blood,
heated in a flash beyond boiling, erupted, jerked and fell, holes blown
entirely through their thick bodies. Often, two or three behind fell
victim as well before a filament died. He spread his fingers and moved
his hands slowly from side to side, spreading death across the whole

line. Blossoms of Fire appeared that were not his weaving, and Death-gates, slightly smaller than Lews Therin's, and Arrows of Fire that must have been Logain's. The other Asha'man were paying attention, but few would be where they could see those last two webs spun.

Trollocs fell by the hundreds, the thousands, riven by lightning bolts and balls of fire, Blossoms of Fire and Deathgates and Arrows of Fire, the earth itself exploding beneath their feet, yet on they raced, roaring and waving their weapons, Myrddraal riding close behind, black-bladed swords in hand. As they reached the outbuildings, some of the Trollocs surrounded them, pounding on the doors with their fists, prying at the boards of the walls with their swords and spears, tossing flaming torches onto the thatched roofs. Saldaeans up there, working their horsebows as fast they could, kicked the torches back down, but some hung up on the edges of the roof, and flames began catching even on damp thatch.

The fires, Rand thought at Lews Therin. *The Saldaeans will burn! Do something!*

Lews Therin made no reply, only wove death as fast as he could and hurled it at the Trollocs, Deathgates and Arrows of Fire. A Myrddraal, riddled by half a dozen red filaments, was flung from its saddle, then another. A third lost its head to an Arrow of Fire in an explosion of boiled blood and flesh, but that one rode on, waving its sword, as if it did not know it was dead. Rand was seeking them out. If the Myrd-draal were all killed, the Trollocs might well turn and run.

Deathgates and Arrows of Fire only, Lews Therin spun now. The mass of Trollocs was too close to the manor house for Blossoms of Fire. Some of the Asha'man apparently did not realize that right away. The room shook to great booms, the whole manor house shook, as if struck by huge sledgehammers, shook as though about to shake apart, and then there were no more explosions, except where a fireball erupted or the ground itself exploded to throw Trollocs like broken toys. The sky seemed to rain lightning. Silver-blue bolts struck continuously so close to the house that the hair on Rand's arms and chest tried to lift, the hair on his head.

Some of the Trollocs succeeded in forcing open the doors to one of the barns and began flooding inside. He shifted his hands, cutting down those still outside with flickering red filaments that blew holes in them. Some had managed to get inside, but those the Saldaeans would have to deal with themselves. On another barn and a stable, flames were beginning to ripple up the thatch, men coughing from the acrid smoke as they shot their bows.

Listen to me, Lews Therin. The fire. You must do something!

Lews Therin said nothing, just spun his webs to kill Trollocs and Myrddraal.

"Logain," Rand shouted. "The fires! Put them out!"

The other man did not answer either, but Rand saw the weaves that pulled the heat from the flames, killing them. They just vanished, leaving behind cold blackened thatch where not even tendrils of smoke rose. Death walked among the Trollocs, but they were so close that even the explosions of fireballs rattled the house, now.

Suddenly there was a Myrddraal afoot beside the window, pale eyeless face as calm as an Aes Sedai's, black sword already stabbing toward him. Two thrown Aiel spears took it in the chest, and a throwing knife blossomed in its throat, but it only staggered before resuming the thrust. Rand bunched his fingers together, and just before the blade reached him, a hundred Arrows of Fire ripped through the Myrddraal, flinging it back twenty paces to lie riddled and leaking black blood onto the ground. Myrddraal seldom died right away, but this one never twitched.

Hurriedly, Rand searched for more targets, but he realized that Lews Therin had stopped channeling. He could still feel the goose bumps that told him Cadsuane and Alivia held the Power, still feel *saidin* in Logain, but the other man was weaving no more webs either. Outside, the ground lay carpeted with bodies and parts of bodies from the fields almost to the manor house walls. Within paces of them. A few horses belonging to Myrddraal still stood, one holding up a foreleg as if it were broken. A headless Myrddraal staggered about, flailing wildly with its sword, and here and there a Trolloc jerked or tried to lift itself and failed, but nothing else moved.

It's done, he thought. *It's done, Lews Therin. You can release* saidin *now.* Harilin and Enaila were standing on the table, veiled and spears in hand. Min stood beside them, her face grim, a throwing knife in either hand. The bond was full of fear, and not for herself, he suspected. They had saved his life, but he had to save it himself, now.

"A close run thing," Logain muttered. "If this had happened before I arrived. . . . A close-run thing." He gave himself a shake and released the Source, turning away from his glassless window. "Did you intend keeping these new weaves for your favorites, like Taim? Those gateways. Where did we send those Trollocs? I just copied your weave exactly."

"It doesn't matter where they went," Rand said absently. His attention was focused on Lews Therin. The madman, the bloody voice in his head, drew a little deeper on the Power. *Let go, man.* "Shadowspawn can't survive passing through a gateway."

I want to die, Lews Therin said. *I want to join Ilyena.*

If you really wanted to die, why did you kill Trollocs? Rand thought. *Why kill that Myrddraal?* "People will find groups of dead Trollocs and maybe Myrddraal without a mark on them," he said aloud.

I seem to remember dying, Lews Therin murmured. *I remember how I did it.* He drew deeper still, and small pains grew in Rand's temples.

"Not too many in any one place, though. The destination shifts every time a Deathgate opens." Rand rubbed at his temples. That pain was a warning. He was close to the amount of *saidin* he could hold without dying or being burnt out. *You can't die yet,* he told Lews Therin. *We have to reach Tarmon Gai'don or the* world *dies.*

"A Deathgate," Logain said, his voice tinged with distaste. "Why are you still holding the Power?" he asked suddenly. "And so much. If you're trying to show me that you're stronger than I am, I already know it. I saw how large your . . . your *Deathgates* were compared to mine. And I'd say you're holding every drop of *saidin* that you can safely."

That certainly caught everyone's attention. Min tucked her knives away and leapt down from the table, the bond suddenly so full of fear it seemed to throb with it. Harilin and Enaila exchanged worried glances, then went back to staring out the windows. They did not trust Trollocs to be dead until the corpses were three days buried. Alivia took a step toward him, frowning, but he shook his head slightly, and she turned back to her window, though her frown remained.

Cadsuane glided down the room, her smooth face sternly composed. "What does he feel?" she demanded of Min. "Don't toy with me, girl. You know the cost of that. I know that he bonded you, and you know I know. Is he afraid?"

"He's never afraid," Min said. "Except for me or. . . ." She set her jaw stubbornly and folded her arms beneath her breasts, fixing Cadsuane with a glare that dared the Green sister to do her worst. By the tangled mix of emotions ranging from fear to shame that she tried to keep out of the bond and failed, she had some idea of what Cadsuane's worst could be.

"I'm standing under your nose," Rand said. "If you want to know how I feel, ask me." *Lews Therin?* he thought. There was no answer, and the *saidin* filling him did not slacken. His temples began to throb.

"Well?" Cadsuane said impatiently.

"I feel right as well water." *Lews Therin?* "But I have a rule for you, Cadsuane. Don't threaten Min again. In fact, leave her alone altogether."

"Well, well. The boy shows some teeth." Golden birds and fish, stars and moons, swayed as she shook her head. "Just don't show too many. And you might ask the young woman whether she wants your protection." Strangely, Min had shifted her frown to him, and the bond was threaded with irritation. Light, it was bad enough that she did not like him worrying about her. Now she seemed to want to take on Cadsuane single-handed, something he would not be eager to do himself.

We can die at Tarmon Gai'don, Lews Therin said, and suddenly, the Power drained out of him.

"He released," Logain said, as if he were suddenly on Cadsuane's side.

"I know," she told him. He whipped his head around in surprise.

"Min can deal with you in your own way if she wishes," Rand said starting for the door. "But don't threaten her." *Yes,* he thought. *We can die at Tarmon Gai'don.*

CHAPTER
20

The Golden Crane

The wind had died away as the rain diminished, but gray clouds still hid the sun. The fine drizzle was enough to dampen Rand's hair, however, and begin soaking into his gold-embroidered black coat as he walked through the dead Trollocs. Logain had spun a shield of Air so that raindrops bounced from it or apparently slid down nothing to cascade around him, but Rand refused to risk Lews Therin seizing *saidin* again. The man had said he could wait until the Last Battle to die, but how far could you trust a madman on anything?

Madman? Lews Therin whispered. *Am I any madder than you?* He cackled with wild laughter.

Now and then Nandera looked over her shoulder at Rand. A tall, sinewy woman, her graying hair hidden beneath her brown *shoufa*, she led the Maidens, those on this side of the Dragonwall, at least, but she had chosen to lead his bodyguard of Maidens personally. Her green eyes, all he could see of her sun-dark face above her black veil, carried little expression, yet he was sure she was worried over him not protecting himself from the rain. Maidens noticed what seemed out of the ordinary. He hoped she would keep quiet.

You have to trust me, Lews Therin said. *Trust me. Oh, Light, I'm pleading with a voice in my head! I* must *be mad.*

Nandera and the rest of the fifty veiled Maidens made a large ring around Rand, almost shoulder-to-shoulder, prodding their spears into every Trolloc and Myrddraal they passed, casually stepping over huge severed arms and legs, severed heads bearing horns or tusks or sharp teeth. Occasionally a Trolloc groaned or feebly tried to crawl away—or to lunge at them, snarling—but not for long. War with Trollocs was like war with rabid dogs. You killed them, or they killed you. There was no parley, no surrender, no middle ground.

Rain had kept the vultures away so far, yet crows and ravens flapped everywhere, black feathers glistening wetly, and if any were the Dark One's eyes, it did not stop them alighting to pluck out Trollocs' eyes or see whether they could wrench loose some other gobbet. Enough of the Trollocs had been torn apart that the birds had rich feasting. None went near any dead Myrddraal, though, and they shunned Trollocs too near a Myrddraal. That indicated nothing beyond caution. Very likely the Myrddraal smelled wrong to the birds. A Myrddraal's blood would etch steel if left on it very long. To ravens and crows, it must have smelled like poison.

The surviving Saldaeans shot the birds with arrows or skewered them on their sinuously curved swords or simply bludgeoned them with shovels or hoes or rakes, anything that could make a handy club—in the Borderlands, leaving a crow or raven alive was unthinkable; there, they were all too often the Dark One's eyes—yet there were too many. Hundreds of black-feathered shapes lay crumpled among the Trollocs, and for every corpse there seemed to be hundreds more squabbling loudly over the softer bits, including pieces of their dead fellows. The Asha'man and Aes Sedai had long since given up trying to kill them all.

"I don't like my men tiring themselves this way," Logain said. *His* men. "Or the sisters, for that matter. Gabrelle and Toveine will be near exhaustion by nightfall." He had bonded the two Aes Sedai, so he should know. "What if there's another attack?"

All around the manor house and outbuildings brief fires flared, so hot that people shielded their eyes against them, as Aes Sedai and Asha'man incinerated Trolloc and Myrddraal dead where they lay. There were too many to afford the labor of gathering them into heaps. With fewer than twenty Aes Sedai, fewer than a dozen Asha'man, and maybe a hundred thousand Trollocs, it was going to be a long job. Very likely, before it was done the stench of decay would be added to the already foul odors in the air, the fetid, coppery smell of Shadowspawn blood, the stink of whatever had been in the Trollocs' intestines when they were ripped open. Best not to think too closely on that. There might not be a farmer or villager left alive between the manor house and the Spine of the World. That had to be where the Trollocs had come from, the Waygate outside Stedding Shangtai. At least Loial's home itself was safe. Neither Trollocs nor Myrddraal would enter a *stedding* unless driven, and it required considerable driving.

"Would you rather let them rot where they are?" Cadsuane inquired, sounding as if she herself had no preference in the matter. She held her green skirts up so the silk did not trail in the blood-soaked mud or the offal that littered the ground, yet she stepped over legs and around heads as casually as did the Maidens. She also had woven a parasol against the rain, as had Alivia, although not until she saw the Green do so. Rand had tried to make the sisters sworn to him teach the Seanchan woman more about the Power, but to their minds, that had nothing to do with their oaths of fealty. She was safe to herself and seemed safe to others, and they were content to leave matters as they were. Nynaeve had refused, too, because of Min's viewing. Cadsuane had coolly informed him that she was not in the business of instructing wilders.

"This truly would be a charnel house then," Min said. Her walk had a fetching sway to it, though she was plainly trying not to think of what lay underfoot while avoiding planting a heeled blue boot on any of it at the same time, and that made her stumble now and again. She was getting wet, too, her ringlets beginning to cling to her head, though the bond carried no hint of vexation. Only anger, and that seemed directed at Logain from the sharp stare she was giving him. "Where would the servants go, and the people who work the fields and stables and barns? How would they live?"

"There won't be another attack," Rand said. "Not until whoever sent this one learns it failed, and maybe not then. This is all they sent. The Myrddraal wouldn't have attacked piecemeal." Logain grunted, but he could not argue with that.

Rand looked back toward the manor house. In some places, dead Trollocs lay right at the foundations. None had made it inside, but. . . . *Logain was right,* he thought, surveying the carnage. It *had* been a close-run thing. Minus the Asha'man and Aes Sedai Logain had brought, the end might well have been different. A very close-run thing. And if there *was* another attack, later. . . ? Plainly someone knew Ishamael's trick. Or that blue-eyed man in his head really could locate him. Another attack would be larger. That, or come from some unexpected direction. Perhaps he should let Logain bring a few more Asha'man.

You should have killed them, Lews Therin wept. *Too late, now. Too late.*

The Source is clean now, fool, Rand thought.

Yes, Lews Therin replied. *But are they? Am I?*

Rand had wondered that about himself. Half of the double wound in his side had come from Ishamael, the other half from Padan Fain's dagger that carried the taint of Shadar Logoth. They often throbbed, and when they did, they seemed alive.

The circle of Maidens parted slightly to let through a white-haired serving man with a long sharp nose who looked even frailer than Ethin. He was trying to shelter beneath a two-tiered Sea Folk parasol missing half its fringe, of all things, but the aged blue silk had several ragged holes worn in it, so small rivulets fell on his yellow coat and one on his head. His thinning hair clung to his skull and dripped. He seemed wetter than if he had gone without. Doubtless one of Algarin's forebears had obtained the thing somehow as a memento, but the obtaining must have been a story in itself. Rand doubted the Sea Folk gave up a clan Wavemistress's parasol lightly.

"My Lord Dragon," the old man said with a bow that spilled more water down his back, "Verin Sedai instructed me to give this to you straightaway." From beneath his coat, he produced a paper, folded and sealed.

Rand hastily stuffed it into a pocket of his own coat against the rain. Ink ran easily. "Thank you, but it could have waited till I returned to the house. Best you get back inside before you're soaked through completely."

"She *did* say straightaway, my Lord Dragon." The fellow sounded offended. "She is Aes Sedai."

At Rand's nod, he bowed again and started slowly back toward the manor house, his back stiff with pride, the parasol showering him with streams of water. She was Aes Sedai. Everyone hopped for Aes Sedai, even in Tear, where they were not much liked. What did Verin have to say that she needed to put in a letter? Thumbing the seal, Rand walked on.

His destination was one of the barns, its thatched roof partially blackened. This was the barn the Trollocs had gotten into. A burly fellow in a rough brown coat and muddy boots, leaning against a jamb in the open doors, straightened and for some reason hastily looked inside over his shoulder as Rand approached, the Maidens spreading out to surround the barn.

He stopped dead in the doorway, Min and the others halting beside him. Logain growled an oath. A pair of lanterns hanging from uprights that supported the loft gave a dim light, enough to see that every single surface was thick with crawling flies, even the straw-covered dirt floor. As many more buzzed around in the air, it seemed.

"Where did they come from?" Rand asked. Algarin might not be wealthy, yet his barns and stables were kept as clean as such places could be. The burly man gave a guilty start. He was younger than most of the servants in the house, but his head was bald halfway back, and creases bracketed his wide mouth, fanned out from his eyes.

"Don't know, my Lord," he muttered, knuckling his forehead with a grimy hand. He focused on Rand so hard that it was plain he did not want to look into the barn. "I stepped to the door for a breath of fresh, and when I turned around, they was all over everything. I thought. . . . I thought maybe they's *dead* flies."

Rand shook his head in disgust. These flies were all too alive. Not every Saldaean defending this barn had died, but all of the Saldaean dead had been gathered here. Saldaeans disliked burials in rain. None of them could say why, but you just did not bury people while it was raining. Nineteen men lay in a neat row on the floor, as neat as it could be when some were missing limbs or had their heads split open. But they had been laid out carefully by their friends and companions, their faces washed, their eyes closed. They were why he had come there. Not to say goodbye or anything sentimental; he had not known any of these men more than to recognize a face here and there. He had come to remind himself that even what seemed a complete victory had its cost in blood. Still, they deserved better than to be crawling with flies.

I need no reminders, Lews Therin growled.

I'm not you, Rand thought. *I have to harden myself.* "Logain, get rid of these bloody things!" he said aloud.

You're harder than I ever was, Lews Therin said. Suddenly he giggled. *If you're not me, then who are you?*

"Now I'm a flaming fly-whisk?" Logain muttered.

Rand rounded on him angrily, but Alivia spoke in that slurred drawl before he could get a word out.

"Let me try, my Lord." She asked, in a manner of speaking, but like an Aes Sedai, she did not await permission. His skin tingled with goose bumps as she embraced *saidar* and channeled.

Flies always took shelter from even the lightest rain because one raindrop was enough to put a fly on the ground, easy prey until its wings dried off, yet suddenly the doorway was billowing with buzzing flies as if the rain were far preferable to the barn. The air seemed solid with them. Rand batted flies away from his face, and Min covered her face with her hands, the bond heavy with distaste, but they were interested only in flight. In moments, they were all gone. The balding man, staring at Alivia with his mouth hanging open, suddenly coughed and spat out two flies onto his hand. Cadsuane gave him a look that snapped his mouth shut and sent his rough knuckle flying to his forehead. Just a look, yet she was who she was.

"So you watch," she said to Alivia. Her dark eyes were fixed on the Seanchan woman's face, but Alivia did not start or stammer. She was much less impressed by Aes Sedai than most people.

"And remember what I see. I must learn somehow if I am to help the Lord Dragon. I have learned more than you are aware of." Min made a sound in her throat, very nearly a growl, and the bond swelled with anger, but the yellow-haired woman ignored her. "You are not angry with me?" she asked Rand, her voice anxious.

"I'm not angry. Learn as much as you can. You're doing very well."

She blushed and dropped her eyes like a girl startled by an unexpected compliment. Fine lines decorated the corners of her eyes, but sometimes it was hard to remember that she was a hundred years older than any living Aes Sedai, rather than half a dozen years younger than himself. He *had* to find someone to teach her more.

"Rand al'Thor," Min said angrily, folding her arms beneath her breasts, "you are *not* going to let that woman—"

"Your viewings are never wrong," he broke in. "What you see always happens. You've tried to change things, and it never worked. You told me so yourself, Min. What makes you think this time can be different?"

"Because it *has* to be different," she told him fiercely. She leaned toward him as though ready to launch herself at him. "Because I *want* it to be different. Because it *will* be different. Anyway, I don't know about everything I've seen. People move on. I was wrong about Moiraine. I saw all sorts of things in her future, and she's dead. Maybe some of the other things I saw never came true either."

It must not be different this time, Lews Therin panted. *You promised!*

A faint scowl appeared on Logain's face, and he shook his head slightly. He could not like hearing Min question her ability. Rand almost regretted telling him about her viewing of him, though it had seemed harmless encouragement at the time. The man had actually asked Aes Sedai to confirm Min's ability, though he had been wise enough to try to keep his doubting from Rand.

"I cannot see what makes this young woman so vehement for you, boy," Cadsuane mused. She pursed her lips in thought, then shook her head, ornaments swaying. "Oh, you're pretty enough, I suppose, but I just cannot see it."

To avoid another argument with Min—she did not call them that; she called them "talking," but he knew the difference—Rand took out Verin's letter and broke the blob of yellow sealing wax impressed with the head of a Great Serpent ring. The Brown sister's spidery hand covered most of the page, a few letters blotted where raindrops had soaked the paper. He walked closer to the nearest lantern. It gave off a faint stink of spoiled oil.

As I said, I have done what I can do here. I believe that I can fulfill my oath to you better elsewhere, so I have taken Tomas and gone to be about it. There are many ways to serve you, after all, and many needs. I am convinced that you can trust Cadsuane, and you certainly should heed her advice, but be wary of other sisters, including those who have sworn fealty to you. Such an oath means nothing to a Black sister, and even those who walk in the Light may interpret it in ways you would disapprove of. You already know that few see that oath as invoking absolute obedience in all things. Some may find other holes. So whether or not you follow Cadsuane's advice, and I repeat that you should, follow mine. Be very wary.

It was signed simply, "Verin."

He grunted sourly. *Few* thought the oath meant absolute obedience? It was more like none. They obeyed, usually, yet the letter was not always the spirit. Take Verin herself. She warned him against the

others doing things he might disapprove of, but she had not said where
she was going or what she intended to do there. Was she afraid he
might not approve? Maybe it was just Aes Sedai concealment. Sisters
kept secrets as naturally as they breathed.

When he held out the letter to Cadsuane, her left eyebrow
twitched slightly. She must have been truly startled to show so much,
but she took the letter and held it where the lantern's light illumi-
nated it.

"A woman of many masks," she said finally, handing the page back.
"But she gives good advice here."

What did she mean about masks? He was about to ask her when
Loial and Elder Haman suddenly appeared in the doorway, each carrying a long-handled axe, with an ornately decorated head, on his shoulder. The white-haired Ogier's tufted ears were laid back, his face grim,
and Loial's ears were flickering. With excitement, Rand guessed. It
could be difficult to tell.

"I trust we are not interrupting?" Elder Haman said, his ears rising
as he looked sadly at the line of bodies.

"You are not," Rand told him, sticking the letter back in his
pocket. "I wish I could come to your wedding, Loial, but—"

"Oh, that's done, Rand," Loial said. He *must* be excited; it was unlike him to interrupt. "My mother insisted. There won't even be time
for much of a wedding feast, maybe none, what with the Stump and
me having to—" The older Ogier laid a hand on his arm. "What?"
Loial said, looking at him. "Oh. Yes. Of course. Well." He scrubbed
under his broad nose with a finger the size of a fat sausage.

Something he was not supposed to be told? Even Ogier had secrets,
it seemed. Rand fingered the letter in his pocket. But then, so did
everyone else.

"I promise you this, Rand," Loial said. "Whatever happens, I will
be there with you at Tarmon Gai'don. Whatever happens."

"My boy," Elder Haman murmured, "I don't think you
should. . . ." He trailed off, shaking his head and rumbling under his
breath, like a distant earthquake.

Rand crossed the straw in three strides and offered his right hand.
Smiling widely, and with an Ogier that meant very wide, Loial took it
in a hand that enveloped his. This close, Rand had to crane his neck to
look up at his friend's face. "Thank you, Loial. I can't tell you how
much hearing that means to me. But I'll need you before then."

"You . . . need me?"

"Loial, I've sealed the Waygates I know, in Caemlyn and Cairhien, Illian and Tear, and I put a very nasty trap on the one that was cut open near Fal Dara, but I couldn't find the one near Far Madding. Even when I know there's a Waygate actually in a city, I can't find it by myself, and then there are all those cities that don't exist anymore. I need you to find the rest for me, Loial, or Trollocs will be able to flood into every country at once, and no one will know they're coming until they're in the heart of Andor or Cairhien."

Loial's smile vanished. His ears trembled and his eyebrows drew down till the ends lay on his cheeks. "I can't, Rand," he said mournfully. "I must leave first thing tomorrow morning, and I don't know when I'll be able to come Outside again."

"I know you've been out of the *stedding* a long time, Loial." Rand tried to make his voice gentle, but it came out hard. Gentleness seemed a fading memory. "I'll speak to your mother. I'll convince her to let you leave after you've had a little rest."

"He needs more than a little rest." Elder Haman planted the butt of his axe haft on the floor, gripping the axe with both hands, and directed a stern look at Rand. Ogier were peaceful folk, yet he looked anything but. "He has been Outside more than five years, far too long. He needs weeks of rest in a *stedding* at the least. Months would be better."

"My mother doesn't make those decisions anymore, Rand. Though truth to tell, I think she's still surprised to realize it. Erith does. My wife." His booming voice put so much pride into that word that he seemed ready to burst with it. His chest certainly swelled, and his smile split his face in two.

"And I haven't even congratulated you," Rand said, clapping him on the shoulder. His attempt at heartiness sounded false in his own ears, but it was the best he could manage. "If you need months, then months you shall have. But I still need an Ogier to find those Waygates. In the morning, I'll take you all to Stedding Shangtai myself. Maybe I can convince someone there to do the job." Elder Haman shifted his frown to his hands on the axe haft and began muttering again, too softly to make out words, like a bumblebee the size of a huge mastiff buzzing in an immense jar in the next room. He seemed to be arguing with himself.

"That might take time," Loial said doubtfully. "You know we don't like to make hasty decisions. I'm not certain they will even let a human

into the *stedding*, because of the Stump. Rand? If I can't come back before the Last Battle. . . . You will answer my questions about what happened while I was in the *stedding*, won't you? I mean, without making
me drag everything out of you?"

"If I can, I will," Rand told him.

If you can, Lews Therin snarled. *You agreed we could finally die at Tarmon Gai'don. You* agreed, *madman!*

"He'll answer questions to your heart's delight, Loial," Min said
firmly, "if I have to stand over him the whole while." Anger suffused
the bond. She really did seem to know what he was thinking.

Elder Haman cleared his throat. "It seems to me that I myself am
more accustomed to Outside than almost anyone except the stone-
masons. Um. Yes. In fact, I think I am likely to be the best candidate
for your task."

"Phaw!" Cadsuane said. "It seems you infect even Ogier, boy." Her
tone was stern, but her face was all Aes Sedai composure, unreadable,
hiding whatever was passing behind those dark eyes.

Loial's ears went rigid with shock, and he almost dropped his axe,
fumbling to catch it. "You? But the Stump, Elder Haman! The Great
Stump!"

"I believe I can safely leave that in your hands, my boy. Your words
were simple yet eloquent. Um. Um. My advice is, don't try for beauty.
Keep the simple eloquence, and you may surprise quite a few. Including your mother."

It seemed impossible that Loial's ears could grow any stiffer, but
they did. His mouth moved, but no words came out. So he was to
speak to the Stump. What was so secret about that?

"My Lord Dragon, Lord Davram has returned." It was Elza Penfell
who escorted Bashere into the barn. She was a handsome woman in a
dark green riding dress; her brown eyes seemed to grow feverish when
they found Rand. She, at least, was one he did not have to worry about.
Elza was fanatical in her devotion.

"Thank you, Elza," he said. "Best you return to help with the
cleanup. There's a long way to go, yet."

Her mouth tightened slightly, and her gaze took in everyone from
Cadsuane to the Ogier with an air of jealousy before she offered a
curtsy and left. Yes, fanatical was the word.

Bashere was a short, slender man in a gold-worked gray coat with
the ivory baton of the Marshal-General of Saldaea, tipped with a

golden wolf's head, tucked behind his belt opposite his sword. His baggy trousers were tucked into turned-down boots that had been waxed till they shone despite a light splattering of mud. His recent work had required as much formality and dignity as he could supply, and he could supply a great deal. Even the Seanchan must have heard his reputation by now. Gray streaked his black hair and the thick mustaches that curled around his mouth like down-turned horns. Dark tilted eyes sad, he walked right past Rand with the rolling gait of a man more accustomed to a saddle than his own feet, walked slowly along the line of dead men, staring intently at each face. Impatient as Rand was, he gave him his time to mourn.

"I've never seen anything like what's outside," Bashere said quietly as he walked. "A big raid out of the Blight is a thousand Trollocs. Most are only a few hundred. Ah, Kirkun, you never did guard your left the way you should. Even then, you need to outnumber them three or four times to be assured you won't go into their cookpots. Out there. . . . I think I saw a foreshadowing of Tarmon Gai'don. A small part of Tarmon Gai'don. Let's hope it really is the Last Battle. If we live through that, I don't think we'll ever want to see another. We will, though. There's always another battle. I suppose that will be the case until the whole world turns Tinker." At the end of the row, he stopped in front of a man whose face was split almost down to his luxuriant black beard. "Ahzkan here had a bright future ahead of him. But you could say the same of a lot of dead men."

Sighing heavily, he turned to face Rand. "The Daughter of the Nine Moons will meet you in three days at a manor house in northern Altara, near the border of Andor." He touched the breast of his coat. "I have a map. She's already near there somewhere, but they say it isn't in lands they control. When it comes to secrecy, these Seanchan make Aes Sedai look as open as village girls." Cadsuane snorted.

"You suspect a trap?" Logain eased his sword in its scabbard, perhaps unconsciously.

Bashere made a dismissive gesture, but he eased his sword, too. "I always suspect a trap. It isn't that. The High Lady Suroth still didn't want me or Manfor to talk to anyone but her. Not anyone. Our servants were mutes, just as when we went to Ebou Dar with Loial."

"Mine had had her tongue cut out," Loial said in tones of disgust, his ears tilting back. His knuckles paled on the haft of his axe. Haman made a shocked sound, his ears going stiff as fence posts.

"Altara just crowned a new King," Bashere went on, "but everybody in the Tarasin Palace seemed to be walking on eggshells and looking over their shoulders, Seanchan and Altaran alike. Even Suroth looked as though she felt a sword hovering above her neck."

"Maybe they're frightened of Tarmon Gai'don," Rand said. "Or the Dragon Reborn. I'll have to be careful. Frightened people do stupid things. What are the arrangements, Bashere?"

The Saldaean pulled the map from inside his coat and walked back to Rand unfolding it. "They're very precise. She will bring six *sul'dam* and *damane*, but no other attendants." Alivia made a noise like an angry cat, and he blinked before going on, no doubt uncertain of a freed *damane*, to say the least. "You can bring five people who can channel. She'll assume any man with you can, but you can bring a woman who can't to make the honors even."

Min was suddenly at Rand's side, wrapping her arm around his.

"No," he said firmly. He was not about to take her into a possible trap.

"We'll talk about it," she murmured, the bond filling with stubborn resolve.

The most dire words a woman can say short of "I'm going to kill you," Rand thought. Suddenly he felt a chill. *Had* it been him? Or Lews Therin? The madman chuckled softly in the back of his head. No matter. In three days, one difficulty would be resolved. One way or another. "What else, Bashere?"

Lifting the damp cloth that lay across her eyes, carefully so she did not catch the bracelet-and-rings *angreal* in her hair—she wore that and her jeweled *ter'angreal* every waking moment now—Nynaeve sat up on the edge of her bed. With men needing Healing from dreadful wounds, some missing a hand or an arm, it had seemed petty to ask Healing for a headache, but the willow bark seemed to have worked as well. Only more slowly. One of her rings, set with a pale green stone that now appeared to glow with a faint internal light, seemed to vibrate continually on her finger though it did not really move. The pattern of vibrations was mixed, a reaction to *saidar* and *saidin* being channeled outside. For that matter, someone could have been channeling inside. Cadsuane was sure it should be able to indicate direction, but she could not say how. Ha! for Cadsuane and her supposed superior knowledge!

She wished she could say that to the woman's face. It was not that Cadsuane intimidated her—certainly not; she stood above Cadsuane— just that she wanted to maintain some degree of harmony. That was the reason she held her tongue around the woman.

The rooms she shared with Lan were spacious, but also drafty, with no casement fitting its window properly, and over the generations the house had settled enough that the doors had been trimmed so they could close all the way, making more gaps to let every breeze whistle through. The fire on the stone hearth danced as though it were outdoors, crackling and spitting sparks. The carpet, so faded she could no longer really make out the pattern, had more holes burned in it than she could count. The bed with its heavy bedposts and worn canopy was large and sturdy, but the mattress was lumpy, the pillows held more feathers that poked through than they did down, and the blankets seemed almost more darns than original material. But Lan shared the rooms, and that made all the difference. That made them a palace.

He stood at one of the windows where he had been since the attack began, staring down now at the work going on outside. Or perhaps studying the slaughter yard the manor house grounds had become. He was so still, he might have been a statue, a tall man in a well-fitting dark green coat, his shoulders broad enough to make his waist appear slender, with the leather cord of his *hadori* holding back his shoulder-length hair, black tinged with white at the temples. A hard-faced man, yet beautiful. In her eyes he was, let anyone else say what they would. Only they had best not say it in her hearing. Even Cadsuane. A ring bearing a flawless sapphire was cold on her right hand. It seemed more likely he was feeling anger than hostility. That ring did have a flaw, in her estimation. It was all very well to know someone nearby was feeling angry or hostile, but that did not mean the emotion was directed at you.

"It's time for me to go back outside and lend a hand again," she said as she stood.

"Not yet," he told her without turning from the window. Ring or no ring, his deep voice was calm. And quite firm. "Moiraine used to say a headache was sign she had been channeling too much. That's dangerous."

Her hand strayed toward her braid before she could snatch it down again. As if he knew more about channeling than she! Well, in some ways he did. Twenty years as Moiraine's Warder had taught him as much as a man could know of *saidar*. "My headache is completely gone. I'm perfectly all right now."

"Don't be petulant, my love. There are only a few hours till twilight. Plenty of work will be left tomorrow." His left hand tightened on the hilt of his sword, relaxed, tightened. Only that hand moved.

Her lips compressed. Petulant? She smoothed her skirt furiously. She was *not* petulant! He seldom invoked his right to command in private—curse those Sea Folk for ever thinking of such a thing!—but when he did, the man was unbending. Of course, she could go anyway. He would not try to stop her physically. She was certain of that. Fairly certain. Only she did not intend to violate her marriage vows in the slightest way. Even if she did want to kick her beloved husband's shins.

Kicking her skirts instead, she went to stand beside him at the window and slip her arm through his. His arm was rock hard, though. His muscles *were* hard, wonderfully so, but this was the hardness of tension, as though he were straining to lift a great weight. How she wished she had his bond, to give her hints of what was troubling him. When she laid hands on Myrelle. . . . No, best not to think of *that* hussy! Greens! They simply could not be trusted with men!

Outside, not far from the house, she could see a pair of those black-coated Asha'man, and the sisters bonded to them. She had avoided that whole lot as much as possible—the Asha'man for obvious reasons, the sisters because they supported Elaida—yet you could not spend time in the same house with people, even a house as large and rambling as Algarin's, and avoid coming to recognize them. Arel Malevin was a Cairhienin who seemed even wider than he actually was because he stood barely chest-high to Lan, Donalo Sandomere a Tairen with a garnet in his left ear and his gray-streaked beard trimmed to a point and oiled, although she doubted very much that his creased, leathery face belonged to a noble. Malevin had bonded Aisling Noon, a fierce-eyed Green who peppered her speech with Borderland oaths that sometimes made Lan wince. Nynaeve wished she understood them, but he refused to explain. Sandomere's captive was Ayako Norsoni, a diminutive White with wavy waist-length black hair who was nearly as brown-skinned as a Domani. She seemed shy, a rarity among Aes Sedai. Both women wore their fringed shawls. The captives almost always did, perhaps as gestures of defiance. But then, they seemed to get on strangely well with the men. Often Nynaeve had seen them chatting companionably, hardly the behavior of defiant prisoners. And she suspected that Logain and Gabrelle were not the only pair sharing a bed outside wedlock. It was disgraceful!

Suddenly fires bloomed below, six enveloping dead Trollocs in front of Malevin and Aisling, seven in front of Sandomere and Ayako, and she squinted against the blinding glare. It was like trying to look at thirteen noonday suns blazing in a cloudless sky. They were linked. She could tell from the way the flows of *saidar* moved, stiffly, as though they were being forced into place rather than guided. Or rather, the men were trying to force them. That never worked with the female half of the Power. It was pure Fire, and the blazes were ferocious, fiercer than she would have expected from Fire alone. But of course they would be using *saidin* as well, and who could say what they were adding from that murderous chaos? The little she could recall of being linked with Rand left her with no desire ever again to go near *that*. In just a few minutes the fires vanished, leaving only low heaps of grayish ash lying on seared earth that looked hard and cracked. That could not do the soil much good.

"You can't find this very entertaining, Lan. What are you thinking?"

"Idle thoughts," he said, his arm hard as stone beneath her hand. New fires flared outside.

"Share them with me." She managed to put a hint of question in that. He seemed amused by the nature of their vows, yet he absolutely refused to follow the smallest instruction when they were alone. Requests, he granted instantly—well, most of the time—but the man would quietly leave his boots muddy till the mud flaked off if she *told* him not to track in mud.

"Unpleasant thoughts, but if you wish. The Myrddraal and Trollocs make me think of Tarmon Gai'don."

"Unpleasant thoughts, indeed."

Still staring out the window, he nodded. There was no expression on his face—Lan could teach Aes Sedai about hiding emotions!—but a touch of heat entered his voice. "It's coming soon, Nynaeve, yet al'Thor seems to think he has forever to dance with the Seanchan. Shadowspawn could be moving down through the Blight while we stand here, down through—" His mouth snapped shut. Down through Malkier, he had almost said, dead Malkier, the murdered land of his birth. She was sure of it. He went on as if he had not paused. "They could strike at Shienar, at the whole Borderlands, next week, or tomorrow. And al'Thor sits weaving his Seanchan schemes. He should send someone to

convince King Easar and the others to return to their duty along the
Blight. He should be marshaling all the force he can gather and taking
it to the Blight. The Last Battle will be there, and at Shayol Ghul. The
war is there."

Sadness welled up in her, yet she managed to keep it out of her
voice. "You have to go back," she said quietly.

At last he turned his head, frowning down at her. His clear blue
eyes were so cold. They held less of death than they had, of that she was
certain, but they were still so cold. "My place is with you, heart of my
heart. Ever and always."

She gathered all of her courage and held on to it hard, so hard that
she ached. She wanted to speak fast, to get the words out before
courage failed, but she forced herself to a steady tone and an even pace.
"A Borderland saying I heard from you once. 'Death is lighter than a
feather, duty heavier than a mountain.' My duty lies here, making sure
Alivia doesn't kill Rand. But I will take you to the Borderlands. Your
duty lies there. You want to go to Shienar? You mentioned King Easar
and Shienar. And it is close to Malkier."

He looked down at her for a long time, but at last he exhaled softly,
and the tension left his arm. "Are you sure, Nynaeve? If you are, then,
yes, Shienar. In the Trolloc Wars, the Shadow used Tarwin's Gap to
move large numbers of Trollocs, just as it did a few years back, when
we sought the Eye of the World. But only if you are completely sure."

No, she was not sure. She wanted to cry, to scream at him that he
was a fool, that his place *was* with her, not dying alone in a futile private war with the Shadow. Only, she could not say any of that. Bond or
no bond, she knew he was torn inside, torn between his love of her and
his duty, torn and bleeding as surely as if he had been stabbed with a
sword. She could not add to his wounds. She could try to make sure he
survived, though. "Would I make the offer if I wasn't sure?" she said
dryly, surprised at how calm she sounded. "I won't like sending you
away, but you have your duty, and I have mine."

Wrapping his arms around her, he hugged her to his chest, gently
at first, then harder, until she thought he might squeeze all the air
from her lungs. She did not care. She hugged him just as fiercely, and
had to pry her hands from his broad back when she was done at last.
Light, she wanted to weep. And knew she must not.

As he began packing his saddlebags, she hurriedly changed into a
riding dress of yellow-slashed green silk and stout leather shoes, then

slipped from the room before he was done. Algarin's library was large, a square, high-ceilinged room lined with shelves. Half a dozen cushioned chairs stood scattered around the floor, and a long table and a tall map-rack completed the furnishings. The stone hearth was cold and the iron stand-lamps unlit, but she channeled briefly to light three of them. A hasty search found the maps she needed in the rack's diamond-shaped compartments. They were as old as most of the books, yet the land did not change greatly in two or three hundred years.

When she returned to their rooms, Lan was in the sitting room, saddlebags on his shoulder, Warder's color-shifting cloak hanging down his back. His face was still, a stone mask. She took only time to get her own cloak, blue silk lined with velvet, and they walked in silence, her right hand resting lightly on his left wrist, out to the dimly lit stable where their horses were kept. The air there smelled of hay and horses and horse dung, as it always did in stables.

A lean, balding groom with a nose that had been broken more than once sighed when Lan told him they wanted Mandarb and Loversknot saddled. A gray-haired woman began work on Nynaeve's stout brown mare, while three of the aging men made a job of getting Lan's tall black stallion bridled and out of his stall.

"I want a promise from you," Nynaeve said quietly as they waited. Mandarb danced in circles so that the plump fellow trying to lift the saddle onto the stallion's back had to run trying to catch up. "An oath. I mean it, Lan Mandragoran. We aren't alone any longer."

"What do you want my oath on?" he asked warily. The balding groom called for two more men to help.

"That you'll ride to Fal Moran before you enter the Blight, and that if anyone wants to ride with you, you'll let him."

His smile was small, and sad. "I've always refused to lead men into the Blight, Nynaeve. There were times men rode with me, but I would not—"

"If men have ridden with you before," she cut in, "men can ride with you again. Your oath on it, or I vow I'll let you ride the whole long way to Shienar." The woman was fastening the cinches on Loversknot's saddle, but the three men were still struggling to get Mandarb's saddle on his back, to keep him from shaking off the saddle blanket.

"How far south in Shienar do you mean to leave me?" he asked. When she said nothing, he nodded. "Very well, Nynaeve. If that's what you want. I swear it under the Light and by my hope of rebirth and salvation."

It was very hard not to sigh with relief. She had managed it, and without lying. She was trying to do as Egwene wanted and behave as though she had already taken the Three Oaths on the Oath Rod, but it was very hard dealing with a husband if you could not lie even when it was absolutely necessary.

"Kiss me," she told him, adding hastily, "That wasn't an order. I just want to kiss my husband." A goodbye kiss. There would be no time for one later.

"In front of everyone?" he said, laughing. "You've always been so shy about that."

The woman was nearly done with Loversknot, and one of the grooms was holding Mandarb as steady as he could while the other two hurriedly buckled the cinches.

"They're too busy to see anything. Kiss me, or I'll think you're the one who's—" His lips on hers shut off words. Her toes curled.

Some time later, she was leaning on his broad chest to catch her breath while he stroked her hair. "Perhaps we can have one last night together in Shienar," he murmured softly. "It may be some time before we're together again, and I'll miss having my back clawed."

Her face grew hot, and she pushed away from him unsteadily. The grooms were done, and staring very pointedly at the straw-covered floor, but they might well be close enough to overhear! "I think not." She was proud that she did not sound breathless. "I don't want to leave Rand alone with Alivia that long."

"He trusts her, Nynaeve. I don't understand it, but there it is, and that's all that matters."

She sniffed. As if any man knew what was good for him.

Her stout mare whickered uneasily as they rode among dead Trollocs to a patch of ground not far from the stable that she knew well enough to weave a gateway. Mandarb, a trained warhorse, reacted not at all to the blood and the stench and the huge corpses. The black stallion seemed as calm as his rider, now that Lan was on his back. She could understand that. Lan had a very calming effect on her, too. Usually. Sometimes, he had exactly the opposite effect. She wished they *could* have one more night together. Her face grew hot again.

Dismounting, she drew on *saidar* without using the *angreal* and wove a gateway just tall enough for her to lead Loversknot through

onto grassland dotted with thickets of black-spotted beech and trees
she did not recognize. The sun was a golden ball only a little down
from its peak, yet the air was decidedly cooler than in Tear. Cold
enough to make her gather her cloak, in fact. Mountains topped with
snow and clouds rose to the east and north and south. As soon as Lan
was through, she let the weave dissipate and immediately wove another gateway, larger, while she climbed into her saddle and settled the
cloak around her again.

Lan led Mandarb a few steps westward, staring. Land ended
abruptly in what was obviously a cliff no more than twenty paces from
him, and from there ocean stretched to the horizon. "What is the
meaning of this?" he demanded, turning back. "This isn't Shienar. It's
World's End, in Saldaea, as far from Shienar as you can get and still be
in the Borderlands."

"I told you I would take you to the Borderlands, Lan, and I have.
Remember your oath, my heart, because I surely will." And with that
she dug her heels in the mare's flanks and let the animal bolt through
the open gateway. She heard him call her name, but she let the gateway
close behind her. She *would* give him a chance to survive.

Only a few hours past midday, less than half a dozen tables were occupied in the large common room of The Queen's Lance. Most of the
well-dressed men and women, with clerks and bodyguards standing
attentively behind them, were there to buy or sell ice peppers, which
grew well in the foothills on the landward side of the Banikhan Mountains, called the Sea Wall by many in Saldaea. Weilin Aldragoran had
no interest in peppers. The Sea Wall had other crops, and richer.

"My final price," he said, waving a hand over the table. Every finger bore a jeweled ring. Not large stones, but fine. A man who sold
gems should advertise. He traded in other things as well—furs, rare
woods for cabinetmakers, finely made swords and armor, occasionally
other things that offered a good return—but gems brought in the
greater part of his profit in any year. "I'll come no lower." The table was
covered with a piece of black velvet, the better to show off a good portion of his stock. Emeralds, firedrops, sapphires, and best of all, dia-
monds. Several of those were large enough to interest a ruler, and none
was small. None held a flaw, either. He was known throughout the
Borderlands for his flawless stones. "Accept it, or someone else will."

The younger of the two dark-eyed Illianers across from him, a clean-shaven fellow named Pavil Geraneos, opened his mouth angrily, but the older, Jeorg Damentanis, his gray-streaked beard practically quivering, laid a fat hand on Geraneos' arm and gave him a horrified look. Aldragoran made no effort to conceal his smile, showing a little tooth.

He had been only a toddler when the Trollocs swept down into Malkier, and he had no memories of that land at all—he seldom even thought of Malkier; the land *was* dead and gone—yet he was glad he had let his uncles give him the *hadori*. At another table, Managan was in a shouting match with a dark Tairen woman wearing a lace ruff and rather inferior garnets in her ears, the pair of them nearly drowning out the young woman playing the hammered dulcimer on the low platform beside one of the tall stone fireplaces. That lean young man had refused the *hadori*, as had Gorenellin, who was near Aldragoran's age. Gorenellin was bargaining hard with a pair of olive-skinned Altarans, one of whom had a nice ruby in his left ear, and there was sweat on Gorenellin's forehead. No one shouted at a man who wore the *hadori* and a sword, as Aldragoran did, and they tried to avoid making him sweat. Such men carried a reputation for sudden, unpredictable violence. If he had seldom been forced to use the sword at his hip, it was widely known that he could and would.

"I do accept, Master Aldragoran," Damentanis said, giving his companion a sidelong glare. Not noticing, Geraneos bared his teeth in what he probably hoped Aldragoran would take for a smile. Aldragoran let it pass. He *was* a merchant, after all. A reputation was a fine thing when it enhanced your bargaining power, but only a fool went looking for fights.

The Illianers' clerk, a weedy, graying fellow and also Illianer, unlocked their iron-strapped coin box under the watchful eyes of their two bodyguards, bulky men with those odd beards that left the upper lip bare, in leather coats sewn with steel discs. Each carried a sword and stout cudgel at his belt. Aldragoran had a clerk at his own back, a hard-eyed Saldaean who did not know one end of a sword from the other, but he never used bodyguards. Guards on his premises, to be sure, but not bodyguards. That only added its bit to his reputation. And of course, he had no need of them.

Once Damentanis had endorsed two letters-of-rights and passed over three leather purses fat with gold—Aldragoran counted the coins but did not bother weighing them; some of those thick crowns from ten different lands would be lighter than others, yet he was willing to accept the inevitable loss—the Illianers carefully gathered up the stones, sorting them into washleather purses that went into the coin box. He offered them more wine, but the stout man declined politely, and they departed with the bodyguards carrying the iron-strapped box between them. How they were to protect anything burdened so was beyond him. Kayacun was far from a lawless town, but there were more footpads abroad than usual of late, more footpads, more murderers, more arsonists, more of every sort of crime, not to mention madness of the sort a man just did not want to think on. Still, the gems were the Illianers' concern now.

Ruthan had Aldragoran's coin box open—a pair of bearers were waiting outside to carry it—but he sat staring at the letters-of-rights and the purses. Half again what he had expected to get. Light coins from Altara and Murandy or no light coins, at least half again. This would be his most profitable year ever. And all due to Geraneos letting his anger show. Damentanis had been afraid to bargain further after that. A wonderful thing, reputation.

"Master Aldragoran?" a woman said, leaning on the table. "You were pointed out to me as a merchant with a wide correspondence by pigeon."

He noticed her jewelry first, of course, a matter of habit. The slim golden belt and long necklace were set with very good rubies, as was one of her bracelets, along with some pale green and blue stones he did not recognize and so dismissed as worthless. The golden bracelet on her left wrist, an odd affair linked to four finger rings by flat chains and the whole intricately engraved, held no stones, but her remaining two bracelets were set with fine sapphires and more of the green stones. Two of the rings on her right hand held those green stones, but the other two held particularly fine sapphires. Particularly fine. Then he realized she wore a fifth ring on that hand, stuck against one of the rings with a worthless stone. A golden serpent biting its own tail.

His eyes jerked to her face, and he suffered his second shock. Her face, framed by the hood of her cloak, was very young, but she wore the ring, and few were foolish enough to do that without the right. He had seen young Aes Sedai before, two or three times. No, her age did not shock him. But on her forehead, she wore the *ki'sain*, the red dot of a married woman. She did not look Malkieri. She did not sound

Malkieri. Many younger folk had the accents of Saldaea or Kandor, Arafel or Shienar—he himself sounded of Saldaea—but she did not sound a Borderlander at all. Besides, he could not recall the last time he had heard of a Malkieri girl going to the White Tower. The Tower had failed Malkier in need, and the Malkieri had turned their backs on the Tower. Still, he stood hurriedly. With Aes Sedai, courtesy was always wise. Her dark eyes held heat. Yes, courtesy was wise.

"How may I help you, Aes Sedai? You wish me to send a message for you via my pigeons? It will be my pleasure." It was also wise to grant Aes Sedai any favors they asked, and a pigeon was a small favor.

"A message to each merchant you correspond with. Tarmon Gai'don is coming soon."

He shrugged uneasily. "That is nothing to do with me, Aes Sedai. I'm a merchant." She was asking for a good many pigeons. He corresponded with merchants as far away as Shienar. "But I will send your message." He would, too, however many birds it required. Only stone-blind idiots failed to keep promises to Aes Sedai. Besides which, he wanted rid of her and her talk of the Last Battle.

"Do you recognize this?" she said, fishing a leather cord from the neck of her dress.

His breath caught, and he stretched out a hand, brushed a finger across the heavy gold signet ring on the cord. Across the crane in flight. How had she come by this? Under the Light, how? "I recognize it," he told her, his voice suddenly hoarse.

"My name is Nynaeve ti al'Meara Mandragoran. The message I want sent is this. My husband rides from World's End toward Tarwin's Gap, toward Tarmon Gai'don. Will he ride alone?"

He trembled. He did not know whether he was laughing or crying. Perhaps both. She was *his* wife? "I will send your message, my Lady, but it has nothing to do with me. I am a merchant. Malkier is dead. Dead, I tell you."

The heat in her eyes seemed to intensify, and she gripped her long, thick braid with one hand. "Lan told me once that Malkier lives so long as one man wears the *hadori* in pledge that he will fight the Shadow, so long as one woman wears the *ki'sain* in pledge that she will send her sons to fight the Shadow. I wear the *ki'sain*, Master Aldragoran. My husband wears the *hadori*. So do you. Will Lan Mandragoran ride to the Last Battle alone?"

He *was* laughing, shaking with it. And yet, he could feel tears rolling down his cheeks. It was madness! Complete madness! But he could not help himself. "He will not, my Lady. I cannot stand surety for anyone else, but I swear to you under the Light and by my hope of rebirth and salvation, he will not ride alone." For a moment, she studied his face, then nodded once firmly and turned away. He flung out a hand after her. "May I offer you wine, my Lady? My wife will want to meet you." Alida was Saldaean, but she definitely would want to meet the wife of the Uncrowned King.

"Thank you, Master Aldragoran, but I have several more towns to visit today, and I must be back in Tear tonight."

He blinked at her back as she glided toward the door gathering her cloak. She had several more towns to visit today, and she had to be back in Tear *tonight*? Truly, Aes Sedai were capable of marvels!

Silence hung in the common room. They had not been keeping their voices low, and even the girl with the dulcimer had ceased plying her hammers. Everyone was staring at him. Most of the outlanders had their mouths hanging open.

"Well, Managan, Gorenellin," he demanded, "do you still remember who you are? Do you remember your blood? Who rides with me for Tarwin's Gap?"

For a moment, he thought neither man would speak, but then Gorenellin was on his feet, tears glistening his eyes. "The Golden Crane flies for Tarmon Gai'don," he said softly.

"The Golden Crane flies for Tarmon Gai'don!" Managan shouted, leaping up so fast he overturned his chair.

Laughing, Aldragoran joined them, all three shouting at the top of their lungs. "The Golden Crane flies for Tarmon Gai'don!"

CHAPTER
21

Within the Stone

The mud of the outer city gave way to paved streets at the walls
of Tear, where the first thing Rand noticed was the absence of
guards. Despite the lofty stone ramparts with their towers, the
city was less defended than Stedding Shangtai, where he and every
other human had been gently but firmly refused entrance at first light.
Here, the archers' balconies on the towers were empty. The iron-
strapped door of the squat gray guardhouse just inside the broad gates
stood wide open, and a hard-faced woman in rough woolens, her
sleeves shoved up her thin arms, sat there at a wooden tub scrubbing
clothes with a washboard. She appeared to have taken up residence;
two small, grubby children sucking their thumbs stared wide-eyed
past her at him and his companions. At their horses, at least.

Tai'daishar was a sight to stare at, a sleek black stallion with a massive chest, a horse that drew attention, yet he had chosen to ride the animal anyway. If the Forsaken could find him as easily as they had at
Algarin's manor house, there was little point to hiding. Or at least to
putting too much effort into it. He wore black riding gloves to conceal
the dragons' heads on his hands and the herons branded into his palms.
His coat was dark gray wool without a stitch of embroidery, the stallion's saddle cloth simple, and his sword's hilt and scabbard had been
covered in unworked boarhide ever since it came into his possession,

nothing to pull a second glance. Cadsuane, in unadorned gray wool, wore the hood of her dark green cloak well up to shield her Aes Sedai face, but Min, Nynaeve and Alivia had no need for hiding. Though Min's flower-embroidered red coat and snug breeches might attract a little notice, not to mention her heeled red boots. He had seen women in Cairhien wearing clothes like that, copying her, yet it seemed unlikely that her fashion had spread to Tear, where modesty held sway. In public, at least. Nynaeve was wearing yellow-slashed blue silk and all of her jewelry, just partly concealed by her blue cloak, but Tear would be full of silks. She had wanted to wear her shawl! That was in her saddlebags, though. A little effort only.

The second thing he noticed was the sound, a rhythmic racketing clatter accompanied periodically by a piercing whistle. Faint at first, it seemed to be coming closer rapidly. Despite the early hour, the streets he could see from the gates were crowded. Half the people in sight appeared to be Sea Folk, the men bare-chested, the women in bright linen blouses, all wearing long sashes more colorful than those worn by Tairen commoners. Every head appeared to be turned toward that sound. Children darted through the throng, dodging carts most often pulled by oxen with wide horns, racing toward the noise. Several well-dressed men and women had dismounted from their sedan chairs and stood with the bearers to watch. A fork-bearded merchant with silver chains across the chest of his coat was half out of the window of a red-lacquered coach, shouting at his driver to manage the nervously dancing team while he strained for a better view.

White-winged pigeons, startled from pointed slate rooftops by a particularly sharp whistle, suddenly wheeled into the air. And two large flocks crashed into each other, pelting the folk below with stunned birds. Every single bird fell. A few people actually stopped staring toward the approaching noise and gaped at the sky. A surprising number snatched up fallen birds and wrung their necks, though, and not just barefoot people in worn woolens. A woman in silk and lace, standing beside one of the sedan chairs, quickly gathered half a dozen before gazing toward the noise with the birds dangling from her hands by their feet.

Alivia made a startled sound. "Is that ill luck or good?" she drawled. "It must be ill. Unless pigeons here are different?" Nynaeve gave her a sour look, but said nothing. She had been very quiet since Lan vanished the day before, a subject on which she was doubly silent.

"Some of those people are going to die of hunger," Min said sadly. The bond quivered with sorrow. "Every last one I can see something about."

How can I hide? Lews Therin laughed. *I am* ta'veren!

You're dead, Rand thought at him sharply. People in front of him were going to starve, and he laughed? There was nothing to be done, of course, not when Min spoke, but laughing was another matter. *I am* ta'veren. *Me!*

What else was happening in Tear because of his presence? His being *ta'veren* did not always have any effect at all, but when it did, the result could blanket an entire city. Best to get on with what he had come for before the wrong people figured out what things like pigeons flying into one another meant. If the Forsaken were sending armies of Trollocs and Myrddraal after him, it was likely that Darkfriends would take any opportunity to put an arrow through his ribs. Making little effort to hide was not the same as making no effort.

"You might as well have brought the Banner of Light and an honor guard of thousands instead of six," Cadsuane murmured dryly, eyeing the Maidens who were trying to pretend they had nothing to do with Rand's party while standing in a wide circle around it, *shoufa* covering their heads and veils hanging down their chests. Two were Shaido, fierce-eyed whenever they looked at him. The Maidens' spears were all on their backs, stuck through the harness of their bowcases, but only because Rand had offered to leave them behind and take someone else otherwise. Nandera had insisted on at least a few Maidens, staring at him with eyes as hard as emeralds. He had never considered refusing. The only child of a Maiden any Maiden had ever known, he had obligations to meet.

He gathered Tai'daishar's reins, and abruptly a large wagon full of machinery came into sight, clanking and hissing, wide iron-studded wheels striking sparks from the gray paving stones as it moved along the street as fast as a man could trot. The machinery seemed to sweat steam; a heavy wooden shaft swung up and down pushing another, vertical shaft, and gray woodsmoke drifted from a metal chimney; but there was no sign of a horse, just an odd sort of tiller in the front to turn the wheels. One of the three men standing in the wagon pulled a long cord, and steam rushed in a shrill whistle out of a tube atop a huge iron cylinder. If the onlookers stared in awe and maybe covered their ears, the fork-bearded merchant's team was in no such mood.

Whinnying wildly, they bolted, scattering people as they ran and nearly pitching the man out on his head. Curses pursued them, and several braying mules that galloped off with their drivers in bouncing carts sawing at the reins. Even a few oxen began to lumber along more quickly. Min's astonishment filled the bond.

Controlling the black with his knees—trained as a warhorse, Tai'daishar responded immediately, though he still snorted—Rand stared in amazement, too. It seemed Master Poel actually had made his steamwagon work. "But how did the thing get to Tear?" he asked the air. The last he had seen, it had been at the Academy of Cairhien, and seizing up every few paces.

"It's called a steamhorse, my Lord," a barefoot, dirty-faced urchin in a ragged shirt said, bouncing on the pavement. Even the sash holding up his baggy breeches seemed as much holes as cloth. "I've seen it nine times! Com here's only seen it seven."

"A steamwagon, Doni," his equally ragged companion put in. "A steam*wagon.*" Neither of them could have been more than ten, and they were gaunt rather than skinny. Their muddy feet, torn shirts and holed breeches meant they came from outside the walls, where the poorest folk lived. Rand had changed a number of laws in Tear, especially those that weighed heavily on the poor, but he had been unable to change everything. He had not even known how to begin. Lews Therin began to maunder on about taxes and money creating jobs, but he might as well have been spilling out words at random for all the sense he made. Rand muted the voice to a buzz, a fly on the other side of a room.

"Four of them hitched together, one behind the other, pulled a hundred wagons all the way from Cairhien," Doni went on, ignoring the other boy. "They covered near a hundred miles every day, my Lord. A hundred miles!"

Com sighed heavily. "There were six of them, Doni, and they only pulled fifty wagons, but they covered *more* than a hundred miles every day. A hundred and twenty some days, I heard, and it was one of the steam-men said it." Doni turned to scowl at him, the pair of them balling up fists.

"Either way, it's a remarkable achievement," Rand told them quickly, before they could begin trading blows. "Here."

Dipping into his coat pocket, he pulled out two coins and tossed one toward each boy without looking to see what they were. Gold glittered in the air before the boys eagerly snatched the coins. Exchanging startled glances, they went running out through the gates as fast as they could go, no doubt fearful he would demand the coins back. Their families could live for months on that much gold.

Min gazed after them with an expression of misery that the bond echoed even after she shook her head and smoothed her face. What had she seen? Death, probably. Rand felt anger, but no sorrow. How many tens of thousands would die before the Last Battle was done? How many would be children? He had no room left in him for sorrow.

"Very generous," Nynaeve said in a tight voice, "but are we going to stand here all morning?" The steamwagon was moving on out of sight quickly, yet her plump brown mare was still blowing anxiously and tossing her head, and she was having difficulty with the animal, placid as it was by nature. She was far from as good a rider as she thought herself. For that matter, Min's mount, an arch-necked gray mare from Algarin's stables, danced so that only Min's firm, red-gloved grip on the reins kept her from running, and Alivia's roan was trying to dance, though the former *damane* controlled the animal as easily as Cadsuane did her bay. Alivia sometimes displayed surprising talents. *Damane* were expected to ride well.

As they rode into the city, Rand took a last glance at the disappearing steamwagon. Remarkable was hardly the word. A hundred wagons or only fifty—only!—incredible was more like it. Would merchants start using those things instead of horses? It hardly seemed likely. Merchants were conservative folk, not known for leaping at new ways of doing things. For some reason, Lews Therin began laughing again.

Tear was not beautiful, like Caemlyn or Tar Valon, and few of its streets could be called particularly broad, but it was large and sprawling, one of the great cities of the world, and, like most great cities, a jumble that had grown up willy-nilly. In those tangled streets, tile-roofed inns and slate-roofed stables, the roof corners slanted sharply, stood alongside palaces with squared white domes and tall, balcony-ringed towers that often came to points, the heights of domes and towers gleaming in the early-morning sun. Smithies and cutlers, seamstresses and butchers, fishmongers and rugweavers' shops rubbed against marble structures with tall bronze doors behind massive white columns, guild halls and bankers and merchants' exchanges.

At this hour, the streets themselves were still cast in deep shadows, yet they bustled with that storied southern industry. Sedan chairs borne by pairs of lean men wove through the crowds almost as quickly as the children who raced about in play while coaches and carriages behind teams of four or six moved as slowly as the carts and wagons, most drawn by large oxen. Porters trudged along, their bundles slung beneath poles carried on two men's shoulders, and apprentices carried rolled carpets and boxes of the masters' handiwork on their backs. Hawkers cried their wares from trays or handbarrows, pins and ribbons, a few with roasted nuts and meat pies, and tumblers or jugglers or musicians performed at nearly every intersection. You would never have thought this city was the site of a siege.

Not everything was peaceful, though. Early morning or not, Rand saw obstreperous drunks being thrown out of inns and taverns and so many fistfights and men wrestling on the pavement that it seemed one pair was not well out of sight before the next came into view. A good many obvious armsmen mingled in the crowd, swords at their hips and the fat sleeves of their woolen coats striped in various House colors, but even those wearing breastplates and helmets made no move to break up the rows. A fair number of the fights involved armsmen, with one another, with Sea Folk, with roughly clad fellows who might have been laborers or apprentices or shoulderthumpers. Soldiers with nothing to do grew bored, and bored soldiers got drunk and fought. He was glad to see the rebels' armsmen bored.

The Maidens, drifting through the throng and still trying to pretend they had no association with Rand, drew puzzled looks and head-scratching, mainly from dark-faced Sea Folk, though a gaggle of children trailed after them gaping. The Tairens, many of whom were not all that much fairer than the Sea Folk, had seen Aiel before, and if they wondered why they had returned to the city, it appeared they had different business at hand this morning, and more important. No one seemed to give Rand or his other companions a second glance. There were other mounted men and women in the streets, most of them outlanders, here a pale Cairhienin merchant in a somber coat, there an Arafellin with silver bells fastened to his dark braids, here a copper-skinned Domani in a barely opaque riding dress barely hidden by her cloak followed by a pair of hulking bodyguards in leather coats sewn with steel discs, there a Shienaran with his head shaved except for a gray topknot and his belly straining his buttons. You could not move ten paces in Tear without seeing outlanders. Tairen commerce had long arms.

Which was not to say that he passed through the city without in-cident. Ahead of him, a running baker's boy tripped and fell, flinging his basket into the air, and when the boy levered himself off the paving stones as Rand rode by, he stopped halfway up with his mouth hanging open, staring at the long loaves standing on end near the basket, propped together in a rough cone. A fellow in his shirt-sleeves, drinking in a second-story window of an inn, overbalanced and toppled toward the street with a shriek that cut off when he landed on his feet not ten paces from Tai'daishar, mug still in hand. Rand left him behind wide-eyed and feeling at himself in wonder-ment. Ripples of altered chance were following Rand, spreading across the city.

Not every event would be as harmless as the loaves, or as beneficial as the man landing on his feet rather than his head. Those ripples could turn what should be a bruiseless tumble into broken bones or a broken neck. Lifelong feuds could be started by men speaking words they had never thought to hear come from their own lips. Women could decide to poison their husbands over trivial offenses they had tolerated com-placently for years. Oh, some fellow might find a rotting sack full of gold buried in his own basement without really knowing why he had decided to dig in the first place, or a man might ask and gain the hand of a woman he had never before had the courage to approach, but as many would find ruination as found good fortune. Balance, Min had called it. A good to balance every ill. He saw an ill to balance every good. He needed to be done in Tear and gone as soon as possible. Gal-loping in those crowded streets was out of the question, but he picked up his pace enough that the Maidens had to trot.

His destination had been in sight since long before he entered the city, a mass of stone like a barren, sheer-sided hill that stretched from the River Erinin into the city's heart, covering at least eight or nine marches, a good square mile or more, and dominating the city's sky. The Stone of Tear was mankind's oldest stronghold, the oldest structure in the world, made with the One Power in the last days of the Breaking itself. One solid piece of stone it was, without a single join, though better than three thousand years of rain and wind had weathered the surface to roughness. The first battlements stood a hundred paces above the ground, though there were arrowslits aplenty lower, and stone spouts for showering attackers with boiling oil or molten lead. No besieger could stop the Stone from being supplied through its own wall-shielded docks, and it contained forges and manufactories to replace or mend every sort of weapon should its armories fall short. Its highest tower, rearing over the very center of the Stone, held the banner of Tear, half red, half gold, with a slanting line of three silver crescents, and so large that it could be made out plainly as it curled in a strong breeze. It had to be strong to move that flag. Lower towers supported smaller versions, but here they alternated with another rippling banner, the ancient symbol of Aes Sedai black-and-white on a field of red. The Banner of Light. The Dragon Banner, some called it, as if there were not another that bore that name. The High Lord Darlin was flaunting his allegiance, it seemed. That was well.

Alanna was in there, and whether or not that was well he would have to learn. He was not as sharply aware of her as before Elayne and Aviendha and Min jointly bonded him—he thought he was not; they had pushed her aside to take primacy somehow, and she had told him she could sense little more of him than his presence—yet she still lay in the back of his head, a bundle of emotions and physical sensations. It seemed a long time since he had been near enough to her to sense those. Once again, the bond with her felt an intrusion, a would-be usurper of his bond to Min and Elayne and Aviendha. Alanna was weary, as if perhaps she had not been getting enough sleep lately, and frustrated, with strong streaks of anger and sulkiness. Were the negotiations going badly? He would find out soon enough. She would be aware he was in the city, aware he was coming closer if little more. Min had tried to teach him a trick called masking that supposedly could hide him from the bond, but he had never been able to make it work. Of course, she admitted she had never been able to make it work either.

Soon he found himself on a street that ran directly to the plaza that surrounded the Stone on three sides, but he had no intention of riding straight there. For one thing, every massive iron-strapped gate would be barred tight. For another, he could see several hundred armsmen at the foot of the street. He expected there would be the same in front of every gate. They hardly gave the impression of men besieging a fortress. They seemed to be lounging about with no order—many had their helmets off and their halberds propped against the buildings lining the street, and serving women from nearby taverns and inns circulated among them selling mugs of ale or wine from trays—yet it was highly unlikely they would remain complacent about anyone trying to enter the Stone. Not that they could stop him, of course. He could sweep aside a few hundred men like so many moths.

He had not come to Tear to kill anyone, though, not unless he had to, so he rode into the stableyard of a tile-roofed inn, three stories of dark gray stone with a prosperous look. The sign out front was freshly painted with, of all things, a rough approximation of the creatures encircling his forearms. The artist apparently had decided the thing was inadequate as described, though, because he had added long, sharp teeth and leathery, ribbed wings. Wings! They almost looked copied from one of those Seanchan flying beasts. Cadsuane looked at the sign and snorted. Nynaeve looked at it and giggled. So did Min!

Even after Rand gave the barefoot stableboys silver to curry the horses, they stared at the Maidens harder than at the coins, but no harder than the patrons stared in The Dragon's beam-ceilinged common room. Conversation trailed off when the Maidens followed Rand and the others inside, spearpoints sticking up above their heads and bullhide bucklers in hand. Men and women, most in plain if good quality wool, turned in their low-backed chairs to stare. They seemed to be middling merchants and solid craftsfolk, yet they gaped like villagers seeing a city for the first time. The serving women, in dark high-necked dresses and short white aprons, stopped trotting and goggled over their trays. Even the woman playing a hammered dulcimer between the two stone fireplaces, cold on this fine morning, fell silent.

A very dark fellow with tightly curled hair, at a square table beside the door, seemed not to notice the Maidens at all. Rand took him for one of the Sea Folk at first, though he wore a peculiar coat without collar or lapels, once white but now stained and wrinkled. "I tell you, I have many, many of the . . . the worms that make . . . yes, make . . . silk on a ship," he said haltingly in an odd, musical accent. "But I must have the . . . the . . . andberry . . . yes, andberry leaves to feed them. We will be rich."

His companion waved a plump, dismissive hand even while staring at the Maidens. "Worms?" he said absently. "Everybody knows silk grows on trees."

Walking deeper into the common room, Rand shook his head as the proprietor advanced to meet him. Worms! The tales people could come up with to try prying coin out of somebody else.

"Agardo Saranche at your service, my Lord, my Ladies," the lean, balding man said with a deep bow, sweeping his hands wide. Not all

Tairens were dark by any means, but he was nearly as fair complected as a Cairhienin. "How may I serve?" His dark eyes kept drifting to the Maidens, and every time they did, he tugged at his long blue coat as though it suddenly felt too tight.

"We want a room with a good view of the Stone," Rand said.

"It *is* worms that make silk, friend," a man drawled behind him. "My eyes on it."

At that familiar accent, Rand spun to find Alivia staring, wide-eyed and her face bloodless, at a man in a dark coat who was just passing through the doorway into the street. With an oath, Rand ran to the door, but there were close to a dozen men in dark coats walking away from the inn, any one of whom might have spoken. There was no way to pick out one man of average height and width seen only from behind. What was a Seanchan doing in Tear? Scouting for another invasion? He would put paid to that soon enough. But he turned from the door wishing he could have laid hands on the man. Knowing would be better than having to guess.

He asked Alivia whether she had gotten a good look at the fellow, but she shook her head silently. Her face was still pale. She was ferocious when she talked of what she wanted to do to *sul'dam*, yet it seemed just hearing the accents of her native land was enough to shake her. He hoped that did not turn out to be weakness in her. She was going to help him, somehow, and he could not afford her to be weak.

"What do you know of the man who just left?" he demanded of Saranche. "The one with the slurred way of talking."

The innkeeper blinked. "Nothing, my Lord. I've never seen him before. You want *one* room, my Lord?" He ran his eyes over Min and the other women, and his lips moved as if he were counting.

"If you're thinking of any impropriety, Master Saranche," Nynaeve said indignantly, tugging at the braid hanging from the cowl of her cloak, "you had best think twice and again. Before I box your ears." Min hissed softly, and one hand drifted toward her other wrist before she checked the motion. Light, but she was quick to reach for her knives!

"What impropriety?" Alivia asked in tones of puzzlement. Cadsuane snorted.

"One room," Rand said patiently. *Women can always find a reason to be indignant,* he thought. Or had that been Lews Therin? He shrugged in discomfort. And a touch of irritation that he only just managed to keep out of his voice. "Your largest with a view of the Stone. We don't want it for long. You'll be able to rent it out again for tonight. You may have to keep our horses a day or two, though."

A look of relief crept over Saranche's narrow face, though patently false rue filled his voice. "I regret that my largest room is taken, my Lord. In fact, all of my large rooms are taken. But I will be more than happy to escort you up the street to The Three Moons and—"

"Phaw!" Cadsuane pushed back her hood enough to reveal her face and some of her golden hair ornaments. She was all cool composure, her gaze implacable. "I think you can find a way to make that room available, boy. I think you had better find a way. Pay him well," she added to Rand, ornaments swaying on their chains. "That was advice, not an order."

Saranche took Rand's fat golden crown with alacrity—it was doubtful the entire inn earned much more in a week—but it was Cadsuane's ageless face that sent him bounding up the staircase at the back of the common room to return in a handful of minutes and show them to a room on the second floor with dark polished paneling and a rumpled bed wide enough for three flanked by a pair of windows filled by the Stone looming over the rooftops. The previous occupant had been hustled out so quickly that he had left a woolen stocking crumpled at the foot of the bed and a carved horn comb on the washstand in the corner. The innkeeper offered to have their saddlebags brought up, and wine, and seemed surprised when Rand refused, but one glance at Cadsuane's face, and he bowed his way out again hurriedly.

The room was fairly large as inn rooms went, yet not compared to most chambers in Algarin's manor house, much less in a palace. Especially not with near a dozen people filling the space. The walls seemed to close in on Rand. His chest suddenly felt tight. Every breath came with difficulty. The bond was suddenly full of sympathy and concern.

The box, Lews Therin panted. *Have to get out of the box!*

Keeping his eyes on the windows—being able to see the Stone was a necessity, and seeing open air between the Dragon and the Stone, the open air above, loosened his breathing a little. Just a little—keeping his eyes fixed on the sky above the Stone, he ordered everyone to stand against the walls. They obeyed with speed. Well, Cadsuane gave him a sharp look before gliding to the wall, and Nynaeve sniffed before flouncing over, but the rest moved quickly. If they thought he wanted space for safety's sake, in a way he did. Having them out of his line of sight made the room seem a little larger. Only a little, yet every inch was a blessed relief. The bond was filled with concern.

Must get out, Lews Therin moaned. *Have to get out.*

Stiffening himself against what he knew would come, watchful of any attempt by Lews Therin, Rand seized the male half of the True Source, and *saidin* flooded into him. Had the madman tried to seize it first? He had brushed it, certainly, touched it, but it was Rand's. Mountains of flame collapsing in fiery avalanches tried to scour him away. Waves that made ice seem warm tried to crush him in raging seas. He gloried in it, suddenly so alive it seemed he had been sleep-walking before. He could hear the breath of everyone in the room, could see that great banner atop the Stone so clearly he almost thought he could make out the weave of the fabric. The double wound in his side throbbed as if trying to rip itself out of his body, but with the Power filling him, he could ignore that pain. He thought he could have ignored a sword thrust.

Yet with *saidin* came the inevitable violent nausea, the almost overwhelming desire to double over and empty himself of every meal he had ever eaten. His knees trembled with it. He fought that as hard as he fought the Power, and *saidin* had to be fought ever and always. A man forced *saidin* to his will, or it destroyed him. The face of the man from Shadar Logoth floated in his head for a moment. He looked furious. And near to sicking up. Without any doubt he was *aware* of Rand in that moment, and Rand of him. Move a hair in any direction, and they would touch. No more than a hair.

"What's the matter?" Nynaeve demanded, moving close and peering up at him in concern. "Your face has gone all gray." She reached for his head, and his skin popped out in goose bumps.

He brushed her hands away. "I'm all right. Stand clear." She stood there giving him one of those looks women carried in their belt pouches. This one said she knew he was lying even if she could not prove it. Did they practice those looks in front of mirrors? "Stand clear, Nynaeve."

"He's all right, Nynaeve," Min said, though her face had a touch of gray about it, too, and she had both red-gloved hands pressed to her middle. She knew.

Nynaeve sniffed at him, wrinkling her nose in disdain, but she finally moved out of his way. Maybe Lan had had enough and run away. No, not that. Lan would not leave her unless she told him to, and then only for as long as was needful. Wherever he was, Nynaeve knew and likely had sent him there for reasons of her own. Aes Sedai and their bloody secrets.

He channeled, Spirit touched with Fire, and the familiar vertical silvery slash appeared at the foot of the bed, seemed to rotate into a dim view of massive columns in darkness. Light from the inn room gave all the illumination. The opening, standing inches above the floor, was no larger than the door to the room, yet as soon as it was fully open, three of the Maidens, already veiled, darted through pulling spears free, and Rand's skin pebbled again as Alivia leaped after them. Protecting him was a self-imposed duty, but one she took as seriously as the Maidens did.

There would be no ambush here, though, no dangers, so he stepped through, and down. At the other end, the gateway sat more than a foot above the huge gray slabs of stone that he had not wanted to damage any more than he already had. This was the Heart of the Stone, and with the Power in him, and the light spilling through the gateway from the room in The Dragon, he could see the narrow hole in one of those stones where he had driven Callandor into the floor. *Who draws it out shall follow after.* He had thought long and hard before sending Narishma to bring Callandor to him. However the Prophecies meant the man was to follow him, Narishma was otherwise occupied today. A forest of immense redstone columns surrounded him, stretching up into the dark that hid the unlit golden lamps and the vaulted ceiling and the great dome. His boots echoed hollowly in the vast chamber, and even the whispers of the Maidens' soft boots. In this space, the sense of confinement vanished.

Min hopped down right behind him—with a throwing knife in either hand, and her head swiveling, eyes searching the darkness—but Cadsuane, standing at the edge of the gateway, said, "I don't jump unless I absolutely have to, boy." She held out a hand, waiting for him to take it.

He handed her down, and she nodded thanks. It could have been meant for thanks. It could have meant "You took your bloody time about it," too. A ball of light appeared over her upturned palm, and a moment later Alivia was balancing a globe of light, too. The pair created a pool of brightness that turned the surrounding darkness deeper. Nynaeve required the same courtesy, and had the grace to murmur thanks—she quickly gained her own ball of light—but when he offered a hand to one of the Maidens—he thought it was Sarendhra, one of the Shaido, though all he could see of her face was blue eyes above her black veil—she grunted contemptuously and leaped down, spear in hand, followed by the other two. He let the gateway close, but held on to *saidin* despite the roiling in his stomach and head. He did not expect to need to channel again before he left the Stone, yet he did not want to give Lews Therin another opportunity to seize the Power, either.

You have to trust me, Lews Therin snarled. *If we're going to make it to Tarmon Gai'don so we can die, you have to trust me.*

You told me once not to trust anyone, Rand thought. *Including you.*

Only madmen trust no one, Lews Therin whispered. Abruptly he began to weep. *Oh, why do I have a madman in my head?* Rand pushed the voice away.

On striding through the tall arch that led from the Heart, he was surprised to find two Defenders of the Stone in ridged helmets and shining breastplates, the puffy sleeves of their black coats striped in black and gold. Swords drawn, they were staring at the archway with expressions that combined confusion with grim resolution. Doubtless they had been startled to see lights and hear footsteps echoing in a room with only one entrance, an entrance they were guarding. The Maidens crouched, spears coming up, spreading out to either side, slowly curling in toward the pair.

"By the Stone, it's him," one of the men said, sheathing his sword hurriedly. Stocky, with a puckered scar that began on his forehead and journeyed across the bridge of his nose and down to his jaw, he bowed deeply, hands in steel-backed gauntlets spreading wide. "My Lord Dragon," he said. "Iagin Handar, my Lord. The Stone stands. I got this that day." He touched the scar on his face.

"An honorable wound, Handar, and a day to remember," Rand told him as the other, leaner man hastily put up his blade and bowed. Only then did the Maidens lower their spears, but their faces remained veiled. A day to remember? Trollocs and Myrddraal inside the Stone. The second time he had truly wielded Callandor, using the Sword that was Not a Sword as it was meant to be used. The dead lying everywhere. A dead girl he could not make live again. Who could forget such a day? "I know I gave orders for the Heart to be guarded while Callandor was there, but why are you still standing guard?"

The two men exchanged puzzled looks. "You gave the order to set guards, my Lord Dragon," Handar said, "and the Defenders obey, but you never said anything about Callandor except that no one was to approach it unless they had proof they came from you." Suddenly the stocky man gave a start and bowed again, more deeply still. "Forgive me, my Lord, if I seem to question you. I don't mean to. Shall I summon the High Lords to your apartments? Your rooms have been kept in readiness for your return."

"No need," Rand told him. "Darlin will be expecting me, and I know where to find him."

Handar winced. The other man suddenly found something interesting on the floor to study. "You may require a guide, my Lord," Handar said slowly. "The corridors. . . . Sometimes the corridors change."

So. The Pattern truly was loosening. That meant the Dark One was touching the world more than he had since the War of the Shadow. If it loosened too much before Tarmon Gai'don, the Age Lace might unravel. An end to time and reality and creation. Somehow he had to bring about the Last Battle before that happened. Only he did not dare. Not yet.

He assured Handar and the other man that he needed no guide, and the pair of them bowed yet again, apparently accepting that the Dragon Reborn could do anything he said he could do. In simple truth, he knew he could locate Alanna—he could have pointed straight at her—and she had moved since he first felt her. To find Darlin and inform him that Rand al'Thor was approaching, he was sure. Min had named her as one he held in his hand, yet Aes Sedai always found a way to play both ends against the middle. They always had schemes of their own, goals of their own. Witness Nynaeve and Verin. Witness any of them.

"They hop when you say toad," Cadsuane said coolly, pushing the cowl of her cloak down her back, as they walked away from the Heart. "That can be bad for you, when too many people jump at your word." *She* had the nerve to say that! Cadsuane bloody Melaidhrin!

"I'm fighting a war," he told her harshly. The nausea had his temper on edge. That was part of the reason he was harsh. "The fewer people who obey, the more chance I'll lose, and if I lose, everybody loses. If I could make everyone obey, I would." There were far too many who did not obey as it was, or obeyed in their own way. Why in the Light would Min feel *pity*?

Cadsuane nodded. "As I thought," she murmured, half to herself. And what was *that* supposed to mean?

The Stone had all the trappings of a palace, from silk tapestries and rich runners in the corridors from Tarabon and Altara and Tear itself to golden stands holding mirrored lamps. Chests standing against the stone walls might be for storing what the servants needed for cleaning, yet they were of rare woods, often elaborately carved and always with gilded banding. Niches held bowls and vases of Sea Folk porcelain, thin as leaves and worth many times their weight in gold, or massive, gem-studded figures, a golden leopard with ruby eyes trying to pull down a silver deer with pearl-covered antlers that stood a pace tall, a golden lion that was even taller, with emerald eyes and firedrops for claws, others set so extravagantly with gems that no metal showed. Servants in black-and-gold livery bowed or curtsied as Rand climbed through the Stone, those who recognized him very deeply indeed. Some eyes widened at sight of the Maidens trailing behind, but their surprise never slowed their courtesies.

All the trappings of a palace, yet the Stone had been designed for war within as well as without. Wherever two corridors crossed, murderholes dotted the ceiling. Between the tapestries, arrowslits pierced the walls high up, angled to cover the corridors in both directions, and no flight of sweeping stairs but had arrowslits placed so the staircase could be swept by arrows or crossbow bolts. Only one assailant had ever succeeded in forcing a way into the Stone, the Aiel, and they had swept over the opposition too quickly for many of those defenses to come into play, but any other enemy that managed to get inside the Stone would pay a price in blood for every hallway. Except that Traveling had changed warfare forever. Traveling and Blossoms of Fire and so much more. That blood price would still be paid, yet stone walls and high towers could no longer hold back an assault. The Asha'man had made the Stone as obsolete as the bronze swords and stone axes men had often been reduced to in the Breaking. Mankind's oldest stronghold was now a relic.

The bond with Alanna led him up and up, until he came to tall, polished doors with golden leopards for door handles. She was on the other side. Light, but his stomach wanted to empty itself. Hardening himself, he pulled open one of the doors and went in, leaving the Maidens to stand guard. Min and the others followed him in.

The sitting room was almost as ornate as his own apartments in the Stone, the walls hung with broad silk tapestries showing scenes of the hunt and battle, the large, patterned Taraboner carpet on the floor worth sufficient gold to feed a large village for a year, the black marble fireplace tall enough for a man to walk into and wide enough to hold eight abreast. Every piece of furnishing, all massively made, was elaborately carved, crusted with gilt and dotted with gems, as were the tall golden stand-lamps, their mirrored flames adding to the light let in by the glass-paned ceiling. A golden bear with ruby eyes and silver claws and teeth, more than a pace high, stood atop a gilded plinth on one side of the room, while an identical plinth held an emerald-eyed, ruby-taloned eagle nearly as tall. Restrained pieces for Tear.

Seated in an armchair, Alanna looked up as he walked in, and held out a golden goblet for one of the two young serving women in black and gold to fill with dark wine from a tall golden pitcher. Slender in a gray riding dress slashed with green, Alanna was beautiful enough that Lews Therin began humming to himself. Rand almost thumbed his earlobe before snatching his hand down, suddenly unsure whether that gesture was his or the madman's. She smiled, but darkly, and as her eyes swept across Min and Nynaeve, Alivia and Cadsuane, the bond carried her suspicion, not to mention anger and sulkiness. The last two heightened for Cadsuane. And there was joy, as well, mixed in with all the rest, when her gaze touched him. Not that it showed in her voice. "Why, who would have expected you, my Lord Dragon?" she murmured, with a hint of asperity in the title. "Quite a surprise, wouldn't you say, my Lord Astoril?" So she had not warned anyone after all. Interesting.

"A very pleasant surprise," an elderly man in a coat with red-and-blue striped sleeves said as he rose to bow, stroking his oiled beard, trimmed to a point. The High Lord Astoril Damara's face was creased, the hair that hung to his shoulders snow white and thinning, but his back was straight and his dark eyes sharp. "I've been looking forward to this day for some time." He bowed again, to Cadsuane, and after a moment, to Nynaeve. "Aes Sedai," he said. Very civil for Tear, where channeling if not Aes Sedai themselves had been outlawed before Rand altered the law.

Darlin Sisnera, High Lord and Steward in Tear for the Dragon Reborn, in a green silk coat with yellow-striped sleeves and gold-worked boots, was less than a head shorter than Rand, with close-cut hair and a pointed beard, a bold nose and blue eyes that were rare in Tear. Those eyes widened as he turned from a conversation with Caraline Damodred near the fireplace. The Cairhienin noblewoman gave Rand a jolt, though he had expected to see her here. The litany he used to forge his soul in fire almost started up in his head before he could stop it. Short and slim and pale, with large dark eyes and a small ruby dangling onto her forehead from a golden chain woven into the black hair falling in waves to her shoulders, she was the very image of her cousin Moiraine. Of all things, she wore a long blue coat, embroidered in golden scrolls except for the horizontal stripes of red, green and white that ran from neck to hem, over snug green breeches and heeled blue boots. It seemed the fashion had traveled after all. She made a curtsy, even so, though it looked odd in that garb. Lews Therin hummed even harder, making Rand wish the man had a face so he could hit him. Moiraine was a memory for hardening his soul, not for humming at.

"My Lord Dragon," Darlin said, bowing stiffly. He was not a man accustomed to offering the first courtesy. He gave no bow for Cadsuane, just a sharp look before he seemed to dismiss her presence entirely. She had kept him and Caraline as "guests" for a time in Cairhien. He was unlikely to forget that, or forgive. At his gesture, the two serving women moved quickly to offer wine. As might have been expected, Cadsuane with her ageless face received the first goblet, but surprisingly, Nynaeve got the second. The Dragon Reborn was one thing, a woman wearing the Great Serpent ring something else again, even in Tear. Throwing her cloak back, Cadsuane retreated to the wall. It was unlike her to be retiring. But then, from there, she could observe everyone at once. Alivia took a place by the door, doubtless for much the same reason. "I am glad to see you better than when I saw you last," Darlin went on. "You've done me great honor. Though I may yet lose my head for it, if your Aes Sedai make no more progress than they have."

"Do not be sulky, Darlin," Caraline murmured, her throaty voice sounding amused. "Men do sulk, do they not, Min?" For some reason, Min barked a laugh.

"What are you doing here?" Rand demanded of the two people he had not expected to see. He took a goblet from one of the serving women while the other hesitated between Min and Alivia. Min won out, perhaps because Alivia's blue dress was plain. Sipping her wine, Min strolled over to Caraline—at a glance from the Cairhienin woman, Darlin moved away, grinning—and the two women stood with their heads together, whispering. Filled with the Power, Rand could catch the occasional word. His name, Darlin's.

Weiramon Saniago, also a High Lord of Tear, was not short, and he stood as straight as a sword, yet there was something of a strutting rooster about him. His gray-streaked beard, trimmed to a point and oiled, practically quivered with pride. "Hail to the Lord of the Morning," he said, bowing. Or rather, he intoned it. Weiramon was a great one for intoning and declaiming. "Why am I here, my Lord Dragon?" He sounded puzzled at the question. "Why, when I heard that Darlin was besieged in the Stone, what could I do but come to his aid? Burn my soul, I tried to talk some of the others into accompanying me. We'd have put a quick end to Estanda and that lot, I vow!" He clutched a fist to demonstrate how he would have crushed the rebels. "But only Anaiyella had the courage. The Cairhienin were a complete lot of lily-hearts!" Caraline paused her talk with Min to give him a look that would have had him hunting for the stab wound had he noticed it. Astoril pursed his lips and commenced a study of his wine.

The High Lady Anaiyella Narencelona also wore a coat and snug breeches with heeled boots, though she had added a white lace ruff, and her green coat was sewn with pearls. A close cap of pearls sat atop her dark hair. A slim, pretty woman, she offered a simpering curtsy, and somehow made it seem she wanted to kiss Rand's hand. Courage was not a word he would have applied to her. Nerve, on the other hand. . . . "My Lord Dragon," she cooed. "I wish we could report complete success, but my Master of the Horse died fighting the Seanchan, and you left most of my armsmen in Illian. Still, we managed to strike a blow in your name."

"Success? A blow?" Alanna's scowl took in Weiramon and Anaiyella both before she twisted back around to face Rand. "They landed at the Stone's docks with one ship, but they put most of their armsmen and all the mercenaries they hired in Cairhien ashore from the rest upriver. With orders to enter the city and attack the rebels." She made a sound of disgust. "The only result was a great many men dead and our negotiations with the rebels thrown back to the beginning." Anaiyella's simper took on a sickly twist.

"My plan was to sortie from the Stone and attack them from both sides," Weiramon protested. "Darlin refused. Refused!"

Darlin was not grinning now. He stood with his feet apart, and looked a man who wished he had a sword in his hand rather than a goblet. "I told you then, Weiramon. If I stripped the Stone of Defenders, the rebels would still have outnumbered us badly. Too badly. They've hired every sell-sword from the Erinin to the Bay of Remara."

Rand took a chair, flinging one arm over the back. The heavy arms had no supports at the front, so his sword was no problem. Caraline and Min seemed to have switched their talk to clothing. At least, they were fingering each other's coats, and he heard words like back-stitch and bias-cut, whatever that meant. Alanna's gaze drifted between him and Min, and he felt disbelief warring with suspicion along the bond. "I left you two in Cairhien because I wanted you in Cairhien," he said. He trusted neither, but they could cause small harm in Cairhien, where they were outlanders without power. Anger heated by nausea entered his voice. "You will make plans to return there as soon as possible. As soon as possible."

Anaiyella's simper grew more sickly, and she cringed slightly.

Weiramon was made of sterner stuff. "My Lord Dragon, I will serve you where you command, but I can serve best on my native soil. I know these rebels, know where they can be trusted and where—"

"As soon as possible!" Rand snapped, slamming his fist down on the chair arm hard enough to make the wood creak loudly.

"One," Cadsuane said, quite clearly and quite incomprehensibly.

"I strongly suggest you do as he says, Lord Weiramon." Nynaeve eyed Weiramon blandly, took a sip of wine. "He has a temper lately, worse than ever, and you don't want it directed at you."

Cadsuane exhaled a heavy breath. "Stay out of this, girl," she said sharply. Nynaeve glared at her, opened her mouth, then grimaced and closed it again. Gripping her braid, she glided across the carpet to join Min and Caraline. She had gotten very good at gliding.

Weiramon studied Cadsuane for a moment, tilting back his head so he was staring down his nose. "As the Dragon Reborn commands," he said finally, "so does Weiramon Saniago obey. My ship can be readied to sail by tomorrow, I wager. Will that suffice?"

Rand nodded curtly. It would have to answer. He was not about to waste a moment making a gateway to send this pair of fools where they belonged today. "There's hunger in the city," he said, eyeing the golden bear—how many days would that much gold feed Tear? The thought of food made his stomach clench—and waited for a response that was quick in coming, if not from the direction he expected.

"Darlin had cattle and sheep herded down to the city," Caraline said with some considerable warmth. Rand was the one getting the dagger look, now. "These days. . . ." She faltered for a moment, though the heat never left her gaze. "These days, meat is inedible two days after slaughter, so he had the animals brought, and wagons full of grain. Estanda and her companions seized it all for themselves."

Darlin gave her a fond smile, but his voice was apologetic. "I've tried three times, but Estanda is greedy, it seems. I saw no point in continuing to supply my enemies. Your enemies."

Rand nodded. At least the man was not ignoring the situation in the city. "There are two boys who live outside the walls. Doni and Com. I don't know any more name than that. About age ten. Once the rebels are settled and you can leave the Stone, I would appreciate it if you found them and kept an eye on them." Min made a sound in her throat, and the bond carried sadness so bleak it almost overwhelmed the burst of love that came with it. So. It must have been death she saw. But she had been wrong about Moiraine. Maybe this viewing could be changed by a *ta'veren*.

No, Lews Therin growled. *Her viewings must not change.* We *have to die!* Rand ignored him.

Darlin appeared puzzled by the request, but he acceded, as what else was he to do when the Dragon Reborn made it?

Rand was about to bring up the purpose of his visit when Bera Harkin, another of the Aes Sedai he had sent to Tear to deal with the rebels, entered the room frowning over her shoulder as if the Maidens had made some difficulty for her. They might well have. The Aiel considered the Aes Sedai sworn to him to be Wise Ones' apprentices, and Maidens took every opportunity to remind apprentices that they were not Wise Ones yet. She was a stocky woman, with brown hair cut close around a square face, and despite her green silks, lacking Aes Sedai agelessness she would have looked a farmwife. A farmwife who ruled her house and farm with a firm hand, though, and would tell a king not to track mud into her kitchen. She was Green Ajah, after all, with every scrap of Green Ajah pride and haughtiness. She frowned at Alivia, too, with all the disdain of Aes Sedai for wilder, and that faded only to coolness when she caught sight of Rand.

"Well, I must say I shouldn't be surprised to see you, considering what's happened this morning," she said. Unpinning her simple silver cloak brooch, she fastened it to her belt pouch and folded the cloak over her arm. "Though it might have been the news that the others are no more than a day west of the Erinin."

"The others?" Rand said quietly. Quietly and steely hard.

Bera did not seem impressed. She went on arranging the folds of her cloak. "The other High Lords and Ladies, of course. Sunamon, Tolmeran, all of them. Apparently they're traveling hot-foot for Tear as fast their armsmen's horses can move."

Rand leaped up so fast that his sword bound for a moment on the chair arm. Only a moment because the gilded wood, weakened by his earlier blow, split with a loud crack, and the arm dropped to the carpet. He never so much as glanced at it. The fools! The Seanchan at the border with Altara, and they were coming back to Tear? "Doesn't anybody remember how to obey?" he thundered. "I want messengers sent to them immediately! They're to return to Illian faster than they left or I'll have the lot of them hanged!"

"Two," Cadsuane said. What in the Light was she counting? "A bit of advice, boy. Ask her what happened this morning. I smell good news."

Bera gave a little start at realizing Cadsuane was in the room. Eyeing her sideways, and cautiously, she stopped fiddling with her cloak. "We've reached agreement," she said as if the question had been asked. "Tedosian and Simaan were wavering, as usual, but Hearne was nearly as adamant as Estanda." She shook her head. "I think Tedosian and Simaan might have come around sooner, but some fellows with strange accents have been promising them gold and men."

"Seanchan," Nynaeve said. Alivia opened her mouth, then closed it without speaking.

"They might be," Bera allowed. "They keep clear of us and look at us like we were mad dogs that might bite any moment. That sounds like what little I've heard of Seanchan. In any case, less than an hour gone, Estanda suddenly began asking whether the Lord Dragon would restore her title and lands, and they all collapsed right behind her. The agreement is this. Darlin is accepted as Steward in Tear for the Dragon Reborn, all laws you made remain unchanged, and they pay for feeding the city for one year as a fine for rebellion. In return, they receive full restoration, Darlin is crowned King of Tear, and they swear fealty to him. Merana and Rafela are preparing the documents for signatures and seals."

"King?" Darlin said incredulously. Caraline swayed over to take his arm.

"Restoration?" Rand growled, hurling his goblet aside in a spray of wine. The bond carried caution, a warning from Min, but he was too angry to pay heed. The sickness twisting his insides twisted his rage, too. "Blood and bloody ashes! I stripped them of lands and titles for rebelling against me. They can stay commoners and swear fealty to me!"

"Three," Cadsuane said, and Rand's skin popped out in goose bumps an instant before something struck him across the bottom like a hard-swung switch. Bera's lips parted in shock, and the cloak slid off her arm to the floor. Nynaeve laughed. She smothered it quickly, but she laughed! "Don't make me have to keep reminding you about manners, boy," Cadsuane went on. "Alanna told me the terms you offered before she left—Darlin as Steward, your laws kept, everything else on the table—and it seems they've been met. You can do as you wish, of course, but another piece of advice. When the terms you offer are accepted, hold to them."

Else no one will trust you, Lews Therin said, sounding entirely sane. For the moment.

Rand glared at Cadsuane, fists clenched hard, on the brink of weaving something that would singe her. He could feel a welt on his bottom, and would feel it more in the saddle. It seemed to pulse, and his anger pulsed with it. She peered back calmly over her wine. Was there a hint of challenge in her gaze, of daring him to channel? The woman spent every moment in his presence challenging him! The trouble was, her advice was good. He *had* given Alanna those terms. He had expected them to bargain harder, gain more, but they had gotten what he actually asked for. More. He had not thought of fines.

"It seems your fortunes have risen, King Darlin," he said. One of the serving women curtsied and handed Rand another goblet full of wine. Her face was as calm as any Aes Sedai's. You might have thought men arguing with sisters was a matter of every day with her.

"All hail King Darlin," Weiramon intoned, sounding half strangled, and after a moment Anaiyella echoed him, as breathless as if she had run a mile. Once, she had talked of herself for a crown in Tear.

"But why would they want me as King?" Darlin said, scrubbing a hand through his hair. "Or anyone. There've been no kings in the

Stone since Moreina died, a thousand years ago. Or did you demand that, Bera Sedai?"

Bera straightened from picking up her cloak and began shaking it out. "It was their . . . 'demand' would be too strong . . . their suggestion. Any of them would have leapt at the chance of a throne, especially Estanda." Anaiyella made a choking sound. "But of course, they knew there was no hope of that. This way, they can swear to you instead of to the Dragon Reborn, making it slightly less distasteful."

"And if you are king," Caraline put in, "it means that Steward in Tear for the Lord Dragon becomes a lesser title." She laughed throatily. "They may even tack on three or four more noble sounding titles to try pushing it down to obscurity." Bera pursed her lips as though she had been about to bring up that very point.

"And would you marry a king, Caraline?" Darlin asked. "I'll accept the crown, if you will. Though I'll have to have a crown made."

Min cleared her throat. "I can tell you how it should look, if you like."

Caraline laughed again and released Darlin's arm, swaying away from him. "I will have to see you in it before I could answer that. Have Min's crown made, and if it makes you look pretty. . . ." She smiled. "Then perhaps I will consider it."

"I wish you both the best," Rand said curtly, "but there are more important matters to go into right now." Min gave him a sharp look, disapproval flooding the bond. *Nynaeve* gave him a sharp look. What was *that* about? "You *will* accept that crown, Darlin, and as soon as those documents are signed, I want you to arrest those Seanchan, then gather every man in Tear who knows one end of sword or halberd from the other. I'll arrange for Asha'man to take you to Arad Doman."

"And me, my Lord Dragon?" Weiramon asked avidly. He all but quivered with eagerness, managing to strut while standing still. "If there is fighting to be done, I can serve you better there than languishing in Cairhien."

Rand studied the man. And Anaiyella. Weiramon was a bungling idiot, and he trusted neither, but he could not see what harm they could do with no more than a handful of followers. "Very well. You two may accompany the High Lord . . . that is, King Darlin." Anaiyella gulped as though she for one would rather return to Cairhien.

"But what am I supposed to do in Arad Doman?" Darlin wanted to know. "The little I've heard of that land, it's a madhouse." Lews Therin laughed wildly in Rand's head.

"Tarmon Gai'don is coming soon," Rand said. The Light send not too soon. "You are going to Arad Doman to get ready for Tarmon Gai'don."

CHAPTER
22

To Make an Anchor Weep

Despite the pitching induced by the long blue rollers, Harine din Togara sat very straight alongside her sister, just ahead of their parasol bearers and the steersman at his long tiller. Shalon seemed intent on studying the twelve men and women working the oars. Or perhaps she was deep in thought. There was plenty to think on of late, not least this meeting Harine had been summoned to, but she let her thoughts drift blindly. Composing herself. Every time the First Twelve of the Atha'an Miere met since she had attained Illian, she had needed to compose herself before attending. When she reached Tear and found Zaida's *Blue Gull* still anchored in the river, she had been sure the woman was in Caemlyn yet, or at least trailing far behind her own wake. A painful mistake, that. Though in truth, very little would have been altered had Zaida been weeks behind. Not for Harine, at least. No. No thoughts of Zaida.

The sun stood only a fist above the horizon in the east, and several vessels of the shorebound were making for the long breakwater that guarded Illian's harbor. One carried three masts and a semblance of a high-rig, all the major sails square, yet he was squat and ill-handled, wallowing through the low rolling seas in fountains of spray rather than slicing them. Most were small and low-rigged, their triangular sails nearly all high-boomed. Some seemed quick enough, but since

the shorebound seldom sailed beyond sight of land and usually anchored at night for fear of shoals, their quickness availed them little.
Cargo that required true speed went to Atha'an Miere ships. At a pre-
mium price, to be sure. It was a small portion of what Atha'an Miere
carried, in part because of the price, in part because few things actually
required their speed. Besides, cargo hire guaranteed some profit, but
when the Cargomaster traded on his own for the ship, all of the profit
went to vessel and clan.

As far as the eye could see to east and west along the coastline,
Atha'an Miere ships lay at anchor, rakers and skimmers, soarers and
darters, most surrounded by bumboats so cluttered they looked like
drunken shore festivals. Rowed out from the city, the bumboats offered
for sale everything from dried fruit to quartered beeves and sheep,
from iron nails and iron stock to swords and daggers, from gaudy trin-
kets of Illian that might catch a deckhand's eye to gold and gems.
Though the gold was usually a thin plate that wore off in a few months
to show the brass beneath and the gems colored glass. They brought
rats, too, if not for sale. Anchored so long, every ship was plagued by
rats, now. Rats and spoilage made sure there was always a market for
the peddlers.

Bumboats also surrounded the massive Seanchan-built vessels,
dozens upon dozens of them, that had been used in the Escape. That
was what it was being called, now, the great Escape from Ebou Dar.
Say the Escape, and no one asked what escape you meant. Great bluff-
bowed things they were, twice the beam of a raker and more, some,
suitable for battering through heavy seas perhaps, but strangely rigged
and with odd ribbed sails too stiff for proper setting. Men and women
were swarming over those masts and yards now, altering the rigging to
something more usable. No one wanted the craft, but the shipyards
would require years to replace all of the vessels lost at Ebou Dar. And
the expense! Overly beamy or not, those ships would see many years of
use. No Sailmistress had any desire to sink into debt, borrowing from
the clan coffers, when most if not all of her own gold was being sal-
vaged by the Seanchan in Ebou Dar, not unless she had no other choice.
Some, unlucky enough to have neither their own ships nor one of the
Seanchan's, did have no other choice.

Harine's twelve passed the heavy wall of the breakwater, thick with
dark slime and long hairy weed that the breakers crashing against the
gray stone failed to dislodge, and the broad, gray-green harbor of Illian

opened up before her, ringed with deep expanses of marsh, just turning from winter brown to green in patches, where long-legged birds waded. A line of mist drifted across the boat on a gentle breeze, dampening her hair before it passed on up the harbor. Small fishing boats were pulling their nets along the edges of the marsh, a dozen sorts of gull and tern wheeling overhead to steal what they could. The city did not interest her beyond the long stone docks, lined with trading craft, but the harbor. . . . That broad, nearly circular expanse of water was the greatest anchorage known, and filled with shipping and river craft, most waiting their turn at the docks. It truly was filled, by hundreds of vessels in every shape and size, and not all of those ships belonged to the shorebound. There were only rakers here, those slender three-masters that could race porpoises. Rakers and three of the ungainly Seanchan monstrosities. They were the vessels of Wavemistresses and of Sailmistresses who formed the First Twelve of each clan, those that could be fitted into the harbor before there was no more room. Even Illian's anchorage had its limits, and the Council of Nine, not to mention this Steward in Illian for the Dragon Reborn, would have made trouble had the Atha'an Miere begun crowding their trade.

Abruptly a strong, icy wind came up out of the north. No, it did not come up; it just suddenly was there full strength, whipping the harbor to choppy whitecaps and carrying a smell of pines and something . . . earthy. She knew little of trees, but much of timbers used in building ships. Though she did not think there were many pines anywhere near to Illian. Then she noticed the mist line. While ships rocked and pitched under that southerly blast, the mist continued its slow drift northward. Keeping her hands on her knees required effort. She wanted very much to wipe the dampness out of her hair. She had thought after Shadar Logoth that nothing ever would shake her again, but she had seen too many . . . oddities . . . of late, oddities that spoke of the world twisting.

As abruptly as it had come, the wind was gone. Murmurs rose, the stroke faltered, and the number four port oar caught a crab, splashing water into the boat. The crew knew winds did not behave that way.

"Steady there," Harine said firmly. "Steady!"

"Give way together, you shorebound ragpickers," her deckmistress shouted from the bow. Lean and leathery, Jadein had leather lungs as well. "Do I need to call the stroke for you?" The twin insults tightened some faces in anger, others in chagrin, but the oars began moving smoothly again.

Shalon was studying the mist, now. Asking what she saw, what she thought, would have to wait. Harine was not sure she wanted the answer heard by any of her crew. They had seen enough to have them frightened already.

The steersman turned the twelve toward one of the bulky Seanchan ships, where any bumboat that ventured near was being chased away before the peddler could get out two words. It was one of the largest of them, with a towering sterncastle that had three levels. Three! And the thing actually had a pair of *balconies* across the stern! She would not care to see what a following sea driven by a cemaros or one of the Aryth Ocean's soheens would do to those. Other twelves and a few eights waited their turn to sidle up to the vessel in the order of precedence of their passengers.

Jadein stood up in the bow and bellowed, "Shodein!" Her voice carried well, and a twelve that was approaching the ship circled away. The others continued their waiting.

Harine did not stand until the crew had backed oars, and drawn them in on the starboard, bringing the twelve to a smooth halt right where Jadein could catch a dangling line and hold the small craft alongside the larger. Shalon sighed.

"Courage, sister," Harine told her. "We have survived Shadar Logoth, though the Light help me, I am unsure *what* we survived." She barked a laugh. "More than that, we survived Cadsuane Melaidhrin, and I doubt anyone else here could do that."

Shalon smiled weakly, but at least she smiled.

Harine scrambled up the rope ladder as easily as she could have twenty years before and was piped aboard by the deckmaster, a squat fellow with a fresh scar running under the leather patch that covered where his right eye had been. Many had taken wounds in the Escape. Many had died. Even the deck of this ship felt strange beneath her bare feet, the planking laid in an odd pattern. The side was manned properly, however, twelve bare-chested men to her left, twelve women in bright linen blouses to her right, all bowing till they were looking straight down at the deck. She waited for Shalon and the parasol bearers to join her before starting forward. The vessel's Sailmistress and Windfinder, at the end of the rows, bowed less deeply while touching hearts, lips and foreheads. Both wore waist-long white mourning stoles that all but hid their many necklaces, as did she and Shalon.

"The welcome of my ship to you, Wavemistress," the Sailmistress said, sniffing her scent box, "and the grace of the Light be upon you until you leave his decks. The others await you in the great cabin."

"The grace of the Light be upon you also," Harine replied. Turane, in blue silk trousers and a red silk blouse, was stocky enough to make her Windfinder, Serile, look slender rather than average, and she had a gimlet eye and a sour twist to her mouth, but neither those nor the sniffing was meant for discourtesy. Turane was not *that* bold. The gaze was the same she gave everyone, her own vessel lay at the bottom of the harbor at Ebou Dar, and the harbor did stink after the clean air of the open salt.

The great cabin ran nearly the whole length of the tall sterncastle, a space clear of any furniture save for thirteen chairs and a table against the bulkhead that held tall-necked wine pitchers and goblets of yellow porcelain, and two dozen women in brocaded silks could not come near filling it. She was the last of the First Twelve of the Atha'an Miere to arrive, and the reaction to her among the other Wavemistresses was what she had come to expect. Lincora and Wallein turned their backs very deliberately. Round-faced Niolle gave her a scowl, then stalked over to refill her goblet. Lacine, so slender that her bosom seemed immense, shook her head as if wondering at Harine's presence. Others went on chatting as if she were not there. All wore the mourning stoles, of course.

Pelanna strode across the deck to her, the long pink scar down the right side of her square face giving her a dangerous look. Her tightly curled hair was nearly all gray, the honor chain across her left cheek heavy with gold medallions recording her triumphs, including one for her part in the Escape. Her wrists and ankles still bore the marks of Seanchan chains, though hidden by her silks now. "I hope you are quite recovered, Harine, the Light willing," she said, tilting her head to one side and clasping her plump, tattooed hands in mock sympathy. "Not still sitting tender, are you? I put a cushion on your chair just in case."

She laughed uproariously, looking to her Windfinder, but Caire gave her a blank look, as if she had not heard, then added a faint laugh. Pelanna frowned. When she laughed at anything, she expected those under her to laugh as well. The stately Windfinder had her own worries, however, a daughter missing among the shorebound, abducted by Aes Sedai. There *would* be repayment for that. One did not need to like Caire or Pelanna to know that was necessary.

Harine favored the pair with a tight smile and brushed by Pelanna closely enough that the woman had to step back or have her feet trodden on, scowling as she did. *Daughter of the sands,* Harine thought sourly.

Mareil's approach brought a genuine smile, however. The tall, slender woman, her shoulder-length hair as much white as black, had been her friend since they began as deckhands together on an aging raker with an iron-handed Sailmistress embittered by her lack of prospects. Learning that Mareil had escaped Ebou Dar, and unharmed, had been a joy. She favored Pelanna and Caire with a frown. Tebreille, her Windfinder, also grimaced at the pair, but unlike them, it was not because Mareil demanded wrist-licking. Sisters, Tebreille and Caire shared a deep concern for Talaan, Caire's daughter, yet beyond that, either would have slit the other's throat for a copper. Or better, in their view, seen her sister reduced to cleaning the bilges. There was no hatred deeper than hatred between siblings.

"Don't let those mud-ducks peck at you, Harine." Mareil's voice was deep for a woman, but melodious. She handed Harine one of the two goblets she carried. "You did what you felt you had to do, and the Light willing, all will come right."

Against her will, Harine's eyes went to the ringbolt set in one of the beams of the overhead. It could have been removed by now. She was sure it remained for the purpose of provoking her. That strange young woman Min had been right. Her Bargain with the Coramoor had been judged deficient, giving away too much and demanding too little in return. In this same cabin, with the rest of the First Twelve and the new Mistress of the Ships watching, she had been stripped and hung by her ankles from that ringbolt, stretched tight to another set in the deck, then strapped until she howled her lungs out. The welts and bruises had faded, but the memory lingered however hard she tried to suppress it. Not howls for mercy or respite, though. Never that, else she would have had no alternative to stepping aside, becoming just a Sailmistress again while someone else was chosen Wavemistress of Clan Shodein. Most of the women in this room believed she should have done so anyway after such a punishment, perhaps even Mareil. But she had the other part of Min's foretelling to bolster her courage. She would be Mistress of the Ships one day. In law, the First Twelve of the Atha'an Miere could choose any Sailmistress as Mistress of the Ships, yet only five times in more than three thousand years had they reached outside their own number. The Aes Sedai said Min's peculiar visions always came true, but she did not intend to gamble.

"All will come right, Mareil, the Light willing," she said. Eventually. She just had to have the courage to ride out whatever came before.

As usual, Zaida arrived without ceremony, striding in followed by Shielyn, her Windfinder, tall and slim and reserved, and Amylia, the bosomy, pale-haired Aes Sedai Zaida had brought back with her from Caemlyn. Ageless face seeming permanently surprised, her startling blue eyes very wide, the Aes Sedai was breathing heavily for some reason. Everyone bowed, but Zaida paid the courtesies no heed. In green brocades and white mourning stole, she was short, with a close cap of graying curls, yet she managed to make herself seem every bit as tall as Shielyn. A matter of presence, Harine had to admit. Zaida had that, and a coolness of thought that being caught by a cemaros on a lee shore could not shake. In addition to returning with the first of the Aes Sedai agreed to in the bargain for use of the Bowl of the Winds, she also had returned with her own bargain, for land in Andor under Atha'an Miere law, and where Harine's Bargain had been judged wanting, Zaida's had found great favor. That and the fact that she had come straight to Illian via one of those peculiar gateways, woven by her own Windfinder, were not the only reasons that she was now Mistress of the Ships, but neither had hurt her cause. Harine herself thought this Traveling overrated. Shalon could make a gateway, now, but making one to the deck of a ship without causing damage, even on still waters like these, especially from the deck of another ship, was chancy at best, and no one could make one large enough to sail a ship through. Very overrated.

"The man has not arrived yet," Zaida announced, taking the chair with its back to the large stern windows and arranging her long, fringed red sash just so, adjusting the angle of the emerald-studded dagger thrust through the sash. She was a very particular woman. It was natural enough to want everything in its place on board a ship— tidiness became a habit as well as a necessity—yet she was exacting even by the usual standards. The remaining chairs, none fastened to the deck in proper fashion, made two rows facing each other, and the Wavemistresses began taking their seats, each woman's Windfinder standing behind her chair. "It appears he intends us to wait on him. Amylia, see that the goblets are all filled." Ah. It seemed the woman had put her foot wrong yet again.

Amylia jumped, then gathered her bronze-colored skirts to her knees and went racing for the table where the wine pitchers sat. Badly wrong, it appeared. Harine wondered how long Zaida would continue to allow her to wear dresses rather than trousers, which were much more practical shipboard. It would surely be a shock to her when they passed beyond sight of land and blouses were abandoned. Of the Brown Ajah, Amylia had wanted to study the Atha'an Miere, but she was given little time for study. Her purpose was to work, and Zaida saw that she did. She was there to teach the Windfinders all that the Aes Sedai knew. She still dithered over that, but shorebound instructors, rare as they were, ranked barely a whisker above the deckhands— in the beginning, the woman apparently had believed her dignity fully equal to Zaida's if not more!—and the deckmaster's flail laid with some frequent regularity across her rump supposedly was changing her mind, if slowly. Amylia had actually tried to desert three times! Strangely, she did not know how to make a gateway, knowledge that carefully was being kept from her, and she should have known she was being watched too closely to bribe her way onto a bumboat. Well, she was unlikely to try again. Reportedly she had been told that a fourth attempt would earn a public strapping this time followed by being hung by her ankles in the rigging. No one would risk that shame, surely. Sailmistresses and even Wavemistresses had been reduced to deckhands and gone willingly after that, eager to lose themselves and their disgrace in the mass of men and women hauling lines and handling sail.

Removing the cushion from the seat of her chair and dropping it disdainfully on the deck, Harine took her place at the bottom of the left-hand row, Shalon at her back. She was the least senior except for Mareil, seated across from her. But then, Zaida would have sat only one chair farther up had she not gained the sixth fat golden earring for each ear and the chains that connected them. Her lobes might still be sore from the piercings. A pleasant thought. "As he makes us wait, perhaps we should make him wait when he finally does appear." With an untouched goblet in hand, she waved away the anxious Aes Sedai, who scurried over to Mareil. Foolish woman. Did she not know she should have served the Mistress of the Ships first and then followed with the Wavemistresses *by seniority*?

Zaida toyed with her piercework scent box, hanging on a very heavy golden chain around her neck. She wore a wide, close-fitting collar of heavy gold links, too, a gift from Elayne of Andor. "He comes from the Coramoor," she said dryly, "whom you were supposed to stick to like a barnacle." Her voice never hardened, but every word cut at Harine. "This man will be as close as I can come to speaking to the Coramoor without dire need, since you agreed he did not have to attend me more than three times in any period of two years. Because of you, I must accept this man's discourtesy if he turns out to be a scabrous drunkard who must run to the rail and empty his stomach every second sentence. The ambassador *I* send to the Coramoor will be someone who knows how to obey her orders." Pelanna tittered and smirked. She thought everyone was like herself.

Shalon squeezed Harine's shoulder reassuringly, but she did not need it. Stay with the Coramoor? There was no way she could explain to anyone, even Shalon, Cadsuane's rude methods of enforcing her will or her total lack of respect for Harine's dignity. She had been an ambassador from the Atha'an Miere in name, and forced to dance to any tune the Aes Sedai piped. She was willing to admit, if only to herself, that she had almost wept with relief when she realized that cursed woman was going to let her leave. Besides, that girl's visions always came true. So the Aes Sedai said, and they could not lie. It was enough.

Turane slipped into the cabin and bowed to Zaida. "The Coramoor's emissary has arrived, Shipmistress. He . . . he stepped out of a gateway on the quarterdeck." That created murmurs among the Windfinders, and Amylia jerked as though she had felt the deckmaster's flail again.

"I hope he did not damage your deck too badly, Turane," Zaida said. Harine sipped wine to hide her small smile. Apparently the man was to be made to wait a little, at least.

"Not at all, Shipmistress." Turane sounded surprised. "The gateway opened a good foot above the deck, and he stepped through from one of the city's docks."

"Yes," Shalon whispered. "I can see how to do that." She thought anything to do with the Power was wonderful.

"That must have a shock, seeing a stone dock above your quarterdeck," Zaida said. "Very well. I will see whether the Coramoor has sent me a scabrous drunkard. Send him in, Turane. But do not rush. Amylia, am I to get any wine before nightfall?"

The Aes Sedai gasped and, making little whimpers as if on the point of tears, rushed to fetch a goblet as Turane bowed and left. Light, what *had* Amylia done? Long moments passed, and Zaida had her wine well before a large man with dark hair curling to his broad shoulders entered the cabin. He certainly was not scabrous, nor did he appear drunk. The high collar of his black coat held a silver pin in the shape of a sword on one side, and on the other a red-and-gold pin shaped like one of the creatures that entwined the Coramoor's forearms. A dragon. Yes, that was what it was called. A round pin fastened to his left shoulder showed three golden crowns against blue enamel. A sigil, perhaps? Was he a shorebound noble? Could the Coramoor actually have done Zaida honor in sending this man? Knowing Rand al'Thor as she did, she doubted it had been intentional. It was not that he tried to dishonor anyone, yet he cared little for the honors of others.

He bowed to Zaida, handling the sword at his side smoothly, but he failed to touch heart and lips and forehead. Still, some shortcomings had to be overlooked with the shorebound. "I apologize if I arrive late, Shipmistress," he said, "but it seemed unnecessary to come before all of your number were here." He must have a very good looking glass to have observed that from the docks.

Studying him up and down with a frown, Zaida sipped her wine. "You have a name?"

"I am Logain," he said simply.

Half the women in the room exhaled sharply, and most of the rest let their jaws drop. More than one slopped wine from her goblet. Not Zaida, and not Harine, but the others. Logain. That was a name known even to the Atha'an Miere.

"May I speak, Shipmistress?" Amylia asked breathily. She was clutching the porcelain pitcher so hard that Harine feared it might shatter in her hands, but the woman had learned enough sense to say no more until Zaida nodded. Then words spilled from her in a breathless rush. "This man was a false Dragon. He was gentled for it. How it is he can channel again, I cannot know, but he channels *saidin*. *Saidin*! He is tainted, Shipmistress. If you deal with him, you will incur the wrath of the White Tower. I know—"

"Enough," Zaida cut in. "You should be well aware by now how much I fear the wrath of the White Tower."

"But—!" Zaida held up a single finger, and the Aes Sedai's mouth snapped shut, her lips twisting in a sickly fashion. That one word might lead to her kissing the deckmaster's sister again, and she knew it.

"What she says is true in part," Logain said calmly. "I am an Asha'-

man, but there is no taint any longer. *Saidin* is clean. The Creator decided to show us mercy, it seems. I have a question for her. Whom do
you serve, Aes Sedai, Egwene al'Vere or Elaida a'Roihan?" Wisely,
Amylia kept her mouth shut.

"For the next year, she serves *me*, Logain," Zaida said firmly. The
Aes Sedai squeezed her pale eyes shut for a moment, and when they
opened again, they were even wider than before, impossible as that
seemed, and they held a look of horror. Was it possible she had believed Zaida might relent and let her go early? "You can confine your
questions to me," the Shipmistress went on, "but first, I have two for
you. Where is the Coramoor? I must send an ambassador to him, and
he must keep her close, in accordance with the Bargain. Remind him
of that. And what message do you bring from him? A request for some
service, I suppose."

"As to where he is, I cannot say." The man smiled slightly, as if he
had made a joke. He smiled!

"I demand," Zaida began, but he cut her off, provoking angry mutters and hot glares from the other women. The fool seemed to think he
was an equal to the Mistress of the Ships!

"He wants his whereabouts kept secret for now, Shipmistress. The
Forsaken have made efforts to kill him. I am willing to take Harine
din Togara with me, however. From what I heard, I think he found her
acceptable."

Harine jerked so hard she spilled wine over the back of her hand,
then took another long swallow. But, no, Zaida would divorce Amel
and marry a ballast stone before she sent Harine din Togara as her ambassador. Still, even the thought of it was enough to make her tongue
stick to the roof of her mouth. Even becoming Mistress of the Ships
might be insufficient recompense for being forced to endure Cadsuane
any longer.

Studying Logain with a stony face, Zaida told Amylia to pour wine
for him. The Aes Sedai flinched, and by the time she reached the table,
she was trembling so hard that the pitcher's spout clattered on the rim
of the goblet. Almost as much wine went onto the deck as inside the
goblet. Strangely, Logain walked over to her and put his hands on hers
to steady her. Was he one of those who could not leave others to do
their own work?

"You've nothing to fear from me, Amylia Sedai," he told her. "It's
been a long time since I ate anyone for breakfast." She stared up at him

with her mouth hanging open as though uncertain whether he was making a joke.

"And the service he requests?" Zaida said.

"Not a request, Shipmistress." He had to straighten the pitcher to keep the goblet from overflowing. Taking the goblet, he stepped away from Amylia, but she stood gaping at his back. Light, but the woman found no end of ways to get into trouble. "A call on your side of the Bargain with the Coramoor. Among other things, you promised him ships, and he needs ships to carry food and other supplies to Bandar Eban from Illian and Tear."

"That can be done," Zaida said, not quite masking her relief, though she shot a frown at Harine. Pelanna glared as well, of course, but so did Lacine and Niolle and several others. Harine suppressed a sigh.

Some of the details of the Bargain were quite onerous, she had to admit, such as the requirement that the Mistress of the Ships be prepared to attend *him* up to three times in any two years. The Jendai Prophecy said the Atha'an Miere were to serve the Coramoor, yet few opinions of how they were to serve included the Mistress of the Ships going running when he called. But the others had not been there, bargaining with Aes Sedai convinced that she had no alternative to making whatever Bargain she could. Truth of the Light, it was a wonder she had gotten as much as she had!

"Supplies for more than a million people, Shipmistress," Logain added as casually as if he were asking for another goblet of wine. "How many more, I cannot say, but Bandar Eban itself is starving. The ships must arrive as soon as possible."

Shock rippled through the cabin. Harine was not alone in taking a long drink of wine. Even Zaida's eyes widened in amazement. "That might require more rakers than we possess," she said at last, unable to keep the incredulity from her voice.

Logain shrugged as though that were of no account. "Even so, that is what he requires of you. Use other ships if you must."

Zaida stiffened in her chair. Required. Bargain or no Bargain, that was imprudent language to use with her.

Turane slipped into the cabin again, and in breach of all protocol, ran to Zaida, her bare feet slapping the deck. Bending close, she whispered into the Shipmistress's ear. Zaida's face slowly took on a look of horror. She half-raised her scent box, then shuddered and let it fall to her bosom.

"Send her in," she said. "Send her in immediately. There is news to make an anchor weep," she went on as Turane raced from the cabin. "I will let you hear it from she who brought it. You must wait," she added when Logain opened his mouth. "You must wait." He had sufficient sense to hold his peace, but not enough to hide his impatience, stalking to the side of the cabin to stand with his mouth tight and his brows drawn down.

The young woman who entered and bowed deeply to Zaida was tall and lean, and she might have been lovely except that her face was haggard. Her blue linen blouse and green trousers looked as if they had been worn for days, and she swayed on her feet with weariness. Her honor chain held only a handful of medallions, as befitted her youth, yet Harine could see that no fewer than *three* commended acts of great courage.

"I am Cemeille din Selaan Long Eyes, Shipmistress," she said hoarsely, "Sailmistress of the darter *Wind Racer*. I sailed as fast as I could, but I fear it is too late for anything to be done. I stopped at every island between Tremalking and here, but I was always too late." Tears began to trickle down her cheeks, yet she seemed unaware of them.

"Tell the First Twelve your sad news in your own way, at your own pace," Zaida said gently. "Amylia, give her wine!" Not gently said at all. The Aes Sedai leaped to obey.

"Almost three weeks ago," Cemeille said, "Amayar on Tremalking began asking the gift of passage to every island. Always a man and a woman to each island. Those who asked for Aile Somera requested they be put off in boats out of sight of land when they were told that the Seanchan hold all of Somera." She took a full goblet from Amylia, nodding her thanks, then drank deeply.

Harine exchanged questioning glances with Mareil, who shook her head slightly. No Amayar had ever requested the gift of passage in Harine's memory, though for them, it truly was a gift, with no gift expected in return. And they avoided the salt, keeping their small fishing boats close to shore, so asking to be put off out of sight of land was as strange as asking passage. But what could be so dire in this?

"All of the Amayar in the ports left, even those owed money from the shipyards or the ropewalks, but no one thought anything of it for two or three days." The wine had not wet Cemeille's throat enough to mitigate her hoarseness. She scrubbed at the tears on her cheeks with the back of her hand. "Not until we realized none had come back. The governor sent people to the Amayar villages, and they found. . . ." She squeezed her eyes shut. "The Amayar were all dead or dying. Men, women"—her voice broke—"children."

Funeral keening rose in the cabin, and Harine was surprised to realize that shrill sound was coming from her mouth, too. Sad enough to make an anchor weep? This should make the heavens sob. No wonder the Sailmistress was hoarse. How many hours, how many days, had she cried since learning of this catastrophe?

"How?" Pelanna demanded when the keening died. Face distraught, she leaned forward in her chair. She was holding her scent box to her nose as if the scent could somehow ward off the stench of this news. "Some sickness? Speak, woman!"

"Poison, Wavemistress," Cemeille replied. She struggled to compose herself, but tears still leaked down her face. "Everywhere I have been, it was the same. They gave their children a poison that put them into a deep sleep from which they did not waken. It seems there was not enough of that to go around, so many of the adults took slower poisons. Some lived long enough to be found and tell the tale. The Great Hand on Tremalking melted. The hill where it stood reportedly is now a deep hollow. It seems the Amayar had prophecies that spoke of the Hand, and when it was destroyed, they believed this signaled the end of time, what they called the end of Illusion. They believed it was time for them to leave this . . . this illusion"—she laughed the word bitterly— "we call the world."

"Have none been saved?" Zaida asked. "None at all?" Tears glistened on her cheeks, too, but Harine could not fault her on that. Her own cheeks were wet.

"None, Shipmistress."

Zaida stood, and tears or no tears, she held the aura of command, and her voice was steady. "The fastest ships must be sent to every island. Even to those of Aile Somera. A way must be found. When the salt first stilled after the Breaking, the Amayar asked our protection from brigands and raiders, and we owe them protection still. If we can find only a handful who still live, we still owe it."

"This is as sad a story as I have ever heard." Logain's voice sounded too loud as he walked back out in front of Zaida. "But your ships are committed to Bandar Eban. If you don't have enough rakers, then you must use your other fast ships, too. All of them if necessary."

"Are you mad as well as heartless?" Zaida demanded. Fists on her hips and feet apart, she seemed to be standing on a quarterdeck. Her glare stabbed at Logain. "We must mourn. We must save who we can, and mourn for the countless thousands we cannot save."

She might as well have smiled for all the effect her glares had on Logain. As he spoke, it seemed to Harine that the space turned chill and the light dimmed. She was not the only woman to hug herself against that cold. "Mourn if you must," he said, "but mourn on the march for Tarmon Gai'don."

CHAPTER
23

Call to a Sitting

With Magla and Salita out for the morning, Romanda had the patched brown tent to herself, a blessed opportunity to read, though the two mismatched brass lamps on the small table gave off a faint yet nose-wrinkling scent of rancid oil. One had to live with such things these days. Some might consider *The Flame, the Blade and the Heart* unseemly for one of her attainments and position—as a girl in Far Madding, she had been forbidden such books—but it made an agreeable change from dry histories and terrifying reports of food spoilage. She had seen a side of beef kept for months as fresh as the day the cow was slaughtered, but now the Keepings were failing one by one. Some had taken to muttering that there must be a flaw in Egwene's creation, yet that was arrant blather. If a weave worked once, then properly done, it always worked, barring something to disrupt the weave, and Egwene's new weaves always worked as claimed. She had to give the woman that. And try as they might, and they had tried very hard, no one could detect any interference. It was as if *saidar* itself were failing. It was unthinkable. And inescapable. Worst of all, no one could think of anything to do! She certainly could not. A brief interlude with tales of romance and adventure was much preferable to contemplating utter futility and the failure of what was by its very nature unfailing.

The novice straightening the tent had sense enough not to comment on her reading, or to glance at the wood-bound book twice. Bodewhin Cauthon was quite pretty, but she was an intelligent girl even so, though she had something of her brother around the eyes and rather more of him in her head than she was willing to admit. Undoubtedly she was already hard on the path to the Green, or perhaps the Blue. The girl wanted to *live* adventure, not just read about it, as if an Aes Sedai's life would not bring her more adventure than she wished without searching for it. Romanda felt no regret over the girl's path. The Yellow would have plenty to choose from among more suitable novices. There could be no question of accepting any of the older women, of course, yet that left a wealth of choice. She tried to focus on the page. She did enjoy the story of Birgitte and Gaidal Cain.

The tent was not particularly large and was quite crowded. It held a trio of hard canvas cots barely softened by thin mattresses stuffed with lumpy wool, three ladderback chairs made by distinctly different hands, a rickety washstand with a cracked mirror and a chipped blue pitcher standing in the white basin, and, along with the table, made steady by a small block of wood under one leg, brassbound chests for clothing, bed linens and personal possessions. As a Sitter, she could have had the space to herself, but she liked being able to keep a close eye on Magla and Salita. Just because they all sat for the Yellow was no reason to trust too far. Magla supposedly was her ally in the Hall yet went her own way much too often, and Salita seldom did anything else. Still, it made for inconvenience aside from crowding. Bodewhin had a great deal of work, mainly putting away the dresses and slippers Salita scattered across the tattered carpets after deciding they would not do. That woman was frivolous enough for a Green. She went through her entire wardrobe every single morning! Likely she thought Romanda would have her serving woman straighten—she always seemed to think Aelmara was as much in her service as Romanda's—but Aelmara had served Romanda for years before she went into retirement, not to mention helping her escape Far Madding after a slight misunderstanding a short time later. There was no possibility she would require Aelmara to look after another sister as well as herself.

She frowned at the book, not seeing a word. Why in the Light had Magla insisted on Salita back in Salidar? In truth, Magla had bandied several names about, each more ridiculous than the last, but had settled on Salita once she decided the plump Tairen had the best chance of being raised to a chair. Romanda had thrown her own support behind Dagdara, a far more suitable candidate, not to mention one she thought she could sway without too much difficulty, yet she herself had been trying for a chair while Magla already held one. That carried weight, and no matter that Romanda had previously held a chair longer than anyone in living memory. Well, it was done, and that was that. What could not be cured must be endured.

Nisao ducked into the tent, the light of *saidar* around her winking out as she did so. In the brief instant before the tentflap fell shut, Sarin, her bald-headed stump of a Warder, was visible outside, a hand resting on his sword hilt and his head swiveling, plainly standing guard.

"May I speak with you alone?" the diminutive sister said. Short enough to make Sarin seem tall, she always minded Romanda of a large-eyed sparrow. There was nothing tiny about her powers of observation or her intellect, however. She had been a natural choice for the council the Ajahs created to try keeping an eye on Egwene, and it was certainly no fault of hers that said council had had little or no restraining effect on the woman.

"Of course, Nisao." Romanda casually closed the book and eased up to tuck it beneath the yellow-tasseled cushion on her chair. It would never do to have word get around that she was reading that. "It must be almost time for your next class, Bodewhin. You don't want to be late."

"Oh, no, Aes Sedai! Sharina would be very upset." Spreading her white skirts in a deep curtsy, the novice darted from the tent.

Romanda compressed her lips. *Sharina* would be upset. That woman was emblematic of all that was wrong with allowing those above eighteen into the novice ranks. Her potential was beyond incredible, but that was beside the point. Sharina Melloy was a disruption. But how to be rid of her? Her and all the other women too old to have had their names written in the novice book in the first place. Provisions were strictly limited for putting a woman out once her name was in the book. Unfortunately, over the years a number of women had been found to have lied about their age to gain entrance to the Tower. By a few years only in most cases, but allowing them to remain had set precedents. And Egwene al'Vere had set another, and worse. There had to be some way to overcome it.

"May I make us private?" Nisao asked.

"If you wish. Have you learned something about the negotiations?" Despite Egwene's capture, talks continued under the pavilion at the foot of the bridge in Darein. Or rather, the semblance of talks. They were a farce, a dumb-show of obstinacy, yet it was necessary to keep a close eye on the negotiators. Varilin had snatched most of that work to herself, claiming Gray Ajah prerogative, but Magla found ways to wriggle into the matter whenever she could, and so did Saroiya and Takima and Faiselle. Worse than the fact that none of them seemed to trust the others to carry out the negotiations—or much at all, for that matter—at times, all of them almost seemed to be negotiating for Elaida. Well, perhaps it was not that bad. They held fast against the woman's ridiculous demand that the Blue Ajah be dissolved and argued, if not nearly with sufficient force, for Elaida stepping down, but if she—and Lelaine, she was forced to admit—did not stiffen their backbones now and then, they might well accede to some of Elaida's other odious conditions. Light, at times it was as if they had forgotten the entire purpose of marching on Tar Valon! "Pour us tea," she went on, gesturing to a painted wooden tray sitting atop two stacked chests that held a silver pitcher and several battered pewter cups, "and tell me what you've heard."

The glow surrounded Nisao briefly while she warded the tent and tied off the weave. "I know nothing of the negotiations," she said, filling two of the cups. "I want to ask you to speak to Lelaine."

Romanda took the proffered cup and used taking a slow swallow to give herself time for thought. At least this tea had not yet turned. Lelaine? What could there be about Lelaine that required warding? Still, anything that gave her leverage against the other woman would be useful. Lelaine seemed entirely too smug of late for her to be entirely comfortable about it. She shifted on the seat cushion. "Regarding what? Why don't you speak to her yourself? We haven't fallen as low as it seems the White Tower has under Elaida."

"I have spoken to her. Or rather, she has spoken to me, and rather forcefully." Nisao sat down, and set her cup on the table while she arranged her yellow-slashed skirts with overly elaborate care. She wore a small frown. It seemed she was fiddling for time, too. "Lelaine demanded that I stop asking questions about Anaiya and Kairen," she said finally. "According to her, their murders are Blue Ajah business."

Romanda snorted, shifting again. The book's wooden cover was a hard lump beneath her, its corners digging into her hip. "That is utter nonsense. But why were you asking questions? I don't recall you being inquisitive about such matters."

The other woman touched her cup to her lips, but if she drank, it was the tiniest sip. Lowering the cup, she almost seemed to grow taller, she sat up so straight. A sparrow becoming a hawk. "Because the Mother ordered me to."

Romanda kept her eyebrows from rising only with an effort. So. In the beginning, she had accepted Egwene for the same reason she suspected every other Sitter had. Certainly Lelaine had done so, once she realized she could not attain the stole and staff herself. A malleable young girl would be a puppet in the hands of the Hall, and Romanda had fully intended to be the one pulling her strings. Later, it had seemed obvious that Siuan was the true puppeteer, and there had been no way to stop her short of rebelling against a second Amyrlin, which surely would have shattered the rebellion against Elaida. She hoped Lelaine had ground her teeth over that half as much as she had. Now Egwene was in Elaida's hands, yet in several meetings she had remained cool and collected, determined in her course of action and that of the sisters outside Tar Valon's walls. Romanda found in herself a grudging respect for the girl. Very grudging, but she could not deny it. It had to be Egwene herself. The Hall kept a tight fist on the dream *ter'angreal*, and though no one could find the one Leane had been loaned before that dire night, she and Siuan had been practically at each other's throats. There was no question of Siuan slipping into *Tel'aran'rhiod* to tell the woman what to say. Was it possible that Nisao had come to the same conclusion about Egwene without seeing her in the Unseen World? That council had stuck very close to her.

"That is reason enough for you, Nisao?" She could hardly slip the book back out without the other woman noticing. She shifted again, but there was no comfortable position on the thing. She was going to have a bruise if this continued.

Nisao twisted her pewter cup about on the tabletop, but she still did not look away. "It is my major reason. In the beginning, I thought she would end up as your pet. Or Lelaine's. Later, when it was clear she had evaded both of you, I thought Siuan must be holding the leash, but I soon learned I was wrong. Siuan has been a teacher, I'm sure, and an advisor, and perhaps even a friend, but I've seen Egwene call her up short. No one has a leash on Egwene al'Vere. She is intelligent, observant, quick to learn and deft. She may become one of the great Amyrlins." The bird-like sister gave a sudden, brief laugh. "Do you realize she will be the longest sitting Amyrlin in history? No one will ever live long enough to top her unless she chooses to step down early." Smiles faded to solemnity, and perhaps worry. Not because she had skirted the edge of violating custom, however. Nisao schooled her face well, but her eyes were tight. "If we manage to unseat Elaida, that is."

Hearing her own thoughts thrown back at her, with emendations, was unnerving. A great Amyrlin? Well! It would take many years to see whether that came about. But whether or not Egwene managed that considerable and unlikely feat, she would discover that the Hall was much less amenable once her war powers expired. Romanda Cassin certainly would be. Respect was one thing, becoming a lapdog quite another. Standing on the pretext of straightening her deep yellow skirts, she drew the book from beneath the cushion as she sat back down and tried to drop it surreptitiously. It hit the carpet with a thud, and Nisao's eyebrows twitched. Romanda ignored that, pulling the book under the edge of the table with her foot.

"We will." She put more confidence than she felt into that. The peculiar negotiations and Egwene's continuing imprisonment gave her pause, forget the girl's claims that she could undermine Elaida from within. Though it seemed half her work had been done by others, if her reporting on the situation in the Tower was accurate. But Romanda believed because she had to believe. She had no intention of living cut off from her Ajah, accepting penance until Elaida thought her *fit* to be fully Aes Sedai again, no intention of accepting Elaida a'Roihan as Amyrlin. Better Lelaine than that, and one argument in her own mind for raising Egwene had been that it kept the stole and staff from Lelaine. No doubt Lelaine had thought the same concerning her. "And I will inform Lelaine in no uncertain terms that you can ask any questions you wish. We *must* solve those murders, and the murder of any sister is every sister's concern. What have you learned so far?" Not a proper question, perhaps, but being a Sitter gave you certain privileges. At least, she had always believed it did.

Nisao displayed no pique at being questioned, no hesitation in answering. "Very little, I fear," she said ruefully, frowning at her winecup. "It seemed there must be some link between Anaiya and Kairen, some reason they two were picked out, but all I've learned so far is that they had been close friends for many years. Blues called them and another

Blue sister, Cabriana Mecandes, 'the Three,' because they were so close. But they were all closemouthed, too. No one recalls any of them talking about their own affairs except with one another. In any event, friendship seems a feeble motive for murder. I hope I can find some reason why anyone would want to murder them, especially a man who can channel, but I confess, it's a small hope."

Romanda furrowed her brow. Cabriana Mecandes. She paid little attention to the other Ajahs—only the Yellow had any truly useful function; how could any of their passions compare to Healing?—yet that name chimed a small gong in the back of her head. Why? It would come to her or not. It could not be important. "Small hopes can grow surprising fruit, Nisao. That's an old saying in Far Madding, and it's true. Continue your investigation. In Egwene's absence, you may report what you learn to me."

Nisao blinked, and her jaw tightened briefly, but whether or not reporting to Romanda sat well with her, there was little she could do but obey. She could hardly claim interference in her affairs. Murder could not be one sister's affair. Besides, Magla might have gotten her ridiculous choice for the third Yellow Sitter, yet Romanda had secured the position of First Weaver for herself easily. After all, she had been head of the Yellow before she retired, and even Magla had been unwilling to stand against her. The position carried much less power than she would have liked, but at least she could count on obedience in most things. From Yellow sisters if not Sitters, at least.

As Nisao untied her ward against eavesdropping and let it dissipate, Theodrin popped into the tent. She was wearing her shawl spread across her shoulders and down her arms to display the long fringe, as newly raised sisters often did. The willowy Domani had chosen Brown after Egwene granted her that shawl, but the Brown had not known what to do with her despite finally accepting her. They had seemed ready to largely ignore her, entirely the wrong thing, so Romanda had taken her in. Theodrin tried to behave as if she really were Aes Sedai, yet she was a bright, levelheaded girl for all that. She spread her brown woolen skirts in a curtsy. A small curtsy, but a curtsy. She was well aware that she had no right to the shawl until she had been tested. And passed. It would have been cruel not to make sure she understood.

"Lelaine has called a sitting of the Hall," she said breathlessly. "I couldn't find out why. I ran to tell you, but I didn't want to intrude while the ward was up."

"And rightly not," Romanda said. "Nisao, if you will excuse me, I must see what Lelaine is about." Gathering her yellow-fringed shawl from atop one of the chests holding her clothing, she arranged it over her arms and checked her hair in the cracked mirror before herding the others outside and seeing them on their way. It was not so much that she thought Nisao would have looked for what had made that thud if left in the tent alone, but it was better to take no chances. Aelmara would replace the book where it belonged, with several similar volumes in the chest that held Romanda's personal possessions. That had a very stout lock with only two keys, one kept in her belt pouch, the other in Aelmara's.

The morning was crisp, yet spring had arrived with a rush. The dark clouds massing behind Dragonmount's shattered peak would deliver rain rather than snow, though not on the camp, it was to be hoped. Many of the tents leaked, and the camp streets were a bog already. Horse carts making deliveries splashed mud from their high wheels as they made new ruts, driven by women for the most part, and a few gray-haired men. Male access to the Aes Sedai camp was strictly limited, now. Even so, nearly every sister she saw glided along the uneven wooden walkways wrapped in the light of *saidar* and followed by her Warder if she had one. Romanda refused to embrace the Source whenever she went outside—someone had to set an example of proper behavior with every sister in the camp on tenterhooks—yet she was very conscious of the lack. Conscious of the lack of a Warder, too. Keeping most men out of the camp was all very well, but a murderer was unlikely to pay any heed to the restriction.

Ahead, Gareth Bryne rode out of a crossing street, a stocky man with mostly gray hair, his breastplate strapped over a buff-colored coat and his helmet hanging from his saddle bow. Siuan was with him, swaying on a plump shaggy mare and looking such a pretty girl that it was almost possible to forget she had been hard-bitten and sharp-tongued as Amyrlin. Easy to forget she was still an accomplished schemer. Blues always were. The mare plodded along, but Siuan nearly fell off before Bryne reached out to steady her. At the edge of the Blue quarters—the camp was laid out in rough approximation of the Ajah quarters in the Tower—he dismounted long enough to help her down, then climbed back into his bay's saddle and left her standing there holding the mare's reins and gazing after him. Now, why would she do that? Blacking the man's boots, doing his laundry. That relationship was abhorrent. The Blue should put an end to it, and to the Pit of Doom with custom. However strong, custom should not be abused to hold all Aes Sedai up to ridicule.

Turning her back on Siuan, she started toward the pavilion that served as their temporary Hall of the Tower. As pleasant as it was to meet in the true Hall, not to mention under Elaida's very nose, few sisters could manage to put themselves to sleep at any hour, so the pavilion must continue to serve. She glided along the walkway without haste. She was not about to be seen hurrying to answer Lelaine's call. What *could* the woman want now?

A gong sounded, magnified with the Power so it carried across the camp clearly—another of Sharina's suggestions—and suddenly the walkways were crowded with novices hurrying to their next class or to chores, all clustered by family. Those families of six or seven always attended class together, did chores together, in fact, did everything together. It was an effective way to manage so many novices—nearly fifty more had wandered into the camp in just the last two weeks, pushing the total back near a thousand in spite of runaways, and almost a quarter of those were young enough to be proper novices, more than the Tower had held in centuries!—yet she wished it were not Sharina's work. The woman had not even suggested it to the Mistress of Novices. She had organized the thing herself and presented it to Tiana whole and complete! The novices, some of them graying or with lines in their faces so that it was difficult to think of them as children despite their white dresses, squeezed to the edge of the walkway to let sisters pass while they offered curtsies, but none stepped into the muddy street to make more room. Sharina again. *Sharina* had spread the word that she did not want to see the girls dirtying their nice white woolens unnecessarily. It was enough to make Romanda grind her teeth. The novices who curtsied to *her* straightened hurriedly and practically ran.

Ahead of her, she spotted Sharina herself, talking to Tiana, who was shrouded in the glow of *saidar*. Doing all of the talking, with Tiana merely nodding now and then. There was nothing disrespectful in Sharina's demeanor, but despite novice white, with her creased face and gray hair in a tight bun on the back of her head, she looked exactly what she was, a grandmother. And Tiana had an unfortunately youthful appearance. Something about her bone structure and large brown eyes overwhelmed the ageless look of Aes Sedai. Lack of disrespect or no, there was too much appearance of a woman instructing her granddaughter to suit Romanda. As she approached them, Sharina offered a proper curtsy—a very proper curtsy, Romanda had to admit—and hurried off the other way to join her own family, waiting for her. Were there fewer lines in her face than there had been? Well, there was no saying what might happen when a woman began with the Power at her age. Sixty-seven and a novice!

"Is she giving you difficulties?" she asked, and Tiana leaped as though an icicle had slid down the back of her dress. The woman lacked the dignity, the gravity, necessary in a Mistress of Novices. At times, she seemed smothered by the number of her charges, too. And she was much too lenient besides, accepting excuses where there could be none.

She recovered quickly, however, falling in beside Romanda, though she smoothed her dark gray skirts unnecessarily. "Difficulties? Of course not. Sharina is the best-behaved novice in the book. Truth to tell, most are well-behaved. The greatest number sent to my study are mothers upset because their daughters are learning faster than they or have a higher potential, or aunts with the same complaint of nieces. They seem to believe the matter can be rectified somehow. They can be surprisingly adamant about it until I set them straight about being adamant with any sister. Although a good many have been sent to me more than once, I fear. A handful still seem surprised that they can be switched."

"Is that so," Romanda said absently. Her eye had caught palehaired Delana hurrying in the same direction, gray-fringed shawl looped over her arms and her so-called secretary striding at her side. Delana wore an almost somber dark gray, but the Saranov trollop was in blue-slashed green silk that left half her bosom on display and fit much too snugly over hips that she rolled blatantly. Of late, the pair of them seemed to have abandoned the story that Halima was merely Delana's servant. Indeed, the woman was gesturing emphatically while Delana merely nodded in the meekest manner imaginable. Meek! It was always a mistake to choose a pillow-friend who did not wear the shawl. Especially if you were fool enough to let her take the lead.

"Sharina isn't only well-behaved," Tiana continued blithely, "she is showing a great skill with Nynaeve's new way of Healing. Like a number of the older novices. Most were village Wise Women of one sort or another, though I don't see how that can have any bearing. One was a noble in Murandy."

Romanda tripped over her own heel and staggered two steps, arms flailing for balance, before she could catch herself and gather her shawl. Tiana put a hand on her arm to steady her, murmuring about the unevenness of the walkway's planking, but she shook it off. *Sharina* had a gift for the new Healing? And a *number* of the older women? She herself had learned the new way, but while it was different enough from the old that the second-learned weave limitation seemed not to apply, she had no great gift for it. Not nearly what she had for the old method.

"And why are *novices* being allowed to practice that, Tiana?"

Tiana flushed, as well she should. Such weaves were much too complex for novices, not to mention dangerous if misapplied. Done improperly, Healing could kill rather than cure. The woman channeling as well as the patient. "I can hardly stop them from seeing Healing done, Romanda," she said defensively, moving her arms as if adjusting a shawl she was not wearing. "There are always broken bones or some fool who's managed to cut himself badly, not to mention all the illness we have to deal with lately. Most of the older women only have to see a weave once to have it down." Abruptly, for a bare instant, red returned to her cheeks. Smoothing her face, she drew herself up, and defensiveness fell away from her voice. "In any event, Romanda, I shouldn't need to remind you that the novices and Accepted are mine. As Mistress of Novices, *I* decide what they can learn and when. Some of those women could test for Accepted today, after only months. When it comes to the Power, at least. If I choose not to make them twiddle their thumbs idly, it is my decision to make."

"Perhaps you should run to see whether Sharina has any further instructions for you," Romanda said coldly.

Spots of crimson staining her cheeks, Tiana turned on her heel and strode away without another word. Not quite forbidden rudeness, but close. Even from behind she was the image of indignation, her back stiff as an iron rod, her steps quick. Well, Romanda was willing to admit she had come near rudeness herself. But with cause.

Trying to put the Mistress of Novices out of her mind, she set out toward the pavilion again, but had to restrain herself to keep from walking as fast as Tiana. Sharina. And *several* of the other older women. Should she rethink her position? No. Of course not. Their names should never have been allowed in the novice book in the first place. Yet their names were there, and it seemed they had mastered this wonderful new Healing. Oh, it was a tangled snarl. She did not want to think about it. Not now.

The pavilion stood at the heart of the camp, a much-patched piece of heavy canvas surrounded by a walkway three times as wide as any of the others. Holding her skirts well up out of the mud, she hurried across to it. She did not mind haste when it got her out of the mud more quickly. Even so, Aelmara would have a time cleaning her shoes. And her petticoats, she thought as she let her skirts down, decently concealing her ankles once more.

Word of the Hall sitting always drew sisters hoping for news of the negotiations or of Egwene, and a good fifty or more were already gathered around the pavilion with their Warders, or standing just inside, behind where their Sitters would sit. Even here, most shone with the Light of the Power. As if they were in any danger surrounded by other Aes Sedai. She found herself with a strong urge to walk around the pavilion boxing ears. That was impossible, of course. Even if custom could be set aside, which she had no desire to do, a chair in the Hall gave no authority for such a thing.

Sheriam, the narrow blue stole of the Keeper vivid on her shoulders, stood out in the crowd, in part because there was a clear space around her. Other sisters were avoiding looking at her, much less approaching her. The flame-haired woman embarrassed many of the sisters, appearing every time the Hall was called to sit as she did. The law was quite clear. Any sister could attend a sitting of the Hall unless it was closed, yet the Amyrlin could not enter the Hall of the Tower without being announced by the Keeper, and the Keeper was not allowed in without the Amyrlin. Sheriam's green eyes were tight, as usual, and she fidgeted in an unbecoming manner, like a novice who knew she was due another visit to the Mistress of Novices. At least she was not embracing the Source, and her Warder was nowhere in sight.

Before stepping beneath the pavilion, Romanda glanced over her shoulder and sighed. The great bulk of black clouds behind Dragonmount was gone. Not drifting apart, simply gone entirely. Very likely there would be another wave of panic among the grooms and laborers, and the serving women. Surprisingly, the novices seemed to take these strange occurrences more in stride. Perhaps that was because they were trying to take their cues from the sisters, but she suspected Sharina's hand again. What *was* she to do about the woman?

Inside, eighteen cloth-covered boxes, colored for the six Ajahs rep-

resented in the camp, made platforms for polished benches, two slanting rows atop the layered carpets, widening toward a box covered with
stripes in all seven colors. Wisely, Egwene had insisted on including
red despite considerable opposition. Where Elaida seemed determined
to divide every Ajah from every other, Egwene was determined to hold
them all together, including the Red. The wooden bench atop that
platform had the Amyrlin's seven-striped stole laid across it. No one
claimed responsibility for placing it there, but no one had removed it,
either. Romanda was uncertain whether it was meant to be a reminder
of Egwene al'Vere, the Amyrlin Seat, an echo of her presence, or a reminder that she was absent and a prisoner. How it was seen doubtless
depended on the sister looking.

She was not the only Sitter taking her time to answer Lelaine's call.
Delana was there, of course, slumped on her bench and rubbing the
side of her nose, her watery blue eyes pensive. Once, Romanda had
considered her levelheaded. Unsuitable for a chair, but levelheaded. At
least she had not allowed Halima to follow her into the Hall and continue her harangue. Or rather, at least Halima had chosen not to. No
one who had heard the woman shouting at Delana possessed any
doubts who gave the orders there. Lelaine herself was already on her
bench, just below the Amyrlin's, a slender, hard-eyed woman in blue-
slashed silk who rationed her smiles tightly. Which made it doubly
odd that now and then she glanced toward the seven-colored stole and
gave a small smile. That smile made Romanda uneasy, and few things
could do that. Moria, in blue wool embroidered with silver, was striding up and down in front of the blue-covered platforms. Was her frown
because she knew why Lelaine had called the Hall and disapproved, or
because she was worried over not knowing?

"I saw Myrelle walking with Llyw," Malind said, hitching up her
green-fringed shawl as Romanda entered the pavilion, "and I don't
think I've ever seen a sister looking so harassed." Despite the sympathy
in her tone, her eyes sparkled and her full lips quirked with amusement. "How did you ever talk her into bonding him? I was there when
someone suggested it to her, and I vow, she turned *pale*. The man could
almost pass for an Ogier."

"I expressed myself forcefully on duty." Faiselle, stocky and square-
faced, was forceful in everything; in truth, a hammer of a woman. She
mocked every tale of seductive Domani. "I pointed out that Llyw had
been becoming more and more dangerous to himself and others since

Kairen died, and I told her it couldn't be allowed to continue. I made her see that as the only sister ever to save two other Warders in the same circumstances, she was the only choice to try doing it again. I'll admit I had to twist her arm a little, but she eventually saw the right of the matter."

"How under the Light could you twist Myrelle's arm?" Malind leaned forward eagerly.

Romanda passed them by. How *could* anyone have twisted Myrelle's arm? No. No gossip.

Janya was on her bench for the Brown, squinting in thought. At least, she was squinting, but the woman always seemed to be thinking of something else even when she was talking to you. Maybe her eyes were bad. The rest of the benches still stood empty, though. Romanda wished she had been more leisurely. She would much rather have been the last to arrive than one of the first.

After a moment's hesitation, she approached Lelaine. "Would you care to give an idea of why you called the Hall?"

Lelaine smiled down at her, an amused smile, yet unpleasant even so. "You might as well wait until we have enough Sitters to proceed. I don't care to repeat myself. I will tell you this much. It will be dramatic." Her eyes drifted to the striped stole, and Romanda felt a chill.

She did not let it show, however, merely taking her bench across from Lelaine. She could not help glancing uneasily at the stole herself. Was this some move to unseat Egwene? It seemed unlikely the other woman could say anything that would convince her to stand for the greater consensus. Or many of the other Sitters, since that would throw them back to the struggle between her and Lelaine for control and weaken their position against Elaida. Yet Lelaine's air of confidence was unnerving. She schooled her features to calmness and waited. There was nothing else to do.

Kwamesa all but darted into the pavilion, her sharp-nosed face chagrined at not being first to arrive, and joined Delana. Salita appeared, dark and cool-eyed in yellow-slashed green embroidered with yellow scrollwork on the bosom, and suddenly there was a rush. Lyrelle glided in, graceful and elegant in brocaded blue silk, to take her place with the Blues, then Saroiya and Aledrin with their heads together, the blocky Domani seeming almost slender alongside the stout Taraboner. As they took their places on the White benches, fox-faced Samalin joined Faiselle and Malind, and tiny Escaralde scurried in. She scurried! The woman was from Far Madding, too. She should know better how to behave.

"Varilin is in Darein, I believe," Romanda said as Escaralde climbed up beside Janya, "but even if some others arrive later, we have more than eleven. Are you content to begin, Lelaine, or do you wish to wait?"

"I am content to begin."

"Do you wish a formal sitting?"

Lelaine smiled again. She was being very free with those this morning. They did nothing to warm her face. "That won't be necessary, Romanda." She rearranged her skirts slightly. "But I ask that what is said here be Sealed to the Hall for the time being." A murmur rose from the growing crowd of sisters standing behind the benches and those outside the pavilion. Even some of the Sitters showed surprise. If the sitting was not formal, what need could there be to restrict knowledge of what was said so closely?

Romanda nodded as though it were the most reasonable request in the world, though. "Let all depart who do not hold a chair. Aledrin, will you make us private?"

Despite dark yellow hair of a silky texture and large, liquid brown eyes, the Taraboner White fell short of pretty, but she had a good head on her shoulders, which was far more important. Standing, she seemed uncertain whether she should speak the formal words, and finally contented herself with weaving the ward against eavesdropping around the pavilion and holding it. The murmuring faded as sisters and Warders passed through that ward, until the last was gone and silence fell. They stood in ranks shoulder-to-shoulder on the walkway watching, however, the Warders all crowded to the rear so everyone could see.

Adjusting her shawl, Lelaine stood. "A Green sister was brought to me when she came asking for Egwene." The Green Sitters stirred, exchanging glances, no doubt wondering why the sister was not brought to them instead. Lelaine affected not to notice. "Not for the Amyrlin Seat, for Egwene al'Vere. She has a proposal that meets some of our needs, though she was reluctant to say very much of it to me. Moria, will you bring her so she can present her proposal to the Hall?" She resumed her seat.

Moria left the pavilion still frowning, and the crowd outside opened enough to let her through. Romanda could see sisters trying to question her, but she ignored them, disappearing across the street and into the Blue Ajah quarters. Romanda had a dozen questions she would have liked to ask in the interval, but informal session or not, questions would have been improper at this point. The Sitters did not wait in silence, however. At every Ajah except the Blue, women stepped down so they could come together and speak in low voices. Except the Blue and the Yellow. Salita climbed down and walked over to Romanda's platform, but Romanda raised a hand slightly as soon as she opened her mouth.

"What is there to discuss until we know what the proposal is, Salita?"

The Tairen Sitter's round face was as unreadable as a stone, but after a moment she nodded and resumed her seat. She was not unintelligent, far from it. Just unsuitable.

At last Moria returned leading a tall woman in dark green, her dark hair pulled back severely from a stern ivory face and held by a silver comb, and everyone climbed back to their benches. Three men with swords at their hips trailed after her through the watching sisters and into the pavilion. Unusual, that. Very unusual when matters had been Sealed to the Hall. Romanda paid them little mind at first, though. She had had no real interest in Warders since her last had died, a good many years earlier. But someone among the Greens gasped, and Aledrin squeaked. She actually squeaked! And she was staring at the Warders. That had to be what they were, and not only because they were heeling the Green. There was no mistaking a Warder's deadly grace.

Romanda took a longer look, and nearly gasped herself. They were disparate men, alike only in the way a leopard was like a lion, but one, a pretty, sun-dark boy with his hair in belled braids, garbed all in black, wore a pair of pins on the tall collar of his coat. A silver sword, and a sinuous, maned creature in red and gold. She had heard enough descriptions to know she was looking at an Asha'man. An Asha'man who had been bonded, apparently. Gathering her skirts, Malind jumped down and rushed out into the crowd of sisters. Surely she was not *frightened*. Although Romanda admitted to a hint of unease herself, if only *to* herself.

"You are not one of us," Janya said, speaking up where she should not as always. She leaned forward, squinting at the new-come sister. "Should I take it you have not come here to join us?"

The Green's mouth twisted in obvious distaste. "You take it

correctly," she said in a strong Taraboner accent. "My name is Merise Haindehl, and me, I will stand with no sister who wishes to contend against other sisters while the world hangs in the balance. Our enemy, it is the Shadow, not women who wear the shawl as we do." Mutters rose in the pavilion, some angry, some, Romanda thought, shamed.

"If you disapprove of what we do," Janya went on, as if she had a right to speak before Romanda, "why do you bring us any sort of proposal?"

"Because the Dragon Reborn, he asked Cadsuane, and Cadsuane, she asked me," Merise replied. The Dragon Reborn? The tension in the Hall was suddenly palpable, but the woman continued as if she were senseless to it. "Properly, it is not my proposal. Jahar, speak to them."

The sun-dark youth stepped forward, and as he passed her, Merise reached up to pat him on the shoulder encouragingly. Romanda's respect for her rose. To bond an Asha'man was accomplishment enough. To pat one as you might a hunting hound took a level of courage and self-confidence she herself was unsure she possessed.

The boy strode to the center of the pavilion staring at the bench where the Amyrlin's stole lay, then turned about slowly, running his gaze over the Sitters with an air of challenge. It came to Romanda that he was unafraid, too. An Aes Sedai held his bond, he was alone and surrounded by sisters, yet if there was a scrap of fear in him, he had it under complete control. "Where is Egwene al'Vere?" he demanded. "I was ordered to lay the offer before her."

"Manners, Jahar," Merise murmured, and his face colored.

"The Mother is unavailable at the moment," Romanda said smoothly. "You can tell us, and we will tell her as soon as we can. This offer comes from the Dragon Reborn?" And Cadsuane. But learning what *that* woman was doing in company with the Dragon Reborn was secondary.

Instead of answering, he snarled and spun to face Merise. "A man just tried to listen in," he said. "Or maybe it was that Forsaken who killed Eben."

"He is right." Aledrin's voice was unsteady. "At least, something touched my warding, and it wasn't *saidar*."

"He's *channeling*?" someone said incredulously. A flurry broke out of Sitters shifting on the benches, and the light of the Power enveloped several.

Abruptly, Delana stood. "I need a breath of fresh air," she said, glowering at Jahar as though she wanted to rip his throat out.

"There's no need to be uneasy," Romanda said, though she was not sure herself, but Delana, wrapped in her shawl, hurried from the pavilion.

Malind passed her coming in, as did Nacelle, a tall slender Malkieri, one of the handful remaining in the Tower. A good many had died in the years after Malkier fell to the Shadow, letting themselves be pulled into schemes to avenge their native land, and replacements had been few and far between since. Nacelle was not particularly intelligent, but then, Greens did not need intelligence, only courage.

"This session has been Sealed to the Hall, Malind," Romanda said sharply.

"Nacelle needs only moments," Malind replied, rubbing her hands together. Irritatingly, she did not even bother to look at Romanda, keeping her eyes on the other Green. "This is her first chance to test a new weave. Go ahead, Nacelle. Try it."

The glow of *saidar* appeared around the slim Green. Shocking! The woman neither asked permission nor told them what weave she intended, although tight strictures held on what uses of the Power were allowed in the Hall. Channeling all of the Five Powers, she wove around the Asha'man something that seemed akin to the weave for detecting residues, a thing Romanda had small facility for. Nacelle's blue eyes widened. "He is channeling," she breathed. "Or at least holding *saidin*."

Romanda's eyebrows climbed. Even Lelaine gasped. Finding a man who could channel was always a matter of reading the residues of what he had done, then arduously narrowing the suspects down to the true culprit. Or rather, it had been. This was truly wondrous. Or would have been before men who could channel started wearing black coats and strutting around openly. Still, it negated one advantage those men had always had over Aes Sedai. The Asha'man seemed not to care. His lip curled in what might have been a sneer.

"Can you tell what he is channeling?" she asked, and disappointingly, Nacelle shook her head.

"I thought I'd be able to, but no. On the other hand. . . . You there, Asha'man. Extend a flow toward one of the Sitters. Nothing dangerous, mind, and do not touch her." Merise glowered at her, fists planted on her hips. Maybe Nacelle failed to realize he was one of her Warders. She certainly gestured at him in peremptory fashion.

A stubborn cast to his eyes, Jahar opened his mouth.

"Do it, Jahar," Merise said. "He is mine, Nacelle, but I will let you give him an order. This once." Nacelle looked shocked. Apparently she *had* failed to realize.

For the Asha'man's part, that stubborn look remained, yet he must have obeyed because Nacelle clapped her hands delightedly and laughed.

"Saroiya," she said excitedly. "You extended a flow toward Saroiya. The Domani White. Am I right?"

Saroiya's coppery skin paled, and gathering her white-fringed shawl around her, she hastily slid back on her bench as far as she could. For that matter, Aledrin edged away on her own bench.

"Tell her," Merise said. "Jahar, he can be stubborn, but he is the good boy for all that."

"The Domani White," Jahar agreed reluctantly. Saroiya swayed as if she were going to fall over, and he glanced at her contemptuously. "It was only Spirit, and it's gone now." Saroiya's face darkened, but whether from anger or embarrassment there was no telling.

"A remarkable discovery," Lelaine said, "and I'm sure that Merise will allow you to test further, Nacelle, but the Hall has business to conclude. I'm certain you agree, Romanda."

Romanda barely managed to stop herself from glaring. Lelaine overstepped herself too often. "If your demonstration is at an end," she said, "you may withdraw, Nacelle." The Malkieri Green was reluctant to go, perhaps because she could tell from Merise's expression that there would be no further testing—really, you would think a Green of all people would be careful with any man who might be another sister's Warder—yet she had no choice, of course. "What proposal does the Dragon Reborn have for us, boy?" Romanda asked once Nacelle was on the other side of the warding.

"This," he said, facing her proudly. "Any sister who is faithful to Egwene al'Vere may bond an Asha'man, to a total of forty-seven. You cannot ask for the Dragon Reborn, nor any man who wears the dragon, but any Soldier or Dedicated you ask cannot refuse." Romanda felt as if all the breath had been squeezed from her lungs.

"You will agree this meets our needs?" Lelaine said calmly. The woman must have known the gist of it from the start, burn her.

"I do," Romanda replied. With forty-seven men who could channel, surely they could expand their circles as far as they would go. Perhaps even a circle that included all of them. If there were limits, they would need to be worked out.

Faiselle popped to her feet, as if this were a formal sitting. "This must be debated. I call for a formal session."

"I see no need for that," Romanda told her without rising. "This is much better than . . . what we previously agreed on." There was no point in saying too much in front of the boy. Or Merise. What was her connection to the Dragon Reborn? Could she be one of the sisters said to have sworn oaths to him?

Saroiya was on her feet before the last word left Romanda's mouth. "There is still the question of covenants, to be sure we are in control. We still have not agreed on those."

"I should think the Warder bond will make any other covenants moot," Lyrelle said dryly.

Faiselle rose hurriedly, and she and Saroiya spoke atop each other. "The taint—" They stopped, staring at each other suspiciously.

"*Saidin* is clean," Jahar said, though no one had addressed him. Merise really should teach the boy how to behave if she was going to bring him before the Hall.

"Clean?" Saroiya said derisively.

"It has been tainted for more than three thousand years," Faiselle put in sharply. "How can be it clean?"

"Order!" Romanda snapped, trying to regain control. "Order!" She stared at Saroiya and Faiselle until they resumed their seats, then turned her attention to Merise. "Can I assume that you have linked with him?" The Green simply nodded once. She really did not like her present company, and did not want to say a word more than necessary. "Can you say that *saidin* is free of the taint?"

The woman did not hesitate. "I can. I took time to be convinced. The male half of the Power, it is more alien than you can imagine. Not the inexorable yet gentle power of *saidar*, but rather a raging sea of fire and ice whipped by a tempest. Yet I am convinced. It is clean."

Romanda let out a long breath. A marvel to balance some of the horrors. "We are not formal, but I call the question. Who stands to accept this offer?" She was on her feet as soon as she finished, but no faster than Lelaine, and Janya beat both of them. In moments, everyone was on her feet save Saroiya and Faiselle. Outside the warding, heads turned as sisters doubtless began discussing what might have just been voted on. "The lesser consensus standing, the offer to bond forty-seven Asha'man is accepted." Saroiya's shoulders slumped, and Faiselle exhaled heavily.

She called for the greater consensus in the name of unity, but it did not surprise her when the pair remained firmly on their benches. After all, they had fought approaching the Asha'man at every turn, struggled despite law and custom to impede it even after it had been decided on. In any event, it was done, and without need of even a temporary alliance. Bonding would last a lifetime, of course, yet it was better than any sort of alliance. That implied too much equality.

"A peculiar number, forty-seven," Janya mused. "May I question your Warder, Merise? Thank you. How did the Dragon Reborn come to that number, Jahar?" A very good question, Romanda thought. In the shock of achieving what they needed without any requirement for partnership, it had eluded her.

Jahar drew himself up as if he had anticipated this, and dreaded answering. His face remained hard and cold, though. "Fifty-one sisters have been bonded by Asha'man already, and four of us are bonded to Aes Sedai. Forty-seven makes the difference. There were five of us, but one died defending his Aes Sedai. Remember his name. Eben Hopwil. Remember him!"

There was a stunned silence from the benches. Romanda felt a lump of ice in her middle. Fifty-one sisters? Bonded by Asha'man? It was an abomination!

"Manners, Jahar!" Merise snapped. "Do not make me tell you again!"

Shockingly, he rounded on her. "They need to know, Merise. They need to know!" Turning back, he ran his gaze along the benches. His eyes seemed hot. He had been dreading nothing. He had been angry, and still was. "Eben was linked with his Daigian and Beldeine, with Daigian controlling the link, so when they found themselves facing one of the Forsaken, all he could do was shout, 'She's channeling *saidin*,' and attack her with his sword. And despite what she did to him, ruined as he was, he managed to hang on to life, hang on to *saidin*, long enough for Daigian to drive her off. So you remember his name! Eben Hopwil. He fought for his Aes Sedai long after he should have been dead!"

When he fell silent, no one spoke until Escaralde finally said, very quietly, "We will remember him, Jahar. But how did fifty-one sisters come to be . . . bonded to Asha'man?" She leaned forward as if his answer would be pitched as low.

The boy shrugged, still angry. It was of no matter to him, Asha'man bonding Aes Sedai. "Elaida sent them to destroy us. The Dragon Reborn has a standing order that no Aes Sedai can be harmed unless she tries to harm one of us first, so Taim decided to capture and bond them before they had the chance."

So. They were Elaida's supporters. Should that make a difference? Somehow it did, a little. But any sisters held by Asha'man brought it all back to a matter of equality, and that was intolerable.

"I have another question for him, Merise," Moria said, and waited until the Green nodded. "Twice now, you did speak as if a woman did channel *saidin*. Why? That do be impossible." Murmurs of agreement rippled around the pavilion.

"It might be impossible," the boy replied coolly, "but she did it. Daigian told us what Eben said, and she couldn't detect anything at all even while the woman was channeling. It had to be *saidin*."

Suddenly that small chime sounded again in the back of Romanda's head, and she knew where she had heard the name Cabriana Mecandes. "We must order the arrest of Delana and Halima immediately," she said.

She had to explain, of course. Not even the Amrylin Seat could order the arrest of a Sitter without explanation. The murders with *saidin* of two sisters who had been close friends of Cabriana, a woman Halima had claimed friendship with as well. A female Forsaken who channeled the male half of the Power. They were hardly convinced, especially Lelaine, not until a thorough search of the camp turned up no trace of either woman. They had been seen walking toward one of the Traveling grounds with Delana and her serving woman both carrying large bundles and scurrying along behind Halima, but they were gone.

CHAPTER
24

Honey in the Tea

E gwene knew from the start that her strange captivity would be
difficult, yet she believed that embracing pain as the Aiel did
would be the easiest part. After all, she had been beaten severely
when she paid her *toh* to the Wise Ones for lying, strapped by one after
another in turn, so she had experience. But embracing pain did not
mean just giving way to it rather than fighting. You had to draw the
pain inside of you and welcome it as a part of you. Aviendha said you
must be able to smile and laugh with joy or sing while the worst of the
pain still gripped you. That was not so easy at all.

That first morning before dawn, in Silviana's study, she did her best
while the Mistress of Novices plied a hard-soled slipper on her bared
bottom. She made no effort to stifle her sobs when they came, or later
her wordless howls. When her legs wanted to kick, she allowed them
to flail until the Mistress of Novices trapped them under one of hers,
awkwardly because of Silviana's skirts, and then she let her toes drum
the floor while her head tossed wildly. She tried to draw the pain inside
her, to drink it in like breath. Pain was as much a part of life as breathing. That was how the Aiel saw life. But, oh, Light, it hurt!

When she was finally allowed to straighten, after what seemed a
very long time, she flinched when her shift and dress fell against her

flesh. The white wool seemed heavy as lead. She attempted to welcome the scalding heat. It was hard, though. So very hard. Still, it seemed that her sobbing stopped very quickly of its own accord, and her flow of tears dried up rapidly. She did not snivel or writhe. She studied herself in the mirror on the wall, with its fading gilt. How many thousands of women had peered into that mirror over the years? Those who were disciplined in this room were always required to study their own reflection afterward and think over why they had been punished, but that was not why she did it. Her face was still red, yet already it looked . . . calm. Despite the painful heat in her bottom, she actually felt calm. Perhaps she should try singing? Perhaps not. Plucking a white linen handkerchief from her sleeve, she carefully dried her cheeks.

Silviana studied her with a look of satisfaction before replacing the slipper in the narrow cabinet opposite the mirror. "I think I got your attention from the start, or I'd have gone harder," she said dryly, patting the bun on the back of her head. "I doubt I will see you again soon in any case. You may like to know that I asked questions as you requested. Melare had already begun asking. The woman *is* Leane Sharif, though the Light knows how. . . ." Trailing off, shaking her head, she pulled her chair back around behind the writing table and sat. "She was most anxious about you, more so than about herself. You may visit her in your free time. If you have any free time. I'll give instructions. She's in the open cells. And now you had better run if you want anything to eat before your first class."

"Thank you," Egwene said, and turned toward the door.

Silviana sighed heavily. "No curtsy, child?" Dipping her pen in the silver-mounted ink jar, she began to write in the punishment ledger, a neat, precise hand. "I will see you at midday. It seems you will eat both of your first two meals back in the Tower standing."

Egwene could have left it there, but in the night, while waiting for the Sitters to gather in the Hall in *Tel'aran'rhiod*, she had decided on the fine line she must walk. She meant to fight, yet she had to do it while appearing to go along. To some extent, at least. Within the limits she set herself. Refusing every order would mean appearing merely obstinate—and perhaps would get her confined to a cell, where she would be useless—but some commands she must not obey if she was to maintain any scrap of dignity. And that, she had to do. More than scraps. She could not allow them to deny who she was, however hard they insisted. "The Amyrlin Seat curtsies to no one," she said calmly, knowing full well the reaction she would get.

Silviana's face hardened, and she took up her pen again. "I will see you at the dinner hour, as well. I suggest you leave without speaking further, unless you wish to end spending the entire day over my knee."

Egwene left without speaking. And without curtsying. A fine line, like a wire suspended over a deep pit. But she had to walk it.

To her surprise, Alviarin was pacing up and down in the hall outside, wrapped in her white-fringed shawl and hugging herself, staring at something in the unseen distance. She knew the woman was no longer Elaida's Keeper, if not why she had been removed so suddenly. Spying in *Tel'aran'rhiod* gave only glimpses and snatches; it was an uncertain reflection of the waking world in so many ways. Alviarin must have heard her yowling, but strangely, Egwene felt no shame. She was fighting an odd battle, and in battle, you took wounds. The normally icy White did not appear so cool today. In fact, she seemed quite agitated, her lips parted and her eyes hot. Egwene offered her no courtesies, yet Alviarin only gave her a baleful glare before entering Silviana's study. A fine line.

A little down the corridor, a pair of Reds stood watching, one round-faced, the other slender, both cool-eyed, with shawls draped along their arms so the long red fringe was displayed prominently. Not the same pair who had been there when she woke, but they were not present by happenstance. They were not precisely guards, and then again, they were not precisely not guards. She did not curtsy to these, either. They watched her without expression.

Before she had taken more than half a dozen steps along the red-and-green floor tiles, she heard a woman's pained howling start up behind her, hardly muffled at all by the heavy door to Silviana's study. So Alviarin was taking a penance, and not doing well to be shrieking at the top of her lungs so soon. Unless she also was trying to embrace pain, which seemed unlikely. Egwene wished she knew *why* Alviarin was undergoing penance, if it *was* an imposed penance. A general had scouts and eyes-and-ears to inform him on his enemy. She had only her own eyes and her own ears, and what little she could learn in the Unseen World. Any scrap of knowledge might prove useful, though, so she must dig for every one possible.

Breakfast or no breakfast, she returned to her tiny room in the novice quarters long enough to wash her face in cool water at the wash-stand and comb her hair. That comb, which had been in her belt pouch, was among the few personal belongings she retained. In the night, the clothes she had been wearing when captured vanished, re-placed by novice white, but the dresses and shifts that hung from pegs on the white wall truly were hers. Stored away when she was raised Ac-cepted, they still carried small tags stitched with her name sewn into their hems. The Tower was never wasteful. You never knew when a new girl would fit an old set of clothes. But having nothing to wear save novice white did not make her a novice, whatever Elaida and the others believed.

Not until she was sure that her face was no longer red and she looked as collected as she felt did she leave. When you had few weapons, your appearance could be one. The same two Reds were wait-ing on the railed gallery to shadow her.

The dining hall where novices ate lay on the lowest level of the Tower, to one side of the main kitchen. It was a large white-walled chamber, plain though the floor tiles showed all the Ajah colors, and filled with tables, each of which could accommodate six or eight women on small benches. A hundred or more white-clad women were sitting at those tables, chattering away over breakfast. Elaida must be very set up over their number. The Tower had not held so many novices in years. Doubtless even news of the Tower breaking had been enough to put the thought of going to Tar Valon into some heads. Egwene was not impressed. These women filled barely half the dining hall if that, and there was another like it one floor up, closed now for centuries. Once she gained the Tower, that second kitchen would be opened again, and the novices still would need to eat by shifts, something un-known since well before the Trolloc Wars.

Nicola caught sight of her as soon as she walked in—the woman appeared to have been watching for her—and nudged the novices to ei-ther side. Silence slid across the tables in a wave, and every head turned as Egwene glided down the central aisle. She looked neither to left nor right.

Halfway to the kitchen door, a short slim novice with long dark hair suddenly stuck out a foot and tripped her. Catching her balance just short of falling on her face, she turned coolly. Another skirmish. The young woman had the pale look of a Cairhienin. This close, Eg-wene could be sure that she would be tested for Accepted unless she had other failings. But the Tower was good at rooting out such things. "What is your name?" she said.

"Alvistere," the young woman replied, her accent confirming her face. "Why do you want to know? So you can carry tales to Silviana? It will do you no good. Everyone will say they saw nothing."

"A pity, that, Alvistere. You want to become Aes Sedai and give up the ability to lie, yet you want others to lie for you. Do you see any inconsistency in that?"

Alvistere's face reddened. "Who are you to lecture me?"

"I am the Amyrlin Seat. A prisoner, but still the Amyrlin Seat." Alvistere's big eyes widened, and whispers buzzed through the room as Egwene walked on to the kitchen. They had not believed she would still claim the title while garbed in white and sleeping among them. As well to disabuse them of that notion quickly.

The kitchen was a large, high-ceilinged room with gray-tiled floors, where the roasting spits in the long stone fireplace were still but the iron stoves and ovens radiated enough heat that she would have begun perspiring immediately had she not known how to ignore it. She had labored in this kitchen often enough, and it seemed certain she would again. Dining halls surrounded it on three sides, for the Accepted and for Aes Sedai as well as novices. Laras, the Mistress of the Kitchens, was waddling about sweaty-faced in a spotless white apron that could have made three novice dresses, waving her long wooden spoon like a scepter as she directed cooks and under-cooks and scullions who scurried for her as fast as they would have for any queen. Perhaps faster. A queen would be unlikely to give anyone a smack with her scepter for moving too slowly.

A great deal of the food seemed to be going onto trays, sometimes worked silver, sometimes carved wood and perhaps gilded, that women carried away through the door to the sisters' main dining hall. Not kitchen serving women with the white Flame of Tar Valon on their bosoms, but dignified women in well-cut woolens with an occasional touch of embroidery, sisters' personal servants who would make the long climb back to the Ajah quarters.

Any Aes Sedai could eat in her own rooms if she wished, though it meant channeling to warm the food again, yet most enjoyed company at meals. At least, they had. That steady stream of women carrying out cloth-covered trays was a confirmation that the White Tower was spiderwebbed with cracks. She should have felt pleasure at that. Elaida stood on a platform that was ready to crumble beneath her. But the Tower *was* home. All she felt was sadness. And anger at Elaida, too. That one deserved to be pulled down simply for what she had done to the Tower since gaining the stole and staff!

Laras gave her one long look, drawing in her chin until she had a fourth, then returned to brandishing her spoon and looking over an under-cook's shoulder. The woman had helped Siuan and Leane escape, once, so her loyalties to Elaida were weak. Would she help another now? She was certainly making every effort to avoid looking in Egwene's direction again. Another under-cook, who likely did not know her from any other novice, a smiling woman still working on her second chin, handed her a wooden tray with a large, stout cup of steaming tea and a thick, white-glazed plate of bread, olives and crumbly white cheese that she carried back into the dining hall.

Silence fell again, and once more every eye centered on her. Of course. They knew she had been summoned to the Mistress of Novices. They were waiting to see whether she would eat standing. She wanted very much to ease herself onto the hard wooden bench, but she made herself sit down normally. Which reignited the flames, of course. Not as strongly as before, yet strong enough to make her shift before she could stop herself. Strangely, she felt no real desire to grimace or squirm. To stand, yes, but not the other. The pain was part of her. She accepted it without struggle. She tried to welcome it, yet that still seemed beyond her.

She tore a piece of bread—there were weevils in the flour here, too, it appeared—and slowly the conversation in the room started up again, quietly because novices were expected not to make too much noise. At her table also the talk resumed, though no one made any effort to include her. That was just as well. She was not here to make friends among the novices. Nor to have them see her as one of themselves. No, her purpose was far different.

Leaving the hall with the novices after returning her tray to the kitchen, she found another pair of Reds waiting for her. One was Katerine Alruddin, vulpine in copiously red-slashed gray, a mass of raven hair falling in waves to her waist and her shawl looped over her elbows.

"Drink this," Katerine said imperiously, extending a pewter cup in one slim hand. "All of it, mind." The other Red, dark and square-faced, adjusted her shawl impatiently and grimaced. Apparently she disliked acting as a serving woman even by association. Or perhaps it was dislike for what was in the cup.

Suppressing a sigh, Egwene drank. The weak forkroot tea looked and tasted like water tinged a faint brown, with just a hint of mint. Almost a memory of mint rather than the taste itself. Her first cup had been soon after waking, the Red sisters on duty eager to be done with shielding and about their own business. Katerine had let the hour slip a little, yet even without this cup, she doubted she would have been able to channel very strongly for some time yet. Certainly not with enough strength to be useful.

"I don't want to be late for my first class," she said, handing the cup back. Katerine took it, though she seemed surprised to realize that she had. Egwene glided on after the novices before the sister could object. Or remember to call her down for failing to curtsy.

That first class, in a plain, windowless room where ten novices occupied benches for thirty or more, was every bit the disaster she expected. Not a disaster for her, however, no matter the outcome. The instructor was Idrelle Menford, a lanky, hard-eyed woman who had already been Accepted when Egwene first came to the Tower. She still wore the white dress with the seven bands of color at hem and cuffs. Egwene took a seat at the end of a bench, once again without consideration for her tenderness. That had lessened, though not very far. Drink in the pain.

Standing on a small dais at the front of the room, Idrelle looked down her long nose with more than a spark of satisfaction at seeing Egwene in white once more. It almost softened her frown, a fixture with Idrelle. "You have all gone beyond making simple balls of fire," she told the class, "but let's see what our new girl is capable of. She used to think a great deal of herself, you know." Several of the novices tittered. "Make a ball of fire, Egwene. Go on, child." A ball of *fire*? That was one of the earliest things novices learned. What *was* she about?

Opening herself to the Source, Egwene embraced *saidar*, let it rush into her. The forkroot allowed only a trickle, a thread where she was accustomed to torrents, yet it was the Power, and trickle or no, it brought all of the life and joy of *saidar*, all the heightened awareness of herself and the room around her. Awareness of herself meant her smarting bottom suddenly felt freshly slippered again, but she did not shift. Breathe in the pain. She could smell the faint aroma of soap from the novices' morning wash, see a tiny vein pulsing on Idrelle's forehead.

Part of her wanted to clout the woman's ear with a flow of Air, but given the amount of the Power she commanded now, Idrelle would barely feel it. Instead, she channeled Fire and Air to produce a small ball of green fire that floated in front of her. A pale, pitiful thing it was, actually transparent.

"Very good," Idrelle said sarcastically. Ah, yes. She had just wanted to begin by showing the novices how weak Egwene's channeling was. "Release *saidar*. Now, class—"

Egwene added a blue ball, then a brown, and a gray, making them spin around one another.

"Release the Source!" Idrelle said brusquely.

A yellow ball joined the others, a white, and finally, a red ball. Quickly she added rings of fire one inside the other around the whirling balls. Red came first this time, because she wanted it smallest, green last and largest. Had she been able to choose an Ajah, it would have been the Green. Seven rings of fire rotated, no two in the same direction, around seven balls of fire that carried out an intricate dance at the heart. Pale and thin they might be, yet it was an impressive display beyond dividing her flows fourteen ways. Juggling with the Power was not all that much easier than juggling with your hands.

"Stop that!" Idrelle shouted. "Stop it!" The glow of *saidar* enveloped the teacher, and a switch of Air struck Egwene hard across the back. "I said stop it!" The switch struck again, then again.

Egwene calmly kept the rings spinning, the balls dancing. After Silviana's hard-swung slipper, it was easy to drink in the pain of Idrelle's blows. If not to welcome it. Would she ever be able to smile while she was being beaten?

Katerine and the other Red appeared in the doorway. "What is going on in here?" the raven-haired sister demanded. Her companion's eyes widened when she saw what Egwene was doing. It was very unlikely that either of them could divide their flows so far.

The novices all popped to their feet and curtsied when the Aes Sedai entered, of course. Egwene remained seated.

Idrelle spread her banded skirts looking flustered. "She won't stop," she wailed. "I told her to, but she won't!"

"Stop that, Egwene," Katerine ordered firmly.

Egwene maintained her weaves until the woman opened her mouth again. Only then did she release *saidar* and stand.

Katerine's mouth snapped shut, and she took a deep breath. Her face retained its Aes Sedai serenity, but her eyes glittered. "You will run to Silviana's study and tell her that you disobeyed your instructor and disrupted a class. Go!"

Pausing long enough to straighten her skirts—when she obeyed, she must not do so with any appearance of eagerness or haste—Egwene squeezed past the two Aes Sedai and glided up the hallway.

"I told you to run," Katerine said sharply behind her.

A flow of Air struck her still sensitive bottom. Accept the pain. Another blow. Drink in the pain like breath. A third, hard enough to stagger her. Welcome the pain.

"Unhand me, Jezrail," Katerine snarled.

"I'll do no such thing," the other sister said with a strong Tairen accent. "You go too far, Katerine. A swat or two is permitted, but punishing her further belongs to the Mistress of Novices. Light, at this rate, you'll leave her unable to walk before she reaches Silviana."

Katerine breathed heavily. "Very well," she said at last. "But she can add disobeying a sister to her list of offenses. I *will* inquire, Egwene, so don't think you can let it slip your mind."

When she stepped into the Mistress of Novices' study, Silviana's eyebrows rose in surprise. "Again so soon? Fetch the slipper from the cabinet, child, and tell me what you've done now."

After two more classes and two more visits to Silviana's study—she refused to be made mock of, and if an Accepted did not want her doing a thing better than the Accepted herself could, the woman should not ask her to do it at all—plus her foreordained midday appointment between, the stern-faced woman decided that she was to have Healing to begin each day.

"Else you'll soon be too bruised to spank without bringing blood. But don't think this means I am going easy on you. If you require Healing *three* times a day, I'll just spank all the harder to make up. If need be, I'll go to the strap or the switch. Because I will make your head straight, child. Believe me on that."

Those three classes, leaving three very embarrassed Accepted, had another result. Her teaching was shifted to sessions alone with Aes Sedai, something normally reserved for Accepted. That meant climbing the long, tapestry-lined spiraling corridors to the Ajah quarters, where sisters stood at the entrances like guards. They were guards, in truth. Visitors from other Ajahs were unwelcome, to say the least. In fact, she never saw any Aes Sedai near the quarters of another Ajah.

Except for Sitters, she seldom saw sisters in the hallways outside the quarters other than in groups, always wearing their shawls, usually with Warders following close behind, but this was not like the fear that gripped the encampment outside the walls. Here it was always sisters of the same Ajah together, and when two groups passed, they cut each other dead if they did not glare. In the worst of summer the Tower remained cool, yet the air seemed feverish and gelid when sisters of different Ajahs came too close. Even the Sitters she recognized walked quickly. The few who realized who she was gave her long, studying looks, but most appeared distracted. Pevara Tazanovni, a plumply pretty Sitter for the Red, almost walked into her one day—she was not going to jump aside, even for Sitters—but Pevara hurried on as if she had not noticed. Another time Doesine Alwain, boyishly slim if elegantly dressed, did the same while deep in conversation with another Yellow sister. Neither glanced at her twice. She wished she had some idea who the other Yellow was.

She knew the names of the ten "ferrets" Sheriam and the others had sent into the Tower to try undermining Elaida, and she very much would have liked to make contact with them, but she did not know their faces, and asking after them would only draw attention to them. She hoped one of them would pull her aside or hand her a note, but none did. Her battle would have to be fought alone except for Leane unless she overheard something that put faces to some of those names.

She did not neglect Leane, of course. Her second night back in the Tower she went down to the open cells after supper despite her bone-deep weariness. Those half-dozen rooms in the first basement were where women who could channel were held if not to be closely confined. Each held a large cage of iron latticework that ran from stone floor to stone ceiling, with a space around it four paces wide and iron stand-lamps to provide light. At Leane's cell, two Browns were sitting on benches against the wall with a Warder, a wide-shouldered man with a beautiful face and touches of white at his temples. He looked up when Egwene walked in, then returned to honing his dagger on a stone.

One of the Browns was Felaana Bevaine, slender with long yellow hair that gleamed as if she brushed it several times a day. She stopped writing in a leather-bound notebook on a lapdesk long enough to say in a raspy voice, "Oh. It's you, is it? Well, Silviana said you can visit, child, but don't give her anything without showing it to Dalevien or me, and don't make any fuss." She promptly returned to her writing. Dalevien, a stocky woman with gray streaking her short dark hair, never looked up from her comparison of the text of two books, one held open on either knee. The glow of *saidar* shone around her, and she was maintaining a shield on Leane, but there was no reason for her to look once it had been woven.

Egwene lost no time in rushing to thrust her hands through the iron lattice and clasp Leane's. "Silviana told me they finally believe who you are," she said, laughing, "but I didn't expect to find you in such luxury."

It was luxury only when held up alongside the small dark cells where a sister might be held for trial, with rushes on the floor for a mattress and a blanket only if you were lucky, yet Leane's accommodations did appear reasonably comfortable. She had a small bed that looked softer than those in the novice quarters, a ladder-back chair with a tasseled blue cushion, and a table that held three books and a tray with the remains of her supper. There was even a washstand, though the white pitcher and bowl both had chips and the mirror was bubbled, and a privacy screen, opaque enough that she would be only a shadowy shape behind it, hid the chamber pot.

Leane laughed, too. "Oh, I am very popular," she said briskly. Even the way she stood seemed languorous, the very image of a seductive Domani despite plain dark woolens, but that brisk voice remained from before she had decided to remake herself as she wanted to be. "I've had a steady stream of visitors all day, from every Ajah except the Red. Even the Greens try to convince me to teach them how to Travel, and they mainly want to get their hands on me because I 'claim' to be Green now." She shivered much too ostentatiously for it to be real. "That would be as bad as being back with Melare and Desala. Dreadful woman, Desala." Her smile faded away like mist in a noonday sun. "They told me they'd put you in white. Better than the alternatives, I suppose. They give you forkroot? Me, too."

Surprised, Egwene glanced toward the sister holding the shield, and Leane snorted.

"Custom. If I weren't shielded, I could swat a fly and not hurt it, but custom says a woman in the open cells is always shielded. But they just let you wander around otherwise?"

"Not exactly," Egwene said dryly. "There are two Reds waiting outside to escort me to my room and shield me while I sleep."

Leane sighed. "So. I'm in a cell, you are being watched, and we're both full of forkroot tea." She cast a sidelong look at the two Browns. Felaana was still intent on her writing. Dalevien turned pages in the two books on her knees and began muttering under her breath. The Warder must have intended to shave with that dagger, he was honing it so keen. His main attention seemed to be on the doorway, though. Leane lowered her voice. "So when do we escape?"

"We don't," Egwene told her, and related her reasons and her plan in a near whisper while watching the sisters out of the corner of her eye. She told Leane everything she had seen. And done. It was hard to tell how many times she had been spanked that day, and how she had behaved during, but necessary to convince the other woman that she would not be broken.

"I can see any sort of raid is out of the question, but I had hoped—" The Warder shifted, and Leane cut off, but he was merely sheathing his dagger. Folding his arms across his chest and stretching his legs out, he leaned back against the wall, his eyes on the doorway. He looked as if he could be on his feet in the blink of an eye. "Laras helped me escape once," she went on softly, "but I don't know that she would do it again." She shivered, and there was nothing fake about it this time. She had been stilled when Laras helped her and Siuan escape. "She did it for Min more than for Siuan or me, anyway. Are you certain about this? A hard woman, Silviana Brehon. Fair, so I hear, but hard enough to break iron. Are you absolutely certain, Mother?" When Egwene said that she was, Leane sighed again. "Well, we'll be two worms gnawing at the root then, won't we." It was not a question.

She visited Leane every night that exhaustion failed to drag her to her bed straight after supper, and found her astonishingly sanguine for a prisoner confined to a cell. Leane's stream of visiting sisters was continuing, and she slipped the tidbits Egwene suggested into every conversation. Those visitors could not order an Aes Sedai punished, even one held in the open cells, though a few grew angry enough to wish they could, and besides, hearing those things from a sister carried more weight than hearing them from one they saw as a novice. Leane could even argue openly, at least until the visitors stalked out. But she reported that many did not. A few agreed with her. Cautiously, hesitantly, perhaps on one point and not others, but they agreed. Almost as important, to Leane at least, some of the Greens decided that since she had been stilled and thus was no longer Aes Sedai for a time, she had the right to ask admission to any Ajah once she was a sister again. Not all by any means, but "few" was better than "none." Egwene began to think that Leane in her cell was having more effect than she was roaming free. Well, free after a fashion. She was not exactly jealous. This was important work they were doing, and it did not matter which of them did it better so long as it got done. But there were times when it made the trek to Silviana's study much harder. Still, she had successes. Of a sort.

That first afternoon, in Bennae Nalsad's cluttered sitting room—books stood in haphazard stacks everywhere on the floor tiles, and the shelves were full of bones and skulls and the preserved skins of animals, birds and snakes along with stuffed examples of some of the smaller specimens; a large brown lizard was perched on the huge skull of a bear, so still you would have thought it stuffed as well until it blinked—that first afternoon, the Shienaran Brown asked her to perform an exhaustive set of weaves one after the other. Bennae sat in a high-backed chair on one side of the brown-streaked marble fireplace, Egwene, with decided discomfort, in one on the other. She had not been invited to sit, but neither had Bennae objected.

Egwene performed each weave as asked until Bennae casually asked for the weave for Traveling, and then she merely smiled and folded her hands in her lap. The sister leaned back and adjusted her deep brown silk skirts a hair. Bennae's eyes were blue and sharp, her dark hair, caught in a silver net, liberally streaked with gray. Ink stains marked two of her fingers, and another smudged the side of her nose. She held a porcelain cup of tea, but she had not offered any to Egwene.

"I think there is little of the Power that remains for you to learn, child, especially considering your wonderful discoveries." Egwene inclined her head, accepting the compliment. Some of those things truly were her discoveries, and it hardly mattered now in any case. "But that hardly means you have nothing to learn. You had few novice classes before you were. . . ." The Brown frowned at Egwene's white dress and cleared her throat. "And fewer lessons as . . . well, later. Tell me if you can, what mistakes did Shein Chunla make that caused the Third War of Garen's Wall? What were the causes of the Great Winter War between Andor and Cairhien? What caused the Weikin Rebellion and how did it end? Most of history seems to be the study of wars, and the important parts of that are how and why they began and how and why ended. A great many wars would never have taken place if people had paid attention to the mistakes others had made. Well?"

"Shein didn't make any mistakes," Egwene said slowly, "but you're right. I do have a lot to learn. I don't even know the names of those other wars." Rising, she poured herself a cup of tea from the silver pitcher on the side table. Aside from the ropework silver tray, the tabletop held a stuffed lynx and the skull of a serpent. That was as big as a *man's* skull!

Bennae frowned, but not for the tea. She hardly seemed to notice that. "What do you mean Shein didn't make any mistakes, child? Why, she bungled the situation as badly as ever I've heard of."

"Well before the Third War of Garen's Wall," Egwene said, returning to her chair, "Shein was doing exactly as the Hall told her and nothing they didn't." She might be lacking in other areas of history, but Siuan had tutored her thoroughly in the mistakes made by other Amyrlins. And this particular question gave her an opening. Sitting down normally took a great effort.

"What *are* you talking about?"

"She tried running the Tower with an iron hand, never a compromise on anything, running roughshod over any opposition. The Hall grew tired of it, but they couldn't settle on a replacement, so rather than deposing her, they did worse. They left her in place and forced a penance on her whenever she tried to issue an order of any kind. Any kind at all." She knew she was going on, sounding as if she were the one giving a lecture, but she had to get it all out. Not easing herself on the hard wood of the chair seat was difficult. Welcome the pain. "The Hall ran Shein and the Tower. But they mishandled a great deal themselves, largely because each Ajah had its own goals and there was no hand to shape them into a goal for the Tower. Shein's reign was marked by wars all over the map. Eventually, the sisters themselves got tired of the Hall's bungling. In one of the six mutinies in Tower history, Shein *and* the Hall were pulled down. I know she supposedly died in the Tower of natural causes, but, in fact, she was smothered in her bed in exile fifty-one years later after the discovery of a plot to put her back on the Amyrlin Seat."

"Mutinies?" Bennae said incredulously. "Six of them? Exiled and *smothered*?"

"It's all recorded in the secret histories, in the Thirteenth Depository. Though I suppose I shouldn't have told you that." Egwene took a sip of tea and grimaced. It was all but rancid. No wonder Bennae had not touched hers.

"*Secret* histories? A *thirteenth* Depository? If such a thing existed, and I think I would know, why should you not have told me?"

"Because by law the existence of the secret histories as well as their contents can be known only to the Amyrlin, the Keeper, and the Sitters. Them and the librarians who keep the records, anyway. Even the law itself is part of the Thirteenth Depository, so I guess I shouldn't have told that either. But if you can gain access somehow, or ask someone who knows and will tell you, you'll find out I'm right. Six times in the history of the Tower, when the Amyrlin was dangerously divisive or dangerously incompetent and the Hall failed to act, sisters have risen up to remove her." There. She could not have planted the seed deeper with a shovel. Or driven it home more bluntly with a hammer.

Bennae stared at her for a long moment, then raised the cup to her lips. She spluttered as soon as the tea touched her tongue, and began dabbing at the spots on her dress with a delicate, lace-edged handkerchief. "The Great Winter War," she said huskily as she set the cup on the floor beside her chair, "began late in the year six hundred seventy-one. . . ." She did not mention secret records or mutinies again, but she did not have to. More than once during the lesson she trailed off, frowning at something beyond Egwene, and Egwene had little doubt what it was.

Later that day, Lirene Doirellin said, "Yes, Elaida made a vital mistake there," pacing up and down in front of her sitting room's fireplace. The Cairhienin sister was only a little shorter than Egwene, but the nervous way her eyes darted gave her the air of a hunted thing, a sparrow fearful of cats and convinced there were lots of cats in the vicinity. Her dark green skirts had only four discreet slashes of red, though she had been a Sitter once. "That proclamation of hers, on top of trying to kidnap him, could not have been better calculated to keep the al'Thor boy as far from the Tower as he can stay. Oh, she has made mistakes, Elaida has."

Egwene wanted to ask about Rand and the kidnapping—kidnapping?—but Lirene left no opening as she went on about Elaida's many mistakes, all the while pacing back and forth, her eyes darting and her hands twisting unconsciously. Egwene was unsure whether or

not that session could be called a success, but at least it was not a failure. And she had learned something.

Not all of her forays went so well, of course.

"This is not a discussion," Pritalle Nerbaijan said. Her tone was utterly calm, yet her tilted green eyes were heated. Her rooms looked
more those of a Green than a Yellow, with several bared swords hanging on the walls and a silk tapestry showing men fighting Trollocs. She
was gripping the hilt of the dagger at her woven silver belt. Not a simple belt knife; a dagger with a blade near a foot long and an emerald
capping its pommel. Why she had agreed to lecture Egwene was a
mystery, given her dislike of teaching. Perhaps because it was Egwene.
"You are here for a lesson on the limits of power. A very *basic* lesson,
suitable for a novice."

Egwene wanted to shift on the three-legged stool that Pritalle had
given her for a seat, but instead she concentrated on the smarting, focused on drinking it in. On welcoming it. The day had already seen
three visits to Silviana, and she could sense a fourth coming, with the
midday meal an hour off yet. "I merely said that if Shemerin could be
reduced from Aes Sedai to Accepted then Elaida's power has no limits.
At least, she thinks it doesn't. But if you accept that, then it really
doesn't."

Pritalle's grip tightened on the dagger's hilt until her knuckles
showed white, yet she seemed unaware. "Since you think you know
better than I," she said coolly, "you can visit Silviana when we finish."
A partial success, perhaps. Egwene did not think Pritalle's anger was
for her.

"I expect proper behavior out of you," Serancha Colvine told her
firmly another day. The word to describe the Gray sister was
"pinched." A pinched mouth, and a pinched nose that constantly
seemed to be detecting a bad smell. Even her pale blue eyes seemed
pinched with disapproval. She might well have been pretty otherwise.
"Do you understand?"

"I understand," Egwene said, sitting down on the stool that had
been placed in front of Serancha's high-backed chair. The morning was
cool, and a small fire burned on the stone hearth. Drink in the pain.
Welcome the pain.

"An incorrect response," Serancha said. "The correct response
would have been a curtsy and 'I understand, Serancha Sedai.' I intend

to make a list of your failures for you to carry to Silviana when we're done. We'll begin again. Do you understand, child?"

"I understand," Egwene said without rising. Aes Sedai serenity or no Aes Sedai serenity, Serancha's face turned purple. In the end, her list covered four pages in a tight, cramped hand. She spent more time writing than she did lecturing! Not a success.

And then there was Adelorna Bastine. The Saldaean Green some-how managed stateliness in spite of being slim and no taller than Eg-wene, and she had a regal, commanding air that might have been intimidating had Egwene let it. "I hear you make trouble," she said, picking up an ivory-backed hairbrush from a small inlaid table beside her chair. "If you try to make trouble with me, you'll learn that I know how to use this."

Egwene did learn, without trying. Three times she went across Adelorna's lap, and the woman did indeed know how to use a hair-brush for more than brushing her hair. That managed to stretch an hour lecture to two.

"May I go now?" Egwene said at last, calmly drying her cheeks as well as she could with a handkerchief that was already damp. Breathe in the pain. Absorb the fire. "I'm supposed to fetch water up for the Red, and I don't want to be late."

Adelorna frowned at her hairbrush before returning it to the table that Egwene had overset twice with her kicking. Then she frowned at Egwene, studying her as if trying to see inside her skull. "I wish Cadsuane were in the Tower," she murmured. "I think she'd find you a challenge." There seemed a touch of respect in her voice.

That day was a turning point in some ways. For one thing, Silviana decided that Egwene was to receive Healing twice each day.

"You seem to *invite* being beaten, child. It's pure stubbornness, and I won't put up with it. You *will* face reality. The next time you visit me, we'll see how you like the strap." The Mistress of Novices folded Egwene's shift over her back, then paused. "Are you *smiling*? Did I say something amusing?"

"I just thought of something funny," Egwene said. "Nothing of consequence." Not of consequence to Silviana, anyway. She had real-ized how to welcome the pain. She was fighting a war, not a single bat-tle, and every time she was beaten, every time she was sent to Silviana, it was a sign that she had fought another battle and refused to yield. The pain was a badge of honor. She howled and kicked as hard as ever during that slippering, but while she was drying her cheeks afterward, she hummed quietly to herself. It was easy to welcome a badge of honor.

Attitudes among the novices began to shift by the second day of her captivity. It seemed that Nicola—and Areina, who was working in the stables and often came to visit Nicola; they seemed so close that Egwene wondered whether they had become pillow-friends, always with their heads together and smiling mysterious smiles—Nicola and Areina had regaled them all with tales of her. Very inflated tales. The two women had made her seem a combination of every legendary sister in the histories, along with Birgitte Silverbow and Amaresu herself, carrying the Sword of the Sun into battle. Half of them seemed in awe of her, the others angry with her for some reason or outright scornful. Foolishly, some tried to emulate her behavior in their classes, but a flurry of visits to Silviana quelled that. At the midday meal of the third day, nearly two dozen novices ate standing up and red-faced with embarrassment, Nicola among them. And Alvistere, surprisingly. That number dropped to seven at supper, and on the fourth day, only Nicola and the Cairhienin girl did so. And that was the end of that.

She expected some might resent the fact that she continued to refuse to bend while they had been put back on the straight and narrow so quickly, but to the contrary, it only seemed to decrease the number who were angry or scornful and increase the respect. No one tried to become her friend, which was just as well. White dress or no white dress, she was Aes Sedai, and it was improper for an Aes Sedai to befriend a novice. There was too much risk the girl would start feeling above herself and get into trouble for it. Novices began coming to her for advice, for help learning their lessons, though. Only a handful at first, but the number grew day by day. She was willing to help them learn, which was usually just a matter of strengthening a girl's confidence or convincing a young woman that caution was wise, or taking them patiently through the steps of a weave that was giving trouble. Novices were forbidden to channel without an Aes Sedai or Accepted present, though they nearly always did in secret anyway, but she *was* a sister. She refused to help more than one at a time, however. Word of groups would surely leak out, and she would not be the only one sent to Silviana. She would make that trip as often as necessary, but she did not want to earn it for others. And as for advice. . . . With the novices kept strictly clear of men, advice was easy. Though strains between pillow-friends could be as harsh as anything men ever caused.

One evening, returning from yet another session with Silviana, she overheard Nicola talking to two novices who could not have been more than fifteen or sixteen. Egwene hardly remembered being that young. It seemed a lifetime ago. Marah was a stocky Murandian with mischievous blue eyes, Namene a tall, slim Domani who giggled incessantly.

"Ask the Mother," Nicola said. A few of the novices had taken to calling Egwene that, though never where anyone not wearing white could hear. They were foolish, but not utter fools. "She's always willing to give advice."

Namene giggled nervously and wriggled. "I wouldn't want to bother her."

"Besides," Marah said, a lilt in her voice, "they say she always gives the same advice, she does."

"And good advice it is, too." Nicola held up one hand to tick off fingers. "Obey the Aes Sedai. Obey the Accepted. Work hard. Then work harder."

Gliding on toward her room, Egwene smiled. She had been unable to make Nicola behave properly while she was openly Amyrlin, but it seemed she might have succeeded while masquerading as a novice herself. Remarkable.

There was one more thing she could do for them: comfort them. Impossible as it seemed at first, the interior of the Tower sometimes changed. People got lost trying to find rooms they had been to dozens of times. Women were seen walking out of walls, or into them, often in dresses of old-fashioned cut, sometimes in bizarre garb, dresses that seemed simply lengths of brightly colored cloth folded around the body, embroidered ankle-length tabards worn over wide trousers, stranger things still. Light, when could any woman have wanted to wear a dress that left her bosom completely exposed? Egwene was able to discuss it with Siuan in *Tel'aran'rhiod*, so she knew that these things were signs of the approach of Tarmon Gai'don. An unpleasant thought, yet there was nothing to be done about it. What was, was, and it was not as if Rand himself was not a herald of the Last Battle. Some of the sisters in the Tower must have known what it all meant, too, but wrapped up in their own affairs they made no effort to comfort novices who were weeping with fright. Egwene did.

"The world is full of strange wonders," she told Coride, a pale-

haired girl who was sobbing facedown on her bed. Only a year younger
than herself, Coride was most definitely still a girl despite a year and a
half in the Tower. "Why be surprised if some of those wonders appear
in the White Tower? What better place?" She never mentioned the
Last Battle to these girls. That was hardly likely to be any comfort.

"But she walked into a wall!" Coride wailed, raising her head. Her
face was red and blotchy, and her cheeks glistened damply. "A wall!
And then none of us could find the classroom, and Pedra couldn't either, and she got cross with us. Pedra never gets cross. She was frightened, too!"

"I'll wager Pedra didn't start crying, though." Egwene sat down on
the edge of the girl's bed, and was pleased that she did not wince.
Novice mattresses were not noted for softness. "The dead can't harm
the living, Coride. They can't touch us. They don't even seem to see us.
Besides, they were initiates of the Tower or else servants here. This was
their home as much as it is ours. And as for rooms or hallways not being where they're supposed to be, just remember that the Tower is a
place of wonders. Remember that, and they won't frighten you."

It seemed feeble to her, but Coride wiped her eyes and swore she
would never be frightened again. Unfortunately, there were a hundred
and two like her, not all so easily comforted. It was enough to make Egwene angrier at the sisters in the Tower than she already had been.

Her days were not all lessons and comforting novices and being
punished by the Mistress of Novices, though the last did take up an unfortunate amount of each day. Silviana had been right to doubt that she
would have much free time. Novices were always given chores. Often it
was make-work, since the Tower had well over a thousand serving men
and women without counting laborers, but physical work helped build
character, so the Tower had always believed. Plus, it helped keep the
novices too tired to think of men, supposedly. She was loaded down
with chores beyond what the novices were given, though. Some were
assigned by sisters who considered her a runaway, others by Silviana in
the hope that weariness would dull the edge of her "rebellion."

Daily, after one meal or another, she scrubbed dirty pots with
coarse salt and a stiff brush in the workroom off the main kitchen.
From time to time Laras would put her head in, but she never spoke.
And she never used her long spoon, even when Egwene was massaging
the small of her back, aching from being head-down in a large kettle,
rather than scrubbing. Laras dealt out smacks aplenty to scullions and

under-cooks who tried to play pranks on Egwene, as was customary
with novices sent to work in the kitchen. Supposedly that was just because, as she announced loudly every time she gave a thwack, they had
plenty of time to play when they were not supposed to be working, but
Egwene noticed that Laras was not so quick when someone goosed one
of the true novices or tipped a cup of cold water down the back of her
neck. It seemed she did have an ally of sorts. If she could only figure
out how to make use of her.

She hauled water in buckets hanging from the ends of a pole balanced across her shoulders, to the kitchen, to the novices' quarters, to
the Accepted's quarters, all the way up to the Ajah's quarters. She carried meals to sisters in their rooms, raked garden paths, pulled weeds,
ran errands for sisters, attended Sitters, swept floors, mopped floors,
scrubbed floors on her hands and knees, and that was only a partial list.
She never shirked at these tasks, and only in part because she would
not give anyone an excuse to call her lazy. In a way, she viewed them as
penance for not having prepared properly before turning the harbor
chain to *cuendillar*. Penances were to be borne with dignity. As much
dignity as anyone can have while scrubbing a floor, anyway.

Besides, visiting the Accepted's quarters gave her a chance to see
how they viewed her. There were thirty-one in the Tower, but at any
given time some were teaching novices and others taking lessons of
their own, so she seldom found more than ten or twelve in their rooms
around the nine-tiered well surrounding a small garden. Word of her
arrival always spread quickly, though, and she never lacked an audience. At first, many of them tried to overwhelm her with orders, especially Mair, a plump blue-eyed Arafellin, and Asseil, a slim Taraboner
with pale hair and brown eyes. They had been novices when she came
to the Tower, and already jealous of her quick rise to Accepted when
she left. With them, every second sentence was fetch that, or carry this
there. For all of them she was the "novice" who had caused so much
difficulty, the "novice" who thought she was the Amyrlin Seat. She carried pails of water till her back ached, uncomplaining, yet she refused
to obey their commands. Which earned her more visits to the Mistress
of Novices, of course. As the days passed, as her continual trips to Silviana's study showed no effect, however, that flow of commands dwindled and finally ceased. Even Asseil and Mair had not really been
trying to be mean, only to behave as they thought they should in the
circumstances, and they were at a loss as to what to do with her.

Some of the Accepted showed signs of fright at the dead walking and the interior of the Tower changing, and whenever she saw a bloodless face or teary eyes she would say the same things she told the novices. Not addressing the woman directly, which might have gotten her back up rather than soothing her, but as if talking to herself. It worked as well with Accepted as with novices. Many gave a start when she began, or opened their mouths as though to tell her to be quiet, yet none did, and she always left a thoughtful expression behind. The Accepted continued to come out onto the stone-railed galleries when she entered, but they watched her in silence as though wondering what she was. Eventually she would teach them what she was. Them and the sisters, too.

Attending Sitters and sisters, a woman in white standing quietly in the corner quickly became part of the furniture even when she was notorious. If they noticed her, they changed their conversation, yet she overheard many snippets, often of plots to avenge some slight given or wrong done by another Ajah. Oddly, most of the sisters seemed to see the other Ajahs inside the Tower as more their enemies than they did the sisters in the camp outside the city, and the Sitters were not much better. It made her want to slap them. True, it boded well for relations when the other sisters returned to the Tower, but still. . . .

She did pick up other things. The unbelievable disaster that had befallen an expedition sent against the Black Tower. Some of the sisters seemed not to believe it, yet they appeared to be trying to convince themselves it could not have happened. More sisters captured after a great battle and somehow forced to swear fealty to Rand. She had already had inklings of that, and she could not like it any more than she did sisters being bonded by Asha'man. Being *ta'veren* or the Dragon Reborn was no excuse. No Aes Sedai had ever before sworn fealty to any man. The sisters and Sitters argued over who was to blame, with Rand and the Asha'man at the head of the list. But one name came up again and again. Elaida do Avriny a'Roihan. They talked of Rand, too, of how to find him before Tarmon Gai'don. They knew it was coming despite their failure to console the novices and Accepted, and they were desperate to lay hands on him.

Sometimes she risked a comment, a mention of Shemerin being stripped of the shawl against all custom, a suggestion that Elaida's edict regarding Rand was the best way in the world to make him dig in his heels. She offered sympathy for the sisters captured by the Asha'-

man, for those taken at Dumai's Wells—with Elaida's name dropped in—or regretted the neglect that saw garbage rotting in the once pristine streets of Tar Valon. There was no need to mention Elaida there; they knew who was responsible for Tar Valon. At times, those comments earned her still more trips to Silviana's study, and more chores besides, yet surprisingly often they did not. She made careful note of the sisters who merely told her to be quiet. Or better still, said nothing. Some even nodded agreement before they caught themselves.

Some of those chores led to interesting encounters.

On the morning of her second day she was using a long-handled bamboo rake to fish detritus from the ponds of the Water Garden. There had been a rainstorm the night before, and the heavy winds had deposited leaves and grasses in the ponds among the bright green lily pads and budding water irises, and even a dead sparrow that she calmly buried in one of the flower beds. A pair of Reds stood on one of the arching pond bridges, leaning on the lacy stone railing and watching her and the fish swirling below them in a flurry of red and gold and white. A half-dozen crows burst up out of one of the leatherleafs and silently winged their way north. Crows! The Tower grounds were supposed to be warded against crows and ravens. The Reds did not seem to have noticed.

She was squatting on her heels beside one of the ponds, washing the dirt from her hands after burying that pitiful bird, when Alviarin appeared, her white-fringed shawl wrapped tightly around her as if the morning were still windy rather than bright and fair. This was the third time she had seen Alviarin, and every time she had been alone rather than in company with other Whites. She had seen clusters of Whites in the hallways, though. Was there a clue in that? If so, she could not imagine to what, unless Alviarin was being shunned by her own Ajah for some reason. Surely the rot had not gone that deep.

Eyeing the Reds, Alviarin approached Egwene along the coarse gravel path that wound among the ponds. "You have fallen far," she said when she was close. "You must feel it keenly."

Egwene straightened and blotted her hands on her skirt, then picked up the rake. "I'm not the only one." She had had another session with Silviana before dawn, and when she left the woman's study, Alviarin had been waiting to go in again. That was a daily ritual for the White, and the talk of the novices' quarters, with every tongue speculating on the why of it. "My mother always says, don't weep over what can't be mended. It seems good advice under the circumstances."

Faint spots of color appeared in Alviarin's cheeks. "But you seem to be weeping a good deal. Endlessly, by all reports. Surely you would escape that if you could."

Egwene caught another oak leaf on the broom and brushed it off into the wooden pail of damp leaves at her feet. "Your loyalty to Elaida isn't very strong, is it?"

"Why do you say that?" Alviarin said suspiciously. Glancing at the two Reds, who appeared to be paying more mind now to the fish than Egwene, she stepped closer, inviting lowered voices.

Egwene fished at a long strand of grass that had to have come all the way from the plains beyond the river. Should she mention the letter this woman had written to Rand practically promising him the White Tower at his feet? No, that piece of information might prove valuable, but it seemed the sort of thing that could only be used once. "She stripped you of the Keeper's stole and ordered your penance. That's hardly an inducement to loyalty."

Alviarin's face remained smooth, yet her shoulders relaxed visibly. Aes Sedai seldom showed so much. She must feel under phenomenal strain to be so little in control of herself. She darted a look at the Reds again. "Think on your situation," she said in near a whisper. "If you want an escape from it, well, you may be able to find one."

"I am content with my situation," Egwene said simply.

Alviarin's eyebrows quirked upward in disbelief, but with another glance at the Reds—one was watching them now rather than the fish— she glided away, a very fast glide on the verge of breaking into a trot.

Every two or three days she would appear while Egwene was doing chores, and while she never openly offered help with an escape, she used that word frequently, and she began to show frustration when Egwene refused to rise to her bait. Bait it was, to be sure. Egwene did not trust the woman. Perhaps it was that letter, surely designed to draw Rand to the Tower and into Elaida's clutches, or maybe it was the way she kept waiting for Egwene to make the first move, to beg possibly. Likely Alviarin would try to set conditions, then. In any case, she had no intention of escaping unless there was no other choice, so she always gave the same response.

"I am content with my situation."

Alviarin began grinding her teeth audibly when she heard that.

On the fourth day, she was on her hands and knees scrubbing blue-and-white floor tiles when the boots of three men accompanied by a sister in elaborately red-embroidered gray silk passed her. A few paces on, the boots stopped.

"That be her," a man's voice said in the accents of Illian. "She did be pointed out to me. I think me I will speak to her."

"She's only another novice, Mattin Stepaneos," the sister told him. "You wanted to walk in the gardens." Egwene dipped her scrub brush in the bucket of soapy water and began another stretch of tiles.

"Fortune stab me, Cariandre, this may be the White Tower, but I do still be the lawful King of Illian, and if I want to speak to her—with you for chaperone; all very proper and decent—then I will speak with her. I did be told she did grow up in the same village with al'Thor." One set of boots, blacked till they glistened, approached Egwene.

Only then did she stand, the dripping brush in one hand. She used the back of the other to brush her hair out of her face. She refrained from knuckling the small of her back, much as she wanted to.

Mattin Stepaneos was stocky and almost entirely bald, with a neatly trimmed white beard in the Illianer fashion and a heavily creased face. His eyes were sharp, and angry. Armor would have suited him better than the green silk coat embroidered with golden bees on the sleeves and lapels. "Just another novice?" he murmured. "I think you be mistaken, Cariandre."

The plump Red, her lips compressed, left the two serving men with the Flame of Tar Valon on their chests and joined the balding man. Her disapproving gaze touched Egwene briefly before shifting to him. "She's a much-punished novice who has a floor to scrub. Come. The gardens should be very pleasant this morning."

"What be pleasant," he said, "do be talking to someone other than Aes Sedai. And only of the Red Ajah at that, since you do manage to keep me from any others. On top of which, the servants you did give me might as well be mutes, and I think me the Tower Guards do have orders to hold their tongues around me as well."

He fell silent as two more Red sisters approached. Nesita, plump and blue eyed and mean as a snake with the itch, nodded companionably to Cariandre while Barasine handed Egwene the by now all too familiar pewter cup. The Red seemed to have custody of her in a way—at least, her watchers and minders were always Reds—and they seldom let much more than the promised hour pass before someone appeared with the cup of forkroot tea. She drained it and handed it back. Nesita seemed disappointed that she did not protest or refuse, but there seemed little point. She had, once, and Nesita had helped pour the vile stuff down her throat using a funnel she had ready in her belt pouch. That would have been a fine show of dignity in front of Mattin Stepaneos.

He watched the silent exchange with puzzled interest, though Cariandre plucked at his sleeve, urging him again to his walk in the gardens. "Sisters bring you water when you thirst?" he asked when Barasine and Nesita glided away.

"A tea they think will improve my mood," she told him. "You look well, Mattin Stepaneos. For a man Elaida had kidnapped." That tale was the talk of the novices' quarters, too.

Cariandre hissed and opened her mouth, but he spoke up first, his jaw tight. "Elaida did save me from murder by al'Thor," he said. The Red nodded approvingly.

"Why would you think yourself in danger from him?" Egwene asked.

The man grunted. "He did murder Morgase in Caemlyn, and Colavaere in Cairhien. He destroyed half the Sun Palace killing her, I did hear. And I did hear of Tairen High Lords poisoned or stabbed to death in Cairhien. Who can say what other rulers he did murder and destroy the bodies?" Cariandre nodded again, smiling. You might have thought him a boy reciting his lessons. Did the woman have *no* understanding of men? He certainly saw it. His jaw grew harder still, and his hands clenched into fists for a moment.

"Colavaere hanged herself," Egwene said, making sure she sounded patient. "The Sun Palace was damaged later by someone trying to kill the Dragon Reborn, maybe the Forsaken, and according to Elayne Trakand, her mother was murdered by Rahvin. Rand has announced his support for her claims to both the Lion Throne and the Sun Throne. He hasn't killed any of the Cairhienin nobles rebelling against him, or the High Lords in rebellion. In fact, he named one of them his Steward in Tear."

"I think that is quite—" Cariandre began, pulling her shawl up onto her shoulders, but Egwene went on right over her.

"Any sister could have told you all that. If she wanted to. If they were speaking to one another. Think why you see only Red sisters.

Have you seen sisters of *any* two Ajahs speaking? You've been kidnapped and brought aboard a sinking ship."

"That is more than enough," Cariandre snapped right atop Egwene's last sentence. "When you finish scrubbing this floor, you will run to the Mistress of Novices and ask her to punish you for shirking. And for showing disrespect to an Aes Sedai."

Egwene met the woman's furious gaze calmly. "I have barely enough time after I finish to get clean before my lesson with Kiyoshi. Could I visit Silviana after the lesson?"

Cariandre shifted her shawl, seemingly taken aback by her calmness. "That is a problem for you to work out," she said at last. "Come, Mattin Stepaneos. You have helped this child shirk long enough."

There was no time to change out of her damp dress or even comb her hair after leaving Silviana's study, not if she were to have any hope of being on time for Kiyoshi without running, which she refused to do. That made her late, and it turned out that the tall, slender Gray was a stickler for both punctuality and neatness, which put her back yelping and kicking under Silviana's hard-swung strap little more than an hour later. Quite aside from embracing pain, something else helped see her through that. The memory of Mattin Stepaneos' thoughtful expression as Cariandre led him off down the corridor and how he twice looked back over his shoulder at her. She had planted another seed. Enough seeds planted, and perhaps what sprouted from them would splinter those cracks in the platform beneath Elaida. Enough seeds would bring Elaida down.

Early on her seventh day of captivity, she was carrying water up the Tower again, to the White Ajah quarters this time, when she suddenly stopped in her tracks feeling as if she had been punched in her stomach hard. Two women in gray-fringed shawls were walking down the spiraling corridor toward her, trailed by a pair of Warders. One was Melavaire Someinellin, a stout Cairhienin in fine gray wool with white flecking her dark hair. The other, with blue eyes and dark honey hair, was Beonin!

"So you're the one who betrayed me!" Egwene said angrily. A thought occurred to her. How *could* Beonin have betrayed her after swearing fealty? "You must be Black Ajah!"

Melavaire drew herself up as much as she could, which was not very far since she was inches shorter than Egwene, and planted her fists on her ample hips as she opened her mouth to deliver a blast. Egwene had

had one lesson from her, and while she was a kindly woman usually, when she became angry, she could be fearsome.

Beonin laid a hand on the other sister's plump arm. "Let me speak to her alone please, Melavaire."

"I trust you will speak sharply," Melavaire said in a stiff voice. "To even *think* of making such a charge. . . ! To even *mention* some things. . . !" Shaking her head in disgust, she retreated a little up the corridor followed by her Warder, squat and even wider than she, a bear of a man though he moved with the expected Warder grace.

Beonin gestured and waited until her own Warder, a lean man with a long scar on his face, joined them. She adjusted her shawl several times. "Me, I betrayed nothing," she said quietly. "I would not have sworn to you except that the Hall, it would have had me birched if it learned the secrets you knew. Perhaps more than once, even. Reason enough to swear, no? I never pretended to love you, yet I maintained that oath until you were captured. But you are no longer Amyrlin, yes? Not as a captive, not when there was no hope of rescuing you, when you refused rescue. And you are a novice once more, so that oath, it has two reasons to hold no longer. The talk of rebellion, it was wild talk. The rebellion is finished. The White Tower, it will soon be whole again, and I will not be sorry to see it so."

Lifting the pole from her shoulders, Egwene set down the pails of water and folded her arms beneath her breasts. She had tried to maintain a calm demeanor since being captured—well, except when she being punished—but this encounter would have tried a stone. "You explain yourself at great length," she said dryly. "Are you trying to convince yourself? It won't do, Beonin. It won't do. If the rebellion is finished, where is the flood of sisters coming to kneel before Elaida and accept her penance? Light, what else have you betrayed? Everything?" It seemed likely. She had visited Elaida's study a number of times in *Tel'aran'rhiod*, but the woman's correspondence box had always been empty. Now she knew why.

Sharp spots of red appeared in Beonin's cheeks. "I tell you, I have betrayed n—!" She finished with a strangled grunt and put a hand to her throat as if it refused to let the lie leave her tongue. That proved she was not Black Ajah; but it proved something more.

"You betrayed the ferrets. Are they all down in the basement cells?"

Beonin's eyes flashed up the corridor. Melavaire was talking with her Warder, his head bent close to hers. Squat or not, he was taller than she. Beonin's Tervail was watching her with a worried expression. The distance was too far for any of the three to have overheard, but Beonin stepped closer and lowered her voice. "Elaida, she is having them watched, though I think the Ajahs, they keep what they see to themselves. Few sisters want to tell Elaida any more than they must. It was necessary, you understand. I could hardly return to the Tower and keep them secret. It would have been discovered eventually."

"Then you'll have to warn them." Egwene could not keep her voice clear of her disdain. This woman split hairs with a razor! She took the thinnest excuse to decide her oath no longer applied, and then she *betrayed* the very women she had helped choose. Blood and bloody ashes!

Beonin remained silent for a long moment, fiddling with her shawl, but at last she said, surprisingly, "I have already warned Meidani and Jennet." They were the two Grays among the ferrets. "I have done what I can for them. The others, they must sink or swim by themselves. Sisters have been assaulted for simply going too near another Ajah's quarters. Me, I will not walk back to my rooms clad only in my shawl and the welts just to try—"

"Think of it as a penance," Egwene cut in. Light! Sisters *assaulted*? Things were even worse than she had thought. She had to remind herself that well-manured ground would help her seeds to grow.

Beonin glanced up the hallway again, and Tervail took a step toward her before Beonin shook her head. Her face was smooth despite the color staining her cheeks, but inside, she must have been in turmoil. "You know I could send you to the Mistress of Novices, yes?" she said in a tight voice. "I hear you spend half of each day squealing for her. I think you would dislike more visits, yes?"

Egwene smiled at her. Not two hours earlier she had managed to smile the moment Silviana's strap stopped falling. This was much harder. "And who can say what I might squeal? About oaths, perhaps?" The color drained from the other woman's cheeks, leaving her face bloodless pale. No, she did not want that getting out. "You may have convinced yourself I am no longer Amyrlin, Beonin, but it's time to start convincing yourself that I still am. You will warn the others, whatever the cost to yourself. Tell them to stay away from me unless I send word otherwise. They've had more than enough attention drawn to them. But from now on, you'll seek me out every day in case I have instructions for them. I have some now." Quickly she listed the things she wanted them to bring up in conversation, Shemerin being stripped of the shawl, Elaida's complicity in the disasters at the Black Tower and Dumai's Wells, all the seeds she had been planting. They would not be planted one by one now, but broadcast by handfuls.

"Me, I cannot speak for other Ajahs," Beonin said when she finished, "but in the Gray, sisters speak of most of these things often. The eyes-and-ears, they are busy of late. Secrets Elaida hoped to hold, they are coming out. I am sure it must be the same in the others. Perhaps it is not necessary for me to—"

"Warn them, and deliver my instructions, Beonin." Egwene lifted the pole back onto her shoulders, shifting it to the most comfortable position she could find. Two or three of the Whites would use a hairbrush or slipper on her *and* send her to Silviana if they thought her slow. Embracing pain, even welcoming it, did not mean seeking it out unnecessarily. "Remember. It's a penance I've set you."

"I will do as you say," Beonin said with obvious reluctance. Her eyes hardened suddenly, but it was not for Egwene. "It would be enjoyable to see Elaida pulled down," she said in an unpleasant voice before hurrying away to join Melavaire.

That shocking meeting, turned into an unexpected victory, left Egwene feeling very good about the day, and no matter that Ferane did turn out to think she had been slow. The White Sitter was plump, but she had an arm as strong as Silviana's.

That night, she dragged herself down to the open cells after supper despite wanting her bed in the worst way. Aside from lessons and howling under Silviana's strap—the last time just before supper— most of the rest of the day had been given to hauling water. Her back and shoulders ached. Her arms ached, her legs. She was swaying on her feet with weariness. Strangely, she had not had one of those wretched headaches since being taken prisoner, nor any of those dark dreams that left her disturbed even though she could never remember them, but she thought she might be heading for a fine headache tonight. That would make telling true dreams difficult, and she had had some fine ones lately, about Rand, Mat, Perrin, even Gawyn, though most dreams of him were just that.

Three White sisters she knew in passing were guarding Leane: Nagora, a lean woman with pale hair worn in a roll on her nape who sat very straight to make up for her lack of stature; Norine, lovely with her large liquid eyes but often as vague as any Brown; and Miyasi, tall and plump with iron-gray hair, a stern woman who brooked no nonsense and saw nonsense everywhere. Nagora, surrounded by the light of *saidar*, held the shield on Leane, but they were arguing over some point of logic that Egwene could not make out from the little she heard. She could not even tell whether there were two sides to the argument, or three. There were no raised voices, no shaken fists, and their faces remained smooth Aes Sedai masks, but the coldness in their voices left no doubt that had they not been Aes Sedai, they would have been shouting if not trading blows. She might as well not have existed for all the attention they paid her entrance.

Watching the three from the edge of her eye, she moved as close to the iron latticework as she could and gripped it with both hands to steady herself. Light, she was tired! "I saw Beonin today," she said softly. "She's here in the Tower. She claimed her oath to me no longer held because I was no longer the Amyrlin Seat."

Leane gasped and stepped near enough that she was brushing the iron bars. "*She* betrayed us?"

"The inherent impossibility of dissimulated structures is a given," Nagora said firmly. Her voice was an icy hammer. "A given."

"She denies it, and I believe her," Egwene whispered. "But she admitted betraying the ferrets. Elaida is only having them watched for the moment, but I told Beonin to warn them, and she said she would. She said she had already warned Meidani and Jennet, but why would she betray them and then tell them about it? And she said she would like to see Elaida pulled down. Why would she flee to Elaida if she still wants her brought down? She as much as admitted no one else has abandoned our cause. I'm missing something, and I'm too tired to see what it is." A yawn that she barely managed to cover with a hand cracked her jaw.

"Dissimulated structures are implied by four of the five axioms of sixth-order rationality," Miyasi said just as firmly. "Strongly implied."

"So-called sixth-order rationality has been discarded as an aberration by anyone with intellect," Norine put in, a touch sharply. "But dissimulated structures are fundamental to any possibility of understanding what is happening right here in the Tower every day. Reality itself is shifting, changing day by day."

Leane glanced at the Whites. "Some always thought Elaida had spies among us. If Beonin was one, her oath to you would have held her until she could convince herself you were no longer Amyrlin. But if her reception here wasn't what she expected, it might have changed her loyalties. Beonin was always ambitious. If she didn't get her due as she sees matters. . . ." She spread her hands. "Beonin always expected her due and perhaps a little more."

"Logic is always applicable to the real world," Miyasi said dismissively, "but only a novice would think the real world can be applied to logic. Ideals *must* be first principles. *Not* the mundane world." Nagora snapped her mouth shut with a dark look, as if she felt words had been snatched right off her tongue.

Coloring faintly, Norine rose and glided away from the benches toward Egwene. The other two followed her with their eyes, and she seemed to feel their gazes, shifting her shawl uncomfortably first one way than another. "Child, you look exhausted. Go to your bed now."

Egwene wanted nothing more than her bed, but she had a question to be answered first. Only she had to be careful. The three Whites were all paying attention now. "Leane, do the sisters who visit you still ask the same questions?"

"I told you to go to your bed," Norine said sharply. She clapped her hands together as if that would somehow make Egwene obey.

"Yes," Leane said. "I see what you mean. Perhaps there can be a measure of trust."

"A small measure," Egwene said.

Norine planted her fists on her hips. There was little coolness in her face or her voice, and no vagueness at all about her. "Since you refuse to go to your bed, you can go to the Mistress of Novices and tell her you disobeyed a sister."

"Of course," Egwene said quickly, turning to go. She had her answer—Beonin had not passed on Traveling, and that meant she likely had not passed on anything else; perhaps there could be a little trust—and besides, Nagora and Miyasi were advancing on her. The last thing she wanted was to be dragged bodily to Silviana's study, something Miyasi at least was quite capable of. She had even stronger arms than Ferane.

On the morning of her ninth day back in the Tower, before first light, Doesine herself came to Egwene's small room to give her her morning dose of Healing. Outside, rain was falling with a dull roar. The two Reds who had been watching over her sleep gave her her forkroot, frowning at Doesine, and hurried away. The Yellow Sitter snorted in contempt when the door closed behind them. She used the old method of Healing that made Egwene gasp as though doused in an icy pond and left her ravenously eager for breakfast. As well as free of the pain in her bottom. That actually felt peculiar; you could adapt to anything over time, and a bruised bottom already seemed normal. But the use of the old way, the way used every time she had been given Healing since being captured, reaffirmed that Beonin had kept some secrets, though how she had managed it was still a mystery. Beonin herself had only said that most sisters thought the tales of new weaves were merely rumors.

"You don't mean to bloody surrender, do you, child?" Doesine said while Egwene was pulling her dress over her head. The woman's language was very much at odds with her elegant appearance, in gold-embroidered blue with sapphires at her ears and in her hair.

"Should the Amyrlin Seat ever surrender?" Egwene asked as her head popped out at the top of her dress. She doubled her arms behind her to do up the buttons of white-dyed horn.

Doesine snorted again, though not in contempt, Egwene thought. "A brave course, child. Still, my wager is that Silviana will bloody well have you sitting straight and walking right before much longer." But she left without calling Egwene down for naming herself the Amyrlin Seat.

Egwene had yet another appointment with the Mistress of Novices before breakfast—she had not missed a day, so far—and following a determined effort to undo Doesine's work in one go, her tears ceased as soon as Silviana's strap stopped falling. When she lifted herself off the end of the writing table, where a leather pad was attached just for bending over, its surface worn down by who knew how many women, and her skirt and shift fell against her fiery skin, she felt no urge to flinch. She accepted the painful heat, welcomed it, warmed herself with it as she would have warmed her hands in front of a fireplace on a cold winter morning. There seemed a strong resemblance between her bottom and a blazing fireplace right at that moment. Yet looking into the mirror, she saw an unruffled face. Red-cheeked, but calm.

"How could Shemerin have been reduced to Accepted?" she asked, wiping her tears away with her handkerchief. "I've inquired, and there's no provision for it in Tower law."

"How often have you been sent to me because of those 'inquiries'?" Silviana asked, hanging the split-tailed strap in the narrow cabinet alongside the leather paddle and the limber switch. "I'd think you would have given over long since."

"I'm curious. How, when there's no provision?"

"No provision, child," Silviana said gently, as if explaining to a child in truth, "but no prohibition, either. A loophole that. . . . Well, we won't go into that. You'd only find a way to get yourself another strapping with it." Shaking her head, she took her seat behind the writing table and rested her hands on the tabletop. "The problem was that Shemerin accepted it. Other sisters told her to ignore the edict, but once she realized pleading wouldn't change the Amyrlin's mind, she moved into the Accepted's quarters."

Egwene's stomach growled loudly, anxious for breakfast, but she was not done. She was actually having a conversation with Silviana. A conversation, however odd the topic. "But why would she run away? Surely her friends didn't stop trying to talk sense into her."

"Some talked sense," Silviana said dryly. "Others. . . ." She moved her hands like the pans of a balance scale, first one up then the other. "Others tried to force her to see sense. They sent her to me nearly as often as you are sent. I treated her visits as private penances, but she lacked your—" She stopped abruptly, leaning back in her chair and studying Egwene over steepled fingers. "Well, now. You actually have me chatting. Not prohibited certainly, yet hardly proper in these circumstances. Go on to breakfast," she said, picking up her pen and opening the silver cap of her ink jar. "I'll mark you down for midday again, since I know you have no intention of curtsying." The faintest hint of resignation tinged her voice.

When Egwene entered the novices' dining hall, the first novice to see her stood, and suddenly there was a loud scraping of benches on the colorful floor tiles as the others rose, too. They stood there at their benches in silence as Egwene walked down the center aisle toward the kitchen. Suddenly Ashelin, a plump, pretty girl from Altara, darted into the kitchen. Before Egwene reached the kitchen door, Ashelin was back with a tray in her hands that held the usual thick cup of steaming tea and plate of bread, olives and cheese. Egwene reached for the tray, but the olive-skinned girl hurried to the nearest table and set it down in front of an empty bench, offering a suggestion of a curtsy as she backed away. Lucky for her, neither of Egwene's escorts this morning had chosen that moment to peer into the dining hall. Lucky for all those novices on their feet.

A cushion rested on the bench in front of Egwene's tray. A tattered thing that was more patches in different colors than original material, but still a cushion. Egwene picked it up and set it on the end of the table before sitting down. Welcoming the pain was easy. She basked in the warmth of her own fires. A soft susurration gusted through the room, a collective sigh. Only when she popped an olive into her mouth did the novices sit.

She almost spat it out again—it was not far short of spoiled—but she was famished after her Healing, so she spat only the pit into the palm of her hand and deposited it on the plate, washing the taste away with a sip of tea. There was honey in the tea! Novices got honey only on special occasions. She tried not to smile as she cleaned her plate, and clean it she did, even picking up crumbs of bread and cheese with a dampened finger. Not smiling was difficult, though. First Doesine—a Sitter!—then Silviana's resignation, now this. The two sisters were far more important than the novices or the honey, but they all indicated the same thing. She was winning her war.

CHAPTER
25

Attending Elaida

Gold-embossed leather folder under her arm, Tarna kept to the central core of the Tower as she climbed toward Elaida's apartments, although it meant using a seemingly endless series of staircases—twice those stairs were not located where she remembered them, but so long as she continued upward, she would reach her destination—rather than the gently spiraling corridors. On the stairs, she met no one but occasional liveried servants who bowed or curtsied before hurrying on about their tasks. In either of the spiraling hallways she would have to pass the entrances to the Ajah quarters and perhaps encounter other sisters. Her Keeper's stole allowed her to enter any Ajah's quarters, yet she avoided all except the Red save when duty called. Among sisters of the other Ajahs she was all too aware that her narrow stole was red, all too aware of hot eyes watching her from cold faces. They did not unnerve her—little did; she took the shifting interior of the Tower in stride—but still. . . . She thought matters had not gone so far that anyone would actually attack the Keeper, yet she took no chances. Retrieving the situation was going to be a long, hard struggle, whatever Elaida thought, and an assault on the Keeper might make it irretrievable.

Besides, not having to watch over her shoulder allowed her to think on Pevara's troubling question, one she had not considered be-

fore suggesting the bonding of Asha'man. Who in the Red actually
could be trusted with the task? Hunting men who could channel led
Red sisters to look askance at all men, and a fair number hated them.
A surviving brother or father might well escape hatred, a favorite
cousin or uncle, but once they were all gone, so was affection. And
trust. And there was another matter of trust. Bonding any man violated custom strong as law. Even with Tsutama's blessings, who might
run to Elaida when bonding Asha'man was broached? She had removed three more names from her mental list of possibilities by the
time she reached the entrance to Elaida's apartments, only two floors
below the top of the Tower. After almost two weeks, her list of those
she could be certain of still contained only a single name, and that one
was impossible for the task.

Elaida was in her sitting room, where the furnishings were all gilt
and ivory inlays and the large patterned carpet was one of Tear's finest
creations. She was sitting in a low-backed chair before the marble fireplace sipping wine with Meidani. Seeing the Gray was no surprise despite the early hour. Meidani dined with the Amyrlin most nights, and
visited often during the day by invitation. Elaida, her six-striped stole
wide enough to cover her shoulders, was regarding the taller woman
over her crystal goblet, a dark-eyed eagle regarding a mouse with big
blue eyes. Meidani, emeralds at her ears and on a wide collar around
her slim throat, seemed very conscious of that gaze. Her full lips
smiled, but they seemed tremulous. The hand not holding her goblet
moved constantly, touching the emerald comb over her left ear, patting her hair, covering her bosom, which was largely exposed by her
snug bodice of brocaded silvery-gray silk. Her bosom was hardly excessive, yet her slenderness made it seem so, and she appeared about to
pop free of the garment. The woman was garbed for a ball. Or a se-
duction.

"The morning reports are ready, Mother," Tarna said, bowing
slightly. Light! She felt as if she had intruded on lovers!

"You won't mind leaving us, Meidani?" Even the smile Elaida directed at the yellow-haired woman was predatory.

"Of course not, Mother." Meidani set her goblet on the small table
beside her chair and leaped to her feet, offering a curtsy that nearly had
her out of her dress. "Of course not." She scurried from the room
breathing hard, her eyes wide.

When the door closed behind her, Elaida laughed. "We were

pillow-friends as novices," she said, rising, "and I believe she wants to renew the relationship. I may let her. She might reveal more on the pillows than she's let slip so far. Which is nothing, truth to tell." She strode to the nearest window and stood staring down toward where her fantastical palace would rise to overtop the Tower itself. Eventually. If sisters could be convinced to work on it again. The heavy rain that had begun during the night was still falling, and it seemed unlikely she could see anything of that palace's foundations, all that had been completed so far. "Help yourself to wine if you wish."

Tarna kept her face smooth with an effort. Pillow-friends were common among novices and Accepted, but girlhood things should be left behind with girlhood. Not all sisters saw it so, certainly. Galina had been quite surprised when Tarna refused her advances after gaining the shawl. She herself found men far more attractive than women. Most seemed heavily intimidated by Aes Sedai, to be sure, especially if they learned you were Red Ajah, but over the years she had come across a few who were not.

"That seems odd, Mother," she said, putting the leather folder down on the side table that held an ornately wrought golden tray bearing a crystal wine pitcher and goblets. "She appears frightened of you." Filling a goblet, she sniffed the wine before sipping. The Keepings seemed to be working. For now. Elaida had finally agreed that that weave, at least, must be shared. "Almost as if she knew that you know about her being a spy."

"Of course she's afraid of me." Sarcasm dripped heavily from Elaida's voice, but then hardened to stone. "I want her afraid. I intend to put her through the mangle. By the time I have her birched, she'll tie herself to the birching frame if I order it. If she knew I knew, Tarna, she'd be fleeing instead of delivering herself into my hands." Still staring out into the rainstorm, Elaida sipped at her wine. "Have you any news of the others?"

"No, Mother. If I could inform the Sitters of why they're to be watched—"

"No!" Elaida snapped, spinning to face her. Her dress was such a mass of intricate red scrollwork that the embroidery all but hid the gray silk beneath. Tarna had suggested that less flaunting of her former Ajah—she had phrased it more diplomatically, but that was what she meant—might help bring the Ajahs together again, yet Elaida's eruption of fury had been sufficient to keep her quiet on the topic since.

"What if some of the Sitters are working with them? I wouldn't put it past them. Those ridiculous talks continue at the bridge despite my orders. No, I wouldn't put it past them at all!"

Tarna inclined her head over her goblet, accepting what she could not change. Elaida refused to see that if the Ajahs disobeyed her order to break off the talks, they were unlikely to spy on their own sisters at her command without knowing why. Saying so would only result in another tirade, though.

Elaida stared at her as if to make sure she was not going to argue. The woman seemed harder than ever. And more brittle. "A pity the rebellion in Tarabon failed," she said at last. "There's nothing to be done about it, I suppose." But she mentioned it frequently, at odd moments, since word came that the Seanchan were reasserting their grip on that country. She was not so resigned as she pretended. "I want to hear some good news, Tarna. Is there any word of the seals on the Dark One's prison? We must make sure no more get broken." As if Tarna did not know that!

"Not that the Ajahs have reported, Mother, and I don't think they would hold that back." She wished she had those last words back as soon as they were spoken.

Elaida grunted. The Ajahs released only trickles of what their eyes-and-ears told them, and she resented that bitterly. Her own eyes-and-ears were concentrated in Andor. "How is the work coming at the harbors?"

"Slowly, Mother." With the flow of trade stifled, the city was already feeling hunger. It would begin starving soon, unless the harbor mouths were cleared. Even cutting away the portion of the Southharbor chain that was still iron had proved not enough to allow sufficient ships in to feed Tar Valon. Once Tarna was able to convince her of the necessity, Elaida had ordered the chain towers dismantled so those huge pieces of *cuendillar* could be removed. Like the city walls, however, the towers had been built and strengthened with the Power, and only the Power could disassemble them. It was far from easy. The original builders had done good work, and *those* wards seemed not to have weakened a hair. "Reds are doing most of the work for the time being. Sisters from other Ajahs come now and then, but only a few. I expect that will change soon, though." They knew the necessity of the work, however much they might resent it—no sister could like having to labor in that fashion; the Reds doing most of it certainly grumbled enough—but the order had come from Elaida, and these days, that resulted in foot-dragging.

Elaida breathed heavily, then took a long drink. She seemed to need it. Her hand gripped the goblet so hard that tendons stood out on its back. She advanced across the patterned silk carpet as if she meant to strike at Tarna. "They defy me again. Again! I *will* have obedience, Tarna. I *will* have it! Write out an order, and once I sign and seal it, post it in every Ajah's quarters." She stopped almost nose-to-nose with Tarna, her dark eyes glittering like a raven's. "The Sitters of any Ajah that fails to send its fair share of sisters to work on the chain towers will take a daily penance from Silviana until the matter is rectified. Daily! And the Sitters of any Ajah that sends sisters to those . . . those *talks* will do the same. Write it out for me to sign!"

Tarna drew a deep breath. Penances might work and they might not, depending on how set the Sitters were, and the Ajah heads—she did not think things had gone so wrong that they might refuse to accept penance at all; that would be an end to Elaida for sure, perhaps an end to the Tower. But posting the order publicly, not allowing the Sitters a scrap to hide behind and maintain their dignity, was the wrong way to go about it. In truth, it might well be the very worst way. "If I may make a suggestion," she began as delicately as she could manage. She had never been known for delicacy.

"You may not," Elaida cut in harshly. She took another long drink, draining her goblet, and glided across the carpet to refill it. She drank too much, of late. Tarna had even seen her drunk once! "How is Silviana doing with the al'Vere girl?" she said as she poured.

"Egwene spends near enough half of every day in Silviana's study, Mother." She was careful to keep her tone neutral. This was the first time Elaida had asked after the young woman since her capture, nine days ago.

"So much? I want her tamed to the Tower's harness, not broken."

"I . . . doubt she will be broken, Mother. Silviana will be careful of that." And then there was the girl herself. That was not for Elaida's ears, though. Tarna had been shouted at more than enough. She had learned to avoid subjects that only resulted in shouting. Advice and suggestions unoffered were no more useless than advice and suggestions untaken, and Elaida almost never took either. "Egwene's stubborn, but I expect she must come around soon." The girl had to. Galina, beating Tarna's block out of her, had not expended a tenth of the effort Silviana was putting into Egwene. The girl had to yield to that soon.

"Excellent," Elaida murmured. "Excellent." She looked over her shoulder, her face a mask of serenity. Her eyes still glittered, though. "Put her name on the roster to attend me. In fact, have her attend me tonight. She can serve supper for Meidani and me."

"It will be as you command, Mother." It seemed yet another visit to the Mistress of Novices was inevitable, but no doubt Egwene would earn just as many of those if she never came near Elaida.

"And now your reports, Tarna." Elaida sat down again and crossed her legs.

Replacing her barely touched goblet on the tray, Tarna took up her folder and sat in the chair Meidani had been using. "The redone wards appear to be keeping rats out of the Tower, Mother," for how long was another question; she checked those wards herself every day, "but ravens and crows have been seen in the Tower grounds, so the wards on the walls must be. . . ."

The midday sun cast dappled light through the leafy branches of the tall trees, mostly oak and leatherleaf and sourgum with a smattering of cottonwoods and massive pines. Apparently there had been a fierce windstorm some years back, because fallen timber, scattered about here and there but all stretched in the same general direction, provided good seating with only a little hatchet work to hack away a few limbs. Sparse undergrowth allowed a good view in all directions, and not far off, a small clear stream splashed over mossy stones. It would have been a good campsite if Mat had not been intent on covering as much ground as he could every day, but it did just as well as a place to rest the horses and eat. The Damona Mountains still lay at least three hundred miles to the east, and he intended to reach them in a week. Vanin said he knew a smugglers' pass—purely by hearsay, of course; just something he had overheard by chance, but he knew right where to find it—that would have them inside Murandy two days after that. Much safer than trying to go north into Andor or south toward Illian. In either direction, the distance to safety would be further and the chance of encountering Seanchan greater.

Mat gnawed the last scrap of meat from a rabbit's hind leg, and tossed the bone on the ground. Balding Lopin darted in, stroking at

his beard in consternation, to pick it up and drop it in the pit he and
Nerim had made in the mulch-covered forest floor, though the pit
would be dug up by animals within a half-hour after their departure.
Mat moved to wipe his hands on his breeches. Tuon, nibbling at a
grouse leg on the other side of the low fire, gave him a very direct look,
her eyebrows raised, while the fingers of her free hand wiggled at Selucia, who had ravaged half a grouse by herself. The bosomy woman did
not reply, but she sniffed. Loudly. Meeting Tuon's gaze, he deliberately
wiped his hands on his breeches. He could have gone over to the
stream, where the Aes Sedai were washing their hands, but no one's
clothing was going to be pristine by the time they reached Murandy in
any case. Besides, when a woman named you Toy all the time, it was
natural to take any chance to let her know you were nobody's toy. She
shook her head and waggled her fingers again. This time, Selucia
laughed, and Mat felt his face heat. He could imagine two or three
things she might have said, none of which he would have enjoyed
hearing.

Setalle, sitting on the end of his log, made sure he heard some of
them anyway. Reaching an agreement with the onetime Aes Sedai
had not shifted her attitudes a hair. "She might have said men are
pigs," she murmured without lifting her eyes from her embroidery
hoop, "or just that you are." Her dark gray riding dress had a high
neck, but she still wore her snug silver necklace with the marriage
knife hanging from it. "She may have said you're a mud-footed country lout with dirt in your ears and hay in your hair. Or she might
have said—"

"I think I see the direction you're going," he told her through gritted teeth. Tuon giggled, though the next instant her face belonged on
an executioner once more, cold and stern.

Pulling his silver-mounted pipe and goatskin tabac pouch from his
coat pocket, he thumbed the bowl full and lifted the lid on the box of
strikers at his feet. It fascinated him the way fire just sprang up, spikes
of it darting in all directions at first, when he scratched the lumpy, red-
and-white head of a striker down the rough side of the box. He waited
until the flame burned away from the head before using it to light his
pipe. Pulling the taste and smell of sulphur into his mouth once had
been enough for him. He dropped the burning stick and ground it
firmly under his boot. The mulch was still damp from the last rain to
fall here, but he took no chances with fire in woods. In the Two Rivers,

men turned out from miles around when the woods caught fire. Sometimes hundreds of marches burned, even so.

"The strikers, they should not be wasted," Aludra said, lifting her eyes from the small stones board balanced atop a nearby log. Thom, stroking his long white mustaches, continued to contemplate the cross-hatched board. He rarely lost at stones, yet she had managed to win two games from him since they left the show. Two out of a dozen or more, but Thom took care with anyone who could defeat him even once. She swept her beaded braids back over her shoulders. "Me, I must be in the same place for two days to make more. Men always find ways to make work for women, yes?"

Mat puffed away, if not contentedly, at least with some degree of pleasure. Women! A delight to look at and a delight to be with. When they were not finding ways to rub salt into a man's hide. It seemed six up and a half dozen down. It truly did.

Most of the party had finished eating—the best part of two grouse and one rabbit were all that remained on the spits over the fire, but they would be taken along wrapped in linen; the hunting had been good during the morning's ride, yet there was no certainty the afternoon would be as profitable, and flatbread and beans made a poor meal. Those who had finished were taking their ease or, in the case of the Redarms, checking the hobbled packhorses, better than sixty of them on four leads. Buying so many in Maderin had been expensive, but Luca had rushed into town to take care of the bargaining himself once he heard about a merchant dead in the street. He almost—almost but not quite—had been ready to give them packhorses from the show's animals to be rid of Mat after that. Many of the animals were loaded with Aludra's paraphernalia and her supplies. Luca had ended up with the greater part by far of Mat's gold, one way and another. Mat had slipped a fat purse to Petra and Clarine, too, but that was friendship, to help them buy their inn a little sooner. What remained in his saddlebags was more than enough to see them comfortably to Murandy, though, and all he needed to replenish it was a common room where dice were being tossed.

Leilwin, with a curved sword hanging from a broad leather strap that slanted across her chest, and Domon, with a shortsword on one side of his belt and a brass-studded cudgel on the other, were chatting with Juilin and Amathera on yet another log close by. Leilwin—he had come to accept that that was the only name she would stomach—made a point of showing that she would not avoid Tuon or Selucia, or lower her eyes when they met, though she had to steel herself visibly to carry it off. Juilin had the cuffs of his black coat turned back, a sign he felt among friends, or at least people he could trust. The onetime Panarch of Tarabon still clutched the thief-catcher's arm tightly, but she met Leilwin's sharp blue eyes with little flinching. In fact, she often seemed to gaze at the other woman with something approaching awe.

Seated cross-legged on the ground and unmindful of the dampness, Noal was playing Snakes and Foxes with Olver and spinning wild tales about the lands beyond the Aiel Waste, about some great coastal city that foreigners were not allowed to leave except by ship and the inhabitants were not allowed to leave at all. Mat wished they would find another game to play. Every time they brought out that piece of red cloth with its spiderweb of black lines, it reminded him of his promise to Thom, reminded him the bloody Eelfinn were inside his head somehow, and maybe the flaming Aelfinn, too. The Aes Sedai came up from the stream, and Joline stopped to talk with Blaeric and Fen. Bethamin and Seta, trailing along behind, hesitated until a gesture from the Green sent them to stand behind the log where Teslyn and Edesina sat, as far apart as they could manage, with uncut branches between, and began reading small leather-bound books taken from their belt pouches. Both Bethamin and Seta stood behind Edesina.

The yellow-haired former *sul'dam* had come round in spectacular, and painful, fashion. Painful for her and for the sisters. When she first hesitantly asked them to teach her, too, at supper the night before, they refused. They were only teaching Bethamin because she had already channeled. Seta was too old to become a novice, she had not channeled, and that was that. So she duplicated whatever it was that Bethamin had done and had all three leaping about the cookfire and squealing in showers of dancing sparks for as long as she could hold onto the Power. They agreed to teach her then. At least, Joline and Edesina did. Teslyn still was having none of any *sul'dam*, former or not. All three of them took a hand in switching her, though, and she had spent the morning continually easing herself in her saddle. She still looked afraid, of the One Power and maybe of the Aes Sedai, but strangely, her face somehow seemed . . . content, too. How to understand that was beyond Mat.

He should have felt content himself. He had avoided a charge of murder, avoided riding blindly into a Seanchan trap that would have killed Tuon, and left the *gholam* behind for good this time. It would be following Luca's show, and Luca had been warned, for whatever good that would do. In well under two weeks he would be over the mountains into Murandy. The need to figure out how to get Tuon back to Ebou Dar safely, no easy task at all now, especially since he would have to guard against Aes Sedai trying to spirit her away, would mean that much longer to look at her face. And to try puzzling out what went on behind those big beautiful eyes. He should have been as happy as a goat in a corn crib. He was far from it.

For one thing, all those sword-cuts he had received in Maderin hurt. Some of them were inflamed, though he had managed to keep that from anyone so far. He hated being fussed over nearly as much as he hated anyone using the Power on him. Lopin and Nerim had sewed him up as well as they could, and he had refused Healing despite attempted bullying by all three Aes Sedai. He had been surprised that Joline, of all people, tried to insist, but she did, and flung up her hands in disgust when he failed to relent. Another surprise had been Tuon.

"Don't be foolish, Toy," she had drawled in his tent, standing over him, arms folded beneath her breasts, while Lopin and Nerim plied their needles and he gritted his teeth. Her proprietary air, very much a woman making sure her property was repaired properly, had been enough to make him grind his teeth, never mind the needles. Or that he was down to his smallclothes! She had just walked in and refused to leave short of manhandling, and he had felt in no condition to manhandle a woman he suspected might be able to break his arm. "This Healing is a wonderful thing. My Mylen knows it, and I taught it to my others, too. Of course, many people are foolish about having the Power touch them. Half my servants would faint at the suggestion, and most of the Blood, too, I shouldn't be surprised. But I wouldn't have expected it of you." If she had a quarter his experience of Aes Sedai, she would have.

They had ridden off up the road from Maderin as if setting out for Lugard, then taken to the forest as soon as the last farms were out of sight. The moment they entered the trees, the dice started up in his head again. That was the other thing that soured his mood, those bloody dice drumming inside his head for two days. There hardly seemed any way they could stop here in the forest. What kind of momentous event could happen in the woods? Still, he had stayed well clear of the small villages they had passed. Sooner or later the dice would stop, though, and he could only wait for it.

Tuon and Selucia headed for the stream to wash, wiggling their fingers at one another rapidly. Talking about him, he was sure. When women started putting their heads together, you could be sure—

Amathera screamed, and every head whipped around toward her. Mat spotted the cause as quickly as Juilin did, a black-scaled snake a good seven feet long wriggling quickly away from the log Juilin was seated on. Leilwin cursed and leaped to her feet drawing her sword, but no faster than Juilin, who tugged his shortsword free of its scabbard and started after the snake so swiftly that his conical red cap fell off.

"Let it go, Juilin," Mat said. "It's heading away from us. Let it go." The thing probably had a den under that log and had been surprised to come out and find people. Luckily, blacklances were solitary snakes.

Juilin hesitated before deciding that comforting a shivering Amathera was more important than chasing a snake. "What kind is it, anyway?" he said, folding her in his arms. He was a city man, after all. Mat told him, and for a moment, he looked as though he meant to go after it again. Wisely, he decided against. Blacklances were quick as lightning, and with a shortsword, he would have needed to get close. Anyway, Amathera was clinging to him so hard he would have had a time getting free of her.

Taking his hat from the butt of his *ashandarei*, which was driven point-down into the ground, Mat settled it on his head. "Daylight's wasting," he said around his pipestem. "Time we were moving on. Don't dawdle over there, Tuon. Your hands are clean enough." He had tried calling her Precious, but since her claim of victory back in Maderin, she refused to acknowledge that he had even spoken when he did.

She did not hurry in the slightest, of course. By the time she returned, drying her small hands on a small piece of toweling that Selucia would drape across the pommel of her saddle to dry, Nerim and Lopin had filled in the refuse pit, wrapped the remains of the meal and tucked them into Nerim's saddlebags, and doused the fire with water brought from the stream in folding leather buckets. *Ashandarei* in hand, Mat was ready to mount Pips.

"A strange man, who lets poisonous serpents go," Tuon said. "From the fellow's reaction, I assume a blacklance *is* poisonous?"

"Very," he told her. "But snakes don't bite anything they can't eat unless they're threatened." He put a foot in the stirrup.

"You may kiss me, Toy."

He gave a start. Her words, not spoken softly, had made them the object of every eye. Selucia's face was so stiffly expressionless her disapproval could not have been plainer. "Now?" he said. "When we stop tonight, we could take a stroll alone—"

"By tonight, I may have changed my mind, Toy. Call it a whim, for a man who lets poisonous snakes go." Maybe she saw one of her omens in that?

Taking off his hat and sticking the black spear back into the ground, he took the pipe from between his teeth and planted a chaste kiss on her full lips. A first kiss was nothing to be rough with. He did not want her to think him pushy, or crude. She was no tavern maid to enjoy a bit of slap and tickle. Besides, he could almost feel all those eyes watching. Someone snickered. Selucia rolled her eyes.

Tuon folded her arms beneath her breasts and looked up at him through her long eyelashes. "Do I remind you of your sister?" she asked in a dangerous tone. "Or perhaps your mother?" Somebody laughed. More than one somebody, in fact.

Grimly, Mat tapped the dottle from his pipe on the heel of his boot and stuffed the warm pipe into his coat pocket. He hung his hat back on the *ashandarei*. If she wanted a real kiss. . . . Had he really thought she would not fill his arms? Slim, she was to be sure, and small, but she filled them very nicely indeed. He bent his head to hers. She was far from the first woman he had kissed. He knew what he was about. Surprisingly—or then again, perhaps not so surprisingly—she did not know. She was a quick pupil, though. Very quick.

When he finally released her, she stood there looking up at him and trying to catch her breath. For that matter, his breath came a little raggedly, too. Metwyn whistled appreciatively. Mat smiled. What would she think of what plainly was her first real kiss ever? He tried not to smile too widely, though. He did not want her to think he was smirking.

She laid fingers against his cheek. "I thought so," she said in that slow honey drawl. "You're feverish. Some of your wounds must be infected."

Mat blinked. He gave her a kiss that had to have curled her toes, and all she said was that his face was hot? He bent his head again—this time, she would bloody well need help to stay standing!—but she put a hand against his chest, fending him off.

"Selucia, fetch the box of ointments I got from Mistress Luca," she commanded. Selucia went scurrying for Tuon's black-and-white mount.

"We don't have time for that now," Mat said. "I'll smear on something tonight." He might as well have kept his mouth shut.

"Strip off, Toy," she said in the same tone she had used with her maid. "The ointment will sting, but I expect you be brave."

"I am *not* going to—!"

"Riders coming," Harnan announced. He was already in his saddle, on a dark bay gelding with white forefeet, holding the lead to one of the strings of packhorses. "One of them's Vanin."

Mat swung up onto Pips for a better vantage. A pair of horsemen were approaching at a gallop, dodging around fallen trees when they had to. Aside from recognizing Chel Vanin's dun, there was no mistaking the man himself. Nobody else who was that wide and sat his saddle like a sack of suet could have maintained his seat at that pace without any apparent effort. The man could have stayed in the saddle on a wild boar. Then Mat recognized the other rider, whose cloak was flailing behind him, and felt as if he had been punched in the belly. He would not have been surprised in the least had the dice stopped then, but they kept bouncing off the inside of his skull. What in the Light was Talmanes bloody well doing in Altara?

The two riders slowed to a walk short of Mat, and Vanin reined in to let Talmanes approach alone. It was not shyness. There was nothing shy about Vanin. He leaned lazily on the tall pommel of his saddle and spat to one side through a gap in his teeth. No, he knew Mat would not be best pleased, and he meant to stay clear.

"Vanin brought me up to date, Mat," Talmanes said. Short and wiry, with the front of his head shaved and powdered, the Cairhienin had the right to wear stripes of color across his chest in considerable number, but a small red hand sewn to the breast of his dark coat was its only decoration unless you counted the long red scarf tied around his left arm. He never laughed and seldom smiled, but he had his reasons. "I was sorry to hear about Nalesean and the others. A good man, Nalesean. They all were."

"Yes, they were," Mat said, keeping a tight rein on his temper. "I assume Egwene never came to you for help getting away from those fool Aes Sedai, but what in the bloody flaming Light are you doing here?" Well, maybe he did not have such a tight rein after all. "At least tell me you haven't brought the whole bloody Band three hundred bloody miles into Altara with you."

"Egwene is still the Amyrlin," the other man said calmly, straightening his cloak. Another red hand, larger, marked that. "You were wrong about her, Mat. She really is the Amyrlin Seat, and she has those Aes Sedai by the scruff of the neck. Though some of them might not know it yet. The last I saw, she and the whole lot of them were off to besiege Tar Valon. She might have it by now. They can make holes in the air like the one the Dragon Reborn made to take us near Salidar." The colors spun in Mat's head, resolving for an instant into Rand talking to some woman with gray hair in a bun atop her head, an Aes Sedai, he thought, but his anger blew the image away like mist.

All that talk of the Amyrlin Seat and Tar Valon attracted the sisters, of course. They heeled their horses up beside Mat and tried to take over. Well, Edesina hung back a little the way she did when Teslyn or Joline had the bit in her teeth, but the other two. . . .

"Who do you be talking about?" Teslyn demanded while Joline was still opening her mouth. "Egwene? There did be an Accepted named Egwene al'Vere, but she be a runaway."

"Egwene al'Vere is the one, Aes Sedai," Talmanes said politely. The man was always polite to Aes Sedai. "And she is no runaway. She is the Amyrlin Seat, my word on it." Edesina made a sound that would have been called a squeak coming from anyone but an Aes Sedai.

"Later for that," Mat muttered. Joline opened her mouth again, angrily. "Later, I said." That was not enough to stop the slender Green, but Teslyn laid a hand on her arm and murmured something, and that was. Joline still glared daggers, though, promising to drag out everything she wanted to know later. "The Band, Talmanes?"

"Oh. No, I only brought three banners of horse and four thousand mounted crossbowmen. I left three banners of horse and five of foot, a little short of crossbows, in Murandy with orders to move north to Andor. And the Mason's Banner, of course. Handy to have masons ready to hand if you need a bridge built or the like."

Mat squeezed his eyes shut for a moment. Six banners of horse and five of foot. And a banner of masons! The Band had only been two banners counting horse *and* foot when he left them in Salidar. He wished he had back half the gold he had handed over to Luca so freely. "How am I supposed to pay that many men?" he demanded. "I couldn't find enough dice games in a year!"

"Well, as to that, I made a small deal with King Roedran. Finished with, now, and not before time—I think he was about ready to turn on us; I will explain later—but the Band's coffers hold a year's pay and more. Besides, sooner or later the Dragon Reborn will give you estates, and grand ones. He has raised men to rule nations, so I hear, and you grew up with him."

This time, he did not fight the colors as they resolved into Rand and the Aes Sedai. It was an Aes Sedai, for sure. A hard woman, she looked. If Rand tried to give him any titles, he would stuff them down Rand's bloody throat is what he would do. Mat Cauthon had no liking for nobles—well, a few like Talmanes were all right; and Tuon; never forget Tuon—and he certainly had no bloody desire to become one! "That's as may be," was all he said, though.

Selucia cleared her throat loudly. She and Tuon moved their horses up beside Mat, and Tuon was so straight in her mare's saddle, so cool-eyed, cold-faced and regal, that he expected Selucia to start proclaiming her titles. She did nothing of the sort. Instead, she shifted on her dun and scowled at him, eyes like blue coals in a fire, then cleared her throat again. Very loudly. Ah.

"Tuon," Mat said, "allow me to present Lord Talmanes Delovinde of Cairhien. His family is distinguished and ancient, and he has added honors to its name." The little woman inclined her head. Perhaps all of an inch. "Talmanes, this is Tuon." So long as she called him Toy, she would get no titles from him. Selucia glared, eyes hotter than ever, impossible as that seemed.

Talmanes blinked in surprise, though, and bowed very low in his saddle. Vanin pulled the sagging brim of his hat lower, half hiding his face. He still avoided looking directly at Mat. So. It seemed the man had already told Talmanes exactly who Tuon was.

Growling under his breath, Mat leaned from the saddle to snatch his hat from the spear and pull up the *ashandarei*. He clapped the hat on his head. "We were ready to move on, Talmanes. Take us to where your men are waiting, and we'll see if we can have as good luck avoiding Seanchan on the way out of Altara as you had on the way in."

"We saw a good many Seanchan," Talmanes said, turning his bay to fall in beside Pips. "Though most of the men we saw seemed to be Altaran. They have camps scattered everywhere, it seems. Luckily, we saw none of those flying creatures I have heard tell of. But there is a problem, Mat. There was a landslide. I lost my rear guard and some of the packhorses. The pass is well and truly blocked, Mat. I sent three men to try climbing over with the orders sending the Band to Andor. One broke his neck, and another his leg."

Mat stopped Pips short. "I'm guessing this is the same pass Vanin was talking about?"

Talmanes nodded, and Vanin, waiting to fall in farther back, said, "Bloody right, it was. Passes don't grow on trees, not in mountains like the Damonas." He was no respecter of rank.

"Then you'll have to find another one," Mat told him. "I've heard you can find your way blindfolded at midnight. It should be easy for you." Flattery never hurt. Besides, he had heard that about the man.

Vanin made a sound like he was swallowing his tongue. "Find another pass?" he muttered. "Find another pass, the man says. You don't just go find another pass in new mountains like the Damonas. Why do you think I only knew the one?" He was shaken to admit that much. Before this, he had been adamant that he had only heard of it.

"What are you talking about?" Mat demanded, and Vanin explained. At great length, for him.

"An Aes Sedai explained it to me, once. You see, there's old mountains. They was there before the Breaking, maybe on the bottom of the sea or the like. They have passes all over, broad and gentle. You can ride into those and as long you keep your head and your direction and have enough supplies, sooner or later you come out the other side. And then there's mountains made during the Breaking." The fat man turned his head and spat copiously. "Passes in those are narrow, twisty things, and sometimes they aren't really what you'd call passes at all. Ride into one of those, and you can wander around till your food runs out trying to find a way to the other side. Loss of that pass is going to hurt a lot of folks who use it for what you might call untaxed goods, and men'll die before they find a new one that gets them all the way through. We go into the Damonas with that pass gone, likely we'll all die, too. Them as doesn't turn back in time and hasn't gotten their heads so turned around they can't find the way back."

Mat looked around, at Tuon, the Aes Sedai, at Olver. They were all depending on him to get them to safety, but his safe route out of Altara was not there any more. "Let's ride," he said. "I have to think." He had to bloody think for all he was worth.

CHAPTER
26

As If the World Were Fog

T oy set a fast pace through the forest, but Tuon rode close behind him—with Selucia at her side, of course—so she could listen in on him and Talmanes. Her own thoughts interfered with eavesdropping, however. So he had grown up with the Dragon Reborn, had he? The Dragon Reborn! And he had denied knowing anything at all of the man. That was one lie of his she had failed to catch, and she was good at catching lies. In Seandar, the undetected lie might be the one that killed you or sent you to the sale block as property. Had she known of his prevarication, she might have slapped his face rather than allowing him to kiss her. Now, *that* had been a shock, one she was not sure she had recovered from yet. Selucia had described being kissed by a man, but the actuality made the other woman's descriptions pale. No, she had to listen.

"You left *Estean* in charge?" Toy erupted, so loudly that a covey of gray doves burst from cover in the thin undergrowth with a mournful whirring sound. "The man's a fool!"

"Not too much of a fool to listen to Daerid," Talmanes replied calmly. He did not seem a man to get overly excited. He kept a careful watch, head swiveling constantly. Every so often he scanned the sky through the thick branches overhead, too. He had only heard of *raken*, yet he watched for them. His words were even crisper and quicker than

552

Toy's, and difficult to follow. These people all spoke so fast! "Carlomin and Reimon are not fools, Mat—at least, Reimon is only a fool sometimes—but neither will they listen to a commoner, no matter how much more he knows about warfare than they do. Edorion will, but I wanted him with me."

That red hand symbol Talmanes wore was intriguing. More than intriguing. Much more. Of an old and distinguished House, was he? But Toy was the one. He remembered Hawkwing's face. That seemed utterly impossible, yet his denial of it had plainly been a lie, as plain as the spots on a leopard. Could the Red Hand be Toy's sigil? But if so, what about his ring? She had almost fainted when she first saw that. Well, she had come as close to it as she had since childhood.

"That's going to change, Talmanes," Toy growled. "I let it go on too long as it is. If Reimon and the others command banners now, that makes them Banner-Generals. And you a Lieutenant-General. Daerid commands five banners, and that makes him a Lieutenant-General, too. Reimon and the others will obey his orders or they can go home. Come Tarmon Gai'don, I'm not going to have my skull split open because they bloody refuse to listen to somebody who doesn't have bloody estates."

Talmanes turned his horse to ride around a patch of briars, and everyone followed. The tangled vines seemed to have particularly long thorns, and hooked besides. "They will not like it, Mat, but they will not go home, either. You know that. Have you any ideas yet how we are to get out of Altara?"

"I'm thinking on it," Toy muttered. "I'm thinking on it. Those crossbowmen. . . ." He exhaled heavily. "That wasn't wise, Talmanes. For one thing, they're used to marching on their own feet. Half of them will have all they can do to stay in the saddle if we're moving fast, and we're going to have to. They can be useful in woods like these, or anywhere they have plenty of cover, but if we're on open ground, with no pikes, they'll be ridden down before they can loose a second flight."

In the distance, a lion coughed. In the distance, but it was still enough to make the horses whicker nervously and dance a few steps. Toy leaned forward on his gelding's neck and appeared to whisper in the animal's ear. It quieted immediately. So that had not been another of his fanciful tales after all. Remarkable.

"I picked men who could ride, Mat," Talmanes said once his bay stopped frisking. "And they all have the new crank." A touch of excitement entered his voice now. Even restrained men tended to warmth over weapons. "Three turns of the crank," his hands moved in a quick circle, demonstrating, "and the bowstring is latched. With a little training, a man can get off seven or eight quarrels in a minute. With a heavy crossbow."

Selucia made a small sound in her throat. She was right to be startled. If Talmanes was telling the truth, and he had no reason to lie that Tuon could find, then she had to obtain one of these marvelous cranks somehow. With one for a pattern, artisans could make more. Archers could shoot faster than crossbowmen, but they took longer to train, too. There were always more crossbowmen than archers.

"*Seven?*" Toy exclaimed incredulously. "That would be more than useful, but I never heard of such thing. Ever." He muttered that as if it had some special significance, then shook his head. "How did you come by it?"

"Seven or eight. There was a mechanic in Murandy who wanted to take a wagonload of things he had invented up to Caemlyn. There is a school of some sort there for scholars and inventors. He needed money for the journey, and he was willing to teach the Band's armorers to make the things. Smother your enemy with arrows at every opportunity. It is always better to kill your enemies far off than close at hand."

Selucia held her hands up so Tuon could see them, slim fingers moving quickly. WHAT IS THIS BAND THEY SPEAK OF? She used the proper form, inferior to superior, yet her impatience was almost palpable. Impatience with everything that was happening. Tuon kept few secrets from her, but some seemed advisable for the present. She would not put it past Selucia to return her to Ebou Dar forcibly, so she would not be breaking her word. A shadow's duties were many, and sometimes required paying the final sacrifice. She did not want to have to order Selucia's execution.

She replied in the imperative form. TOY'S PERSONAL ARMY, OBVIOUSLY. LISTEN AND WE MAY LEARN MORE.

Toy commanding an army seemed very odd. He was charming at times, even witty and amusing, but often a buffoon and always a rapscallion. He had seemed very much in his element as Tylin's pet. Yet he had seemed in his element among the show's performers, too, and with the *marath'damane* and the two escaped *damane*, and in the hell. That had been such a disappointment. Not even one fight! Events later had not compensated for that. Getting swept up in a street brawl was hardly the same as seeing fights in a hell. Which admittedly had been far more boring than rumor heard in Ebou Dar had made it seem. Toy had displayed an unexpected side of himself in that street brawl. A formidable man, though with a peculiar weakness. For some reason, she found that strangely endearing.

"Good advice," he said absently, tugging at the black scarf tied around his neck. She wondered about the scar he took such pains to hide. That he did was understandable. Why had he been hanged, and how had he survived? She could not ask. She did not mind lowering his eyes a little—in fact, it was enjoyable making him writhe; it took so little effort—but she did not want to destroy him. At least, not for the moment.

"Do you not recognize it?" Talmanes said. "It is from your book. King Roedran has two copies in his library. He has it memorized. The man thinks it will make him a great captain. He was so pleased with how our bargain worked out that he had a copy printed and bound for me."

Toy gave the other man a mystified look. "My book?"

"The one you told us about, Mat. *Fog and Steel*, by Madoc Comadrin."

"Oh, that book." Toy shrugged. "I read it a long time ago."

Tuon gritted her teeth. Her fingers flashed. WHEN WILL THEY STOP TALKING OF BOOKS AND GO BACK TO INTERESTING THINGS?

PERHAPS IF WE LISTEN WE MAY LEARN MORE, Selucia replied. Tuon glared at her, but the woman wore such an innocent look that she could not maintain her scowl. She laughed—softly, so as not to let Toy realize how close behind him she was—and Selucia joined in. Softly.

Toy had fallen silent, though, and Talmanes seemed content to leave it so. They rode in silence save for the sounds of the forest, birds singing, strange black-tailed squirrels chittering on branches. Tuon set herself to watching for omens, but nothing caught her eye. Bright-feathered birds darted among the trees. Once they spotted a herd of perhaps fifty tall, lean cattle with very long horns that stuck out almost straight to either side. The animals had heard them coming and were squared up, facing them. A bull tossed his head and pawed at the ground. Toy and Talmanes led the careful way around the herd, keeping their distance. She looked over her shoulder. The Redarms—why were they called that? She would have to ask Toy—the Redarms were leading the packhorses, but Gorderan had raised his crossbow, and the others had arrows nocked to their bows. So these cattle were dangerous. There were few omens concerning cattle, and she was relieved when the herd dwindled behind them. She had not come all this way to be killed by a cow. Or to see Toy killed by one.

After a time, Thom and Aludra came up to ride beside her. The woman glanced at her once, then looked straight ahead. The Taraboner's face, framed by those brightly beaded braids, was always wooden when she looked at her or Selucia, so clearly she was one of those who refused to accept the Return. She was watching Toy, and she looked . . . satisfied. As if something had been confirmed for her, perhaps. Why had Toy brought her along? Surely not for her fireworks. Those were pretty enough, but they could not compare with Sky Lights performed by even a half-trained *damane*.

Thom Merrilin was much more interesting. Patently, the white-haired old man was an experienced spy. Who had sent him to Ebou Dar? The White Tower seemed the most obvious candidate. He spent little time around the three who called themselves Aes Sedai, but a well-trained spy would not give himself away in that fashion. His presence troubled her. Until the last Aes Sedai was leashed, the White Tower was something to be wary of. Despite everything, she still had troubling thoughts at times that somehow, Toy was part of a White Tower plot. That was impossible unless some of the Aes Sedai were omniscient, yet the thought sometimes came to her.

"A strange coincidence, wouldn't you say, Master Merrilin?" she said. "Encountering part of Toy's army in the middle of an Altaran forest."

He stroked his long mustaches with a knuckle, failing to mask a small smile. "He's *ta'veren*, my Lady, and you can never tell what will happen around a *ta'veren*. It's always . . . interesting . . . when you travel with one of those. Mat has a tendency to find what he needs when he needs it. Sometimes before he knows he needs it."

She stared at him, but he seemed serious. "He's tied to the Pattern?" That was how the word would translate. "What is that supposed to mean?"

The old man's blue eyes widened in astonishment. "You don't know? But it's said Artur Hawkwing was the strongest *ta'veren* anyone had ever seen, perhaps as strong as Rand al'Thor. I'd have thought you of all people would. . . . Well, if you don't, you don't. *Ta'veren* are people the Pattern shapes itself around, people who were spun out by the Pattern itself to maintain the proper course of the weaving, perhaps to correct flaws that were creeping in. One of the Aes Sedai could explain better than I." As if she would have conversation with a *marath'damane*, or worse, a runaway *damane*.

"Thank you," she told him politely. "I think I've heard enough." *Ta'veren.* Ridiculous. These people and their endless superstitions! A small brown bird, surely a finch, flew out of a tall oak and circled widdershins three times above Toy's head before flying on. She had found her omen. Stay close to Toy. Not that she had any intention of doing otherwise. She had given her word, playing the game as it had to be played, and she had never broken her word in her life.

Little more than an hour after setting out, as a bird warbled ahead, Selucia pointed out the first sentry, a man with a crossbow up in the thick branches of a spreading oak cupping a hand to his mouth. Not a bird, then. More birdcalls heralded their advance, and soon they were riding through a tidy encampment. There were no tents, but the lances were neatly stacked, the horses picketed on scattered lines among the trees, near to the blankets of the men who would ride them, with a saddle or packsaddle at every animal's head. It would not take long for them to break camp and be on the march. Their fires were small and gave off little smoke.

As they rode in, men in dull green breastplates with that red hand on their coatsleeves and red scarves tied to their left arms began rising to their feet. She saw grizzled faces with scars and fresh young faces, all with their eyes on Toy and expressions she could only call eager. A growing murmur of voices rose, rustling through the trees like a breeze.

"It's Lord Mat."

"Lord Mat is back."

"Lord Mat's found us."

"Lord Mat."

Tuon exchanged glances with Selucia. The affection in those voices was unfeigned. That was rare, and often went with a commander who had a slack hand at discipline. But then, she expected any army of Toy's to be a ragtag affair, full of men who spent their time drinking and gambling. Only, these men looked no more ragtag than any regiment that had crossed a mountain range and ridden several hundred miles. No one looked unsteady on his feet with drink.

"Mostly we camp during the day and move at night to avoid being seen by the Seanchan," Talmanes said to Toy. "Just because we have seen none of those flying beasts does not mean some might not be around. Most of the Seanchan seem to be farther north or farther south, but apparently they have a camp not thirty miles north of here, and rumor says there is one of the creatures there."

"You seem pretty well informed," Toy said, studying the soldiers they passed. He nodded suddenly, as if he had reached a decision. He seemed grim and . . . could it be resigned?

"I am that, Mat. I brought half the scouts, and I also signed some Altarans who were fighting the Seanchan. Well, most of them seem to have been stealing horses more than anything else, but some were willing to give that up for a chance to really fight them. I think I know where most of the Seanchan camps are from the Malvide Narrows south to here."

Suddenly a man began to sing in a deep voice, and others joined in, the song spreading rapidly.

> *There're some delight in ale and wine,*
> *and some in girls with ankles fine,*
> *but my delight, yes, always mine,*
> *is to dance with Jak o' the Shadows.*

Every man in the camp was singing, now, thousands of voices roaring the song.

> *We'll toss the dice however they fall,*
> *and snuggle the girls be they short or tall,*
> *then follow Lord Mat whenever he calls,*
> *to dance with Jak o' the Shadows.*

They finished with shouts, laughing and clapping one another on the shoulder. Who under the Light was this Jak o' the Shadows?

Reining in, Toy raised the hand holding his odd spear. That was all, yet silence spread through the soldiers. So he was not soft with discipline. There were a few other reasons for soldiers to be fond of their officers, but the most common seemed unlikely to apply to Toy, of all people.

"Let's not let them know we're here until we want them to know,"

Toy said loudly. He was not orating, just making sure his voice carried. And the men heard, repeating his words over their shoulders to be passed back to men beyond the sound of his voice. "We're a long way from home, but I mean to get us home. So be ready to move, and move fast. The Band of the Red Hand can move faster than anybody else, and we're going to have to prove it." There was no cheering, but plenty of nods. Turning to Talmanes, he said, "Do you have maps?"

"The best to be found," Talmanes replied. "The Band has its own mapmaker, now. Master Roidelle already had good maps of everything from the Aryth Ocean to the Spine of the World, and since we crossed the Damonas, he and his assistants have been making new maps of the country we crossed. They even marked a map of eastern Altara with what we have learned of the Seanchan. Most of those camps are temporary, though. Soldiers heading somewhere else."

Selucia shifted in her saddle, and Tuon signed PATIENCE in high imperative form, a command. She kept her face smooth, but inside, she was furious. Knowing where soldiers were gave clues to where they were going. There had be some way to burn that map. That would be as important as laying hands on one of the crossbow cranks.

"I'll want to talk with Master Roidelle, too," Toy said.

Soldiers came to take the horses, and for a while all seemed confusion and milling about. A gap-toothed fellow took Akein's reins, and Tuon gave him explicit instructions on caring for the mare. He returned her a sour look along with his bow. Commoners in these lands seemed to believe themselves equal to everyone. Selucia gave the same sort of instructions to the lanky young man who took Rosebud. She thought that an appropriate name for a dresser's horse. The young man stared at Selucia's chest, until she slapped him. Hard. He only grinned and led the dun away rubbing his cheek. Tuon sighed. That was all very well for Selucia, but for herself, striking a commoner would lower her eyes for months.

Soon enough, though, she was settled on a folding stool with Selucia at her back, and stout Lopin presented them with tin cups full of dark tea, bowing quite properly to Selucia as well as to her. Not deeply enough, but the balding man did try. Her tea was honeyed to perfection, lightly, but then, he had served her often enough to know how she liked it. Activity bustled about them. Talmanes had a brief reunion with gray-haired Nerim, who apparently was his serving man, and happy to be reunited with him. At least, the thin man's normally mournful countenance actually flashed a momentary smile. That sort of thing should have been done in private. Leilwin and Domon allowed Master Charin to lead Olver off to explore the camp with Juilin and Thera—Thom and Aludra went too, to stretch their legs—then deliberately took stools close by. Leilwin even went so far as to stare unblinking at Tuon for a long moment. Selucia made a low sound very like a growl, but Tuon ignored the provocation and gestured Mistress Anan to bring her stool over beside her. Eventually, the traitors would be punished, and the thief, the property restored to its rightful owners, and the *marath'damane* leashed, but those things had to wait on what was more important.

Three more officers appeared, young noblemen with that red hand on their dark silk coats, and had their own reunion with Toy, with a great deal of laughing and hitting each other on the shoulder, which they seemed to take as a sign of fondness. She soon had them sorted out. Edorion was the dark, lean man with the serious expression except when smiling, Reimon the broad-shouldered fellow who smiled a great deal, and Carlomin the tall, slender one. Edorion was clean-shaven, while Reimon and Carlomin both had dark beards that were trimmed to points and glistened as if oiled. All three made much over the Aes Sedai, bowing deeply. They even bowed to Bethamin and Seta! Tuon shook her head.

"I've told you often enough it's a different world than you're used to," Mistress Anan murmured, "but you still don't quite believe it, do you?"

"Just because a thing is a certain way," Tuon replied, "doesn't mean it should be that way, even if it has been for a long time."

"Some might say the same of your people, my Lady."

"Some might." Tuon let it rest there, though she usually enjoyed her private conversations with the woman. Mistress Anan argued against leashing *marath'damane*, as might be expected, and even against keeping *da'covale* of all things, yet they were discussions rather than arguments, and Tuon had made her concede a few points. She had hopes of bringing the woman around eventually. Not today, though. She wanted her mind focused on Toy.

Master Roidelle appeared, a graying, round-faced man whose bulk strained his dark coat, followed by six fit-appearing younger men each carrying a long, cylindrical leather case. "I brought all the maps of Altara I have, my Lord," he told Talmanes in a musical accent as he bowed. Did everyone in these lands speak as if racing to get the words out? "Some cover the whole country, they do, some no more than a hundred square miles. The best are my own, of course, those I made these past weeks."

"Lord Mat will tell you what he wants to see," Talmanes said. "Shall we leave you to it, Mat?"

But Toy was already telling the mapmaker what he wanted, the map marked with the Seanchan camps. In short order it was sorted out from the others in one of the cases and spread on the ground with Toy squatting on his heels beside it. Master Roidelle sent one of his assistants running to fetch him a stool. He would have burst his coat buttons trying to imitate Toy, and likely have fallen over besides. Tuon stared at that map hungrily. How to get her hands on it?

Exchanging glances and laughing as if being snubbed were the funniest thing in the world, Talmanes and the other three men strolled toward Tuon. The Aes Sedai gathered around the map on the ground until Toy told them to quit peering over his shoulder. They moved off a little, Bethamin and Seta heeling them at a distance, and began talking quietly among themselves, occasionally glancing in his direction. If Toy had been paying any heed to their expressions, especially Joline's, he might have been worried in spite of the incredible *ter'angreal* Mistress Anan said he carried.

"We're about here, right?" he said, marking a spot with his finger. Master Roidelle murmured that they were. "So this is the camp where the *raken* supposedly is? The flying beast?" Another murmur of assent. "Good. What kind of camp is it? How many men are there?"

"Reportedly it's a supply camp, my Lord. For resupplying patrols." The young man returned with another folding stool, and the stout man eased himself down with a grunt. "Supposedly about a hundred soldiers, mostly Altaran, and about two hundred laborers, but I'm told there can be as many as five hundred more soldiers at times." A careful man, Master Roidelle.

Talmanes made one of those odd bows, with one foot forward, and the other three mirrored him. "My Lady," Talmanes said, "Vanin told me of your circumstances, and the promises Lord Mat made. I just want to tell you, he keeps his word."

"That he does, my Lady," Edorion murmured. "Always." Tuon motioned him to step aside so she could continue to watch Toy, and he did so with a surprised glance at Toy and another for her. She gave him a

stern look. The last thing she wanted was for these men to start imagining things. Not everything had fallen out as it had to, yet. There was
still a chance this could all go awry.

"Is he a lord or is he not?" she demanded.

"Excuse me," Talmanes said, "but would you say that again? I apologize. I must have dirt in my ears." She repeated herself carefully, but
it still took them a minute to puzzle out what she had said.

"Burn my soul, no," Reimon said finally with a laugh. He stroked
his beard. "Except to us. Lord enough for us."

"He dislikes nobles for the most part," Carlomin said. "I count it
an honor to be among the few he doesn't dislike."

"An honor," Reimon agreed. Edorion contented himself with
nodding.

"Soldiers, Master Roidelle," Toy said firmly. "Show me where the
soldiers are. And more than any few hundred."

"What is he doing?" Tuon said, frowning. "He can't think to *sneak*
this many men out of Altara even if he knows where every last soldier
is. There are always patrols, and sweeps by *raken*." Again they took
their time before answering. Perhaps she should try speaking very fast.

"We've seen no patrols in better than three hundred miles, and
no—*raken*?—no *raken*," Edorion said quietly. He was studying her. Too
late to stop his imaginings.

Reimon laughed again. "If I know Mat, he's planning us a battle.
The Band of the Red Hand rides to battle again. It's been too long, if
you ask me."

Selucia sniffed, and so did Mistress Anan. Tuon had to agree with
them. "A battle won't get you out of Altara," she said sharply.

"In that case," Talmanes said, "he's planning us a war." The other
three nodded agreement as if that were the most normal thing under
the Light. Reimon even laughed. He seemed to think everything was
humorous.

"Three thousand?" Toy said. "You're sure? Sure enough, man. Sure
enough will do. Vanin can locate them if they haven't moved too far."

Tuon looked at him, squatting there by the map, moving his fingers over its surface, and suddenly she saw him in a new light. A buffoon? No. A lion stuffed into a horse-stall might look like a peculiar
joke, but a lion on the high plains was something very different. Toy
was loose on the high plains, now. She felt a chill. What sort of man

had she entangled herself with? After all this time, she realized, she had hardly a clue.

The night was cool enough to send a small shiver through Perrin whenever the breeze gusted despite his fur-lined cloak. A halo around the fat crescent moon said there would be more rain before long. Thick clouds drifting across the moon made the pale light dim and strengthen, dim and strengthen, yet it was enough for his eyes. He sat Stepper just inside the edge of the trees and watched the cluster of four tall gray stone windmills in a clearing atop the ridge, their pale sails gleaming and shadowed by turns as they rotated. The machinery of the windmills groaned loudly. It seemed doubtful the Shaido even knew they should grease the works of the things. The stone aqueduct was a dark bar stretching east on high stone arches past abandoned farms and rail-fenced fields—the Shaido had planted, too early, with this much rain—toward another ridge and the lake beyond. Malden lay one more ridge west. He eased the heavy hammer in its loop on his belt. Malden and Faile. In a few hours, he would add a fifty-fourth knot to the leather cord in his pocket.

He cast his mind out. *Are you ready, Snowy Dawn?* he thought. *Are you close enough yet?* Wolves avoided towns, and with Shaido hunting parties in the surrounding forest during the day, they stayed farther from Malden than usual.

Patience, Young Bull, came the reply, touched with irritation. But then, Snowy Dawn was irascible by nature, a scarred male of considerable age for a wolf who had once killed a leopard by himself. Those old injuries sometimes kept him from sleeping very long at a stretch. *Two days from now, you said. We will be there. Now let me try to sleep. We must hunt well tomorrow, since we cannot hunt the day after.* They were images and smells rather than words, of course—"two days" was the sun crossing the sky twice, and "hunt" a pack trotting with noses into the breeze blended with the scent of deer—but Perrin's mind converted the images to words even as he saw them in his head.

Patience. Yes. Haste spoiled the work. But it was hard now that he was so close. Very hard.

A form appeared from the dark door at the base of the nearest windmill and waved an Aiel spear back and forth overhead. The groaning had convinced him the windmills must still be deserted—they had been when the Maidens scouted them earlier, and no one would put up with that noise any longer than they had to—but he had sent Gaul and some of the Maidens to be sure one way or another.

"Let's go, Mishima," he said, gathering his reins. "It's done." One way or another.

"How can you make out anything?" the Seanchan muttered. He avoided looking at Perrin, whose golden eyes would be glowing in the night. That had made the scarred man jump the first time he saw it. He did not smell amused tonight. He smelled tense. But he called softly over his shoulder. "Bring the carts ahead. Quickly, now. Quickly. And be quiet about it, or I'll have your ears!"

Perrin heeled his dun stallion forward without waiting on the others, or the six high-wheeled carts. Liberally greased axles made them as silent as carts could be. They still sounded noisy to him, the cart horses' hooves squelching in the mud, the carts themselves creaking as wood flexed and rubbed, but he doubted anyone else could have heard them fifty paces off, and maybe not closer. At the top of the gentle slope he dismounted and let Stepper's reins fall. A trained warhorse, the stallion would stand there as if hobbled so long as his reins hung down. The windmill heads squealed, turning slightly as the breeze shifted. The slowly spinning arms were long enough that Perrin could have touched one by jumping when it swung low. He stared toward the last ridge that hid Malden. Nothing grew there taller than a bush. Nothing moved in the darkness. Just one ridge between him and Faile. The Maidens had come outside to join Gaul, all of them still veiled.

"There was no one," Gaul said, not quietly. This close, the grinding of the windmills' gears would have swallowed quiet words.

"The dust has not been disturbed since I was here last," Sulin added.

Perrin scratched his beard. Just as well. Had they needed to kill Shaido, they could have carried away the bodies, but the dead would have been missed, and it would have drawn attention to the windmills and aqueduct. It might have started someone thinking about the water.

"Help me get the lids off, Gaul." There was no need for him to do that. It would save only minutes, but he needed to be doing something. Gaul simply stuck his spear through the harness holding his bowcase to join the others on his back.

The aqueduct ran along the ground on the ridgetop, between the four windmills, and stood shoulder-high on Perrin, less on Gaul, who climbed over. Just beyond the last pair of windmills, bronze handles on either side allowed them to lift off heavy pieces of stone two feet wide and five feet long until they had cleared a stretch of six feet. What the opening was used for, he did not know. There was another like it on the other side. Maybe to work on the flaps that made sure water flowed only one way, or to get inside to repair any leaks. He could see small ripples of motion as it streamed toward Malden, filling more than half the stone channel.

Mishima joined them and dismounted to stand peering uncertainly at Sulin and the Maidens. He probably believed the night hid his expression. He smelled wary, now. He was followed quickly by the first of the red-coated Seanchan soldiers scrambling up the muddy slope, each carrying two middling-sized jute sacks. Middling, but not heavy. Each contained only ten pounds. Eyeing the Aiel suspiciously, the wiry woman set her sacks down and slashed one open with her dagger. A handful of fine dark grains spilled on the muddy ground.

"Do that over the opening," Perrin said. "Make sure every grain goes into the water."

The wiry woman looked to Mishima, who said firmly, "Do as Lord Perrin commands, Arrata."

Perrin watched as she emptied the sack into the aqueduct, hands lifted over her head. The dark grains floated away toward Malden. He had dropped a pinch into a cup of water, hating to waste even that, and they took some time to absorb enough water to sink. Long enough to reach the big cistern in the town, he hoped. And if not, they could steep in the aqueduct itself. The cistern would still turn to forkroot tea eventually. The Light send it would be strong enough. With luck, maybe even strong enough to affect the *algai'd'siswai*. The Wise Ones who could channel were his target, but he would take any advantage he could gain. The Light send it did not grow strong faster than he expected. If those Wise Ones began staggering too soon, they might puzzle out the cause before he was ready. But all he could do was go ahead as if he knew exactly. That, and pray.

By the time the second sack was being poured into the stone channel, the others began crowding up the slope. First came Seonid, a short woman holding her dark divided skirts up out of the mud. Shifting his attention from the Maidens to her, Mishima made one of those small gestures to ward off evil. Strange that they could believe a thing like that worked. The soldiers lined up with their sacks stared at her, wide-eyed for the most part, and shifted their feet. The Seanchan were none too easy about working with Aes Sedai. Her Warders, Furen and Teryl, were at her heels, each with a hand resting on his sword hilt. They were just as uneasy about the Seanchan. The one was dark with gray streaking his curly black hair, the other fair and young, with curled mustaches, yet they were alike as two beans, tall, lean and hard. Rovair Kirklin came a little behind them, a compact man with dark receding hair and a glum expression. He did not like being separated from Masuri. All three of the men had small bundles containing food strapped to their backs and fat waterskins hanging from their shoulders. A lanky man rested his sacks on the side of the opening as the wiry woman headed downslope to fetch more. The carts were piled high with them.

"Remember," Perrin told Seonid, "the biggest danger will be getting from the cistern to the fortress. You'll have to use the guardwalk on the wall, and there might be Shaido in the town even at this hour." Galina had seemed unsure on that. Thunder boomed hollowly in the distance, then again. "Maybe you'll have rain to hide you."

"Thank you," she said icily. Her moonshadowed face was a mask of Aes Sedai serenity, but her scent spiked with indignation. "I would not have known any of that if you had not told me." The next moment her expression softened, and she laid a hand on his arm. "I know you are worried about her. We will do what can be done." Her tone was not exactly warm—it never was—but not so chill as before, and her scent had mellowed to sympathy.

Teryl lifted her up onto the edge of the aqueduct—the Seanchan emptying forkroot into the thing, a tall fellow with almost as many scars as Mishima, nearly dropped his sack—and she grimaced faintly before swinging her legs over and lowering herself into the water with a small gasp. It must have been cold. Ducking her head, she moved out of sight toward Malden. Furen climbed in after her, then Teryl, and finally Rovair. They had to bend sharply to fit under the roof of the aqueduct.

Elyas clapped Perrin on the shoulder before hoisting himself up. "Should have trimmed my beard short like yours to keep it out of that," he said, gazing down at the water. That graying beard, ruffled by the breeze, spread across his chest. For that matter, his hair, gathered at the back of his neck with a leather cord, hung to his waist. He carried a small bundle of food and a waterskin, too. "Still, a cold bath helps a man keep his mind off his troubles."

"I thought that was for keeping your mind off women," Perrin said. He was in no mood for joking, but he could not expect everyone to be as grim as he was.

Elyas laughed. "What else causes a man's troubles?" He disappeared into the water, and Tallanvor replaced him.

Perrin caught his dark coatsleeve. "No heroics, mind." He had been of two minds about letting the man be part of this.

"No heroics, my Lord," Tallanvor agreed. For the first time in a long time, he looked eager. The smell of him quivered with eagerness. But there was an edge of caution in it, too. That caution was the only reason he was not back in their camp. "I won't put Maighdin at risk. Or the Lady Faile. I just want to see Maighdin that much quicker."

Perrin nodded and let him go. He could understand that. Part of him wanted to climb into the aqueduct, too. To see Faile again that much quicker. But every piece of the work had to be done properly, and he had other tasks. Besides, if he were actually inside Malden, he was not sure he could restrain himself from trying to find her. He could not catch his own scent, of course, but he doubted there was any caution in it now. The windmill heads turned again with loud squeaks as the wind shifted back. At least it never seemed to die up here. Any stoppage of the water flow would be disastrous.

The ridgetop was becoming crowded, now. Twenty of Faile's hangers-on were waiting their turn at the aqueduct, all that remained save the two who were spying on Masema. The women wore men's coats and breeches and had their hair cut short except for a tail at the back in imitation of the Aiel, though no Aiel would have worn a sword as they did. Many of the Tairen men had shaved their beards because Aiel did not wear them. Behind them fifty Two Rivers men carried halberds and unstrung bows, their bowstrings safely tucked away inside their coats and each with three bristling quivers tied to his back along with a parcel of food. Every man in the camp had volunteered for this, and Perrin had had to let them choose lots. He had considered doubling the number, or more. Hangers-on and Two Rivers men had their bundles of food and their waterskins. The constant flow of Seanchan soldiers continued, carrying full sacks up the slope and empty sacks back down. They were disciplined. When a man slipped in the mud and fell, as happened with some regularity, there was no cursing or even mutters. They just got up and went ahead.

Selande Darengil, wearing a dark coat with six horizontal stripes of color across the chest, stopped to offer Perrin her hand. She only came up to his chest, but Elyas claimed she handled the sword at her hip credibly. Perrin no longer thought she and the others were fools—well, not all the time—in spite of their attempts to copy Aiel ways. With differences, of course. The tail of dark hair at Selande's nape was tied with a length of dark ribbon. There was no fear in her scent, only determination. "Thank you for allowing us to be part of this, my Lord," she said in that precise Cairhienin accent. "We will not let you down. Or the Lady Faile."

"I know you won't," he said, shaking her hand. There had been a time when she had been pointed about serving Faile, and not him. He shook the hand of every one of them before they climbed into the aqueduct. They all smelled determined. So did Ban al'Seen, who commanded the Two Rivers men going into Malden.

"When Faile and the others come, wedge the outer doors shut, Ban." Perrin had told him this before, but he could not help repeating himself. "Then see if you can get them back up the aqueduct." That fortress had not kept the Shaido out the first time, and if anything went wrong, he doubted it would keep them out this time either. He did not mean to renege on his bargain with the Seanchan—the Shaido were going to pay for what they had done to Faile, and besides, he could not leave them behind to continue ravaging the countryside— but he wanted her out of harm's way as soon as possible.

Ban propped his bowstave and halberd against the aqueduct and hoisted himself up to reach a hand down inside. When he lowered himself back to the ground, he wiped his damp hand on his coat then rubbed the side of his prominent nose. "Below the water, it's coated with something feels like pond slime. We're going to have a hard enough time getting down that last slope without sliding the whole way, Lord Perrin, much less trying to climb it again. I expect the best thing is to wait in that fortress till you reach us."

Perrin sighed. He had thought of sending ropes, but they would have needed nearly two miles of it to span that last slope, a lot to be carried, and if any Shaido spotted the butt end of it in the Malden end of the aqueduct, they would search every nook and cranny in the town.

A small risk, perhaps, yet the bitter loss that might result made it loom large. "I'll be there as fast as I can, Ban. I promise you that."

He shook hands with every one of them, too. Lantern-jawed Tod al'Caar and Leof Torfinn, with a white streak through his hair where a scar ran, given to him by Trollocs. Young Kenly Maerin, who was making a stab at growing a beard again unfortunately, and Bili Adarra, who was almost as wide as Perrin if a hand shorter. Bili was a distant cousin, and some of the closest kin Perrin had living. He had grown up with many of these men, though some were a few years older than he. Some were a few years younger, too. By now, he knew the men from down to Deven Ride and up to Watch Hill as well as he did those from around Emond's Field. He had more reason than Faile alone to reach that fortress as fast as he could.

Had al'Lora, a lean fellow with thick mustaches like a Taraboner, was the last of the Two Rivers men. As he climbed into the aqueduct, Gaul appeared, face still veiled and four spears gripped in the hand that held his bull-hide buckler. He put a hand on the edge of the aqueduct and leapt up to sit on the stone coping.

"You're going in?" Perrin said in surprise.

"The Maidens can do any scouting you need, Perrin Aybara." The big Aiel glanced over his shoulder toward the Maidens. Perrin thought he scowled, though it was hard to be sure because of the black veil that hid all but his eyes. "I heard them talking when they thought I was not listening. Unlike your wife and the others, Chiad is properly *gai'shain*. Bain, too, but I care nothing about her. Chiad still has the rest of her year and a day to serve after we rescue her. When a man has a woman as *gai'shain*, or a woman a man, sometimes a marriage wreath is made as soon as white is put off. It is not uncommon. But I heard the Maidens say they would reach Chiad first, to keep her from me." Behind him, Sulin's finger flashed in Maiden handtalk, and one of the others slapped a hand over her mouth as if stifling laughter. So they had been goading him. Maybe they were not so hard against his suit for Chiad as they pretended. Or maybe there was something Perrin was missing. Aiel humor could be rough.

Gaul slipped into the water. He had to bend almost parallel to the surface to get under the aqueduct's top. Perrin stared at the opening. So easy to follow Gaul. Turning away was hard. The line of Seanchan soldiers still snaked up and down the slope.

"Mishima, I'm going back to my camp. Grady will take you to yours when you're done here. Do what you can to blur the tracks before you go."

"Very well, my Lord. I've told off some men to scrape grease from the axles and grease these windmills. They sound as if they could seize up any minute. We can do those at the far ridge, too."

Taking up Stepper's reins, Perrin looked up at the slow-turning sails. Slow, but steady. They had never been made to turn fast. "And if some Shaido decide to come out here tomorrow and wonder where the fresh grease came from?"

Mishima regarded him for a long moment, his face half-hidden by moonshadows. For once, he did not seem put off by glowing yellow eyes. His scent. . . . He smelled as if he saw something unexpected. "The Banner-General was right about you," he said slowly.

"What did she say?"

"You'll have to ask her, my Lord."

Perrin rode down the slope and back to the trees thinking how easy it would be to turn around. Gallenne could handle everything from here. It was all laid out. Except that the Mayener believed every battle climaxed with a grand charge of horse. And preferably began with one, too. How long would he stick to the plan? Arganda was more sensible, but he was so anxious for Queen Alliandre that he might well order that charge, as well. That left himself. The breeze gusted hard, and he pulled his cloak around him.

Grady, elbows on his knees, was in a small clearing sitting on a half-worked mossy stone that was partially sunken into the ground and no doubt left over from building the aqueduct. A few others like it stood around. The breeze kept his scent from Perrin's nose. He did not look up until Perrin drew rein in front of him. The gateway they had used to come here still stood open, showing another clearing among tall trees, not far from where the Seanchan were now camped. It might have been easier to have had them set up close to Perrin's camp, but he wanted to keep the Aes Sedai and Wise Ones as far from the *sul'dam* and *damane* as possible. He was not afraid of the Seanchan breaking Tylee's word, but the Aes Sedai and Wise Ones practically came down with the pip just thinking about *damane*. Probably the Wise Ones and Annoura would stay their hands for the time being. Probably. Masuri, he was not so sure of. In a number of ways. Better to keep a few leagues between them for as long as it could be managed.

"Are you all right, Grady?" The man's weathered face seemed to have new lines in it. That might have been a trick of moonshadows cast by the trees, but Perrin did not think so. The carts had passed through the gateway easily, but was it a little smaller than the first he had seen Grady make?

"Just tired a little, my Lord," Grady said wearily. He remained seated with his elbows on his knees. "All this Traveling we've been doing lately. . . . Well, I couldn't have held the gateway open long enough for all those soldiers to ride through yesterday. That's why I've taken to tying them off."

Perrin nodded. Both of the Asha'man were tired. Channeling took strength out of a man as surely as swinging a hammer all day at a forge. More so, in truth. The man with the hammer could keep going far longer than any Asha'man. That was why the aqueduct was the route into Malden and not a gateway, why there would be no gateway to bring Faile and the others out again, much as Perrin wished there could be. The two Asha'man only had so much more left in them until they could rest, and that little had to be used where it was needed most. Light, but that was a hard thought. Only, if Grady or Neald fell one gateway short of what was needed, a lot of men were going to die. A hard decision.

"I'm going to need you and Neald the day after tomorrow." That was like saying he needed air. Without the Asha'man, everything became impossible. "You're going to be busy then." Another gross understatement.

"Busy as a one-armed man plastering a ceiling, my Lord."

"Are you up to it?"

"Have to be, don't I, my Lord."

Perrin nodded again. You did what had to be done. "Send me back to our camp. After you return Mishima and his people to his, you and the Maidens can sleep there if you'd like." That would spare Grady a little against two days from now.

"Don't know about the Maidens, my Lord, but I'd as soon come on home tonight." He turned his head to look at the gateway without rising, and it dwindled in the reverse of how it had opened, the view through it seeming to rotate as it narrowed, finishing with a vertical slash of silvery blue light that left a faint purplish bar in Perrin's vision when it winked out. "Those *damane* fair make my skin crawl. They don't want to be free."

"How would you know that?"

"I talked to some of them when none of those *sul'dam* was close by. Soon as I brought up maybe they'd like those leashes off, just hinting like, they started screaming for the *sul'dam*. The *damane* were crying, and the *sul'dam* petting them and stroking them and glaring daggers at me. Fair made my skin crawl."

Stepper stamped an impatient hoof, and Perrin patted the stallion's neck. Grady was lucky those *sul'dam* had let him go with a whole hide. "Whatever happens with the *damane*, Grady, it won't be this week, or next. And it won't be us who fixes it. So you let the *damane* be. We have a job of work in front of us that needs doing." And a deal with the Dark One to do it. He pushed the thought away. Anyway, it had grown hard to think of Tylee Khirgan being on the Dark One's side. Or Mishima. "You understand that?"

"I understand, my Lord. I'm just saying it makes my skin crawl."

At last another silvery blue slash appeared, widening into an opening that showed a clearing among large, widely spaced trees and a low stone outcrop. Leaning low on Stepper's neck, Perrin rode through. The gateway winked out behind him, and he rode on through the trees until he came to the large clearing where the camp lay, near what had once been the tiny village of Brytan, a collection of flea-riddled hovels that the most rain-soaked night could not tempt a man into. The sentries up in the trees gave no warnings, of course. They recognized him.

He wanted nothing so much as he wanted his blankets right then. Well, Faile, certainly, but lacking her, he wanted to be alone in the dark. Likely, he would fail to find sleep again, but he would spend the night as he had so often before, thinking of her, remembering her. Short of the ten-pace wide thicket of sharpened stakes that surrounded the camp, though, he reined in. A *raken* was crouched just outside the stakes, its long gray neck lowered so a woman in a hooded brown coat could scratch its leathery snout. Her hood hung down her back, revealing short-cropped hair and a hard, narrow face. She looked at Perrin as if she recognized him, but went right on scratching. The saddle on the creature's back had places for two riders. A messenger had come, it seemed. He turned into one of the narrow, angled lanes through the stakes that had been left to allow horses through. Just not quickly.

Most everybody had turned in already. He sensed movement on the horselines, in the heart of the camp, likely some of the Cairhienin grooms or farriers, but the patched canvas tents and small huts of woven evergreen branches, now long since brown, lay dark and quiet. Nothing moved among the low Aiel tents, and only a few sentries walking up and down in the nearest Mayener section of the camp. The Mayeners and Ghealdanin put little trust in the Two Rivers men in the trees. His tall, red-striped tent was alight, however, and the shadows of a number of people shifted on the tent walls. When he climbed down in front of the tent, Athan Chandin appeared to take the reins and knuckle his forehead while he hunched a sort of bow. Athan was a good bowshot or he would not have been here, but he had a truckling manner. Perrin went in unpinning his cloak.

"There you are," Berelain said brightly. She must have dressed hastily, because her long black hair looked as though it had had just a lick and a promise from a brush, but her high-necked gray riding dress appeared neat and fresh. Her serving women never let her don anything unless it was freshly ironed. She held out a silver winecup for Breane to refill from a long-necked wine pitcher, which the Cairhienin woman did with a grimace. Faile's maid disliked Berelain with a passion. Berelain seemed not to notice, though. "Forgive me for entertaining in your tent, but the Banner-General wanted to see you, and I thought I'd keep her company. She's been telling us about some Whitecloaks."

Balwer was standing unobtrusively in a corner—the bird-like little man could be as unnoticeable as a lizard on a branch when he wished to be—but his scent sharpened at the mention of Whitecloaks.

Tylee, her shoulders straining a coat like that of the flier, made a straight-legged bow while keeping one eye on Annoura. She seemed to believe the Aes Sedai might turn into ravening wild dogs at any moment. Perrin thought she smelled of distress, though none showed on her dark face. "My Lord, I have two pieces of news I felt I had to bring you immediately. Have you begun putting the forkroot into the town's water?"

"I have," he said worriedly, tossing his cloak down atop one of the brass-banded chests. Tylee sighed. "I told you I would. I'd have done it two days ago if that fool woman in Almizar hadn't dragged her heels so. What's happened?"

"Forgive me," Lini announced, "but I was roused from my blankets, and I would like to return to them. Does anyone require anything else of me tonight?" There were no curtsies or 'my Lords' from the frail-appearing woman with her white hair in a loose braid for sleeping. Unlike with Berelain, her brown dress looked hastily donned, unusual for her. Her scent was crisp and sharp with disapproval. She was one of those who believed the ridiculous tale that Perrin had slept with Berelain on the very night after Faile had been captured. She managed to avoid looking at him while her gaze swept around the tent's interior.

"I'll have some more wine," Aram announced, holding out his cup. Grim-faced and haggard in a red-striped coat, his eyes hollow, he was attempting to lounge in one of the folding camp chairs, but the sword strapped to his back made leaning against the gilt-edged back impossible. Breane started toward him.

"He's had enough," Lini said sharply, and Breane turned away. Lini had a firm hand with Faile's servants.

Aram muttered an oath and leaped to his feet, tossing his cup down on the flowered carpet that served as a floor. "I might as well go somewhere I won't have some old woman nagging at me every time I take a drink." He gave Perrin a sullen glare before stalking out of the tent. Doubtless on his way to Masema's camp. He had pleaded to be one of the party sent into Malden, but his hot head could not be trusted with that.

"You can go, Lini," Berelain said. "Breane can look after us well enough." A snort was the acknowledgment Lini gave—she made it sound almost delicate—before she stalked out, stiff-backed and reeking of disapproval. And still not looking at Perrin.

"Forgive me, my Lord," Tylee drawled in careful tones, "but you seem to run your household more . . . loosely . . . than I'm accustomed to."

"It's our way, Banner-General," Perrin said, picking up Aram's cup. No need to dirty another. "Nobody around here is property." If that sounded sharp, so be it. He had come to like Tylee after a fashion, but these Seanchan had ways that would make a goat gag. He took the pitcher from Breane—she actually tried to hold onto it for a moment, frowning at him as if she would deny him a drink—and poured for himself before handing it back. She snatched the pitcher out of his hand. "Now, what happened? What about these Whitecloaks?"

"I sent *raken* out scouting as far as they could go just before dawn, and again just after sunset. One of the fliers tonight turned back sooner than expected. She saw seven thousand Children of the Light on the move not fifty miles from my camp."

"On the move toward you?" Perrin frowned at his wine instead of drinking. "Seven thousand seems a very exact count to make in the dark."

"It seems these men, they are deserters," Annoura broke in. "At least, the Banner-General sees them so." In gray silk, she appeared as neat as if she had spent an hour dressing. Her thrusting nose made her look like a crow wearing beaded braids as she peered at Tylee, and the Banner-General a particularly interesting bit of carrion. She held a winecup, but it seemed untouched. "I have heard rumors that Pedron Niall died fighting the Seanchan, but apparently Eamon Valda, who replaced Niall, swore fealty to the Seanchan Empress." Tylee mouthed, "may she live forever," under her breath; Perrin doubted anyone but himself heard. Balwer opened his mouth, too, but closed it again without speaking. The Whitecloaks were a bugbear to him. "Something over a month ago, however," the Gray sister went on, "Galad Damodred killed Valda and led seven thousand Whitecloaks to leave the Seanchan cause. A pity he became enmeshed with Whitecloaks, but perhaps some good has come of it. In any case, it appears there is a standing order that these men are all to be killed as soon as found. I have summed it up nicely, yes, Banner-General?"

Tylee's hand twitched as if it wanted to make one of those signs against evil. "That's a fair summing up," she said. To Perrin, not Annoura. The Seanchan woman seemed to find speaking to an Aes Sedai difficult. "Except the part about good coming of it. Oath-breaking and desertion can never be called good."

"I take it they're not moving toward you, or you'd have said." Perrin put a hint of question into that, though there was no question in his mind.

"North," Tylee answered. "They're heading north." Balwer half opened his mouth again, then shut it with a click of teeth.

"If you have advice," Perrin told him, "then give it. But I don't care how many Whitecloaks desert the Seanchan. Faile is the *only* thing I care about. And I don't think the Banner-General will give up the chance to collar three or four hundred more *damane* to chase after them." Berelain grimaced. Annoura's face remained smooth, but she took a long swallow of her wine. None of the Aes Sedai felt very complacent about that part of the plan. None of the Wise Ones did, either.

"I will not," Tylee said firmly. "I think I'll take some wine after all." Breane took a deep breath before moving to comply, and a hint of fear entered her scent. Apparently the tall dark woman intimidated her.

"I won't deny I would enjoy a chance to strike a blow at the White-cloaks," Balwer said in that dry-as-dust voice, "but in truth, I feel I owe this Galad Damodred a debt of gratitude." Perhaps his grudge was against this Valda personally. "In any case, you have no need of my advice here. Events are in motion in Malden, and if they weren't, I doubt you'd hold back even a day. Nor would I have advised it, my Lord. If I may be so bold, I am quite fond of the Lady Faile."

"You may," Perrin told him. "Banner-General, you said two pieces of news?"

The Seanchan took the proffered winecup from Breane and looked at him so levelly it was clear she was avoiding a glance at the others in the tent. "May we speak alone?" she asked quietly.

Berelain glided across the carpet to rest a hand on his arm and smile up at him. "Annoura and I don't mind leaving," she said. Light, how could anyone believe there was anything between him and her? She was as beautiful as ever, true, yet the scent that had minded him of a hunting cat was so long gone from her smell that he barely remembered it. The bedrock of her scent was patience and resolve, now. She had come to accept that he loved Faile and only Faile, and she seemed as determined to see Faile freed as he was.

"You can stay," he said. "Whatever you have to say, Banner-General, you can say in front of everyone here."

Tylee hesitated, glancing at Annoura. "There are two large parties of Aiel heading toward Malden," she said at last, reluctantly. "One to the southeast, one to the southwest. The *morat'raken* estimate they could be there in three days."

Suddenly, everything seemed to ripple in Perrin's sight. He felt *himself* ripple. Breane gave a cry and dropped the pitcher. The world rippled again, and Berelain clutched his arm. Tylee's hand seemed frozen in that odd gesture, thumb and forefinger forming a crescent. Everything rippled for a third time, and Perrin felt as if he were made of fog, as if the world were fog with a high wind coming. Berelain shuddered, and he put a comforting arm around her. She clung to him, trembling. Silence and the scent of fear filled the tent. He could hear voices being raised outside, and they sounded afraid, too.

"What was that?' Tylee demanded finally.

"I don't know." Annoura's face remained serene, but her voice was unsteady. "Light, I have no idea."

"It doesn't matter what it was," Perrin told them. He ignored their stares. "In three days, it will all be over. That's all that matters." Faile was all that mattered.

The sun stood short of its noonday peak, but Faile already felt harassed. The water for Sevanna's morning bath—she bathed twice a day, now!—had not been hot enough, and Faile had been beaten along with everyone else, although she and Alliandre had only been there to scrub the woman's back. More than twenty wetlander *gai'shain* had begged to be allowed to swear fealty just since sunrise. Three had suggested rising up, pointing out that there were more *gai'shain* in all these tents than Shaido. They had seemed to listen when she pointed out that nearly all of the Aiel knew how to use a spear, while most of the wetlanders were farmers or craftsfolk. Few had ever held a weapon, and fewer still used one. They had seemed to listen, but this was the first day anyone had suggested such a thing right after swearing. Usually they took several days to work themselves around to it. The pressure was building. Toward a slaughter unless she could thwart it. And now this. . . .

"It is only a game, Faile Bashere," Rolan said, towering over her as they walked along one of the muddy streets that wound through the Shaido tents. He sounded amused, and a very small smile curved his lips. A beautiful man to be sure.

"A kissing game, you said." She shifted the lengths of striped toweling folded over her arm to draw his attention. "I have work to do, and no time for games. Especially kissing games."

She could see a few Aiel, several of them men staggering drunk even at this hour, but most of the people in the street were wetlanders wearing dirty *gai'shain* robes or children splashing happily in the mud puddles left by the night's heavy rain. The street was thronged with men and women in mud-stained white carrying baskets or buckets or pots. Some actually went about chores. There were so many *gai'shain* in the camp that there really was not enough work to go around. That would not stop a Shaido from ordering what were seen as idle hands to some work or other if those hands stuck out of white sleeves, however, even if it was make-work. To avoid having to dig useless holes in muddy fields or scrub pots that were already clean, a good many of the *gai'shain* had taken to carrying something that made them look as if they were working. That did not help anyone avoid the real work, but it did help avert the other kind. Faile did not have to worry about that with most of the Shaido, not so long as she wore those thick golden chains around her waist and neck, but the necklace and belt were inadequate for deterring Wise Ones. She had scrubbed clean pots for some of them. And sometimes had been punished for not being available when Sevanna wanted her. Thus the toweling.

"We could start with a kissing game children play," he said, "though the forfeits in that are sometimes embarrassing. In the game adults play, the forfeits are fun. Losing can be as pleasant as winning."

She could not help laughing. The man certainly was persistent. Suddenly she saw Galina hurrying through the crowd in her direction, holding her white silk robes up out of the mud, eyes searching avidly. Faile had heard the woman was allowed clothing again as of this morning. Of course, she had never been without the tall necklace and wide belt of gold and firedrops. A cap of hair less than an inch long covered her head, and of all things, a large red bow was pinned in it. It seemed unlikely that was by the woman's choice. Only a face Faile could not put an age to convinced her that Galina really was Aes Sedai. Beyond that, she was unsure of anything about her except the danger she presented. Galina spotted her and stopped dead, hands kneading her robes. The Aes Sedai eyed Rolan uncertainly.

"I'll have to think on it, Rolan." She was not about to chase him away until she was sure of Galina. "I need time to think."

"Women always want time to think. Think on forgetting your troubles in the pleasure of a harmless game."

The finger he drew softly down her cheek before walking away made her shiver. To Aiel, touching someone's cheek in public was as much as a kiss. It surely had felt like a kiss to her. Harmless? Somehow, she doubted that any game that involved kissing Rolan would end with just kissing. Luckily, she would not have to find out—or hide anything from Perrin—if Galina proved true. If.

The Aes Sedai darted to her as soon as Rolan was gone. "Where is it?" Galina demanded, seizing her arm. "Tell me! I know you have it. You must have it!" The woman sounded almost pleading. Therava's treatment of her had shattered that fabled Aes Sedai composure.

Faile shook off her grip. "First tell me again that you will take my friends and me with you when you go. Tell me straight out. And tell me when you are going."

"Don't you *dare* talk to me that way," Galina hissed.

Faile saw black flecks floating in her vision before she realized that she had been slapped. To her surprise, she slapped the other woman back as hard as she could, staggering her. She refrained from putting a hand to her stinging face, but Galina rubbed her own cheek, her eyes wide with shock. Faile steeled herself, perhaps for a blow with the Power or something worse, but nothing happened. Some of the passing *gai'shain* stared at them, but none stopped or even slowed. Anything that looked like a gathering of *gai'shain* would draw Shaido eyes, and earn punishments for everyone involved.

"Tell me," she said again.

"I will take you and your friends with me," Galina practically snarled, snatching her hand down. "I leave tomorrow. *If* you have it. If not, Sevanna will know who you are within the hour!" Well, that was certainly speaking straight out.

"It's hidden in the town. I'll get it for you now."

But as she turned, Galina grabbed her arm again. The Aes Sedai's eyes darted, and she lowered her voice as if suddenly concerned about being overheard. She sounded frightened. "No. I'll take no chances on anyone seeing. You'll give it to me tomorrow morning. In the town. We'll meet there. In the south end of the town. I'll mark the building. With a red scarf."

Faile blinked. The southern half of Malden was a burned-out shell. "Why there?" she asked incredulously.

"Because no one goes there, fool! Because no one will see us!" Galina's eyes were still darting. "Tomorrow morning, early. Fail me, and you'll regret it!" Gathering the skirts of her silk robe, she scurried away into the crowd.

Faile frowned as she watched the woman go. She should have felt exultation, but she did not. Galina seemed almost a wild thing, unpredictable. Still, Aes Sedai could not lie. There seemed no way for her to wriggle out of her promise. And if she found one, there were still her own plans for an escape, though those seemed no further along, if much more dangerous, than they had when first begun. Which left Rolan. And his kissing games. Galina had to prove true. She had to.

CHAPTER
27

A Plain Wooden Box

T he midday Altaran sun was warm, though a gusting breeze
sometimes whipped Rand's cloak. They had been on the hilltop
for two hours, now. A great mass of dark clouds creeping down
from the north above blue-gray haze spoke of rain to come, and a cool-
ing. Andor lay only a few miles in that direction across low, forested
hills of oak and pine, leatherleaf and sourgum. That border had seen
countless generations of cattle raids going in both directions. Was
Elayne watching it rain in Caemlyn? That lay a good hundred and fifty
leagues east, too far for her to be more than a faint presence in the back
of his head. Aviendha, in Arad Doman, was fainter still. He had not
considered that the Wise Ones would take her along. Still, she would
be safe among tens of thousands of Aiel, as safe as Elayne behind Caemlyn's walls. Tai'daishar stamped a hoof and tossed his head, eager to be
moving. Rand patted the big black's neck. The stallion could reach the
border in under an hour, but their way was west today. A short way
west in just a short while, now.

He had to impress at today's meeting, and he had chosen his garb
with care. The Crown of Swords sat on his head for more reason than
making an impression, though. Half the small swords nestled among
the wide band of laurel leaves pointed down, making it uncomfortable
to wear, giving constant reminders of its weight, in gold and in re-

sponsibility. A small chip in one of those laurel leaves dug at his temple to remind him of the battle against the Seanchan where it had been made. A battle lost when he could not afford to lose. His dark green silk coat was embroidered in gold on the sleeves, shoulders and high collar, a gold-inlaid buckle in the shape of a dragon fastened his swordbelt, and he had the Dragon Scepter in hand, a two-foot length of spearhead with a long green-and-white tassel below the polished steel point. If the Daughter of the Nine Moons recognized it for part of a Seanchan spear, she must also see the dragons that Maidens had carved winding around the remaining haft. Today, he wore no gloves. The golden-maned dragonheads on the backs of his hands glittered metallically in the sun. However high she stood among the Seanchan, she would know whom she faced.

A fool. Lews Therin's wild laughter echoed inside his head. *A fool to walk into a trap.* Rand ignored the madman. It might be a trap, but he was ready to spring it if it was. It was worth the risk. He needed this truce. He could crush the Seanchan, but at what cost in blood, and in time he might not have? He glanced north again. The sky above Andor was clear except for a few high white clouds, drifting wisps. The Last Battle was coming. He had to take the risk.

Min, toying with the reins of her gray mare nearby, was feeling smug, and that irritated him. She had inveigled a promise from him in a weak moment and refused to release him. He could just break it. He should break it. As if she had heard his thoughts, she looked at him. Her face, surrounded by dark shoulder-length ringlets, was smooth, but the bond suddenly carried suspicion and hints of anger. She seemed to be trying to suppress both, yet she adjusted the cuffs of her ornately embroidered red coat the way she did when checking her knives. Of course, she would not use one of her blades on him. Of course not.

A woman's love can be violent, Lews Therin murmured. *Sometimes they hurt a man worse than they think they have, worse than they mean to. Sometimes, they're even sorry afterwards.* He sounded sane for the moment, but Rand shoved the voice down.

"You should let us scout farther out, Rand al'Thor," Nandera said. She and the two dozen other Maidens on the sparsely wooded hilltop wore their black veils up. Some had their bows in hand and arrows nocked. The rest of the Maidens were among the trees well out from the hill, keeping watch against unpleasant surprises. "The land is clear

all the way to the manor house, but this still smells of a trap to me."
There had been a time when words like "manor" and "house" sounded
awkward on her tongue. She had been a long time in the wetlands now,
though.

"Nandera speaks truth," Alivia muttered sullenly, heeling her roan
gelding closer. Apparently the golden-haired woman still resented the
fact that she would not be going with him, but her reaction to hearing
her native accents in Tear made that impossible. She admitted having
been shaken, but claimed it had been the surprise of the thing. He
could not chance it, though. "You cannot trust any of the High Blood,
especially not a daughter of the Empress, may she—" Her mouth
snapped shut, and she smoothed her dark blue skirts unnecessarily, grimacing at what she had almost said. He trusted her, literally with his
life, but she had too many deep-buried instincts to risk putting her
face-to-face with the woman he was going to meet. The bond carried
anger with no effort to suppress it, now. Min disliked seeing Alivia
near him.

"It smells of a trap to me, too," Bashere said, easing his sinuously
curved sword in its scabbard. He was plainly clad, in burnished helmet
and breastplate, his gray silk coat alone marking him out from the
eighty-one Saldaean lancers arrayed around the hilltop. His thick,
down-curved mustaches almost bristled behind the face-bars of his helmet. "I'd give ten thousand crowns to know how many soldiers she has
out there. And how many *damane*. This Daughter of the Nine Moons is
the heir to their throne, man." He had been shocked when Alivia revealed that. No one in Ebou Dar had mentioned it to him, as if it were
of no importance. "They may claim their control ends far south of here,
but you can wager she has at least a small army to see to her safety."

"And if our scouts find this army," Rand replied calmly, "can we be
sure they won't be seen?" Nandera made a scornful sound. "Best not to
assume you're the only one with eyes," he told her. "If they think we're
planning to attack them or kidnap the woman, everything falls apart."
Maybe that was why they had kept their secret. The Imperial heir
would be a more tempting target for a kidnapping than a mere high-
ranking noblewoman. "You just keep watch to make sure they don't
catch *us* by surprise. If it all goes wrong, Bashere, you know what to
do. Besides, she may have an army, but so do I, and not so small."
Bashere had to nod at that.

Aside from the Saldaeans and the Maidens, the hilltop was

crowded with Asha'man and Aes Sedai and Warders, better than twenty-five all told, and as formidable a group as any small army. They mingled with surprising ease, and few outward signs of tension. Oh, Toveine, a short, coppery-skinned Red, was scowling at Logain, but Gabrelle, a dusky Brown with sooty green eyes, was talking with him quite companionably, perhaps even coquettishly. That might have been the reason for Toveine's scowl, though disapproval seemed more likely than jealousy. Adrielle and Kurin each had an arm around the other's waist, though she was tall enough to overtop the Domani Asha'man, and beautiful where he was plain and had gray at his temples. Not to mention that he had bonded the Gray against her will. Beldeine, new enough to the shawl that she simply looked like any young Saldaean woman with slightly tilted brown eyes, reached out every now and then to touch Manfor, and he smiled at her whenever she did. Her bonding of him had been a shock, but apparently the yellow-haired man had been more than willing. Neither had asked Rand his opinion before the bonding.

Strangest of all perhaps were Jenare, pale and sturdy in a gray riding dress embroidered with red on the skirts, and Kajima, a clerkish fellow in his middle years who wore his hair like Narishma, in two braids with silver bells at the ends. She laughed at something Kajima said, and murmured something that made him laugh in turn. A *Red* joking with a man who could channel! Maybe Taim had effected a change for the better, whatever he had intended. And maybe Rand al'Thor was living in a dream, too. Aes Sedai were famous for their dissembling. But could a Red dissemble that far?

Not everyone felt agreeable today. Ayako's eyes seemed almost black as she glared at Rand, but then, considering what happened to a Warder when his Aes Sedai died, the dark-complected little White had reason to fear Sandomere going into possible danger. The Asha'man bond differed from the Warder bond in some respects, but in others it was identical, and no one yet knew the effects of an Asha'man's death on the woman he had bonded. Elza was frowning at Rand, too, one hand on the shoulder of her tall, lean Warder Fearil as if she were gripping a guard dog's collar and thinking of loosing him. Not against Rand, certainly, but he worried for anyone she thought might be threatening him. He had given her orders about that, and her oath should see them obeyed, yet Aes Sedai could find loopholes in almost anything.

Merise was speaking firmly to Narishma, with her other two

Warders sitting their horses a little way off. There was no mistaking the way the stern-faced woman gestured as she spoke, leaning close to him so she could speak in a low voice. She was instructing him about something. Rand disliked that in the circumstances, yet there seemed little he could do. Merise had sworn no oaths, and she would ignore him when it came to one of her Warders. Or much of anything else, for that matter.

Cadsuane was watching Rand, too. She and Nynaeve were wearing all of their *ter'angreal* jewelry. Nynaeve was making a good try at Aes Sedai calm. She seemed to practice that a great deal since sending Lan wherever she had sent him. Half the hilltop separated her plump brown mare from Cadsuane's bay, of course. Nynaeve would never admit it, but Cadsuane intimidated her.

Logain rode up between Rand and Bashere, his black gelding prancing. The horse was almost the exact shade of his coat and cloak. "The sun is almost straight overhead," he said. "Time we go down?" There was only a mere hint of question in that. The man chafed at taking orders. He did not wait on a reply. "Sandomere!" he called loudly. "Narishma!"

Merise held Narishma by his sleeve for another moment of instructions before letting him ride over, which made Logain scowl. Sun-dark Narishma with his dark, belled braids looked years younger than Rand, though he was a few years older in truth. Sitting his dun as straight as a sword, he nodded to Logain as to an equal, producing another scowl. Sandomere spoke a quiet word to Ayako before mounting his dapple, and she touched his thigh once he was in the saddle. Wrinkled, with receding hair and a gray-streaked beard trimmed to a point and oiled, he made her appear youthful rather than ageless. He wore the red-and-gold dragon on his high black collar, now, as well as the silver sword. Every Asha'man on the hill did, even Manfor. He had only recently been raised to Dedicated, but he had been one of the first to come to the Black Tower, before there was a Black Tower. Most of the men who had begun with him were dead. Even Logain had not denied he deserved it.

Logain had enough sense not to call Cadsuane or Nynaeve, but they rode to join Rand anyway, placing themselves to either side of him, each briefly eyeing him, faces so smooth they might have been thinking anything. Their eyes met, and Nynaeve looked away quickly. Cadsuane gave a faint snort. And Min came, too. His "one more" to balance the honors. A man should never give promises in bed. He opened his mouth, and she arched an eyebrow, looking at him very directly. The bond felt full of . . . something dangerous.

"You stay behind me once we get there," he told her, not at all what he had intended to say.

Danger faded to what he had come to recognize as love. There was wry amusement in the bond, too, for some reason. "I will if I want to, you wool-headed sheepherder," she said with more than a little asperity, just as if the bond would not tell him her true feelings. Hard as those might be to decipher.

"If we're going to do this fool thing, let's get it done with," Cadsuane said firmly, and heeled her dark bay down the hill.

A short distance from the hill, farms began to appear along a meandering dirt road through the forest, hard-packed by long years of use but still carrying a slick of mud from the last rainfall. The chimneys of thatched stone houses smoked with the midday meal-cooking. Sometimes girls and women sat out in the sun at their spinning wheels. Men in rough coats walked in the stone-walled fields checking their sprouting crops amid boys hoeing weeds. The pastures held brown-and-white cattle or black-tailed sheep, usually watched by a boy or two with bows or slings. There were wolves in these forests, and leopards and other things that enjoyed the taste of beef and mutton. Some people shaded their eyes to peer at the passersby, doubtless wondering who these finely dressed folk were who had come to visit the Lady Deirdru. Surely there could be no other reason for their presence, heading toward the manor house and so far from anywhere important. No one seemed agitated or frightened, though, just going about their day's work. Rumors of an army in the region surely would have upset them, and rumors of that sort spread like wildfire. Strange. The Seanchan could not Travel and arrive without news speeding ahead of them. It was very strange.

He felt Logain and the other two men seize *saidin*, filling themselves with it. Logain held almost as much as he could have himself, Narishma and Sandomere somewhat less. They were the strongest among the other Asha'man, though, and both had been at Dumai's Wells. Logain had proven he could handle himself in other places, other battles. If this was a trap, they would be ready, and the other side would never know it until too late. Rand did not reach for the Source. He could feel Lews Therin lurking in his head. This was no time to give the madman a chance to get hold of the Power.

"Cadsuane, Nynaeve, you'd better embrace the Source now," he said. "We're getting close."

"I've been holding *saidar* since back on that hill," Nynaeve told him. Cadsuane snorted and gave him a look that called him an idiot.

Rand stilled a grimace before it could begin. His skin felt no tingling, no goosebumps. They had masked their ability, and with it, shielded him from sensing the Power in them. Men had had few advantages over women when it came to channeling, but now they had lost those few while women retained all of theirs. Some of the Asha'man were trying to puzzle out how to duplicate what Nacelle had created, to find a weave that would allow men to detect women's weaves, but so far without success. Well, it would have to be dealt with by someone else. He had all he could manage on his plate at the moment.

The farms continued, some alone in a clearing, others clustered three or four or five together. If they followed the road far enough they would reach the village of King's Crossing in a few miles, where a wooden bridge spanned a narrow river called the Reshalle, but well short of that the road passed by a large clearing marked by a pair of tall stone gateposts, though there were neither gates nor fence. A hundred paces or more beyond it, at the end of a mud-slicked clay lane, lay Lady Deidre's manor, two stories of thatch-roofed gray stone saved from looking a large farmhouse only by the gateposts and the tall twinned doors at the front. The stables and outbuildings had the same practical appearance, sturdy and unornamented. There was no one in sight, no stablemen, no servant on her way to fetch eggs, no men in the fields that flanked the lane. The house's tall chimneys stood smokeless. It *did* smell of a trap. But the countryside was quiet, the farmers unruffled. There was only one way to find out.

Rand turned Tai'daishar in through the gateposts, and the others followed. Min did not heed his warning. She pushed her gray in between Tai'daishar and Nynaeve's mare and grinned at him. The bond carried nervousness, but the woman grinned!

When he was halfway to the house, the doors opened, and two women came out, one in dark gray, the other in blue with red panels on her breast and ankle-length skirts. Sunlight glinted off the silvery leash connecting them. Two more appeared, and two more, until three pairs stood in a row to either side of the door. As he reached the three-quarter point, another woman stepped into the doorway, very dark and very small, dressed in pleated white, her head covered by a transparent scarf that fell over her face. The Daughter of the Nine Moons. She had been described to Bashere right down to her shaven head. A tension in his shoulders he had not been aware of melted. That she was actually here did away with the possibility of a trap. The Seanchan would not risk the heir to their throne in anything so dangerous. He drew rein and dismounted.

"One of them is channeling," Nynaeve said, just loudly enough for him to hear, as she climbed down from her saddle. "I can't see anything, so she's masked her ability and inverted the weave—and I wonder how the Seanchan learned *that*!—but she's channeling. Only one; there isn't enough for it to be two." Her *ter'angreal* could not tell whether it was *saidin* or *saidar* being channeled, but it was unlikely to be a man.

I told you it was trap, Lews Therin groaned. *I told you!*

Rand pretended to check his saddle girth. "Can you tell which one?" he asked quietly. He still did not reach for *saidin*. There was no telling what Lews Therin might do in these circumstances if he managed to grab control again. Logain was fiddling with his girth, too, and Narishma was watching Sandomere check one of the dapple's hooves. They had heard. The small woman was waiting in the doorway, very still but no doubt impatient and likely offended by their apparent interest in their horses.

"No," Cadsuane replied grimly. "But I can do something about it. Once we're closer." Her golden hair ornaments swayed as she tossed her cloak back as though unmasking a sword.

"Stay behind me," he told Min, and to his relief, she nodded. Her face wore a small frown, and the bond carried worry. Not fear, though. She knew he would protect her.

Leaving the horses standing, he started toward the *sul'dam* and *damane* with Cadsuane and Nynaeve a little distance to either side of him. Logain, hand resting on his sword hilt as if that were his real weapon, strode along on the other side of Cadsuane, Narishma and Sandomere beyond Nynaeve. The small dark woman began walking toward them slowly, holding her pleated skirts up off the damp ground.

Abruptly, no more than ten paces away, she . . . flickered. For an instant, she was taller than most men, garbed all in black, surprise on her face, and though she still wore the veil, her head was covered with short-cut wavy black hair. Only an instant before the small woman returned, her step faltering as she let her white skirts fall, but another flicker, and the tall dark woman stood there, her face twisted in fury behind the veil. He recognized that face, though he had never seen it before. Lews Therin had, and that was enough.

"Semirhage," he said in shock before he could stop the word, and suddenly everything seemed to happen at once.

He reached for the Source and found Lews Therin clawing for it, too, each of them jostling the other aside from reaching it. Semirhage flicked her hand, and a small ball of fire streaked toward him from her fingertips. She might have shouted something, an order. He could not leap aside; Min stood right behind him. Frantically trying to seize *saidin*, he flung up the hand holding the Dragon Scepter in desperation. The world seemed to explode in fire.

His cheek was pressed against the damp ground, he realized. Black flecks shimmered in his vision, and everything seemed faintly hazy, as if seen through water. Where was he? What had happened? His head felt stuffed with wool. Something was prodding him in the ribs. His sword hilt. The old wounds were a hard knot of pain just above that. Slowly, he realized he was looking at the Dragon Scepter, or what was left of it. The spearpoint and a few inches of charred haft lay three paces away. Small, dancing flames were consuming the long tassel. The Crown of Swords lay beyond it.

Abruptly it came to him that he could feel *saidin* being channeled. His skin was goose bumps all over from *saidar* being wielded. The manor house. Semirhage! He tried to push himself up, and collapsed with a harsh cry. Slowly he pulled a left arm that seemed all pain up where he could see his hand. See where his hand had been. Only a mangled, blackened ruin remained. A stub sticking out of a cuff that gave off thin streamers of smoke. But the Power was still being channeled around him. His people were fighting for their lives. They might be dying. Min! He struggled to rise, and fell again.

As though thinking of her had summoned her, Min was crouching over him. Trying to shield him with her body, he realized. The bond was full of compassion and pain. Not physical pain. He would have known if she had the smallest injury. She was feeling pain for him. "Lie still," she said. "You've. . . . You've been hurt."

"I know," he said hoarsely. Again, he reached for *saidin*, and for a wonder, this time Lews Therin did not try to interfere. The Power filled him, and that gave him the strength to push himself to his feet one-handed, preparing several very nasty weaves as he did so. Careless of his muddy coat, Min gripped his good arm as though she were trying to hold him upright. But the fighting was over.

Semirhage was standing stiffly with her arms at her sides, her skirts pressed against her legs, doubtless wrapped up in flows of Air. The hilt of one of Min's knives stood out from her shoulder, and she must have been shielded, too, but her dark, beautiful face was contemptuous. She had been a prisoner before, briefly, during the War of the Shadow. She had escaped from high detention by frightening her jailers to the point that they actually smuggled her to freedom.

Others had been injured more seriously. A short dark *sul'dam* and tall pale-haired *damane*, linked by an *a'dam*, lay sprawled on the ground, staring up at the sun with already glazed eyes, and another pair were on their knees and clinging to one another, blood running down their faces and matting their hair. The other pairs stood as stiffly as Semirhage, and he could see the shields on three of the *damane*. They looked stunned. One of the *sul'dam*, a slender, dark-haired young woman, was weeping softly. Narishma's face was bloodied, too, and his coat appeared singed. So did Sandomere's, and a bone jutted through his left coatsleeve, white smeared with red, until Nynaeve firmly pulled his arm straight and guided the bone back into place. Grimacing in pain, he gave a guttural groan. She cupped her hands around his arm over the break, and moments later he was flexing his arm and moving his fingers and murmuring thanks. Logain appeared untouched, as did Nynaeve and Cadsuane, who was studying Semirhage the way a Brown might study an exotic animal never before seen.

Suddenly gateways began opening all around the manor house, spilling out mounted Asha'man and Aes Sedai and Warders, veiled Maidens and Bashere riding at the head of his horsemen. An Asha'man and Aes Sedai in a ring of two could make a gateway considerably larger than those Rand could alone. So someone had managed to give the signal, a red sunburst in the sky. Every Asha'man was full of *saidin*, and Rand assumed the Aes Sedai were equally full of *saidar*. The Maidens began spreading out into the trees.

"Aghan, Hamad, search the house!" Bashere shouted. "Matoun, form the lancers! They'll be on us as soon as they can!" Two soldiers thrust their lances into the ground and leapt down to run inside drawing their swords while the others began arraying themselves in two ranks.

Ayako flung herself from her saddle and rushed to Sandomere not even bothering to hold her skirts out of the mud. Merise rode to Narishma before swinging down right in front of him and taking his head in her hands without a word. He jerked, his back arching and nearly pulling his head free, as she Healed him. She had little facility with Nynaeve's method of Healing.

Ignoring the turmoil, Nynaeve gathered her skirts in bloodied hands and hurried to Rand. "Oh, Rand," she said when she saw his arm, "I'm so sorry. I. . . . I'll do what I can, but I can't fix it the way it was." Her eyes were filled with anguish.

Wordlessly, he held out his left arm. It throbbed with agony. Strangely, he could still feel his hand. It seemed he should be able to make a fist with the fingers that were no longer there. His goose bumps intensified as she drew more deeply on *saidar*, the tendrils of smoke vanished from his cuff, and she gripped his arm above the wrist. His entire arm began tingling, and the pain drained away. Slowly, blackened skin was replaced by smooth skin that seemed to ooze down until it covered the small lump that had been the base of his hand. It was a miraculous thing to see. The scarlet-and-gold scaled dragon grew back, too, as much as it could, ending in a bit of the golden mane. He could *still* feel the whole hand.

"I'm so sorry," Nynaeve said again. "Let me delve you for any other injuries." She asked, but did not wait, of course. She reached up to cup his head between her hands, and a chill ran through him. "There's something wrong with your eyes," she said with a frown. "I'm afraid to try fixing that without studying on it. The smallest mistake could blind you. How well can you see? How many fingers am I holding up?"

"Two. I can see fine," he lied. The black flecks were gone, but everything still seemed seen through water, and he wanted to squint against a sun that appeared to glare ten times brighter than it had. The old wounds in his side were knotted with pain.

Bashere climbed down from his compact bay in front of him and frowned at the stump of his left arm. Unbuckling his helmet, he took it off and held it under his arm. "At least you're alive," he said gruffly. "I've seen men hurt worse."

"Me, too," Rand said. "I'll have to learn the sword all over again, though." Bashere nodded. Most forms required two hands. Rand bent to pick up the crown of Illian, but Min released his arm and hurriedly handed the crown to him. He settled it on his head. "I'll have to work out new ways to do everything."

"You must be in shock," Nynaeve said slowly. "You've just suffered a grievous injury, Rand. Maybe you'd better lie down. Lord Davram, have one your men bring a saddle to put his feet up."

"He's not in shock," Min said sadly. The bond was full of sadness. She had taken hold of his arm as if to hold him up again. "He lost a hand, but there's nothing to do about it, so he's left it behind already."

"Wool-headed fool," Nynaeve muttered. Her hand, still smeared with Sandomere's blood, drifted toward the thick braid hanging over her shoulder, but she yanked it back down. "You've been hurt badly. It's all right to grieve. It's all right to feel stunned. It's normal!"

"I don't have time," he told her. Min's sadness threatened to overflow the bond. Light, he was all right! Why did she feel so sad?

Nynaeve muttered half under her breath about "woolhead" and "fool" and "man-stubborn," but she was not finished. "Those old wounds in your side have broken open," she almost growled. "You aren't bleeding badly, but you *are* bleeding. Maybe I can finally do something about them."

But as hard as she tried—and she tried three times—nothing changed. He still felt the slow trickle of blood sliding down his ribs. The wounds were still a throbbing knot of pain. Finally, he pushed her hand gently away from his side.

"You've done what you can, Nynaeve. It's enough."

"Fool." She did growl, this time. "How can it be enough when you're still bleeding?"

"Who is the tall woman?" Bashere asked. He understood, at least. You did not waste time on what could not be mended. "They didn't try passing *her* off as the Daughter of the Nine Moons, did they? Not after telling me she was a little thing."

"They did," Rand replied, and explained briefly.

"Semirhage?" Bashere muttered incredulously. "How can you be sure?"

"She's Anath Dorje, not . . . not what you called her," a honey-skinned *sul'dam* said loudly in a twangy drawl. Her dark eyes were tilted, and her hair was streaked with gray. She looked the eldest of the *sul'dam*, and the least frightened. It was not that she did not look afraid, but she controlled it well. "She's the High Lady's Truthspeaker."

"Be silent, Falendre," Semirhage said coldly, looking over her shoulder. Her gaze promised pain. The Lady of Pain was good at delivering on her promises. Prisoners had killed themselves on learning it was she who held them, men and women who managed to open a vein with teeth or fingernails.

Falendre did not seem to see it, though. "You don't command me," she said scornfully. "You're not even *so'jhin*."

"How *can* you be sure?" Cadsuane demanded. Those golden moons and stars, birds and fishes, swung as she moved her piercing gaze from Rand to Semirhage and back.

Semirhage saved him the effort of thinking up a lie. "He's insane," she said coolly. Standing there stiff as a statue, Min's knife hilt still sticking out beside her collarbone and the front of her black dress glistening with blood, she might have been a queen on her throne. "Graendal could explain it better than I. Madness was her specialty. I will try, however. You know of people who hear voices in their heads? Sometimes, very rarely, the voices they hear are the voices of past lives. Lanfear claimed he knew things from our own Age, things only Lews Therin Telamon could know. Clearly, he is hearing Lews Therin's voice. It makes no difference that his voice is real, however. In fact, that makes his situation worse. Even Graendal usually failed to achieve reintegration with someone who heard a real voice. I understand the descent into terminal madness can be . . . abrupt." Her lips curved in a smile that never touched her dark eyes.

Were they looking at him differently? Logain's face was a carved mask, unreadable. Bashere looked as though he still could not believe. Nynaeve's mouth hung open, and her eyes were wide. The bond. . . . For a long moment, the bond was full of . . . numbness. If Min turned away from him, he did not know whether he could stand it. If she turned away, it would be the best thing in the world for her. But compassion and determination as strong as mountains replaced numbness, and love so bright he thought he could have warmed his hands over it. Her grip on his arm tightened, and he tried to put a hand over hers. Too late, he remembered and snatched the nub of his hand away, but not before it had touched her. Nothing in the bond wavered by a hair.

Cadsuane moved closer to the taller woman and looked up at her. Facing one of the Forsaken seemed to faze her no more than facing the Dragon Reborn did. "You're very calm for a prisoner. Rather than deny the charge, you give evidence against yourself."

Semirhage shifted that cold smile from Rand to Cadsuane. "Why should I deny myself?" Pride dripped from every word. "I am Semirhage." Someone gasped, and a number of the *sul'dam* and *damane* started trembling and weeping. One *sul'dam*, a pretty, yellow-haired woman, suddenly vomited down the front of herself, and another, stocky and dark, looked as if she might.

Cadsuane simply nodded. "I am Cadsuane Melaidhrin. I look forward to long talks with you." Semirhage sneered. She had never lacked courage.

"We thought she was the High Lady," Falendre said hurriedly, and haltingly at the same time. Her teeth seemed near to chattering, but she forced words out. "We thought we were being honored. She took us to a room in the Tarasin Palace where there was a . . . a hole in the air, and we stepped through to this place. I swear it on my eyes! We thought she was the High Lady."

"So, no army rushing toward us," Logain said. You could not have told from his tone whether he was relieved or disappointed. He bared an inch of his sword and thrust it back into its scabbard hard. "What do we do with them?" He jerked his head toward the *sul'dam* and *damane*. "Send them to Caemlyn like the others?"

"We send them back to Ebou Dar," Rand said. Cadsuane turned to stare at him. Her face was a perfect mask of Aes Sedai serenity, yet he doubted she was anywhere near serene inside. The leashing of *damane* was an abomination that Aes Sedai took personally. Nynaeve was anything but serene. Angry-eyed, gripping her braid in a tight, blood-daubed fist, she opened her mouth, but he spoke over her. "I need this truce, Nynaeve, and taking these women prisoner is no way to get one. Don't argue. That's what they'd call it, including the *damane*, and you know it as well as I do. They can carry word that I want to meet the Daughter of the Nine Moons. The heir to the throne is the only one who can make a truce stand."

"I still don't like it," she said firmly. "We could free the *damane*. The others will do as well for carrying messages." The *damane* who had not been weeping before burst into tears. Some of them cried to the *sul'dam* to save them. Nynaeve's face took on sickly cast, but she threw up her hands and gave over arguing.

The two soldiers Bashere had sent into the house came out, young men who walked with a rolling motion, more accustomed to saddles than their own feet. Hamad had a luxuriant black beard that fell below the edge of his helmet and a scar down his face. Aghan wore thick mustaches like Bashere's and carried a plain wooden box with no lid under his arm. They bowed to Bashere, free hands swinging their swords clear.

"The house is empty, my Lord," Aghan said, "but there's dried blood staining the carpets in several rooms. Looks like a slaughter yard, my Lord. I think whoever lived here is dead. This was sitting by the front door. It didn't look like it belonged, so I brought it along." He held out the box for inspection. Within lay coiled *a'dam* and a number of circlets made of segmented black metal, some large, some small.

Rand started to reach in with his left hand before he remembered. Min caught the movement and released his right arm so he could scoop up a handful of the black metal pieces. Nynaeve gasped.

"You know what these are?" he asked.

"They're *a'dam* for men," she said angrily. "Egeanin said she was going to drop the thing in the ocean! We *trusted* her, and she gave it to somebody to copy!"

Rand dropped the things back into the box. There were six of the larger circlets, and five of the silvery leashes. Semirhage had been prepared no matter who he brought with him. "She really thought she could capture all of us." That thought should have made him shiver. He seemed to feel Lews Therin shiver. No one wanted to fall into Semirhage's hands.

"She shouted for them to shield us," Nynaeve said, "but they couldn't because we were all holding the Power already. If we hadn't been, if Cadsuane and I hadn't had our *ter'angreal*, I don't know what would have happened." She *did* shiver.

He looked at the tall Forsaken, and she stared back, utterly composed. Utterly cold. Her reputation as a torturer loomed so large that it was easy to forget how dangerous she was otherwise. "Tie off the shields on the others so they'll unravel in a few hours, and send them to somewhere near Ebou Dar." For a moment, he thought Nynaeve was going to protest again, but she contented herself with giving her braid a strong tug and turning away.

"Who are you to ask for a meeting with the High Lady?" Falendre demanded. She emphasized the title for some reason.

"My name is Rand al'Thor. I'm the Dragon Reborn." If they had wept at hearing Semirhage's name, they wailed at hearing his.

* * *

Ashandarei slanted across his saddle, Mat sat Pips in the darkness among the trees and waited, surrounded by two thousand mounted crossbowmen. The sun was not long down, and events should be in motion. The Seanchan were going to be hit hard tonight in half a dozen places. Some small and some not so small, but hard in every case. Moonlight filtering through the branches overhead gave just enough illumination for him to make out Tuon's shadowed face. She had insisted on staying with him, which meant Selucia was at her side on her dun, of course, glaring at him as usual. There were not enough moon-shadows to obscure that, unfortunately. Tuon must be unhappy about what was to happen tonight, yet nothing showed on her face. What was she thinking? Her expression was all the stern magistrate.

"Your scheme do entail a good deal of luck," Teslyn said, not for the first time. Even shadowed, her face looked hard. She shifted in her saddle, adjusting her cloak. "It be too late to change everything, but this part can be abandoned certainly." He would have preferred to have Bethamin or Seta, neither bound by the Three Oaths and both knowing the weaves *damane* used for weapons, something that horrified the Aes Sedai. Not the weaves; just that Bethamin and Seta knew them. At least, he thought he would. Leilwin had flatly refused to fight any Seanchan except to defend herself. Bethamin and Seta might have done the same, or found at the last minute that they could not act against their countrymen. In any case, the Aes Sedai had rejected allowing the two women to be involved, and neither had opened her mouth once that was said. That pair were too meek around Aes Sedai to say boo to a goose.

"Grace favor you, Teslyn Sedai, but Lord Mat *is* lucky," Captain Mandevwin said. The stocky one-eyed man had been with the Band since the first days in Cairhien, and he had earned the gray streaks in his hair, hidden now beneath his green-painted helmet, an open-faced footman's helmet, in battles against Tear and Andor before that. "I remember times we were outnumbered, with enemies on every side, and he danced the Band around them. Not to slip away, mind, but to beat them. Beautiful battles."

"A beautiful battle is one you don't have to fight," Mat said, more sharply than he intended. He did not like battles. You could get holes poked in you in a battle. He just kept getting caught in them, that was all. Most of that dancing around *had* been trying to slip away. But there would be no slipping away tonight, or for many days to come. "Our part of it is important, Teslyn." What was keeping Aludra, burn her? The attack at the supply camp must be under way already, just strong enough that the soldiers defending it would think they could hold until help arrived, strong enough to make them sure they needed help. The others would be full strength from the start, to overwhelm the defenders before they knew what was on them. "I mean to bloody the Seanchan, bloody them so hard and fast and often that they're re-acting to what we're doing instead of making their own plans." As soon as the words left his tongue he wished he had phrased that an-other way.

Tuon leaned close to Selucia, and the taller woman put her scarf-covered head down to exchange whispers. It was too dark for their bloody finger-talk, but he could not hear a word they were saying. He could imagine. She had promised not to betray him, and that had to cover trying to betray his plans, yet she must wish she had that prom-ise back. He should have left her with Reimon or one of the others. That would have been safer than letting her stay with him. He could have if he had tied her up, her and Selucia both. And probably Setalle as well. That bloody woman still took Tuon's side every time.

Mandevwin's bay stamped a hoof, and he patted the animal's neck with a gauntleted hand. "You cannot deny there is battle luck, when you find a weakness in your enemy's lines that you never expected, that should not be there, when you find him arrayed to defend against at-tack from the north only you are coming from the south. Battle luck rides on your shoulder, my Lord. I have seen it."

Mat grunted and resettled his hat on his head irritably. For every time a banner got lost and blundered into a bloody chink in the en-emy's defenses, there were ten when it just was not bloody where you expected when you bloody well needed it. That was the truth of bat-tle luck.

"One green nightflower," a man called from above. "Two! Both green!" Scrapings told of him climbing down hurriedly.

Mat heaved a small sigh of relief. The *raken* was away and headed west. He had counted on that—the nearest large body of soldiers loyal to the Seanchan lay west—and even cheated by riding as far west as he dared. Just because you were sure your opponent would react in a cer-tain way did not mean he would. Reimon would be overrunning the supply camp any minute, smothering the defenders with ten times their number and securing much-needed provisions.

"Go, Vanin," he said, and the fat man dug his heels in, sending his dun off into the night at a canter. He could not outpace the *raken*, but so long as he brought word in time. . . . "Time to move, Mandevwin."

A lean fellow dropped the last distance from a lower limb, carefully cradling a looking glass that he handed up to the Cairhienin.

"Get mounted, Londraed," Mandevwin said, stuffing the looking glass into the cylindrical leather case tied to his saddle. "Connl, form the men by fours."

A short ride took them to a narrow hard-packed road, winding through low hills, that Mat had avoided earlier. There were few farms and fewer villages in this area, but he did not want to spread rumors of large parties of armed men. Not until he wanted them to spread, anyway. Now he needed speed, and rumor could not outrun him in tonight's business. Most of the farmhouses they trotted by were dark shapes in the moonlight, lamps and candles already extinguished. The thud of hooves and the creak of saddle leather were the only sounds aside from the occasional thin, reedy cry of some night bird or an owl's hooting, but two thousand or so horses made a fair amount of noise. They passed through a small village where only a handful of thatch-roofed houses and the tiny stone inn showed any light, but people stuck their heads out of doors and windows to gape. Doubtless they thought they were seeing soldiers loyal to the Seanchan. There seemed to be few of any other kind remaining in most of Altara. Somebody raised a cheer, but he was a lone voice.

Mat rode alongside Mandevwin with Tuon and the other women behind, and now and then he looked over his shoulder. Not to make sure she was still there. Strange as it was, he had no doubt she would keep her word not to escape, even now. And not to make sure she was keeping up. The razor had an easy stride, and she rode well. Pips could not have outrun Akein had he tried. No, he just liked looking at her, even by moonlight. Maybe especially by moonlight. He had tried kissing her again the night before, and she had punched him in the side so hard that at first he thought she had broken one of his shortribs. But she had kissed him just before they started out this evening. Only once, and said not to be greedy when he attempted a second. The woman melted in his arms while he was kissing her, and turned to ice the moment she stepped back. What was he to make of her? A large owl passed overhead, wings flapping silently. Would she see some omen in that? Probably.

He should not be spending so much time thinking about her, not tonight. In truth, he *was* depending on luck to some extent. The three thousand lancers Vanin had found, mostly Altarans with a few Seanchan, might or might not be those Master Roidelle had marked on his map, though they had not been too far from where he placed them, but there was no telling for sure in which direction they had moved since. Northeast, almost certainly, toward the Malvide Narrows, and the Molvaine Gap beyond. It seemed that except for the last stretch, the Seanchan had taken to avoiding the Lugard Road for moving soldiers, doubtless to conceal their numbers and destinations in the country roads. Certain was not absolutely sure, however. If they had not moved too far, this was the road they would use to reach that supply camp. If. But if they had ridden farther than he expected, they might use another road. No danger there; just a wasted night. Their commander might decide to cut straight across the hills, too. That could prove nasty if he decided to join this road at the wrong point.

About four miles beyond the village, they came to a place where two gently sloping hills flanked the road, and he called a halt. Master Roidelle's own maps were fine, but those he had from other men were the work of masters, too. Roidelle acquired only the best. Mat recognized this spot as if he had seen it before.

Mandevwin wheeled his horse around. "Admar, Eyndel, take your men up the north slope. Madwin, Dongal, the south slope. One man in four to hold horses."

"Hobble the horses," Mat said, "and put the feedbags on to stop whinnying." They were facing lancers. If it all turned sour and they tried to run, those lancers would ride them down like they were hunting wild pigs. A crossbow was no good from horseback, especially if you were trying to get away. They had to win here.

The Cairhienin stared at him, any expression hidden by the facebars of his helmet, but he did not hesitate. "Hobble the horses and put on their nosebags," he ordered. "Every man on the line."

"Tell off some to keep watch north and south," Mat told him. "Battle luck can run against you as easily as in your favor." Mandevwin nodded and gave the order.

The crossbowmen divided and rode up the thinly treed slopes, their dark coats and dull green armor fading into the shadows. Bur-

nished armor was all very well for parades, but it could reflect moonlight as well as sunlight. According to Talmanes, the hard part had
been convincing the lancers to give up their bright breastplates and
the nobles their silvering and gilding. The foot had seen sense straight
off. For a time there was the rustle of men and horses moving across the
mulch, moving through brush, but finally silence fell. From the road,
Mat could not have told there was anyone on either slope. Now he just
had to wait.

Tuon and Selucia kept him company, and so did Teslyn. A gusting
breeze had sprung up from the west that tugged at cloaks, but of
course, Aes Sedai could ignore such things, though Teslyn held hers
shut. Selucia let the gusts take her cloak where it would, oddly, but
Tuon took to holding hers closed with one hand.

"You might be more comfortable among the trees," he told her.
"They'll cut the wind."

For a moment, she shook with silent laughter. "I'm enjoying
watching you take your ease on your hilltop," she drawled.

Mat blinked. Hilltop? He was sitting Pips in the middle of the
bloody road with flaming gusts cutting through his coat like winter
was coming back. What was she talking about, hilltop?

"Have a care with Joline," Teslyn said, suddenly and unexpectedly.
"She be . . . childish . . . in some ways, and you do fascinate her the
way a shiny new toy do fascinate a child. She will bond you if she can
decide how to convince you to agree. Perhaps even if you do no realize
you be agreeing."

He opened his mouth to say there was no bloody flaming chance of
that, but Tuon spoke first.

"She cannot have him," she said sharply. Drawing a breath, she
went on in amused tones. "Toy belongs to me. Until I am through
playing with him. But even then, I won't give him to a *marath'damane*.
You understand me, Tessi? You tell Rosi that. That's the name I intended to give her. You can tell her that, too."

The sharp gusts might not have affected Teslyn, but she shivered at
hearing her *damane* name. Aes Sedai serenity vanished as rage contorted her face. "What I do understand—!"

"Give over!" Mat cut in. "Both of you. I'm in no mood to listen to
the pair of you trying to jab each other with needles." Teslyn stared at
him, indignation plain even by moonlight.

"Why, Toy," Tuon said brightly, "you're being masterful again."

She leaned over to Selucia and whispered something that made the bosomy woman give a loud guffaw.

Hunching his shoulders and pulling his cloak around him, he leaned on the high pommel of his saddle and watched the night for Vanin. Women! He would give up all of his luck—well, half—if he could understand women.

"What do you think you can achieve with raids and ambushes?" Teslyn said, again not for the first time. "The Seanchan will only send enough soldiers to hunt you down." She and Joline had kept trying to stick their noses into his planning, and so had Edesina to a lesser extent, until he chased them away. Aes Sedai thought they knew everything, and while Joline at least did know something of war, he had not needed advice. Aes Sedai advice sounded an awful lot like telling you what to do. This time, he decided to answer her.

"I'm counting on them sending more soldiers, Teslyn," he said, still watching for Vanin. "The whole army they have in the Molvaine Gap, in fact. Enough of it, anyway. They're more likely to use that than any other. Everything Thom and Juilin picked up says their big push is aimed at Illian. I think the army in the Gap is to guard against anything coming at them out of Murandy or Andor. But they're the stopper in the jar for us. I mean to pull that stopper out so we can pass through."

After several minutes of silence, he looked over his shoulder. The three women were just sitting their horses and watching him. He wished he had enough light to make out their expressions. Why were they bloody staring? He settled back to looking for Vanin, yet it seemed he could feel their eyes on his back.

Perhaps two hours by the shifting of the fat crescent moon went by, with the wind slowly picking up strength. It was enough to take the night beyond cool into cold. Periodically he tried to make the women take shelter among the trees, but they resisted stubbornly. He had to remain, to catch Vanin without having to shout—the lancers would be close behind the man; perhaps very close if their commander was a fool—but they did not. He suspected that Teslyn refused because Tuon and Selucia did. That made no sense, but there it was. As for why Tuon refused, he could not have said unless it was because she liked to listen to him arguing himself hoarse.

Eventually the wind brought the sound of a running horse, and he sat up straight in his saddle. Vanin's dun cantered out of the night, the bulky man as always an improbable sight in a saddle.

Vanin drew rein and spat through a gap in his teeth. "They're a mile or so behind me, but there's maybe a thousand more than there was this morning. Whoever's in charge knows his business. They're pushing hard without blowing their horses."

"If you be outnumbered two to one," Teslyn said, "perhaps you will reconsider—"

"I don't intend to give them a stand-up fight," Mat broke in. "And I can't afford to leave four thousand lancers loose to make trouble for me. Let's join Mandevwin."

The kneeling crossbowmen on the slope of the northern hill made no sound when he rode through their line with the women and Vanin, just shuffled aside to let them through. He would have preferred at least two ranks, but he needed to cover a wide front. The sparse trees did cut the wind, but not by much, and most of the men were huddled in their cloaks. Still, every crossbow he could see was drawn, with a bolt in place. Mandevwin had seen Vanin arrive and knew what it meant.

The Cairhienin was pacing just behind the line until Mat appeared and swung down from Pips. Mandevwin was relieved to hear that he no longer needed to keep a watch to his rear. He merely nodded thoughtfully at hearing of a thousand more lancers than expected and sent a man racing off to bring the watchers down from the crest to take their places in the line. If Mat Cauthon took it in stride, so would he. Mat had forgotten that about the Band. They trusted him absolutely. Once, that had almost made him break out in a rash. Tonight, he was glad of it.

An owl hooted twice, somewhere behind him, and Tuon sighed.

"Is there an omen in that?" he asked, just for something to say.

"I'm glad you are finally taking an interest, Toy. Perhaps I will be able to educate you yet." Her eyes were liquid in the moonlight. "An owl hooting twice means someone will die soon." Well, that put a bloody end to conversation.

Soon enough, the Seanchan appeared, four abreast and leading their horses at a trot, lances in hand. Vanin had been right about their commander knowing his job. Cantered for a time then led at a trot, horses could cover a lot of ground quickly. Fools tried to gallop long distances and ended with dead or crippled horses. Only the first forty or so wore the segmented armor and strange helmets of Seanchan. A pity, that. He had no idea how the Seanchan would feel about casualties to their Altaran allies. Losses to their own would catch notice, though.

When the middle of the column was right in front of him, a deep voice on the road suddenly shouted, "Banner! Halt!" Those two words carried the familiar slurred drawl of the Seanchan. The men in segmented armor stopped sharply. The others straggled to a halt.

Mat drew breath. Now that had to be *ta'veren* work. They could hardly have been better placed if he had given the order himself. He rested a hand on Teslyn's shoulder. She flinched slightly, but he needed to get her attention quietly.

"Banner!" the deep voice shouted. "Mount!" Below, soldiers moved to obey.

"Now," Mat said quietly.

The foxhead went cold on his chest, and suddenly a ball of red light was floating high above the road, bathing the soldiers below in an unearthly glow. They had only a heartbeat to gape. Along the line below Mat, a thousand crossbow strings gave what sounded like one loud snap, and a thousand bolts streaked into the formation, punching through breastplates at that short range, knocking men from their feet, sending horses rearing and screaming, just as a thousand more struck from the other side. Not every shot struck squarely, but that hardly mattered with a heavy crossbow. Men went down with shattered legs, with legs ripped half off. Men clutched at the stumps of ruined arms trying to stem the flow of blood. Men screamed as loudly as the horses.

He watched a crossbowman nearby as the fellow bent to fasten the paired hooks of the bulky, boxlike crank, hanging from a strap at the front of his belt, to his crossbow string. As the man straightened, the cord streamed out of the crank, but once he was erect, he set the crank on the butt of the upended crossbow, moved a small lever on the side of the box, and began to work the handles. Three quick turns with a rough whirring sound, and the string caught on the latch.

"Into the trees!" the deep voice shouted. "Close with them before they can reload! Move!"

Some tried to mount, to ride into the attack, and others dropped reins and lances to draw swords. None made it as far as the trees. Two thousand more bolts slashed into them, cutting men down, punching through men to kill men behind or topple horses. On the hillside, men began working their cranks furiously, but there was no need. On the road, a horse kicked feebly here and there. The only men moving were frantically trying to use whatever they had to hand for tourniquets to keep from bleeding to death. The wind brought the sound of running horses. Some might have riders. There were no more shouts from the deep voice.

"Mandevwin," Mat shouted, "we're done here. Mount the men. We have places to be."

"You must stay to offer aid," Teslyn said firmly. "The rules of war do demand it."

"This is a new kind of war," he told her harshly. Light, it was silent on the road, but he could still hear the screaming. "They'll have to wait for their own to give them aid."

Tuon murmured something half under her breath. He thought it was, "A lion can have no mercy," but that was ridiculous.

Gathering his men, he led them down the north side of the hill. There was no need to let the survivors see how many they were. In a few hours they would join up with the men from the other hill, and in a few hours more, with Carlomin. Before sunrise they were going to hit the Seanchan again. He intended to make them *run* to pull that bloody stopper for him.

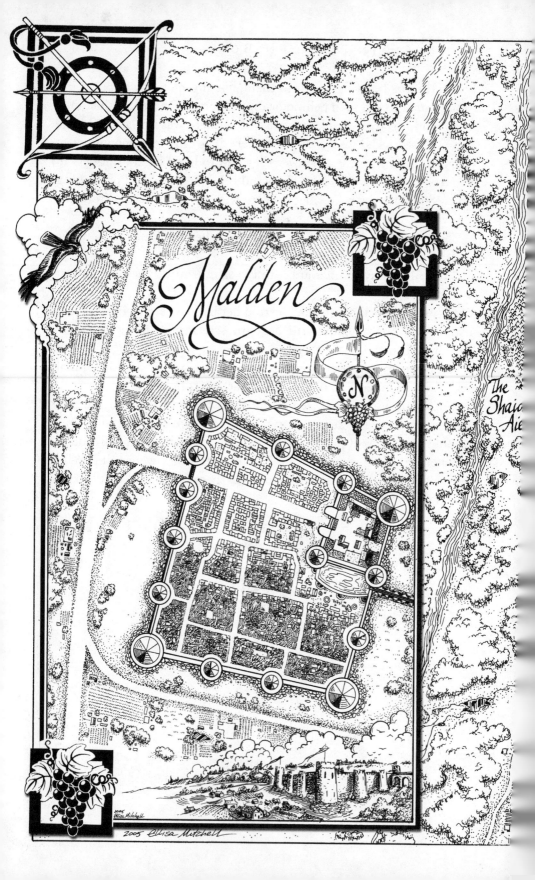

Malden

The Shai...
Aie...

2005
Ellisa Mitchell

2005 Ellisa Mitchell

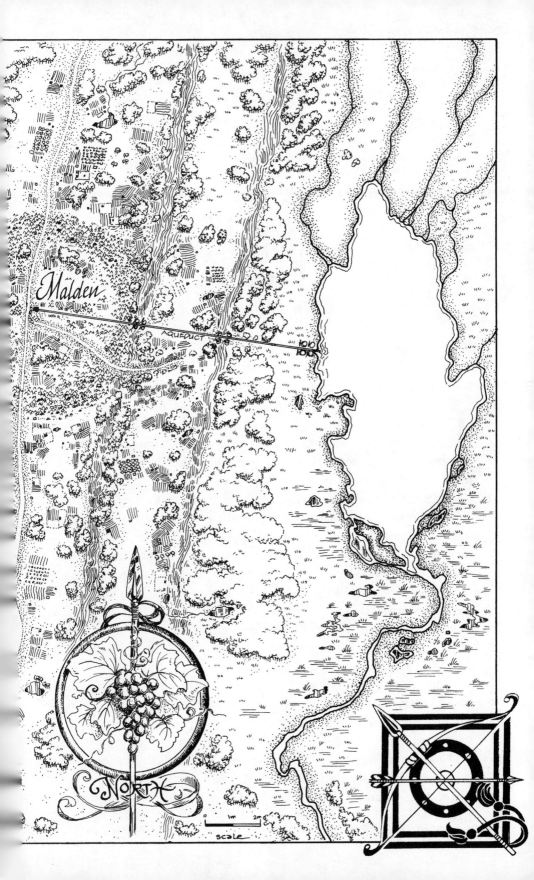

Malden

AQUEDUCT

1010
100

NORTH

1m   2m
scale

CHAPTER
28

In Malden

Just before first light, Faile was fastening the wide belt of golden links around her waist for the last time when Dairaine entered the small, already crowded peaked tent where they all slept. Outside, the sky would be starting to turn gray, but inside, it might still have been night. Faile's eyes had adapted to the darkness, though. The slender little woman with black hair that spilled to her waist in waves was frowning around her yawns. She had stood just below the High Seat of her House in Cairhien, but she had been wakened in the night because Sevanna could not sleep and wanted to be read to. Sevanna enjoyed Dairaine's voice, and likely the tales she carried of supposed misdeeds among Sevanna's *gai'shain*. The Cairhienin woman was never chosen out as one of those who had failed to please. Her hands went to her golden collar, then hesitated when she took in Faile, Alliandre and Maighdin, already dressed and on their feet.

"I forgot to put the book back in the proper place," she said in a voice like crystal chimes, turning back toward the tentflap. "Sevanna will have me beaten if she sees it out of place when she wakes."

"She's lying," Maighdin growled, and Dairaine darted for outside.

That was enough to convince Faile. She grabbed the woman's cowl and hauled her back into the tent. Dairaine opened her mouth to scream, but Alliandre clapped her hand over it, and the three of them

wrestled the woman to the blanket-strewn ground-cloth. It took all
three. Dairaine was small, but she writhed like a snake, tried to claw at
them, to bite. While the other two held the woman down, Faile produced the second knife she had secured, a quite serviceable dagger with
a ridged steel hilt and a blade longer than her hand, and began slicing
strips from one of the blankets.

"How did you know?" Alliandre said, struggling to contain one of
Dairaine's arms while keeping her mouth covered without being bitten. Maighdin had taken care of the woman's legs by sitting on them
and had her other arm twisted to her shoulder blades. Dairaine still
managed to twist, if uselessly.

"She was frowning, but when she spoke, her face went smooth. I
could just make it out. If she were really worried about being beaten,
she'd have frowned harder, not stopped." The golden-haired woman
was not a very skilled lady's maid, yet she was a very observant one.

"But what made her suspicious?"

Maighdin shrugged. "Maybe one of us looked surprised, or guilty.
Though I can't say how she could have noticed without any light."

Soon enough they had Dairaine trussed up with her ankles and
wrists tied together behind her back. She would not wriggle far like
that. A wadded length torn from her shift and tied in place with another piece of blanket served for a gag that let her emit only grunts.
She twisted her head to glare up at them. Faile could not see her face
very well, but the woman's expression had to be either glaring or
pleading, and Dairaine only pleaded with Shaido. She used her position as one of Sevanna's *gai'shain* to bully *gai'shain* who were not, and
her tale-carrying to bully those who were. The trouble was, they could
not leave her here. Someone might come at any moment to summon
one of them to serve Sevanna.

"We can kill her and hide the body," Alliandre suggested, smoothing her long hair. It had become disarrayed in the struggle.

"Where?" Maighdin said, combing her own sun-gold hair with her
fingers. She did not sound a lady's maid speaking to a queen. Prisoners
were equals in their captivity or else they aided their captors. It had
taken time to teach Alliandre that. "It has to be somewhere she won't
be found for at least a day. Sevanna might send men after Galina to
bring us back if we're suspected of killing one of her *belongings*." She
vested that word with all the scorn it would bear. "And I don't trust
Galina not to let them bring us back." Dairaine began struggling

against her bonds again and grunting harder than ever. Maybe she had
decided to plead after all.

"We aren't going to kill her," Faile told them. She was being neither squeamish nor merciful. There simply was nowhere they could be
sure a body would remain hidden long enough, not that they could
reach without being seen. "I'm afraid our plans have changed a little.
Wait here."

Ducking outside, where the sky was indeed beginning to pearl, she
found what had made Dairaine suspicious. Bain and Chiad were there
in their plain white robes as expected, to escort them as far as the
meeting place. Rolan and his friends might not be done breakfasting
yet—she hoped they were not; they might do something foolish and
ruin everything—and Bain and Chiad had volunteered to divert any
men who tried to interfere with them. She had not been able to make
herself ask how they intended to do that. Some sacrifices deserved a veil
of secrecy. And all of a heart's gratitude. Two *gai'shain* holding wicker
baskets were not enough to rouse suspicion in the Cairhienin woman,
but thirty or forty *gai'shain* were, crowding the narrow muddy lane
through the *gai'shain* tents. Aravine's plump plain face watched her
from a white cowl, and Lusara's beautiful one. Alvon was there with his
son Theril in their robes of muddy tentcloth, and Alainia, a plump
Amadician silversmith in dirty coarse white linen, and Dormin, a
stocky Cairhienin bootmaker, and Corvila, a lean weaver from right
here in Altara, and. . . . They represented not a tenth part of those who
had sworn to her, but a gathering of *gai'shain* this large would have
planted suspicion in a stone. At least when added to the three of them
being dressed. Dairaine likely had heard who had been summoned to
Sevanna this morning. How had they learned she was leaving today? It
was too late to worry about that. If any Shaido knew, they would all
have been dragged from the tent before this.

"What are you doing here?" she demanded.

"We wanted to see you go, my Lady," Theril said in his rough,
barely intelligible accents. "We were very careful to come by ones and
twos." Lusara nodded happily, and she was not the only one.

"Well, we can say goodbye now," Faile said firmly. No need to tell
them how close they had come to ruining the escape. "Until I come
back for you." If her father would not give her an army, then Perrin
would. His friendship with Rand al'Thor would provide it. Light,
where *was* he? No! She had to be glad he had not caught up yet, had

not gotten himself killed trying to sneak into the camp and rescue her. She had to be glad, and not think of what might be delaying him. "Now go before someone sees you here and runs to tell tales. And don't talk to *anyone* about this." Her adherents were safe enough, otherwise she would already be chained, but there were too many like Dairaine among the *gai'shain*, and not only among the long-held Cairhienin. Some people naturally set to licking wrists wherever they were.

They bowed or curtsied or knuckled their foreheads, just as if nobody might be poking their heads out to see, and scattered in every direction with chagrined expressions. They really had expected to watch her leave! She had no time to fritter away on exasperation. Hurrying to Bain and Chiad, she hastily explained the situation inside the tent.

They exchanged glances when she finished and put down the baskets to free fingers for Maiden handtalk. She avoided looking at their hands, since they plainly wanted privacy. Not that she could have understood much in any case. Their hands moved very fast. Flame-haired Bain with her dark blue eyes stood nearly half a hand taller than she, gray-eyed Chiad just a finger taller. They were her close friends, but they had adopted each other as first-sisters, and that created bonds closer than any friendship.

"We will take care of Dairaine Saighan," Chiad said at last. "But it means you must go into the town alone."

Faile sighed, but there was no helping it. Perhaps Rolan *was* already awake. He could be watching her that minute. He always seemed to appear out of nowhere when she needed him. Surely he would not interfere with her leaving, not when he had promised to take her when he himself left. Yet he still had hopes, so long as she wore white. Him and his kissing games! He might want to keep her in *gai'shain* robes a little longer. When men wanted to help, they always thought their way was the only way.

Bain and Chiad ducked into the small peaked tent, and Alliandre and Maighdin came out. There really was not room inside for five. Maighdin went around the side of the tent and returned with a basket like those the other women had been carrying. Dirty *gai'shain* robes bulged out of the top of each, making them appear loads of laundry, but beneath were dresses that came near enough fitting, a hatchet, a sling, cords for making snares, flint and steel, packets of flour, meal, dried beans, salt and yeast, a few coins they had been able to find, everything they would need to make their way west to find Perrin.

Galina would take them out of the camp, but there was no saying which direction her "Aes Sedai business" would take her then. They had to be self-reliant from the start. Faile would not put it past the Aes Sedai to abandon them as soon as she was able.

Maighdin stood over her basket with an air of determination, her jaw set and her eyes firm, but Alliandre's face was wreathed in smiles.

"Try not to look so happy," Faile told her. Wetlander *gai'shain* seldom smiled, and never so joyfully.

Alliandre tried to moderate her expression, but every time she smoothed her smiles away, they crept back. "We're escaping today," she said. "It's hard not to smile."

"You'll stop if some Wise One sees you and decides to find out why you're happy."

"We're hardly likely to meet a Wise One among the *gai'shain* tents or in Malden," the woman said through a smile. Determined or not, Maighdin nodded agreement.

Faile gave up. In truth, she felt a little giddy herself in spite of Dairaine. They were escaping today.

Bain came out of the tent, holding the tentflap for Chiad, who was carrying on her back a blanket-wrapped bundle just large enough to be a small woman doubled-up. Chiad was strong, but she had to lean forward a little to support the weight.

"Why is she so still?" Faile asked. She had no fear they had killed Dairaine. They were fierce about following the rules for *gai'shain*, and violence was forbidden. But that blanket could have been full of wood for all that it moved.

Bain spoke softly, an amused light in her eyes. "I stroked her hair and told her I would be very upset if I had to hurt her. Simple truth, considering how much *toh* even slapping her would cost me." Chiad chuckled. "I think Dairaine Saighan thought we were threatening her. I think she will be very quiet and very still until we let her go." She shook with silent laughter. Aiel humor was still a mystery to Faile. She knew they would be punished severely for this, though. Aiding an escape attempt was dealt with as harshly as trying to escape.

"You have all my gratitude," she said, "you and Chiad both, now and forever. I have great *toh*." She kissed Bain lightly on the cheek, which made the woman blush as red as her hair, of course. Aiel were almost prudishly restrained in public. In some ways.

Bain glanced at Chiad, and a faint smile appeared on her lips.

"When you see Gaul, tell him Chiad is *gai'shain* to a man with strong hands, a man whose heart is fire. He will understand. I need to help her carry our burden to a safe place. May you always find water and shade, Faile Bashere." She touched Faile's cheek lightly with her fingertips. "One day, we will meet again."

Going over to Chiad, she took one end of the blanket, and they hurried away carrying it between them. Gaul might understand, but Faile did not. Not the heart of fire, anyway, and she doubted that Manderic's hands interested Chiad in the slightest. The man had bad breath and started getting drunk as soon as he woke unless he was going on a raid or hunting. But she put Gaul and Manderic out of her mind and shouldered her basket. They had wasted too much time already.

The sky was beginning to take on the appearance of actual daylight, and *gai'shain* were stirring among the wildly diverse tents of the camp close on Malden's walls, scurrying off to be about some chore or at least carrying something to give a semblance of working, but none paid any mind to three women in white carrying baskets of laundry toward the town's gates. There always seemed to be laundry to be done, even for Sevanna's *gai'shain*. There were far too many wetlander *gai'shain* for Faile to know everyone, and she saw no one she knew until they came on Arrela and Lacile, shifting from foot to foot with baskets on their shoulders. Taller than most Aiel women and dark, Arrela kept her black hair cut as short as any Maiden and strode like a man when she walked. Lacile was short and pale and slim, and had red ribbons tied in her hair, which was not much longer. Her walk was graceful in robes, and had been a scandalous sway when she had worn breeches. Their sighs of relief were nearly identical, though.

"We thought something had happened," Arrela said.

"Nothing we couldn't handle," Faile told her.

"Where are Bain and Chiad?" Lacile asked anxiously.

"They have another task," Faile said. "We go alone."

They exchanged glances, and their sighs were far from relieved this time. Of course Rolan would not interfere. Not with them getting away. Of course not.

The iron-strapped gates of Malden stood open, shoved back against the granite walls, as they had since the city fell. Rust had turned the broad iron straps brown, and the hinges were so rusty that pushing the gates shut again might be impossible. Pigeons nested in the gray stone towers flanking them, now.

They were the first to arrive. At least, Faile could see no one ahead of them down the street. As they walked through the gates, she retrieved her dagger from the pocket inside her sleeve and held it with the blade pressed against her wrist, pointing up her arm.

The other women made similar motions, if not so deftly. Without Bain and Chiad, and hoping that Rolan and his friends were otherwise occupied, they had to provide their own protection. Malden was not as dangerous for a woman—for a *gai'shain* woman; Shaido who tried to prey on their own got short shrift—not as dangerous as the Shaido portion of the camp, yet women had been assaulted there, sometimes by groups of men. The Light send if they were accosted, it was only by one or two. One or two they might catch by surprise and kill before they realized these *gai'shain* had teeth. If there were more than two, they would do what they could, but an Aiel weaver or potter was as dangerous as most trained armsmen. Baskets or no baskets, they walked on their toes, heads swiveling, ready to spring in any direction.

This part of the town had not been burned, yet it had a look of desolation. Broken dishes and pottery crunched beneath their soft white boots. Bits of clothing, cut off men and women made *gai'shain*, still littered the gray paving stones. Those sorry, bedraggled rags had lain first in the snow and then in the rain for well over a month, and she doubted any ragpicker would have gathered them, now. Here and there lay children's toys, a wooden horse or a doll whose paint was beginning to flake, dropped by the very young who had been allowed to flee, like the very old, the ill and infirm. Slate-roofed buildings of wood or stone along the street showed gaping holes where their doors and windows had been. Along with anything the Shaido considered valuable or useful, the town had been stripped of every easily removable piece of wood, and only the fact that tearing down houses was less efficient than cutting firewood in the surrounding forests had spared the wooden structures themselves. Those openings minded Faile of eye sockets in skulls. She had walked along this street countless times, yet this morning, they seemed to be watching her. They made her scalp crawl.

Halfway across the town, she looked back toward the gates, no more than a hundred and fifty paces behind. The street was still empty for the moment, but soon the first white-clad men and women would materialize with their water buckets. Fetching water was a task that began early and lasted all day. They had to hurry, now. Turning down a narrower side street, she started to walk faster, although she had trouble keeping her basket balanced. The others must have been having the same difficulty, yet no one complained. They had to be out of sight before those *gai'shain* appeared. There was no reason for any *gai'shain* entering the town to leave the main street until they reached the cistern below the fortress. An attempt to curry favor or just a careless word could send Shaido into the town hunting for them, and there was only one way out, short of climbing onto the walls and dropping ten paces to the ground hoping that no one broke a leg.

At a now signless inn, three stories of stone and empty windows, she darted into the common room followed by the others. Lacile set down her basket and pressed herself against the doorframe to keep watch up the street. The beam-ceilinged room was bare to the dusty floorboards, and the stone fireplaces were missing their andirons and firetools. The railing had been stripped from the staircase at the back of the room, and the door to the kitchen was gone, too. The kitchen was just as empty. She had checked. Pots and knives and spoons were useful. Faile lowered her basket to the floor and hurried to the side of the staircase. It was a sturdy piece of work, of heavy timbers and made to last for generations. Tearing it down would have been nearly as hard as tearing down a house. She felt underneath, along the top of the wide outer support, and her hand closed on the wrist-thick, not quite glassy rod. It had seemed as good a hiding place as she could find, a place no one would have any reason to look, but she was surprised to find she had been holding her breath.

Lacile remained by the doorway, but the others hurried to Faile without their baskets.

"At last," Alliandre said, gingerly touching the rod with her fingertips. "The price of our freedom. What is it?"

"An *angreal*," Faile said, "or perhaps a *ter'angreal*. I don't know for certain, except that Galina wants it very badly, so it must be one or the other."

Maighdin put her hand on the rod boldly. "It could be either," she murmured. "They often have an odd feel. So I've been told, anyway." She claimed never to have been to the White Tower, but Faile was not so sure as she once had been. Maighdin could channel, but so weakly and with so much difficulty that the Wise Ones saw no danger in letting her walk free. Well, as free as any *gai'shain* was. Her denials might well be a matter of shame. Faile had heard that women who had been

put out of the Tower because they could not become Aes Sedai sometimes denied ever having gone in order to hide their failure.

Arrela gave a shake of her head and backed away a step. She was
Tairen, and despite traveling with Aes Sedai, she was still uncomfortable over the Power or anything to do with it. She looked at the
smooth white rod as if at a red adder and licked her lips. "Galina
might be waiting on us. She might get angry if we make her wait
long."

"Is the way still clear, Lacile?" Faile asked as she stuck the rod far
down into her basket. Arrela exhaled heavily, clearly as relieved at having the thing out of her sight as she had been to see Faile earlier.

"Yes," the Cairhienin replied, "but I do not understand why." She
still stood so that one eye could peek around the corner of the doorframe. "The first *gai'shain* should be coming for water by now."

"Maybe something has happened in the camp," Maighdin said.
Suddenly, her face was grim and her knife was in her hand, a wooden-
handled affair with a chipped and pitted blade.

Faile nodded slowly. Maybe something such as Dairaine having
been found already. She could not tell where Faile and the others had
been going, but she might have recognized some among the waiting
gai'shain. How long would they hold out if put to the question? How
long would Alvon hold out if Theril were? "There's nothing we can do
about it, in any case. Galina will get us out."

Even so, when they left the inn, they ran, carrying the baskets in
front of them and trying to hold up their long robes so they did not
trip. Faile was not the only one to look over her shoulder frequently
and stumble. She was not sure whether or not she was relieved to finally see *gai'shain* carrying buckets on yokes drift across the crossing of
the town's main street. She certainly did not slow down.

They did not have far to run. In moments, the smell of charred
wood that had faded from the rest of Malden began to grow. The
southern end of Malden was a ruin. They halted at the edge of the devastation and edged around a corner so they would not be seen by anyone glancing down the street. From where they stood to the southern
wall, near two hundred paces, marched roofless shells with blackened
stone walls interspersed with piles of charred beams washed clean of
ash by the rains. In places, not even the heaviest timbers remained.
Only on the south side of this street were there any structures even
close to whole. This was where the fire that raged after the Shaido took

the city had been finally stopped. Half a dozen buildings stood without roofs, though the lower floors looked intact, and twice as many were leaning piles of black timbers and half-burned boards that appeared on the edge of collapse.

"There," Maighdin said, pointing east along the street. A long length of red cloth fluttered in the breeze where she pointed. It was tied to a house that seemed ready to fall in. Walking to it slowly, they rested their baskets on the paving stones. The red cloth fluttered again.

"Why would she want to meet us *here?*" Alliandre muttered. "That could cave in if anybody sneezed." She rubbed at her nose as though the word had given her the urge.

"It is quite sound. I inspected it." Galina's voice behind them jerked Faile's head around. The woman was striding toward them, plainly from one of the sound buildings on the north side of the street. After so long seeing her in that belt and collar of gold and firedrops, she looked odd without them. She still wore her white silk robes, but the absence of the jewelry was convincing. Galina had not somehow managed to turn truth on its head. She was leaving today.

"Why not in one of the sound buildings?" Faile demanded. "Or right here?"

"Because I don't want anyone to see it in my hands," Galina said, walking past her. "Because no one will look inside that ruin. Because I say so." She stepped through what had been a doorway, ducking under a heavy, charred roof beam that slanted across the opening, and immediately turned to her right and began descending stairs. "Don't dawdle."

Faile exchanged looks with the other women. This was more than passing strange.

"If she'll get us out of here," Alliandre growled, snatching up her basket, "I'm willing to hand her the thing in a privy." Still, she waited on Faile to pick up her own basket and lead the way.

Charred timbers and blackened boards hung low over the stone stairs that led downward, but Galina's ease at entering reassured Faile. The woman would not risk being buried alive or crushed at the very moment she finally gained the rod. Bars and beams of light filtering through gaps in the wreckage gave enough illumination to show that the basement was quite clear despite the treacherous nature of what lay above. Large barrels stacked along one stone wall, most scorched and with staves sprung from the heat, said this had been an inn or a tavern.

Or perhaps a wine merchant's shop. The area around Malden had produced a great deal of mediocre wine.

Galina stood in the middle of the grit-covered stone floor, in a
small beam of light. Her face was all Aes Sedai calm, her agitation of
the previous day completely subdued. "Where is it?" she said coolly.
"Give it to me."

Faile set her basket down and shoved her hand deep inside. When
she brought out the white rod, Galina's hands twitched. Faile extended
the rod toward her, and she reached for it almost hesitantly. If she had
not known better, Faile would have said she was afraid to touch it.
Galina's fingers closed around the rod, and she exhaled heavily. She
jerked the rod away before Faile could release it. The Aes Sedai seemed
to be trembling, but her smile was . . . triumphant.

"How do you intend to get us away from the camp?" Faile asked.
"Should we change our clothes now?"

Galina opened her mouth, then suddenly raised her free hand,
palm out. Her head tilted toward the stairs as if listening. "It may be
nothing," she said softly, "but it's best if I check. Wait here and be
quiet. Be quiet," she hissed when Faile started to speak. Lifting the
hem of her silk robes, the Aes Sedai scurried to the stairs and started
up like a woman uneasy about what she might find at the top. Her feet
passed out of sight behind the sagging boards and beams.

"Did any of you hear anything?" Faile whispered. They all shook
their heads. "Maybe she's holding the Power. I've heard that can—"

"She wasn't," Maighdin interrupted. "I've never seen her
embracing—"

Suddenly, wood groaned overhead, and with a thunderous crash
charred beams and boards collapsed, sending out blinding billows of
black dust and grit that sent Faile into paroxysms of coughing. The
smell of charring suddenly was as thick in the air as it had been the day
Malden burned. Something falling from above hit her shoulder hard,
and she crouched, trying to protect her head. Someone cried out. She
heard other falling objects hit the basement's stone floor, boards or
pieces of boards. Nothing made a loud enough noise to be a roof beam
or a heavy joist.

Eventually—it seemed like hours; it might have been minutes—
the rain of debris stopped. The dust began to thin. Quickly she looked
around for her companions, and found them all huddling on the floor
with their arms around their heads. There seemed to be more light

than before. A little more. Some of the gaps overhead were wider, now. A trickle of blood ran down Alliandre's face from her scalp. Everyone was dusted with black from head to foot.

"Is anyone injured?" Faile asked, finishing with a cough. The dust had not cleared completely, and her throat and tongue felt coated with it. The stuff tasted like charcoal.

"No," Alliandre said, touching her scalp gingerly. "A scrape, that's all." The others denied injury as well, though Arrela seemed to be moving her right arm carefully. No doubt they had all suffered bruises, and Faile thought her left shoulder was going to be black and blue shortly, but she would not count that a real injury.

Then her eyes fell on the stairs, and she wanted to weep. Wreckage from above filled the whole space where the staircase had been. They might have been able to squeeze through some of the gaps overhead. Faile thought she could reach them standing on Arrela's shoulders, but she doubted she could pull herself through with one good arm. Or that Arrela could. And if either managed, she would be in the middle of a burned-out ruin and likely as not to make the rest of the thing fall in, too.

"No!" Alliandre moaned. "Not now! Not when we were so close!" Rising, she rushed as near to the rubble as she could get, almost pressing against it, and began to shout. "Galina! Help us! We're trapped! Channel and lift the boards away! Clear a path for us to get out! Galina! Galina! Galina!" She sagged against the tangle of timbers, shoulders shaking. "Galina," she wept. "Galina, help us."

"Galina's gone," Faile said bitterly. The woman would have answered if she was still above or had any intention of aiding them. "With us trapped down here, maybe dead, she has the perfect excuse for leaving us behind. Anyway, I don't know whether an Aes Sedai could move some of those timbers if she tried." She did not want to mention the possibility that Galina had arranged that excuse herself. Light, she should never have slapped the woman. It was too late for self-recrimination, though.

"What are we going to do now?" Arrela asked.

"Dig ourselves out," Faile and Maighdin said at the same instant. Faile looked at the other woman in surprise. Her maid's dirty face wore a queen's resolve.

"Yes," Alliandre said, straightening. She turned around, and if runnels of tear-tracks marked the dust on her face, no new tears appeared. She really was a queen, and could not like being shamed by the courage of a lady's maid. "We'll dig ourselves out. And if we fail. . . . If we fail, I will not die wearing *this*!" Unfastening her golden belt, she flung it contemptuously into a corner of the basement. Her golden collar followed.

"We'll need those to make our way through the Shaido camp," Faile said gently. "Galina may not be taking us out, but I intend leaving today." Dairaine made that imperative. Bain and Chiad could not keep her hidden long. "Or as soon we can dig out, anyway. We'll pretend we've been sent to pick berries." She did not want to step on her liege-woman's bold gesture, though. "However, we don't need to wear them now." Removing her belt and collar, she righted her basket and set them atop the dirty *gai'shain* robes. The others emulated her. Alliandre retrieved her own belt and collar with a rueful laugh. At least she could laugh again. Faile wished she could.

The jumble of charred timbers and half-burned boards filling the staircase resembled one of those blacksmith's puzzles her Perrin enjoyed. Almost everything seemed to be propping up something else. Worse, the heavier timbers might be beyond all of them working together. But if they could clear enough for them to be able to crawl through, writhing between the thick beams. . . . It would be dangerous, that crawl. But when a dangerous path was your only route to safety, you had to take it.

A few boards came away easily and were piled at the back of the basement, but after that everything had to be chosen with care, examined to see whether anything would fall if it were removed, hands feeling back as far as they could go into the tangle, groping for nails that might have caught, trying not think about the whole pile shifting and trapping an arm, crushing it. Only then could they begin pulling, sometimes two of them together, tugging harder and harder until the piece suddenly gave. That work went slowly, with the great pile occasionally groaning, or shifting slightly. Everyone darted back, holding their breath, when that happened. Nobody moved again until they were sure the snarl of timbers was not going to collapse. The work became the focus of their world. Once, Faile thought she heard wolves howling. Wolves generally made her think of Perrin, but not this time. The work was all.

Then Alliandre wrenched a charred board free, and with a great groan, the mass began to shift. Toward them. Everyone ran toward the back of the basement as the pile fell in with a deafening rumble, sending up more billows of dust.

When they stopped coughing and could see again, dimly, with dust still hanging in the air, perhaps a quarter of the basement was filled. All of their work undone, and worse, the jumble was leaning toward them precariously. Groaning, it sagged a little more toward them and stopped. Everything about it said the first board pulled free would bring the whole mass down on their heads. Arrela began to cry softly. Tantalizing gaps admitted sunlight and allowed them to see the street, the sky, but nothing anyone could wriggle through, even Lacile. Faile could see the red scarf Galina had used to mark the building. It fluttered for a moment in the breeze.

Staring at the scarf, she seized Maighdin's shoulder. "I want you to try to make that scarf do something the wind wouldn't make it do."

"You want to attract attention?" Alliandre said hoarsely. "It's far more likely to be Shaido than anyone else."

"Better that than dying down here of thirst," Faile replied, her voice harsher than she wanted. She would never see Perrin again, then. If Sevanna had her chained, she would at least be alive for him to rescue. He would rescue her; she knew it. Her duty now was to keep the women who followed her alive. And if that meant captivity, so be it. "Maighdin?"

"I might spend all day trying to embrace the Source and never succeed," the sun-haired woman said in dull tones. She stood slumped, staring at nothing. Her face suggested that she saw an abyss beneath her feet. "And if I do embrace it, I can almost never weave anything."

Faile loosened her grip on Maighdin and smoothed her hair instead. "I know it's difficult," she said soothingly. "Well, in truth, I don't know. I've never done it. But you have. And you can do it again. Our lives depend on you, Maighdin. I know the strength that's in you. I've seen it time and again. There is no surrender in you. I know you can do it, and so do you."

Slowly, Maighdin's back straightened, and despair slid off her face. She might still see the abyss, but if she fell, she would fall without flinching. "I'll try," she said.

For a long while she stared up at the scarf, then shook her head dejectedly. "The Source is there, like the sun just beyond the edge of

sight," she whispered, "but every time I try to embrace it, it's like trying to catch smoke with my fingers."

Faile hastily pulled the *gai'shain* robes from her basket and another,
careless of the gold belts and collars falling to the stone floor. "Sit
down," she said, arranging the robes in a pile. "Make yourself comfortable. I know you can do it, Maighdin." Pressing the other woman
down, she folded her legs and sat beside her.

"You can do it," Alliandre said softly, sitting down on Maighdin's
other side.

"Yes, you can," Lacile whispered, joining them.

"I know you can," Arrela said as she lowered herself to the floor.

Time passed, with Maighdin staring at the scarf. Faile whispered
encouragement and held onto hope hard. Suddenly the scarf went
rigid, as if something had pulled it taut. A wondrous smile appeared
on Maighdin's face as the scarf began to swing back and forth like a
pendulum. Six, seven, eight times it swung. Then it fluttered in the
breeze and fell limp.

"That was marvelous," Faile said.

"Marvelous," Alliandre said. "You're going to save us, Maighdin."

"Yes," Arrela murmured, "you're going to save us, Maighdin."

There were many kinds of battle. Sitting on the floor, whispering
encouragement, Maighdin fighting to find what she could seldom find,
they fought for their lives while the scarf swung, then fell to the
breeze, swung and fell limp. But they fought on.

Galina kept her head down and tried not to hurry as she made her way
out of Malden, past the streams of white-clad men and women carrying
empty buckets into the town and full buckets back out. She did not
want to attract attention, not without that cursed belt and necklace.
She had donned the things when she dressed in the night, while Therava was still asleep, but it had been such a pleasure to remove them and
hide them with the clothes and other things she had secreted away for
her escape that she could not resist. Besides, Therava would have been
angered to wake and find her missing. She would have ordered a watch
for her "little Lina," and everyone marked her by those jewels. Well,
they would pay to help her return to the Tower, now, return to her
rightful place. That arrogant Faile and the other fools were dead or as

good as, and she was free. She stroked the rod, hidden in her sleeve, and shivered with delight. Free!

She did hate leaving Therava alive, but if anyone had entered the woman's tent and found her with a knife through her heart, Galina would have been the first suspect. Besides. . . . Images rose in her head, of her bending stealthily over the sleeping Therava, the woman's own belt knife in hand, of Therava's eyes snapping open, meeting hers in the darkness, of her screaming, of her hand opening nervelessly to drop the knife, of her begging, of Therava. . . . No. No! It would not have been that way. Certainly not! She had left Therava alive of necessity, not because she was. . . . Not for any other reason.

Suddenly wolves howled, wolves in every direction, a dozen or more. Her feet stopped of their own accord. A motley collection of tents surrounded her, walled tents, peaked tents, low Aiel tents. She had walked right through the *gai'shain* portion of the camp without realizing it. Her eyes rose to the ridge west of Malden, and she flinched. Thick fog curled along the whole length of it, concealing the trees as far as she could see in either direction. The town walls hid the ridge to the east, yet she was sure there would be thick fog there, too. The man had come! The Great Lord preserve her, she had been just in time. Well, he would not find his fool wife even if he managed to survive whatever he was about to try, nor would he find Galina Casban.

Thanking the Great Lord that Therava had not forbidden her to ride—the woman had much preferred dangling the possibility that she might be allowed, if she groveled sufficiently—Galina hurried toward her hidden stores. Let the fools who wanted to die here, die. She was free. Free!

CHAPTER 29

The Last Knot

Perrin stood just below the ridgetop, near the edge of the fog, and studied the encampment and stone-walled town below. Two hundred paces of fairly steep slope sparsely dotted with low brush down to level ground, perhaps seven hundred more of cleared ground to the first tents, then better than a mile to the town. It seemed so close, now. He did not use his looking glass. A glint off the lens from the sun just peeking over the horizon, a fingernail edge of golden-red, might ruin everything. The grayness around him curled but did not really move with the breeze, even when it gusted and made his cloak stir. The dense mist on the far ridge, obscuring the windmill there, seemed too still as well, if you studied it a while. How long before someone among those tents noticed? There was nothing to be done for it. The fog felt like any fog, damp and a little cool, but somehow Neald had fixed these mists in place before he went off to his other tasks. The sun would not burn them off even at noonday, or so the Asha'man claimed. Everything would be done by noon, one way or another, but Perrin hoped the man was right. The sky was clear, and the day looked to be warm for early spring.

Only a few Shaido seemed to be outside in the camp, relatively speaking, but thousands of white-clad figures bustled about among the tents. Tens of thousands. His eyes ached to find Faile among them, his heart ached to see her, but he could as well try to pick out one particular pin from a barley-basket of them spilled on the ground. Instead, he stared at the town's gates, standing wide open as they had every time he had gazed on them. Invitingly wide. They called to him. Soon, Faile and her companions would know it was time to head for those gates, and the towered fortress that bulked at the north end of the town. She might be at chores, if the Maidens were right about how the prisoners would be treated as *gai'shain*, but she would know to slip away and go to the fortress. She and her friends, and likely Alyse as well. Whatever her scheme with the Shaido, the Aes Sedai would not want to remain on a battleground. A second sister in the fortress might come in handy. The Light send it did not come to that.

He had planned with care for every eventuality he could imagine down to outright disaster, yet this was no blacksmith's puzzle however much he wished it were. The twisted iron pieces of a blacksmith's puzzle moved only in certain ways. Move them in the right way, and the puzzle came apart. People could move in a thousand ways, sometimes in directions you never believed possible till it happened. Would his plans stand up when the Shaido did something unexpected? They would do it, almost certainly, and all he could do in return was hope it would not lead to that disaster. With a last, longing look at Malden's gates, he turned and walked back up the ridge.

Inside the fog, even he could not see ten paces, but he soon found Dannil Lewin among the trees on the ridgetop. Lean to the point of skinny, with a pickaxe for a nose and thick mustaches in the Taraboner style, Dannil stood out even when you could not see his face clearly. Other Two Rivers men were shapes beyond him, growing dimmer and dimmer with distance. Most were squatting or sitting on the ground, resting while they had the chance. Jori Congar was trying to entice some of the others into a game of dice, but he was quiet about it, so Perrin let it pass. No one was accepting the offer anyway. Jori was uncommon lucky with his dice.

Dannil made a leg when he saw Perrin and murmured, "My Lord." The man had been spending too much time with Faile's people. He called it acquiring polish, whatever that was supposed to mean. A man was not a piece of brass.

"Make sure nobody does anything woolhead foolish like I just did, Dannil. Sharp eyes below might spot movement near the edge of the fog and send men to investigate."

Dannil coughed discreetly into his hand. Light, he was getting as bad as any of thóse Cairhienin and Tairens. "As you say, my Lord. I'll keep everybody back."

"My Lord?" Balwer's dry voice said out of the mist. "Ah, there you are, my Lord." The little stick of a man appeared, followed by two larger shapes, though one was not much taller. They halted at a gesture from him, indistinct forms in the fog, and he came on alone. "Masema has put in an appearance below, my Lord," he said quietly, folding his hands. "I thought it best to keep Haviar and Nerion out of his sight, and his men's, under the circumstances. I don't believe he is suspicious of them. I think he has anyone he is suspicious of killed. But out of sight, out of mind is best."

Perrin's jaw tightened. Masema was supposed to be beyond the eastern ridge with his army, if it could be called that. He had counted those men—and a few women—as they shuffled uneasily through gateways made by the two Asha'man, and they were twenty thousand if they were one. Masema had always been vague about their numbers, and Perrin had not had an accurate count until last night. Ragged and dirty, only one here or there wore a helmet much less a breastplate, but every hand had gripped sword or spear or axe, halberd or crossbow, the women included. The women among Masema's followers were worse than the men by far, and that was saying something. For the most part the lot of them were only good for terrorizing people into swearing to follow the Dragon Reborn—the colors whirled in his head and were shattered by his anger—that and murdering them if they refused. They had a better purpose today. "Maybe it's time for Haviar and Nerion to start staying away from Masema's people for good," he said.

"If you wish it, my Lord, but in my judgment, they still are as safe as any man can be doing what they do, and they're eager." Balwer tilted his head, a curious sparrow in a branch. "They haven't been corrupted, if that's what you fear, my Lord. That's always a danger when you send a man to pretend to be what he isn't, but I have a keen nose for the signs."

"Keep them close, Balwer." After today, with luck, there might not be much of Masema's army left to spy on in any case. There might not even be a Masema to worry about.

Perrin scrambled down the brushy reverse slope, past where the Mayener and Ghealdanin lancers were waiting beside their horses in the thick mist, streamered lances propped on their shoulders or steel heads driven into the ground. The Winged Guards' red-painted helmets and breastplates might have been safe enough on the ridgetop, but not the Ghealdanin's burnished armor, and since Gallenne and Arganda both bristled if one was favored over the other, both waited here. The fog extended quite some distance—Neald claimed that was intentional, but the man had smelled surprised, and pleased, when he realized what he had done—so Perrin was still walking through grayness when he reached the bottom of the ridge, where all of the high-wheeled carts stood in a line with horses hitched. The dim figures of the Cairhienin cart drivers moved about them, checking harness, tightening the ropes that held the canvas covers on.

Masema was waiting, and Perrin wanted nothing so much as to chew off the man's arm, but he spotted the stout shape of Basel Gill beside one of the carts and headed that way. Lini was with him, wrapped in a dark cloak, and Breane with her arm around the waist of Lamgwin, Perrin's hulking manservant. Master Gill snatched off his brimmed hat to reveal thin graying hair combed back over a bald spot that it failed to cover. Lini sniffed and pointedly avoided looking at Perrin while pretending to adjust her cowl. She smelled of anger and fear. Master Gill just smelled of fear.

"It's time for you to start north, Master Gill," Perrin said. "When you reach the mountains, follow them until you strike the Jehannah Road. With luck, we'll catch you up before you reach the mountains, but if not, send Alliandre's servants off to Jehannah, then you head east through the pass, then north again. We'll be as close behind you as we can." If his plan did not go too far awry. Light, he was a blacksmith, not a soldier. But even Tylee had finally agreed it was a good plan.

"I will not leave this spot until I know that Maighdin is safe," Lini told the fog, her thin voice a reed of iron. "And the Lady Faile, of course."

Master Gill rubbed a hand back over his head. "My Lord, Lamgwin and I were thinking maybe we could help out. The Lady Faile means a great deal to us, and Maighdin . . . Maighdin is one of our own. I know one end of a sword from the other, and so does Lamgwin." He was wearing one belted around his bulk, yet if he had handled a sword these past twenty years, Perrin would eat the whole great length of that belt. Breane's grip on Lamgwin tightened, but the big man patted her shoulder and rested his other hand on the hilt of a shortsword. The fog obscured his scarred face and sunken knuckles.

He was a tavern brawler, though a good man even so, but never a swordsman.

"You're my *shambayan*, Master Gill," Perrin said firmly. "It's your duty to get the cart drivers and grooms and servants to safety. Yours and Lamgwin's. Now go on with you and see to it." The stout man nodded reluctantly. Breane breathed a small sigh of relief when Lamgwin knuckled his forehead in acquiescence. Perrin doubted that the man could have heard the sigh, though Lamgwin put his arm around her and murmured comforting words.

Lini was not so compliant. Back stiff as a rod, she addressed the fog again. "I will not leave this spot until I know—"

Perrin slapped his hands together with a loud crack, startling her into looking at him in surprise. "All you can do here is catch the ague from standing in the damp. That and die, if the Shaido manage to break through. I'll bring Faile out. I'll bring Maighdin and the others out." He would, or die himself in the attempt. There was no point saying that, though, and reason not to. They had to believe in their bones that he would be following with Faile and the rest. "And you are going north, Lini. Faile will be upset with me if I let anything happen to you. Master Gill, you make sure she rides with you if you have to tie her up and put her in the back of a cart."

Master Gill jerked, crumpling his hat between his hands. He smelled of alarm, suddenly, and Lini of pure indignation. Amusement filled Lamgwin's scent, and he rubbed at his nose as though concealing a smile, but strangely, Breane was indignant, too. Well, he had never claimed to understand women. If he could not understand the woman he was married to, which he could not half the time, then it was unlikely he ever would understand the rest of them.

In the end, Lini actually climbed up beside the driver of a cart without having to be forced, though she slapped away Master Gill's hand when he tried to assist her, and the line of carts began to trundle off northward though the fog. Behind one of the carts, laden with the Wise Ones' tents and possessions, marched a cluster of white-clad *gai'shain*, meek even now, men and women with their cowls up and their eyes lowered. They were Shaido, taken at Cairhien, and in a few months they would put off white and return to their clan. Perrin had had them watched, discreetly, despite the Wise Ones' assurances that they would adhere to *ji'e'toh* in this regard whatever others they abandoned, yet it appeared the Wise Ones were right. They still numbered seventeen. None had tried to run off and warn the Shaido beyond the ridge. The carts' axles had been greased liberally, but they still creaked and squealed to his ears. With luck, he and Faile *would* catch up to them shy of the mountains.

As the strings of spare horses began to pass him, on long leads held by mounted grooms, a Maiden appeared in the mist coming down the line of carts. Slowly she resolved into Sulin, *shoufa* around her neck to bare her short white hair and black veil hanging down onto her chest. A fresh slash across her left cheek would add another scar to her face unless she accepted Healing from one of the sisters. She might not. Maidens seemed to have odd attitudes about Wise Ones' apprentices, or maybe it was just that these apprentices were Aes Sedai. They even saw Annoura as an apprentice, though she was not.

"The Shaido sentries to the north are dead, Perrin Aybara," she said. "And the men who were going out to replace them. They danced well, for Shaido."

"You took casualties?" he asked quietly.

"Elienda and Briain woke from the dream." She might have been speaking of the weather rather than two deaths among women she knew. "We all must wake eventually. We had to carry Aviellin the last two miles. She will need Healing." So. She would accept it.

"I'll send one of the Aes Sedai with you," he said, looking around in the fog. Aside from the line of horses passing him, he could see nothing. "As soon as I can find one."

They found him almost as he spoke, Annoura and Masuri striding out of the fog leading their horses with Berelain and Masema, his shaven head glistening damply. Even in the mist, there was no mistaking the rumpled nature of the man's brown coat, or the crude darn on the shoulder. None of the gold his followers looted stuck to his hands. It all went to the poor. That was the only good that could be said of Masema. But then, a fair number of the poor that gold went to feed had been made poor by having their possessions stolen and their shops or farms burned by Masema's people. For some reason, Berelain was wearing the coronet of the First of Mayene this morning, the golden hawk in flight above her brow, though her riding dress and cloak were plain dark gray. Beneath her light, flowery perfume, her scent was patience and anxiety, as odd a combination as Perrin had ever smelled. The six Wise Ones were with them, too, dark shawls draped over their arms, folded kerchiefs around their temples holding back their long hair. With all their necklaces and bracelets of gold and ivory, they made Berelain appear simply dressed for once. Aram was one of their number as well, the wolfhead pommel of his sword rising above one red-striped shoulder, and the fog could not hide the absence of his habitual glower. The man gravitated toward Masema and seemed almost to bask in some light that Masema gave off. Perrin wondered whether he should have sent Aram with the carts. But if he had, he was sure Aram would have leaped off and sneaked back as soon as he was out of Perrin's sight.

He explained Aviellin's need to the two Aes Sedai, but to his surprise, when Masuri said she would come, fair-haired Edarra raised a hand that stopped the slim Brown in her tracks. Annoura shifted uncomfortably. She was no apprentice, and uneasy over Seonid and Masuri's relationship with the Wise Ones. They tried to include her in it, and sometimes succeeded.

"Janina will see to it," Edarra said. "She has more skill than you, Masuri Sokawa."

Masuri's mouth tightened, but she kept silent. The Wise Ones were quite capable of switching an apprentice for speaking up at the wrong time, even if she did happen to be an Aes Sedai. Sulin led Janina, a flaxen-haired woman who never seemed to be ruffled by anything, off into the fog, Janina striding as quickly as Sulin despite her bulky skirts. So the Wise Ones had learned Healing, had they? That might be useful later in the day; the Light send it was not needed often.

Watching the pair disappear into the murk, Masema grunted. The thick mist hid the ever-burning intensity of his deep-set eyes and obscured the triangular white scar on his cheek, but his scent was full in Perrin's nose, hard and sharp as a freshly stropped razor yet twitching in a frenzy. That smell of madness sometimes made him think his nose must bleed from breathing it.

"Bad enough you use these blasphemous women who do what only the Lord Dragon, blessed be his name, may do," Masema said, his voice full of the heat that the fog concealed in his eyes.

The colors spinning in Perrin's head turned into a brief image of Rand and Min and a tall man in a black coat, an Asha'man, and he felt a shock right down to his boots. Rand's left hand was gone! No matter. Whatever had happened, had happened. And today his business lay elsewhere.

"... but if they know Healing," Masema continued, "it will be that much harder to kill the savages. A pity you won't let the Seanchan leash all of them."

His sidelong glance at Annoura and Masuri said he included them, despite the fact both had visited him in secret more than once. They regarded him with Aes Sedai calm, though Masuri's slim hands moved once as if to smooth her brown skirts. She said she had changed her mind and now believed the man must be killed, so why was she meeting him? Why was Annoura? Why did Masema allow them? He more than hated Aes Sedai. Perhaps answers could be found now that Haviar and Nerion no longer needed protection.

Behind Masema, the Wise Ones stirred. Fire-haired Carelle, who looked as if she possessed a temper though she did not, actually stroked the hilt of her belt knife, and Nevarin, who could have given Nynaeve lessons in getting angry, gripped hers. Masema should have felt those eyes boring into his back, but his scent never shifted. Insane he might be, but never a coward.

"You wanted to speak to Lord Perrin, my Lord Prophet," Berelain said gently, though Perrin could smell the strain of her smile.

Masema stared at her. "I am simply the Prophet of the Lord Dragon, not a lord. The Lord Dragon is the only lord, now. His coming has shattered all bonds and destroyed all titles. King and queens, lords and ladies, are but dust beneath his feet."

Those whirling hues threatened again, but Perrin crushed them. "What are you doing here?" he demanded. There was no way to soften moments with Masema. The man was as hard as a good file. "You're supposed to be with your men. You risked being seen by coming here, and you'll risk it again going back. I don't trust your people to hold for five minutes without you there to stiffen their spines. They'll run as soon as they see the Shaido coming their way."

"They are not my people, Aybara. They are the Lord Dragon's people." Light, being around Masema meant having to stomp on those colors every few minutes! "I left Nengar in charge. He has fought more battles than you have dreamed of. Including against the savages. I also gave the women orders to kill any man who tries to run and have let it be known that I will hunt down anyone who escapes the women. They will hold to the last man, Aybara."

"You sound as if you're not going back," Perrin said.

"I intend to stay close to you." Fog might hide the heat in Masema's eyes, but Perrin could *feel* it. "A pity if any misfortune should befall you just as you reclaim your wife."

So a small part of his plan had unraveled already. A hope really, rather than part of the plan. If all else went well, the Shaido who managed to flee would carve a way through Masema's people without more than slowing a step, but instead of taking a Shaido spear through his ribs, Masema would be . . . keeping an eye on him. Without any doubt, the man's bodyguard was not far off in the fog, two hundred or so ruffians better armed and better mounted than the rest of his army. Perrin did not look at Berelain, but the scent of her worry had strengthened. Masema had reason to want both of them dead. He would warn Gallenne that his primary task today would be protecting Berelain from Masema's men. And he would have to watch his own back.

Off in the fog, a brief flash of silver-blue light appeared, and he frowned. It was too early yet for Grady. Two figures coalesced out of the mist. One was Neald, not strutting for once. In fact, he stumbled. His face looked tired. Burn him, why was he wasting his strength this way? The other was a young Seanchan in lacquered armor with a single thin plume on the peculiar helmet he carried beneath his arm. Perrin recognized him, Gueye Arabah, a lieutenant Tylee thought well of. The two Aes Sedai gathered their skirts as if to keep him from brushing against them, though he went nowhere near them. For his part, he missed a step when he came close enough to make out their faces, and Perrin heard him swallow hard. He smelled skittish, of a sudden.

Arabah's bow included Perrin and Berelain, and he frowned slightly at Masema as though wondering what such a ragged fellow was doing in their company. Masema sneered, and the Seanchan's free hand drifted toward his sword hilt before he stopped it. They seemed touchy folk, Seanchan did. But Arabah did not waste time. "Banner-General Khirgan's compliments, my Lord, my Lady First. *Morat'raken* report those bands of Aiel are moving faster than expected. They will arrive some time today, possibly as soon as noon. The group to the west is perhaps twenty-five or thirty thousand, the one to the east larger by a third. About half of them are wearing white, and there will be children, of course, but that is still a lot of spears to have behind you. The Banner-General wishes to know if you would like to discuss altering the deployments. She suggests moving a few thousand of the Altaran lancers to join you."

Perrin grimaced. There would be at least three or four thousand *al-gai'd'siswai* with each of those bands. A lot of spears to have at his back for certain sure. Neald yawned. "How are you feeling, Neald?"

"Oh, I'm ready to do whatever needs doing, I am, my Lord," the man said with just a hint of his usual jauntiness.

Perrin shook his head. The Asha'man could not be asked to make one gateway more than necessary. He prayed that they would not fall one short. "By noon, we'll be done here. Tell the Banner-General we go ahead as planned." And pray that nothing else went amiss. He did not add that aloud, though.

Out in the fog, wolves howled, an eerie cry that rose all around Malden. It was truly begun, now.

"You're doing wonderfully, Maighdin," Faile croaked. She felt light-headed, and her throat was dry from encouraging the woman. Every-one's throat was dry. By the slant of the light coming through the gaps overhead, it was near midmorning, and they had been talking without cease for most of that. They had tried tapping the unbroken barrels, but the wine inside was too rancid even for wetting lips. Now they were taking turns with the encouragement. She was sitting alongside her sun-haired maid while the others rested against the back wall, as far from that leaning jumble of boards and timbers as they could get. "You're going to save us, Maighdin."

Above them, the red scarf was just visible through that narrow gap in the tangle. It had hung limply for some time, now, except when the breeze caught it. Maighdin stared at it fixedly. Her dirty face glistened with sweat, and she breathed as if she had been running hard. Sud-denly the scarf went taut and began to swing, once, twice, three times. Then the breeze sent it fluttering, and it fell. Maighdin continued to stare.

"That was beautiful," Faile said hoarsely. The other woman was getting tired. More time was passing between each success, and the successes were lasting a shorter time. "It was—"

Abruptly a face appeared beside the scarf, one hand gripping the length of red. For a moment, she thought she must be imagining it. Aravine's face framed by her white cowl.

"I see her!" the woman said excitedly. "I see the Lady Faile and Maighdin! They're alive!" Voices raised a cheer, quickly stilled.

Maighdin swayed as if she might fall over, but a beautiful smile wreathed her face. Faile heard weeping behind her, and wanted to weep with joy herself. Friends had found them, not Shaido. They might escape yet.

Pushing herself to her feet, she moved closer to the leaning pile of charred rubble. She tried to work moisture into her mouth, but it was thick. "We're all alive," she managed in husky voice. "How in the Light did *you* find us?"

"It was Theril, my Lady," Aravine replied. "The scamp followed you despite your orders, and the Light bless him for it. He saw Galina leave, and the building fall in, and he thought you were dead. He sat down and cried." A voice protested in rough Amadician accents, and Aravine turned her head for a moment. "I know someone who's been crying when I see him, boy. You just be thankful you stopped to cry. When he saw the scarf move, my Lady, he came running for help."

"You tell him there's no shame in tears," Faile said. "Tell him I've seen my husband cry when tears were called for."

"My Lady," Aravine said hesitantly, "he said Galina pulled on a timber when she came out. It was set like a lever, he said. He said she made the building collapse."

"Why would she do that?" Alliandre demanded. She had helped Maighdin to her feet and half supported her to reach Faile's side. Lacile and Arrela joined them, alternating between tears and laughter. Alliandre's face was a thunderhead.

Faile grimaced. How often in the last few hours had she wished she had that slap back? Galina had *promised*! Could the woman be Black Ajah? "That doesn't matter now. One way or another, I'll see her repaid." How was another matter. Galina *was* Aes Sedai, after all. "Aravine, how many people did you bring? Can you—?"

Large hands took Aravine by the shoulders and moved her aside. "Enough talk." Rolan's face appeared in the gap, *shoufa* around his neck and veil hanging onto his chest. Rolan! "We cannot clear anything with you standing there, Faile Bashere. This thing may fall in when we start. Go to the other end and huddle against the far wall."

"What are you doing here?" she demanded.

The man chuckled. He chuckled! "You still wear white, woman. Do as you are told, or when I have you out of there, I will smack your bottom soundly. And then maybe we will soothe your tears with a kissing game."

She showed him her teeth, hoping he did not take it for a grin. But he was right about them needing to move away, so she led her companions across the board-strewn stone floor to the far end of the basement where they crouched against the wall. She could hear voices muttering outside, likely discussing exactly how to go about clearing a path without making the rest of the building collapse on her head.

"All this for nothing," Alliandre said bitterly. "How many Shaido do you suppose are up there?"

Wood scraped loudly, and with a groan, the leaning pile of rubble leaned inward a little more. The voices began again.

"I haven't any idea," Faile told her. "But they must all be *Mera'din*, not Shaido." The Shaido did not mingle with the Brotherless. "There might be some hope in that." Surely Rolan would let her go once she learned about Dairaine. Of course, he would. And if he remained stubborn. . . . In that case, she would do whatever was necessary to convince him. Perrin would never have to find out.

Wood scraped on wood again, and once more the heap of burned timbers and boards tilted inward a little further.

The fog hid the sun, but Perrin estimated it must be near midmorning. Grady would be coming soon. He should have been there by now. If the man had grown too tired to make another gateway. . . . No. Grady would come. Soon. But his shoulders were as tight as if he had been working a forge for a full day and longer.

"I tell you, I don't like this one bit," Gallenne muttered. In the thick mist, his red eyepatch was just another shadow. His heavy-chested bay nosed his back, impatient to be moving, and he patted the animal's neck absently. "If Masema really wants to kill the Lady First, I say we finish him now. We outnumber him. We can overwhelm his bodyguard in minutes."

"Fool," Arganda growled, glancing off to his right as if he could see Masema and his men through the curling grayness. Unlike the Mayener, he had put on his silvered helmet with its three fat white plumes. It and his breastplate, worked in gold and silver, glistened with condensation. Fog or no fog, his armor seemed almost to glow. "You think we can kill two hundred men without making a sound? Shouts will be heard the other side of this ridge. You have your ruler where you can surround her with nine hundred men and maybe get her away. Alliandre is still in that bloody town, and surrounded by Shaido."

Gallenne bristled, hand going to his sword hilt, as though he might practice on Arganda before moving on to Masema.

"We're not killing anybody but Shaido today," Perrin said firmly. Gallenne grunted, but he did not try to argue. He stank of discontent, though. Protecting Berelain would keep the Winged Guards out of the fighting.

Off to the left, a bluish flash appeared, dimmed by the thick mist, and the tightness in Perrin's shoulders loosened. Grady appeared in the fog, peering about him. His step picked up when he saw Perrin, but it was unsteady. Another man was with him, leading a tall, dark horse. Perrin smiled for the first time in a long while.

"It's good to see you, Tam," he said.

"Good to see you, too, my Lord." Tam al'Thor was still a blocky man who looked ready to work from sunup to sundown without slacking, but the hair on his head had gone completely gray since Perrin had seen him last, and he had a few more lines on his bluff face. He took in Arganda and Gallenne with a steady gaze. Fancy armor did not impress him.

"How are you holding up, Grady?" Perrin asked.

"I'm holding up, my Lord." The weathered man's voice sounded bone weary. Shadowed by the fog as it was, his face still looked older than Tam's.

"Well, as soon as you're done here, join Mishima. I want somebody keeping an eye on him. Somebody who makes him too nervous to think they can change what they agreed to." He would have liked to tell Grady to tie off this gateway. It would make a short path to take Faile back to the Two Rivers. But if things went wrong today, it would make a short path for the Shaido, too.

"Don't know as I could make a cat nervous right now, my Lord, but I'll do what I can."

Frowning, Tam watched Grady vanish into the gray murk. "I could wish I'd had some other way to get here," he said. "Fellows like him visited the Two Rivers a while back. One called himself Mazrim Taim, a name we'd all heard. A false Dragon. Only now he wears a black coat with fancy embroidery and calls himself the M'Hael. They talked everywhere about teaching men to channel, about this Black Tower." He freighted the words with sourness. "The Village Councils tried to put a stop to it, and the Women's Circles, but they ended up taking above forty men and boys with them. Thank the Light some listened to sense, or I think they'd have had ten times that." His gaze shifted to Perrin. "Taim said Rand sent him. He said Rand is the Dragon Reborn." There was a touch of questioning in that, perhaps a hope for denial, perhaps a demand to know why Perrin had kept silent.

Those hues whirled in Perrin's head, but he batted them away and answered by not answering. What was, was. "Nothing to be done about it now, Tam." According to Grady and Neald, the Black Tower did not just let men go once they signed on.

Sadness entered Tam's scent, though he let nothing show on his face. He knew the fate of men who could channel. Grady and Neald claimed the male half of the Source was clean, now, but Perrin could not see how that could be. What was, was. You did the job you were given, followed the road you had to follow, and that was that. There was no point complaining about blisters, or rocks underfoot.

Perrin went on. "This is Bertain Gallenne, Lord Captain of the Winged Guards, and Gerard Arganda, First Captain of the Legion of the Wall." Arganda shrugged uncomfortably. That name carried political weight in Ghealdan, and apparently Alliandre had not felt strong enough to announce that she was reconstituting the Legion. Balwer had a nose for sniffing out secrets, though. This one made sure Arganda would not go wild trying to reach his queen. "Gallenne, Arganda, this is Tam al'Thor. He's my First Captain. You studied the map, Tam, and my plan?"

"I studied them, my Lord," Tam said dryly. Of course he would have. "It looks a good plan to me. As good as any till the arrows start flying."

Arganda put a booted foot in his roan's stirrup. "So long as he's *your* First Captain, my Lord, I have no objections." He had offered plenty earlier. Neither he nor Gallenne had been pleased that Perrin was putting someone over them.

From up the slope came a black-winged mocker's shrill cry of alarm. Only one. If it had been a real bird, the call would have been repeated.

Perrin scrambled up the slope as fast he could. Arganda and Gallenne passed him on their mounts, but they divided to ride to their men, disappearing into the thick gray haze. Perrin continued to the top and beyond. Dannil was standing almost at the edge of the fog, peering toward the Shaido encampment. He pointed, but the reason for the alarm was obvious. A large group of *algai'd'siswai* was leaving the tents, maybe four hundred or more. The Shaido sent out raiding parties frequently, but this one was aimed straight at Perrin. They were just walking, but it would not take them long to reach the ridge.

"It's time to let them see us, Dannil," he said, unpinning his cloak and draping it over a low bush. He would come back for it later. If he could. It would only get in his way, now. Dannil sketched a bow before hurrying back into the trees as Aram appeared, sword already in hand. He smelled eager. The cloak pin Perrin put into his pocket carefully. Faile had given him that. He did not want to lose it. His fingers found the leather cord he had knotted for every day of her captivity. Pulling it out, he let it fall to the ground without glancing at it. This morning had seen the last knot.

Tucking his thumbs behind the wide belt that supported his hammer and belt knife, he strolled out of the fog. Aram advanced up on his toes, already in one of those sword stances. Perrin just walked. The morning sun, indeed halfway to its noon peak, was in his eyes. He had considered taking the eastern ridge and putting Masema's men here, but it would have meant that much farther to reach the town gates. A foolish reason, yet those gates drew him as a lodestone drew iron filings. He eased his heavy hammer in its loop on his belt, eased his belt knife. That had a blade as long as his hand.

The appearance of two men, apparently walking idly toward them, was enough to halt the Shaido. Well, perhaps not so idly, considering Aram's sword. They would have to be blind to miss the sun glinting off his long blade. They must have been wondering whether they were watching madmen. Halfway down the slope, he stopped.

"Relax," he told Aram. "You're going to tire yourself out that way."

The other man nodded without taking his eyes from the Shaido and planted his feet firmly. His scent was that of a hunter after dangerous quarry and determined to pull it down.

After a moment, half a dozen of the Shaido started toward them, slowly. They had not veiled. Likely they were hoping he and Aram would not be frightened into running. Among the tents, people were pointing at the two fools on the slope.

The sound of running boots and hooves and snorting horses made him look over his shoulder. Arganda's Ghealdanin appeared out of the fog first, in their burnished breastplates and helmets, riding behind a

rippling red banner that bore the three six-pointed silver stars of
Ghealdan, and then the Winged Guards in their red armor behind the
golden hawk on a field of blue of Mayene. Between them, Dannil began arraying the Two Rivers men in three ranks. Every man carried a
pair of bristling quivers at his belt and also a bundle of shafts that he
stuck point down into the slope before slicing the binding cords. They
wore their swords and shortswords, but the halberds and other
polearms had been left on the carts this morning. One of them had
brought along the red wolfhead banner, but the staff was stuck aslant
into the ground behind them. No one could be spared to carry the
thing. Dannil carried a bow, too.

Masema and his bodyguard of lancers took position on the Winged
Guards' right, their poorly handled horses plunging and rearing. Their
armor showed patches of speckled brown where rust had been scraped
away instead of properly cleaned. Masema himself was out in front, a
sword at his hip but helmetless and without a breastplate. No, he did
not lack courage. He was glaring at the Mayeners, where Perrin could
just make out Berelain in the middle of that forest of lances. He could
not get a clear view of her face, but he imagined it was still frosty. She
had objected strenuously to her soldiers being held back from the
fighting, and he had needed to be very firm to make her see reason.
Light, the woman had half suggested she might *lead* them in a charge!

The Wise Ones and the two Aes Sedai filed down between the
Ghealdanin and the Two Rivers men accompanied by the Maidens,
each of whom had long strips of red cloth tied around her upper arms
and dangling to the wrist. He could not pick out Aviellin, but by their
number she must be among them, newly Healed or not. Black veils
covered their faces except for their eyes, yet he did not need to see their
faces or catch their scents to know they were indignant. The markings
were necessary to avoid accidents, but Edarra had had to put her foot
down to make them wear the things.

Bracelets of gold and ivory rattled as Edarra adjusted her dark
shawl. With smooth sun-dark cheeks that seemed darker because of
her pale-yellow hair, she looked little older than Perrin, but her blue
eyes held an unshakable calm. He suspected she was far older than she
appeared. Those eyes had seen a great deal. "I think it will begin soon,
Perrin Aybara," she said.

Perrin nodded. The gates called to him.

The appearance of near enough two thousand lancers and two

hundred-odd bowmen was sufficient to make the Shaido below raise their veils and spread out while more began rushing from the tents to join them in a thick, lengthening line. Pointing fingers along that line, pointing spears, made him look back again.

Tam was on the slope, now, and more Two Rivers men were pouring out of the fog with longbows in hand. Some tried to mingle with the men who had followed Perrin, to reunite with brothers, sons, nephews, friends, but Tam chivvied them away, trotting his black gelding up and down as he arranged them in three ever-expanding ranks to either side of the horsemen. Perrin spotted Hu Barran and his equally lanky brother Tad, the stablemen from the Winespring Inn, and square-faced Bar Dowtry, only a few years older than he himself was, who was making a name for himself as a cabinetmaker, and skinny Thad Torfinn, who seldom left his farm except to come into Emond's Field. Oren Dautry, lean and tall, stood between Jon Ayellin, who was hulking and bald, and Kev Barstere, who finally had gotten out from under his mother's thumb if he was here. There were Marwins and al'-Dais, al'Seens and Coles, Thanes and al'Caars and Crawes, men from every family he knew, men he did not recognize, from down to Deven Ride or up to Watch Hill or Taren Ferry, all grim-faced and burdened with pairs of bristling quivers and extra sheaves of arrows. And among them stood others, men with coppery skins, men with transparent veils across the lower half of their faces, fair-skinned men who just did not have the look of the Two Rivers. They carried shorter bows, of course—it took a lifetime to learn the Two Rivers longbow—but every face he could make out looked as determined as any Two Rivers man. What in the Light were the outlanders doing here? On and on the streams of running men continued until finally those three long lines held at least three thousand men, maybe four.

Tam walked his horse down the slope to Perrin and sat studying the swelling Shaido ranks below, yet he seemed to hear Perrin's unspoken question. "I asked for volunteers from the Two Rivers men and picked the best bowshots, but those you took in started coming forward in groups. You gave them and their families homes, and they said they were Two Rivers men too, now. Some of those bows won't carry much more than two hundred paces, but the men I chose hit what they aim at."

Below, the Shaido began beating their spears rhythmically against their bull-hide bucklers. RAT-tat-tat-tat! RAT-tat-tat-tat! RAT-tat-

tat-tat! The sound rose like thunder. The flow of veiled shapes running out from the tents slowed to a trickle that dwindled further and then ceased. All of the *algai'd'siswai* had been drawn out, it seemed. That was the plan, after all. There must have been twenty thousand of them, near enough, all pounding their bucklers. RAT-tat-tat-tat! RAT-tat-tat-tat! RAT-tat-tat-tat!

"After the Aiel War, I hoped never to hear that again," Tam said loudly, to be heard. That noise could get on a man's nerves. "Will you give the command, Lord Perrin?"

"You do it." Perrin eased his hammer again, his belt knife. His eyes kept going from the Shaido to the town gates, and the dark mass of the fortress inside the town. Faile was in there.

"Soon now we will know," Edarra said. About the tea, she meant. If they had not waited long enough, they were all dead. Her voice was calm, though. Aram shifted, up on his toes again, sword upright before him in both hands.

Perrin could hear Tam calling as he rode along the lines of bowmen. "Longbows, nock! Shortbows, hold till you're close! Longbows, nock! Shortbows, hold till you're close! Don't draw, you fool! You know better! Longbows . . . !"

Below, perhaps a quarter of the Shaido turned and began trotting north, paralleling the ridge, still beating their bucklers. Another quarter began trotting south. They intended to sweep around and catch the men on the slope from either side. Flanking, Tylee called it. A ripple passed through those remaining as they began sticking their spears through the harness holding their bowcases, hanging their bucklers on their belts, unlimbering their bows.

"Very soon," Edarra murmured.

A fireball larger than a man's head arched out from the tents toward the ridge, then another, twice the size, and more, streams of them. Sailing high, the first turned down. And exploded with loud roars a hundred paces overhead. In rapid succession, the others began exploding harmlessly, too, but more followed, spheres of flame speeding toward the ridge in a continuous flow. Forked silver lightning stabbed down from a cloudless sky and erupted with booming crashes of thunder and great showers of sparks without ever coming near the ground.

"Perhaps fifteen or twenty Wise Ones escaped the tea," Edarra said, "otherwise more would have joined in by now. I can see only nine women channeling. The rest must be among the tents." She disliked the agreement he had with the Seanchan almost as much as the Aes Sedai did, yet her voice was calm. In her book, the Shaido had violated *ji'e'toh* to such a degree that it was questionable whether they could be called Aiel any longer. To her, they were something that had to be cut out of the body of the Aiel, and their Wise Ones were the worst of the sickness for allowing it. Masuri drew her arm back, but Edarra laid a hand on her shoulder. "Not yet, Masuri Sokawa. We will tell you when." Masuri nodded obediently, though she smelled of impatience.

"Well, I for one feel in danger," Annoura said firmly, drawing her arm back. Edarra looked at her levelly. After a moment, the Aes Sedai lowered her arm. Her beaded braids clicked together as she twisted her head away from the Wise One's stare. Her scent was of strong unease. "Perhaps I can wait a little longer," she muttered.

The fireballs hurtling across the sky continued to explode far above, the lightning jabbed toward the ridge, but the Shaido below were not waiting. With a shout, the main mass began trotting quickly toward the ridge. And singing at the tops of their lungs. Perrin doubted anyone else on the slope could make out more than a roar, but his ears caught words faintly. They were singing in parts.

> *Wash the spears . . .*
>   *. . . while the sun climbs high.*
> *Wash the spears . . .*
>   *. . . while the sun falls low.*
> *Wash the spears . . .*
>   *. . . who fears to die?*
> *Wash the spears . . .*
>   *. . . no one I know!*

He shut the sound out, ignoring it while his eyes drifted beyond the onrushing mass of veiled figures to the gates of Malden. Iron filings to a lodestone. The shapes below seemed to have slowed half a step, though he knew they had not. Everything seemed to slow down for him at times like this. How long before they came in range? They had covered little more than half the distance to the ridge.

"Longbows, raise! On my signal!" Tam shouted. "Longbows, raise! On my signal!"

Perrin shook his head. It was too soon. Thousands of bowstrings

snapped behind him. Arrows arced over his head. The sky seemed
black with them. Seconds later another flight followed, then a third.
Fireballs burned swathes through them, but it was still thousands of
arrows that fell in a deadly hail onto the Shaido. Of course. He had forgotten to factor in the bowmen's elevation. That gave them a little
more distance. Trust Tam to see it right away. Not every arrow struck
a man, of course. Many plunged into the ground. Perhaps half struck
algai'd'siswai, piercing arms or legs, striking bodies. Wounded Shaido
hardly slowed, even when they had to struggle up from the ground.
They left hundreds lying still, though, and the second flight put down
hundreds more, as did the third, with the fourth and fifth already on
the way. The Shaido kept coming, leaning forward as if trotting into a
driving rain while their Wise Ones' balls of fire and lightnings exploded far overhead. They were no longer singing. Some raised their
bows and shot. An arrow grazed Perrin's left arm, but the rest fell
short. Not by far, though. Another twenty paces, and—

The sudden sharp sound of Seanchan horns pulled his gaze north
and south just in time to see the ground erupt in fountains of fire
among the flanking parties. Spears of lightning stabbed into them. The
damane were being kept back in the trees, for the time, but they did
deadly work. Again and again, explosions of fire or lightning hurled
men like twigs. Those *algai'd'siswai* could have no idea where the attack
was coming from. They began to run toward the trees, toward their
killers. Some of the fireballs coming out of the camp began flying toward the forests where the *damane* were, and lightnings jabbed toward
the trees, but with as little effect as they had against the ridge. Tylee
claimed *damane* were used for all sorts of tasks, but the truth was, they
were weapons of war, and they and the *sul'dam* were very good at it.

"Now," Edarra said, and fireballs began raining down on the Shaido
below. The Wise Ones and Aes Sedai made throwing motions with
both arms as fast as they could, and every time, a ball of flame seemed
to rise from their fingertips. Many of those exploded too soon, of
course. The Shaido Wise Ones were working to defend their own. But
the *algai'd'siswai* were much nearer to the ridge, so they had less time
to react. Fireballs burst among the Shaido, hurling men aside, flinging
severed arms and legs into the air. Silver-blue lightning bolts forked
down, and most of those struck, too. The hair on Perrin's arms stirred.
The hair on his head tried to stand. The air seemed to crackle with the
lightnings' discharges.

Even as they flung death at the men below, Edarra and the others continued to parry the Shaido Wise Ones' attacks, and all the while, the Two Rivers men worked their bows as fast as they could. A trained man could loose twelve shafts in a minute, and the range was shorter now. The Shaido lacked no more than two hundred paces of reaching the bottom of the ridge. Their arrows still fell short of Perrin, but the Two Rivers arrows were striking home every time at this range. Each bowman was picking his own target, of course, so Perrin saw *algai'd'-siswai* fall pierced by two, three, even four shafts.

Flesh could only take so much. The Shaido began to fall back. It was not a rout. They did not flee. Many shot arrows back at the ridge despite no hope of making the range. But they turned as if on a command and ran, trying to outpace the Two Rivers shafts and the rain of fire and lightning that pursued them. The flankers were falling back, too, as lancers appeared out of the trees forming ranks a thousand horses wide, advancing slowly while fire and lightning harried the Shaido.

"By ranks," Tam shouted, "advance three paces and loose!"

"Advance at a walk!" Arganda bellowed.

"With me!" Masema shouted.

Perrin was supposed to make that slow advance with the others, but he began to walk down the slope faster and faster. The gates tugged at him. His blood was becoming fire. Elyas claimed it was a natural feeling when you were in danger of your life, but he could not see it. He had almost drowned in the Waterwood once, and he had felt nothing like this thrill that was surging through him now. Someone behind shouted his name, but he trotted on, picking up speed. Freeing his hammer from its belt loop, he drew his belt knife with his left hand. Aram was running beside him, he realized, but his own focus was on the gates, on the Shaido who still stood between him and Faile. Fire, lightning and arrows fell among them like hail, and they were no longer turning to fire their own arrows, though they often looked over their shoulders. But many were supporting wounded, men who dragged a leg or clutched a side with a Two Rivers shaft jutting from it, and he was catching up.

Abruptly, half a dozen veiled men turned back gripping spears and started toward him and Aram at the run. Not using their bows meant they had expended their arrows. He had heard tales of champions, of men who decided the future by single combat between two armies that would abide by the outcome. The Aiel had no such tales. He did not slow down, though. His blood *was* fire. *He* was fire.

A Two Rivers shaft took one Shaido in the middle of his chest, and even as he fell, three more were feathered with at least a dozen arrows each. But now he and Aram were too close to the remaining two. Anyone but the very best bowshots would risk hitting him or Aram if he fired. Aram flowed toward one of the Shaido as if dancing, his blade a bright blur, but Perrin had no time to watch anyone else fight if he had wanted to. A veiled man who overtopped him by a head stabbed at him with a short spear held near its base. Blocking the spear with his belt knife, Perrin swung his hammer. The Shaido tried to stop it with his buckler, but he altered the swing slightly, and heard the bones in the man's forearm snap under ten pounds of steel swung by a blacksmith's arm. He was inside the spear, now, and without slowing, he slashed across the man's throat with his knife. Blood gouted, and he was running again while the man was falling. He had to reach Faile. Fire in his blood, fire in his heart. Fire in his head. No one and nothing would keep him from Faile.

CHAPTER

30

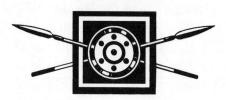

Outside the Gates

Faile tried to estimate the time by the slant of light falling through the gaps in the ruined building overhead; it seemed still short of noon. All that had been cleared was a small space at the very top of the basement stairs. Any of them could have passed through it, if they dared to try climbing the slanting pile of blackened rubble, but that still looked as though it might fall in any moment. The tangled heap still creaked alarmingly at times. The only good thing was that it had not started raining on their heads. How long that would last was a question. She had been hearing thunder for some time, quite a lot of it, and slowly coming closer. The booms were almost continuous. A storm that fierce might be enough to make the building finish collapsing. Light, she was thirsty.

Rolan suddenly appeared in the opening and lay down on the stone landing. He was not wearing the harness that held his bow case. Carefully he wriggled his way out *onto* the rubble. The pile groaned softly under his weight. Kinhuin, a green-eyed man a good hand or more shorter than he, knelt to grip his ankles. There were only three of the Brotherless up there, it seemed, but that was three too many.

Head and shoulders sticking over the edge of the rubble, Rolan lowered one arm. "There is no more time, Faile Bashere. Take my hand."

644

"Maighdin first," Faile said thickly, waving away the sun-haired woman's weary protests. Light, but her mouth was coated with grit and too dry to spit any of it out. "Arrela and Lacile next. I'll go last." Alliandre nodded approvingly, but Arrela and Lacile tried to object, too. "Be quiet and do as I say," she told them firmly. Thunder crashed and crashed. The storm that produced that much thunder would bring a deluge, not simple rainfall.

Rolan laughed. How could the man *laugh* at a time like this? He only stopped when the charred timbers beneath him groaned again from his shaking. "You still wear white, woman. So be quiet and do as *I* say." There was a touch of mocking in his tone at that, but not when he added, "No one will be taken out before you." That sounded like cast iron.

"My Lady," Alliandre said quietly, hoarsely, "I believe he means it. I will send the others out in the order you gave."

"Stop pouting and give me your hand," Rolan commanded.

She was *not* pouting! The man could be as infuriatingly stubborn as her Perrin. Only, in Perrin, it was intriguing, not really infuriating. Raising her right hand as high as it would go, she let Rolan's hand envelope hers. He lifted her easily, till her face was just below his.

"Catch hold of my coat." There was no hint of strain in his voice despite the awkward angle of his arm. "You will have to climb over me."

She swung her left hand up and caught a fistful of the rough wool, holding on hard. The pain in her shoulder told her it was bruised as badly as she feared. When he released her other hand, she gasped at the jolt of agony and quickly grabbed his coat with that one, too. Grasping her waist in both hands, he boosted her higher, so she was lying on his broad back. Thunder boomed and boomed without ceasing. The rain must start falling soon. That would make getting the others out more difficult.

"I like feeling your weight on me, Faile Bashere, but maybe you could climb a little faster so I can bring the others out." He pinched her bottom, and she laughed in spite of herself. The man just would not stop trying!

The climb over him was slower than she could have hoped for. She did not believe anything was broken in her shoulder, but it *hurt*. Once, she thought she kicked Rolan in the head. Pinch her, would he?

At last she was outside and past Kinhuin, on her feet under the sky once more. Her first sight of the building from outside made her swallow, and then cough vigorously as bits of grit entered her throat. The charred timbers were tilting to an alarming degree, ready to crash into the basement. The third Brotherless, Jhoradin, a blue-eyed man with red-gold hair and a face that fell not far short of prettiness, was watching Kinhuin and Rolan, but every so often he glanced at the building as if expecting to see it fall. He was squat for an Aiel, not quite as tall as Perrin but half again as wide. There must have been at least a hundred of her people in the street, staring at her anxiously, some of their white robes stained with soot from their efforts at digging her out. A hundred! She could not find it in her heart to upbraid them, however. Especially after Aravine thrust a plump waterskin into her hands. The first mouthful went to wash away grit and dust, though she wanted desperately to swallow it anyway, but after that, she held up the skin and all but poured water down her throat. Her bruised shoulder protested. She ignored it and drank and drank.

Suddenly she became aware of lightning striking outside the town to the west and lowered the waterskin to stare. Close outside the town. Out of a cloudless sky. And sometimes not striking. Many of those forked silvery bolts erupted with thunderous roars far above the ground. Balls of fire hurtled across the sky, sometimes bursting in air with a boom like thunder. Someone was fighting a battle with the Power! But who? Could Perrin have found enough Aes Sedai or Asha'man to attack the camp? But something was very odd. She knew how many Wise Ones in the camp could channel, and there did not seem to be enough lightning or fireballs. Perhaps it was not Perrin after all. There were factions among the Wise Ones. Not just between those supporting or opposing Sevanna, but between septs with old alliances or animosities. Maybe one of those factions was fighting another. That seemed highly unlikely, but less so than Perrin finding enough Aes Sedai to attack and the Wise Ones not fighting back with everything they could muster.

"When the lightnings started, Rolan said there was a battle," Aravine said when Faile asked her. "That's all. Nobody wanted to go find out more until we knew you were safe."

Faile ground her teeth in frustration. Even if she did not have to deal with Rolan, whatever was going on outside the walls might make escaping that much more difficult. If only she knew what it was, she might be able to see how to avoid it. Or use it. "No one is to go anywhere, Aravine. It might be dangerous." And they might inadvertently lead Shaido back when they returned. Light, what was going on?

Maighdin staggered out past Kinhuin rubbing her hip. "He pinched me!" Her voice was thick, but indignation came through. Faile felt a stab of. . . . Not jealousy. Certainly not that. The bloody man could pinch any woman he wanted to. He was not Perrin.

Grimacing, she handed the sun-haired woman the waterskin, and Maighdin washed out her mouth hurriedly before beginning to gulp thirstily. She was not so sun-haired at the moment, her curls all sweat-matted and as coated with dust as her sweaty face. She was not even pretty at the moment.

Arrela came out of the ruin rubbing her bottom and looking grim as death, but she eagerly took the waterskin that Aldin offered. The tall young Amadician, a square-shouldered fellow who looked more a soldier than the bookkeeper he was, gazed at her avidly as she drank. Arrela did not like men that way, but Aldin refused to accept that he could not convince her to marry him. Lacile appeared—rubbing *her* bottom!—and Jhoradin handed her another waterskin, drawing a finger down her dirty cheek. She smiled up at him before beginning to drink. Already preparing her way back into his blankets if Rolan proved obstinate. At least, Faile thought that was what she was doing.

At last Alliandre stalked past Kinhuin, and if she was not rubbing herself, her expression of frosty ire told the tale plainly enough. Kinhuin backed out of the opening and stood while Rolan began working his way back across the dangerous pile of timbers.

"My Lady," Aravine called anxiously, and Faile turned to find the plump-faced woman kneeling on the paving stones and lifting Maighdin's head onto her lap. Maighdin's eyelids fluttered but never came more than half open. Her lips moved weakly, but only mumbles emerged.

"What happened?" Faile said, hurrying to kneel beside them.

"I don't know, my Lady. She was drinking as if she intended to empty the skin, and suddenly she staggered. The next I knew, she just collapsed." Aravine's hands fluttered like falling leaves.

"She must be very tired," Faile said, smoothing her maid's hair and trying not to think of how they were to get the woman out of the camp if she could not walk. It would be done if they had to carry her. Light, she felt a touch wobbly herself. "She saved us, Aravine." The Amadician woman nodded gravely.

"I will hide you somewhere safe until tonight, Faile Bashere," Rolan said, fastening the last buckles of his bow case harness. His brown *shoufa* was already wrapped around his head. "Then I will take you to the forest." Taking three short spears from Jhoradin, he thrust them up through the harness behind so the long spearpoints, glinting in the sun, stuck up above his head.

Faile almost collapsed beside Maighdin with relief. There would be no need to conceal anything from Perrin. But she could not afford weakness, not now. "Our supplies," she began, and as if the sound of her voice were the last straw, the building gave a squealing groan and fell in with a crash that drowned out the explosions for a moment.

"I will see that you have what you need," Rolan told her, raising the black veil across his face. Jhoradin handed him another spear and his buckler, which he hung on his belt knife before seizing her right arm and drawing her to her feet. "We must move quickly. I do not know who we are dancing the spears with, but the *Mera'din* will dance today."

"Aldin, will you carry Maighdin?" was all she managed to get out before Rolan strode away pulling her with him.

She looked over her shoulder to see Aldin lifting a limp Maighdin in his arms. Jhoradin had Lacile by her arm as firmly as Rolan had her. The three Brotherless were leading a parade of white-garbed men and women. And one boy. Theril wore a grim expression. Fumbling in her sleeve, no easy matter with Rolan's big hand on her arm, she closed her fingers around the ridged hilt of her dagger. Whatever was happening outside the walls, she might have need of that blade before nightfall.

Perrin ran along the winding street through the tents. No one moved in his sight, but through the roar of exploding fireballs and lightnings, he could hear other sounds of battle. Steel clashing on steel. Men shouting, as they killed or died. Men screaming. Blood ran down the left side of his face from a gash in his scalp, and he could feel it oozing down his right side from where a spear had grazed him, oozing down his left thigh from a spear that had bitten deeper. Not all of the blood on him was his own. A face appeared at the opening to a low, dark tent and drew back hurriedly. A child's face, and frightened, not the first he had seen. The Shaido were being pressed so hard that a good many children had been left behind. They would be a problem for later, though. Over the tents, he could see the gates little more than a hundred paces ahead. Beyond them lay the fortress and Faile.

Two veiled Shaido darted out from beside a dirty brown wall-tent, spears at the ready. But not for him. They were looking at something off to the left. Without slowing, he ran into them. Both were larger than he, but the force of his rush carried them all to the ground, and he fell already fighting. His hammer smashed into the bottom of one man's chin while he stabbed and stabbed at the other man, blade biting deep. The hammer rose and crushed the first man's face, splashing blood, rose and fell again while he stabbed. The man with the ruined face twitched once as Perrin rose. The other lay staring at the sky.

A hint of motion at the corner of his left eye made him throw himself to the right. A sword whisked through the air where his neck would have been. Aram's sword. The onetime Tinker had taken wounds, too. Blood coated half his face like a strange mask, there were blood-wet rents in his red-striped coat, and his eyes looked almost glazed, like those of a corpse, but he still seemed to be dancing with that blade in his hands. His scent was the scent of death, a death he sought.

"Have you gone mad?" Perrin growled. Steel rang against steel as he blocked that sword away with the head of his hammer. "What are you doing?" He blocked another slice of the blade, tried to grapple the other man, and barely danced back in time to get away with only a gash across his ribs.

"The Prophet explained it to me." Aram sounded in a daze, yet his sword moved with liquid ease, blows barely diverted with hammer or belt knife as Perrin backed away. All he could do was hope he did not trip over a tent rope or come up against a tent. "Your eyes. You're really Shadowspawn. It was you who brought the Trollocs to the Two Rivers. He explained it all. Those eyes. I should have known the first time I saw you. You and Elyas with those Shadowspawn eyes. I have to rescue the Lady Faile from you."

Perrin gathered himself. He could not keep moving ten pounds of steel as quickly as Aram moved a sword that weighed a third of that. Somehow, he had to get close, get beyond that blade blurring with the speed of its motion. He could not do so without getting cut, and likely badly, but if he waited much longer, the man was going to kill him. Something caught his heel, and he staggered backward, nearly falling.

Aram darted in, sword chopping down. Suddenly, he stiffened, eyes going wide, and the blade dropped from his hands. He toppled forward to lie on his face, two arrows jutting from his back. Thirty paces beyond him, a pair of veiled Shaido already had arrows nocked and drawn again. Perrin leaped sideways, behind a green, peaked tent, rolling to his feet quickly. At the corner of the tent, an arrow poked through the canvas, still quivering. Crouching, he made his way past the green tent and then a faded blue one, a low tent of dingy brown, hammer in one hand, knife in the other. This was not the first time he had played this game today. Cautiously, he peeked around the edge of the brown tent. The two Shaido were nowhere to be seen. They might be stalking him in turn, or off hunting someone else already. The game had turned both ways before. He could see Aram, lying where he had fallen. A scrap of breeze ruffled the dark fletchings on the arrows sticking up from his back. Elyas had been right. He should never have let Aram pick up that sword. He should have sent him away with the carts, or made him go back to the Tinkers. So many things he should have done. Too late, now.

The gates called to him. He glanced over his shoulder. So close, now. Still crouching, he began to run again along those twisting streets, wary of those two Shaido or any others that might be lurking. The sounds of battle were ahead of him, now, coming from north and south, but that did not mean there would be no stragglers.

Rounding a corner only a few paces from the wide-open gates, he found them filled with people. Most were garbed in dirty white robes, but three were veiled *algai'd'siswai*, one of them a hulking fellow who would have dwarfed Lamgwin. That one had Faile's arm in his fist. She looked as if she had been rolled in the dirt.

With a roar, Perrin rushed forward raising his hammer, and the huge man flung Faile back and ran toward him, spear coming up as he plucked his buckler from his belt.

"Perrin!" Faile screamed.

The big Shaido seemed to hesitate for a heartbeat, and Perrin took advantage of it. His hammer hit the side of the man's head so hard that his feet left the ground as he fell. Another was right behind him, though, spear ready to stab. Suddenly the man grunted, surprise in the green eyes above his black veil, and dropped to his knees peering over his shoulder at Faile, who stood close. Slowly he fell forward, revealing a ridged steel hilt rising from his back. Perrin looked hastily for the third, and found him also lying on his face, with two wooden knife hilts sticking out of his back. Lacile was leaning against Arrela, weeping. No doubt she had found actually killing someone not so easy as she had supposed.

Alliandre was at the front of the crowd, too, and Maighdin right behind her, carried by a tall young man in white, but Perrin had eyes only for Faile. Letting knife and hammer fall, he stepped over the dead men and gathered her in his arms. The smell of her filled his nose. It filled his head. She smelled strongly of charred wood, of all things, but he could still smell *her*.

"I've dreamed of this moment so long," he breathed.

"I have, too," she said against his chest, hugging him hard. Her scent was full of joy, but she was trembling.

"Did they hurt you?" he asked gently.

"No. They. . . . No, Perrin, they didn't hurt me." There were other smells mixed in with her joy, though, laced through it inextricably. The dull, aching scent of sadness and the greasy aroma of guilt. Shame, like thousands of hair-fine needles pricking. Well, the man was dead, and a woman had the right to keep her secrets if she wanted.

"All that matters is that you're alive, and we're together again," he told her. "That's all that matters in the world."

"All that matters," she agreed, hugging him even harder. Hard enough that she actually groaned with the effort. But the next instant, she had pushed back and was examining his wounds, fingering open tears in his coat to look at them. "These don't look too bad," she said briskly, though all of those emotions still lay tangled in her joy. She reached up to part his hair and tugged until he bent his head so she could examine the slash along his scalp. "You'll need Healing, of course. How many Aes Sedai did you bring? How did you—? No, that's of no matter right now. There are enough of them to defeat the Shaido, and that is what's important."

"This lot of Shaido," he said, straightening to look down at her. Light, dirt or no dirt, she was so beautiful. "There'll be another six or seven thousand spears here in . . ." he glanced at the sun; it seemed it should be higher, "less than two hours, maybe. We need to finish up here and be moving before then, if we can. What's wrong with Maighdin?" She was limp as a feather pillow against the young man's chest. Her eyelids were fluttering without opening fully.

"She tired herself out saving our lives," Faile said, abandoning his injuries and turning to the other people in white. "Aravine, all of you, start gathering up *gai'shain*. Not just those sworn to me. Everybody in white. We leave no one we can reach behind. Perrin, what direction is safest?"

"North," he told her. "North is safe."

"Start them moving north," Faile went on. "Gather carts, wagons, packhorses, and load them with whatever you think we'll need. Hurry!" People started moving. Running. "No, you stay here, Aldin. Maighdin still needs to be carried. You stay, too, Alliandre. And Arrela. Lacile needs a shoulder to cry on for a while."

Perrin grinned. Put his wife down in the middle of a house engulfed in flames, and she would calmly set about putting the fire out. She *would* put it out, too. Bending, he cleaned his belt knife on the green-eyed man's coat before sheathing it. His hammer needed a good wiping, too. He tried not to think about what he was smearing on the man's coat. The fire was fading from his blood. There was no thrill remaining, only tiredness. His wounds were beginning to throb. "Will you send someone to he fortress to let Ban and Seonid know they can come out now?" he said as he slipped the hammer's haft back through the loop on his belt.

Faile stared at him in amazement. "They're in the *fortress*? How? Why?"

"Alyse didn't tell you?" He had always been slow to anger until Faile was taken. Now, he felt fury bubbling up in him. Bubbles like white-hot iron. "She said she was taking you with her when she left, but she promised to tell you to go to the fortress when you saw fog on the ridges and heard wolves howl by daylight. I'd swear she said it straight out. Burn me, you can't trust Aes Sedai an inch."

Faile glanced toward the western ridge, where the fog still clung thickly, and grimaced. "Not Alyse, Perrin. Galina. If that wasn't a lie, too. It has to be her. And she has to be Black Ajah. Oh, how I wish I knew her real name." She moved her left arm and winced. She *had* been hurt. Perrin found himself wanting to kill the big Shaido all over again. Faile did not let her injury slow her, though. "Theril, come out from there. I see you peeking around the gate."

A skinny young man edged shyly around the corner of the gate. "My father told me to stay and keep an eye on you, my Lady," he said in an accent so rough that Perrin could barely understand.

"That's as may be," Faile said firmly, "but you run to the fortress as fast as you can and tell whoever you find there that Lord Perrin says they're to come. Run, now." The boy knuckled his forehead and ran.

In a quarter of an hour or so he reappeared, still running, followed by Seonid and Ban and all the others. Ban made a leg to Faile and murmured smoothly how pleased he was to see her again before ordering the Two Rivers men to set up a guard ring around the gate, bows at the ready and halberds stuck in the ground. He used his normal voice for that. He was another who was trying to acquire polish. Selande and Faile's other hangers-on rushed around her, all babbling with excitement and saying how worried they had been when she failed to appear after the wolves howled.

"I'm going to Masuri," Kirklin announced in tones that dared challenge. He did not wait for one, though, simply drawing his sword and running off along the wall to the north.

Tallanvor gave a cry when he saw Maighdin being held by the tall young man and had to be convinced that she was only exhausted. He still took her away from the fellow and held her against his own chest, whispering to her.

"Where is Chiad?" Gaul demanded. On learning that she had never been with them, he lifted the veil across his face. "The Maidens tricked me," he said grimly, "but I will find her before them."

Perrin caught his arm. "There are a lot of men out there who'll take you for a Shaido."

"I have to find her first, Perrin Aybara." There was something in the Aiel's voice, something in his scent, that Perrin could only call heartache. He understood the sorrow of thinking the woman you loved might be lost to you forever. He let go of Gaul's sleeve, and the man darted through the line of bowmen, spear and buckler in hand.

"I'll go with him." Elyas grinned. "Maybe I can keep him out of trouble." Drawing the long knife that had given him his name among the wolves, Long Tooth, he went running after the tall Aielman. If the two of them could not make their way safely out there, then no one could.

"If you are done jabbering, perhaps you will stand still for Healing," Seonid told Perrin. "You look as if you need it." Furen and Teryl were heeling her, hands on their sword hilts and eyes trying to watch in every direction. The ring of Two Rivers men were all very well, their attitude seemed to say, but Seonid's safety was their charge. They looked like leopards heeling a house cat. Only she was no house cat.

"See to Faile first," he said. "Her arm is hurt." Faile was talking with Alliandre, both of them so angry they should have had tails to bristle. No doubt angry over Alyse or Galina or whatever her name was.

"I do not see *her* bleeding like a stuck pig." Seonid lifted her hands to cup his head, and that too familiar chill hit him, like suddenly being immersed in a winter pond on the brink of freezing. He gasped and jerked, arms flailing out of his control, and when she released him, his wounds were gone, if not the blood smeared on his face and staining his coat and breeches. He also felt he could eat a whole deer by himself.

"What was that?" The diminutive Green turned away from him toward Faile. "Did you mention Galina Casban?"

"I don't know her last name," Faile said. "A round-faced Aes Sedai with a plump mouth and black hair and big eyes. Pretty in a way, but an unpleasant woman. Do you know her? I think she must be Black Ajah."

Seonid stiffened, hands knotting in her skirts. "That sounds like Galina. A Red, and decidedly unpleasant. But why would you make such an accusation? It is not a charge to bring against a sister lightly, even against one as disagreeable as Galina."

As Faile explained, beginning with the first meeting with Galina, Perrin's anger grew again. The woman had blackmailed her, threatened her, lied to her, then tried to murder her. His fists clenched so tight that his arms shook. "I'll break her neck when I get my hands on it," he growled when she fell silent.

"That is not your right," Seonid said sharply. "Galina must be tried before three sisters sitting as a court, and for this charge, they must be Sitters. The entire Hall of the Tower might sit for it. If she is found guilty, she will be stilled and executed, but justice in this lies with Aes Sedai."

"If?" he said incredulously. "You heard what Faile said. Can you have any doubt?" He must have looked threatening, because Furen and Teryl glided in to flank Seonid, their hands resting lightly on sword hilts, their eyes hard on his face.

"She's right, Perrin," Faile said gently. "When Jac Coplin and Len Congar were accused of stealing a cow, you knew they were thieves, but you made Master Thane prove they had stolen it before you let the Village Council have them strapped. It's just as important with Galina."

"The Village Council wouldn't have strapped them without a trial whatever I'd said," he muttered. Faile laughed. She laughed! Light, it was good to hear again. "Oh, all right. Galina belongs to the Aes Sedai. But if they don't take care of her, I will if I ever find her again. I don't like people hurting you."

Seonid sniffed at him, her scent disapproving. "Your arm is injured, my Lady?"

"See to Arrela first, please," Faile said. The Aes Sedai rolled her eyes in exasperation and took Faile's head between her hands. Faile shivered and exhaled, hardly more than a heavy sigh. Not a bad injury, then, and gone now in any case. She thanked Seonid while leading her to Arrela.

Suddenly Perrin realized he could not hear the explosions any longer. In fact, he could not recall hearing one for some time. That had to be good. "I need to find out what's happening. Ban, you keep a close guard on Faile."

Faile protested his going alone, and by the time he finally agreed to take ten of the Two Rivers men, a rider in lacquered armor had appeared rounding the northern corner of the town wall. Three thin blue plumes marked her as Tylee. As she rode closer, he realized she had a nude woman draped across her tall bay in front of the saddle. A woman bound at ankles and knees, wrists and elbows. Her long golden hair almost brushed the ground, and there were jeweled necklaces and ropes of pearls caught in it. A strand of large green stones and gold slid free and fell to the dirt as Tylee reined in. Removing her peculiar helmet with gauntleted hands, she rested it on the woman's upturned bottom.

"A remarkable weapon, those bows of yours," she drawled, eyeing the Two Rivers men. "I wish we had the like. Kirklin told me where to find you, my Lord. They've begun surrendering. Masema's men held to the point of suicide—most of them are dead or dying, I think—and the *damane* turned that ridge into a deathtrap only a madman would walk into. Best of all, the *sul'dam* have already fitted *a'dam* to over two hundred women. That 'cold tea' of yours was enough that most of them could not stand without help. I'll have to send for *to'raken* to fly them all out."

Seonid made a sound in her throat. Her face was smooth, but her scent was dagger-sharp fury. She stared at Tylee as though trying to stare a hole through her. Tylee paid her no mind at all except to shake her head slightly.

"After my people and I are gone," Perrin said. His agreement was with her. He did not want to risk testing it with anyone else. "What are our losses aside from Masema's men?"

"Light," Tylee replied. "Between your archers and the *damane*, they never really managed to close with us. I've never seen a battle plan come off so smoothly. If we have a hundred dead between us, I'll be surprised."

Perrin winced. He supposed those were light casualties under the circumstances, but some would be Two Rivers men. Whether or not he knew them, they were his responsibility. "Do you know where Masema is?"

"With what's left of his army. He's no coward, I'll say that for him. He and his two hundred—well, about one hundred, now—cut a path all the way through the Shaido to the ridge."

Perrin ground his teeth. The man was back surrounded by his rabble. It would be his word against Masema's about why Aram had tried to kill him, and in any event, it was unlikely the man's followers would surrender him for trial. "We need to start moving before the others get here. If the Shaido think rescue is at hand, they might decide to forget they surrendered. Who's your prisoner?"

"Sevanna," Faile said in a cold voice. The smell of her hatred was nearly as strong as it had been while speaking of Galina.

The golden-haired woman twisted herself upward, shaking hair out of her face and losing several more necklaces in the process. Her eyes, glaring at Faile, were green fire above a strip of cloth that had been tied for a gag. She stank of rage.

"Sevanna of the Jumai Shaido." Satisfaction was strong in Tylee's voice. "She told me so proudly. She's no coward, either. Met us wearing nothing but a silk robe and her jewels, but she managed to spear two of my Altarans before I took it away from her." Sevanna snarled through her gag and struggled as if to throw herself from the horse. Until Tylee smacked her bottom, anyway. After that, she contented herself with glaring at everyone in sight. She was nicely rounded, though he should not be noticing something like that with his wife there. Except that Elyas said she would expect him to notice, so he made himself study her openly.

"I claim the contents of her tent," Faile announced, shooting him a sharp look. Maybe he was not supposed to be that open. "She has a huge chest of jewels in there, and I want them. Don't look at me like a looby, Perrin. We have a hundred thousand people to feed, clothe and help get back to their homes. A hundred thousand at least."

"I want to come with you, my Lady, if you'll have me," the young fellow who had been holding Maighdin piped up. "I won't be the only one, if you'll have us."

"Your lady wife, I presume, my Lord," Tylee said, eyeing Faile.

"She is. Faile, allow me to present Banner-General Tylee Khirgan, in service to the Empress of Seanchan." Perhaps he was acquiring some of that polish himself. "Banner-General, my wife, Lady Faile ni Bashere t'Aybara." Tylee bowed in her saddle. Faile made a small curtsy, inclined her head slightly. Dirty face or no dirty face, she was regal. Which made him think of the Broken Crown. Discussion of that little matter would have to come later. No doubt it would be a prolonged discussion. He thought he might not find it so hard to raise his voice, the way she apparently wanted, this time. "And this is Alliandre Maritha Kigarin, Queen of Ghealdan, Blessed of the Light, Defender of Garen's Wall. And my liege woman. Ghealdan is under my protection." Fool thing to say, but it had to be said.

"Our agreement doesn't speak to that, my Lord," Tylee said carefully. "I don't decide where the Ever Victorious Army goes."

"Just so you know, Banner-General. And tell those above you they can't have Ghealdan." Alliandre smiled at him so widely, so gratefully, he almost wanted to laugh. Light, Faile was smiling, too. A proud smile. He rubbed the side of his nose. "We really do need to begin moving before those other Shaido arrive. I don't want to find myself with them in front of me and all those prisoners behind me thinking about picking up a spear again."

Tylee chuckled. "I have a little more experience with these people than you, my Lord. Once they surrender, they won't fight again or try to escape for three days. Besides, I have some of my Altarans making bonfires out of their spears and bows just to make sure. We have time to make our deployments. My Lord, I hope I never have to face you in the field," she said, pulling the steel-backed gauntlet from her right hand. "I would be honored if you'd call me Tylee." She bent over Sevanna to offer her hand.

For a moment, Perrin could only stare. It was a strange world. He had gone to her thinking he was making a deal with the Dark One, and the Light knew, some of what the Seanchan did was beyond repugnant, but the woman was stalwart and true to her word.

"I'm Perrin, Tylee," he said, clasping her hand. A very strange world.

*   *   *

Stripping off her shift, Galina tossed it down atop the silk robe and bent to pick up the riding dress she had pulled from Swift's saddle-bags. The thing had been sewn for a slightly larger woman, but it would suffice until she could sell one of those firedrops.

"Stand as you are, Lina," came Therava's voice, and suddenly Galina could not have straightened if the forest around her had been on fire. She could scream, though. "Be silent." She choked as her throat swallowed the scream convulsively. She could still weep, silently, and tears began to fall on the mulch of the forest floor. A hand slapped her rudely. "Somehow, you have the rod," Therava said. "You would not be out here, else. Give it to me, Lina."

There was no question even of resisting. Straightening, Galina dug the rod out of her saddlebags and handed it to the hawk-eyed woman, tears sliding down her cheeks.

"Stop sniveling, Lina. And put on your necklace and collar. I will have to punish you for taking them off."

Galina flinched. Even Therava's command could not shut off her tears, and she knew she would be punished for that, too. Golden neck-lace and collar came out of the saddlebags and went onto her. She stood there wearing only her pale woolen stockings and soft laced white boots, and the weight of the firedrop-studded collar and belt seemed enough to bear her to the ground. Her eyes fastened themselves to the white rod in Therava's hands.

"Your horse will do for a pack animal, Lina. As for you, you are for-bidden to ride ever again."

There had to be some way to get that rod again. There had to be! Therava turned the thing over and over in her hands, taunting her.

"Stop playing with your pet, Therava. What are we going to do?" Belinde, a slender Wise One with hair bleached almost white by the sun, strode up to glare at Therava with pale blue eyes. She was bony, with a face well suited to glaring.

That was the first Galina realized that Therava was not alone. Sev-eral hundred men, women and children stood among the trees behind them, some of the men carrying women slung over their shoulders of all things. She covered herself with her hands, her face heating. Those long days of enforced nakedness had not inured her to being unclothed in front of men. Then she noticed another oddity. Only a handful were *algai'd'siswai*, with bow cases on their backs and quivers at their hips, but every man and every woman except the Wise Ones among them was carrying at least one spear. They had their faces veiled, too, with a scarf or just a scrap of cloth. What could it mean?

"We are returning to the Three-fold Land," Therava said. "We will send runners to find every sept that can be found and tell them to abandon their wetlander *gai'shain*, abandon everything they must, and make their way by stealth back to the Three-fold Land. We will rebuild our clan. The Shaido will rise from the disaster Sevanna led us to."

"That will take generations!" Modarra protested. Slim and quite pretty, but even taller than Therava, as tall as most Aielmen, she stood up to Therava unflinchingly. Galina could not understand how she did that. The woman made her flinch with a glance.

"Then we will take generations," Therava said firmly. "We will take whatever time is necessary. And we will never leave the Three-fold Land again." Her gaze shifted to Galina. Who flinched. "You will never touch this again," she said, raising the rod briefly. "And you will never try to escape me again. She has a strong back. Load her, and let us be on our way. They may try to pursue us."

Burdened with waterskins and pots and kettles till she almost felt decently covered, Galina staggered through the forest at Therava's heels. She did not think of the rod, or escape. Something had broken in her. She was Galina Casban, Highest of the Red Ajah, who sat on the Supreme Council of the Black Ajah, and she was going to be Therava's plaything for the rest of her life. She was Therava's little Lina. For the rest of her life. She knew that to her bones. Tears rolled silently down her face.

CHAPTER
31

The House on Full Moon Street

T hey must stay together," Elayne said firmly. "The two of you shouldn't be out by yourselves, for that matter. Always three or four together anywhere in Caemlyn. That's the only way to be safe." Just two of the mirrored stand-lamps were lit, six flames filling the sitting room with a dim light and the scent of lilies—so much of the lamp oil had gone bad that it was always perfumed, now—but a crackling fire on the hearth was beginning to take away some of the early hour's coolness.

"There are times a woman wants a little privacy," Sumeko replied calmly, as if yet another Kinswoman had not just died from wanting privacy. Her voice was calm, at least, but plump hands smoothed her dark blue skirts.

"If you won't put the fear of the Light into them, Sumeko, I will," Alise said, her usually mild face stern. She looked the elder of the two, with touches of gray in her hair compared to the glossy black hair that fell below Sumeko's stout shoulders, yet she was the younger by better than two hundred years. Alise had been intrepid when Ebou Dar fell and they were forced to flee the Seanchan, but her hands moved on her brown skirts, too.

It was long past the bedtime that Essande's niece Melfane de-creed, but tired as she was all the time, once Elayne woke, she could never get back to sleep, and warm goat's milk did not help. Warm goat's milk tasted worse than cool. She was going to make Rand bloody al'Thor drink warm bloody goat's milk till it came out of his ears! Right after she found out what had hurt him badly enough that she sensed a small jolt of pain while everything else in that small knot in the back of her head that was him remained as vague as a stone. It had been all a stone again ever since, so he was all right, yet something had hurt him deeply for her to sense anything at all. And why was he Traveling so often? One day, he was far to the southeast, the next to the northwest and even more distant, the day after that somewhere else. Was he running from whoever had hurt him? But she had her own worries at the moment.

Unable to sleep and restless, she had dressed herself in the first thing that came to hand, a dark gray riding dress, and gone for a walk to enjoy the stillness of the palace in the small hours of the morning, when even the servants were abed and flickering stand-lamps were the only things that moved in the hallways aside from her. Her and her bodyguards, but she was learning to ignore their presence. She did enjoy the solitude, until the two women encountered her and delivered the sad news that would have awaited sunrise otherwise. She had brought them back to her smaller sitting room to discuss the matter behind a ward against listeners.

Sumeko shifted her bulk in her armchair to glare at Alise. "Reanne let you press boundaries, but as Eldest, I expect—"

"You're not Eldest, Sumeko," the smaller woman said coolly. "You have the authority here, but by the Rule, the Knitting Circle consists of the thirteen eldest of us in Ebou Dar. We aren't in Ebou Dar any longer, so there is no Knitting Circle."

Sumeko's round face grew hard as granite. "At least you admit I have the authority."

"And I expect you to use it to prevent any more of us being murdered. Suggesting isn't enough, Sumeko, no matter how strongly you say you suggest. It isn't enough."

"Arguing will get us nowhere," Elayne said. "I know you're on edge. I am, too." Light, three women murdered with the One Power in the last ten days, and very likely seven more before that, were enough to put an anvil on edge. "But snapping at each other is the worst thing we can do. Sumeko, you need to put your foot down. I don't care how much anyone wants privacy, *no* one can be by herself for a minute.

Alise, use your persuasion." Persuasion was not exactly the word. Alise did not persuade. She simply expected people to do as she said, and they nearly always did. "Convince the others that Sumeko is right. Between the two of you, you have to—"

The door opened to admit Deni, who closed it again behind her and bowed, one hand on her sword hilt, the other on her long cudgel. The red-lacquered breastplates and helmets, trimmed in white, had been delivered only yesterday, and the stocky woman had been smiling ever since she donned hers, but she looked solemn behind the face-bars now. "Pardon for interrupting, my Lady, but there's an Aes Sedai here demanding to see you. A Red, by her shawl. I told her you were likely sleeping, but she was ready to come in and wake you herself."

A Red. There were reports of Reds in the city from time to time, though not so often as once—most Aes Sedai in the city went without their shawls, concealing their Ajahs—yet what would a Red want with her? Surely they all knew by now that she stood with Egwene and against Elaida. Unless someone was finally trying to bring her to book for the bargain with the Sea Folk.

"Tell her that I'm—"

The door opened again, bumping Deni's back, pushing her out of the way. The woman who entered, vine-woven shawl draped along her arms so the long red fringe displayed itself to advantage, was tall and slim and copper-skinned. She would have been pretty, except that her mouth was compressed until her full lips seemed thin. Her riding dress was so dark it might have been black, but the pale light of the stand-mirrors picked up hints of red, and the divided skirts were slashed with brighter red. Duhara Basaheen never made any secret of her Ajah. Once, Sumeko and Alise would have been on their feet and curtsying for an Aes Sedai in a flash, but now they remained seated, studying her. Deni, normally placid, in appearance at least, scowled and fingered her cudgel.

"I see the tales of you gathering wilders are true," Duhara said. "A great pity, that. The two of you get out. I wish to speak with Elayne privately. If you're wise, you will leave tonight, heading in different directions, and tell any others like you to do the same. The White Tower looks amiss on wilders gathering together. When the Tower looks on something amiss, thrones have been known to tremble." Neither Sumeko nor Alise moved. Alise actually arched an eyebrow.

"*They* can stay," Elayne said coldly. With the Power in her, her emotions were not bouncing. They were steady in an icy anger. "*They* are welcome here. *You*, on the other hand. . . . Elaida tried to have me *kidnapped*, Duhara. Kidnapped! *You* can leave."

"A poor welcome, Elayne, when I came to the palace as soon as I arrived. And after a journey that would be as torturous to describe as it was to endure. Andor has always had good relations with the Tower. The Tower intends to see they remain good. Are you sure you want these wilders to hear everything I have to say to you? Very well. If you insist." Gliding to one of the carved sideboards, she wrinkled her nose at the silver pitcher holding goat's milk and poured herself a cup of dark wine before taking a chair across from Elayne. Deni made a move as if to try dragging her out, but Elayne shook her head. The Domani sister ignored the Kinswomen as if they had ceased to exist. "The woman who drugged you has been punished, Elayne. She was flogged in front of her own shop with everyone in her village watching." Duhara sipped her wine, waiting for Elayne to respond.

She said nothing. She knew very well that Ronde Macura had been flogged for failure rather than for feeding her that vile tea, but saying so would make Duhara wonder how she knew, and that might lead to things that needed to remain hidden.

The silence stretched, and finally the other woman went on. "You must know that the White Tower wants very much for you to mount the Lion Throne. To achieve that end, Elaida has sent me to be your advisor."

In spite of herself, Elayne laughed. *Elaida* had sent her an advisor? It was ludicrous! "I have Aes Sedai to advise me when I need advice, Duhara. You *must* know I oppose Elaida. I wouldn't accept a pair of stockings from that woman."

"Your so-called advisors are rebels, child," Duhara said chidingly, with a heavy dose of distaste on the word "rebels." She gestured with the silver winecup. "Why do you think you have so many Houses opposing you, so many standing aside? They surely know you don't really have the backing of the Tower. With me as your advisor, that changes. I might be able to put the crown on your head inside a week. At most, it should take no more than a month or two."

Elayne met the other woman's gaze with a level gaze of her own. Her hands wanted to make fists, but she kept them still in her lap. "Even *were* that so, I'd refuse you. I expect to hear any day that Elaida has been deposed. The White Tower will be whole again, and no one will be able to claim I lack its backing then."

Duhara studied her wine for a moment, her face a mask of Aes Sedai serenity. "It won't be entirely smooth going for you," she said as if Elayne had not spoken. "This is the part I thought you wouldn't want the wilders to hear. And that guard. Does she think I'm going to attack you? No matter. Once you have the crown firmly on your head, you will have to appoint a regent, because you must return to the Tower then, to complete your training and eventually be tested for the shawl. You need have no fear of being birched as a runaway. Elaida accepts that Siuan Sanche ordered you to leave the Tower. Your pretense of being Aes Sedai is another matter. That, you will pay for with tears." Sumeko and Alise stirred, and Duhara took notice of them again. "Ah, you didn't know that Elayne is really only one of the Accepted?"

Elayne rose and stared down at Duhara. Usually, someone seated held the advantage over someone standing, but she made her stare hard and her voice harder. She wanted to slap the woman's face! "I was raised Aes Sedai by Egwene al'Vere on the day she herself was raised Amyrlin. I chose the Green Ajah and was admitted. Don't you *ever* say I'm not Aes Sedai, Duhara. Burn me if I'll stand still for it!"

Duhara's mouth pinched down till her lips seemed a gash. "Think, and you will see the reality of your situation," she said finally. "Think hard, Elayne. A blind woman could see how much you need me, and the White Tower's blessing. We will talk again later. Have someone show me to my rooms. I am more than ready for my bed."

"You'll have to find a room at an inn, Duhara. Every bed in the palace already has three or four people sleeping in it." If dozens of beds had been free, she would not have offered Duhara one. Turning her back, she walked to the fireplace and stood warming her hands. The gilded pendulum clock on the scroll-carved marble mantel chimed three times. Perhaps as many hours remained till sunrise. "Deni, have someone escort Duhara to the gates."

"You won't fend me off so easily, child. No one fends off the White Tower easily. Think, and you'll see I'm your only hope." Silk whisked against silk as she left the room, and the door clicked shut behind her. It seemed very possible Duhara would cause trouble trying to make herself needed, but one problem at a time.

"Did she put doubts in your minds?" Elayne said, turning from the fire.

"None," Sumeko replied. "Vandene and the other two accept you as Aes Sedai, so you must be." Conviction was strong in her voice, but then, she had reason to want to believe. If Elayne were a liar, her dreams of returning to the Tower, of joining the Yellow Ajah, died.

"But this Duhara believes she was speaking the truth." Alise spread her hands. "I'm not saying I doubt you. I don't. But the woman believes."

Elayne sighed. "The situation is . . . complicated." That was like saying water was moist. "I am Aes Sedai, but Duhara doesn't believe. She can't, because that would be admitting Egwene al'Vere truly is the Amyrlin Seat, and Duhara won't do that until Elaida has been brought down." She hoped Duhara would believe then. Accept, at least. The Tower *had* to be made whole. "Sumeko, you will *order* the Kinswomen to stay in groups? Always?" The stout woman muttered that she would. Unlike Reanne, Sumeko had no flair for leadership, or liking for it, either. A pity no older Kinswoman had appeared to take the burden from her. "Alise, you'll make sure they obey?" Alise's agreement was firm and quick. She would have been the perfect candidate if the Kin did not determine their rankings by age. "Then we've done what we can. It's long past time you were in your beds."

"Long past time for you, too," Alise said as she stood. "I could send for Melfane."

"No need to rob her of sleep, too," Elayne said hastily. And firmly. Melfane was short and stout, a merry woman with a ready laugh, and unlike her aunt in other ways, as well. Merry or not, the midwife was a tyrant who would not be pleased to learn that she was awake. "I'll sleep when I can."

Once they left, she released *saidar* and took up a book from several on the second sideboard, yet another history of Andor, but she could not concentrate. Bereft of the Power, she felt grumpy. Burn her, she was so weary that her eyes felt grainy. She knew that if she lay down, though, she would stare at the ceiling till the sun rose. In any case, she had stared at the page for only minutes when Deni appeared again.

"Master Norry is here, my Lady, with that Hark fellow. Said he'd heard you were up and wondered if you could spare him a few minutes."

He had *heard* she was up? If he was having her *watched* . . . ! The import broke through her grumpiness. Hark. He had not brought Hark since that first visit, ten days ago. No, eleven days, now. Ebullience replaced peevishness. Telling Deni to send them in, she followed the woman as far as the anteroom, where a patterned carpet covered most of the red-and-white floor tiles. Here, too, only a pair of stand-lamps were lit, giving off a dim, wavering light and a scent of roses.

Master Norry looked more than ever a white-crested wading bird with his long, spindly shanks, and tufts of hair sticking up behind his ears, but for once, he almost seemed excited. He was actually rubbing his hands together. He was not carrying his leather folder tonight; even in the dim light, the ink stains on his crimson tabard showed. One had turned the tuft of the White Lion's tail black. He offered a stiff bow, and the nondescript Hark imitated him awkwardly, then knuckled his forehead for good measure. He was wearing a darker brown than he had previously, but the same belt and buckle. "Forgive the hour, my Lady," Norry began in that dry voice.

"How *did* you know I was awake?" she demanded, emotions bouncing again.

Norry blinked, startled by the question. "One of the cooks mentioned sending up warm goat's milk for you when I went to get some for myself, my Lady. I find warm goat's milk very soothing when I can't sleep. But she mentioned wine, too, so I assumed you had visitors and might still be awake."

Elayne sniffed. She still wanted to snap at someone. Keeping that out of her voice required an effort. "I suppose you've success to report, Master Hark?"

"I followed him like you said, my Lady, and he's been to the same house three nights, counting this one. It's on Full Moon Street in the New City, it is. Only place he ever goes except taverns and common rooms. He drinks some, he does. Dices a lot, too." The man hesitated, dry-washing his hands nervously. "I can go now, right, my Lady? You'll take off whatever it was you put on me?"

"According to the tax rolls," Norry said, "the house is owned by the Lady Shiaine Avarhin, my Lady. She seems to be the last of the House."

"What else can you tell me about the place, Master Hark? Who else lives there besides this Lady Shiaine?"

Hark rubbed his nose uneasily. "Well, I don't know as they lives there, my Lady, but there's two Aes Sedai there tonight. I saw one of them letting Mellar out while the other was coming in, and the one who was coming in said, 'A pity there are only two of us, Falion, the way Lady Shiaine works us.' Only, she said Lady like she didn't mean it, she did. Funny. She was carrying a stray cat, a thing scrawny as she was." He bobbed a sudden, nervous bow. "Begging your pardon, my Lady. Didn't mean no offence, speaking of an Aes Sedai that way, but it took me a minute to realize she *was* Aes Sedai, it did. There was good light from the entry hall, there was, but she was so thin and plain, with a wide nose, that nobody would take her for Aes Sedai without some study."

Elayne laid a hand on his arm. Excitement bubbled in her voice, and she let it. "What were their accents?"

"Their accents, my Lady? Well, the one with the cat, she's from right here in Caemlyn I'd say. The other. . . . Well, she didn't say above two sentences, but I'd say she was Kandori. Called the other Marillin, if that helps, my Lady."

Laughing, Elayne capered a few steps. She knew who had set Mellar on her now, and it was worse than she had feared. Marillin Gemalphin and Falion Bhoda, two Black sisters who had fled the Tower after doing murder. That had been to facilitate theft, but it was the murders that would see them stilled and beheaded. It had been to find them, and the others with them, that she, Egwene and Nynaeve had been sent out of the Tower. The Black Ajah had planted Mellar next to her, to spy most likely, but still a chilling thought. Worse than she had feared, and yet, finding the two now was like completing the circle.

Hark was staring at her with his mouth hanging open, she realized. Master Norry was studiously examining the lion's stained tail. She stopped dancing and folded her hands. Fool men! "Where is Mellar now?"

"In his rooms, I believe," Norry said.

"My Lady, you'll take it off now?" Hark said. "And I can go? I did what you asked."

"First you have to lead us to this house," she said, darting past him to the twinned doors. "Then we'll talk." Putting her head out into the corridor, she found Deni and seven more Guardswomen lined up on either side of the doors. "Deni, send someone to fetch the Lady Birgitte as fast as possible, and someone else to wake the Aes Sedai and ask them to come, too, with their Warders and prepared to take a ride. Then you go and wake however many Guardswomen you think you need to arrest Mellar. You needn't be too gentle about it. The charges are murder and being a Darkfriend. Lock him in one of the basement storerooms with a strong guard." The stocky woman smiled broadly and began giving orders as Elayne went back inside.

Hark was wringing his hands and shifting from one foot to the other anxiously. "My Lady, what do you mean we'll talk? You promised to take this thing off me if I followed the man, you did. And I did, so you have to keep your word."

"I never said I'd remove the Finder, Master Hark. I said you'd be exiled to Baerlon instead of hanging, but wouldn't you rather remain in Caemlyn?"

The man widened his eyes, trying to look sincere. And failing. He even smiled. "Oh, no, my Lady. I've been dreaming about the fresh country air in Baerlon, I has. I'll wager there's never a worry about getting rotten meat in your stew there. Here, you got to sniff careful before you eat anything. I'm looking forward to it, I am."

Elayne put on the stern face her mother had always worn passing judgment. "You'd be out of Baerlon two minutes behind the Guardsmen who escorted you there. And then you'd hang for breaking your exile. Much better for you to remain in Caemlyn and take on a new line of work. Master Norry, could you use a man with Hark's talents?"

"I could, my Lady," Norry replied without even a pause for thought. A satisfied smile touched his thin lips, and Elayne realized what she had done. She had given him a tool to encroach on Mistress Harfor's ground. But there was no undoing it, now.

"The work won't be so remunerative as your former 'trade,' Master Hark, but you won't hang for it."

"Not so what, my Lady?" Hark said, scratching his head.

"It won't pay so well. What do you say? Baerlon, where you'll surely cut a purse or bolt, and hang for either one, or Caemlyn, where you'll have steady work and no fear of the hangman. Unless you take up cutting purses again."

Hark swayed on his feet, scrubbing the back of his hand across his mouth. "I needs a drink, I does," he muttered hoarsely. Very likely he believed the Finder would allow her to know if he cut a purse. If so, she had no intention of disabusing him.

Master Norry scowled at the man, but when he opened his mouth, she said, "There's wine in the small sitting room. Let him have one cup, then join me in the large sitting room."

The large sitting room was dark when she walked in, but she channeled to light the mirrored stand-lamps against the dark-paneled walls, and the kindling of the fires neatly laid on the facing hearths. Then she took a seat in one of the low-backed chairs around the scroll-edged table and released *saidar* again. Since her experiment at holding the Power all day, she had not held it longer than necessary. Her mood swung from joyful excitement to morose worry and back. On the one hand, she was done with having to put up with Mellar, and soon she would have her hands on two Black sisters. Questioning them might lead to the rest, or at least reveal their plans. And if not, this Shiaine would have her own secrets. Anyone who was "working" two Dark-friend sisters would have secrets worth knowing. On the other hand, what would Duhara do to try forcing her acceptance as an advisor? Duhara would try to meddle somehow, but she could not see how. Burn her, she did not need any more difficulties between her and the throne. With a little luck, tonight would not only snare two Black sisters, it might uncover a third, a murderer ten times over. Back and forth she went, from Falion and Marillin to Duhara, even after Master Norry and Hark joined her.

Hark, a silver cup in his hand, tried to take a seat at the table, but Master Norry tapped him on the shoulder and jerked his head toward a corner. Sullenly, Hark went where he was directed. He must have begun drinking as soon as the cup was filled, because he emptied it in one long pull then stood turning it over in his hands and staring at it. Suddenly he gave a start and directed an ingratiating grin at her. Whatever he saw on her face made him flinch. Scuttling to the long table against the wall, he set the cup down with exaggerated care, then scuttled back to his corner.

Birgitte was the first to arrive, the bond filled with weary discontent. "A ride?" she said, and when Elayne explained, she began raising objections. Well, some of it was objections; the rest was just insults.

"What hare-brained, crack-pated scheme are you talking about, Birgitte?" Vandene said as she entered the room. She wore a riding dress that hung loose on her. One of her sister's, it would have fit her perfectly while Adeleas was alive, but the white-haired woman had lost weight. Her Jaem, wiry and gnarled, took one look at Hark and placed himself where he could watch the man. Hark ventured a smile, but it faded when Jaem's expression remained hard as iron. The

Warder's graying hair was thin, but there was nothing soft about him.

"She intends to try capturing two Black sisters tonight," Birgitte replied, shooting a hard look at Elayne.

"Two Black sisters?" Sareitha exclaimed walking through the door. She gathered her dark cloak around her as though the words had given a chill. "Who?" Her Warder Ned, a tall, broad-shouldered young man with yellow hair, eyed Hark and touched his sword hilt. *He* chose a spot where he could watch the man, too. Hark shifted his feet. He might have been thinking of trying to run.

"Falion Bhoda and Marillin Gemalphin," Elayne said. Sareitha's mouth hardened.

"What about Falion and Marillin?" Careane asked as she glided into the room. Her Warders were disparate men, a tall, gangly Tairen, a blade-slender Saldaean, and a broad-shouldered Cairhienin. They exchanged glances, and Tavan, the Cairhienin, leaned against the wall watching Hark while Cieryl and Venr stood in the doorway. Hark's mouth took on a sickly twist.

There was nothing for it but to explain again from the beginning. Which Elayne did with a rising impatience that had nothing to do with her shifting moods. The longer this took, the more chance that Falion and Marillin might be gone by the time she reached the house on Full Moon Street. She *wanted* them. She intended to *have* them! She should have made Birgitte wait until everyone had gathered.

"A good plan, I think," Vandene said when she finished. "Yes, it will do nicely." Others were not so agreeable.

"It isn't a plan, it's bloody madness!" Birgitte said sharply. Arms folded beneath her bosom, she scowled down at Elayne, the bond such a turmoil of emotions that Elayne could barely make them out. "The four of you enter the house alone. Alone! That isn't a plan. It's flaming insanity! Warders are supposed to guard their Aes Sedai's backs. Let us come with you." The other Warders put in emphatic agreements, but at least she was not trying to stop the whole thing any more.

"There are four of us," Elayne told her. "We can watch our own backs. And sisters do *not* ask their Warders to face other sisters." Birgitte's face darkened. "If I need you, I'll shout so loud you'd be able to hear me if you were back here in the palace. The Warders remain outside!" she added when Birgitte opened her mouth. The bond filled with frustration, but Birgitte's jaw snapped shut.

"Perhaps this man can be trusted," Sareitha said, glancing at Hark with no trust at all, "but even if he heard correctly, nothing says there are still only two sisters in the house. Or any. If they have gone, there's no danger, but if others have joined them, we might as well put our necks in a noose and spring the trap ourselves."

Careane folded her sturdy arms and nodded. "The danger is too great. You yourself told us that when they fled the Tower, they stole a number of *ter'angreal*, some very dangerous indeed. I've never been called a coward, but I don't fancy trying to sneak up on someone who might have a rod that can make balefire."

"He could hardly have misheard something as simple as 'there are only two of us,'" Elayne replied firmly. "And they spoke as if they didn't expect any others." Burn her, considering her standing with respect to them, they should have been jumping to obey rather than arguing. "In any case, this isn't a discussion." A pity both objected. If only one had, it could have been a clue. Unless they both were Black Ajah. A bone-freezing thought, that, yet her plan took the possibility into account. "Falion and Marillin won't know we are coming until it's too late. If they're gone, we'll arrest this Shiaine, but we are going."

It was a larger party than Elayne had expected that rode out of the Queen's Stableyard behind her and Hark. Birgitte had insisted on bringing fifty Guardswomen, though all they would be doing was missing sleep, a column of twos in red-lacquered helmets and breast-plates, black in the night, that snaked along the palace behind the Aes Sedai and Warders. Reaching the front of the palace, they skirted the edge of the Queen's Plaza, the great oval crowded now with rude shelters that housed sleeping Guardsmen and nobles' armsmen. Men were billeted everywhere room could be found, but there were insufficient basements and attics and spare rooms near enough the palace, and the parks where circles of Kinswomen would take the men to the places where they were needed. The fighting they did was afoot, on the walls, so their horses were all picketed in nearby parks and in the larger palace gardens. A few sentries shifted as they passed, heads swiveling to follow, but with her hood up, all they could be sure of was that a large contingent of Guardswomen were escorting a party through the night. The sky to the east was still dark, but it must be less than two hours till first light. The Light send dawn would see Falion and Marillin in custody. And one more. At least one more.

Winding streets led over and around the hills past narrow, tile-covered towers that would glitter with a hundred colors when the sun rose and glittered faintly in the cloud-dappled moonlight, past silent shops and lightless inns, simple stone houses with slate roofs and small palaces that might have fit in Tar Valon. The ring of horseshoes on the paving stones and the faint creak of saddle leather sounded loud in the silence. Except for an occasional dog that slunk away into the deeper shadows of alleys, nothing else moved. The streets were dangerous at this hour, but no footpad would be mad enough to come in sight of so large a party. Half an hour after leaving the Royal Palace, Elayne rode Fireheart through the Mondel Gate, a wide, twenty-foot-high arch in the Inner City's tall white wall. Once there would have been Guardsmen on duty there, to keep the peace, but the Queen's Guards were spread too thin now for that.

Almost as soon as they were into the New City, Hark turned east into a warren of streets that meandered in every direction through the city's hills. He rode awkwardly, on a bay mare that had been found for him. Cutpurses seldom spent time in the saddle. Some of the streets were quite narrow here, and it was in one of those that he finally drew rein, surrounded by stone houses of two or three or even four stories. Birgitte raised a hand to halt the column. The sudden silence seemed deafening.

"It's just around that corner there, it is, my Lady, the other side of the street," Hark said in a near whisper, "but if we go riding out there, they might hear us or see us. Pardon, my Lady, but if these Aes Sedai are what you says they are, I don't want them seeing me." He scrambled down from his saddle clumsily and looked up her, wringing his hands, his moonshadowed face anxious.

Dismounting, Elayne led Fireheart to the corner and peeked around the corner of a narrow, three-story house. The houses along the other street stood dark except for one, four substantial stories of stone with the closed gate of a stableyard beside it. Not an ornate building, but large enough for a wealthy merchant or banker. Bankers and merchants were unlikely to be awake at this hour, however.

"There," Hark whispered hoarsely, pointing. He stood far back, so he had to learn forward to point. He really did fear being seen. "The one with the light on the second floor, it is."

"Best to find out if anyone else is awake in there," Vandene said, peering past Elayne. "Jaem? Don't go inside the house."

Elayne expected the lean old Warder to sneak across the street, but he just strolled out holding his cloak close around him against the early morning chill. Even the dangerous grace of a Warder appeared to have deserted him. Vandene seemed to sense her surprise.

"Skulking draws the eye and creates suspicion," she said. "Jaem is just a man walking, and if it's early to be out in the streets, he isn't sneaking, so anyone who sees him will think of some mundane reason for him to be out."

Reaching the stableyard gate, Jaem pulled it open and walked through as if he had a perfect right. Long minutes passed before he came back out, shutting the gate carefully behind him, and strolled back along the street. He rounded the corner and the leopard-like grace reappeared in his step.

"All the windows are dark except that one," he told Vandene quietly. "The kitchen door is unlatched. So is the back door. That lets onto an alley. Trusting, for Darkfriends. Or else dangerous enough they don't worry about burglars. There's a big fellow sleeping in the barn, up in the loft. Big enough to scare any burglar, but he's so drunk he didn't wake while I was tying him up." Vandene raised a questioning eyebrow. "I thought I'd better be safe. Drunks sometimes wake when you least expect. You wouldn't want him seeing you go in and start making noise." She nodded approval.

"It's time to get ready," Elayne said. Moving back from the corner and handing her reins to Birgitte, she tried to embrace the Source. It was like trying to catch smoke with her fingers. Frustration and anger welled up, all the things you needed to suppress if you were to channel. She tried again, and failed again. Falion and Marillin were going to get away. To come this close. . . . They had to be in that lighted room. She knew it. And they were going to escape. Sadness replaced anger, and suddenly *saidar* flowed into her. She barely stifled a sigh of relief. "I'll meld the flows, Sareitha. Vandene, you meld for Careane."

"I don't understand why we have to link," the Tairen Brown muttered, but she put herself on the edge of embracing the Power. "With two of them and four of us, we outnumber them, but linked, it's two and two." A clue? Perhaps she wished it to be three and three?

"Two strong enough to overwhelm them even if they're holding the Power, Sareitha." Elayne reached through her as if she were an *angreal*, and the glow of *saidar* surrounded the other woman as the link was completed. In truth, it surrounded both of them, but she could only see the part around Sareitha—until she wove Spirit around her. Then the glow vanished. She placed the same weave on herself and pre- pared four shields and several other weaves, all inverted. She felt al- most giddy with excitement, but she did not intend to be caught by surprise. Frustration still pulsed along the bond, but for the rest, Bir- gitte felt like a drawn arrow. Elayne touched her arm. "We will be all right." Birgitte snorted and flung her thick braid back over her shoul- der. "Keep an eye on Master Hark, Birgitte. It would be a shame if he had to be hanged because he was tempted to run." Hark squeaked.

She exchanged glances with Vandene, who said, "We might as well be about it."

The four of them walked up Full Moon Street, slowly, as if out for a stroll, and slipped into the shadow-shrouded stableyard. Elayne opened the kitchen door slowly, but the hinges were well-oiled, emit- ting not a squeak. The brick-walled kitchen was lit only by a tiny fire in the wide stone fireplace where a kettle hung steaming, yet that was enough for them to cross the floor without bumping into the table or chairs. Someone sighed, and she pressed a warning finger to her lips. Vandene frowned at Careane, who looked embarrassed and spread her hands.

A short hall led to stairs at the front of the house. Gathering her skirts, Elayne started up, silent on slippered feet. She was careful to keep Sareitha where she could see her. Vandene was doing the same with Careane. They could do nothing with the Power, but that hardly meant they could do nothing. On the second flight of stairs, she began hearing the murmur of voices. Light spilled from an open door.

". . . . don't care what you think," a woman said in that room. "You leave the thinking to me and do as you're told."

Elayne moved to the door. It was a sitting room, with gilded stand- lamps and rich carpets on the floor and a tall fireplace of blue marble, but she had eyes only for the three women in it. Only one, a sharp- faced woman, was seated. That must be Shiaine. The other two stood with their backs to the door, heads bowed like penitents. The sharp- faced woman's eyes widened when she saw her in the doorway, but Elayne gave her no time to open her mouth. The two Black sisters cried out in alarm as shields went onto them, and flows of Air bound their arms to their sides, tightened their skirts around their legs. More flows of Air fastened Shiaine to her gilded armchair.

Elayne drew Sareitha into the room with her and moved to where she could see all of their faces. Sareitha tried to step back. She might only have been trying to give her the place of prominence, but Elayne caught her sleeve again, keeping her in view, too. Vandene and Careane joined them. Marillin's narrow face held Aes Sedai calm, but Falion snarled silently.

"What is the meaning of this?" Shiaine demanded. "I recognize you. You're Elayne Trakand, the Daughter-Heir. But that gives you no right to invade my home and assault me."

"Falion Bhoda," Elayne said calmly, "Marillin Gemalphin, Shiaine Avarhin, I arrest you as Darkfriends." Well, her voice was calm. Inside, she wanted to skip with glee. And Birgitte thought this would be dangerous!

"That is ridiculous," Shiaine said in icy tones. "I walk in the Light!"

"Not if you walk with these two," Elayne told her. "To my certain knowledge they've proven themselves Black Ajah in Tar Valon, Tear and Tanchico. You don't hear them denying it, do you? That's because they know I—"

Suddenly sparks danced all over her from head to toe. She twitched helplessly, muscles spasming, *saidar* slipping from her grasp. She could see Vandene and Careane and Sareitha jerking as sparks flickered across them as well. Only a moment it lasted, but when the sparks vanished, Elayne felt as if she had been fed through a mangle. She had to hold on to Sareitha to stay on her feet, and Sareitha clung to her as hard. Vandene and Careane were supporting one another, swaying, each with her chin on the other's shoulder. Falion and Marillin wore startled expressions, but the light of the Power enveloped them in heartbeats. Elayne felt the shield fasten on to her, saw them settle on the other three. There was no need for binding. Any of them would have fallen over without support. She would have shouted if she could have. If she thought that Birgitte and the others could do more than die.

Four women Elayne recognized entered the room. Asne Zeramene and Temaile Kinderode. Chesmal Emry and Eldrith Jhondar. Four Black sisters. She could have wept. Sareitha groaned softly.

"Why did you wait so long?" Asne demanded of Falion and Marillin. The Saldaean's dark tilted eyes were angry. "I used this so they wouldn't feel us embrace *saidar*, but why did you just stand there?" She waved a small, bent black rod, perhaps an inch in diameter, that had a strangely dull look. The thing seemed to fascinate her. "A 'gift' from Moghedien. A weapon from the Age of Legends. I can kill a man at a hundred paces with this, or just stun him if I want to put him to the question."

"I can kill a man if I can see him," Chesmal said scornfully. Tall and handsome, she was the image of icy arrogance.

Asne sniffed. "But *my* target could be surrounded by a hundred sisters, and not one would know what killed him."

"I suppose it has its uses," Chesmal admitted in grudging tones. "Why *did* you just stand there?"

"They had us shielded," Falion said bitterly.

Eldrith's breath caught, and she put a plump hand to a round cheek. "That's impossible. Unless. . . ." Her dark eyes sharpened. "They've discovered a way to hide the glow, to hide their weaves. Now, that would be most useful."

"You have my thanks for your timely rescue," Shiaine said, rising, "but do you have a reason for coming here tonight? Did Moridin send you?"

Asne channeled a flow of Air that struck Shiaine's cheek with a loud crack, staggering her. "Keep a civil tongue in your mouth, and perhaps we'll let you leave with us. Or we can leave you behind dead." Shiaine's cheek was reddened, but her hands remained at her sides. Her face was expressionless.

"Elayne's the only one we need," Temaile said. She was pretty in a fox-faced way, almost a fragile child in appearance despite her ageless face, but her blue eyes held an unhealthy light. She touched her lips with the tip of her tongue. "I'd enjoy playing with the others, but they'd be a burden we don't need."

"If you're going to kill them," Marillin said as though discussing the price of bread, "spare Careane. She is one of us."

"A gift from Adeleas," Vandene murmured, and Careane's eyes went very wide. Her mouth opened, but no sound came out. The two women sagged and fell to the carpet. Vandene began trying to push herself up, but Careane lay staring at the ceiling, the hilt of Vandene's belt knife protruding from beneath her breastbone.

The glow surrounded Chesmal, and she touched Vandene with a complex weave of Fire, Earth and Water. The white-haired woman collapsed as if her bones had melted. The same weave touched Sareitha, and she pulled Elayne down atop her as she fell. Sareitha's eyes were already glazing.

"Their Warders will be coming now," Chesmal said. "A little more killing to do."

Run, Birgitte, Elayne thought, wishing the bond could carry words. *Run!*

CHAPTER
32

To Keep the Bargain

Birgitte was leaning against the stone wall of the three-story house, thinking sadly of Gaidal, when the bundle of emotions and physical sensations in the back of her head, her awareness of Elayne, suddenly spasmed. That was the only word for it. Whatever it was lasted just a moment, but afterward, the bond was full of . . . limpness. Elayne was conscious, but unsteady. She was unafraid, however. Still, Birgitte threw back her cloak and moved to the corner to peer up Full Moon Street. Elayne could be too brave for her own good. The hardest thing about being Elayne's Warder was keeping her from endangering herself beyond need. Nobody was indestructible, but the bloody woman thought she bloody well was. Her sigil should have been an iron lion rather than a golden lily. That light shone in the window, spilling a pale pool into the narrow street, and there was not a sound except for a cat yowling somewhere in the night.

"Sareitha feels . . . muzzy," Ned Yarman muttered beside her. The tall young Warder's boyish face was a grim shadowed mask inside the hood of his cloak. "She feels weak."

Birgitte became aware of the other Warders crowding her close, stone-faced and hard-eyed. That was clear enough even by moonlight. Something had happened to all of the Aes Sedai, it seemed. But what? "The Lady Elayne said she'd shout if she needed us," she told them, as much to reassure herself as anything else. Even if *both* Careane and Sarei-tha were Darkfriends, they would have been helpless to do anything linked, and apparently whatever had happened had happened to them, as well. Burn her, she should have insisted that she and the other Warders go along.

"Careane won't be pleased if we interfere needlessly," Venr Kosaan said quietly. Blade slim and dark, with touches of white in his tightly curled black hair and short beard, he appeared completely at ease. "I say we wait. She feels confident, whatever's going on."

"More so that she did going in," Cieryl Arjuna added, earning him a sharp glance from Venr. Still short of his middle years, Cieryl seemed all bones, though his shoulders were wide.

Birgitte nodded. Elayne was confident, too. But then, Elayne would feel self-assured walking an unraveling rope stretched over a pit full of sharp stakes. A dog began barking in the distance, and the yowl-ing cat went silent, but other dogs answered the first in a spreading ripple that faded away as suddenly as it had begun.

They waited, with Birgitte fretting in silence. Suddenly, Venr growled an oath and shed his cloak. The next instant, his blade was in his hand and he was running up the street followed by Cieryl and Ta-van, cloaks billowing behind, their blades bared, too. Before they had gone two steps, Jaem gave a wild cry. Unsheathing his sword, he threw his cloak down and raced after the other three at a speed that belied his age. Bellowing with rage, Ned ran, too, the steel in his fist glittering in the moonlight. Fury stabbed through the bond, like the battle fury that took some men. And sadness, too, but still no fear.

Birgitte heard the soft rasp of swords being unsheathed behind her and spun, cloak flaring. "Put those up! They're no use here."

"I know what the Warders running in means as well as you, my Lady," Yurith said in courtly accents, obeying smoothly. And with clear reluctance. Lean and as tall as most men, the Saldaean denied be-ing nobly born, but whenever the conversation came around to what she had done before swearing the oath as a Hunter for the Horn, she always gave one of her rare smiles and changed the subject. She was skilled with that sword, however. "If the Aes Sedai are dying—"

"Elayne is alive," Birgitte cut in. Alive, and in trouble. "*She's* our concern, now, but we'll need a lot more swords to rescue her." And more than swords. "Somebody collar that man!" Two Guardswomen seized Hark's coat before he could slip away into the darkness. Apparently he had no wish to stay near where Aes Sedai had died. Neither did she. "Gather the . . . the extra horses and follow me," she said, swinging into Arrow's saddle. "And ride like fire!" She suited her words, digging her heels into the rangy gray gelding's flanks without waiting.

It was a wild gallop through dark, twisting streets where people were just beginning to appear. She reined Arrow around the few carts and wagons out this early, but men and women had to leap from her path, often shaking fists and shouting curses. She only urged the gelding for more speed, her cloak flapping behind. Before she reached the Mondel Gate, Elayne was moving. She had been uncertain at first, but there could be no mistaking it now. Elayne was moving northeast at about walking speed. The bond said she was too wobbly to walk far, maybe to walk at all, but a wagon would make the same pace. The sky was turning gray. How long before she could gather what was needed? In the Inner City, the street spiraled inward, rising past towers glittering in a hundred colors toward the golden domes and pale spires of the Royal Palace, atop the highest of Caemlyn's hills. As she galloped around the rim of the Queen's Plaza, soldiers stared at her. They were being fed from black kettles atop pushbarrows, cooks ladling some sort of brown stew onto tin plates, and every man she could see wore his breastplate and had his helmet hanging from his sword hilt. Good. Every moment saved was a moment toward saving Elayne.

Two lines of Guardswomen were practicing the sword in the Queen's Stableyard when she galloped in, but the lath blades stopped rattling when she flung herself out of the saddle, let Arrow's reins drop and ran toward the colonnade. "Hadora, run tell the Windfinders to meet me in the Map Room right away!" she shouted without slowing. "All of them! Sanetre, you do the same for Captain Guybon! And have another horse saddled for me!" Arrow was played out for today. She was past the columns by that time, but she did not look back to see whether they were obeying. They would be.

She raced through tapestry-hung hallways and up sweeping marble stairs, got lost and shouted curses as she retraced her steps at a run. Liveried serving men and women gaped as they dodged out of her way. At last she reached the lion-carved doors of the Map Room, where she paused only long enough to tell the two burly Guardsmen on duty to admit the Windfinders as soon as they appeared, then went in. Guybon was already there, in his burnished breastplate with the three golden knots on his shoulder, and Dyelin, delicately holding her blue silk skirts up as she moved, the pair of them frowning at the huge mosaic map, where well over a dozen red discs marked the city's northern wall. Never before had there been so many assaults at once, not even ten, but Birgitte spared the discs barely a glance.

"Guybon, I need every horse and halberd you can muster," she said, unpinning her cloak and tossing it down on her long writing table. "The crossbowmen and archers will have to handle anything that crops up by themselves for a few hours. Elayne's been captured by Darkfriend Aes Sedai, and they're trying to carry her out of the city." Some of the clerks and messengers began murmuring, but Mistress Anford silenced them with a sharp order to see to their work. Birgitte eyed the colorful map in the floor, measuring distances. Elayne seemed to be moving toward the Sunrise Gate and the road to the River Erinin, but even if they used one of the smaller gates, they had gone too far to be aiming at anything but the eastern wall. "They'll probably have her through the gates by the time we're ready to move. We're going to Travel to just this side of the ridge east of the city." And take what was going to happen out of the streets, away from people's homes. It would be better out in the open in any case. In that tangle of streets, with horsemen and halberdmen jammed together, there would be too many people to get in the way, too much chance of accidents.

Guybon nodded, already issuing terse orders that brown-clad clerks copied down hastily for him to sign and pass to young messengers in red-and-white who went running as soon as the paper was in hand. The boys' faces were frightened. Birgitte had no time for her own fear. Elayne felt none, and she was a prisoner. Sadness, yes, but no fear.

"We certainly need to rescue Elayne," Dyelin said calmly, "but she'll hardly thank you if you give Arymilla Caemlyn by doing it. Not counting the men in the towers and holding the gates, almost half the trained soldiers and armsmen in the city are on the northern wall. If you strip away the rest, one more attack will gain a stretch of the wall. Crossbows and bows alone won't stop them. Once they have that, Arymilla's forces will pour into the city, enough to overwhelm what you propose to leave. You will have neatly reversed our positions, and worsened yours. Arymilla will have Caemlyn, and Elayne will be outside without enough armsmen to get back in. Unless these Darkfriends have somehow smuggled an army inside Caemlyn, a few hundred men will do as well as thousands."

Birgitte scowled at her. She had never been able to like Dyelin. She did not know why, exactly, but Dyelin had just made her bristle at first sight. She was fairly certain the other woman felt the same about her. She could never say "up" without Dyelin saying "down." "You care about putting Elayne on the throne, Dyelin. I care about keeping her alive to mount that throne. Or not, so long as she's alive. I owe her my life, and I won't let hers trickle away in Darkfriend hands." Dyelin sniffed and went back to studying the red discs as if she could see the soldiers fighting, her frown deepening the lines at the corners of her eyes.

Birgitte clasped her hands behind her back and forced herself to stand still. She wanted to pace with impatience. Elayne was still trundling toward the Sunrise Gate. "There's something you need to know, Guybon. We'll be facing at least two Aes Sedai, likely more, and they may have a weapon, a *ter'angreal* that makes balefire. Have you ever heard of that?"

"Never. It sounds dangerous, though."

"Oh, it is. Dangerous enough that it's prohibited for Aes Sedai. In the War of the Shadow, even Darkfriends stopped using it." She barked a bitter laugh. All she knew of balefire now was what Elayne had told her. It had come from her in the first place, yet that only made matters worse. Would all of her memories go? She did not think she had lost any recently, but how would she know if she had? She could remember bits of the founding of the White Tower, pieces of what she and Gaidal had done to help it be founded, but nothing before that. All of her earlier memories were yesterday's smoke.

"Well, at least we'll have Aes Sedai of our own," Guybon said, signing another order.

"They're all dead, except for Elayne," she told him flatly. There was no way to gild that. Dyelin gasped, her face growing pale. One of the clerks clasped her hands to her mouth, and another knocked over his ink jar. The ink fanned across the tabletop in a black stream and began dripping onto the floor. Rather than reprimanding the man, Mistress Anford steadied herself with a hand on another clerk's writing table. "I hope to make up for that," Birgitte went on, "but I can't promise anything except that we're going to lose men today. Maybe a lot of men."

Guybon straightened. His expression was thoughtful, his hazel eyes steady. "That will make for an interesting day," he said finally. "But we'll get the Daughter-Heir back, whatever the cost." A solid man, Charlz Guybon, and brave. He had demonstrated that often enough on the walls. Too good looking for her taste, of course.

Birgitte realized she had begun pacing back and forth across the mosaic and stopped. She knew nothing of being a general, whatever Elayne thought, but she knew that showing nerves could infect others with them. Elayne was alive. That was all that was important. Alive and moving farther away by the minute. The left-hand door opened, and one of the burly Guardsmen announced that Julanya Fote and Keraille Surtovni had returned. Guybon hesitated, looking to her, but when she said nothing, he told the man to admit them.

They were very different women, in appearance at least, though each carried a wooden walking staff. Julanya was plump and pretty, with touches of white in her dark hair, while Keraille was short and slim, with tilted green eyes and fiery red curls. Birgitte wondered whether those were their real names. These Kinswomen changed names as easily as other women changed stockings. They wore plain woolens suitable for country peddlers, which each had been in the past, and each was a keen observer, skilled at taking care of herself. They could talk their way out of most situations, but their simple belt knives were not the only blades they carried and they could surprise a strong man with what they could do with those walking staffs. Both offered curtsies. Julanya's skirts and cloak were damp and splashed with mud around the hem.

"Ellorien, Luan and Abelle began breaking camp early this morning, my Lady," she said. "I only stayed long enough to make sure of their direction—north—before coming to report."

"The same is true with Aemlyn, Arathelle and Pelivar, my Lady," Keraille added. "They're coming for Caemlyn."

Birgitte did not need to examine the large map spread out on the table with its markers. Depending on how muddy the roads were, how much rain they had to contend with, they could reach the city by that afternoon. "You've done well, both of you. Go find yourselves hot baths. Do you think they've had a change of heart?" she asked Dyelin once the two women had left.

"No," the woman replied without hesitation, then sighed and shook her head. "I fear the most likely thing is that Ellorien has convinced the others to support her for the Lion Throne. They may be thinking to defeat Arymilla and take over the siege. They have half again her numbers, and double ours." She let that hang. There was no need to say the rest. Even using Kinswomen to shift men, they would be hard pressed to hold the wall against that many.

"First we get Elayne back, then we can worry about that lot," Birgitte said. Where were those bloody Windfinders?

No sooner did she have the thought than they were padding into the room behind Chanelle, a riotous rainbow of silks. Except for Renaile, last in line in her linens, yet a red blouse, green trousers and a deep yellow sash made her bright enough, though even Rainyn, a round-cheeked young woman with just half a dozen golden medallions dangling onto her cheek, made Renaile's honor chain look bare. Renaile's face wore an expression of stoic endurance.

"I do not appreciate being threatened!" Chanelle said angrily, sniffing the golden scent box on its golden chain around her neck. Her dark cheeks were flushed. "That Guardswoman said if we did not run, she would kick—! Never mind what she said, exactly. It was a threat, and I will not be—!"

"Elayne has been captured by Darkfriend Aes Sedai," Birgitte cut in. "I need you to make a gateway for the men who are going to rescue her." A murmur rose among the other Windfinders. Chanelle gestured sharply, but only Renaile fell silent. The others just lowered their voices to whispers, to her obvious displeasure. By the medallions crowding their honor chains, several of them matched Chanelle's rank.

"Why did you summon all of us for one gateway?" she demanded. "I keep the bargain, you can see. I brought everyone as you ordered. But why do you need more than one?"

"Because you're all going to form a circle and make a gateway big enough to take thousands of men and horses." That was one reason.

Chanelle stiffened, and she was not alone. Kurin, her face like a black stone, practically quivered with outrage, and Rysael, normally a very dignified woman, did quiver. Senine, with her weathered face and old marks indicating she once had worn more than six earrings, and fatter ones, fingered the jeweled dagger thrust behind her green sash.

"Soldiers?" Chanelle said indignantly. "That is forbidden! Our bargain says we will take no part in your war. Zaida din Parede Black Wing commanded it so, and now that she is Mistress of the Ships, that command carries even greater weight. Use the Kinswomen. Use the Aes Sedai."

Birgitte stepped close to the dark woman, looking her straight in the eyes. The Kin were useless for this. None of them had ever used the Power as a weapon. They might not even know how. "The other Aes Sedai are dead," she said softly. Someone behind her moaned, one of the clerks. "What is your bargain worth if Elayne is lost? Arymilla certainly won't honor it." Keeping her voice steady saying that took effort. It wanted to shake with anger, shake with fear. She needed these women, but she could not let them know why or Elayne *would* be lost. "What will Zaida say if you ruin her bargain with Elayne?"

Chanelle's tattooed hand half-lifted the piercework scent box to her nose again, then let it fall among her many jeweled necklaces. From what Birgitte knew of Zaida din Parede, she would be more than displeased with anyone who wrecked that bargain, and it was beyond doubtful that Chanelle wished to face the woman's anger, yet she only looked pensive. "Very well," she said after a moment. "For transport only, though. It is agreed?" She kissed the fingertips of her right hand, prepared to seal the bargain.

"You only need do what you want," Birgitte said, turning away. "Guybon, it's time. They must have her to the gate by now."

Guybon buckled on his sword, took up his helmet and steel-backed gauntlets, and followed her and Dyelin out of the Map Room trailed by the Windfinders, with Chanelle loudly insisting that they would provide a gateway only. Birgitte whispered instructions to Guybon before leaving him striding toward the front of the palace while she hurried to the Queen's Stableyard where she found a hammer-nosed dun gelding wearing her saddle and waiting, the reins held by a young groom with her hair in a braid not much different from her own. She also found all hundred and twenty-one Guardswomen armored and mounted. Climbing into the dun's saddle, she motioned them to follow her. The sun was a golden ball clear of the horizon in a sky with only a few high white clouds. At least they would not have rain to contend with, too. Even a wagon might have been able to slip away in some of the heavy rainstorms Caemlyn had seen lately.

A thick snake of men ten and twelve abreast spanned the Queen's Plaza, now, stretching out of sight in both directions, horsemen in helmets and breastplates alternating with men in every sort of helmet imaginable carrying shouldered halberds, most wearing mail shirts or jerkins sewn with steel discs and only rarely a breastplate, each group large or small headed by the banner of its House. Or the banner of a mercenary company. The sell-swords would have too many watchers to try slacking off today. Minus the crossbowmen and archers, there would be close on twelve thousand men in that column, two thirds of them mounted. How many would be dead before noon? She pushed that thought out of her mind. She needed every one of them to convince the Sea Folk. Any man who died today could die as easily on the wall tomorrow. Every man of them had come to Caemlyn prepared to die for Elayne.

At the head of the column were better than a thousand Guardsmen, helmets and breastplates gleaming in the sun, steel-tipped lances slanted precisely, the first of them waiting behind the banner of Andor, the rearing White Lion on a field of scarlet, and Elayne's banner, the Golden Lily on blue, at the edge of one of Caemlyn's many parks. It had been a park, anyway, but oaks hundreds of years old had been cut down and hauled away along with all the other trees and the flowering bushes, their roots dug out to clear a smooth space a hundred paces wide. The graveled paths and grassy ground had long since been trampled to mud by hooves and boots. Three other parks around the palace had received the same treatment, to make places for weaving gateways.

Guybon and Dyelin were already there, along with all the lords and ladies who had answered Elayne's call, from young Perival Mantear to Brannin Martan and his wife, all mounted. Perival wore helmet and breastplate like every other male present. Brannin's were plain and dull and slightly dented where the armorer's hammer had failed its task, tools of his trade as surely as the plain-hilted sword scabbarded at his side. Perival's were as gilded as Conail's and Branlet's, worked with the silver Anvil of Mantear where theirs were lacquered with Northan's Black Eagles and Gilyard's Red Leopards. Pretty armor, for being seen in. Birgitte hoped the women had sense enough to keep those boys out of any fighting. Looking at some of those women's faces, grim and determined, she hoped they had sense enough to stay clear themselves. At least none was wearing a sword. The simple truth was, a woman had to be more skilled than a man to face him with a sword. Stronger arms made too much difference, otherwise. Much better to use a bow.

The Windfinders were grimacing as they shifted their bare feet uneasily on ground still muddy from yesterday's downpour. Wet, they were more than accustomed to, but not mud.

"This man will not tell me where the gateway is to reach," Chanelle said furiously, pointing to Guybon as Birgitte dismounted. "I want to be done so I can wash my feet."

"My Lady!" a woman's voice called from back down the street. "My Lady Birgitte!" Reene Harfor came running up the line of Guardsmen, her red skirts held high, exposing her stockinged legs to the knee. Birgitte did not think she had ever seen the woman so much as trot. Mistress Harfor was one of those women who always did everything perfectly. Every time they met she made Birgitte conscious of every last mistake she herself had ever made. Two men in red-and-white livery were running behind her, carrying a litter between them. When they came closer, Birgitte saw that it held a lanky, helmetless Guardsman with an arrow piercing his right arm and another jutting from his right thigh. Blood trickled down both shafts, so he left a thin trail of drops on the paving stones. "He insisted on being brought to you or Captain Guybon immediately, my Lady," Mistress Harfor said breathlessly, fanning herself with one hand.

The young Guardsman struggled to sit up until Birgitte pressed him back down. "Three or four companies of mercenaries are attacking the Far Madding Gate, my Lady," he said, pain wracking his face and tinging his voice. "From inside the city, I mean. They placed archers to shoot anyone who tried to wave the signal flags for help, but I managed to get away, and my horse lasted just long enough."

Birgitte growled an oath. Cordwyn, Gomaisen and Bakuvun would be among them, she was ready to wager. She should have pressed Elayne to put them out of the city as soon as they made their demands. She did not realize she had spoken aloud until the wounded Guardsman spoke up.

"No, my Lady. Leastwise, not Bakuvun. Him and a dozen or so of his men dropped by to toss . . . uh, to pass the time, and the lieutenant figures they're the only reason we've managed to hold on. If they are still holding. They were using battering rams on the tower doors when I looked back. But there's more, my Lady. There's men massing in Low Caemlyn outside the gates. Ten thousand, maybe twice that. Hard to tell, the way those streets twist."

Birgitte winced. Ten thousand men would be enough to carry an assault from the outside whether or not the mercenaries were held off unless she sent everything, and she could not. What in the Light was she to do? Burn her, she could plan a raid to rescue someone from a fortress or scout in country held by the enemy with confidence that she knew what she was doing, but this was a battle, with the fate of Caemlyn and maybe the throne in the balance. Still, she had it to do. "Mistress Harfor, take this man back to the palace and see his wounds tended, please." There was no point in asking the Windfinders for Healing. They had already made it clear that was taking part in the war, in their view. "Dyelin, leave me all of the horse and a thousand halberdmen. You take the rest and all of the crossbowmen and archers available. And every man you can scrape together who can hold a sword. If the gate is still holding when the Kinswomen get you there, make sure it continues to hold. If it's fallen, take it back. And hold that bloody wall till I can get there."

"Very well," Dyelin said as if those were the easiest orders in the world to carry out. "Conail, Catalyn, Branlet, Perival, you come with me. Your foot will fight better with you there." Conail looked disappointed, no doubt seeing himself riding in a gallant charge, but he gathered his reins and whispered something that made the two younger boys chuckle.

"So will my horse fight better," Catalyn protested. "I want to help rescue Elayne."

"You came to help her secure the throne," Dyelin said sharply, "and you'll go where you're needed to see to that, or you and I will have another talk later." Whatever that meant, Catalyn's plump face reddened, but she sullenly followed Dyelin and the others when they rode away.

Guybon looked at Birgitte, yet he said nothing, though likely he was wondering why she was not sending more. He would not challenge her publicly. The problem was, she did not know how many Black sisters would be with Elayne. She needed every Windfinder, needed them to believe they were all necessary. Had there been time, she would have stripped the sentries from the outer towers, stripped even the gates.

"Make the gateway," she told Chanelle. "To just this side of the ridge east of the city, right on top of the Erinin Road and facing away from the city."

The Windfinders gathered in a circle, doing whatever they had to do to link and taking their bloody time about it. Suddenly the vertical silver-blue slash of a gateway appeared, widening into an opening, five paces tall and covering the whole width of the cleared ground, that showed a wide road of hard-packed clay climbing the gentle slope of the ten-span high ridge on its way to the River Erinin. Arymilla had camps beyond that ridge. Given the news, they might be empty—with luck, they were—but she could not concern herself with them now in any event.

"Forward and deploy as ordered!" Guybon shouted, and spurred his tall bay through followed by the gathered nobles and the Guardsmen ten abreast. The Guardsmen began curling off to the left and out of sight while the nobles took a position a little up the ridge. Some began peering toward the city through looking glasses. Guybon dismounted and ran, crouching, to peer over the crest through his. Birgitte could almost feel the impatience of the Guardswomen waiting behind her.

"You did not need a gateway this large," Chanelle said, frowning at the column of horsemen flowing into the gateway. "Why——?"

"Come with me," Birgitte said, taking the Windfinder by her arm. "I want to show you something." Pulling the dun along by his reins, she began drawing the woman toward the gateway. "You can come back once you've seen it." If she knew the least thing about Chanelle, she was the one guiding the circle. For the rest, she was counting on human nature. She did not look back, yet she nearly sighed with relief when she heard the other Windfinders murmuring among themselves behind her. Following.

Whatever Guybon had seen, it was good news, because he straightened up before running back down to his horse. Arymilla must have stripped her camps to the bone. Make it twenty thousand at the Far Madding Gate, then, if not more. The Light send it was holding. The Light send everywhere was holding. But Elayne first. First and above all else.

When she reached Guybon, who was back on his bay, the Guardswomen arrayed themselves in three lines behind Caseille off to one side. The whole hundred-pace width of the gateway was filled with men and horses now, trotting as they hurried left and right to join the others already forming in three ranks that grew to either side of the road. Good. There would be no easy way for the Windfinders to duck back through for a little while. A wagon with an arched canvas cover and a four-horse team, surrounded by a small mounted party, was halted in the road just beyond the last buildings of Low Caemlyn, perhaps a mile distant. Beyond it, people bustled in the open brick markets that lined the road, going about their lives as best they could, but they might as well not have existed. Elayne was in that wagon. Birgitte raised her hand without taking her eyes from the vehicle, and Guybon put his brass-mounted looking glass in her palm. Wagon and riders leaped closer when she raised the tube to her eye.

"What did you want me to see?" Chanelle demanded.

"In a moment," Birgitte replied. There were four men, three of them mounted, but more important were the seven women on horseback. It was a good looking glass, but not good enough for her to make out an ageless face at that distance. Still, she had to assume all seven were Aes Sedai. Eight against seven might have seemed almost even odds, but not when the eight were linked. Not if she could make the eight take part.

What were the Darkfriends thinking, seeing thousands of soldiers and armsmen appear from behind what would seem to them a heat haze hanging in the air? She lowered the glass. Noblemen were beginning to ride down as their armsmen came out and went to join the lines.

However surprised the Darkfriends were, they did not dither long. Lightning began flashing down out of a clear sky, silver-blue bolts that struck the ground with thunderous crashes and threw men and horses like splashed mud. Horses reared and plunged and screamed, but men fought to control their mounts, to hold their places. No one ran. The booming thunder that accompanied those blasts struck Birgitte like blows, staggering her. She could feel her hair stirring, trying to rise out of her braid. The air smelled . . . sharp. It seemed to tingle. Again lightning lashed the ranks. In Low Caemlyn, people were running. Most were running away, but some fools actually ran to where they could have a better view. The ends of narrow streets opening onto the countryside began filling with spectators.

"If we're going to face that, we might as well be moving and make it harder for them," Guybon said, gathering his reins. "With your permission, my Lady?"

"We'll lose fewer if you're moving," Birgitte agreed, and he spurred down the ridge.

Caseille halted her horse in front of Birgitte and saluted, an arm across her chest. Her narrow face was grim behind the face-bars of her lacquered helmet. "Permission for the Bodyguard to join the line, my Lady?" You could hear the capital. They were not just any bodyguard, they were the Daughter-Heir's Bodyguard and would be the Queen's Bodyguard.

"Granted," Birgitte said. If anyone had a right, these women did.

The Arafellin whirled her horse and galloped down the slope followed by the rest of the Bodyguard to take their place in those lightning-torn ranks. A company of mercenaries, perhaps two hundred men in black-painted helmets and breastplates, riding behind a red banner bearing a running black wolf, halted when they saw what they were riding into, but men behind the banners of half a dozen Houses pushed past them, and they had no choice but to go on. More noblemen rode down to lead their men, Brannin and Kelwin, Laerid and Barel, others. None hesitated once he saw his own banner appear. Sergase was not the only woman to move her horse a few paces as if she, too, meant to join with her armsmen when her banner came out of the gateway.

"At a walk!" Guybon shouted, to be heard over the explosions. All along the line, other voices echoed him. "Advance!" Wheeling his bay, he rode slowly toward the Darkfriend Aes Sedai while lightning boomed and crashed and men and horses flew in fountains of earth.

"What did you want me to see?" Chanelle demanded again. "I want to be away from this place." Small danger of that for the moment. Men were still coming out of the gateway, galloping or running to catch up. Fireballs fell among the ranks, too, now, adding their own eruptions of dirt, arms, legs. A horse's head spun lazily into the air.

"This," Birgitte said, gesturing to the scene in front of them. Guybon had begun to trot, pulling the others with him, the three ranks holding steady in their advance, others coming as hard as they could to join them. Abruptly a leg-thick bar of what appear to be liquid white fire shot out from one of the women beside the wagon. It quite literally carved a gap fifteen paces wide in the lines. For a heartbeat, shimmering flecks floated in the air, the shapes of men and horses struck, and then were consumed. The bar suddenly jerked up into the air, higher and higher, then winked out leaving dim purple lines across Birgitte's vision. Balefire, burning men out of the Pattern so that they were dead before it struck them. She swung the looking glass up to her eye long enough to spot the woman holding a slim black rod that appeared to be perhaps a pace long.

Guybon began to charge. It was too soon, but his only hope was to close while he still had men alive. His only hope but one. Over the thunderous explosions of fireballs and lightning rose a ragged cry of, "Elayne and Andor!" Ragged, but full-throated. The banners were all streaming. A brave sight, if you could ignore how many were falling. A horse and rider struck squarely by a fireball simply disintegrated, men and horses all around them going down as well. Some managed to rise again. A riderless horse stood on three legs, tried to run and fell over thrashing.

"This?" Chanelle said incredulously. "I have no desire to watch men die." Another bar of balefire sliced a breach of nearly twenty paces in the charging ranks before knifing down into the ground, cutting a trench halfway back to the wagon before it vanished. There were a good many dead, though not so many as it seemed there should be. Birgitte had seen the same in battles during the Trolloc Wars where the Power had been used. For every man who lay still, two or three were staggering to their feet or trying to stem a flow of blood. For every horse stiff-legged in death, two more stood on wobbly legs. The hail of fire and lightning continued unabated.

"Then stop it," Birgitte said. "If they kill all the soldiers, or just enough to make the rest break, then Elayne is lost." Not forever. Burn her, she would track her for the rest of her life to see her free, but the Light only knew what they might do to her in that time. "Zaida's bargain is lost. *You* will have lost it."

The morning was not warm, yet sweat beaded on Chanelle's forehead. Fireballs and lightning erupted among the riders following Guybon. The woman holding the rod raised her arm again. Even without using the looking glass, Birgitte was sure it was pointed straight at Guybon. He had to see it, but he never swerved a hair.

Suddenly another bolt of lightning slashed down. And struck the woman holding the rod. She flew in one direction, her mount in another. One of the wagon team sagged to the ground while the others danced and reared. They would have run except for their dead tracemate. The other horses around the wagon were rearing and plunging, too. The rain of fire and lightning ceased as the Aes Sedai fought to control their horses, to maintain their saddles. Rather than trying to calm his team, the man on the driver's seat leaped down and drew his sword as he began to run toward the charging horsemen. The onlookers in Low Caemlyn were running again, too, this time away.

"Take the others alive!" Birgitte snapped. She did not much care whether they lived—they would die soon enough for being Darkfriends and murderers—but Elayne was in that bloody wagon!

Chanelle nodded stiffly, and around the wagon, riders began toppling from their fractious mounts to lie struggling on the ground as if bound hand and foot. Which they were, of course. The running man fell on his face and lay writhing. "I shielded the women, too," Chanelle said. Even holding the Power, they would have been no match for a circle of eight.

Guybon raised his hand, slowing the charge to a walk. It was remarkable how short a time it all had taken. He was less than halfway to the wagon. Men mounted and afoot were still pouring out of the gateway. Swinging into the dun's saddle, Birgitte galloped toward Elayne. *Bloody woman,* she thought. The bond had never once carried any hint of fear.

CHAPTER
33

Nine Out of Ten

T he Darkfriends had taken no chances with Elayne. Aside from shielding her, Temaile had taken seemingly malicious pleasure in tying her in a tight knot with her head between her knees. Her muscles already ached from the cramped position. The gag, a dirty piece of rag with a vile, oily taste, tied so tightly that it dug into the corners of her mouth, had been meant to keep her from shouting for help at the gates. Not that she would have; all that would have done was sentence the men guarding the gates to death. She could feel the six Black sisters holding *saidar* until they were through the gate. But the blindfold had been an unnecessary touch. She thought they wanted to add to her sense of helplessness, yet she refused to feel helpless. After all, she was perfectly safe until her babies were born, and so were her babies. Min had said so.

She knew she was in a wagon or cart by the sound of harness and the feel of rough boards beneath her. They had not bothered to pad the floorboards with a blanket. A wagon, she thought. There seemed to be more than one horse pulling it. The wagon box smelled of old hay so strongly that she wanted to sneeze. Her situation seemed hopeless, but Birgitte would not fail her.

She felt Birgitte leap from somewhere miles behind her to perhaps a mile ahead, and she wanted to laugh. The bond said Birgitte was aimed at her target, and Birgitte Silverbow never missed. When the channeling started on both sides of the wagon, the desire to laugh faded. Determination held rock-steady in the bond, but there was something else as well, now, a strong distaste and a rising . . . not anger, but close. Men would be dying out there. Instead of laughing, Elayne wanted to weep for them. They deserved someone to weep for them, and they were dying for her. As Vandene and Sareitha had died. Sadness for them welled up in her again. No guilt, though. Only by letting Falion and Marillin walk free could they have been spared, and neither would have countenanced that. There had been no way to anticipate the arrival of the others, or that strange weapon Asne had.

A thunderous crash came close at hand, and her conveyance was jolted so violently that she bounced on the floorboards. Her knees and shins were going to be bruised from that. She sneezed in the dust that had risen with her, sneezed again. She could feel individual hairs lifting where they were not held down by the gag and blindfold. The air smelled peculiar. A lightning strike, it appeared. She hoped Birgitte had managed to involve the Windfinders, unlikely as that seemed. The time would come when the Kin would have to use the Power as a weapon—no one could stand aside from Tarmon Gai'don—but let them preserve their innocence a little longer. Moments later, the shield on her vanished.

Unable to see, she could not channel to any real purpose, but she could sense weaves near her, some of Spirit, some of Air. Without seeing the weaves, she was unable to know what they were, yet she could make a reasonable guess. Her captors were themselves captives now, shielded and bound. And all she could do was wait impatiently. Birgitte was coming closer rapidly, yet now she felt anxious to have that bloody web of ropes off her.

The wagon box creaked as someone heaved herself in. Birgitte. The bond carried a flash of joy. In moments, the ropes fell away from her and Birgitte's hands went to the knot of the gag. Moving a little stiffly, Elayne untied the blindfold herself. Light, she was going to ache like fury until she could ask for Healing. That reminded her that she would have to ask the Windfinders, and the sadness rose all over again for Vandene and Sareitha.

Once she could spit out the gag, she wanted to ask for water to wash away the oily taste, but instead, she said, "What kept you?" Her laughter at the other woman's sudden consternation was cut short by another sneeze. "Let's get out of here, Birgitte. The Kin?"

"Windfinders," Birgitte answered, holding open the canvas flap at the back of the wagon. "Chanelle decided she'd rather not report losing her bargain to Zaida."

Elayne sniffed in disdain, a mistake. Sneezing repeatedly, she climbed down from the wagon as quickly as she could manage. Her legs were as stiff as her arms. Burn her, but she wanted a hot bath. And a hairbrush. Birgitte's white-collared red coat looked somewhat rumpled, but Elayne suspected she made her warder appear fresh from the dressing room.

When her feet hit the ground, mounted Guardsmen in a thick ring around the wagon raised a loud cheer, shaking their lances in the air. Guardswomen whooped, too, apparently almost every last one of them. Two of the men bore Andor's White Lion and her Golden Lily. That brought a smile. The Queen's Guards were sworn to defend Andor, the Queen and the Daughter-Heir, yet the decision to carry her personal banner had to have been Charlz Guybon's. Sitting a tall bay with his helmet resting on the saddlebow, he bowed to her, a broad smile on his lips. The man *was* a pleasure to look at. Perhaps he would do for a third Warder. Beyond the Guards rose House banners and banners of mercenary companies, banner after banner. Light, how many men had Birgitte brought? That could be answered later, though. First Elayne wanted to see her prisoners.

Asne lay spreadeagled on the road, her empty eyes staring at the sky; the shield on her was unneeded. The others lay as still, bound with flows of Air that held their arms to their sides and snugged their divided skirts against their legs. A *much* more comfortable position than she had been in. Most seemed remarkably composed considering their situation, though Temaile scowled at her and Falion appeared about to sick up. Shiaine's mud-smeared face would have done credit to any Aes Sedai. The three men bound with Air were anything but composed. They writhed and struggled, glaring at the riders surrounding them as if they wanted nothing more than to attack them all. That was enough to identify them as Asne's Warders, though not necessarily as Darkfriends. Whether they were or not, they would still have to be imprisoned, to protect others from the death-rage that Asne's death had filled them with. They would do anything to kill whomever they held responsible.

"How did they find us?" Chesmal demanded. If she had not been lying in the road with a dirty face, no one would have thought her a prisoner.

"My Warder," Elayne said, smiling at Birgitte. "One of them."

"A *woman* Warder?" Chesmal said disdainfully.

Marillin shook in her bonds with silent laughter for a moment. "I'd heard that," she said when the shaking ceased, "but it seemed too incredible to be true."

"You heard this, and you never mentioned it?" Temaile said, twisting around to transfer her scowl to Marillin. "You great fool!"

"You forget yourself," Marillin said sharply, and the next instant they were arguing about whether Temaile should defer to her! In truth, Temaile should—Elayne could sense their relative strengths—yet it hardly seemed a topic they would argue over now!

"Somebody gag these women," Elayne ordered. Caseille dismounted, handing her reins to another Guardswoman, and strode over to begin cutting a strip from Temaile's skirts with her dagger. "Load them into the wagon and cut away that dead horse. I want to get back inside the walls before Arymilla's people beyond the ridge feel tempted." The last thing she needed now was a pitched battle. Whatever the outcome, Arymilla could afford to lose more men than she. "Where are the Windfinders, Birgitte?"

"Still on the ridge. I think they believe they can deny taking part if they don't get too near the carnage. But you don't have to worry about being attacked here. The camps beyond the ridge are empty." Caseille hoisted Temaile over her shoulder and staggered over to heave her into the wagon like a sack of grain. Guardswomen were picking up the other women, too. They wisely left the struggling Warders to the Guardsmen. It required two to handle each of them. A pair of tall Guardsmen were unfastening the dead horse's harness.

"All I saw were camp followers, grooms and the like," Charlz put in.

"I think all of her camps may be empty," Birgitte went on. "She sent heavy assaults against the northern wall this morning to draw as many of our men as possible, and she has twenty thousand or more in Low Caemlyn below the Far Madding Gate. Some of the mercenaries changed colors and are attacking it from inside, but I sent Dyelin with everything I could spare. As soon as you're safe inside the walls, I'll take the rest to help her. To add to the good news, Luan and the rest of that lot are riding north. They could be here this afternoon."

Elayne's breath caught. Luan and the rest would have be dealt with when they appeared, but the other news . . . ! "Do you remember what Mistress Harfor reported, Birgitte? Arymilla and the others all intend to be with the first party to ride into Caemlyn. They must be outside the Far Madding Gate, too. How many men do you have here?"

"What's the butcher's bill, Guybon?" Birgitte asked, eyeing Elayne warily. The bond carried wariness, too. Great wariness.

"I don't have a full tally yet, my Lady. Some of the bodies. . . ." Charlz grimaced. "I'd say as many as five or six hundred dead, though, perhaps a few more. Twice as many wounded one way and another. As nasty a few minutes as I've ever seen."

"Call it ten thousand, Elayne," Birgitte said, thick braid swaying as she shook her head. She tucked her thumbs behind her belt, and determination filled the bond. "Arymilla has to have at least twice that at the Far Madding Gate, maybe three times if she's really stripped her camps. If you're thinking what I think you're thinking. . . . I told Dyelin to retake the gate if it had fallen, but it's more likely she's fighting Arymilla inside the city. If, by some miracle, the gate is holding, you're talking better than two to one odds against us."

"If they're through the gate," Elayne said stubbornly, "it's unlikely they closed it behind them. We'll take them in the rear." It was not all stubbornness. Not entirely. She had not trained with weapons, but she had received all of the other lessons Gawyn had gotten from Gareth Bryne. A queen had to understand the battle plans her generals gave her rather than simply accept them blindly. "If the gate is holding, we'll have them trapped between us and the wall. Numbers won't count so much in Low Caemlyn. Arymilla won't be able to line up any more men across a street than we can. We *are* going to do it, Birgitte. Now somebody find me a horse."

For a moment, she thought the other woman was going to refuse, which ratcheted up her stubbornness, but Birgitte exhaled heavily. "Tzigan, catch up that tall gray mare for Lady Elayne."

It seemed that everyone around them except the Darkfriends sighed. They must have thought they were going to see a display of Elayne Trakand's fabled temper. Knowing that almost sparked one. Burn her bouncing moods!

Stepping closer, Birgitte lowered her voice. "But you'll ride surrounded by your bodyguard. This isn't some fool story with a queen carrying her banner into battle to lead her troops. I know one of your ancestors did that, but you're not her, and you don't have a broken army to rally."

"Why, that was exactly my plan," Elayne said sweetly. "*How ever did you guess?*"

Birgitte snorted with laughter and muttered "Bloody woman" not quite softly enough to escape detection. Affection flowed in the bond, though.

It was not so simple, of course. Men had to be told off to help the wounded. Some could walk, but many could not. Too many had tourniquets around the bloody stump of an arm or a leg. Charlz and the nobles gathered around Elayne and Birgitte to hear the plan of attack, which *was* simple of necessity, but then Chanelle refused to change the gateway until Elayne agreed that this time they need provide transport only and sealed the agreement with them both kissing their fingertips and pressing them to the other's lips. Only then did the gateway dwindle to a vertical silvery slash and widen again into a hundred-pace-wide view of Caemlyn from the south.

There were no people in the brick markets lining the wide road that ran north from the gateway to the Far Madding Gate, but a great mass of men, mounted and afoot, crowded the road out of bowshot from the walls. The first of them was only a few hundred paces from the gateway. It appeared that they spilled into the side streets, too. The mounted men were to the front with a thicket of banners, but cavalry or infantry, they were all looking toward the gates of Caemlyn itself. The closed gates. Elayne could have shouted for joy.

She rode through first, but Birgitte was taking no chances. Her bodyguard gathered around her, herding her off to one side. Birgitte was right by her side, but somehow they did not seem to be herding *her*. Fortunately, no one tried to object to her pushing the gray forward until only a single line of Guardswomen was between her and the road. *That* line might as well have been a stone wall. The gray was indeed tall, however, so she could see without standing in the stirrups. She should have lengthened those. They were just a little short for her. That made this Chesmal's horse, since she was the only one who came close to her own height. A horse could not be tainted by its rider—just because Chesmal was Black Ajah did not make the *horse* evil—but she felt uncomfortable on the animal for more than short stirrups. The gray would be sold, the gray and all the other horses the Darkfriends had been riding, and the money distributed to the poor.

Cavalry and foot came out of the gateway behind Charlz, enough to fill it from side to side. Followed by the White Lion and the Golden Lily,

he started up the road at a trot with five hundred Guardsmen, spread out
to cover the width of the road. Other parties of similar size split off and
vanished into the streets of Low Caemlyn. When the last men exited the
gateway, it dwindled and vanished. Now, there was no quick escape if
anything went wrong. Now, they had to win, or Arymilla would as good
as have the throne whether or not she had Caemlyn.

"We need Mat Cauthon's bloody luck today," Birgitte muttered.

"You said something like that before," Elayne said. "What do you
mean?"

Birgitte gave her a peculiar look. The bond carried . . . amusement! "Have you ever seen him dicing?"

"I hardly spend much time in places where there's dicing, Birgitte."

"Let's just say he's luckier than any other man I've ever met."

Shaking her head, Elayne put Mat Cauthon out of her mind.
Charlz's men were shutting off her view as they rode forward. Not
charging yet, trying to make no more noise than absolutely necessary.
With a little luck, her men would have Arymilla's surrounded before
they knew what was happening. And then they would hit Arymilla
from every side. Mat was the luckiest man Birgitte had ever met? In
that case, he must be very lucky indeed.

Suddenly Charlz's Guardsmen were moving faster, their steel-
tipped lances swinging down. Someone must have looked back. Shouts
rose, cries of alarm and one thunderous shout she heard repeated from
many directions. "Elayne and Andor!"

There were other cries, as well. "The Moons!" and "The Fox!" "The
Triple Keys!" and "The Hammer!" and "The Black Banner!" Others,
for lesser Houses. But from her side came only the one, repeated again
and again. "Elayne and Andor!"

Suddenly she was shaking, half laughing, half weeping. The Light
send she was not consigning those men to their deaths for nothing.

The cries faded, largely replaced by the clash of steel on steel, by
shouts and screams as men killed or died. Abruptly she realized the
gates were swinging out. And she could not see! Kicking her feet free
of the stirrups, she clambered up to stand on the high-cantled saddle.
The gray shifted nervously, unaccustomed to being a stepstool, but not
enough to disturb her balance. Birgitte muttered a particularly pungent oath, but the next moment she was standing on her saddle, too.
Hundreds of crossbowmen and archers were pouring out of the Far
Madding Gate, but were they her men, or the renegade mercenaries?

For answer, archers began firing at Arymilla's massed cavalry as fast as they could nock and draw. The first crossbows went up and loosed a volley. Immediately those men began working their cranks to rewind their crossbows, but others rushed past them to loose a second flight of bolts that cut down men and horses like scythes reaping barley. More archers spilled out of the gate, firing as fast as they could. A third rank of crossbowmen ran forward to fire, a fourth, a fifth, and then men wielding halberds were pushing past the crossbowmen still running out of the gate. A halberd was a fearsome weapon, combining spear-point and axe blade with a hook for pulling men out of the saddle. Horsemen with no room to charge their lances, their swords outreached by the halberd's long haft, began falling. Men in red coats and burnished breastplates were galloping out of the gate now, Guardsmen swinging to left and right to find another way to get at Arymilla's ranks. The flow of them went on and on, unceasing. How in the Light could Dyelin have so many of the Guards? Unless. . . . Burn the woman, she must have scooped up the half-trained men! Well, half-trained or not, they would be anointed in blood today.

Suddenly three figures in gilded helmets and breastplates rode through the gates, swords in hand. Two of them were very small. The shouts that rose when they appeared were thin with distance, but still audible over the din of battle. "The Black Eagles!" and "The Anvil!" and "The Red Leopards!" Two mounted women appeared in the gate, struggling until the taller managed to pull the other's horse back out of sight.

"Blood and bloody ashes!" Elayne snapped. "Conail's old enough, I suppose, but Branlet and Perival are boys! Somebody should have kept them out of that!"

"Dyelin held them back long enough," Birgitte said calmly. The bond carried bone-deep calm. "Longer than I thought she could hold Conail. And she did manage to keep Catalyn out of it. Anyway, the boys have a few hundred men between them and the forefront, and I don't see anyone trying to make room for them to squeeze forward." It was true. The three were waving their swords impotently at least fifty paces from where men were dying. But then, fifty paces was a short range for bow or crossbow.

Men began appearing on the rooftops, first dozens then hundreds, archers and crossbowmen climbing over the roof peaks, working their way across the slates like spiders until they could shoot down into the packed mass below. One slipped and fell, his body lying atop the men in the street and jerking as it was stabbed repeatedly. Another suddenly reared up, a shaft sticking out of his side, and toppled from his perch. He also lay atop the men in the street, twitching as he was stabbed again and again.

"They're jammed together too tightly," Birgitte said excitedly. "They can't raise a bow much less draw one. I'll wager the dead don't even have room to fall down. It won't be long, now."

But the slaughter continued for a good half-hour before the first shouts of "Quarter!" rose. Men began hanging their helmets on sword hilts and raising them overhead, risking death in the hope of life. Footmen stripped off helmets and held their hands up empty. Horsemen flung down lances, helmets, swords, and raised their hands. It spread like a fever, the cry bellowing from thousands of throats. "Quarter!"

Elayne sat down on her saddle properly. It was done. Now to learn how well it had been done.

The fighting did not stop immediately, of course. Some tried to fight on, but they fought alone and died or were pulled down by men around them who were no longer ready to die. At last, however, even the most diehard began shedding weapons and armor, and if not every voice cried for quarter, the roar was still thunderous. Weaponless men shorn of helmets and breastplates and any other armor they might have worn began staggering through the line of Guardsmen, hands above their heads. Halberdmen herded them like sheep. They had something of the stunned look of sheep in a slaughter yard. The same thing must have been being repeated on dozens of Low Caemlyn's narrow streets, and at the gates, because the only shouts she heard were for quarter, and those were beginning to dwindle as men realized it was being granted.

The sun lacked no more than an hour of its noonday peak by the time the nobles were all separated out. The lesser were escorted inside the city, where they would be held for ransom. To be paid once the throne was secure. The first of the greater nobles to be brought to her, escorted by Charlz and a dozen Guardsmen, were Arymilla, Naean and Elenia. Charlz had a bloody gash down his left sleeve, and a dent in his shining breastplate that must have been made by a hammer blow, but his features were composed behind the face-bars of his helmet. She heaved a huge sigh of relief to see the three women. Among the dead or among the captives, the others would be found. She had decapitated her opposition. At least until Luan and the others arrived. The Guardswomen in front of her at last moved aside so she could confront her prisoners.

The three were garbed as if they had intended to attend Arymilla's coronation that very day. Her red silk dress was sewn with seed pearls on the bosom and embroidered with rearing white lions marching up the sleeves. Swaying in her saddle, she had the same stunned look in her brown eyes that her soldiers had. Naean, slim and straight-backed in blue with the silver Triple Keys of Arawn climbing her sleeves and silver scrollwork across her bosom, her gleaming black hair caught in a silver net set with sapphires, seemed subdued rather than numb. She even managed a sneer, though it was weak. Honey-haired Elenia, in green elaborately embroidered with gold, shared her glares between Arymilla and Elayne. The bond carried equal measures of triumph and disgust. Birgitte's dislike of these women was as personal as Elayne's own.

"You will be my guests in the palace for the time being," Elayne told them. "I hope your coffers are deep. Your ransoms will pay for this war you've caused." That was malicious of her, but she felt spiteful all of a sudden. Their coffers were not deep at all. They had borrowed far more than they could repay in order to hire mercenaries. And bribe mercenaries. They faced ruin without any ransom. With, they faced devastation.

"You cannot believe it ends this way," Arymilla said hoarsely. She sounded as if she were trying to convince herself. "Jarid is still in the field with a considerable force. Jarid and others. Tell her, Elenia."

"Jarid will try to preserve what he can of Sarand from this disaster you've forced us into," Elenia snarled. They began shouting at one another, but Elayne ignored them. She wondered how they would enjoy sharing a bed with Naean.

Next to appear under escort was Lir Baryn, and moments later Karind Anshar. As slender as a blade, and as strong, Lir wore a thoughtful expression rather than defiant or sullen. His green coat, embroidered with the silver Winged Hammer of House Baryn on the high collar, bore the marks of the breastplate he was no longer wearing, and his dark hair was matted with sweat. More glistened on his face. He had not gotten so sweaty watching other men fight. Karind was garbed as grandly as the other women, in shimmering blue silk heavy with silver braid and pearls in her gray-streaked hair. Her square face looked resigned, especially after Elayne told them about their ransoms. Neither had borrowed as heavily as the other three so far as she knew, but that ransom would still cut deep.

Then two Guardsmen appeared with a woman a little older than

Elayne, in simple blue, a woman she thought she recognized. A single enameled brooch, a red star and silver sword on glittering black, appeared to be her only jewelry. But why was Sylvase Caeren being brought to her? A pretty woman with alert blue eyes that held steady on Elayne's face, she was Lord Nasin's heir, not the High Seat of Caeren.

"Caeren stands for Trakand," Sylvase said shockingly as soon as she reined in. The bond echoed Elayne's startlement. Arymilla gaped at Sylvase as if she were mad. "My grandfather suffered a seizure, Arymilla," the young woman said calmly, "and my cousins fell over themselves affirming me as High Seat. I will publish it, Elayne, if you wish."

"That might be best," Elayne said slowly. Publication would make her support irrevocable. This would not be the first time a House had switched sides, even without the death of a High Seat, but best to be certain. "Trakand welcomes Caeren warmly, Sylvase." Best not to be too distant, either. She knew little of Sylvase Caeren.

Sylvase nodded, accepting. So she had at least a degree of intelligence. She knew she would not be fully trusted until she demonstrated her loyalty by sending out the proclamations of support. "If you trust me a little, may I have custody of Arymilla, Naean and Elenia? In the Royal Palace, of course, or wherever you choose to house me. I believe my new secretary, Master Lounalt, may be able to convince them to throw their support to you."

For some reason, Naean gave a loud cry and would have fallen from her saddle if a Guardsman had not grabbed her arm to support her. Arymilla and Elenia both appeared ready to sick up.

"I think not," Elayne said. No proposed conversation with a secretary produced those reactions. It seemed Sylvase had a hard core to her. "Naean and Elenia have published their support of Arymilla. They'll hardly destroy themselves by recanting." That truly would destroy them. Smaller Houses sworn to them would begin falling away until their own House dwindled in importance. They themselves might not survive as High Seats much beyond announcing that they now stood for Trakand. And as for Arymilla. . . . Elayne would not allow Arymilla to change her tune. She would refuse the woman's support if it were offered!

Something grim entered Sylvase's gaze as she glanced at the three women. "They might, with the proper persuasion." Oh, yes; a very hard core. "But as you wish, Elayne. Be very careful of them, though. Treachery is in their blood and bones."

"Baryn stands for Trakand," Lir announced suddenly. "I, too, will publish it, Elayne."

"Anshar stands for Trakand," Karind said in firm tones. "I will send the proclamations out today."

"Traitors!" Arymilla cried. "I'll see you dead for this!" She fumbled at her belt, where a dagger's scabbard hung, jeweled and empty, as if she intended to see to the matter herself. Elenia began to laugh, but she did not sound amused. It sounded almost like weeping.

Elayne drew a deep breath. Now she had nine of the ten Houses needed. She was under no illusions. Whatever Sylvase's reasons, Lir and Karind were trying to salvage what they could by cutting themselves loose from a lost cause and hitching themselves to one that suddenly appeared to be rising. They would expect her to give them preferment for standing for her before she had the throne while forgetting that they had ever supported Arymilla. She would do neither. But neither could she reject them out of hand. "Trakand welcomes Baryn." Never warmly, though. Never that. "Trakand welcomes Anshar. Captain Guybon, get the prisoners into the city as soon as you can. Armsmen for Caeren, Baryn and Anshar will be restored their weapons and armor once the proclamations have been sent out, but they can have their banners back now." He saluted her and wheeled his bay, already shouting orders.

As she heeled the gray toward Dyelin, who was riding out of a side street followed by Catalyn and the three young fools in their gilded armor, Sylvase, Lir and Karind fell in behind her and Birgitte. She felt no disquiet having them at her back, not with a hundred Guardswomen at theirs. They would be watched very closely until those proclamations were sent. Including Sylvase. Elayne's mind was already casting itself ahead.

"You're awfully quiet," Birgitte said softly. "You've just won a great victory."

"And in a few hours," she replied, "I'll learn whether I have to win another."

CHAPTER
34

A *Cup of* Kaf

Furyk Karede pressed his gauntleted fist to his heart, returning the sentry's salute, and ignored the fact that the man spat as he rode past. He hoped the eighty men and twenty-one Ogier behind him ignored it, too. They had better, if they knew what was good for them. He was here for information, and a killing would make getting it more difficult. Since his manservant Ajimbura had planted his knife in a Standardbearer's heart over a perceived insult to his master—in truth, a real insult, but Ajimbura should have held his temper the way he himself had—since then, he had taken to leaving the wiry little hill-tribesman in the forest with the *sul'dam* and *damane* and some of the Guards to watch over the packhorses when he entered a camp. He had come a long way from Ebou Dar chasing the wind, almost four weeks of haring after rumors, until the news brought him here to this camp in east central Altara.

The neat rows of pale tents and horselines stood in a forest clearing large enough for *raken* to land, but there was no sign of *raken* or fliers, no ground company with its wagons and *raken*-grooms. But then, he had not seen a *raken* in the skies for some time now. Supposedly almost all had been sent west. Why, he did not know and did not care. The High Lady was his goal and his entire world. A tall thin message pole cast its long shadow in the early morning sun, though, so there must be *raken* somewhere about. He thought the camp might contain a thousand men, not counting farriers and cooks and the like. Interestingly, every last soldier he could see wore familiar armor from home rather than those solid breastplates and barred helmets. Practice was to pad out most forces with men from this side of the ocean. It was interesting that they were all armored, too. A rare commander kept his soldiers in armor unless he expected action soon. From the rumors he had picked up, that might be the case here.

Three flagstaffs marked the command tent, a tall, walled affair of pale canvas with air vents along the peak that doubled as smoke holes. No smoke issued from them now, for the morning was only a little cool, though the sun hung not far above the horizon. On one flagstaff the blue-bordered Imperial Banner hung in limp folds, hiding the spread-winged golden hawk clutching lightning in its talons. Some commanders hung it from a horizontal staff so it was always visible in full, but he thought that ostentatious. The other two banners, on shorter flanking staffs, would be of the regiments these men belonged to.

Karede dismounted in front of that tent and removed his helmet. Captain Musenge emulated him, revealing a grim expression on his weathered face. The other men climbed down too, to rest their horses, and stood by their animals. The Ogier Gardeners leaned on their long-hafted, black-tasseled axes. Everyone knew they would not be staying long.

"Keep the men out of trouble," he told Musenge. "If that means accepting insults, so be it."

"There'd be fewer insults if we killed a few of them," Musenge muttered. He had been in the Deathwatch Guards even longer than Karede, though his hair was unbroken black, and he would suffer insults to the Empress, might she live forever, as gladly as insults to the Guards.

Hartha scratched one of his long gray mustaches with a finger the size of a fat sausage. The First Gardener, commander of all the Ogier in the High Lady Tuon's bodyguard, was almost as tall as a man in the saddle, and wide with it. His red-and-green lacquered armor contained enough steel to make armor for three or four humans. His face was as dour as Musenge's, yet his booming voice was calm. Ogier were always calm except in battle. Then they were as cold as deep winter in Jeranem. "After we rescue the High Lady we can kill as many of them as need killing, Musenge."

Recalled to his duty, Musenge flushed for having allowed himself to stray. "After," he agreed. ·

Karede had schooled himself too hard over the years, had been schooled too hard by his trainers, to sigh, but had he been other than a Deathwatch Guard, he might have done so now. Not because Musenge wanted to kill someone and almost anyone would do. Rather it was because the insults he had walked away from these past weeks chafed him as much as they did Musenge and Hartha. But the Guards did whatever was necessary to carry out their assignments, and if that meant walking away from men who spat on the ground at the sight of armor in red and the dark green most called black, or dared to murmur about lowered eyes in his hearing, then walk away he must. Finding and rescuing the High Lady Tuon was all that mattered. Everything else was dross beside that.

Helmet under his arm, he ducked into the tent to find what must have been most of the camp's officers gathered around a large map spread out on a folding camp table. Half wore segmented breastplates lacquered in horizontal red and blue stripes, the other half red and yellow. They straightened and stared when he walked in, men from Khoweal or Dalenshar with skin blacker than charcoal, honey-brown men from N'Kon, fair-haired men from Mechoacan, pale-eyed men from Alqam, men from every part of the Empire. Their stares held not the wariness often tinged with admiration that he had always been used to, but very nearly challenges. It seemed everyone believed the filthy tale of Guards' involvement with a girl pretending to be the High Lady Tuon and extorting gold and jewels from merchants. Likely they believed that other, whispered tale about the girl, not merely vile but horrific. No. That the High Lady was in danger of her life from the Ever Victorious Army itself went beyond horrific. That was a world gone mad.

"Furyk Karede," he said coolly. His hand wanted to go to his sword hilt. Only discipline kept it at his side. Discipline and duty. He had accepted sword thrusts for duty. He could accept insults for it. "I wish to speak to the commander of this camp." For a long moment the silence stretched.

"Everybody out," a tall lean man barked at last in the sharp accents of Dalenshar. The others saluted, gathered their helmets from another table and filed out. Not one offered Karede a salute. His right hand twitched once, *feeling* a phantom hilt against his palm, and was still.

"Gamel Loune," the lean man introduced himself. Missing the top of his right ear, he had a slash of solid white there through his tight black curls and flecks of white elsewhere. "What do you want?" There was the barest touch of wariness in that. A hard man, and self-controlled. He would have had to be to earn the three red plumes decorating the helmet atop his sword-rack. Weak men without mastery of themselves did not rise to Banner-General. Karede suspected the only reason Loune was willing to talk to him was that his own helmet bore three black plumes.

"Not to interfere in your command." Loune had cause to fear that. Ranks in the Deathwatch Guard stood half a step higher than those outside. He could have co-opted the man's command had he needed to, though he would have been required to explain his reasons later. They would have had to be good reasons for him to avoid losing his head. "I understand there have been . . . difficulties in this part of Altara recently. I want to know what I am riding into."

Loune grunted. " 'Difficulties.' That's one word for it."

A stocky man in a plain brown coat, a narrow beard dangling from the point of his chin, entered the tent, carrying a heavily carved wooden tray with a silver pitcher and two sturdy white cups, the sort that would not break easily while being carried about in wagons. The scent of freshly brewed *kaf* began to suffuse the air.

"Your *kaf*, Banner-General." Setting the tray on the edge of table holding the map, he carefully filled one cup with the black liquid while watching Karede from the corner of his eye. Somewhere in his middle years, he wore a pair of long knives at his belt, and his hands had a knifeman's calluses. Karede sensed close kin to Ajimbura, in spirit but not blood. Those dark brown eyes never came from the Kaensada Hills. "I waited till the others left since there's hardly enough for you any more. Don't know when I'm going to get more, I don't."

"Will you take *kaf*, Karede?" Loune's reluctance was obvious, but he could hardly fail to offer. For an insult that large, Karede would have been forced to kill him. Or so the man would think.

"With pleasure," Karede replied. Placing his helmet alongside the tray, he doffed his steel-backed gauntlets and laid them beside it.

The serving man filled the second cup, then started toward a corner of the tent, but Loune said, "That will be all for now, Mantual." The stocky man hesitated, eyeing Karede, before making a bow to Loune, touching eyes and lips with his fingertips, and departing.

"Mantual is over-protective of me," Loune explained. Clearly he did not want to explain, but he did want to avoid what might be taken for open insult. "Odd fellow. Attached himself to me years ago in Pujili, wormed his way into becoming my manservant. I think he'd stay if I stopped paying him." Yes, very close kin to Ajimbura.

For a time they simply sipped *kaf*, balancing the cups on fingertips and enjoying the pungent bitterness. It seemed to be a pure Ijaz Mountains brew, and if so, very expensive. Karede's own supply of black beans, most definitely not Ijaz Mountains, had run out a week ago, and he had been surprised at how much he missed having *kaf*. He never used to mind going without anything at need. The first cups done, Loune refilled them.

"You were going to tell me about the difficulties," Karede prompted now that conversation would not be impolite. He always tried to be polite even with men he was going to kill, and rudeness here would dam up the man's tongue.

Loune set his cup down and leaned his fists on the table, frowning at the map. Small red wedges supporting tiny paper banners were scattered across it, marking Seanchan forces on the move, and red stars indicating forces holding in place. Little black discs marking engagements peppered the map, but strangely, no white discs to indicate the enemy. None.

"Over the last week," Loune said, "there have been four sizeable engagements and upwards of sixty ambushes, skirmishes and raids, many quite large, all spread out across three hundred miles." That encompassed almost the entire map. His voice was stiff. Plainly, given a choice, he would have told Karede nothing. That half-step gave him none, however. "There must be six or eight different armies involved on the other side. The night after the first large engagement saw nine major raids, each forty to fifty miles from the site of the battle. Not small armies, either, at least not taken altogether, but we can't find them, and nobody has any eyeless idea where they came from. Whoever they are, they have *damane*, those Aes Sedai, with them, and maybe those cursed Asha'man. Men have been torn apart by explosions our *damane* say weren't caused by the Power."

Karede sipped his *kaf*. The man was not thinking. If the enemy had Aes Sedai and Asha'man, they could use the thing called Traveling to move as far as they wished in a step. But if they could do that, why had they not used it to step all the way to safety with their prize? Perhaps not all Aes Sedai and Asha'man could Travel, yet that begged another question. Why had they not sent those who could? Maybe the only Aes Sedai were the *damane* stolen from the Tarasin Palace. Reportedly, none of them had had any idea how to Travel. That made sense. "What do the prisoners say about who sent them?"

Loune's laugh was bitter. "Before you can have eyeless prisoners, you need an eyeless victory. What we've had are a string of eyeless defeats." Picking up his cup, he took a sip. His voice loosened as if he had forgotten the colors of Karede's armor. He was just a soldier talking his trade, now. "Gurat thought he had some of them two days ago. He lost four banners of horse and five of foot almost to the last man. Not all dead, but most of the wounded are the next thing to it. Pincushioned with crossbow bolts. Mostly Taraboners and Amadicians, but that isn't supposed to matter, is it. Had to be twenty thousand or more crossbowmen to put out that volume. Thirty thousand, maybe. And yet they manage to hide from the *morat'raken*. I know we've killed some—the reports claim it, at least—but they don't even leave their dead behind. Some fools have begun whispering that we're fighting spirits." Fools he might consider them, but the fingers of his left hand hooked in a sign to ward off evil. "I'll tell you one thing I know, Karede. Their commanders are very good. Very, very good. Every man to face them has been fought off his feet, outmaneuvered and outfought completely."

Karede nodded thoughtfully. He had speculated that the White Tower must have tasked one of its best to kidnap the High Lady Tuon, but he had not been thinking along the lines of what people this side of the ocean called the great captains. Perhaps Thom Merrilin's real name was Agelmar Jagad or Gareth Bryne. He looked forward to meeting the man, not least to ask him how he had known she would be coming to Ebou Dar. He might hide Suroth's involvement, but then again, he might not. On the heights, today's ally could be tomorrow's sacrifice. Except for the Gardeners, the Deathwatch Guards were *da'covale* to the Empress herself, might she live forever, yet they lived on the heights. "There must be some plan for finding them and pinning them. Are you in charge of it?"

"No, praise be to the Light!" Loune said fervently. He took a long drink as though wishing it were brandy. "General Chisen is bringing his entire army back through the Malvide Narrows. Apparently the Tarasin Palace decided this was important enough to risk thrusts out of Murandy or Andor, though from what I've heard, neither one is capable of striking at anyone at the moment. I just have to wait here until Chisen arrives. We'll see a different result then, I think. More than half Chisen's men will be veterans from home."

Abruptly Loune seemed to recall who he was talking to. His face turned to dark wood, a hard mask. It did not matter. Karede was convinced this was the work of Merrilin or whatever his name was. And he knew why the man was doing what he was doing. Under different circumstances, he would have told Loune his reasoning, but the High Lady would not be safe until she was back in the Tarasin Palace among those who knew her face. If the man failed to believe him on the key point, that she *was* the High Lady, he would have increased her danger for nothing.

"I thank you for the *kaf*," he said, setting the cup down and taking up his helmet and gauntlets. "The Light see you safe, Loune. We will meet in Seandar someday."

"The Light see you safe, Karede," Loune said after a moment, plainly surprised by the polite farewell. "We will meet in Seandar someday." The man had shared *kaf*, and Karede had no quarrel with him. Why should he be surprised?

Karede did not speak to Musenge until they had ridden out of the camp, the Ogier Gardeners striding along just ahead of the human Guards. Hartha was walking on Karede's other side, his long axe propped on his shoulder, his head nearly level with theirs.

"We head northeast," he said, "for the Malvide Narrows." If he remembered the maps correctly, and he seldom forgot any map he had more than glimpsed, they could reach it in four days. "The Light shine on us that we arrive before the High Lady." If they did not, the pursuit would continue, all the way to Tar Valon if necessary. The thought of turning back without the High Lady never occurred to him. If he had to bring her out of Tar Valon, he would.

C H A P T E R
35

The Importance of Dyelin

T hey want *safe conduct?*" Elayne said incredulously. "To enter *Caemlyn?*" Lightning flashed outside the windows, and thunder boomed. Outside, a deluge fell on Caemlyn, a hammering downpour. The sun must have been well above the horizon, but the stand-lamps were lit against twilight darkness.

The slender young man standing in front of her low-backed chair colored with embarrassment, yet he continued to look her in the eye. He was little more than a boy, really, his smooth cheeks likely shaved as much for form as because he needed a razor very often. Very properly, Hanselle Renshar, Arathelle's grandson, wore neither sword nor armor, but the marks of breastplate straps remained on his green coat, imprinted by long wear. A large damp spot on his left shoulder showed where his cloak had leaked through. Odd, the things you noticed at times like this. "I was instructed to ask for it, my Lady," he said, his voice steady.

Dyelin, arms folded beneath her breasts, grunted sourly. She was not far from scowling. Mistress Harfor, resplendent as always in her crimson tabard with the White Lion spotless on her formidable bosom, sniffed audibly. Hanselle colored again. They were in Elayne's smaller sitting room, where a small fire on the marble hearth took away most of the morning's chill and lamp oil scented the air with roses. She wished Birgitte was there. From the mild irritation flowing through the bond, she was dealing with reports. Her annoyance was not great enough for it to be anything more urgent.

The arrival of Luan and the others below the city two days ago with their sixty thousand armsmen had occasioned more than a little excitement, and impromptu celebrations in the streets by the citizens, once it became clear they were not going to occupy the camps abandoned when Jarid Sarand left. Taking with him men from Houses that now sided with Elayne, though they could not know it yet. The Light only knew what trouble *that* bloody man was going to cause. But Hanselle's message put a new complexion on the huge encampment just a mile south of Low Caemlyn. If Arathelle, Luan and the others knew about the city being supplied from Tear and Illian through gateways, and surely everyone in Andor knew by this time, perhaps they had decided a siege would accomplish nothing. Safe conduct was a matter of battle lines. Perhaps they intended to call for Caemlyn's surrender to avoid a grand assault. The proclamations of support, carried by Kinswomen rather than riders, had been posted from Aringill to the mining villages in the Mountains of Mist, or soon would be, but even with Sumeko and other Kinswomen wearing themselves out in Healing, the armsmen of Caeren, Anshar and Baryn who had not been carried off by Jarid did not bring her numbers anywhere near sixty thousand. Small bands of armsmen were beginning to flow into the city as word spread that it was safe to approach Caemlyn, but not enough yet. It might be a week or more before sizeable parties appeared. Those had been staying clear of the city for fear of Arymilla's army. The outcome of a massive assault was not a foregone conclusion—men atop a wall had considerable advantage over those trying to scale it—but it would be a near run thing at best, and no hope for more help soon. Dyelin had paid another visit to Danine Candraed in the west, but the woman still dithered. Elayne had nine Houses where she needed ten, everything hung in the balance, and Danine could not bloody decide whether or not to stand for Trakand.

"Why do they wish to speak with me?" She managed to keep Birgitte's irritation from tinging her voice. Birgitte's and her own.

Hanselle reddened yet again. He seemed to do that easily. Burn her, they truly had sent a boy! "I was not informed, my Lady. I was simply told to ask for safe conduct." He hesitated. "They will not enter Caemlyn without it, my Lady."

Rising, she went to her writing desk, removed a smooth sheet of good white paper from the rosewood paper-box and dipped a pen in the silver-mounted crystal ink jar. Precise letters flowed onto the page without her usual flourishes. She was short and to the point.

Lord Luan Norwelyn, Lady Arathelle Renshar, Lord Pelivar Coelan, Lady Aemlyn Carand, Lady Ellorien Traemane and Lord Abelle Pendar may feel safe in entering Caemlyn and be assured that they and their retinues may depart the city at any time they wish. I will receive them informally this afternoon in the Grand Hall as befits their stations. We must speak of the Borderlanders.

Elayne Trakand
Daughter-Heir of Andor
High Seat of House Trakand

She tried to maintain calm, but the steel nib dug into the paper with the last letters. Safe conduct. She channeled a sealing candle alight, and her hand trembled as she dribbled golden yellow wax onto the page. They implied she would try to hold them by force. No, more than implied! They as good as said it! She pressed her seal, a blossoming lily, into the wax as if trying to drive it through the tabletop.

"Here," she said, handing the sheet to the young man. Her voice was ice, and she made no effort to warm it. "If this fails to make them feel safe, perhaps they might try wrapping themselves in swaddling." Thunder boomed for punctuation.

He colored once more, this time plainly in anger, but wisely confined himself to offering thanks as he folded the page. He was carefully tucking it inside his coat when Mistress Harfor showed him out. She would escort him to his horse personally. A messenger from nobles as powerful as Luan and the others had to be given a certain level of honor.

Suddenly Elayne's anger turned to sadness. She could not have said *what* she was sad over. Her moods often seemed to change without cause. Perhaps for all those who had died and all those who would. "Are you *certain* you don't want to be queen, Dyelin? Luan and that lot would stand for you in a heartbeat, and if I stand for you, those who've stood for me will stand with me. Burn me, Danine would probably stand for you."

Dyelin took a chair, spreading her blue skirts carefully, before answering. "I'm *absolutely* certain. Running my own House is work enough for me without adding all of Andor to it. Besides, I disapprove of the throne changing Houses without good cause—the lack of a Daughter-Heir, or worse, one who's a fool or incompetent, cruel or greedy. You're none of those things. Continuity provides stability, and stability brings prosperity." She nodded; she liked that turn of phrase. "Mind, had you died before returning to Caemlyn and making your claim, I would have entered my own, but the simple truth is, you'll make a better ruler than I would. Better for Andor. In part that's because of your connection to the Dragon Reborn." Dyelin's raised eyebrow invited Elayne to expound on that connection. "But in large part," she went on when Elayne said nothing, "it's you yourself. I watched you grow up, and by the time you were fifteen I knew you'd be a good queen, perhaps as good as Andor has ever had."

Elayne's face grew hot, and tears welled in her eyes. Burn her bouncing moods! Only she knew she could not blame her pregnancy this time. Praise from Dyelin was like praise from her mother, never grudging, but never given unless she felt it was deserved.

Her morning was busy, and she had only Caemlyn and the palace to deal with rather than all of Andor. Mistress Harfor reported that the spies in the palace who could be confirmed as reporting to Arymilla or her allies had grown very quiet and still, like mice that feared a cat might be watching.

"At least it's safe to dismiss them now, my Lady," Reene said in tones of great satisfaction. She disliked having spies in the Royal Palace as much as Elayne did, perhaps more. Daughter-Heir or Queen might live in the palace, but in the First Maid's eyes, it belonged to her. "All of them." Spies for others had been left in place so that no one would suspect that Reene knew.

"Keep them all on and continue to watch them," Elayne told her. "They're the most likely to take coin from someone else, and we know who they are." A spy who was known could be kept from learning anything they should not, and you could make sure they learned exactly what you wanted them to. That went for the Ajah eyes-and-ears Mistress Harfor had uncovered, too. The Ajahs had no right to spy on her, and if she occasionally spoon-fed them false information, it would be their own fault if they acted on it. She could not do that too often or they would realize she had uncovered their spies, but she could at need.

"As you say, my Lady. The world has changed, hasn't it?"

"I'm afraid it has, Mistress Harfor."

The round woman nodded sadly, but she quickly returned to business. "One of the windows in the Grand Hall has developed a leak, my Lady. I'd have seen to anything minor without bothering you, but this is a crack in the glass, which means calling in. . . ." The list of problems that needed Elayne's approval and papers that needed her signature went on.

Master Norry reported on wagonloads of grain and beans and trade goods in that dusty voice of his, and announced with some surprise that the number of arsons had not decreased. Seventeen buildings had burned in the night. He had been sure the capture of Arymilla would see an end to that, and he was rueful over being wrong. He brought death warrants in the names of Rhys a'Balaman and Aldred Gomaisen for her to sign and seal. Mercenaries who turned their colors could expect no more unless their new masters prevailed. Evard Cordwyn had died at the gate or he would have gone to the gallows, too. Hafeen Bakuvun had sent a petition asking a reward for his actions at the Far Madding Gate, yet that was easy enough to reject. The presence of the Domani mercenary and his men might well have been the difference in the gate holding until Dyelin arrived, but they had been earning their pay, no more.

"The prisoners are still being closemouthed, I fear," Norry said, sliding the refused petition back into his leather folder. He seemed to feel that if he did that quickly enough it was the same as never having removed it. "The Darkfriend Aes Sedai, I mean, my Lady. And the other two. Very closemouthed except for . . . um . . . invective. Mellar is the worst with that, shouting about what he intends to do to the women who arrested him," Deni had taken her instuctions literally; the Guardswomen had pummeled Mellar severely, leaving him a mass of bruises from head to foot, "but the Aes Sedai can be quite . . . um . . . vituperative, as well. I fear it may be necessary to put them to the question if we hope to learn anything useful."

"Don't call them Aes Sedai," she snapped. Hearing "Aes Sedai" linked with "Darkfriend" made her stomach writhe. "Those women have given up any right to be called Aes Sedai." She had taken their Great Serpent rings herself and had them melted down. That was Egwene's prerogative, not hers, and she might well be reprimanded for it, but she could not restrain herself. "Ask the Lady Sylvase for the use of her secretary." She had no questioners among her people, and accord-

ing to Aviendha, an unskilled questioner was likely to kill the one being put unsuccessfully to the question. When *was* her sister going to
be allowed to visit? Light, she missed Aviendha. "I suspect he's no such
thing." Lightning lit up the windows of the sitting room, the glassed
casements rattling with the boom of its thunder.

Norry pressed his fingertips together, holding the folder against
his ink-stained tabard with the heels of his hands and frowning
gravely. "Few people keep a private questioner, my Lady. It suggests . . . um . . . a dark side. But then, as I understand matters, her
grandfather chased away every man who showed interest in her until
men stopped showing interest, and she has been virtually a prisoner
since reaching her majority. That would tend to give anyone a dark
view of the world. She may not . . . um . . . be as trustworthy as you
could wish, my Lady."

"Do you think you can bribe some of her servants to be my eyes-
and-ears?" How easy it was to ask that. Spies had become a part of her
life, as much as masons or glaziers.

"That should be possible, my Lady. I will know for certain in a day
or two." Once, he would have been horrified by the very idea of having anything to do with spying. All things changed eventually, it
seemed. His hands shifted on the folder, almost but not quite opening
it. "I fear the sewers in the southern part of the New City need attention urgently."

Elayne sighed. Not everything changed. Burn her, once she did
have all of Andor, she suspected she would seldom have an hour to herself. What *did* Luan and the others want?

Not long after midmorning, Melfane Dawlish appeared and had
Essande and Neris strip Elayne to the skin so she could be weighed in
a huge, wooden-armed balance scale the midwife had brought along, a
daily ritual. The brass pan was padded with a blanket, thank the Light!
The stout little woman listened to her heart though a hollow wooden
tube pressed to her chest and back, thumbed back her eyelids to examine her eyes, and smelled her breath. She had Elayne make water, then
held the glass jar up to the light of a stand-lamp to study it. She
smelled that, too, and even dipped a finger in and licked it! It was another daily ritual. Elayne averted her eyes, pulling her flower-
embroidered silk robe tight around her, but she still shuddered. This
time, Melfane noticed.

"I can tell some sickness from changes in the taste, my Lady. Anyway, there's worse things. My boy Jaem, the one who carried the scale for me, his first paid job of work was mucking out in a stable. He claimed everything he ate tasted like—" Her round belly shook with laughter. "Well, you can imagine, my Lady." Elayne could, and was glad she was not prone to nausea. She shuddered again anyway. Essande seemed quite composed, hands folded at her waist and watching her niece with approval, but Neris looked about to sick up. "Pity he can't learn my craft, but no one would buy herbs from a man. Or have a man midwife." Melfane laughed uproariously at that ridiculous notion. "Wants to be apprenticed to an armorer, of all things. Old for it, but there it is. Now, you be sure to read to your babe." She was more than doubtful of Elayne's claim that she would have a boy and a girl. She would not accept it until she could hear their heartbeats, and that would be some few weeks yet. "And have musicians play for her. She'll learn the sound of your voice. Learn to like reading and music, too. It helps in other ways besides. Makes the child brighter."

"You say that every time, Mistress Dawlish," Elayne said peevishly. "I *can* remember, you know. And I *am* doing it."

Melfane laughed again, a twinkle in her dark eyes. She accepted Elayne's bouncing moods the way she accepted rain and lightning. "You'd be surprised how many don't believe a babe in the womb can hear, but I can see the difference in those who get read to and those who don't. Do you mind if I have a few words with my aunt before I go, my Lady? I brought her a pie and an ointment for her joints." Essande's face reddened. Well, now that her lie was exposed, she would accept Healing or Elayne would know the reason why.

At the end of the midday meal, Elayne brought up the intentions of Luan and the others with Birgitte. It was a wonderful meal, and she ate ravenously. Melfane had lambasted the cooks and every other woman in earshot for the bland diet they had been feeding her. Today there were small pond trout grilled to perfection, cabbage rolls stuffed with crumbly white ewe's milk cheese, broad beans with pinenuts, and a tangy apple tart. Another reason it was marvelous was that nothing had the faintest hint of spoiling. To drink, there was good black tea with mint that made her tense for a moment until she realized it really was mint. The only thing Melfane had forbidden was wine, however well watered. Birgitte had even given up drinking herself, though it seemed impossible it could have any effect through the bond. Elayne refrained from pointing that out. Birgitte had been drinking too much to dull the pain of losing her Gaidal. Elayne understood even if she did not approve. She could not imagine what she would do if Rand died.

"I don't know," Birgitte said after wolfing down the last of her tart. "My best guess is they've come to ask you to help them move against the Borderlanders. The one bloody thing that's sure is that they didn't bloody come to throw their support to you."

"That's my best guess, too." Elayne picked up crumbs of cheese with a damp fingertip and popped them into her mouth. She could have eaten as much again as had been on her plate, but Melfane had announced her strict intention to limit her weight gain. Just enough and not too much. Perhaps a cow being fattened for market felt like this. "Unless they're going to demand I surrender Caemlyn."

"There's always that," Birgitte said, sounding almost cheerful. The bond said she was anything but. "We still have watchers in the towers, though, and Julanya and Keraille have gotten work as laundresses in their camp, so we'll know if they begin to move against the city before the first man sets out."

Elayne wished she did not sigh so often. Burn her, she had Arymilla, Naean and Elenia under guard and definitely *not* enjoying sharing a bed—she knew the thought should not give her pleasure but it did—and she had gained three more allies, if not necessarily the most solid. At least they were tied to her inextricably, now. She should have been feeling triumphant.

That afternoon, Essande and Sephanie dressed her in dark green slashed with emerald on the skirts and embroidered with silver across the bosom, down the sleeves and around the hem. For jewelry, she wore her Great Serpent ring and a large silver pin enameled blue except for the shape of Trakand's Keystone. The pin made her morose. Inside the House it was said that Trakand was the keystone that held Andor together. She had not done a very good job of it so far.

She and Birgitte took turns reading aloud to her babes. From histories, of course; if Melfane was right, she did not want to direct them to frivolous tales. Dry stuff, it was. A plump man in red and white played the flute while a lean woman in livery played the twelve-string bittern, producing lively, joyous tunes. At least when crashes of thunder did not drown them out. Bards did not grow on trees, and Birgitte had been uncertain about allowing anyone from outside the palace near Elayne, but Mistress Harfor had found a number of accomplished musicians who had leapt at the chance to put on livery. Their pay was con-

siderably better in the palace than in a common room, and their clothing was provided with it. Elayne thought of trying to hire a gleeman,
but that made her think of Thom. Was he dry? Was he even alive? All
she could do was pray. The Light send it so. Please.

Mistress Harfor came to announce the arrival of Luan, Arathelle
and the others, and Elayne donned the coronet of the Daughter-Heir, a
simple gold band that held a single golden rose surrounded by thorns
above her brows. Caseille, along with eight Guardswomen, fell in behind her, Birgitte and Essande as they left her apartments, boots thud-
ding loudly on the floor tiles in step. Nine Guardswomen had been
among the dead when she was rescued from the Darkfriends, and that
seemed to have bonded the others together even more tightly. They
got lost twice finding their way to the Grand Hall, but no one so much
as murmured. What were shifting corridors when you had faced
Power-wrought fire and lightning? The great arched doors of the
Grand Hall, carved with tall lions on both sides, stood open, and Caseille took the Guardswomen to stand in front of them while she, Birgitte and Essande went in.

The tall windows in the walls were dark with rain except when
lightning flashed, but the mirrored stand-lamps, against the walls and
around the white columns that marched in rows along the sides of the
chamber, were all lit. A loud, steady plunk-plunk-plunk echoed in the
vast space, drops falling into a prosaic wooden bucket standing beneath one of the colored windows set in the ceiling twenty paces overhead, where one of the rearing White Lions had beads of water
glistening along a crack, near scenes of battle and the faces of Andor's
earliest queens. As always in this hall, Elayne felt those women judging her as she crossed the red-and-white floor tiles. They had built Andor with the sharpness of their minds and the blood of their sons and
husbands, beginning with a single city and molding a strong nation
out of the rubble of Artur Hawkwing's empire. They had a right to
judge any woman who sat on the Lion Throne. She suspected their vis-
ages had been placed there so every queen would feel her actions
judged by history.

The throne itself sat atop a white marble dais at the far end of the
chamber, carved and gilded and sized for a woman, yet massive on its
lion-pawed legs. The White Lion, formed from moonstones set in a
field of glittering rubies on its tall back, would stand above the head of
the tallest woman who sat on that throne. Dyelin was already standing

at the foot of the dais's steps, watching Sylvase converse with Conail and Catalyn while Branlet and Perival listened closely. Perival raked his fingers through his hair and nodded. Did Dyelin have questions about Sylvase, too? Lir and Karind stood apart from the rest, and apart from each other as well. Neither even glanced at the other. Having been allies against Elayne, they would not want her to think they were allied still. Essande went to join the serving men and women in the liveries of the eight other Houses, gathered around a table that held tall silver pitchers of wine and tea. That was what informal meant in this context. Each of them would bring a single servant in attendance. For a formal meeting, Elayne would have provided all of the servants, and the Grand Hall would have been crowded with every noble in Caemlyn, every noble from the encampment below Caemlyn.

"Ellorien may well be provocative, Elayne," Dyelin said for about the fifth time since hearing of the safe conduct request. Her face was cool and calm, yet she must have been feeling her nerves. Her hands smoothed unnecessarily at her gold-embroidered skirts.

"I won't let her provoke me," Elayne replied. "Neither will anyone else. I mean you, Conail, and you, Lir." Conail, in gold-worked blue, colored as quickly as Hanselle had. He had gotten into a fight with a mercenary he thought had spoken disparagingly of Elayne and almost killed the man. It was well for him the other man had begun drawing his sword first. Even mercenaries deserved justice, and Andor was not Tear, where nobles could kill commoners with impunity. Well, before Rand changed so many of their laws. Burn him, why *was* he leaping about so?

"I stood for you, Elayne, and that means I always stand up for you," Lir said smoothly. He looked every inch the self-confident courtier in silver-embroidered green silk with House Baryn's silver Winged Hammer on the collar, yet he was too smooth by half, Lir was. "But I'll hold my temper whatever Ellorien says." The bond surged with fleeting contempt. Trying to demonstrate how loyal he was to Elayne, Lir had fought with mercenaries three times. In two days. The man had to have been *searching* for fights to manage that.

"If she tries to goad us, why should we bite our tongues?" Catalyn demanded. Her red dress, embroidered with broad bands of gold at the hem and on the sleeves, did not suit her coloring, especially when her plump cheeks were crimson with anger. Her chin was raised. Perhaps she wore that large enameled pin bearing Haevin's Blue Bear where she did so she would be forced to keep her chin high and look down her nose at everyone. "I've never allowed anyone to poke at me and walk away unscathed."

"An ox responds to the goad and does as the ox-herd wants," Dyelin said drily. "The same way you will be doing what Ellorien wants if you respond to her goads." The crimson remained in Catalyn's cheeks, no doubt from embarrassment, now.

Reene Harfor appeared in the doorway. "My Ladies," she said loudly, her voice echoing in the nearly empty chamber. "My Lords."

This was informality, when two sides met and there was no knowing how far apart they were. Mistress Harfor announced the newly arrived lords and ladies in strict order of precedence, though among the Houses gathered here, there was not a great deal between them. Luan Norwelyn, hard-faced and more gray-haired than when Elayne last saw him, his blue coat undecorated except for Norwelyn's Silver Salmon on the high collar. Arathelle Renshar, her face creased and her brown hair thick with gray, in a red riding dress ornately worked with gold and a large ruby-studded pin that displayed the three Golden Hounds. Pelivar Coelan, tall and lean, his dark hair receding till he almost looked as if he had shaved the front of his head like a Cairhienin, in silver-embroidered blue with twinned red roses worked on his collar, the Roses of Coelan. Aemlyn Carand, plump in gray silk with the three Golden Arrows climbing her sleeves and so thick on her bosom she looked like a bristling quiver. Ellorien Traemane, not so plump as Elayne recalled but still pretty in green-slashed blue embroidered with golden-antlered white stags, the White Stag of Traemane, on the sleeves. Abelle Pendar, his angular face stern beneath gray hair, in dark gray with the three Golden Stars on his collar. They walked up the Grand Hall together, trailed by their servants, but not grouped as announced. Ellorien and Abelle walked with Luan, Pelivar and Aemlyn with Arathelle, two paces between the groups. So. They asked for safe conduct as one, yet they were not one. That made a demand for surrender a little less likely. Even open enemies could act in concert at times. Divided skirts and snug breeches glistened damply. The finest cloak could not protect a person completely in a downpour like this. They would not be in their best tempers.

"Be welcome," she told them as their servants peeled away to join the others. "Will you take wine, or tea? The wine is hot and spiced. This seems a wintery day for spring."

Luan opened his mouth, but Ellorien spoke first. "At least you're not sitting on the throne." Her face might have been carved from marble, and her voice was that hard and cold. "I half expected you to be." Thunder rolled overhead.

Luan looked pained. Arathelle rolled her eyes as if she were hearing something she had heard all too often before. Lir stirred, but Elayne fixed him with a steady look, and he gave a small, apologetic bow.

"I have no right to sit on the throne, Ellorien," she replied calmly. Light, please let her mood hold steady now. "Yet." There was an unintended touch of bite in that. Perhaps she was not so calm as she wished to be.

Ellorien sneered. "If you're waiting for Danine to make your ten, you'll have a long wait. Danine spent the last Succession visiting her manors. She never declared for anyone."

Elayne smiled, but it was difficult. A Succession was when one House succeeded another on the throne. "I will have tea."

Ellorien blinked, but it sparked the others to announce what they would take. Only Elayne, Birgitte, Branlet and Perival took tea. Everyone sniffed at their cups, whether silver cups of wine or porcelain teacups, before taking a sip. Elayne felt no insult. Food and wine could be fine in the kitchens and tainted by the time it reached the table. There was never any telling where or when spoilage would strike. The tea had a faint tang of ginger, but not enough to overwhelm the taste of good Tremalking black.

"I see you've gathered most of your support among the children and Arymilla's leavings," Ellorien said. Catalyn turned as red as her dress, and Branlet straightened angrily, until Perival put a hand on his arm and shook his head. A level-headed boy, Perival, and bright beyond his years. Lir managed to restrain himself this time, but Conail started to say something sharp before Elayne's firm look snapped his teeth shut. Karind merely returned Ellorien's spiteful stare stolidly. Karind was not very intelligent, but little ruffled her.

"You must have had a reason for asking this meeting," Elayne said. "If it was merely to offer insults. . . ." She let that trail off. She had her own reasons for wanting this meeting. If they had asked for her to come to them, she would have. *Without* asking for safe conduct. Feeling a pulse of anger through the bond, she took a firm rein on hers. Birgitte wore a scowl directed at Ellorien like a dagger. If they began feeding one another's temper. . . . That did not bear thinking about, not here, not now.

Ellorien opened her mouth again, and this time, Luan cut her off. "We've come to ask for a truce, Elayne." A flash of lightning lit the northern windows, and those in the ceiling, but the interval to thunder said it had been some distance off.

"A truce? Are we at war, Luan? Has someone declared for the throne that I haven't heard of?" Six sets of eyes swung to Dyelin, who grunted.

"Fools. I told you and told you, and you wouldn't believe me. Perhaps you'll believe this. When Sylvase, Karind and Lir sent their proclamations of support, I sent my own. Taravin stands for Trakand, and the whole of Andor will know it soon enough."

Ellorien colored angrily and managed to make even that seem cold. Aemlyn took a long drink, looking thoughtful. Arathelle allowed a touch of disappointment to touch her face before it returned to a mask nearly as hard as Ellorien's.

"Be that as it may," Luan said, "we still want . . . if not a truce, then a temporary agreement." He drank a small swallow from his winecup and shook his head sadly. "Even gathering everything we can, we'll have a difficult time defeating the Borderlanders, but if we fail to act together, they'll carve up Andor once they decide to move. Frankly, I'm surprised they've remained in one place this long. Their men ought to be well rested by now even after a thousand-league march." Lightning lit the southern windows brightly, and thunder crashed so loudly it seemed the glass panes should shiver. Close, that one.

"I expected them to be into Murandy by now myself," Elayne said. "But I believe their reason for sitting in one place is a fear of sparking a war if they come too near Caemlyn. They seem to be trying to find a way to Murandy using country roads. You know what condition *those* are in this time of year. They want no war with us. When I gave them permission to cross Andor, they told me they were looking for the Dragon Reborn."

Ellorien spluttered, and chips of ice should have come from her mouth. "When you *what*? You prate of how you have no right to sit on the throne—*yet*—and then you arrogate to yourself the right of—!"

"Of an Aes Sedai, Ellorien." Elayne held up her right hand so they could not miss the golden Great Serpent encircling the third finger. Her own voice was frosty despite all she could do. "I did not speak as Daughter-Heir or even High Seat of House Trakand. I spoke as Elayne Aes Sedai of the Green Ajah. Had I not, they would have come anyway.

They were very short of food and fodder. Had I tried to stop them, had anyone tried to stop them, there *would* have been war. They are determined to find the Dragon Reborn. It would have been a war Andor had faint chance of winning. You speak of acting together, Luan? Gather all of Andor's strength, and we could nearly match their numbers, but two in three of ours would be men who can handle a halberd or spear but spend most of their days behind a plow. Every man of theirs is a long-serving armsman who would not be surprised to face Trollocs any day of his life. Instead of a war that would soak Andor in blood and cripple her for a generation, we have the Borderlanders crossing our nation peacefully. I have them watched. They pay for the food and fodder they need, and pay well." Another time, with other listeners, she would have laughed over that. Andoran farmers would try to pry high prices out of the Dark One. "The worst they've done is flog a few horse-thieves, and if they should have been handed over to a magistrate, I can't fault the Borderlanders for it. Now tell me, Ellorien. What would you have done differently, and how?"

Ellorien blinked, icily sullen, then sniffed dismissively and sipped at her wine.

"And what do you plan for this Black Tower?" Abelle asked quietly. "I . . . suspect you have a plan for them, too." Did he suspect her other reason for letting the Borderlanders cross Andor? Let him, so long as he did not give it voice. So long as he kept silent, her motives seemed purely for Andor's good. That was hypocritical, no bones about it, but realistic as well. She had spoken truthfully concerning her other reasons, but that one, spoken aloud, could cost her. She still needed one more House, and it looked as if Candraed had to be it, but Danine would never move if she thought Elayne was trying to force her into it.

"Nothing," she told him. "I send Guardsmen periodically to ride around the Black Tower grounds and remind them they *are* in Andor and subject to Andor's laws, but aside from that, I can do no more than I could if the White Tower were somehow transported to Caemlyn." For a long moment they stared at her, all six of them unblinking.

"Pendar stands for Trakand," Abelle said suddenly, and right atop him, Luan said, "Norwelyn stands for Trakand." Lightning flashed overhead, brightening the colored windows in the ceiling.

Elayne kept herself from swaying with an effort. Birgitte's face was smooth, but the bond carried amazement. It was done. She had eleven, and the throne was hers.

"The more who stand for her, the better for Andor." Dyelin sounded a touch dazed herself. "Stand with me for Trakand."

There was another pause, longer, full of exchanged glances, but then, one by one, Arathelle, Pelivar and Aemlyn announced that their Houses stood for Trakand. Doing so for Dyelin, though. Elayne would have to remember that. Perhaps she could win their loyalty in time, but for the present, they supported her for Dyelin's sake.

"She has the throne," Ellorien said, as cold as ever. "The rest is fluff and feathers."

Elayne tried to make her voice warm. "Will you dine with us this evening, Ellorien? At least remain until the rain abates."

"I have my own cooks," Ellorien replied, turning away toward the doors. Her serving woman came running to take her cup and return it to the table. "As soon as the rain stops, I will be leaving for Sheldyn. I've been away too long."

"Tarmon Gai'don is coming soon, Ellorien," Elayne said. "You won't be able to remain on your estates then."

Ellorien paused, looking over her shoulder. "When Tarmon Gai'-don comes, Traemane rides for the Last Battle, and we ride behind the Lion of Andor." Thunder boomed as she strode out of the Grand Hall with her serving woman at her heels.

"Will you all join me in my apartments?" Elayne asked the others.

Behind the Lion of Andor, but not a word about behind Elayne Trakand. Nearly half her support was suspect one way or another, Jarid Sarand was still on the loose with a not inconsiderable force, and she would have trouble from Ellorien eventually. It was never this way in stories. In stories, everything was always wrapped up neatly by the end. Real life was much . . . messier. Still, she had the throne at last. There was still the coronation, but that was a formality now. As she led the procession from the Grand Hall, chatting with Luan and Pelivar, thunder rolled overhead like martial drums beating the march for Tarmon Gai'don. How long before Andor's banners had to march to the Last Battle?

CHAPTER
36

Under an Oak

T he sun stood well above the mountains as Karede rode through the trees toward the so-called Malvide Narrows, perhaps two leagues ahead. The five-mile-wide gap in the mountains carried the road from Ebou Dar to Lugard, a mile south of him. Well short of the Narrows, though, he would find the camp Ajimbura had located for him. Ajimbura had not been fool enough to try entering the camp, so Karede still did not know whether he was riding into a deathtrap for nothing. No, not for nothing. For the High Lady Tuon. Any Death-watch Guard was ready to die for her. Their honor was duty, and duty often meant death. The sky held only billowing white clouds with no threat of rain. He had always hoped to die in sunlight.

He had brought just a small party. Ajimbura on his white-footed chestnut to show the way, of course. The wiry little man had cut off his white-streaked red braid, a measure of his great devotion. The hill tribes took those braids as trophies from those they killed in their end-less feuds, and to be without one was to be disgraced in the eyes of all the tribes and families, a self-proclaimed coward. That devotion was to Karede rather than the High Lady or the Crystal Throne, but Karede's own devotion was such that it came to the same thing. Two of the Guards rode at Karede's back, their red-and-green armor buffed till it shone, like his own. Hartha and a pair of Gardeners strode along with their long-hafted axes on their shoulders, easily keeping pace with the horses. Their armor glistened as well. Melitene, the High Lady's *der'-sul'dam*, her long, graying hair tied with a bright red ribbon today, was on a high-stepping gray, the silvery length of an *a'dam* connecting her left wrist to Mylen's neck. There had been little that could be done to make those two appear more impressive, but the *a'dam* and Melitene's blue dress, the red panels on skirts and bosom holding silver forked lightning bolts, should draw the eye. Taken altogether, no one should notice Ajimbura at all. The rest were back with Musenge, in case it truly was a deathtrap.

He had considered using another *damane* than Mylen. The tiny woman with the face he could never put an age to almost bounced in her saddle with eagerness to lay eyes on the High Lady again. She was not properly composed. Still, she could do nothing without Melitene, and she was useless as a weapon, a fact that had made her hang her head when he pointed it out to the *der'sul'dam*. She had needed consoling, her *sul'dam* petting her and telling her what beautiful Sky Lights she made, how wonderful her Healing was. Even thinking about that made Karede shudder. Taken in the abstract, it might seem a wonderful thing, wounds undone in moments, but he thought he would need to be near death before he would let anyone touch him with the Power. And yet, if it could have saved his wife Kalia. . . . No, the weapons had been left with Musenge. If there was a battle today, it would be of a different sort.

The first birdcall he heard seemed no different from others he had heard that morning, but it was repeated ahead, and then again. Just one call each time. He spotted a man up in a tall oak with a crossbow that tracked him as he rode. Seeing him was not easy; his breastplate and open-faced helmet were painted a dull green that faded into the tree's foliage. A length of red cloth tied around his left arm helped, though. If he really wanted to hide, he should have removed that.

Karede motioned to Ajimbura and the wiry little man grinned at him, a wizened, blue-eyed rat, before allowing his chestnut to fall back behind the Guards. His long knife was under his coat today. He should pass for a servant.

Soon enough Karede was riding into the camp itself. It had no tents or shelters of any kind, but there were long horselines laid out in orderly fashion, and many more men in green breastplates. Heads turned to watch his party pass, but few men were on their feet, and fewer held a crossbow. A fair number of them were asleep on their blankets, doubtless tired from all the hard riding they had been doing by night. So the birdcall had told them he was not enough to present a danger. They had the look of well-trained soldiers, but he had expected as much. What he had not expected was how few they were. Oh, the trees might be hiding some, but surely the camp held no more than seven or eight thousand men, far too few to have carried out the campaign Loune had described. He felt a sudden tightness in his chest. Where were the rest? The High Lady might be with one of the other bands. He hoped Ajimbura was taking note of the numbers.

Before he had gone far, a short man mounted on a tall dun met him and reined in where he had to stop or ride the man down. The front half of his head was shaved, and appeared to be powdered, of all things. He was no popinjay, though. His dark coat might be silk, yet he wore the same dull green breastplate as the common soldiers. His eyes were hard and expressionless as he scanned Melitene and Mylen, the Ogier. His face did not change as his gaze returned to Karede. "Lord Mat described that armor to us," he said in accents even quicker and more clipped than those of the Altarans. "To what do we owe the honor of a visit from the Deathwatch Guard?"

Lord Mat? Who under the Light was Lord Mat? "Furyk Karede," Karede said. "I wish to speak with man who calls himself Thom Merrilin."

"Talmanes Delovinde," the man said, finding manners. "You want to talk to *Thom*? Well, I see no harm in it. I will take you to him."

Karede heeled Aldazar after Delovinde. The man had made no mention of the obvious, that he and the others could not be allowed to leave and carry word of this army's location. He had some manners. At least, they would not be allowed to leave unless Karede's mad plan worked. Musenge gave him only one chance in ten of success, one in five of living. Personally, he himself believed the odds longer, but he had to make the attempt. And Merrilin's presence argued in favor of the High Lady's presence.

Delovinde dismounted at an oddly domestic scene among the trees, people on camp stools or blankets around a small fire beneath a spreading oak where a kettle was heating. Karede stepped down from his saddle, motioning the Guards and Ajimbura to dismount as well. Melitene and Mylen remained on their mounts for the advantage of height. Of all people, Mistress Anan, who had once owned the inn where he stayed in Ebou Dar, was sitting on one of the three-legged stools reading a book. She no longer wore one of those revealing dresses he had enjoyed looking at, but her close-fitting necklace still dangled that small, jeweled knife onto her impressive bosom. She closed her book and gave him a small nod as if he had returned to the Wandering Woman after an absence of a few hours. Her hazel eyes were quite composed. Perhaps the plot was even more intricate than the Seeker Mor had thought.

A tall, lean white-haired man with mustaches nearly as long as Hartha's was sitting cross-legged on a striped blanket across a stones board from a slender woman with her hair in many beaded braids. He quirked an eyebrow at Karede, shook his head and returned to perusing the crosshatched board. She glared pure hatred at Karede and those behind him. A gnarled old fellow with long white hair was lying on another blanket with a remarkably ugly young boy, playing some game or other on a piece of red cloth spiderwebbed with black lines. They sat up, the boy studying the Ogier with interest, the man with one hand hovering as if to reach for a knife beneath his coat. A dangerous man, and wary. Perhaps he was Merrilin.

Two men and two women sitting together on camp stools had been conversing when Karede rode up, but as he was stepping down, a stern-faced woman stood and fixed her blue eyes on his in very nearly a challenge. She wore a sword on a wide leather strap slanting across her chest, the way some sailors did. Her hair was close-cropped rather than cut in the style of the low Blood, her fingernails were short and none were lacquered, but he was certain she was Egeanin Tamarath. A heavy-set man with hair as short as hers and one of those odd Illianer beards stood beside her, one hand on the hilt of a shortsword, staring at Karede as if he intended to second her challenge. A pretty woman with dark, waist-long hair and the same rosebud mouth as the Taraboner stood, and for a moment it seemed she might kneel or prostrate herself, but then she straightened and looked him right in the eyes. The last man, a lean fellow in a peculiar red cap who looked carved from dark wood, gave a loud laugh and flung his arms around her. The grinning stare *he* gave Karede could only be called triumphant.

"Thom," Delovinde said, "this is Furyk Karede. He wants to talk with a man who 'calls himself' Thom Merrilin."

"With me?" the lean, white-haired man said, rising awkwardly. His right leg appeared slightly stiff. An old battle injury, perhaps?

"But I don't 'call myself' Thom Merrilin. It's my name, though I'm surprised you know it. What do you want of me?"

Karede removed his helmet, but before he could open his mouth, a pretty woman with large brown eyes rushed up, pursued by two others. All three had those Aes Sedai faces, one minute looking twenty, the next twice that, the third somewhere in the middle. It was very disconcerting.

"That's Sheraine!" the pretty woman cried, staring at Mylen. "Release her!"

"You do no understand, Joline," one of the women with her said angrily. Thin-lipped, with a narrow nose, she looked as if she could chew rocks. "She do no be Sheraine any longer. She would have betrayed us, given a chance."

"Teslyn is right, Joline," the third woman said. Handsome rather than pretty, she had long black hair that fell in waves to her waist. "She would have betrayed us."

"I don't believe it, Edesina," Joline snapped. "You will free her immediately," she told Melitene, "or I'll—" Suddenly she gasped.

"I did tell you," Teslyn said bitterly.

A young man in a wide-brimmed black hat galloped up on a dark, blunt-nosed chestnut with a deep chest and flung himself out of the saddle. "What's bloody going on here?" he demanded, striding up to the fire.

Karede ignored him. The High Lady Tuon had ridden up with the young man, on a black-and-white horse with markings like none he had ever seen. Selucia was at her side, on a dun, her head wrapped in a scarlet scarf, but he had eyes only for the High Lady. Short black hair covered her head, but he could never mistake that face. She spared him only one expressionless glance before returning to a study of the young man. Karede wondered whether she recognized him. Probably not. It had been a long time since he had served in her bodyguard. He did not look over his shoulder, but he knew that the reins of Ajimbura's chestnut were now held by one of the Guards. Apparently unarmed and his distinctive braid gone, he should have no problem leaving the camp. The sentries would never see the little man. Ajimbura was a good runner as well as stealthy. Soon, Musenge would know that the High Lady was indeed here.

"She has us shielded, Mat," Joline said, and the young man snatched off his hat and strode to Melitene's horse as if he intended to seize the bridle. He was long-limbed, though he could not be called tall, and he wore a black silk scarf tied around his neck and dangling onto his chest. That made him the one everyone had called Tylin's Toy, as if being the queen's plaything were the most important feature of him. Likely it was. Playthings seldom had another side to them. Strange, but he hardly seemed handsome enough for that. He did look fit, though.

"Release the shield," he told her as if he expected obedience. Karede's eyebrows rose. *This* was the plaything? Melitene and Mylen gasped almost as one, and the young man barked a laugh. "You see, it doesn't work on me. Now you bloody well release the shields, or I'll bloody well haul you out of the saddle and paddle your bottoms." Melitene's face darkened. Few people dared speak so to a *der'sul'dam*.

"Release the shields, Melitene," Karede said.

"The *marath'damane* was on the point of embracing *saidar*," she said instead of obeying. "There's no telling what she might have—"

"Release the shields," he said firmly. "And release the Power."

The young man gave a satisfied nod, then suddenly spun, pointing a finger at the three Aes Sedai. "Now don't you bloody well start! She's let go of the Power. You do it, too. Go ahead!" Again he nodded, for all the world as if he was sure they had obeyed. From the way Melitene was staring at him, perhaps he was. Maybe he was an Asha'man? Perhaps Asha'man could detect a *damane*'s channeling somehow. That hardly seemed likely, but it was all Karede could think of. Yet that hardly squared with how Tylin reportedly had treated the young man.

"One of these days, Mat Cauthon," Joline said acidly, "someone will teach you to show proper respect to Aes Sedai, and I hope I am there to see it."

The High Lady and Selucia laughed uproariously. It was good to see she had managed to keep her spirits up in captivity. Doubtless her maid's companionship had helped. But it was time to get on, too. Time to take his mad gamble.

"General Merrilin," Karede said, "you fought a short but remarkable campaign and achieved miracles at keeping your forces undetected, but your luck is about to run out. General Chisen deduced your real purpose. He has turned his army around and is marching for the Malvide Narrows as fast as he can. He will be here in two days. I have ten thousand men not far from here, enough to pin you until he arrives. But the High Lady Tuon would be in danger, and I want to avoid that. Let me leave with her, and I will allow you and your men to depart unhindered. You can be well the other side of the mountains, into the Molvaine Gap, before Chisen arrives, and into Murandy before he can catch you. The only other choice is annihilation. Chisen has enough men to wipe you out. It won't be a battle. A hundred thousand men against eight thousand will be a slaughter."

They heard him out, every face as blank as if they were stunned. They schooled themselves well. Or perhaps they were stunned at Merrilin's plan apparently unraveling at the last instant.

Merrilin stroked one of his white mustaches with a long finger. He seemed to hiding a smile. "I fear you have mistaken me, Banner-General Karede." For the space of a sentence his voice became extremely resonant. "I am a gleeman, a position higher than court-bard to be sure, but no general. The man you want is Lord Matrim Cauthon." He made a small bow toward the young man, who was settling his flat-topped hat back on his head.

Karede frowned. Tylin's *Toy* was the general? Were they playing a game with him?

"You have about a hundred men, Deathwatch Guards, and maybe twenty Gardeners," Cauthon said calmly. "From what I hear, that could make an even fight against five times their number for most soldiers, but the Band aren't most soldiers, and I have a sight more than six hundred. As for Chisen, if that's the fellow who pulled back through the Narrows, even if he has figured out what I was up to, he couldn't get back in less than five days. My scouts' last reports had him pushing southwest along the Ebou Dar Road as fast he could march. The real question is this, though. Can you get Tuon to the Tarasin Palace safely?"

Karede felt as if Hartha had kicked him in the belly, and not only because the man had used the High Lady's name so casually. "You mean to let me take her away?" he said incredulously.

"If she trusts you. If you can get her to the palace safely. She's in danger till she reaches that. In case you don't know it, your whole bloody Ever Victorious flaming Army is ready to slit her throat or bash in her head with a rock."

"I know," Karede said, more calmly than he felt. Why would this man just release the High Lady after the White Tower had gone to all the trouble of kidnapping her? Why, after fighting that short, bloody campaign? "We will die to the man if that is what is needed to see her safe. It will be best if we set out immediately." Before the man changed his mind. Before Karede woke from this fever-dream. It surely seemed a fever-dream.

"Not so fast." Cauthon turned toward the High Lady. "Tuon, do you trust this man to see you safe to the palace in Ebou Dar?" Karede stifled an impulse to wince. General and lord the man might be, but he had no right to use the High Lady's name so!

"I trust the Deathwatch Guards with my life," the High Lady replied calmly, "and him more than any other." She favored Karede with a smile. Even as a child, smiles from her had been rare. "Do you by any chance still have my doll, Banner-General Karede?"

He bowed to her formally. The manner of her speaking told him she was still under the veil. "Forgiveness, High Lady. I lost everything in the Great Fire of Sohima."

"That means you kept it for ten years. You have my commiseration on the loss of your wife, and of your son, though he died bravely and well. Few men will enter a burning building once. He saved five people before he was overcome."

Karede's throat tightened. She had followed news of him. All he could do was bow again, more deeply.

"Enough of that," Cauthon muttered. "You're going to knock your head on the ground if you keep that up. As soon as she and Selucia can get their things together, you take them out of here and ride hard. Talmanes, roust the Band. It isn't that I don't trust you, Karede, but I think I'll sleep easier beyond the Narrows."

"Matrim Cauthon is my husband," the High Lady said in a loud, clear voice. Everyone froze where they stood. "Matrim Cauthon is my husband."

Karede felt as if Hartha had kicked him again. No, not Hartha. Aldazar. What madness was this? Cauthon looked like a man watching an arrow fly toward his face, knowing he had no chance to dodge.

"Bloody Matrim Cauthon is my husband. That *is* the wording you used, is it not?"

This had to be a fever-dream.

It took a minute before Mat could speak. Burn him, it seemed to take a bloody hour before he could move. When he could, he snatched off his hat, strode to Tuon and seized the razor's bridle. She looked down at him, cool as any queen on a bloody throne. All those battles with the flaming dice rattling away in his head, all those skirmishes and raids, and they had to stop when she said a few words. Well, at least this time he knew what had happened that was bloody fateful for Mat bloody Cauthon. "Why? I mean, I knew you were going to sooner or later, but why now? I like you, maybe more than like you, and I enjoy kissing you," he thought Karede grunted, "but you haven't behaved like a woman in love. You're ice half the time and spend most of the rest digging under my skin."

"Love?" Tuon sounded surprised. "Perhaps we will come to love one another, Matrim, but I have always known I would marry to serve the Empire. What do you mean, you *knew* that I was going to speak the words?"

"Call me Mat." Only his mother had ever called him Matrim, when he was in trouble, and his sisters when they were carrying tales to get him in trouble.

"Your name is Matrim. What did you mean?"

He sighed. The woman never wanted much. Just her own way. Like just about every other woman he had ever known. "I went through a *ter'angreal* to somewhere else, another world maybe. The people there aren't really people—they look like snakes—but they'll answer three questions for you, and their answers are always true. One of mine was that I'd marry the Daughter of the Nine Moons. But you haven't answered my question. Why now?"

A faint smile on her lips, Tuon leaned down from her saddle. And rapped him hard on the top of his head with her knuckles! "Your superstitions are bad enough, Matrim, but I won't tolerate lies. An amusing lie, true, but still a lie."

"It's the Light's own truth," he protested, clapping his hat on. Maybe it would give him some protection. "You could learn for yourself if you could make yourself talk to an Aes Sedai. They could tell you about the Aelfinn and the Eelfinn."

"It could be the truth," Edesina piped up as if she were being helpful. "The Aelfinn can be reached through a *ter'angreal* in the Stone of Tear, so I understand, and supposedly they give true answers." Mat glared at her. A fat lot of help she was, with her "so I understands" and "supposedlies." Tuon continued to stare at him as if Edesina had not opened her mouth.

"I answered your question, Tuon, so you answer mine."

"You know that *damane* can tell fortunes?" She gave him a stern look, likely expecting him to call it superstition, but he nodded curtly. Some Aes Sedai could Foretell the future. Why not a *damane*? "I asked Lidya to tell mine just before I landed at Ebou Dar. This is what she said. 'Beware the fox that makes the ravens fly, for he will marry you and carry you away. Beware the man who remembers Hawkwing's face, for he will marry you and set you free. Beware the man of the red hand, for him you will marry and none other.' It was your ring that caught my eye first." He thumbed the long ring unconsciously, and she smiled. A small smile, but a smile. "A fox apparently startling two ravens into flight and nine crescent moons. Suggestive, wouldn't you say? And just now you fulfilled the second part, so I knew for certain it was you." Selucia made a sound in her throat, and Tuon waggled fingers at her. The bosomy little woman subsided, adjusting her head scarf, but the look she shot at Mat should have been accompanied by a dagger in her hand.

He laughed mirthlessly. Blood and bloody ashes. The ring was a carver's try-piece, bought only because it stuck on his finger; he would give up those memories of Hawkwing's face along with every other old memory, if it would get the bloody snakes out of his head; and yet those things had gained him a wife. The Band of the Red Hand would never have existed without those old memories of battles.

"Seems to me being *ta'veren* works on me as much as it does on anybody else." For a moment, he thought she was going to rap him again. He gave her his best smile. "One more kiss before you leave?"

"I'm not in the mood at the moment," she said coolly. That hanging magistrate was back. All prisoners to be condemned immediately. "Perhaps later. You could return to Ebou Dar with me. You have an honored place in the Empire, now."

He did not hesitate before shaking his head. There was no honored place waiting for Leilwin or Domon, no place at all for the Aes Sedai or the Band. "The next time I see Seanchan, I expect it will be on the field somewhere, Tuon." Burn him, it would be. His life seemed to run that way no matter what he did. "You're not my enemy, but your Empire is."

"Nor are you my enemy, husband," she said coolly, "but I live to serve the Empire."

"Well, I suppose you'd better get your things. . . ." He trailed off at the sound of a cantering horse approaching.

Vanin reined in a rangy gray beside Tuon, eyed Karede and the other Deathwatch Guards, then spat through a gap in his teeth and leaned on the high pommel of his saddle. "There's ten thousand or so soldiers at a little town about five miles west of here," the fat man told Mat. "Only one man Seanchan, near as I could learn. Rest are Altarans, Taraboners, Amadicians. All mounted. Thing is, they're asking after fellows wearing armor like that." He nodded toward Karede. "And rumor says the one of them that kills a girl that sounds a lot like the High Lady gets himself a hundred thousand crowns gold. Their mouths are dripping for it."

"I can slip past them," Karede said. His bluff face looked fatherly. His voice sounded like a drawn sword.

"And if you can't?" Mat asked quietly. "It can't be chance they're this close. They've caught some sniff of you. One more smell might be all it takes to kill Tuon." Karede's face darkened.

"Do you intend to go back on your word?" A drawn blade that might be used soon. Worse, Tuon was watching, looking at Mat like that hanging magistrate in truth. Burn him, if she died, something would shrivel up inside him. And the only way to stop it, to be sure it was stopped, was to do what he hated worse than work. Once, he had thought that fighting battles, much as he hated it, was still better than work. Near enough nine hundred dead in the space of a few days had changed his mind.

"No," he said. "She goes with you. But you leave me a dozen of your Deathwatch Guards and some of the Gardeners. If I'm going to take these people off your back, I need them to think I'm you."

Tuon abandoned most of the clothing Matrim had bought for her, since she would need to travel light. The little cluster of red silk rosebuds he had given her she tucked away in her saddlebags, folded in a linen cloth, as carefully as if were blown glass. She had no farewells to make except for Mistress Anan—she really would miss their discussions—so she and Selucia were ready to ride quickly. Mylen smiled so broadly at the sight of her that she had to pat the little *damane*. It seemed that word of what had happened had spread, because as they rode through the camp with the Deathwatch Guards, men of the Band stood and bowed to her. It was very like reviewing regiments in Seandar.

"What do you make of him?" she asked Karede once they were away from the soldiers and beginning to canter. There was no need to say which "he" she meant.

"It is not my place to make judgments, High Lady," he said gravely. His head swivelled, keeping watch on the surrounding trees. "I serve the Empire and the Empress, may she live forever."

"As do we all, Banner-General. But I ask your judgment."

"A good general, High Lady," he replied without hesitation. "Brave, but not overly brave. He won't get himself killed just to show how brave he is, I think. And he is . . . adaptable. A man of many layers. And if you will forgive me, High Lady, a man in love with you. I saw how he looked at you."

In love with her? Perhaps. She thought she might be able to come to love him. Her mother had loved her father, it was said. And a man of many layers? Matrim Cauthon made an onion look like an apple! She rubbed a hand over her head. She still was not accustomed to the feel of hair on her head. "I will need a razor first thing."

"It may be best to wait until Ebou Dar, High Lady."

"No," she said gently. "If I die, I will die as who I am. I have removed the veil."

"As you say, Highness." Smiling, he saluted, gauntleted fist striking over his heart hard enough that steel clanged on steel. "If we die, we will die as who we are."

CHAPTER
37

Prince of the Ravens

L eaning on the tall pommel of his saddle, *ashandarei* slanted across
Pips' neck, Mat frowned at the sky. The sun was well past its
noon height. If Vanin and those Deathwatch Guards did not return soon, he might find himself fighting a battle with the sun in the
crossbowmen's eyes, or worse, in twilight. Worst of all, dark clouds
loomed over the mountains to the east. The gusting wind was out of
the north. No help there. Rain would put the weasel in the henyard.
Bowstrings fared poorly in rain. Well, any rain was a few hours off,
with luck, but he had never noticed his luck saving him from getting
soaked in a downpour. He had not dared wait until tomorrow. Those
fellows hunting Tuon might have gotten another whiff of Karede's
men, and then he would have had to try attacking them, or laying an
ambush, and carry it out before they could catch Karede. Better to
have them come to him, at a place of his choosing. Finding the proper
spot had not been difficult, between Master Roidelle's collection of
maps on the one hand and Vanin and the other scouts on the other.

Aludra was fussing over one of her tall, metal-bound lofting tubes,
beaded braids hiding her face as she examined something at the broad
wooden base. He wished she had been willing to remain with the pack
animals like Thom and Mistress Anan. Even Noal had been willing to
stay, if only to help Juilin and Amathera make sure Olver did not run off

to watch the battle. The boy was dead eager, which could soon lead to plain dead. Matters had been bad enough when only Harnan and the other three had been corrupting Olver, but now he had half the men teaching him how to use a sword or dagger or fight with his hands and feet, and apparently filling his head with tales of heroes from the way he had been behaving, begging to go on raids with Mat and the like. Aludra was near as bad. Anybody could have used one of those strikers to light the fuse once she had loaded that tube, but she insisted on doing it herself. She was a fierce woman, Aludra was, and none too pleased at finding herself on the same side as Seanchan, however temporary the arrangement was. It seemed wrong to her that they would see some of her handiwork without being on the receiving end. Leilwin and Domon sat their horses nearby keeping an eye on her, as much to make sure she did nothing foolish as to protect her. Mat hoped Leilwin did nothing foolish herself. Since there was apparently only one Seanchan with the people they would fight today, she had decided it was all right to be there, and the way she glared at Musenge and the other Deathwatch Guards, it seemed she might think she had something to prove to them.

The three Aes Sedai, standing together with their reins in hand, cast dark looks at the Seanchan, too, as did Blaeric and Fen, who caressed their sword hilts perhaps unconsciously. Joline and her two Warders had been the only ones aghast at Sheraine's willing departure with Tuon—what an Aes Sedai felt on any subject was usually how her Warders felt on it, too—but the memory of being leashed had to be too fresh for Edesina or Teslyn to feel comfortable around Seanchan soldiers. Bethamin and Seta stood very meekly, hands folded at their waists, a little apart from the sisters. Bethamin's light-colored bay nudged her shoulder with his nose, and the tall, dark woman half reached up to stroke the animal before snatching her hand back down and resuming her humble pose. They still would take no part. Joline and Edesina had made that plain, yet it seemed they wanted the two women under their eyes to make sure of it. The Seanchan women plainly were looking at anything *but* the Seanchan soldiers. For that matter, Bethamin, Seta *and* Leilwin might as well not have existed for all of Musenge and that lot. Burn him, there were so many tensions in the air he could almost feel that hanging rope around his neck again.

Pips stamped a hoof, impatient at standing in one place so long, and Mat patted his neck then scratched the scar forming on his own jaw. Tuon's ointments had stung as badly as she had said they would, but they worked. His new collection of scars did itch yet, though. Tuon. His wife. He was *married*! He had known it was coming, had known for a long time, but just the same. . . . Married. He should have felt . . . different . . . somehow, but he still felt like himself. He intended to keep it that way, burn him if he did not! If Tuon expected Mat Cauthon to settle down, to give up gambling or some such, she had another think coming. He supposed he would have to give over chasing after women, much less catching them, but he would still enjoy dancing with them. And looking at them. Just not when he was with her. Burn him if he knew when that would be. He was not about to go anywhere she had the upper hand, her and her talk of cupbearers and running grooms and marrying to serve the Empire. How was marrying him supposed to serve the flaming Empire?

Musenge left the other ten men and five Ogier in red-and-black armor and trotted his black gelding up to Mat. The horse had good lines, built for speed and endurance both, as far as Mat could tell without a thorough examination. Musenge looked built for endurance, a stocky, stolid man, his face worn but hard, his eyes like polished stones. "Forgiveness, Highness," he drawled, banging a gauntleted fist against his breastplate, "but shouldn't the men be back to work?" He slurred his words worse than Selucia, almost to unintelligibility. "Their rest break has stretched a long time. I doubt they can complete the wall before the traitor arrives as it is." Mat had wondered how long it would take him to mention that. He had expected it earlier.

Open-faced helmets off but breastplates strapped on, the crossbowmen were sitting on the ground behind a long curving wall, perhaps a third of a circle made of earth thrown up out of the four-foot deep trench fronting it, with a thicket of sharpened stakes driven into the ground in front of that and extending a little beyond the ends of the trench. They had finished that in short order. Infantry needed to be as handy with shovel, mattock and axe as they were with weapons. Even cavalry did, but making horsemen believe was harder. Footmen knew it was better to have something between you and the enemy if you could. The tools lay scattered along the trench, now. Some of the men were dicing, others just taking their ease, even napping. Soldiers slept any chance they got. A few were reading books, of all things. Reading! Mandevwin moved among them, fingering his eyepatch and now and then bending to say a few words to a bannerman. The only lancer present, standing beside his horse, every line of him saying he had nothing to do with the crossbowmen, held no lance, but rather a long banner-staff cased for half its length in leather.

It was perfect terrain for what Mat had in mind. Near two miles of grassy meadow dotted with wildflowers and a few low bushes stretched from the wall to the tall trees at the western end. To the north was a blackwater swamp, full of oaks and odd, white-flowering trees that seemed half thick roots, with a lake clinging to its western edge and forest below the lake. A small river flowed south out of the swamp, half a mile behind Mat, before curving away to the west on his left. A small river, but wide enough and deep enough that horses would have to swim it. The far bank lay beyond bowshot. There was only one way for any attacker to get at the wall. Come straight for it.

"When they arrive, I don't want them stopping to count how many men in red and black are here," he replied. Musenge winced slightly for some reason. "I want them to see an unfinished wall and tools thrown down because we learned they were close. The promise of a hundred thousand crowns gold has to have their blood up, but I want them too excited to think straight. They'll see us vulnerable, our defenses incomplete, and with any luck, they'll rush in straight away. They'll figure close to half of them will die when we loose, but that will just raise the chances for one of the others to get that gold. They'll only expect us to manage one volley." He slapped his hands together, and Pips shifted. "Then the trap closes."

"Still, Highness, I wish we had more of your crossbowmen. I've heard you may have as many as thirty thousand." Musenge had heard him tell Tuon he would fight the Seanchan, too. The man was probing for information.

"I have fewer than I did," Mat said with a grimace. His victories had hardly been bloodless, only remarkably close to it. Near four hundred crossbowmen lay in Altaran graves, and close to five hundred of the cavalry. A small enough butcher's bill, considering, yet he liked it best when the butcher presented no bill. "But what I have is enough for the day."

"As you say, Highness." Musenge's voice was so neutral he could have been commenting on the price of beans. Strange. He did not look like a diffident man. "I have always been ready to die for her." There was no need for him to say which "her" he meant.

"I guess I am, too, Musenge." Light, he thought he meant that! Yes, he did mean it. Did that mean he was in love? "Better to live for her, though, wouldn't you say?"

"Should you not be donning your armor, Highness?"

"I don't intend getting close enough to the fighting to need armor. A general who draws his sword has put aside his baton and become a common soldier."

He was only quoting Comadrin again—he seemed to do that a lot when discussing soldiering, but then, the man had known just about everything there was to know about the craft—just quoting, yet it appeared to impress the weathered man, who saluted him again and asked bloody permission before riding back to his men. Mat was tempted to ask what that "Highness" foolishness was about. Likely it was just some Seanchan way of calling him a lord, but he had not heard anything like it in Ebou Dar, and he had been surrounded by Seanchan there.

Five figures appeared out of the forest at the foot of the meadow, and he did not need a looking glass to know them. The two Ogier in armor striped bright red and black would have told him even if Vanin's bulk had not. The mounted men were at a flat gallop, yet the Ogier kept pace, long arms swinging, axes swinging like a sawmill's drive-shaft.

"Sling-men get ready!" Mat shouted. "Everybody else go pick up a shovel!" The appearance had to be just right.

As most of the crossbowmen scattered to pick up tools and make a show of working on the trench and wall, fifty others strapped on their helmets and lined up in front of Aludra. Tall men, they still carried the shortswords they called cat-gutters, but instead of crossbows, they were armed with four-foot long sling-staffs. He would have liked more than fifty, but Aludra only had so much of her powders. Each man wore a cloth belt sewn with pockets slung across his breastplate, and each pocket held a stubby leather cylinder larger than a man's fist with a short length of dark fuse sticking out of the end. Aludra had not come up with a fancy name for them yet. She would, though. She was one for fancy names. Dragons, and dragons' eggs.

One by one the men held up long pieces of slow-match for her to light with a striker. She did it quickly, using each striker until the long wooden stick had burned down nearly to her fingertips, but she never winced, just dropped the thing and lit another while telling the sling-men to be faster, she was getting low on strikers. Light, but she was tight with the things. She had five more boxes that Mat knew of. As each man turned away from her, he put the smoking slow-match between his teeth and secured one of the cylinders to his sling-staff as he walked to the wall. There were wide intervals between sling-men. They had to cover the whole length of the wall.

"Time to get your people in place, Musenge," Mat said loudly.

The Deathwatch Guards formed a single line abreast with the Gardeners on the end. Anybody who took one glance through a looking glass would know what they were. Light, all they needed was to see Ogier in armor and the sun glinting off all that red and black. And if they stopped to think how few of the Guards there were, they would still see they had Mat outnumbered, and there would be only one way to find out whether Tuon was with him.

Vanin galloped behind the wall, flung himself out of the saddle and immediately began walking his lathered dun to cool the animal down. As soon as he passed the wall, crossbowmen began dropping the tools and running to put on helmets and pick up crossbows. Those had been laid so that the men formed three spaced ranks with gaps where the sling-men stood. It no longer mattered if anyone was watching from the forest. What they saw would seem natural.

Mat trotted Pips to Vanin and dismounted. The two human Deathwatch Guards and the two Ogier went to join the others. The horses' nostrils flared with their heavy breathing, but the Ogier were panting no harder. One was Hartha, a stone-eyed fellow who apparently ranked very close to Musenge.

Vanin scowled at the men who had not gotten down to walk their horses. A horsethief he might be, reformed or not, but he disliked mistreating horseflesh. "They went up like one of her nightflowers when they glimpsed us," he said, nodding toward Aludra. "We made sure they got a good look at that fancy armor, then high-tailed it as soon as they started getting mounted. They're coming hard behind us. Harder than they should." He spat on the ground. "I didn't get a good look at their animals, but I doubt they're all good for that run. Some'll founder before they get here."

"The more the better," Mat said. "The fewer who make it, the better in my book." All he needed was to give Tuon a day or two head start on them, and if that came from their ruining horses, if they rode out of the trees and decided he had too many men to take on, he would take that over a battle any day. After today's six-mile gallop, they would need to rest their horses a few days before they were fit to travel any distance at all. Vanin directed that scowl at him. Others might go around calling him my Lord and Highness, but not Chel Vanin.

Mat laughed and clapped him on the shoulder before swinging back into Pips' saddle. It was good there was someone who did not think he was a fool noble, or at least, did not care whether or not he was. He rode to join the Aes Sedai, who were mounted now.

Blaeric and Fen, the one on a bay gelding, the other on a black, gave him stares almost as dark as those they had directed at Musenge. They still suspected he had something to do with what had happened to Joline. He thought of telling Fen that his stub of a topknot looked ridiculous. Fen shifted in his saddle and stroked his sword hilt. Then again, maybe not.

". . . . what I told you," Joline was telling Bethamin and Seta, shaking an admonitory finger. Her dark bay gelding looked a war-horse, but was not. The animal had a good turn of speed, yet its temperament was mild as milk-water. "If you even think about embracing *saidar*, you'll regret it."

Teslyn grunted sourly. She patted her white-faced chestnut mare, a much more feisty creature than Joline's mount, and spoke to the air. "She does train wilders and expects them to behave once out of her sight. Or perhaps she does think the Tower will accept over-age novices." Spots of color appeared in Joline's cheeks, but she straightened in her saddle without saying anything. As usual when those two got into a conflict, Edesina concentrated on something else, in this case brushing imaginary dust from her divided skirts. Enough tension to choke on.

Suddenly riders poured out of the trees at the far end of the meadow in a torrent that swelled into a spreading lake of steel-tipped lances as they drew rein, no doubt in surprise at what lay before them. It seemed that not as many horses had foundered as Mat had hoped for. Pulling the looking glass from its scabbard tied to his saddle's pommel, he raised it to his eye. The Taraboners were easy to pick out, with mail veils hiding their faces to the eyes, but the others wore every sort of helmet, rounded or conical, with face-bars and without. He even saw a few ridged Tairen helmets, though that did not mean there were Tairens among them. Most men used whatever armor they could find. *Don't think,* he thought. *The woman is here. That hundred thousand gold crowns is waiting. Don't bloody—*

A shrill Seanchan bugle sounded, thin with the distance, and the horsemen began advancing at a walk, already spreading out to extend beyond the wall's edges.

"Uncase the banner, Macoll," Mat ordered. So these flaming sons of goats thought they were coming to murder Tuon, did they? "This time, we'll let them know who's killing them. Mandevwin, you have the command."

Mandevwin turned his bay to face front. "Stand ready!" he shouted, and under-officers and bannermen echoed the cry.

Macoll pulled the leather case off, carefully fastening it to his saddle, and the banner streamed on the wind, a red-fringed white square with a large, open red hand in the center, and beneath it, embroidered in red, the words *Dovie'andi se tovya sagain. It's time to toss the dice,* Mat thought, translating. And so it was. He saw Musenge eyeing it. He seemed very calm for a man with ten thousand lances coming toward him.

"Are you ready, Aludra?" Mat called.

"Of course I am ready," she replied. "I only wish I had my drag- ons!" Musenge shifted his attention to her. Burn her, she needed to watch her tongue! Mat wanted those dragons to be a shock when the Seanchan first faced them.

Perhaps twelve hundred paces from the wall, the ranks of lancers began to trot, and at six hundred they began to gallop, but not as hard as they might have. Those horses were tired after a long run already. They lumbered. None of the lances had come down, yet. They would not until the last hundred paces. Some of those carried streamers that floated behind them in the air, a large knot of red here, a clump of green or blue there. They might have been House colors, or perhaps they marked mercenary companies. All those hooves made a noise like distant thunder rolling.

"Aludra!" Mat shouted without looking back. A hollow thump and an acrid sulphur smell announced the lofting tube sending its nightflower aloft, and a loud pop the blooming of a ball of red streaks overhead. Some of the galloping horsemen pointed to it as if in amaze- ment. None looked behind them to see Talmanes leading the three banners of horse out of the forest below the lake. Their lances had been left with the pack animals, but every man would have his horsebow out. Spreading out in a single line, they began following the galloping riders, increasing speed as they came. Their horses had been ridden far last night, but not pressed too hard, and they had been rested all morn- ing. The distance between the two groups of riders began to narrow.

"Front rank!" Mandevwin shouted when the horsemen were four hundred paces away. "Loose!" Above a thousand bolts flashed out, dark streaks in the air. Immediately the front rank bent to fasten their cranks to their crossbows and the second rank raised their weapons. "Second rank!" Mandevwin shouted. "Loose!" Another thousand quar- rels streaked for the oncoming horsemen.

At that range, they could not punch through a breastplate despite heads designed to do just that, but men with shattered legs toppled from their saddles and men with ruined arms reined in frantically to try stemming the flow of blood. And the horses. . . . Ah, Light, the poor horses. Horses fell by the hundreds, some kicking and screaming, struggling to stand, others not moving at all, many of them tripping more animals. Catapulted riders tumbled across the meadow grass until they were trampled by the riders behind.

"Third rank! Loose!" Mandevwin shouted, and as soon as those bolts were away, the front rank straightened. "Front rank!" Mandevwin called. "Loose!" And another thousand bolts added to the carnage. "Second rank! Loose!"

It was not so one-sided as an ambush, of course. Some of the galloping horsemen had flung down their lances and uncased their horsebows. Arrows began to fall among the crossbowmen. Shooting accurately from a galloping horse was no easy task, and the range was too far at the start for the arrows to kill, but more than one man struggled to work his crossbow with a shaft jutting from an arm. The wall protected their legs, yet. Too far to kill unless your target's luck had run out. Mat saw a man fall with an arrow in his eye, another with a shaft taken in the throat. There were other gaps in the ranks, as well. Men shuffled forward quickly to fill them.

"You could join in any time, Joline," he said.

"Third rank! Loose!"

The Aes Sedai shook her head irritably. "I must be in danger. I don't feel in danger yet." Teslyn nodded. She was watching the charge as if it were a parade, and a not very interesting one at that.

"If you would allow Seta and me," Bethamin began, but Joline looked over her shoulder coldly, and the Seanchan woman subsided and dropped her eyes to her hands on the reins. Seta smiled nervously, but it slid off her face under Joline's stare.

"Front rank! Loose!"

Mat rolled his eyes to the heavens and muttered a prayer that was half curse. The bloody women did not feel in danger! *He* felt as though his bloody head was on the chopping block!

"Second rank! Loose!"

Talmanes had come in range, now, and announced himself with a volley from four thousand bows at three hundred paces that cleared saddles. Closing the distance, they fired again. Again. The enemy ranks seemed to ripple with the shock. Some men whirled about and charged at Talmanes' line with lances coming down. Others began returning his hail of arrows with their own. Most continued on, though.

"Form square!" Mandevwin shouted a heartbeat before Mat could. He hoped the man had not left it too bloody late.

The Band was well-trained, though. The men on the flanks fell back at the run, as calmly as if arrows were not pelting them, clanging off breastplates and helmets. And sometimes not. Men fell. The three ranks never lost cohesion, though, as they bent into a hollow box with Mat at its center. Musenge and the other human Deathwatch Guards had their swords out, and the Ogier were hefting their long axes.

"Sling-men!" Mandevwin shouted. "Loose at will! Front rank, west! Loose!" Sling-men along the western rank shifted their sling-staffs so they could touch the fuses coming from the stubby cylinders to the slow-matches held in their teeth and, as the volley lanced out from the crossbows, whipped their slings back and then forward. The dark cylinders flew more than a hundred paces to land among the onrushing horsemen. The sling-men were already fitting more of the cylinders to their slings before the first fell. Aludra had marked each fuse with pieces of thread to indicate different burning times, and each cylinder erupted with a roar in a burst of flame, some on the ground, some as high as a mounted man's head. The explosion was not the real weapon, though a man struck in the face was suddenly headless. He stayed upright in the saddle for three strides before toppling. No, Aludra had wrapped a layer of hard pebbles around the powder inside each cylinder, and those pierced flesh deeply when they hit. Shrieking horses fell to thrash on the ground. Riders fell to lie still.

An arrow tugged at Mat's left sleeve, another pierced his right sleeve, only the fletchings keeping it from going through cleanly, and a third ripped open the right shoulder of his coat. He put a finger behind the scarf around his neck and tugged. The bloody thing felt awfully tight of a sudden. Maybe he *should* consider wearing armor at times like this. The enemy flanks were beginning to curl in, now, preparing to envelop the crossbowmen behind the wall. Talmanes' men still peppered their rear with arrows, but several hundred men had been forced to drop their bows to defend themselves with swords, and it was unlikely that all of the horses with empty saddles out there had belonged to Taraboners or Amadicians. He had left a gap in the center of his line, a path for anyone who decided to flee, yet no one was taking the offering. They could smell that hundred thousand crowns gold.

"I think," Joline said slowly. "Yes, I feel in danger, now." Teslyn simply drew back her hand and threw a sphere of fire larger than a horse's head. The explosion hurled dirt and pieces of men and horses into the air. It was about bloody time!

Facing in three directions, the Aes Sedai began hurling fireballs as fast as they could swing their arms, but the devastation they wrought did nothing to slow the attack. Those men should have been able to see there was no woman matching Tuon's description inside the square by this time, but their blood was no doubt on fire, the scent of riches in their nostrils. A man could live the rest of his life like a noble with a hundred thousand crowns gold. The square was encircled, and they fought to close on it, fought and died as volleys from the crossbows lashed them and sling-men killed them. Another wall began to rise, made of dead and dying men and horses, a wall that some tried to ride over and joined in the attempt. More scrambled down from their saddles and tried to clamber over. Crossbow bolts hurled them back. This close, bolts penetrated breastplates like hot knives going into butter. On they came, and died.

The silence seemed to come suddenly. Not quite silence. The air was full of the sound of panting men who had been working those cranks as fast as they could. And there was moaning from the wounded. A horse was still shrieking, somewhere. But Mat could see no one on his feet between the wall of dead and Talmanes, no one in the saddle except men in green helmets and breastplates. Men who had lowered their bows and swords. The Aes Sedai folded their hands on the high pommels of their saddles. They were breathing hard, too.

"It is done, Mat!" came Talmanes' shout. "Those who are not dead are dying. Not one of the fools tried to escape."

Mat shook his head. He had expected them to be half-mad with the lust for gold. They had been completely mad with it.

It would be necessary to haul away dead men and horses for Mat and the others to get out, and Talmanes set men to work, fastening ropes to horses to drag them aside. No one wanted to climb over that. No one but the Ogier.

"I want to see if I can find the traitor," Hartha said, and he and the other six Gardeners shouldered their axes and walked over the mound of bodies as if it were dirt.

"Well, at least we settled this," Joline said, patting her face with a lace-edged handkerchief. Sweat dotted her forehead. "You owe a debt, Mat. Aes Sedai do not become involved in private wars as a rule. I shall have to think on how you can pay it." Mat had a pretty good idea what she would come up with. She was mad herself if she thought he would agree.

"Crossbows settled this, *marath'damane*," Musenge said. His helmet, breastplate and coat were off, his left shirt-sleeve ripped away so one of the other Guards could wrap a bandage around where an arrow had gone through. The sleeve had come away very neatly, as if the stitching had been weak. He had a raven tattooed on his shoulder. "Crossbows and men with heart. You never had more than this, did you, Highness." That was not a question. "This and whatever losses you suffered."

"I told you," Mat said. "I had enough." He was not going to reveal anything more to the man than he could not avoid, but Musenge nodded as if he had confirmed everything.

By the time an opening could be cleared so that Mat and the others could ride through, Hartha and the Gardeners had returned. "I found the traitor," Hartha said, holding up a severed head by its hair.

Musenge's eyebrows climbed at the sight of that dark, hook-nosed face. "She will be very interested to see this," he said softly. Softly as the sound of sword being drawn is soft. "We must carry it to her."

"You know him?" Mat asked.

"We know him, Highness." Musenge's face, suddenly seeming carved from stone, said he would say no more on the subject.

"Look, would you stop calling me that? My name is Mat. After today, I'd say you have a right to use it." Mat surprised himself by sticking out his hand.

That stone mask crumpled in astonishment. "I could not do that, Highness," he said in scandalized tones. "When she married you, you became Prince of the Ravens. To speak your name would lower my eyes forever."

Mat took off his hat and scrubbed fingers through his hair. He had told everyone who would listen that he did not like nobles, did not want to be one, and he had meant it. He still meant it. And now he bloody was one! He did the only thing he could. He laughed until his sides ached.

EPILOGUE

Remember the Old Saying

The red-walled room, its ceiling painted fancifully with birds and fish cavorting among clouds and waves, bustled with brown-clad clerks scurrying along the aisles between the long tables that covered the floor. None seemed to be trying to listen—most seemed stunned, with cause—but Suroth disliked their presence. They had to overhear some of what was being said, and it was potentially dire news. Galgan had insisted, though. They needed to work to keep their minds off the disastrous news from home, and they were all trusted men and women. He insisted! At least the white-haired old man was not dressed as a soldier, this morning. His voluminous blue trousers and short, high-collared red coat with rows of gold buttons embossed with his sigil were the height of Seandar fashion, which meant the height of fashion for the Empire. When he wore armor, or even just his red uniform, he sometimes looked at her as if she were a soldier under his command!

Well, once Elbar brought word that Tuon was dead, she could have Galgan killed. His cheeks were smeared with ashes, as were hers. The ship Semirhage had promised had brought word of the Empress's death and the Empire was racked by rebellion in every quarter. There was no Empress, no Daughter of the Nine Moons. To commoners, the world trembled on the brink of destruction. To some of the Blood, too. With

Galgan and a few more dead, there would be none to object to Suroth Sabelle Meldarath proclaiming herself Empress. She tried not to think of the new name she would take. Thinking on a new name beforehand was bad luck.

A frown creasing his face, Galgan looked down at the map spread out before them, and placed a red-lacquered fingernail atop mountains on the southern coast of Arad Doman. Suroth did not know what the mountains were called. The map showed all of Arad Doman and held three markers, one red wedge and two white circles, spaced out in a long line north to south. "Has Turan gotten an accurate count of how many men came out of these mountains to join Ituralde when he crossed into Arad Doman, Yamada?"

Efraim Yamada wore the ashes, too, since he was of the Blood, if only the low Blood, his hair cut in the bowl-and-tail rather than a narrow crest across an otherwise shaved scalp. Only the commoners around the table, whatever their rank, were without. Graying and tall in a blue-and-gold breastplate, with broad shoulders and lean hips, Yamada still held some of the beauty of his youth. "He reports at least one hundred thousand, Captain-General. Perhaps half again that."

"And how many came out after Turan crossed the border?"

"Possibly two hundred thousand, Captain-General."

Galgan sighed and straightened. "So Turan has one army ahead of him and another behind, very likely the whole of Arad Doman's strength, and between them he is outnumbered." The fool! Stating the blindingly obvious.

"Turan should have stripped Tarabon of every sword and lance!" Suroth snapped. "If he survives this debacle, I will have his head!"

Galgan quirked a white eyebrow at her. "I hardly think Tarabon is loyal enough to support that just yet," he said drily. "Besides, he has *damane* and *raken*. They should offset his lesser numbers. Speaking of *damane* and *raken*, I've signed the orders raising Tylee Khirgan to Lieutenant-General and the low Blood, since you've dithered over it, and orders to return most of those *raken* to Amadicia and Altara. Chisen still hasn't found whoever created that little mess in the north, and I don't like the notion that whoever it was is lying in wait to spring out as soon as Chisen returns to the Molvaine Gap."

Suroth hissed, gripping her pleated blue skirts in her fists before she could stop her hands. She would not let the man make her show emotion! "You overstep yourself, Galgan," she said coldly. "I command the Forerunners. For the time being, I command the Return. You will sign no orders without my approval."

"You commanded the Forerunners, who have been subsumed into the Return," he replied calmly, and Suroth tasted bitterness. The news from the Empire had emboldened him. With the Empress dead, Galgan intended to make himself the first Emperor in nine hundred years. It seemed he would have to die by tonight. "As for you commanding the Return—" He cut off at the sound of heavy boots from the corridor.

Suddenly Deathwatch Guards filled the doorway, armored and hands on their sword hilts. Hard eyes stared out of their red-and-green helmets to survey the room. Only when they were satisfied did they step aside to reveal that the corridor was filled with Deathwatch Guards, human and Ogier. Suroth barely noticed them. She had eyes only for the small dark woman in pleated blue with a shaven head and ashes on her cheeks. The news was all over the city. She could not have reached the palace without hearing of her mother's death, her family's deaths, but her face was a stern mask. Suroth's knees hit the floor automatically. Around her the Blood knelt, the commoners prostrated themselves.

"The Light's blessings for your safe return, Highness," she said in chorus with the rest of the Blood. So Elbar had failed. No matter. Tuon would not take a new name or become empress until the mourning was finished. She could still die, clearing the way for a new empress.

"Show them what Captain Musenge brought me, Banner-General Karede," Tuon said.

A tall man with three dark plumes on his helmet bent to carefully empty a large lump from a canvas bag onto the green floor tiles. The gagging smell of decay began to permeate the room. Dropping the bag, he strode across the floor to stand beside Suroth.

It took her a moment to recognize Elbar's hook-nosed face in that rotting mass, but as soon as she did, she fell forward, prostrating herself, kissing the floor tiles. Not in desperation, though. She could recover from this. Unless they had put Elbar to the question. "My eyes are lowered, Highness, that one of mine has offended you so deeply that you took his head."

"Offended me." Tuon seemed to be weighing the words. "It might be said he offended me. He tried to kill me."

Gasps filled the room, and before Suroth could more than open her mouth, the Deathwatch Guard Banner-General planted a boot on her bottom, seized her crest in his fist, and hauled her upper body clear of the floor. She did not struggle. That would only have added to the indignity.

"My eyes are deeply lowered that one of mine should be a traitor, Highness," she said hoarsely. She wished she could have spoken naturally, but the cursed man had her back arched till it was a wonder she could speak at all. "Had I even suspected, I would have had him put to the question myself. But if he tried to implicate me, Highness, he lied to protect his true master. I have some thoughts on that which I would share with you in private, if I may be allowed." With a little luck, she could lay this to Galgan. His usurpation of her authority would help.

Tuon looked over Suroth's head. She met Galgan's eyes, and Abaldar's and Yamada's, and those of everyone of the Blood, but not Suroth's. "It is well known that Zaired Elbar was Suroth's man completely. He did nothing that she did not order. Therefore Suroth Sabelle Meldarath is no more. This *da'covale* will serve the Deathwatch Guard as they wish until her hair has grown enough for her to be decent when she is sent to the block for sale."

Suroth never thought of the knife she had intended to use to open her veins, a knife beyond reach in her apartments. She could not think at all. She started screaming, a wordless howl, before they even began cutting her clothing off.

The Andoran sun was warm after Tar Valon. Pevara removed her cloak and began tying it behind her saddle as the gateway winked shut, hiding the view of the Ogier grove in Tar Valon. None of them had wanted anyone to see them leaving. They would return to the grove for the same reason, unless matters went very badly. In which case, they might never return. She had thought this task must be carried out by someone who combined the highest diplomatic skills with the courage of a lion. Well, she was no coward, at least. She could say that much of herself.

"Where did you learn the weave for bonding a Warder?" Javindhra asked abruptly, stowing her own cloak in similar fashion.

"You should recall that I once suggested Red sisters would be well served by having Warders." Pevara snugged her red riding gloves, showing no concern for the question. She had expected it before this. "Why would you be surprised I know the weave?" In truth, she had needed to ask Yukiri, and had been hard pressed to dissemble her reason for asking. She doubted that Yukiri was suspicious, though. A Red bonding a Warder was as likely as a woman flying. Except, of course, that that was why she had come to Andor. Why they had all come.

Javindhra was there only at Tsutama's command, given when Pevara and Tarna could not come up with enough names to suit the Highest. The angular Sitter did not bother to hide her displeasure over that, not from Pevara, although she had buried it deeply around Tsutama. Tarna was there, of course, pale-haired and icy cold, her Keeper's stole left behind but her divided gray skirts embroidered in red to the knee. For Elaida's Keeper to have a Warder would be difficult, though the men were to be housed in the city, away from the Tower, yet it had all been her idea in the first place, and she was, if not eager, then determined to take part in this first experiment. Besides, the need for numbers was paramount, because they had found only three other sisters willing to entertain the idea. The primary task of the Red for so long, finding men who could channel and bringing them to the Tower to be gentled, tended to sour women on all men, so the clues had been few and far between. Jezrail was a square-faced Tairen who kept a painted miniature of the boy she had almost married instead of coming to the Tower. His grandchildren would be grandparents now, but she still spoke of him fondly. Desala, a beautiful Cairhienin with large dark eyes and an unfortunate temper, when given the chance would dance any number of men to exhaustion in a night. And Melare, plump and witty, with a love of conversation, sent money to Andor to pay for her grandnephews' education as she had for her nephews and nieces.

Weary of searching out such tiny clues, weary of probing delicately to learn whether they meant what they might, Pevara had convinced Tsutama that six would be enough to begin. Too, a larger party might cause some unfortunate reaction. After all, the whole Red Ajah appearing at this so-called Black Tower, or even half, might well make the men think themselves under attack. There was no telling how sane they all still were. That was one thing they had agreed on, behind Tsutama's back. They would bond no men who showed any signs of madness. That was, if they were allowed to bond any.

Ajah eyes-and-ears in Caemlyn had sent copious reports on the Black Tower, and some had even found employment inside it, so they had no difficulty locating the well-worn dirt track that led down from the city to a grandiose double-arched black gate, near fifty feet tall and ten spans

wide, topped by crenelations over a down-pointing central spike of stone
and flanked by a pair of thick, crenelated black towers that stood at least
fifteen spans high. There were no actual gates to close up the opening, and
the black stone wall that stretched out of sight east and west, marked at
intervals by the foundations of bastions and towers, was nowhere higher
than four or five paces that she could see. Weeds grew along the uneven
top, and grasses ruffled by the breeze. Those unfinished walls, looking as
if they might never be finished, made the gate seem ludicrous.

The three men who stepped out into the opening were not at all ludicrous, however. They wore long black coats, and swords at their hips.
One, a lean young fellow with curled mustaches, had a silver pin in the
shape of a sword on his high collar. One of the Dedicated. Pevara resisted the instinct to think of him as equivalent to an Accepted and the
other two as novices. Novices and Accepted were kept safe and guided
until they knew enough of the Power to become Aes Sedai. By all reports, Soldiers and Dedicated were considered ready for battle almost
as soon as they learned to channel. And they were forced from the first
day, pressed to seize as much of *saidin* as they could, made to use it almost continually. Men died from that, and they called it "training
losses," as if they could hide death behind bland words. The thought of
losing novices or Accepted in that fashion curdled Pevara's stomach,
but it seemed that the men took it in stride.

"A fine morning to you, Aes Sedai," the Dedicated said with a small
bow as they reined in before him. A very small bow, never taking his
eyes from them. His accents were those of Murandy. "Now what would
six sisters be wanting here at the Black Tower this fine morning?"

"To see the M'Hael," Pevara replied, managing to avoid choking on
the word. It meant "leader" in the Old Tongue, but the implication of
taking that alone as a title gave the word much stronger meaning, as if
he led everyone and everything.

"Ah, to see the M'Hael, is it? And of what Ajahs should I say?"

"The Red," Pevara replied and watched him blink. Very satisfying.
But not very helpful.

"The Red," he said flatly. He had not remained startled very long.
"Well, then. Enkazin, al'Seen, you keep watch while I see what the
M'Hael has to say to this."

He turned his back, and the vertical silvery slash of a gateway appeared in front of him, widening into an opening no larger than a door.
Was that as large as he could make? There had been some discussion

about whether to bond men who were as strong as possible or those who were weak. The weak might be more easily controlled, while the strong might—would definitely—be more useful. They had reached no consensus; each sister would have to decide for herself. He darted through the gateway and closed it before she had a chance to see more than a white stone platform with steps leading up one side and a squared-off black stone that might have been one of the building blocks for the wall, polished till it shone in the sun, sitting atop it.

The two who remained stayed in the middle of the double arch as if to bar the sisters from riding in. One was a Saldaean, a skinny broad-nosed man just short of his middle years who had something of the look of a clerk about him, a bit of a stoop as from hunching for long hours over a writing table, the other a boy, little more than a child, who raked dark hair out of his eyes with his fingers though the breeze quickly put it back again. Neither seemed the slightest uneasy over confronting six sisters alone. If they *were* alone. Were there others in those towers? Pevara refrained from glancing at the tower tops.

"You there, boy," Desala said in a voice like chimes. Chimes tinged with anger. The surest way to set off her temper was to harm a child. "You should be at home with your mother studying your letters. What are you doing here?" The boy flushed bright red and raked hair from his face again.

"Saml's all right, Aes Sedai," the Saldaean said, patting the boy's shoulder. "He's a quick learner, and you don't need to show him anything twice before he knows it." The boy stood up very straight, pride on his face, and tucked his thumbs behind his sword belt. A sword, at his age! True, a noble's son would have been learning the sword for several years at Saml al'Seen's age, but he would not be allowed to wear the thing about!

"Pevara," Tarna said coolly, "no children. I knew they had children here, but no children."

"Light!" Melare breathed. Her white mare sensed her agitation and tossed her head. "Certainly no children!"

"That would be an abomination," Jezrail said.

"No children," Pevara agreed quickly. "I think we should wait to say more until we see Master . . . the M'Hael." Javindhra sniffed.

"No children what, Aes Sedai?" Enkazin asked, frowning. "No children what?" he said again when no one answered.

He no longer appeared so much like a clerk. The stoop remained, but something in his tilted eyes suddenly seemed . . . dangerous. Was he holding the male half of the Power? The possibility sent a chill down Pevara's spine, but she resisted the desire to embrace *saidar*. Some men who could channel seemed able to sense when a woman was holding the Power. Enkazin looked like he might be hasty, now.

They waited in silence except for the occasional stamp of a hoof, Pevara schooling herself to patience, Javindhra grumbling under her breath. Pevara could not make out the words, but she knew grumbling when she heard it. Tarna and Jezrail took books from their saddlebags and read. Good. Let these Asha'man see that they were unconcerned. Only, not even the boy seemed impressed. He and the Saldaean just stood there in the middle of the gate watching, hardly blinking.

After perhaps half an hour, a larger gateway opened and the Murandian strode through. "The M'Hael will be receiving you at the palace, Aes Sedai. Go on through." He jerked his head toward the opening.

"You will show us the way?" Pevara said, dismounting. The gateway was larger, but she would have had to crouch to ride through.

"There'll be someone the other side to guide you." He barked a laugh. "The M'Hael doesn't associate with the likes of me." Pevara filed that away to chew over later.

As soon as the last of them was through, near the white stone platform with its mirror-bright black stone, the gateway winked shut, but they were not alone. Four men and two women in rough woolens took the reins of their horses, and a dark, heavyset man with both the silver sword and a sinuous red-and-gold figure, a dragon, on his tall black collar gave them a minimal bow.

"Follow me," he said curtly in a Tairen accent. His eyes were like augers.

The palace the Murandian had spoken of was just that, two stories of white marble topped with pointed domes and spires in the style of Saldaea, separated from a large space of bare, hard-packed ground by the white platform. It was not large among palaces, but most nobles lived in buildings far smaller and less grand. Broad stone stairs rose to a wide landing in front of tall twinned doors. Each bore a gauntleted fist gripping three lightning bolts, carved large and gilded. Those doors swung open before the Tairen reached them, but there were no servants in evidence. The man must have channeled. Pevara felt that chill again. Javindhra muttered under her breath. With a sound of prayer, this time.

The palace might have belonged to any noble with a taste for tapestries showing battles and red-and-black floor tiles, except that there were no servants in evidence. He had servants, though unfortunately no Red Ajah eyes-and-ears among them, but did he expect them to remain out of sight when not needed or had he ordered them from the halls? Perhaps to avoid having anyone see six Aes Sedai arrive. That line of reasoning ran toward thoughts she would rather not consider. She had acknowledged the dangers before leaving the White Tower. There was no point dwelling on them.

The chamber the Tairen led them to was a throne room, where a ring of spiral-cut black columns supported what must have been the palace's largest dome, its interior layered with gilt and half filled with gilded lamps hanging on gilded chains. Tall mirrored stand-lamps stood along the curved walls, too. Perhaps a hundred men in black coats were standing to either side of the room. Every man she could see wore the sword and the dragon, men with hard faces, leering faces, cruel faces. Their eyes focused on her and the other sisters.

The Tairen did not announce them, but rather simply joined the mass of Asha'man and left them to make their own way across the room. The floor tiles were red and black here, too. Taim must particularly like those colors. The man himself was lounging on what could only be called a throne, a massive chair as heavily carved and gilded as any throne she had seen, atop a white marble dais. Pevara focused on him, and not only to avoid feeling all those eyes of men who could channel following her. Mazrim Taim drew the eye. He was tall, with a strongly hooked nose and an air of physical strength about him. An air of darkness, too. He sat there with his ankles crossed and one arm hanging over the heavy arm of the throne, yet he seemed ready to explode into violence. Interestingly, though his black coat was embroidered with blue-and-gold dragons that twined around the sleeves from elbows to cuffs, he did not wear the collar pins.

"Six sisters of the Red Ajah," he said when they stopped short of the dais. His eyes. . . . She had only thought the Tairen's eyes were augers. "Plainly you didn't come to try gentling us all." Chuckles rippled around the room. "Why *did* you come asking to speak to me?"

"I am Pevara Tazanovni, Sitter for the Red," she said. "This is Javindhra Doraille, also a Red Sitter. The others are Tarna Feir, Desala Nevanche—"

"I didn't ask your names," Taim cut in coldly. "I asked why you came here."

This was not going well. She managed not to take a deep breath, but she wanted to. Outwardly, she was cool and calm. Inside, she wondered whether she would end the day forcibly bonded. Or dead. "We want to discuss bonding Asha'man as Warders. After all, you've bonded fifty-one sisters. Against their will." As well to let him know they were aware of that from the start. "We do not propose bonding any man against his will, however."

A tall, golden-haired man standing near the dais sneered at her. "Why should we allow Aes Sedai to take any m—" Something unseen struck the side of his head so hard that his feet left the floor tiles before he fell in a heap, eyes closed and blood trickling from his nostrils.

A lean man with receding gray-streaked hair and a forked beard bent to touch a finger to the fallen man's head. "He's alive," he said as he straightened, "but his skull's cracked and his jaw's broken." He might have been talking about the weather. None of the men made any move to offer Healing. Not one!

"I have some small skill in Healing," Melare said, gathering her skirts and already moving toward the fallen man. "Enough for this, I think. With your permission."

Taim shook his head. "You do not have my permission. If Mishraile survives till nightfall, he'll be Healed. Perhaps the pain will teach him to guard his tongue. You say *you* want to bond Warders? *Reds?*"

That last word carried a great deal of contempt, which Pevara chose to ignore. Tarna's eyes could have turned the sun to an icicle, though. Pevara laid a cautionary hand on the other woman's arm as she spoke. "Reds have experience with men who can channel." Mutters rose among the watching Asha'man. Angry mutters. She ignored that, too. "We are not afraid of them. Custom can be as hard to change as law, harder at times, but it has been decided to change ours. Henceforth, Red sisters may bond Warders, but only men who can channel. Each sister may bond as many as she feels comfortable with. Given the Green, for example, I think that is unlikely to be more than three or four."

"Very well."

Pevara blinked in spite of herself. "'Very well'?" She must have misunderstood him. He could not have been convinced so easily.

Taim's eyes seemed to bore into her head. He spread his hands, and it was a mocking gesture. "What would you have me say? Fair is fair? Equal shares? Accept 'very well' and ask who will let you bond them. Besides, you must remember the old saying. Let the lord of chaos rule." The chamber erupted with men's laughter.

Pevara had never heard any saying like that. The laughter made the hair on the back of her neck try to stand.

The End

of the Eleventh Book of

The Wheel of Time

GLOSSARY

A Note on Dates in This Glossary. The Toman Calendar (devised by
Toma dur Ahmid) was adopted approximately two centuries after the
death of the last male Aes Sedai, recording years After the Breaking of
the World (AB). So many records were destroyed in the Trolloc Wars
that at their end there was argument about the exact year under the old
system. A new calendar, proposed by Tiam of Gazar, celebrated freedom from the Trolloc threat and recorded each year as a Free Year (FY).
The Gazaran Calendar gained wide acceptance within twenty years after the Wars' end. Artur Hawkwing attempted to establish a new calendar based on the founding of his empire (FF, From the Founding),
but only historians now refer to it. After the death and destruction of
the War of the Hundred Years, a third calendar was devised by Uren
din Jubai Soaring Gull, a scholar of the Sea Folk, and promulgated by
the Panarch Farede of Tarabon. The Farede Calendar, dating from the
arbitrarily decided end of the War of the Hundred Years and recording
years of the New Era (NE), is currently in use.

Aelfinn: A race of beings, largely human in appearance but with
snake-like characteristics, who will give true answers to three
questions. Whatever the question, their answers are always correct, if frequently given in forms that are not clear, but questions

concerning the Shadow can be extremely dangerous. Their true location is unknown, but they can be visited by passing through a *ter'angreal*, once a possession of Mayene but in recent years held in the Stone of Tear. There are reports that they can also be reached by entering the Tower of Ghenjei. They speak the Old Tongue, mention treaties and agreements, and ask if those entering carry iron, instruments of music or devices that can make fire. *See also* Eelfinn.

Amayar, the: The land-dwelling inhabitants of the Sea Folk islands. Known to few people other than the Atha'an Miere, the Amayar are the craftsmen who make what is known as Sea Folk porcelain. Followers of the Water Way, which prizes acceptance of what is rather than what might be wished for, they are very uncomfortable at sea and only venture onto the water in small boats for fishing, never leaving sight of land. Their way of life is very peaceful, and requires very little oversight from the governors appointed from among the Atha'an Miere. Since Atha'an Miere governors have little desire to go far from the sea, the Amayar essentially run their villages according to their own rules and customs.

Arad Doman: A nation on the Aryth Ocean, currently racked by civil war and by wars against those who have declared for the Dragon Reborn. Its capital is Bandar Eban. In Arad Doman, those who are descended from the nobility at the time of the founding of the nation, as opposed to those raised later, are known as the bloodborn. The ruler (king or queen) is elected by a council of the heads of merchant guilds (the Council of Merchants), who are almost always women. He or she must be from the noble class, not the merchant, and is elected for life. Legally the king or queen has absolute authority, except that he or she can be deposed by a three-quarter vote of the Council. The current ruler is King Alsalam Saeed Almadar, Lord of Almadar, High Seat of House Almadar. His present whereabouts are much shrouded in mystery.

Area, units of: (1) Land: 1 ribbon = 20 paces × 10 paces (200 square paces); 1 cord = 20 paces × 50 paces (1000 square paces); 1 hide = 100 paces × 100 paces (10,000 square paces); 1 rope = 100 paces × 1000 paces (100,000 square paces); 1 march = 1000 paces × 1000 paces (¼ square mile). (2) Cloth: 1 pace = 1 pace and 1 hand × 1 pace and 1 hand.

armsmen: Soldiers who owe allegiance or fealty to a particular lord or lady.

Asha'man: (1) In the Old Tongue, "Guardian" or "Guardians," but always a guardian of justice and truth. (2) The name given, both collectively and as a rank, to the men who have come to the Black Tower, near Caemlyn in Andor, in order to learn to channel. Their training largely concentrates on the ways in which the One Power can be used as a weapon, and in another departure from the usages of the White Tower, once they learn to seize *saidin*, the male half of the Power, they are required to perform all chores and labors with the Power. When newly enrolled, a man is termed a Soldier; he wears a plain black coat with a high collar, in the Andoran fashion. Being raised to Dedicated brings the right to wear a silver pin, called the Sword, on the collar of his coat. Promotion to Asha'man brings the right to wear a Dragon pin, in gold and red enamel, on the collar opposite the Sword. Although many women, including wives, flee when they learn that their men actually can channel, a fair number of men at the Black Tower are married, and they use a version of the Warder bond to create a link with their wives. This same bond, altered to compel obedience, has recently been used to bond captured Aes Sedai as well. Some Asha'man have been bonded by Aes Sedai, although the traditional Warder bond is used. The Asha'man are led by Mazrim Taim, who has styled himself the M'Hael, Old Tongue for "leader."

Balwer, Sebban: Formerly secretary to Pedron Niall (the Lord Captain Commander of the Children of the Light) in public, and secretly Niall's spymaster. After Niall's death, Balwer aided the escape of Morgase (once Queen of Andor) from the Seanchan in Amador for his own reasons, and was employed as secretary to Perrin t'Bashere Aybara and Faile ni Bashere t'Aybara. His duties expanded, however, and he now directs *Cha Faile* in their activities, acting as a spymaster for Perrin, though Perrin doesn't think of him so. *See Cha Faile.*

Band of the Red Hand: *See Shen an Calhar.*

Blood, the: Term used by the Seanchan to designate the nobility. There are four degrees of nobility, two of the High Blood and two of the low, or lesser, Blood. The High Blood let their fingernails grow to a length of one inch and shave the sides of their heads, leaving a crest down the center, narrower for men than for women. The length of this crest varies according to fashion. The low Blood also grow their fingernails long, but they shave the sides and back of the head leaving what appears to be a bowl of hair, with a wide tail at the back allowed to grow longer, often to the shoulder for men or to the waist for women. Those of the highest level of the High Blood are called High Lady or High Lord and lacquer the first two fingernails on each hand. Those of the next level of the High Blood are called simply Lord or Lady and lacquer only the nails of the forefingers. Those of the low Blood also are called simply Lady or Lord, but those of the higher rank lacquer the nails of the last two fingers on each hand, while those on the lowest level lacquer only the nails of the little fingers. The Empress and immediate members of the Imperial family shave their heads entirely and lacquer all of their fingernails. One can be raised to the Blood as well as born to it, and this is frequently a reward for outstanding accomplishment or service to the Empire.

calendar: There are 10 days to the week, 28 days to the month and 13 months to the year. Several feast days are not part of any month; these include Sunday (the longest day of the year), the Feast of Thanksgiving (once every four years at the spring equinox) and the Feast of All Souls Salvation, also called All Souls Day (once every ten years at the autumn equinox). While the months have names— Taisham, Jumara, Saban, Aine, Adar, Saven, Amadaine, Tammaz, Maigdhal, Choren, Shaldine, Nesan and Danu—these are seldom used except in official documents and by officials. For most people, using the seasons is good enough.

Captain-General: (1) The military rank of the leader of the Queen's Guard. This position is currently held by Lady Birgitte Trahelion. (2) The title given to the head of the Green Ajah, though known only to members of the Green. This position is currently held by Adelorna Bastine in the Tower, and Myrelle Berengari among the rebel Aes Sedai contingent under Egwene al'Vere. (3) A Seanchan rank, the highest in the Ever Victorious Army except for Marshal-General, which is a temporary rank sometimes given to a Captain-General put in charge of a war.

Cha Faile: (1) In the Old Tongue, "the Falcon's Talon." (2) Name taken by the young Cairhienin and Tairen nobles, attempted followers of *ji'e'toh*, who have sworn fealty to Faile ni Bashere t'Aybara. In secret, they act as her personal scouts and spies. Since her capture by the Shaido, they continue their activities under the guidance of Sebban Balwer.

Children of the Light: Society of strict ascetic beliefs, owing allegiance to no nation and dedicated to the defeat of the Dark One and the destruction of all Darkfriends. Founded during the War of the Hundred Years by Lothair Mantelar to proselytize against an increase in Darkfriends, they evolved during the war into a completely military society. They are extremely rigid in their beliefs, and certain that only they know the truth and the right. They consider Aes Sedai and any who support them to be Darkfriends. Known disparagingly as Whitecloaks, a name they themselves despise, they were formerly headquartered in Amador, Amadicia, but were forced out when the Seanchan conquered the city. Their sign is a golden sunburst on a field of white. *See also* Questioners.

Corenne: In the Old Tongue, "the Return." The name given by the Seanchan both to the fleet of thousands of ships and to the hundreds of thousands of soldiers, craftsmen and others carried by those ships, who came behind the Forerunners to reclaim the lands stolen from Artur Hawkwing's descendants. The *Corenne* is led by Captain-General Lunal Galgan. *See also Hailene, Rhyagelle.*

cuendillar: A supposedly indestructible substance created during the Age of Legends. Any known force used in an attempt to break it, including the One Power, is absorbed, making *cuendillar* stronger. Although the making of *cuendillar* was thought lost forever, new objects made from it have surfaced. It is also known as heartstone.

currency: After many centuries of trade, the standard terms for coins are the same in every land: crowns (the largest coin in size), marks and pennies. Crowns and marks can be minted of gold or silver, while pennies can be silver or copper, the last often called simply a copper. In different lands, however, these coins are of different sizes and weights. Even in one nation, coins of different sizes and weights have been minted by different rulers. Because of trade, the coins of many nations can be found almost anywhere, and for that reason, bankers, moneylenders and merchants all use scales to determine the value of any given coin. Even large numbers of coins are weighed.

The heaviest coins come from Andor and Tar Valon, and in those two places the relative values are: 10 copper pennies = 1 silver penny; 100 silver pennies = 1 silver mark; 10 silver marks = 1 silver crown; 10 silver crowns = 1 gold mark; 10 gold marks = 1 gold crown. By contrast, in Altara, where the larger coins contain less gold or silver, the relative values are: 10 copper pennies = 1 silver penny; 21 silver pennies = 1 silver mark; 20 silver marks = 1 silver crown; 20 silver crowns = 1 gold mark; 20 gold marks = 1 gold crown.

The only paper currency is "letters-of-rights," which are issued by bankers, guaranteeing to present a certain amount of gold or silver when the letter-of-rights is presented. Because of the long distances between cities, the length of time needed to travel from one to another, and the difficulties of transactions at long distance, a letter-of-rights may be accepted at full value in a city near to the bank which issued it, but it may be accepted only at a lower value in a city farther away. Generally, someone intending to be traveling for a long time will carry one or more letters-of-rights to exchange for coin when needed. Letters-of-rights are usually accepted only by bankers or merchants, and would never be used in shops.

da'covale: (1) In the Old Tongue, "one who is owned," or "person who is property." (2) Among the Seanchan, the term often used, along with property, for slaves. Slavery has a long and unusual history among the Seanchan, with slaves having the ability to rise to positions of great power and open authority, including authority over those who are free. It is also possible for those in positions of great power to be reduced to *da'covale*. *See also so'jhin.*

Deathwatch Guard, the: The elite military formation of the Seanchan Empire, including both humans and Ogier. The human members of the Deathwatch Guard are all *da'covale*, born as property and chosen while young to serve the Empress, whose personal property they are. Fanatically loyal and fiercely proud, they often display the ravens tattooed on their shoulders, the mark of a *da'covale* of the Empress. The Ogier members are known as Gardeners, and they are not *da'covale*. The Gardeners are as fiercely loyal as the human Deathwatch Guards, though, and are even more feared. Human or Ogier, the Deathwatch Guards not only are ready to die for the Empress and the Imperial family, but believe that their lives are the property of the Empress, to be disposed of as she wishes. Their helmets and armor are lacquered in dark green (so dark that it is often mistakenly called black) and blood-red, their shields are lacquered black, and their swords, spears, axes and halberds carry black tassels. *See also da'covale.*

Defenders of the Stone, the: The elite military formation of Tear. The current Captain of the Stone (commander of the Defenders) is Rodrivar Tihera. Only Tairens are accepted into the Defenders, and officers are usually of noble birth, though often from minor Houses or minor branches of strong Houses. The Defenders are tasked to hold the great fortress called the Stone of Tear, in the city of Tear, to defend the city, and to provide police services in place of any City Watch or the like. Except in times of war, their duties seldom take them far from the city. Then, as with other such elite formations, they are the core around which the army is formed. The uniform of the Defenders consists of a black coat with padded sleeves striped black-and-gold with black cuffs, a burnished breastplate and a rimmed helmet with a faceguard of steel bars. The Captain of the Stone wears three short white plumes on his helmet, and on the cuffs of his coat three intertwined golden braids on a white band. Captains wear two white plumes and a single line of golden braid on white cuffs, lieutenants one white plume and a single line of black braid on white cuffs, and under-lieutenants one short black plume and plain white cuffs. Bannermen have gold-colored cuffs on their coats, and squadmen have cuffs striped black-and-gold.

Delving: (1) Using the One Power to diagnose physical condition and illness. (2) Finding deposits of metal ores with the One Power. That this has long been a lost ability among Aes Sedai may account for the name becoming attached to another ability.

Depository: A division of the Tower Library. There are twelve publicly know Depositories, each having books and records pertaining to a particular subject, or to related subjects. A Thirteenth Depository, known only to some Aes Sedai, contains secret documents, records and histories which may be accessed only by the Amyrlin Seat, the Keeper of the Chronicles and the Sitters in the Hall of the Tower. And, of course, by that handful of librarians who maintain the depository.

der'morat-: (1) In the Old Tongue, "master handler." (2) Among the Seanchan, the prefix applied to indicate a senior and highly skilled handler of one of the exotics, one who trains others, as in *der'-morat'raken*. *Der'morat* can have a fairly high social status, the highest of all held by *der'sul'dam*, the trainers of *sul'dam*, who rank with fairly high military officers. *See also morat-.*

Eelfinn: A race of beings, largely human in appearance but with fox-like characteristics, who will grant three wishes, although they ask for a price in return. If the person asking does not negotiate a price, the Eelfinn choose it. The most common price in such circumstances is death, but they still fulfill their part of the bargain, although the manner in which they fulfill it is seldom the manner the one asking expects. Their true location is unknown, but it was possible to visit them by means of a *ter'angreal* that was located in Rhuidean. That *ter'angreal* was taken by Moiraine Damodred to Cairhien, where it was destroyed. It is also reported that they may be reached by entering the Tower of Ghenjei. They ask the same questions as the Aelfinn regarding fire, iron and musical instruments. *See also* Aelfinn.

Fain, Padan: Former Darkfriend, now more and worse than a Darkfriend, and an enemy of the Forsaken as much as he is of Rand al'Thor, whom he hates with a passion. Last seen in Far Madding in company with Toram Riatin, who died there.

Fel, Herid: The author of *Reason and Unreason* and other books. Fel was a student (and teacher) of history and philosophy at the Academy of Cairhien. He was discovered in his study torn limb from limb.

First Reasoner: The title given to the head of the White Ajah. This position is currently held by Ferane Neheran, an Aes Sedai in the White Tower. Ferane Sedai is one of only two Ajah heads to sit in the Hall of the Tower at present.

First Weaver: The title given to the head of the Yellow Ajah. This position is currently held by Suana Dragand in the White Tower. Suana Sedai is one of only two Ajah heads to sit in the Hall of the Tower at present. Among the rebel Aes Sedai, Romanda Cassin holds this position.

forcing; forced: When someone with the ability to channel handles as much of the One Power as they can over long periods of time and channels continually, they learn faster and gain strength more rapidly. This is called forcing, or being forced, by Aes Sedai, who abjure the practice with novices and Accepted because of the danger of death or being burned out.

Forerunners, the: *See Hailene.*

Forsaken, the: The name given to thirteen powerful Aes Sedai, men and women both, who went over to the Shadow during the Age of Legends and were trapped in the sealing of the Bore into the Dark One's prison. While it has long been believed that they alone abandoned the Light during the War of the Shadow, in fact others did as well; these thirteen were only the highest-ranking among them. The Forsaken (who call themselves the Chosen) are somewhat reduced in number since their awakening in the present day. Some of those killed have been reincarnated in new bodies and given new names, but much is as yet unknown about their identities and locations.

Hailene: In the Old Tongue, "Forerunners," or "Those Who Come Before." The term applied by the Seanchan to the massive expeditionary force sent across the Aryth Ocean to scout out the lands where Artur Hawkwing once ruled. Now under the command of the High Lady Suroth, its numbers swollen by recruits from conquered lands, the *Hailene* has gone far beyond its original goals, and has in fact been succeeded by the *Corenne*. *See Corenne, Rhyagelle*.

Hand: In Seanchan, Hand refers to a primary assistant or one of a hierarchy of imperial functionaries. A Hand of the Empress is of the First Rank, and Lesser Hands will be found at lower ranks. Some Hands operate in secret, such as those who guide the Seekers and Listeners; others are known and display their rank by wearing the appropriate number of golden hands embroidered on their clothing.

Hanlon, Daved: A Darkfriend, formerly commander of the White Lions in service to the Forsaken Rahvin while he held Caemlyn using the name Lord Gaebril. From there, Hanlon took the White Lions to Cairhien under orders to further the rebellion against the Dragon Reborn. The White Lions were destroyed by a "bubble of evil," and Hanlon was ordered back to Caemlyn and, under the name Doilin Mellar, ingratiated himself with Elayne, the Daughter-Heir. According to rumor, he did considerably more than ingratiate himself.

heart: The basic unit of organization in the Black Ajah. In effect, a cell. A heart consists of three sisters who know each other, with each member of the heart knowing one additional sister of the Black who is unknown to the other two of her heart.

Illuminators, Guild of: A society that held the secret of making fireworks. It guarded this secret very closely, even to the extent of doing murder to protect it. The Guild gained its name from the grand displays, called Illuminations, that it provided for rulers and sometimes for greater lords. Lesser fireworks were sold for use by others, but with dire warnings of the disaster that could result from attempting to learn what was inside them. The Guild once had chapter houses in Cairhien and Tanchico, but both are now destroyed. In addition, the members of the Guild in Tanchico resisted the invasion by the Seanchan and were made *da'covale*, and the Guild as such no longer exists. However, individual Illuminators still exist outside of Seanchan rule and work to make sure that the Guild will be remembered. *See also da'covale.*

Ishara: The first Queen of Andor (circa FY 994–1020). At the death of Artur Hawkwing, Ishara convinced her husband, one of Hawkwing's foremost generals, to raise the siege of Tar Valon and accompany her to Caemlyn with as many soldiers as he could break away from the army. Where others tried to seize the whole of Hawkwing's empire and failed, Ishara took a firm hold on a small part and succeeded. Today, nearly every noble House in Andor contains some of Ishara's blood, and the right to claim the Lion Throne depends both on direct descent from her and on the number of lines of connection to her that can be established.

Kaensada: An area of Seanchan that is populated by less-than-civilized hill tribes. These tribes fight a great deal among themselves, as do individual families within the tribes. Each tribe has its own customs and taboos, the latter of which often make no sense to anyone outside that tribe. Most of the tribesmen avoid the more civilized residents of Seanchan.

Kin, the: Even during the Trolloc Wars, more than two thousand years ago (circa 1000–1350 AB), the White Tower continued to maintain its standards, putting out women who failed to measure up. One group of these women, fearing to return home in the midst of the wars, fled to Barashta (near the present-day site of Ebou Dar), as far from the fighting as was possible to go at that time. Calling themselves the Kin, and Kinswomen, they kept in hiding and offered a safe haven for others who had been put out. In time, their approaches to women told to leave the Tower led to contacts with runaways, and while the exact reasons may never be known, the Kin began to accept runaways, as well. They made great efforts to keep these girls from learning anything about the Kin until they were sure that Aes Sedai would not swoop down and retake them. After all, everyone knew that runaways were always caught sooner or later, and the Kin knew that unless they held themselves secret, they themselves would be punished severely.

Unknown to the Kin, Aes Sedai in the Tower were aware of their existence almost from the very first, but prosecution of the wars left no time for dealing with them. By the end of the wars, the Tower realized that it might not be in their best interests to snuff out the Kin. Prior to that time, a majority of runaways actually had managed to escape, whatever the Tower's propaganda, but once the Kin began helping them, the Tower knew exactly where any runaway was heading, and they began retaking nine out of ten. Since Kinswomen moved in and out of Barashta (and later Ebou Dar) in an effort to hide their existence and their numbers, never staying anywhere more than ten years lest someone notice that they did not age at a normal speed, the Tower believed they were few, and they certainly were keeping themselves low. In order to use the Kin as a trap for runaways, the Tower decided to leave them alone, unlike any other similar group in history, and to keep the very existence of the Kin a secret known only to full Aes Sedai.

The Kin do not have laws, but rather rules (called "the Rule") based in large part on the rules for novices and Accepted in the White Tower, and in part on the necessity of maintaining secrecy. As might be expected given the origins of the Kin, all of their members maintain their rules very firmly.

Recent open contacts between Aes Sedai and Kinswomen, while known only to a handful of sisters, have produced a number of shocks, including the facts that there are twice as many Kinswomen as Aes Sedai and that some have lived more than a hundred years longer than any Aes Sedai since before the Trolloc Wars. The effect of these revelations, both on Aes Sedai and on Kinswomen, is as yet a matter for speculation. *See also* Knitting Circle, the.

Knitting Circle, the: The leaders of the Kin. Since no member of the Kin has ever known how Aes Sedai arrange their own hierarchy—knowledge passed on only when an Accepted has passed her test for the shawl—they put no store in strength in the Power but give great weight to age, with the older woman always standing above the younger. The Knitting Circle (a title chosen, like the Kin, because it is innocuous) thus consists of the thirteen oldest Kinswomen resident in Ebou Dar, with the oldest given the title of Eldest. By the rules, all will have to step down when it is time for them to move on, but so long as they are resident in Ebou Dar, they have supreme authority over the Kin, to a degree that any Amyrlin Seat would envy. Since the Kin have left Ebou Dar, the Knitting Circle does not technically exist. *See also* Kin, the.

Lance-Captain: In most lands, noblewomen do not personally lead their armsmen into battle under normal circumstances. Instead, they hire a professional soldier, almost always a commoner, who is responsible both for training and leading their armsmen. Depending on the land, this man can be called a Lance-Captain, Sword-Captain, Master of the Horse or Master of the Lances. Rumors of closer relationships than Lady and servant often spring up, perhaps inevitably. Sometimes they are true.

Legion of the Dragon, the: A large military formation, all infantry, giving allegiance to the Dragon Reborn, trained by Davram Bashere along lines worked out by himself and Mat Cauthon, lines which depart sharply from the usual employment of foot. While many men simply walk in to volunteer, large numbers of the Legion are scooped up by recruiting parties from the Black Tower, who first gather all of the men in an area who are willing to follow the Dragon Reborn, and only after taking them through gateways near Caemlyn winnow out those who can be taught to channel. The remainder, by far the greater number, are sent to Bashere's training camps.

Legion of the Wall: Formerly an elite military formation of Ghealdan which provided not only a core to any army that was raised from the Ghealdanin nobilty's armsmen but also provided a bodyguard for the ruler of Ghealdan, and policed Jehannah, the capital, in place of a City Watch. After they were slaughtered and the survivors dispersed by the followers of the Prophet Masema, the nobles of the Crown High Council decided that without the Legion, their own power and their influence over any ruler was increased, so they managed to stop the Legion from being re-formed. The current Queen, Alliandre Maritha Kigarin, has plans to do just that, however; plans which would have an explosive effect if they became known to the Crown High Council.

Length, units of: 10 inches = 1 foot; 3 feet = 1 pace; 2 paces = 1 span; 1000 spans = 1 mile; 4 miles = 1 league.

Listeners: A Seanchan spy organization. Almost anyone in the household of a Seanchan noble, merchant or banker may be a Listener, including *da'covale* occasionally, though seldom *so'jhin*. They take no active role, merely watching, listening and reporting. Their reports are sent to Lesser Hands who control both them and the Seekers and decide what should be passed on to the Seekers for further action. *See also* Seekers, Hand.

marath'damane: In the Old Tongue, "those who must be leashed," and also "one who must be leashed." The term applied by the Seanchan to any woman capable of channeling who has not been collared as a *damane*.

march: *See* Area, units of

Master of the Horse; Master of the Lances: *See* Lance-Captain.

Mellar, Doilin: *See* Hanlon, Daved.

Mera'din: In the Old Tongue, "the Brotherless." The name adopted, as a society, by those Aiel who abandoned clan and sept and went to the Shaido because they could not accept Rand al'Thor, a wetlander, as the *Car'a'carn*, or because they refused to accept his revelations concerning the history and origins of the Aiel. Deserting clan and sept for any reason is anathema among the Aiel, therefore their own warrior societies among the Shaido were unwilling to take them in, and they formed this society, the Brotherless.

morat-: In the Old Tongue, "handler." Among the Seanchan, it is used for those who handle exotics, such as *morat'raken*, a *raken* handler or rider, also informally called a flier. *See also der'morat-*.

Prophet, the: More formally, the Prophet of the Lord Dragon. Once known as Masema Dagar, a Shienaran soldier, he underwent a revelation and decided that he had been called to spread the word of the Dragon's Rebirth. He believes that nothing—nothing!—is more important than acknowledging the Dragon Reborn as the Light made flesh and being ready when the Dragon Reborn calls, and he and his followers will use any means to force others to sing the glories of the Dragon Reborn. Those who refuse are marked for death, and those who are slow may find their homes and shops burned and themselves flogged. Forsaking any name but "the Prophet," he has brought chaos to much of Ghealdan and Amadicia, large parts of which he controlled, although with him gone, the Seanchan are reestablishing order in Amadicia and the Crown High Council in Ghealdan. He joined with Perrin Aybara, who was sent to bring him to Rand, and has, for reasons unknown, stayed with him even though this delays his going to the Dragon Reborn. He is followed by men and women of the lowest sort; if they were not so when they were pulled in by his charisma, they have become so under his influence.

Queen's Guards, the: The elite military formation in Andor. In peacetime the Guard is responsible for upholding the Queen's law and keeping the peace across Andor. The uniform of the Queen's Guard include a red undercoat, gleaming mail and plate armor, a brilliant red cloak and a conical helmet with a barred faceguard. High-ranking officers wear knots of rank on their shoulder and golden lion-head spurs. A recent addition to the Queen's Guards is the Daughter-Heir's personal bodyguard, which is composed entirely of women with the sole exception of its captain, Doilin Mellar. These Guardswomen wear much more elaborate uniforms than their male counterparts, including broad-brimmed hats with white plumes, red-lacquered breastplates and helmets trimmed in white and lace-edged sashes bearing the White Lion of Andor.

Questioners, the: An order within the Children of the Light. They refer to themselves as the Hand of the Light—they intensely dislike being called Questioners—and their avowed purposes are to discover the truth in disputations and uncover Darkfriends. In the search for truth and the Light, their normal method of inquiry is torture; their normal manner is that they know the truth already and must only make their victim confess to it. At times they act as if they are entirely separate from the Children and the Council of the Anointed, which commands the Children. The head of the Questioners is the High Inquisitor, at present Rhadam Asunawa, who sits on the Council of the Anointed. Their sign is a blood-red shepherd's crook.

Redarms: Soldiers of the Band of the Red Hand, who have been chosen out for temporary police duty to make sure that other soldiers of the Band cause no trouble or damage in a town or village where the Band has stopped. So named because, while on duty, they wear very broad red armbands that reach from cuff to elbow. Usually chosen from among the most experienced and reliable men. Since any damages must be paid for by the men serving as Redarms, they work hard to make sure all is quiet and peaceful. A number of former Redarms were chosen to accompany Mat Cauthen to Ebou Dar. *See also Shen an Calhar.*

Return, the: *See Corenne.*

***Rhyagelle*, the:** Old Tongue for "Those Who Come Home." Another name for the Seanchan who have returned to the lands once held by Artur Hawkwing. *See also Corenne, Hailene.*

Sea Folk hierarchy: The Atha'an Miere, the Sea Folk, are ruled by the Mistress of the Ships to the Atha'an Miere. She is assisted by the Windfinder to the Mistress of the Ships, and by the Master of the Blades. Below this come the clan Wavemistresses, each assisted by her Windfinder and her Swordmaster. Below each Wavemistress are the Sailmistresses (ship captains) of her clan, each assisted by her Windfinder and her Cargomaster. The Windfinder to the Mistress of the Ships has authority over all Windfinders to clan Wavemistresses, who in turn have authority over all the Windfinders of her clan. Likewise, the Master of the Blades has authority over all Swordmasters, and they in turn over the Cargomasters of their clans. Rank is not hereditary among the Sea Folk. The Mistress of the Ships is chosen, for life, by the First Twelve of the Atha'an Miere, the twelve most senior clan Wavemistresses. A clan Wavemistress is elected by the twelve seniormost Sailmistresses of her clan, called simply the First Twelve, a term which is also used to designate the senior Sailmistresses present anywhere. She can also be removed by a unanimous vote of her clan's First Twelve. In fact, anyone other than the Mistress of the Ships can be demoted, even all the way down to deckhand, for malfeasance, cowardice or other crimes. Also, the Windfinder to a Wavemistress or Mistress of the Ship who dies will, of necessity, have to serve a lower ranking woman, and her own rank thus decreases to the lowest level, equivalent to one who was first raised from apprentice to Windfinder on the day she herself put off her higher honors. The Atha'an Miere, who have until recently kept their distance from Aes Sedai by various means and diversions, are aware that women who can channel have much longer lifespans than other people, though life at sea is dangerous enough that they seldom live out their entire lifespan, and thus they know that a Windfinder may rise to a height and fall to the depths to begin again many times before she dies.

Seandar: The Imperial capital of Seanchan, located in the northeast of the Seanchan continent. It is also the largest city in the empire.

Seekers: More formally, Seekers for Truth, they are a police/spy organization of the Seanchan Imperial Throne. Although most Seekers are *da'covale* and the property of the Imperial family, they have wide-ranging powers. Even one of the Blood can be arrested for failure to answer any question put by a Seeker, or for failure to cooperate fully with a Seeker, this last defined by the Seekers themselves, subject only to review by the Empress. Their reports are sent to Lesser Hands, who control both them and the Listeners. Most Seekers feel that the Hands do not pass on as much information as they should. Unlike the Listeners', the Seekers' role is active. Those Seekers who are *da'covale* are marked on either shoulder with a raven and a tower. Unlike the Deathwatch Guards, Seekers are seldom eager to show their ravens, in part because it necessitates revealing who and what they are. *See also* Hand, Listeners.

sei'mosiev: In the Old Tongue, "lowered eyes," or "downcast eyes." Among the Seanchan, to say that one has "become *sei'mosiev*" means that one has "lost face." *See also sei'taer.*

sei'taer: In the Old Tongue, "straight eyes," or "level eyes." Among the Seanchan, it refers to honor or face, to the ability to meet someone's eyes. It is possible to "be" or "have" *sei'taer*, meaning that one has honor and face, and also to "gain" or "lose" *sei'taer. See also sei'mosiev.*

Shara: A mysterious land to the east of the Aiel Waste which is the source of silk and ivory, among other trade goods. The land is protected both by inhospitable natural features and by man-made walls. Little is known about Shara, as the people of that land work to keep their culture secret. The Sharans deny that the Trolloc Wars touched them, despite Aiel statements to the contrary. They deny knowledge of Artur Hawkwing's attempted invasion, despite the accounts of eyewitnesses from the Sea Folk. The little information that has leaked out reveals that the Sharans are ruled by a single absolute monarch, a Sh'boan if a woman and a Sh'botay if a man. That monarch rules for exactly seven years, then dies. The rule then passes to the mate of that ruler, who rules for seven years and then dies. This pattern has repeated itself since the time of the Breaking of the World. The Sharans believe that the deaths are the "Will of the Pattern."

There are channelers in Shara, known as the Ayyad, who are tattooed on their faces at birth. The women of the Ayyad enforce the Ayyad laws stringently. A sexual relationship between Ayyad and non-Ayyad is punishable by death for the non-Ayyad, and the Ayyad is also executed if force on his or her part can be proven. If a child is born of the union, it is left exposed to the elements, and dies. Male Ayyad are used as breeding stock only. They are not educated in any fashion, not even how to read or write, and when they reach their twenty-first year or begin to channel, whichever comes first, they are killed and the body cremated. Supposedly, the Ayyad channel the One Power only at the command of the Sh'boan or Sh'botay, who is always surrounded by Ayyad women.

Even the name of the land is in doubt. The natives have been known to call it many different names, including Shamara, Co'-dansin, Tomaka, Kigali and Shibouya.

Shen an Calhar: In the Old Tongue, "the Band of the Red Hand." (1) A legendary group of heroes who had many exploits, finally dying in the defense of Manetheren when that land was destroyed during the Trolloc Wars. (2) A military formation put together almost by accident by Mat Cauthon and organized along the lines of military forces during what is considered the height of the military arts, the days of Artur Hawkwing and the centuries immediately preceding.

Sisnera, Darlin: A High Lord in Tear, he was formerly in rebellion against the Dragon Reborn, but now serves as Steward for the Dragon Reborn in Tear.

Snakes and Foxes: A game that is much loved by children until they mature enough to realize that it can never be won without breaking the rules. It is played with a board that has a web of lines with arrows indicating direction. There are ten discs inked with triangles to represent the foxes, and ten discs inked with wavy lines to represent the snakes. The game is begun by saying "Courage to strengthen, fire to blind, music to dazzle, iron to bind," while describing a triangle with a wavy line through it with one's hand. Dice are rolled to determine moves for the players and the snakes and foxes. If a snake or fox lands on a player's piece, he is out of the game, and as long as the rules are followed, this always happens.

so'jhin: The closest translation from the Old Tongue would be "a height among lowness," though some translate it as meaning "both sky and valley" among several other possibilities. *So'jhin* is the term applied by the Seanchan to hereditary upper servants. They are *da'covale*, property, yet occupy positions of considerable authority and often power. Even the Blood step carefully around *so'jhin* of the Imperial family, and speak to *so'jhin* of the Empress herself as to equals. *See also* Blood, the; *da'covale*.

Standardbearer: A Seanchan rank equivalent to Bannerman.

Stump: A public meeting among the Ogier. The meeting can be within or between *stedding*. It is presided over by the Council of Elders of a *stedding*, but any adult Ogier may speak, or may choose an advocate to speak for him. A Stump is often held at the largest tree stump in a *stedding*, and may last for several years. When a question arises that affects all Ogier, a Great Stump is held, and Ogier from all *stedding* meet to address the question. The various *stedding* take turns hosting the Great Stump.

Succession: In general, when one House succeeds another on the throne. In Andor, the term is widely used for the struggle for the throne that arose upon Mordrellen's death. Tigraine's disappearance had left Mantear without a Daughter-Heir, and two years passed before Morgase, of House Trakand, took the throne. Outside of Andor, this conflict was known as the Third War of Andoran Succession.

Sword-Captain: *See* Lance-Captain.

Taborwin, Breane: Once a bored noblewoman in Cairhien, she lost her wealth and status and is now not only a servant, but in a serious romantic relationship with a man whom once she would have scorned.

Taborwin, Dobraine: A lord in Cairhien. He presently serves as Steward for the Dragon Reborn in Cairhien.

Tarabon: A nation on the Aryth Ocean. Once a great trading nation, a source of rugs, dyes and the Guild of Illuminators' fireworks among other things, Tarabon has fallen on hard times. Racked by anarchy and civil war compounded by simultaneous wars against Arad Doman and the Dragonsworn, it was ripe for the picking when the Seanchan arrived. It is now firmly under Seanchan control, the chapter house of the Guild of Illuminators has been destroyed and the Illuminators themselves have been made *da'covale*. Most Taraboners appear grateful that the Seanchan have restored order, and since the Seanchan allow them to continue living their lives with minimal interference, they have no desire to bring on more warfare by trying to chase the Seanchan out. There are, however, some lords and soldiers who remain outside the Seanchan sphere of influence and are fighting to reclaim their land.

weight, units of: 10 ounces = 1 pound; 10 pounds = 1 stone; 10 stone = 1 hundredweight; 10 hundredweight = 1 ton.

Winged Guards, the: The personal bodyguards of the First of Mayene, and the elite military formation of Mayene. Members of the Winged Guards wear red-painted breastplates and helmets shaped like rimmed pots that come down to the nape of the neck in the back, and carry red-streamered lances. Officers have wings worked on the sides of their helmets, and rank is denoted by slender plumes.

Wise Woman: Honorific used in Ebou Dar for women famed for their incredible abilities at healing almost any injury. A Wise Woman is traditionally marked by a red belt. Some have noted that many, indeed most, Ebou Dari Wise Women are not even from Altara, much less Ebou Dar, but only few have recently learned that all Wise Women are in fact Kinswomen and use various versions of Healing, giving out herbs and poultices largely as a cover. With the flight of the Kin from Ebou Dar after the Seanchan took the city, no Wise Women remain there. *See also* Kin, the.

About the Author

Robert Jordan was born in 1948 in Charleston, South Carolina, where he now lives with his wife, Harriet, in a house built in 1797. He taught himself to read when he was four with the incidental aid of a twelve-years-older brother, and was tackling Mark Twain and Jules Verne by five. He is a graduate of the Citadel, the Military College of South Carolina, with a degree in physics. He served two tours in Vietnam with the U.S. Army; among his decorations are the Distinguished Flying Cross with bronze oak leaf cluster, the Bronze Star with "V" and bronze oak leaf cluster, and two Vietnamese Gallantry Crosses with Palm. A history buff, he has also written dance and theater criticism. He enjoys the outdoor sports of hunting, fishing and sailing, and the indoor sports of poker, chess, pool, and pipe collecting. He has been writing since 1977 and intends to continue until they nail shut his coffin.

The Dead Sea
The Wheel of Time
Aile Dashar
Aryth Ocean
Bandar Eban
North
Arad Doman
Katar
Toman Head
Almoth Plain
Falme
Tanchico
Tarabon
Elmora
Jehannah
Amador
Amadicia
Aryth Ocean
the Shadow Coast
Windbiter's Finger
Tremalking
Qaim